THE YEAR'S
BEST SCIENCE
FICTION

EIGHTH ANNUAL COLLECTION

ALSO BY GARDNER DOZOIS

Anthologies

A Day in the Life
Another World
Best Science Fiction Stories of the Year, Sixth Annual Collection
Best Science Fiction Stories of the Year, Seventh Annual Collection
Best Science Fiction Stories of the Year, Eighth Annual Collection
Best Science Fiction Stories of the Year, Ninth Annual Collection
Best Science Fiction Stories of the Year, Tenth Annual Collection
Future Power (with Jack Dann)
Aliens! (with Jack Dann)
Unicorns! (with Jack Dann)
Magicats! (with Jack Dann)
Bestiary! (with Jack Dann)
Mermaids! (with Jack Dann)
Sorcerers! (with Jack Dann)
Demons! (with Jack Dann)
Dogtales! (with Jack Dann)
Ripper! (with Susan Casper)
Seaserpents! (with Jack Dann)
Dinosaurs! (with Jack Dann)
Little People! (with Jack Dann)
The Best of Isaac Asimov's Science Fiction Magazine
Time-Travellers from Isaac Asimov's Science Fiction Magazine
Transcendental Tales from Isaac Asimov's Science Fiction Magazine
Isaac Asimov's Aliens
The Year's Best Science Fiction, First Annual Collection
The Year's Best Science Fiction, Second Annual Collection
The Year's Best Science Fiction, Third Annual Collection
The Year's Best Science Fiction, Fourth Annual Collection
The Year's Best Science Fiction, Fifth Annual Collection
The Year's Best Science Fiction, Sixth Annual Collection
The Year's Best Science Fiction, Seventh Annual Collection

Fiction

Strangers
The Visible Man (collection)
Nightmare Blue (with George Alec Effinger)
Slow Dancing Through Time (with Jack Dann, Michael Swanwick, Susan Casper and
  Jack C. Haldeman II)

Nonfiction

The Fiction of James Tiptree, Jr.

THE YEAR'S BEST SCIENCE FICTION

**EIGHTH
ANNUAL
COLLECTION**

Gardner Dozois, Editor

ST. MARTIN'S PRESS   NEW YORK

For
SCOTT and SUZI BAKER
—for all the help in Paris
and for
MARGARET S. M. FLINN
—for all the help at home

Library of Congress Catalog Card Number: 85-645716

First Edition: July 1991

10 9 8 7 6 5 4 3 2 1

PAPERBACK 0-312-06009-2
HARDCOVER 0-312-06008-4

CONTENTS

ACKNOWLEDGMENTS

The editor would like to thank the following people for their help and support: first and foremost, Susan Casper, for doing much of the thankless scut work involved in producing this anthology; Michael Swanwick, Janet Kagan, Ellen Datlow, Virginia Kidd, Sheila Williams, Ian Randal Strock, Scott L. Towner, Tina Lee, David Pringle, Kristine Kathryn Rusch, Dean Wesley Smith, Pat Cadigan, Arnie Fenner, David S. Garnett, Charles C. Ryan, Chuq von Rospach, James Turner, Lucius Shepard, Susan Allison, Ginjer Buchanan, Lou Aronica, Amy Stout, Beth Meacham, Claire Eddy, David G. Hartwell, Bob Walters, Tess Kissinger, Jim Frenkel, Michael G. Adkisson, Steve Pasechnick, Lawrence Person, Don Webb, Andy Watson, Michael Sumbera, Glen Cox, Mark Van Name, Don Keller, Chris Napolitano, Robert Killheffer, Greg Cox, and special thanks to my own editor, Gordon Van Gelder.

Thanks are also due to Charles N. Brown, whose magazine *Locus* (Locus Publications, P.O. Box 13305, Oakland, CA 94661, $48.00 for a one year subscription [twelve issues] via first class mail, $35.00 second class) was used as a reference source throughout the Summation, and to Andrew Porter, whose magazine *Science Fiction Chronicle* (Science Fiction Chronicle, P.O. Box 2730, Brooklyn, N.Y. 11202–0056, $27.00 for a one year subscription [twelve issues]; $33.00 first class) was also used as a reference source throughout.

SUMMATION
1990

Charles Dickens had it right: "It was the best of times, it was the worst of times." Well, not really—science fiction has seen both better years and worse years than 1990. But certainly if you were scanning the sky for omens this year—as many people *were*, standing posed as we are on the brink of a new decade . . . and, at that, not only the last decade of the century, but the last decade of the millennium as well, with all the End-of-the-World panic *that* is likely to be whipping up—it was possible to find any number of them, both' positive *and* negative, and whether you predicted a bleak future or a hopeful future depended on what weight you were willing to give to *which* omen as you added up the auguries.

This was as true of the wide world outside as it was of the insular little world of science fiction publishing. 1990 was a year that saw positive social reform sweep like a warm thawing breeze through the long-frozen landscapes of Eastern Europe . . . *and* saw a massive, bitterly fought ground war break out in the Middle East. It was a year that saw a higher degree of public awareness of ecological issues than ever before, in the West, at least . . . *and* perhaps-irreversible ecological damage on a scale never before imagined. That saw record bull markets on Wall Street . . . *and* ever-increasing legions of the homeless sleeping on hot-air grates on the street. A year in which there seemed to be an increased emphasis on the importance of literacy and the arts, certainly over the apathetic seventies and eighties . . . *and* a year in which free expression and First Amendment rights were under ever-escalating attacks by fanatics of both the right *and* the left, making enforced censorship of the arts a more real and palpable threat than it has been since the fifties and sixties.

It would be possible to go on in this fashion for pages—but you get the idea.

And as it was in the bigger world outside, so it was in the teapot-tempest microcosm of the science fiction publishing industry. Actually, as far as actual substantive change was concerned, 1990 was a rather quiet year for SF, with most of the real changes coming in the magazine market—but the omens both dark and light were certainly there in the wind to be read, and, as I said, whether you are cautiously hopeful about the future of SF or paint a bleak scenario of approaching collapse and economic retrenchment depends on how you interpret them; plenty of evidence could be assembled to support *either* forecast. The major slump many feared would hit SF publishing this year did *not* actually occur, for instance; in fact, there was a six percent gain in the total number of books published in the related SF/fantasy/horror fields in 1990 over 1989, according to the newsmagazine *Locus*. At the same time, many publishers were clearly worried by the recession, cutting back on their advertising budgets, staging unadmitted buying slowdowns and even unacknowledged buying freezes, being cautious, being wary, going slow, and I suspect that a lot of intense thought is being given behind the scenes to what can be done to retrench, reorganize, save money, and cut the fat out of publishing lines, should the recession deepen into a depression. A major collapse in the overextended horror market was predicted for next year by many industry insiders . . . at the same time that Dell was launching a major new horror imprint, Abyss Books. Specialty SF bookstores—a form of bookstore that only began to proliferate in the early seventies—continued to spread . . . at the same time that the longest-running such store, California's *A Change of Hobbit*, was forced out of business, and other specialty stores were reporting a weak year and poor sales (while yet *other* specialty stores said that they were doing better than ever). A high degree of creativity is expressing itself through many unorthodox channels, with the small press market more prominent, more lively, and more important to the field than it has ever been before . . . at the same time that sharecropper stuff, shared-world anthologies, and seemingly never-ending series are gobbling up an ever-increasing amount of precious rack-display space in bookstores, to the point where it is becoming rare to find an adult SF novel that is complete in itself, and, according to *Locus*, 147 out of a total of 256 adult SF novels were parts of series or set in already established universes—fifty-seven percent of the adult total, up considerably from last year's thirty-nine percent, and a *very* disturbing trend indeed.

So, cast your own runes, and make your own forecasts. I myself remain cautiously optimistic that SF will not only survive but prosper in the nineties, although things may well look considerably bleaker in the immediate next few years, before they begin to brighten. (In fact, I would go as far as to forecast that a new surge of creative energy and evolutionary/revolutionary furor, with a consequent economic Boom, will hit the field in the mid-nineties, just as it did in the mid-eighties, when dozens of new young writers—some "cyberpunk," some not—seemed to appear out of nowhere all at once, and many older writers were suddenly revitalized by the new currents of creative energy surging through the genre. . . . but only time will tell.)

So, as we plunge into the nineties, keep your fingers crossed, keep your eyes open—and hope for the best.

* * *

It was a year of changes in the magazine market, some negative, some positive. The recent big hike in postage rates will hurt all of the magazines to one extent or another, particularly the ones with small operating budgets and/or profit margins, and all of them will have to adapt to it somehow, by cutting corners and reducing costs, if they are to survive. A decrease in advertising revenue, mostly caused by book publishers cutting back on ads because of the recession, has also weakened many of the magazines. Another big hike in postage costs could wipe out the SF magazine market altogether, except for big-budget magazines like *Omni*—and I remain convinced that *that* would eventually spell the death of the genre *as* a genre, cutting it off at its roots, eliminating most of the continuity from one literary generation to another, and making it much more difficult for new young writers to develop their talents successfully (the magazines have been the training ground for new SF writers for generations now, and I don't think that anything could adequately replace them, not even the original anthology series). Let's all hope that this bleak scenario does *not* come to pass.

Also on the downhill side, the promising new magazine *Starshore* seemingly died after three issues, money problems caused *Aboriginal SF* to cut back on its national distribution because of heavy returns and to downgrade the quality of its paper from an all-slick format to middle grade non-slick paper (it still retains slick covers, however), and several of the new semiprozines are either dead or seemingly in trouble.

On the upbeat side, *Amazing* seems to have risen from the grave yet again, after I'd read memorial services over it here last year—a Lazarus trick it's managed to pull off several times during the fifteen years I've been editing Best of the Year anthologies. Plans have been announced for *Amazing* to be reborn in 1991 in a large-size, full-color, slick-paper format, something *Amazing*'s owner TSR probably should have tried years ago—it'll be interesting to see whether TSR will be willing to sink enough money in backing into the magazine over a long-enough period of time to give the new *Amazing* a real chance to establish itself. *Amazing*'s current editor, Patrick L. Price, has been let go, and will not be associated with the new *Amazing*—this is somewhat disappointing, since Price was doing quite a good job as editor, publishing some excellent fiction, and the magazine was livelier under his editorship than it had been in years (also somewhat unfair, since TSR is only *now* implementing some of the long-needed changes that *Price* had been agitating for for years, and that he will not survive to see any benefits from . . . but that's the publishing world for you). *Amazing*'s new editor is Kim Mohan, and it will be interesting to see how well he does at filling Price's shoes; I wish him well. *The Magazine of Fantasy and Science Fiction* will also have a new editor in 1991, for the first time in twenty-five years, as longtime editor Edward L. Ferman steps down, to be replaced by current *Pulphouse* editor Kristine Kathryn Rusch (Ferman will continue as publisher, and will art direct the magazine from his home in Connecticut; the editorial office will move to Rusch's address in Oregon). It's sad to see Ed Ferman stepping down after a *very* distinguished career as a magazine editor, but Kristine Kathryn Rusch is a good editor too, and I suspect that she will infuse some needed new blood into the magazine. *F & SF*'s continued survival is important to the genre, and the passing-on of the torch to a young editor like Rusch will, we hope, help to assure that the magazine will be around for years to come. Rusch will step down as editor of *Pulphouse* (see the original anthology section below for details), to be replaced by Dean Wesley Smith, and *Pulphouse*, currently a hardcover anthology series, will be transformed under his editorship to a *weekly* SF magazine called *Pulphouse: A Weekly Magazine* (the idea of a *weekly* SF magazine seems like a very dubious one to me . . . but then, I had my doubts about the feasibility of the original *Pulphouse* concept in the first place, and turned out to be wrong there, so who knows?).

The British magazine *Interzone* went monthly in May, but so far the increased frequency of publication has not hurt the quality of the fiction they publish—in fact, *Interzone* seemed stronger than ever to me, and may have published more good stuff this year than it ever has before. *Interzone* and *Aboriginal SF* have come up with a bizarre promotional scheme which calls for them to swap editorial content for an issue, with *Aboriginal SF* publishing the contents of *Interzone*'s June 1991 issue as their July–August issue, while the contents of the May–June *Aboriginal SF* will be published as *Interzone*'s July issue. I suppose that the idea behind this is to attract new potential subscribers for each magazine on the *other* magazine's side of the Atlantic, but the whole thing sounds kind of screwy to me, and I hope that it doesn't backfire for them—I could easily see the regular readership of *both* magazines being puzzled, disappointed, and annoyed by the switch, and they might both end up *losing* subscribers as a result; let's hope not.

There was no sign this year of the promised *Shadows Magazine*, a new horror magazine to be edited by veteran horror editor Charles L. Grant, a project that had been talked about last year; we'll have to wait and see if it ever materializes. I saw the first issue of a magazine called *Unique*, a large-format slick pop-culture magazine that said it was also going to be using a fair proportion of SF, fantasy, and horror fiction, but I could never find the announced second issue, and so I don't know whether or not the magazine still exists; maybe more information will be available next year.

As most of you probably know, I, Gardner Dozois, am also editor of *Isaac Asimov's Science Fiction Magazine*. And that, as I've mentioned before, does pose a problem for me in compiling this summation, particularly the magazine-by-magazine review that follows. As *IAsfm* editor, I could be said to have a vested interest in the magazine's success, so that anything negative I said about another SF magazine (particularly another digest-sized magazine, my direct competition), could be perceived as an attempt to make my own magazine look good by tearing down the competition. Aware of this constraint, I've decided that nobody can complain if I only say *positive* things about the competition . . . and so, once again, I've limited myself to a listing of some of the worthwhile authors published by each.

Omni published first-rate fiction this year by Ted Chiang, Kate Wilhelm, Terry Bisson, Jonathan Carroll, Pat Cadigan, and others. *Omni*'s fiction editor is Ellen Datlow.

The Magazine of Fantasy and Science Fiction featured good fiction by John Kessel, Robert Reed, Bruce Sterling, R. Garcia y Robertson, Alan Brennert, Stephen Kraus, Bradley Denton, and others. *F & SF*'s longtime editor was Edward Ferman; starting next year, *F & SF*'s new editor will be Kristine Kathryn Rusch.

Isaac Asimov's Science Fiction Magazine featured critically acclaimed work by James Patrick Kelly, Joe Haldeman, Pat Cadigan, Judith Moffett, Greg Egan, Molly Gloss, Connie Willis, Kim Stanley Robinson, Terry Bisson, Ian R. MacLeod, Robert Silverberg, Nancy Kress, Alexander Jablokov, Mike Resnick, Walter Jon Williams, Pat Murphy, and others. *IAsfm*'s editor is Gardner Dozois.

Analog featured good work by Nancy Kress, Stephen Kraus, Michael F. Flynn, Charles Sheffield, Lois McMaster Bujold, Bernard Deitchman, W. R. Thompson, Robert R. Chase, and others. *Analog*'s longtime editor is Stanley Schmidt.

Amazing featured good work by John Brunner, J. R. Dunn, Kristine Kathryn Rusch, Gregory Benford, Phillip C. Jennings, N. Lee Wood, Martha Soukup, Ian McDonald, and others. *Amazing*'s editor was Patrick L. Price; starting next year, *Amazing*'s new editor will be Kim Mohan.

Interzone featured excellent work by Greg Egan, Ian MacLeod, Greg Bear, Brian Stableford, Lisa Tuttle, Richard Calder, Pat Murphy, Kim Newman, Thomas M. Disch, Gwyneth Jones, and others. *Interzone*'s editor is David Pringle.

Aboriginal Science Fiction featured interesting work by Kristine Kathryn Rusch, Michael Swanwick, Sarah Smith, Rory Harper, and others. The editor of *Aboriginal Science Fiction* is Charles C. Ryan.

Weird Tales published good work by Ian McLeod, David J. Schow, John Brunner, Jonathan Carroll, Gerald Pearce, and others. *Weird Tales*'s editors are George H. Scithers and Darrell Schweitzer.

Short SF continued to appear in many magazines outside genre boundaries, including markets as *outré* as *Penthouse Hot Talk*, an "erotic letters" magazine. *Playboy* in particular continues to run a good deal of SF, under fiction editor Alice K. Turner.

(Subscription addresses follow for those magazines hardest to find on the news stands: *The Magazine of Fantasy and Science Fiction*, Mercury Press, Inc., Box 56, Cornwall, CT, 06753, annual subscription—twelve issues— $26.00 in U.S.; *Isaac Asimov's Science Fiction Magazine*, Davis Publications, Inc., P.O. Box 7058, Red Oak, IA, 51566—$34.95 for thirteen issues; *Interzone*, 124 Osborne Road, Brighton, BN1 6LU, United Kingdom, $52.00 for an airmail one year—twelve issues—subscription; *Analog*, Davis Publications, Inc., P.O. Box 7061, Red Oak, IA, 51591, $34.95 for thirteen issues; *Amazing*, TSR, Inc., P.O. Box 5695, Boston, MA 02206, $30.00 for twelve issues; Aboriginal Science Fiction, P.O. Box 2449, Woburn, MA 01888-0849, $15.00 for 6 issues in U.S.; *Weird Tales*, Terminus Publishing Company, P.O. Box 13418, Philadelphia, PA, 19101-3418, $16.00 for 4 issues in U.S.)

There were some shake-ups in the fiction semiprozine market this year, although things remained fairly lively. Mark Ziesing and Andy Watson's very strange *Journal Wired* published two eclectic issues in 1990, containing some worthwhile fiction by Jonathan Lethem, Lewis Shiner, and others, as well as author interviews and a good deal of critical ranting of various degrees of coherency and interest, but died at the beginning of 1991; by press time, there were rumors that it was going to be reborn in a different form, and then counter-rumors that it was *not* going to be—if it is gone, I'll miss it. There were also rumors flying at press time that Michael G. Adkisson's *New Pathways* might have died, but I called one of the staff just before sitting down to write this portion of the Summation, and he assured me that the rumors were not true, and that *New Pathways* was still alive. I'm relieved to hear that, since it is the most consistently interesting of all the weirdly eclectic mixed fiction and review semiprozines that started to appear in the eighties. There were three issues of *New Pathways* published in 1990; in addition to the usual reviews, comix, and Weird Stuff, they published some good fiction by Jonathan Lethem, Don Webb (the year's *second* most erotic story, about a woman who has Great Sex with a dildo-sized flying saucer), Lewis Shiner, and others. There were only two issues of *Nova Express*— edited by Michael Sumbera, with help by Glen Cox and Dwight Brown— out this year, although I'm told that another one was in the mail at about the time that I sat down to write this Summation; although the fiction they publish has been unimpressive to date, *Nova Express* is a lively and irreverent magazine full of interesting features, reviews, and interviews, and deserves your support. A (mostly) all-fiction semiprozine called *Strange Plasma*, edited by Steve Pasechnick, published two issues this year, and although nothing in it was quite up to the best of the stuff in last year's debut issue, it did feature interesting work by R. A. Lafferty, Gene Wolfe, Cherry Wilder, and Carol Emshwiller.

There are also a slew of horror semiprozines, on both sides of the Atlantic, and there seem to be more of them all the time, in spite of all the talk about the coming disastrous crash of the horror market. Counting *Weird Tales* as a professional market (although there is some argument about that under the Hugo-eligibility rules), the most visible of them are probably *Midnight Graffiti*—which only published one issue this year, though—*Grue*, and the British magazine *Fear*, although that is very difficult to find on the American side of the Atlantic; *Cemetery Dance, Haunts, 2 A.M., Eldritch Tales, Deathrealm,* and the long-running *Weirdbook* are some of the other horror semiprozines, along with the hardcover anthology continuation of the prominent British semiprozine, *Fantasy Tales*. A new horror semiprozine, *Iniquities: The Magazine of Great Wickedness and Wonder*, started at the beginning of 1991, and has already had the dubious distinction of being barred from entering Canada by offended customs officials. There was no issue of *Whispers* once again this year. There is also a semiprozine aimed at the High Fantasy market, *Marion Zimmer Bradley's Fantasy Magazine*, but, to date, the fiction published there has yet to reach reliable levels of quality.

As ever, *Locus* and *SF Chronicle* remain your best bet among the semiprozines if you are looking for news and/or an overview of the genre. *Thrust*, recently renamed *Quantum*, is the longest-running of those semiprozines that concentrate primarily on literary criticism, and one of the most consistently good. The last issue of Mark Van Name's *Short Form* that I saw reviewed more short fiction than some of last year's issues, but still didn't review enough of it to justify the magazine's name; I'd like to see more short fiction reviews in the magazine, since they remain vanishingly rare. There were only two issues of Stephen Brown's *Science Fiction Eye* this year, and I don't imagine that the magazine will ever be able to stick to a regular publication schedule, but I suppose that in a way it really doesn't matter—the two issues they did produce were jammed to bursting with interesting material, passionately opinionated and avidly controversial, and all that probably counts more than punctuality; Bruce Sterling's column alone is probably worth the price of the magazine, and the Sterling column in the August 1990 issue, "My Rihla," is especially good, as fascinating and full of surprising insights as the best of his fiction. *The New York Review of Science Fiction*—whose editorial staff includes Kathryn Cramer, L. W. Currey, Samuel R. Delany, David G. Hartwell, Greg Cox, Robert Killheffer, John J. Ordover, and Gordon Van Gelder—has established itself as perhaps the most reliable of the criticalzines, producing twelve issues right on time this year; the level of criticism here is erratic—some of it is obtuse and bloodless, while other articles are literate, interesting, and intelligent; I like the Reading Lists they solicit from well-known professionals, and the occasional touch of humor (they even produced an issue parodying *themselves*, which takes guts and a certain amount of grace). Another contender entered the ring in the criticalzine arena this year, *Science Fiction Review*, a continuation by other hands (mostly Elton Elliott's) of Dick Geis's famous fanzine of the same name, with some editorial contribution by Geis himself; the three issues they published this year were fat and full of interesting material, although I think they'd do better omitting the short fiction they run to make room for more reviews and commentary. There is also a new critical magazine called *Monad*, edited by Damon Knight; only one issue has appeared to date.

(*Locus*, Locus Publications, P.O. Box 13305, Oakland, CA 94661, $48.00 for a one-year first class subscription, $35.00 second class, 12 issues; *Science Fiction Chronicle*, Algol Press, P.O. Box 2730, Brooklyn, NY 11202–0056, $27.00 for 1 years, 12 issues, $33.00 first class; *Quantum* (formerly *Thrust*), Thrust Publications, 8217 Langport Terrace, Gaithersburg, MD 20877, $9.00 for 4 issues; *Science Fiction Eye*, P.O. Box 43244, Washington, DC 20010–9244, $10.00 for one year; *Short Form*, Hatrack River Publications, P.O. Box 18184, Greensboro, NC 27419–8184, one year subscription (six issues), $24.00; *New Pathways*, MGA Services, P.O. Box 863994, Plano, TX 75086–3994, $25.00 for 6 issue subscription; *Nova Express*, White Car PubLications, P.O. Box 27231, Austin TX 78755–2231, $10.00 for a one-year (four issue) subscription; *Strange Plasma*, Edgewood Press, P.O. Box 264, Cambridge, MA 02238, $8.00 for three issues; *The New York Review of Science Fiction*, Dragon Press, P.O. Box 78, Pleasantville, NY, 10570, $24.00 per year (twelve issues); *Science Fiction Review*, SFR Publications, P.O. Box 20340, Salem, OR 97307, $25.00 for 4 issues; *Grue Magazine*, Hells Kitchen Productions, Box 370, Times Square Sta., New York, NY 10108, $13.00 for three issues; *Fear*, Box 20, Ludlow, Shropshire, SY8 1DB, United Kingdom, $65.00 for 12 issues; *Midnight Graffiti*, 13101 Sudan Road, Poway, CA 92064, one year for $19.95; *Monad*, Pulphouse Publishing, Box 1227, Eugene, OR 97440, $5.00 for single issues or $18.00 for four issues.)

Nineteen ninety was a weaker year overall than last year in the original anthology market, with fewer memorable one-shot nonseries anthologies and fewer good theme anthologies. The best one-shot theme SF anthology of the year was undoubtedly *Alien Sex* (Dutton), a mixed original-and-reprint anthology edited by *Omni* fiction editor Ellen Datlow. There is a first-rate original story here by Pat Murphy, as well as good original work by Lewis Shiner, Geoff Ryman, Lisa Tuttle, Scott Baker, and others, including a real shocker by K.W. Jeter, but the original stuff, good as it is, is overshadowed by the classic reprints here, wonderful stories such as James Tiptree, Jr.'s "And I Awoke and Found Me Here on the Cold Hill's Side," Leigh Kennedy's "Her Furry Face," Pat Cadigan's "Roadside Rescue," and Connie Willis's "All My Darling Daughters" . . . together with other good reprint stuff by Edward Bryant, Harlan Ellison, Bruce McAllister, Larry Niven, and others, it makes up into a—dare I say it?—highly *desirable* package, and makes an intriguing companion piece to the *last* round of SF/sex anthologies, *Eros In Orbit* and *Strange Bedfellows*, which came out back in the seventies. (Interestingly the most *erotic* new story of the year, Nancy Collins' surprisingly upbeat "The Two-Headed Man," is to be found in *Pulphouse Nine*, not in *Alien Sex*.) Another good anthology was *Time Gate II* (Baen), edited by Robert Silverberg with Bill Fawcett; it's not as strong as last year's *Time Gate*, lacking Silverberg's own Hugo-winning story, for one thing, but it does feature some powerful work, most notably by Gregory Benford. A good Alternate History anthology—although not as strong as the two Benford/ Greenberg Alternate History anthologies from last year—is *Beyond the Gate of Worlds* (Tor), edited by Robert Silverberg; again, the strongest story in the book is Silverberg's own, the evocative novella "Lion Time in Timbuctoo," but the anthology also features good work by John Brunner and Chelsea Quinn Yarbro. *Semiotext[e] SF* (Autonomedia), edited by Rudy Rucker, Peter Lamborn Wilson, and Robert Anton Wilson, was a relentlessly self-hyped anthology of "material which had been rejected by the commercial SF media," theoretically repressed stories that had supposedly been too controversial, too radical, too *good*, to be published in the SF magazines and anthologies. The editors describe their own book as "a book of colossal importance not only for the future of SF, but for the future in general," and bill themselves as "the *Dangerous Visions* for the 90s"—but the only thing that is *really* exceptional here is the hype. Far from being too radical, too brilliant, too daring, most of the material here is just plain bad—and much of it has nothing to do with SF by an even remotely reasonable definition. I also wonder how much of the charge that the magazines are too timid to buy controversial material is a self-fulfilling prophecy. For instance, I don't know where *else* Bruce Sterling submitted his "We See Things Differently," the one really first-rate story in the book, but he certainly didn't submit it to me at *IAsfm*, because I would have bought it if he had. Actually, the despised "commercial media" published some pretty controversial stuff this year, including stuff as "dangerous" or more so than most of the stories in *Semiotext[e] SF*. Also worthwhile was *Catfantastic II* (DAW), edited by Andre Norton and Martin H. Greenberg.

Turning to the SF anthology series, 1990 saw the debut of an important new anthology series with the publication of *Universe 1* (Doubleday Foundation), edited by Robert Silverberg and Karen Haber. This is supposedly the continuation of the long-running *Universe* series edited by the late Terry Carr, but, somewhat confusingly, the publisher has chosen to number this volume *Universe 1*, even though Terry Carr had gotten up to *Universe 17* before his untimely death; this will bewilder bibliographers and librarians for years to come. All that to the side, what's the fiction like? Well, perhaps not surprisingly, the stuff here reminds me more in style and tone and ambiance of the kind of story you would have found in a volume of Silverberg's *previous* anthology series, *New Dimensions*, than it really does of stuff you would have found in Carr's *Universe*—but that is no mean recommendation, since Silverberg's *New Dimensions* was undoubtedly the strongest anthology series of the mid-seventies. This is a strong anthology, too, with first-rate stories by Ursula K. Le Guin and Bruce Sterling, and good stuff by Kim Stanley Robinson, Geoffrey A. Landis, M. J. Engh, Richard R. Smith, Gregor Hartmann, James Patrick Kelly, Damian Kilby, and others. There are some minor stories here, of course, but at five hundred pages and twenty stories for $8.95, it's a great value for your money, and I hope that Silverberg and Harber go on to produce *another* seventeen volumes of *Universe*, at the least. *Universe* and *Full Spectrum*, another anthology series produced within the Bantam Spectra/Doubleday Foundation group, are among the most solid and substantial SF original anthology series to come along in some while, and it's a shame that Bantam can't be persuaded to issue a volume of *each* series every year, instead of alternating them every other year, the way they're doing it now.

Another important new anthology series is *Pulphouse* (Pulphouse Publishing), edited by Kristine Kathryn Rusch, a quarterly hardcover anthology—billed as a "hardback magazine"—that is primarily available by subscription. Each issue of *Pulphouse* has a specific theme; of the *Pulphouses* this year, *Pulphouse Seven* was devoted to Horror, *Pulphouse Eight* was the Science Fiction issue, and *Pulphouse Nine* was devoted to Dark Fantasy. Some of these themed issues work better than others. *Pulphouse Seven*, for instance, the Horror issue, was the weakest of the year's *Pulphouses*, although it did feature interesting work by Marina Fitch, Don Webb, Edward Bryant, Charles de Lint, and others, as well as a smug and childishly petulant essay/ rant by David J. Schow. I'm not sure of just what distinction they're making here between "Horror" and "Dark Fantasy," because for me *Pulphouse Nine*, the so-called "Dark Fantasy" issue, actually functioned better as a horror anthology than the Horror issue did; it's a stronger anthology than *Seven*, at any rate, with powerful stories by Joe R. Lansdale and Nancy Collins, and good stuff by Marina Fitch, Mary Rosenblum, William F. Wu, Melinda M. Snodgrass, and others. The strongest *Pulphouse* overall this year was *Pulphouse Eight*, the Science Fiction issue, which is a good anthology by any standard, containing a first-rate story by Greg Egan, and good stuff by Patricia

Anthony, Kij Johnson, Jonathan Lethem, Thomas F. Monteleone, R. Garcia y Robertson, L. Timmel Duchamp, S. P. Somtow, and others. As mentioned above, Kristine Kathryn Rusch is stepping down as editor of *Pulphouse* to take over the editorial helm of *The Magazine of Fantasy and Science Fiction*, but apparently she has already completed future issues through *Pulphouse Twelve*, which will be the last *Pulphouse* to be published in hardcover anthology format as a "hardback magazine." After that, the editorship will be assumed by Dean Wesley Smith, *Pulphouse*'s publisher, and the format will be changed to that of an actual magazine rather than a hardcover anthology; a *weekly* magazine, in fact, to be called *Pulphouse: A Weekly Magazine*. As the editor of a monthly magazine, I must admit that the idea of trying to produce a *weekly* magazine fills me with terror, and I wonder if it is really a feasible concept; it also takes *Pulphouse* out of the economics of the small press hardcover market, where it has done quite well, and into the economics of the magazine market instead, which is quite a different thing. Still, I wish them well—the field can use all the short fiction markets it can get—and all of the *Pulphouse* projects (all of which will retain Rusch as editor except for the weekly magazine—including the Axolotl novella line, the Author's Choice Monthly line, the new Short Story Paperbacks line, and a new Bantam/Pulphouse novella series to be co-edited by Rusch and Betsy Mitchell . . . Good Lord, is she going to be *busy!*) deserve your support. (For information about them, contact: Pulphouse Publishing, Box 1227, Eugene, OR 97440.)

There didn't seem to be any issues of George Zebrowski's *Synergy* this year, as far as I could tell, anyway, and I wonder if the series still exists. There was only one issue of James Baen's *New Destinies* (Baen). *L. Ron Hubbard Presents Writers of the Future Vol. VI* (Bridge), edited by Algis Budrys, features work by some writers who may well become established professionals someday, but they are not established *yet*, and the book that you will hold in your hand here and now is mostly undistinguished novice work. There was a second edition of a new British anthology series this year, *Zenith 2* (Sphere), edited by David S. Garnett; it featured a brilliant novella by Michael Moorcock, as well as good work by Ian McDonald, Lisa Tuttle, John Gribbin, and others. Clearly the *Zenith* series deserved life, but it was denied it—canceled by its publisher this year. I caught up with the newest edition of another British anthology series this year, an anthology I had missed last year, *Other Edens III* (Unwin), edited by Christopher Evans and Robert Holdstock; it featured a first-rate story by Ian McDonald, as well as good fiction by Keith Roberts, Brian Aldiss, Lisa Tuttle, Christopher Evans, and others . . . but this series too has been canceled by its publisher. Taken along with the cancelation of David Garnett's *Orbit Science Fiction Yearbook* series, that seems to be pretty much the end of the brief British anthology renaissance everyone was talking about a year or two ago—almost all of the new British anthology series died in 1990. (There was a *More Tales From the Forbidden Planet* (Titan Books) released this year, edited by Roz Kaveney, but that's a special case, more an occasional one-shot rather than an actual anthology series; it was a good deal weaker than the original volume a few years back, but had some interesting stuff by Rachel Pollack, David Langford, R. M. Lamming, and others.) One ray of hope: David Garnett, obviously not a man who is easily discouraged, has announced that he will be editing a revival of the famous British SF magazine *New Worlds* in paperback anthology form, with the blessing and at least partial participation of former *New Worlds* editor Michael Moorcock, the anthology series to be published by Gollancz. I wish it well, and hope that it has better luck surviving than most other recent British anthology series.

Shared-world anthologies this year included: *Liavek 5: Festival Week* (Ace), edited by Will Shetterly and Emma Bull; *Wild Cards 7* (Bantam), edited by George R.R. Martin; *Tales of the Witch World III* (Tor), edited by Andre Norton; *Sword & Sorceress VI* (DAW), edited by Marion Zimmer Bradley; *Warworld II* (Baen), edited by Jerry Pournelle; and two "Fleet" anthologies, *Total War* (Ace), edited by David Drake and Bill Fawcett and *The Farstars War* (Roc), edited by Bill Fawcett.

In the horror market, the best original one-shot horror anthology was probably *Walls of Fear* (Morrow), edited by Kathryn Cramer (especially if you consider Datlow's *Alien Sex* to be a science fiction anthology instead—which it mostly *was*, although stories like Jeter's "The First Time" are clearly horror stories, not SF). *Walls of Fear* was a literate and intelligent anthology, containing a first-rate story by M. J. Engh, and good stuff by Karl Edward Wagner, Jonathan Carroll, Gene Wolfe, Susan Palwick, Edward Bryant, and others. *Women of Darkness II* (Tor), edited by Kathryn Ptacek, was not as impressive, although it featured interesting work by Melanie Tem, Tanith Lee, and Nina Kiriki Hoffman, as well as by newer talents such as Poppy Z. Brite and Patricia Ramsey-Jones. A promising new horror anthology series debuted this year, *Borderlands* (Avon), edited by Thomas F. Monteleone. *Borderlands*, appropriately enough, seems to be sitting right in the middle of two hostile aesthetic camps, as far as the acrimonious Splatterpunk/"quiet horror" war that is raging in the horror industry is concerned: Some of it is gross enough for anybody (although the shock stuff here tends to be more sexual than gory), while the rest of it is "quiet" but scary stuff reminiscent of the kind of thing Charles L. Grant used in his *Shadows* anthologies—the kingpiece here is a strong story by Harlan Ellison, and the anthology also contains interesting work by Poppy Z. Brite, Chet Williamson, Karl Edward Wagner, Joe R. Lansdale, and others. *Pulphouse Seven* and *Pulphouse Nine*, discussed above, also function as horror anthologies.

Nineteen ninety didn't strike me as a particularly strong year for novels overall—although, as usual, there were so *many* novels published that it was certainly possible to find good ones if you spent a bit of effort looking for them. *Locus* estimates that the total number of books published this year was up by eight percent over 1989, although most of that gain came in the collections, anthologies, and critical book categories, rather than in the novel category, which actually declined somewhat overall. (The greatest increase came in the trade paperback category, which was up thirty-four percent; last year it was up by fifty percent, which means that category has enjoyed an overall increase of one hundred percent since 1988—clearly, as hardcovers become more expensive to produce and to buy, trade paperbacks are becoming an increasingly attractive option for both the publisher and the consumer). *Locus* estimates that there were 281 new SF novels (a rise of less than one percent from last year), 204 new fantasy novels (down twenty-eight percent from last year's total of 277), and 168 new horror novels (down five percent from last year's count of 176—although, with many publishers cutting back on horror, *next* year may well see a dramatic drop in the number of horror titles). That brings the number of new SF/fantasy/horror novels published in 1990—according to *Locus*—to 653; down somewhat from last year's total of 732, but, even so (and even if you restricted yourself to the science fiction novels alone), the novel field has clearly expanded far beyond the ability of any one reviewer to keep up with it. Busy as I am with enormous amounts of reading at shorter lengths, I don't even try anymore, and I must admit that I was unable to find time to read the majority of new novels released this year.

So, once again, I am going to limit myself here to mentioning those novels that have gotten a lot of attention and acclaim this year. They include: *Pacific Edge*, Kim Stanley Robinson (Tor); *Queen of Angels*, Greg Bear (Warner); *The Fall of Hyperion*, Dan Simmons (Doubleday Foundation); *Voyage to the Red Planet*, Terry Bisson (Morrow); *The Hemingway Hoax*, Joe Haldeman (Morrow); *Tehanu: The Last Book of Earthsea*, Ursula K. Le Guin (Atheneum); *Clarke County, Space*, Allen Steele (Ace); *Second Contact*, Mike Resnick (Tor); *Redshift Rendezvous*, John E. Stith (Ace); *The Difference Engine*, William Gibson and Bruce Sterling (Gollancz); *Brain Rose*, Nancy Kress (Morrow); *The World at the End of Time*, Frederik Pohl (Del Rey); *Arachne*, Lisa Mason (Morrow); *Cortez on Jupiter*, Ernest Hogan (Tor); *Castleview*, Gene Wolfe (Tor); *The Blood of Roses*, Tanith Lee (Legend); *Summertide*, Charles Sheffield (Del Rey); *The Child Garden*, Geoff Ryman (St. Martin's); *Raising the Stones*, Sheri S. Tepper (Doubleday Foundation); *Lucid Dreams*, Charles L. Harness (Avon); *The Hollow Earth*, Rudy Rucker (Morrow); *White Jenna*, Jane Yolen (Tor); *The World Next Door*, Brad Ferguson (Tor); *Only Begotten Daughter*, James Morrow (Morrow); *Winterlong*, Elizabeth Hand (Bantam Spectra); *The Shield of Time*, Poul Anderson (Tor); *In the Country of the Blind*, Michael F. Flynn (Baen); *Thomas the Rhymer*, Ellen Kushner (Morrow); *Good Omens*, Neil Gaiman and Terry Pratchett (Workman); *Mary Reilly*, Valerie Martin (Doubleday); *The Ghost from the Grand Banks*, Arthur C. Clarke (Bantam Spectra); *Moon Dance*, S.P. Somtow (Tor); *Fire*, Alan Rodgers (Bantam); *Beyond the Fall of Night*, Arthur C. Clarke and Gregory Benford (Putnam); *Drink Down the Moon*, Charles de Lint (Ace); *Carmen Dog*, Carol Emshwiller (Mercury House); and *Nightfall* (a novel-length version of the famous story), Isaac Asimov and Robert Silverberg (Doubleday Foundation).

Associational novels that might be of interest to SF readers this year included *Slam* (Doubleday), by Lewis Shiner, and *Dotty*, by R. A. Lafferty (available from United Mythologies Press, Box 390, Sta. A, Weston, Ont., Canada M9N 3N1—$17.00 postpaid).

Morrow had a strong year this year, as did Tor and Doubleday Foundation.

There's no one novel here that is clearly dominant, as has been the case in other years, so it's anyone's guess what will win the Hugo and the Nebula in 1991. It'll be interesting to see if Dan Simmons' *The Fall of Hyperion*, the sequel to *Hyperion*, can take the Hugo this year, as *Hyperion* did last year.

Of the first novels, the biggest stir was probably made by the novel debuts of Lisa Mason, Ernest Hogan, Elizabeth Hand, and Michael F. Flynn, although none of them managed to attract the kind of attention that some first novels—William Gibson's *Neuromancer*, for instance—have attracted in years gone by.

Special mention should probably be made here of the series of novella-length books that are being published in Britain by Legend and that will later be published in the United States by St. Martin's Press. They are really novellas by word-count—according to SFWA's Nebula rules, anyway—but they are being sold as individual books and reviewed as such, so I suppose that they might just as well be mentioned in the novel section. At any rate, whether you think of them as novels or novellas, the Legend series has to date produced some of the most memorable fiction of the year: Among them, *Heads*, by Greg Bear; *Kalimantan*, by Lucius Shepard; *Griffin's Egg*, by Michael Swanwick; and *Outnumbering the Dead*, by Frederik Pohl are particularly worthy of notice. These books will probably be available in the best-stocked speciality bookstores, or you can wait for the American editions; but, one way or the other, they're well worth seeking out. Having mentioned the Legend books, I suppose that it's only fair to mention some of the other good novellas in book form that saw print this year: notably *A Short, Sharp Shock*, by Kim Stanley Robinson, from Ziesing, and *Bully!*, by Mike Resnick and *Lion Time in Timbuctoo*, by Robert Silverberg, both from Axolotl. (The Tor Doubles are published *as* novellas, not as individual books, so it doesn't seem appropriate for me to mention them here.) Coming next year will be a new line of original novellas published as individual books, co-published by Bantam and Axolotl Press and edited by busy editor Kristine Kathryn Rusch in conjunction with Betsy Mitchell.

This was a stronger year for short-story collections overall than it was for novels, with several collections published that deserve to be in the library of any serious student of the field.

The three best collections of the year were: *Her Smoke Rose Up Forever*, James Tiptree, Jr. (Arkham House), *The Leiber Chronicles*, Fritz Leiber (Dark Harvest), and *The Adventures of Doctor Eszterhazy*, Avram Davidson (Owls-wick Press). The Tiptree and the Leiber function pretty well as one-volume overviews of the authors' careers, and the Davidson, although it is representative of only one part of Davidson's output, is a marvelous book that I've been wanting to see preserved in hardcover for many years now (I've already gone through two copies of the earlier paperback version of this, read them—literally—to pieces . . . and *this* book collects the *later* Eszterhazy stories as well, making it the only complete Eszterhazy collection; not to be missed). Also excellent are several collections that serve as one-volume overviews of the short fiction-writing careers to date of some *younger* authors: *Points of Departure*, Pat Murphy (Bantam Spectra); *The Ends of the Earth*, Lucius Shepard (Arkham House); *Maps in a Mirror: The Short Fiction of Orson Scott Card*, Orson Scott Card (Tor); and *Facets*, Walter Jon Williams (Tor). Other first-rate collections this year include: *Chateau d'If and Other Stories*, Jack Vance (Underwood-Miller); *N-Space*, Larry Niven (Tor); *Distant Signals and Other Stories*, Andrew Weiner (Porçepic); *Her Pilgrim Soul*, Alan Brennert (Tor); and *Prayers to Broken Stones*, Dan Simmons (Dark Harvest). Also worthwhile: *Four Past Midnight*, Stephen King (Viking); *Lunar Activity*, Elizabeth Moon (Baen); *The Gateway Trip*, Frederik Pohl (Del Rey); *Tales from Distant Earth*, Arthur C. Clarke (Bantam Spectra); *Future Crime*, Ben Bova (Tor); *The Atrocity Exhibition*, J. G. Ballard (Re/Search); *The Start of the End of it All and Other Stories*, Carol Emshwiller (The Women's Press); *Lost Angels*, David J. Schow (Onyx); and *Houses Without Doors*, Peter Straub (Dutton). There was also a new edition of a long-out-of-print collection by Keith Roberts, *Anita*, from Owlswick Press. Mentioned without comment is *Slow Dancing Through Time* (Ursus/Ziesing), a collection of stories by Gardner Dozois in collaboration (in various combinations) with Jack Dann, Michael Swanwick, Susan Casper, and Jack C. Haldeman II.

As is clear from a look at the list above, small press publishers such as

Arkham House, Ziesing, Dark Harvest, Ursus Press, Owlswick Press, Underwood-Miller, and several others, continue to publish the bulk of the year's outstanding collections—although Tor deserves credit this year for publishing collections a good deal more frequently than is customary these days for a trade publishing house (Tor also deserves credit for the Tor Double line, which is bringing some of the best novella work in the field back into print after years of almost total unavailability to the ordinary reader).

Special mention should also be made of Pulphouse Publishing, which for the last year or so has maintained an ambitious program of publishing a new short story collection every *month*—admittedly they are slender books, more like chapbooks than the kind of handsome hardcover editions produced by publishers like Ziesing or Ursus or Arkham House, but they are also cheaper, and are getting some very worthwhile material into print. This year Pulphouse started an even *more* ambitious program with the Short Story Paperback line, individual short stories (both reprint and original) published in chapbook form as individual books, and priced at $1.95 apiece. I tend to doubt that a sufficient number of people are going to be willing to part with two bucks for a book containing a single short story, when they can buy a paperback anthology containing a dozen stories for $3.95, but who knows? At any rate, I wish Pulphouse Publishing well with all of their many projects—anything which increases the availability of short SF to the general public, or which increases the *interest* of the public in reading short fiction, has my support, and is, I believe, vital to the future health of the genre.

Nineteen ninety was another unexceptional year in the reprint anthology market, although, as always, there were some solid values for your money. As usual, your best bets in the reprint anthology market were the various "Best of the Year" anthologies, and the annual Nebula Award anthology. This year, there were three "Best" anthologies covering science fiction (my own, Donald Wollheim's, and a British series called *The Orbit Science Fiction Yearbook*, edited by David S. Garnett), three covering horror (Karl Edward Wagner's long-established *Year's Best Horror Stories*, a new British series called *Best New Horror*, edited by Ramsey Campbell and Stephen Jones, and a new anthology concentrating on horror published in small-press semiprozines, Peter Enfantino's *Quick Chills*), and one mammoth volume covering both horror *and* fantasy (Ellen Datlow and Terri Windling's *The Year's Best Fantasy and Horror*). *Next* year, we are slated to lose two of the "Best" anthology series covering science fiction, as David Garnett's *Orbit Yearbook* has been canceled, and Donald Wollheim's long-running series died along with its creator. This thinning-out of the competition in the science fiction "Best" anthology market should make me happy, I suppose, but it does not—science fiction is a broad and various enough field that there is certainly room for more than *one* editor selecting the best stuff of the year, and I'd like to see other SF "Best" anthology series come along, reflecting perspectives and tastes *other* than my own: Surely that would be the healthiest thing for the genre as a whole, as well. I'd also like to see another new "Best" series devoted entirely to fantasy, rather than seeing fantasy squeezed down to just the Windling half of the Windling/Datlow anthology. As for the proliferation of horror "Bests," two new series since 1989, I suspect that the much-discussed coming "crash" in the horror market, which has been forecast for next year by several industry pundits, *if* it does indeed arrive, may sink several of the new horror "Best" series; only time will tell. At any rate, these "Best" anthologies, and the annual Nebula Award volume, are the most solid values for your money in the reprint anthology market. Other solid values this year include: *Isaac Asimov Presents the Great SF Stories: 20* (DAW), edited by Isaac Asimov and Martin H. Greenberg; *Isaac Asimov Presents the Great SF Stories: 21* (DAW), edited by Isaac Asimov and Martin H. Greenberg; and *The Mammoth Book of Vintage Science Fiction: Short Novels of the 1950s* (Robinson; Carroll & Graf), edited by Isaac Asimov, Martin H. Greenberg, and Charles G. Waugh. *Project Solar Sail* (Roc), edited by Arthur C. Clarke and David Brin, was an interesting mixed reprint/original/nonfiction anthology of stories about the use of solar sails for spaceflight, but it's intriguing to note that the best story in the book, in spite of more modern selections, is Clarke's own "Sunjammer," from all the way back in 1965; it also bemuses me that they *didn't* reprint one of the best solar sail stories ever written, Cordwainer Smith's "The Lady Who Sailed the *Soul.*" Also interesting: *Western Ghosts* (Rutledge Hill Press), edited by Frank D. McSherry, Jr., Charles G. Waugh, and Martin H. Greenberg; *The Fantastic World War II* (Baen), edited by Frank McSherry, Jr.; *Christmas on Ganymede and Other Stories* (Avon), edited by Martin H. Greenberg; *The Women Who Walk Through Fire* (The Crossing Press), edited by Susanna J. Sturgis; and *Space Dreadnoughts* (Ace), edited by David Drake. Noted without comment is *Dinosaurs!* (Ace), edited by Jack Dann and Gardner Dozois.

Horror saw the publication of the highly controversial reprint anthology *Splatterpunks: Extreme Horror* (St. Martin's), edited by Paul M. Sammon, which, on the whole, was a bit too gooshey for my taste; *Intensive Scare* (DAW), edited by Karl Edward Wagner, a good anthology of "medical horror stories" (perhaps the most shuddery kind—as anyone who's spent time in a hospital can attest!); and *Cults of Horror* (DAW), edited by Martin H. Greenberg and Charles G. Waugh.

This was another solid but unexciting year in the SF–oriented nonfiction SF reference book field. Your best bets for reference this year were: *Science

Fiction, Fantasy, & Horror: 1989 (Locus Press), edited by Charles N. Brown and William G. Contento; and *Science Fiction and Fantasy Book Review Annual 1989* (Meckler), edited by Robert A. Collins and Robert Latham. There were also two "Reader's Guides"—*Fantasy Literature: A Reader's Guide* (Garland) and *Horror Literature: A Reader's Guide* (Garland), both edited by Neil Barron—and a critical study, *Understanding American Science Fiction: The Formative Period, 1926–1970* (University of South Carolina), by Thomas D. Clareson.

The update of Peter Nicholls' *Science Fiction Encyclopedia*, which has been rumored for some time now, is reportedly underway, and is promised for next year—I look forward to it, since it is a reference source that is urgently needed; the old edition has never really been adequately replaced in the years since its first publication in 1975.

In the general nonfiction field, the books I enjoyed the most were also those hardest to classify: Dougal Dixon's playful and beautifully illustrated book of, I guess, "speculative biology," *Man After Man: An Anthropology of the Future* (St. Martin's), is a highly inventive look, filled with spectacular renderings, at the bizarre kinds of creatures that humankind *might* evolve into after a few million more years of relentless evolution—and, from the pages of *IAsfm*, a collection of Norman Spinrad's feisty, highly controversial, and often startlingly insightful essays on science fiction, *Science Fiction in the Real World* (Southern Illinois University). Brian W. Aldiss's book of literary reminiscences, *Bury My Heart at W. H. Smith's* (Hodder & Stoughton), was published in Britain, but may never get a trade publication in the United States—too bad, since many of his American fans would find it fascinating. There was an interesting study of portrayals of Dracula, *Hollywood Gothic* (Norton), by David J. Skal, a collection of the unsettling but queasily fascinating art of H. R. Giger, *H. R. Giger's Biomechanics* (Morpheus), and two how-to-write books, the *Science Fiction Writers of America Handbook: The Professional Writer's Guide to Writing Professionally* (Writers Notebook Press), edited by Kristine Kathryn Rusch and Dean Wesley Smith, and *How to Write Science Fiction and Fantasy* (Writer's Digest), by Orson Scott Card.

I remain unimpressed by the majority of genre films, and only force my way into most of them now out of a sense of duty—however, my growing disenchantment is apparently *not* reflected in the taste of the movie-going audience at large, since 1990 was another good year at the box office for genre movies. The surprise hits of the year, both relatively low-budget films (by Hollywood standards) were *Teenage Mutant Ninja Turtles*, a kid's movie with some sly touches to be appreciated by the adults, and *Ghost*, a somewhat sappy New Age-ish variant on a subgenre of films (dead husband/wife returns as ghost) common in the forties which has enjoyed a surprisng resurgence of popularity in the last few years. *Total Recall* had great special effects and production values, and there were a few good moments of authentically Philip K. Dickian material in it—lost, unfortunately, in a sea of chop-sock-pow James Bondian violence. (I'm still waiting for someone to do a Phil Dick movie *right*; the few touches of authentically Dickian aesthetics that shine through the murk in films such as *Bladerunner, Total Recall,* and *Dark Star* prove that Dick's style and content *can* be brought to the screen in an adult and intelligently complex manner . . . *if* anyone were brave enough to trust the *audience* to be adult enough to appreciate it! So far, no one has been.) *Back to the Future III* was a pleasant and harmless entertainment, although for full appreciation of the complex plot you probably would have needed to have seen the first two movies again just prior to sitting down for this one. *Dick Tracy* was loaded with colorful and inventive set dressing and production design, but not with much verve or tension, and Warren Beatty is just not *tough* enough to be impressive as Tracy, a comic strip character who would often shoot criminals in cold blood rather than bring them to trial, with the explanation that he was "saving the taxpayers' money." *The Hunt for Red October* was suspenseful and professionally slick, although only marginally a genre film at best. *The Handmaid's Tale* was a mild box-office disappointment, and neither *RoboCop II* nor *Gremlins II* did as well as they were expected to, either. *The Jetsons: The Movie* was just that, an episode of the old TV cartoon writ large. I strongly suspect that the less said about *Ghost Dad*, the better, although I was not able to actually bring myself to go see it. I have heard people talk enthusiastically about *Edward Scissorhands, The Witches, Tremors, Jacob's Ladder,* and *Jesus of Montreal*, but I didn't have time to see any of *them*, either, so you're on your own—probably you should give them the benefit of the doubt and make an attempt to catch them. *Robot Jox*, a movie with a screenplay by Joe Haldeman, was supposedly released this year, but if it played through Philadelphia at all, it must have done so *fast*, because I never even saw a listing for it, let alone the movie itself. There was also supposedly a movie version of Fredric Brown's *Martians, Go Home*, but that too must have gone through town "like green corn through the hired man," as they used to say in New England. There were lots of horror/slasher/serial killer/exploding head movies, but I find I can no longer physically force myself into the theater to see them, so you're on your own with them, too.

On television, The Sci-Fi Channel, the proposed new cable channel, was again talked about all year, with expensive glossy ads for it appearing in magazines like *Playboy* and *Omni*, but, once again, it had not actually materialized by the time I had to sit down to write this Summation; maybe next year. Either *Star Trek: The Next Generation* has improved or I'm more forgiving of it now, but I enjoyed it more this year than I did the last two years—it's still fundamentally silly, of course, by the standards of print science fiction, but it has been entertaining, with fairly adult character development in a few of the shows, the production values are quite good, and the special effects occasionally stunning for television, light years ahead of those in the original *Star Trek* series; one or two of the cast can actually even *act* . . . although not all of them, by any means. *Alien Nation* has died and *Quantum Leap* is rumored to be ailing. *The Flash* seems to be doing pretty well so far in the ratings, but I can't work up much enthusiasm for it. I like *The Simpsons* well enough—but apparently not nearly as much as I'm *supposed* to like it, judging from the nationwide cult hysteria it has whipped up. I have yet to buy a Bart Simpson T-shirt, for instance, in spite of countless blandishments to do so on every street corner and in every shopping mall. Grump, grump.

The Forty-eighth World Science Fiction Convention, ConFiction, was held in The Hague, Holland, from August 23 to August 27, 1990, and drew an estimated attendance of 3,000. The 1990 Hugo Awards, presented at Noreascon Three, were: Best Novel, *Hyperion*, by Dan Simmons; Best Novella, "The Mountains of Mourning," by Lois McMaster Bujold; Best Novelette, "Enter a Soldier. Later: Enter Another," by Robert Silverberg; Best Short Story, "Boobs," by Suzy McKee Charnas; Best Nonfiction, *The World Beyond the Hill*, by Alexei Panshin and Cory Panshin; Best Professional Editor, Gardner Dozois; Best Professional Artist, Don Maitz; Best Original Artwork, "Rimrunners," by Don Maitz; Best Dramatic Presentation, *Indiana Jones and the Last Crusade*; Best Semiprozine, *Locus*; Best Fanzine, *The Mad 3 Party*, edited by Leslie Turek; Best Fan Writer, David Langford; Best Fan Artist, Stu Shiffman; plus the John W. Campbell Award for Best New Writer to Kristine Kathryn Rusch.

The 1989 Nebula Awards, presented at a banquet at the Hyatt Regency Embarcadero Hotel in San Francisco, California, on April 28, 1990, were: Best Novel, *The Healer's War*, by Elizabeth Ann Scarborough; Best Novella, "The Mountains of Mourning," by Lois McMaster Bujold; Best Novelette, "At the Rialto," by Connie Willis; and Best Short Story, "Ripples in the Dirac Sea," by Geoffrey A. Landis.

The World Fantasy Awards, presented at the Sixteenth Annual World Fantasy Convention in Chicago, Illinois, on November 4, 1990, were: Best Novel, *Lyonesse: Madouc*, by Jack Vance; Best Novella, "Great Work of Time," by John Crowley; Best Short Story, "The Illusionist," by Steven Millhauser; Best Collection, *Richard Matheson: Collected Stories*, by Richard Matheson; Best Anthology, *The Year's Best Fantasy: Second Annual Collection*, edited by Ellen Datlow and Terri Windling; Best Artist, Thomas

Canty; Special Award (Professional), Mark Ziesing Publications; Special Award (Nonprofessional), *Grue Magazine,* edited by Peggy Nadramia; plus a Life Achievement Award to R. A. Lafferty.

The 1990 Bram Stoker Awards, presented in Providence, Rhode Island, during the weekend of June 22–24, 1990, by The Horror Writers of America, were: Best Novel, *Carrion Comfort,* by Dan Simmons; Best First Novel, *Sunglasses After Dark,* by Nancy A. Collins; Best Collection, *Richard Matheson: Collected Stories,* by Richard Matheson; Best Novella/Novelette, "On the Far Side of the Cadillac Desert With Dead Folks," by Joe R. Lansdale; Best Short Story, "Eat Me," by Robert R. McCammon; Best Nonfiction, *Harlan Ellison's Watching,* by Harlan Ellison and *Horror: The 100 Best Books,* edited by Stephen Jones and Kim Newman (tie).

The 1989 John W. Campbell Memorial Award–winner was *The Child Garden,* by Geoff Ryman.

The 1989 Theodore Sturgeon Award was won by "The Edge of the World," by Michael Swanwick.

The 1989 Philip K. Dick Memorial Award–winner was *Subterranean Gallery,* by Richard Paul Russo.

The Arthur C. Clarke award was won by *The Child Garden,* by Geoff Ryman.

* * *

Dead in 1990 were: **Donald A. Wollheim**, 76, editor, publisher, author, anthologist, fan, one of the major shaping forces on modern science fiction for more than fifty years—among many other accomplishments, he edited the first mass market SF anthology, the first all-original SF anthology, and the first anthology series, masterminded the first SF convention, helped establish SF as a legitimate part of the paperback publishing scene in the fifties as editor of Ace Books, edited one of the longest-running "Best of the Year" anthology series, and, in the seventies, was the founder and first editor of a successful new publishing house, DAW Books; **Wilmar H. Shiras**, 82, author of the classic story "In Hiding" and its sequels, collected in *Children of the Atom;* **Roald Dahl**, 74, well-known writer of macabre fiction and children's books; **Lawrence Durrell**, 78, British novelist, author of the "Alexandria Quartet"; **Joseph Payne Brennan**, 71, poet and writer of supernatural fiction; **Walker Percy**, 73, author of *Love in the Ruins,* winner of the National Book Award; **Manuel Puig**, 57, magic realist writer; **Win Gijsen**, 57, prominent Dutch SF author; **Anya Seton**, 86, writer of Gothics and of historical novels; **José Durand**, 64, magic realist writer; **Charles Spain Verral**, 85, veteran author and illustrator; **Carl Sherrell**, 60, fantasy writer and commercial artist; **Henrik Dahl Juve**, 89, veteran pulp writer; **Helen Hoke Watts**, 86, writer and anthologist; **John Fuller**, 76, author of "unexplained phenomena" books such as *Incident at Exeter;* **Stephen Frances**, 72, writer and publisher; **Lisa Novak**, 30, Bantam Spectra editor, murdered along with her husband, **Greg Peretz**; **Donald Hutter**, 57, veteran book editor; **Ed Emshwiller**, 65, Hugo-winning SF artist and well-known experimental filmmaker; **Harry Altshuler**, 77, well-known literary agent; **Arthur "Atom" Thomson**, 62, well-known fan artist and cartoonist; **B. Klíban**, 55, famous cartoonist, creator of such bestselling cartoon books as *Cat*, *Tiny Footprints*, and *Whack Your Porcupine*; **Jim Henson**, 53, internationally renowned puppeteer, creator of *The Muppets*; **Mary Martin**, 76, musical comedy star, probably best known to the genre audience for her role as *Peter Pan*; **David Rappoport**, 38, British film actor, probably best-known to the genre audience for his role in *Time Bandits*; **Gertrude Asimov**, 73, former wife of writer Isaac Asimov; **Cora Walters**, 75, mother of SF illustrator Robert Walters; **Rick Sneary**, 63, longtime fan and fanzine publisher; **Elizabeth Pearse**, 61, longtime fan and art show director; and **Don C. Thompson**, 63, longtime fan, fanzine publisher, and DenVention II co-chairman.

JAMES PATRICK KELLY

Mr. Boy

▼

F. Scott Fitzgerald told us long ago that the rich were not like you and me, but it takes the pyrotechnic and wildly inventive story that follows, one of the year's most powerful and exciting novellas, to demonstrate just *how* unlike us they could eventually become . . .

Like his friend and frequent collaborator John Kessel, James Patrick Kelly made his first sale in 1975, and went on to become one of the most respected and prominent new writers of the '80s. Although his most recent solo novel, *Look into the Sun*, was well-received, Kelly has had more impact to date as a writer of short fiction than as a novelist, and, indeed, Kelly stories such as "Solstice," "The Prisoner of Chillon," "Glass Cloud," "Rat," and "Home Front" must be ranked among the most inventive and memorable short works of the decade. Kelly's first solo novel, the mostly ignored *Planet of Whispers*, came out in 1984. It was followed by *Freedom Beach*, a novel written in collaboration with John Kessel. His story "Friend," also in collaboration with Kessel, was in our Second Annual Collection; his "Solstice" was in our Third Annual Collection; his "The Prisoner of Chillon" was in our Fourth Annual Collection; his "Glass Cloud" was in our Fifth Annual Collection; and his "Home Front" was in our Sixth Annual Collection. Born in Mineola, New York, Kelly now lives in Durham, New Hampshire, the setting for several of his stories, where he's reported to be at work on a third solo novel, *Wildlife*.

1

▼
Mr. Boy

JAMES PATRICK KELLY

I was already twitching by the time they strapped me down. Nasty pleasure and beautiful pain crackled through me, branching and rebranching like lightning. Extreme feelings are hard to tell apart when you have endorphins spilling across your brain. Another spasm shot down my legs and curled my toes. I moaned. The stiffs wore surgical masks that hid their mouths, but I knew that they were smiling. They hated me because my mom could afford to have me stunted. When I really was just a kid I did not understand that. Now I hated them back; it helped me get through the therapy. We had a very clean transaction going here. No secrets between us.

Even though it hurts, getting stunted is still the ultimate flash. As I unlived my life, I overdosed on dying feelings and experiences. My body was not big enough to hold them all; I thought I was going to explode. I must have screamed because I could see the laugh lines crinkling around the stiffs' eyes. You do not have to worry about laugh lines after they twank your genes and reset your mitotic limits. My face was smooth and I was going to be twelve years old forever, or at least as long as Mom kept paying for my rejuvenation.

I giggled as the short one leaned over me and pricked her catheter into my neck. Even through the mask, I could smell her breath. She reeked of dead meat.

Getting stunted always left me wobbly and thick, but this time I felt like last Tuesday's pizza. One of the stiffs had to roll me out of recovery in a wheelchair.

The lobby looked like a furniture showroom. Even the plants had been newly waxed. There was nothing to remind the clients that they were bags of blood and piss. You are all biological machines now, said the lobby, clean as space station lettuce. A scattering of people sat on the hard chairs. Stennie and Comrade were fidgeting by the elevators. They looked as if they were thinking of rearranging the furniture—like maybe into a pile in the middle of the room. Even before they waved, the stiff seemed to know that they were waiting for me.

Comrade smiled. *"Zdrast'ye."*

"You okay, Mr. Boy?" said Stennie. Stennie was a grapefruit yellow steno-nychosaurus with a brown underbelly. His razor-clawed toes clicked against the slate floor as he walked.

"He's still a little weak," said the stiff, as he set the chair's parking brake. He strained to act nonchalant, not realizing that Stennie enjoys being stared at. "He needs rest. Are you his brother?" he said to Comrade.

Comrade appeared to be a teenaged spike neck with a head of silky black hair that hung to his waist. He wore a window coat on which twenty-three different talking heads chattered. He could pass for human, even though he was really a Panasonic. *"Nyet,"* said Comrade. "I'm just another one of his hallucinations."

The poor stiff gave him a dry nervous cough that might have been meant as a chuckle. He was probably wondering whether Stennie wanted to take me home or eat me for lunch. I always thought that the way Stennie got reshaped was more funny-looking than fierce—a python that had rear-ended an ostrich. But even though he was a head shorter than me, he did have enormous eyes and a mouthful of serrated teeth. He stopped next to the wheelchair and rose up to his full height. "I appreciate everything you've done." Stennie offered the stiff his spindly three-fingered hand to shake. "Sorry if he caused any trouble."

The stiff took it gingerly, then shrieked and flew backwards. I mean, he jumped almost a meter off the floor. Everyone in the lobby turned and Stennie opened his hand and waved the joy buzzer. He slapped his tail against the slate in triumph. Stennie's sense of humor was extreme, but then he was only thirteen years old.

Stennie's parents had given him the Nissan Alpha for his twelfth birthday and we had been customizing it ever since. We installed blue mirror glass and Stennie painted scenes from the Late Cretaceous on the exterior body armor. We ripped out all the seats, put in a wall-to-wall gel mat and a fridge and a microwave and a screen and a mini-dish. Comrade had even done an illegal operation on the carbrain so that we could override in an emergency and actually steer the Alpha ourselves with a joystick. It would have been cramped, but we would have lived in Stennie's car if our parents had let us.

"You okay there, Mr. Boy?" said Stennie.

"Mmm." As I watched the trees whoosh past in the rain, I pretended that the car was standing still and the world was passing me by.

"Think of something to do, okay?" Stennie had the car and all and he was fun to play with, but ideas were not his specialty. He was probably smart for a dinosaur. "I'm bored."

"Leave him alone, will you?" Comrade said.

"He hasn't said anything yet." Stennie stretched and nudged me with his foot. "Say something." He had legs like a horse: yellow skin stretched tight over long bones and stringy muscle.

"*Prosrees!* He just had his genes twanked, you jack." Comrade always took good care of me. Or tried to. "Remember what that's like? He's in damage control."

"Maybe I should go to socialization," Stennie said. "Aren't they having a dance this afternoon?"

"You're talking to me?" said the Alpha. "You haven't earned enough learning credits to socialize. You're a quiz behind and forty-five minutes short of E-class. You haven't linked since . . ."

"Just shut up and drive me over." Stennie and the Alpha did not get along. He thought the car was too strict. "I'll make up the plugging quiz, okay?" He probed a mess of empty juice boxes and snack wrappers with his foot. "Anyone see my comm anywhere?"

Stennie's schoolcomm was wedged behind my cushion. "You know," I said, "I can't take much more of this." I leaned forward, wriggled it free and handed it over.

"Of what, *poputchik?*" said Comrade. "Joyriding? Listening to the lizard here?"

"Being stunted."

Stennie flipped up the screen of his comm and went on line with the school's computer. "You guys help me, okay?" He retracted his claws and tapped at the oversized keyboard.

"It's extreme while you're on the table," I said, "but now I feel empty. Like I've lost myself."

"You'll get over it," said Stennie. "First question: Brand name of the first wiseguys sold for home use?"

"NEC-Bots, of course," said Comrade.

"Geneva? It got nuked, right?"

"*Da.*"

"Haile Selassie was that king of Egypt who the Marleys claim is god, right? Name the Cold Wars: Nicaragua, Angola . . . Korea was the first." Typing was hard work for Stennie; he did not have enough fingers for it. "One was something like Venezuela. Or something."

4

"Sure it wasn't Venice?"

"Or Venus?" I said, but Stennie was not paying attention.

"All right, I know that one. And that. The Sovs built the first space station. Ronald Reagan—he was the president who dropped the bomb?"

Comrade reached inside of his coat and pulled out an envelope. "I got you something, Mr. Boy. A get well present for your collection."

I opened it and scoped a picture of a naked dead fat man on a stainless steel table. The print had a DI verification grid on it, which meant this was the real thing, not a composite. Just above the corpse's left eye there was a neat hole. It was rimmed with purple which had faded to bruise blue. He had curly gray hair on his head and chest, skin the color of dried mayonnaise and a wonderfully complicated penis graft. He looked relieved to be dead. "Who was he?" I liked Comrade's present. It was extreme.

"CEO of Infoline. He had the wife, you know, the one who stole all the money so she could download herself into a computer."

I shivered as I stared at the dead man. I could hear myself breathing and feel the blood squirting through my arteries. "Didn't they turn her off?" I said. This was the kind of stuff we were not even supposed to imagine, much less look at. Too bad they had cleaned him up. "How much did this cost me?"

"You don't want to know."

"Hey!" Stennie thumped his tail against the side of the car. "I'm taking a quiz here and you guys are drooling over porn. When was the First World Depression?"

"Who cares?" I slipped the picture back into the envelope and grinned at Comrade.

"Well, let me see then." Stennie snatched the envelope. "You know what I think, Mr. Boy? I think this corpse jag you're on is kind of sick. Besides, you're going to get in trouble if you let Comrade keep breaking laws. Isn't this picture private?"

"Privacy is twentieth century thinking. It's all information, Stennie, and information should be accessible." I held out my hand. "But if *glasnost* bothers you, give it up." I wiggled my fingers.

Comrade snickered. Stennie pulled out the picture, glanced at it and hissed. "You're scaring me, Mr. Boy."

His schoolcomm beeped as it posted his score on the quiz and he sailed the envelope back across the car at me. "Not Venezuela, Viet Nam. Hey, *Truman* dropped the plugging bomb. Reagan was the one who spent all the money. What's wrong with you dumbscuts? Now I owe school another fifteen minutes."

"Hey, if you don't make it look good, they'll know you had help." Comrade laughed.

5

"What's with this dance anyway? You don't dance." I picked Comrade's present up and tucked it into my shirt pocket. "You find yourself a cush or something, lizard boy?"

"Maybe." Stennie could not blush but sometimes when he was embarrassed the loose skin under his jaw quivered. Even though he had been reshaped into a dinosaur, he was still growing up. "Maybe I am getting a little. What's it to you?"

"If you're getting it," I said, "it's got to be microscopic." This was a bad sign. I was losing him to his dick, just like all the other pals. No way I wanted to start over with someone new. I had been alive for twenty-five years now. I was running out of things to say to thirteen-year-olds.

As the Alpha pulled up to the school, I scoped the crowd waiting for the doors to open for third shift. Although there were a handful of stunted kids, a pair of gorilla brothers who were football stars and Freddy the Teddy, a bear who had furry hands instead of real paws, the majority of students at New Canaan High looked more or less normal. Most working stiffs thought that people who had their genes twanked were freaks.

"Come get me at 5:15," Stennie told the Alpha. "In the meantime, take these guys wherever they want to go." He opened the door. "You rest up, Mr. Boy, okay?"

"What?" I was not paying attention. "Sure." I had just seen the most beautiful girl in the world.

She leaned against one of the concrete columns of the portico, chatting with a couple other kids. Her hair was long and nut-colored and the ends twinkled. She was wearing a loose black robe over mirror skintights. Her schoolcomm dangled from a strap around her wrist. She appeared to be seventeen, maybe eighteen. But of course, appearances could be deceiving.

Girls had never interested me much, but I could not help but admire this one. "Wait, Stennie! Who's that?" She saw me point at her. "With the hair?"

"She's new—has one of those names you can't pronounce." He showed me his teeth as he got out. "Hey Mr. Boy, you're *stunted*. You haven't got what she wants."

He kicked the door shut, lowered his head and crossed in front of the car. When he walked he looked like he was trying to squash a bug with each step. His snaky tail curled high behind him for balance, his twiggy little arms dangled. When the new girl saw him, she pointed and smiled. Or maybe she was pointing at me.

"Where to?" said the car.

"I don't know." I sank low into my seat and pulled out Comrade's present again. "Home, I guess."

* * *

I was not the only one in my family with twanked genes. My mom was a three-quarters scale replica of the Statue of Liberty. Originally she wanted to be full-sized, but then she would have been the tallest thing in New Canaan, Connecticut. The town turned her down when she applied for a zoning variance. Her lawyers and their lawyers sued and countersued for almost two years. Mom's claim was that since she was born human, her freedom of form was protected by the Thirtieth Amendment. However, the form she wanted was a curtain of reshaped cells which would hang on a forty-two meter high ferroplastic skeleton. Her structure, said the planning board, was clearly subject to building codes and zoning laws. Eventually they reached an out-of-court settlement, which was why Mom was only as tall as an eleven story building.

She complied with the town's request for a setback of five hundred meters from Route 123. As Stennie's Alpha drove us down the long driveway, Comrade broadcast the recognition code which told the robot sentries that we were okay. One thing Mom and the town agreed on from the start: no tourists. Sure, she loved publicity, but she was also very fragile. In some places her skin was only a centimeter thick. Chunks of ice falling from her crown could punch holes in her.

The end of our driveway cut straight across the lawn to Mom's granite-paved foundation pad. To the west of the plaza, directly behind her, was a utility building faced in ashlar that housed her support systems. Mom had been bioengineered to be pretty much self-sufficient. She was green not only to match the real Statue of Liberty but also because she was photosynthetic. All she needed was a yearly truckload of fertilizer, water from the well, and a hundred and fifty kilowatts of electricity a day. Except for emergency surgery, the only time she required maintenance was in the fall, when her outer cells tended to flake off and had to be swept up and carted away.

Stennie's Alpha dropped us off by the doorbone in the right heel and then drove off to do whatever cars do when nobody is using them. Mom's greeter was waiting in the reception area inside the foot.

"Peter." She tried to hug me but I dodged out of her grasp. "How are you, Peter?"

"Tired." Even though Mom knew I did not like to be called that, I kissed the air near her cheek. Peter Cage was her name for me; I had given it up years ago.

"You poor boy. Here, let me see you." She held me at arm's length and brushed her fingers against my cheek. "You don't look a day over twelve. Oh, they do such good work—don't you think?" She squeezed my shoulder. "Are you happy with it?"

I think my mom meant well, but she never did understand me. Especially when she talked to me with her greeter remote. I wormed out of her grip and fell back onto one of the couches. "What's to eat?"

"Doboys, noodles, fries—whatever you want." She beamed at me and then bent over impulsively and gave me a kiss that I did not want. I never paid much attention to the greeter; she was lighter than air. She was always smiling and asking five questions in a row without waiting for an answer and flitting around the room. It wore me out just watching her. Naturally everything I said or did was cute, even if I was trying to be obnoxious. It was no fun being cute. Today Mom had her greeter wearing a dark blue dress and a very dumb white apron. The greeter's umbilical was too short to stretch up to the kitchen. So why was she wearing an apron? "I'm really, really glad you're home," she said.

"I'll take some cinnamon doboys." I kicked off my shoes and rubbed my bare feet through the dense black hair on the floor. "And a beer."

All of Mom's remotes had different personalities. I liked Nanny all right; she was simple but at least she listened. The lovers were a challenge because they were usually too busy looking into mirrors to notice me. Cook was as pretentious as a four star menu; the housekeeper had all the charm of a vacuum cleaner. I had always wondered what it would be like to talk directly to Mom's main brain up in the head, because then she would not be filtered through a remote. She would be herself.

"Cook is making you some nice broth to go with your doboys," said the greeter. "Nanny says you shouldn't be eating dessert all the time."

"Hey, did I ask for broth?"

At first Comrade had hung back while the greeter was fussing over me. Then he slid along the wrinkled pink walls of the reception room toward the plug where the greeter's umbilical was attached. When she started in about the broth I saw him lean against the plug. Carelessly, you know? At the same time he stepped on the greeter's umbilical, crimping the furry black cord. She gasped and the smile flattened horribly on her face as if her lips were two ropes someone had suddenly yanked taut. Her head jerked toward the umbilical plug.

"E-Excuse me." She was twitching.

"What?" Comrade glanced down at his foot as if it belonged to a stranger. "Oh, sorry." He pushed away from the wall and strolled across the room toward us. Although he seemed apologetic, about half the heads on his window coat were laughing.

The greeter flexed her cheek muscles. "You'd better watch out for your toy, Peter," she said. "It's going to get you in trouble someday."

Mom did not like Comrade much, even though she had given him to me when I was first stunted. She got mad when I snuck him down to Manhattan a couple of years ago to have a chop job done on his behavioral regulators. For a while after the operation, he used to ask me before he broke the law. Now he was on his own. He got caught once and she warned me he was out of control. But she still threw money at the people until they went away.

"Trouble?" I said. "Sounds like fun." I thought we were too rich for trouble. I was the trust baby of a trust baby; we had vintage money and lots of it. I stood and Comrade picked up my shoes for me. "And he's not a toy; he's my best friend." I put my arms around his shoulder. "Tell Cook I'll eat in my rooms."

I was tired after the long climb up the circular stairs to Mom's chest. When the roombrain sensed I had come in, it turned on all the electronic windows and blinked my message indicator. One reason I still lived in my mom was that she kept out of my rooms. She had promised me total security and I believed her. Actually I doubted that she cared enough to pry, although she could easily have tapped my windows. I was safe from her remotes up here, even the housekeeper. Comrade did everything for me.

I sent him for supper, perched on the edge of the bed, and cleared the nearest window of army ants foraging for meat through some Angolan jungle. The first message in the queue was from a gray-haired stiff wearing a navy blue corporate uniform. "Hello, Mr. Cage. My name is Weldon Montross and I'm with Datasafe. I'd like to arrange a meeting with you at your convenience. Call my DI number, 408-966-3286. I hope to hear from you soon."

"What the hell is Datasafe?"

The roombrain ran a search. "Datasafe offers services in encryption and information security. It was incorporated in the state of Delaware in 2013. Estimated billings last year were 340 million dollars. Headquarters are in San Jose, California, with branch offices in White Plains, New York and Chevy Chase, Maryland. Foreign offices. . . ."

"Are they trying to sell me something or what?"

The room did not offer an answer. "Delete," I said. "Next?"

Weldon Montross was back again, looking exactly as he had before. I wondered if he were using a virtual image. "Hello, Mr. Cage. I've just discovered that you've been admitted to the Thayer Clinic for rejuvenation therapy. Believe me when I say that I very much regret having to bother you during your convalescence and I would not do so if this were not a matter of importance. Would you please contact Department of Identification number 408-966-3286 as soon as you're able?"

"You're a pro, Weldon, I'll say that for you." Prying client information

9

out of the Thayer Clinic was not easy, but then the guy was no doubt some kind of op. He was way too polite to be a salesman. What did Datasafe want with me? "Any more messages from him?"

"No," said the roombrain.

"Well, delete this one too and if he calls back tell him I'm too busy unless he wants to tell me what he's after." I stretched out on my bed. "Next?" The gel mattress shivered as it took my weight.

Happy Lurdane was having a smash party on the twentieth but Happy was a boring cush and there was a bill from the pet store for the iguanas that I paid and a warning from the SPCA that I deleted and a special offer for preferred customers from my favorite fireworks company that I saved to look at later and my dad was about to ask for another loan when I paused him and deleted and last of all there was a message from Stennie, time stamped ten minutes ago.

"Hey Mr. Boy, if you're feeling better I've lined up a VR party for tonight." He did not quite fit into the school's telelink booth; all I could see was his toothy face and the long yellow curve of his neck. "Bunch of us have reserved some time on Playroom. Come in disguise. That new kid said she'd link, so scope her yourself if you're so hot. I found out her name but it's kind of unpronounceable. Tree-something Joplin. Anyway it's at seven, meet on channel 17, password is warhead. Hey, did you send my car back yet? Later." He faded.

"Sounds like fun." Comrade kicked the doorbone open and backed through, balancing a tray loaded with soup and fresh doboys and a mug of cold beer. "Are we going?" He set it onto the nightstand next to my bed.

"Maybe." I yawned. It felt good to be in my own bed. "Flush the damn soup, would you?" I reached over for a doboy and felt something crinkle in my jacket pocket. I pulled out the picture of the dead CEO. About the only thing I did not like about it was that the eyes were shut. You feel dirtier when the corpse stares back. "This is one sweet hunk of meat, Comrade." I propped the picture beside the tray. "How did you get it, anyway? Must have taken some operating."

"Three days worth. Encryption wasn't all that tough but there was lots of it." Comrade admired the picture with me as he picked up the bowl of soup. "I ended up buying about ten hours from IBM to crack the file. Kind of pricey but since you were getting stunted, I had nothing else to do."

"You see the messages from that security op?" I bit into a doboy. "Maybe you were a little sloppy." The hot cinnamon scent tickled my nose.

"Ya v'rot ego ebal!" He laughed. "So some stiff is cranky? Plug him if he can't take a joke."

I said nothing. Comrade could be a pain sometimes. Of course I loved the picture, but he really should have been more careful. He had made a mess and left it for me to clean up. Just what I needed. I knew I would only get mad if I thought about it, so I changed the subject. "Well, do you think she's cute?"

"What's-her-face Joplin?" Comrade turned abruptly toward the bathroom. "Sure, for a *perdunya*," he said over his shoulder. "Why not?" Talking about girls made him snippy. I think he was afraid of them.

I brought my army ants back onto the window; they were swarming over a lump with brown fur. Thinking about him hanging on my elbow when I met this Tree-something Joplin made me feel weird. I listened as he poured the soup down the toilet. I was not myself at all. Getting stunted changes you; no one can predict how. I chugged the beer and rolled over to take a nap. It was the first time I had ever thought of leaving Comrade behind.

"VR party, Mr. Boy." Comrade nudged me awake. "Are we going or not?"

"Huh?" My gut still ached from the rejuvenation and I woke up mean enough to chew glass. "What do you mean *we?*"

"Nothing." Comrade had that blank look he always put on so I would not know what he was thinking. Still I could tell he was disappointed. "Are you going then?" he said.

I stretched—*ouch!* "Yeah, sure, get my joysuit." My bones felt brittle as candy. "And stop acting sorry for yourself." This nasty mood had momentum; it swept me past any regrets. "No way I'm going to lie here all night watching you pretend you have feelings to hurt."

"*Tak tochno.*" He saluted and went straight to the closet. I got out of bed and hobbled to the bathroom.

"This is a costume party, remember," Comrade called. "What are you wearing?"

"Whatever." Even his efficiency irked me; sometimes he did too much. "You decide." I needed to get away from him for a while.

Playroom was a new virtual reality service on our local net. If you wanted to throw an electronic party at Versailles or Monticello or San Simeon, all you had to do was link—if you could get a reservation.

I came back to the bedroom and Comrade stepped up behind me, holding the joysuit. I shrugged into it, velcroed the front seam and eyed myself in the nearest window. He had synthesized some kid-sized armor in the German Gothic style. My favorite. It was made of polished silver, with great fluting and scalloping. He had even programmed a little glow into the image so that on the window I looked like a walking night light. There was an armet helmet with a red ostrich plume; the visor was tipped up so I could see my face. I raised my arm and the joysuit translated the movement to the window so that my armored image waved back.

"Try a few steps," he said.

Although I could move easily in the lightweight joysuit, the motion interpreter made walking in the video armor seem realistically awkward. Comrade had scored the sound effects, too. Metal hinges rasped, chain mail rattled softly, and there was a satisfying *clunk* whenever my foot hit the floor.

"Great." I clenched my fist in approval. I was awake now and in control of my temper. I wanted to make up but Comrade was not taking the hint. I could never quite figure out whether he was just acting like a machine or whether he really did not care how I treated him.

"They're starting." All the windows in the room lit up with Playroom's welcome screen. "You want privacy, so I'm leaving. No one will bother you."

"Hey Comrade, you don't have to go . . ."

But he had already left the room. Playroom prompted me to identify myself. "Mr. Boy," I said, "Department of Identification number 203-966-2445. I'm looking for channel 17; the password is warhead."

A brass band started playing "Hail to the Chief" as the title screen lit the windows:

> The White House
> 1600 Pennsylvania Avenue
> Washington, DC, USA
> copyright 2096, Playroom Presentations
> REPRODUCTION OR REUSE STRICTLY PROHIBITED

and then I was looking at a wraparound view of a VR ballroom. A caption bar opened at the top of the windows and a message scrolled across. *This is the famous East Room, the largest room in the main house. It is used for press conferences, public receptions and entertainments.* I lowered my visor and entered the simulation.

The East Room was decorated in bone white and gold; three chandeliers hung like cut glass mushrooms above the huge parquet floor. A band played skitter at one end of the room but no one was dancing yet. The band was Warhead, according to their drum set. I had never heard of them. Someone's disguise? I turned and the joysuit changed the view on the windows. Just ahead Satan was chatting with a forklift and a rhinoceros. Beyond some blue cartoons were teasing Johnny America. There was not much furniture in the room, a couple of benches, an ugly piano, and some life-sized paintings of George and Martha. George looked like he had just been peeled off a cash card. I stared at him too long and the closed caption bar informed me that the painting had been painted by Gilbert Stuart and was the only White House object dating from the mansion's first occupancy in 1800.

"Hey," I said to a girl who was on fire. "How do I get rid of the plugging tour guide?"

"Can't," she said. "When Playroom found out we were kids they turned on all their educational crap and there's no override. I kind of don't think they want us back."

"Dumbscuts." I scoped the room for something that might be Stennie. No luck. "I like the way your hair is burning." Now that it was too late, I was sorry I had to make idle party chat.

"Thanks." When she tossed her head, sparks flared and crackled. "My mom helped me program it."

"So, I've never been to the White House. Is there more than this?"

"Sure," she said. "We're supposed to have pretty much the whole first floor. Unless they shorted us. You wouldn't be Stone Kinkaid in there, would you?"

"No, not really." Even though the voice was disguised, I could tell this was Happy Lurdane. I edged away from her. "I'm going to check the other rooms now. Later."

"If you run into Stone, tell him I'm looking for him."

I left the East Room and found myself in a long marble passageway with a red carpet. A dog skeleton trotted toward me. Or maybe it was supposed to be a sheep. I waved and went through a door on the other side.

Everyone in the Red Room was standing on the ceiling; I knew I had found Stennie. Even though what they see is only a simulation, most people lock into the perceptual field of a VR as if it were real. Stand on your head long enough—even if only in your imagination—and you get airsick. It took kilohours of practice to learn to compensate. Upside down was one of Stennie's trademark ways of showing off.

The Red Room is an intimate parlor in the American Empire style of 1815–20 . . .

"Hi," I said. I hopped over the wainscotting and walked up the silk-covered wall to join the three of them.

"You're wearing German armor." When the boy in blue grinned at me, his cheeks dimpled. He was wearing shorts and white knee socks, a navy sweater over a white shirt. "Augsburg?" said Little Boy Blue. Fine blond hair drooped from beneath his tweed cap.

"Try Wolf of Landshut," I said. Stennie and I had spent a lot of time fighting VR wars in full armor. "Nice shorts." Stennie's costume reminded me of Christopher Robin. Terminally cute.

"It's not fair," said the snowman, who I did not recognize. "He says this is what he actually looks like." The snowman was standing in a puddle which was dripping onto the rug below us. Great effect.

"No," said Stennie, "what I said was I would look like this if I hadn't done something about it, okay?"

I had not known Stennie before he was a dinosaur. "No wonder you got twanked." I wished I could have saved this image, but Playroom was copy-protected.

"You've been twanked? No joke?" The great horned owl ruffled in alarm. She had a girl's voice. "I know it's none of my business, but I don't understand why anyone would do it. Especially a kid. I mean, what's wrong with good old fashioned surgery? And you can be whoever you want in a VR." She paused, waiting for someone to agree with her. No help. "Okay, so I don't understand. But when you mess with your genes, you change who you are. I mean, don't you like who you are? *I* do."

"We're so happy for you." Stennie scowled. "What is this, mental health week?"

"We're rich," I said. "We can afford to hate ourselves."

"This may sound rude . . ." The owl's big blunt head swiveled from Stennie to me. ". . . but I think that's sad."

"Yeah well, we'll try to work up some tears for you, birdie," Stennie said.

Silence. In the East Room, the band turned the volume up.

"Anyway, I've got to be going." The owl shook herself. "Hanging upside-down is fine for bats, but not for me. Later." She let go of her perch and swooped out into the hall. The snowman turned to watch her go.

"You're driving them off, young man." I patted Stennie on the head. "Come on now, be nice."

"Nice makes me puke."

"You *do* have a bit of an edge tonight." I had trouble imagining this dainty little brat as my best friend. "Better watch out you don't cut someone."

The dog skeleton came to the doorway and called up to us. "We're supposed to dance now."

"About time." Stennie fell off the ceiling like a drop of water and splashed headfirst onto the beige Persian rug. His image went all muddy for a moment and then he re-formed, upright and unharmed. "Going to skitter, tin man?"

"I need to talk to you for a moment," the snowman murmured.

"You *need* to?" I said.

"Dance, dance, dance," sang Stennie. "Later." He swerved after the skeleton out of the room.

The snowman said, "It's about a possible theft of information."

Right then was when I should have slammed it into reverse. Caught up with Stennie or maybe faded from Playroom altogether. But all I did was raise my hands over my head. "You got me, snowman; I confess. But society is to blame, too, isn't it? You will tell the judge to go easy on me? I've had a tough life."

14

"This is serious."

"You're Weldon—what's your name?" Down the hall, I could hear the thud of Warhead's bass line. "Montross."

"I'll come to the point, Peter." The only acknowledgment he made was to drop the kid voice. "The firm I represent provides information security services. Last week someone operated on the protected database of one of our clients. We have reason to believe that a certified photograph was accessed and copied. What can you tell me about this?"

"Not bad, Mr. Montross sir. But if you were as good as you think you are, you'd know my name isn't Peter. It's Mr. Boy. And since nobody invited you to this party, maybe you'd better tell me now why I shouldn't just go ahead and have you deleted?"

"I know that you were undergoing genetic therapy at the time of the theft so you could not have been directly responsible. That's in your favor. However, I also know that you can help me clear this matter up. And you need to do that, son, just as quickly as you can. Otherwise there's big trouble coming."

"What are you going to do, tell my mommy?" My blood started to pump; I was coming back to life.

"This is my offer. It's not negotiable. You let me sweep your files for this image. You turn over any hardcopies you've made and you instruct your wiseguy to let me do a spot reprogramming, during which I will erase his memory of this incident. After that, we'll consider the matter closed."

"Why don't I just drop my pants and bend over while I'm at it?"

"Look, you can pretend if you want, but you're not a kid anymore. You're twenty-five years old. I don't believe for a minute that you're as thick as your friends out there. If you think about it, you'll realize that you can't fight us. The fact that I'm here and I know what I know means that all your personal information systems are already tapped. I'm an op, son. I could wipe your files clean any time and I will, if it comes to that. However, my orders are to be thorough. The only way I can be sure I have everything is if you cooperate."

"You're not even real, are you, Montross? I'll bet you're nothing but cheesy old code. I've talked to elevators with more personality."

"The offer is on the table."

"Stick it!"

The owl flew back into the room, braked with outstretched wings and caught onto the armrest of the Dolley Madison sofa. "Oh, you're still here," she said, noticing us. "I didn't mean to interrupt. . . ."

"Wait there," I said. "I'm coming right down."

"I'll be in touch," said the snowman. "Let me know just as soon as you change your mind." He faded.

I flipped backward off the ceiling and landed in front of her; my video armor rang from the impact. "Owl, you just saved the evening." I knew I was showing off, but just then I was willing to forgive myself. "Thanks."

"You're welcome, I guess." She edged away from me, moving with precise little birdlike steps toward the top of the couch. "But all I was trying to do was escape the band."

"Bad?"

"And loud." Her ear tufts flattened. "Do you think shutting the door would help?"

"Sure. Follow me. We can shut lots of doors." When she hesitated, I flapped my arms like silver wings. Actually, Montross had done me a favor; when he threatened me some inner clock had begun an adrenalin tick. If this was trouble, I wanted more. I felt twisted and dangerous and I did not care what happened next. Maybe that was why the owl flitted after me as I walked into the next room.

The sumptuous State Dining Room can seat about 130 for formal dinners. The white and gold decor dates from the administration of Theodore Roosevelt.

The owl glided over to the banquet table. I shut the door behind me. "Better?" Warhead still pounded on the walls.

"A little." She settled on a huge bronze doré centerpiece with a mirrored surface. "I'm going soon anyway."

"Why?"

"The band stinks, I don't know anyone and I hate these stupid disguises."

"I'm Mr. Boy." I raised my visor and grinned at her. "All right? Now you know someone."

She tucked her wings into place and fixed me with her owlish stare. "I don't like VRs much."

"They take some getting used to."

"Why bother?" she said. "I mean, if anything can happen in a simulation, nothing matters. And I feel dumb standing in a room all alone jumping up and down and flapping my arms. Besides, this joysuit is hot and I'm renting it by the hour."

"The trick is not to look at yourself," I said. "Just watch the screens and use your imagination."

"Reality is less work. You look like a little kid."

"Is that a problem?"

"Mr. Boy? What kind of name is that anyway?"

I wished she would blink. "A made up name. But then all names are made up, aren't they?"

"Didn't I see you at school Wednesday? You were the one who dropped off the dinosaur."

"My friend Stennie." I pulled out a chair and sat facing her. "Who you probably hate because he's twanked."

"That was him on the ceiling, wasn't it? Listen, I'm sorry about what I said. I'm new here. I'd never met anyone like him before I came to New Canaan. I mean, I'd heard of reshaping and all—getting twanked. But where I used to live, everybody was pretty much the same."

"Where was that, Squirrel Crossing, Nebraska?"

"Close." She laughed. "Elkhart; it's in Indiana."

The reckless ticking in my head slowed. Talking to her made it easy to forget about Montross. "You want to leave the party?" I said. "We could go into discreet."

"Just us?" She sounded doubtful. "Right now?"

"Why not? You said you weren't staying. We could get rid of these disguises. And the music."

She was silent for a moment. Maybe people in Elkhart, Indiana, did not ask one another into discreet unless they had met in Sunday school or the Four H Club.

"Okay," she said finally, "but I'll enable. What's your DI?"

I gave her my number.

"Be back in a minute."

I cleared Playroom from my screens. The message *Enabling discreet mode* flashed. I decided not to change out of the joysuit; instead I called up my wardrobe menu and chose an image of myself wearing black baggies. The loose folds and padded shoulders helped hide the scrawny little boy's body.

The message changed. *Discreet mode enabled. Do you accept, yes/no?*

"Sure," I said.

She was sitting naked in the middle of a room filled with tropical plants. Her skin was the color of cinnamon. She had freckles on her shoulders and across her breasts. Her hair tumbled down the curve of her spine; the ends glowed like embers in a breeze. She clutched her legs close to her and gave me a curious smile. Teenage still life. We were alone and secure. No one could tap us while we were in discreet. We could say anything we wanted. I was too croggled to speak.

"You *are* a little kid," she said.

I did not tell her that what she was watching was an enhanced image, a virtual me. "Uh . . . well, not really." I was glad Stennie could not see me. Mr. Boy at a loss—a first. "Sometimes I'm not sure what I am. I guess you're not going to like me either. I've been stunted a couple of times. I'm really twenty-five years old."

She frowned. "You keep deciding I won't like people. Why?"

"Most people are against genetic surgery. Probably because they haven't got the money."

"Myself, I wouldn't do it. Still, just because you did doesn't mean I hate you." She gestured for me to sit. "But my parents would probably be horrified. They're realists, you know."

"No fooling?" I could not help but chuckle. "That explains a lot." Like why she had an attitude about twanking. And why she thought VRs were dumb. And why she was naked and did not seem to care. According to hard-core realists, first came clothes, then jewelry, fashion, makeup, plastic surgery, skin tints, and *hey jack*, here we are up to our eyeballs in the delusions of 2096. Gene twanking, VR addicts, people downloading themselves into computers—better never to have started. They wanted to turn back to worn-out twentieth century modes. "But you're no realist," I said. "Look at your hair."

She shook her head and the ends twinkled. "You like it?"

"It's extreme. But realists don't decorate!"

"Then maybe I'm not a realist. My parents let me try lots of stuff they wouldn't do themselves, like buying hairworks or linking to VRs. They're afraid I'd leave otherwise."

"Would you?"

She shrugged. "So what's it like to get stunted? I've heard it hurts."

I told her how sometimes I felt as if there were broken glass in my joints and how my bones ached and—more showing off—about the blood I would find on the toilet paper. Then I mentioned something about Mom. She had heard of Mom, of course. She asked about my dad and I explained how Mom paid him to stay away but that he kept running out of money. She wanted to know if I was working or still going to school and I made up some stuff about courses in history I was taking from Yale. Actually I had faded after my first semester. Couple of years ago. I did not have time to link to some boring college; I was too busy playing with Comrade and Stennie. But I still had an account at Yale.

"So that's who I am." I was amazed at how little I had lied. "Who are you?"

She told me that her name was Treemonisha but her friends called her Tree. It was an old family name; her great-great-grandsomething-or-other had been a composer named Scott Joplin. Treemonisha was the name of his opera.

I had to force myself not to stare at her breasts when she talked. "You like *opera*?" I said.

"My dad says I'll grow into it." She made a face. "I hope not."

The Joplins were a franchise family; her mom and dad had just been transferred to the Green Dream, a plant shop in the Elm Street Mall. To hear her talk, you would think she had ordered them from the Good Fairy.

They had been married for twenty-two years and were still together. She had a brother, Fidel, who was twelve. They all lived in the greenhouse next to the shop where they grew most of their food and where flowers were always in bloom and where everybody loved everyone else. Nice life for a bunch of mall drones. So why was she thinking of leaving?

"You should stop by sometime," she said.

"Sometime," I said. "Sure."

For hours after we faded, I kept remembering things about her I had not realized I had noticed. The fine hair on her legs. The curve of her eyebrows. The way her hands moved when she was excited.

It was Stennie's fault: after the Playroom party he started going to school almost every day. Not just linking to E-class with his comm, but actually showing up. We knew he had more than remedial reading on his mind, but no matter how much we teased, he would not talk about his mysterious new cush. Before he fell in love we used to joyride in his Alpha afternoons. Now Comrade and I had the car all to ourselves. Not as much fun.

We had already dropped Stennie off when I spotted Treemonisha waiting for the bus. I waved, she came over. The next thing I knew we had another passenger on the road to nowhere. Comrade stared vacantly out the window as we pulled onto South Street; he did not seem pleased with the company.

"Have you been out to the reservoir?" I said. "There are some extreme houses out there. Or we could drive over to Greenwich and look at yachts."

"I haven't been anywhere yet, so I don't care," she said. "By the way, you don't go to college." She was not accusing me or even asking—merely stating a fact.

"Why do you say that?" I said.

"Fidel told me."

I wondered how her twelve year old brother could know anything at all about me. Rumors maybe, or just guessing. Since she did not seem mad, I decided to tell the truth.

"He's right," I said, "I lied. I have an account at Yale but I haven't linked for months. Hey, you can't live without telling a few lies. At least I don't discriminate. I'll lie to anyone, even myself."

"You're bad." A smile twitched at the corners of her mouth. "So what *do* you do then?"

"I drive around a lot." I waved at the interior of Stennie's car. "Let's see . . . I go to parties. I buy stuff and use it."

"Fidel says you're rich."

"I'm going to have to meet this Fidel. Does money make a difference?"

When she nodded, her hairworks twinkled. Comrade gave me a knowing glance but I paid no attention. I was trying to figure out how she could make insults sound like compliments when I realized we were flirting. The idea took me by surprise. *Flirting.*

"Do you have any music?" Treemonisha said.

The Alpha asked what groups she liked and so we listened to some mindless dance hits as we took the circle route around the Laurel Reservoir. Treemonisha told me about how she was sick of her parents' store and rude customers and especially the dumb Green Dream uniform. "Back in Elkhart, Daddy used to make me wear it to school. Can you believe that? He said it was good advertising. When we moved, I told him either the khakis went or I did."

She had a yellow and orange dashiki over midnight blue skintights. "I like your clothes," I said. "You have taste."

"Thanks." She bobbed her head in time to the music. "I can't afford much because I can't get an outside job because I have to work for my parents. It makes me mad, sometimes. I mean, franchise life is fine for Mom and Dad; they're happy being tucked in every night by GD, Inc. But I want more. Thrills, chills—you know, adventure. No one has adventures in the mall."

As we drove, I showed her the log castle, the pyramids, the private train that pulled sleeping cars endlessly around a two mile track and the marble bunker where Sullivan, the assassinated president, still lived on in computer memory. Comrade kept busy acting bored.

"Can we go see your mom?" said Treemonisha. "All the kids at school tell me she's awesome."

Suddenly Comrade was interested in the conversation. I was not sure what the kids at school were talking about. Probably they wished they had seen Mom but I had never asked any of them over—except for Stennie.

"Not a good idea." I shook my head. "She's more flimsy than she looks, you know, and she gets real nervous if strangers just drop by. Or even friends."

"I just want to look. I won't get out of the car."

"Well," said Comrade, "if she doesn't get out of the car, who could she hurt?"

I scowled at him. He knew how paranoid Mom was. She was not going to like Treemonisha anyway, but certainly not if I brought her home without warning. "Let me work on her, okay?" I said to Treemonisha. "One of these days. I promise."

She pouted for about five seconds and then laughed at my expression. When I saw Comrade's smirk, I got angry. He was just sitting there watching us. Looking to cause trouble. Later there would be wisecracks. I had had about enough of him and his attitude.

By that time the Alpha was heading up High Ridge Road toward Stamford.

"I'm hungry," I said. "Stop at the 7-11 up ahead." I pulled a cash card out and flipped it at him. "Go buy us some doboys."

I waited until he disappeared into the store and then ordered Stennie's car to drive on.

"Hey!" Treemonisha twisted in her seat and looked back at the store. "What are you doing?"

"Ditching him."

"Why? Won't he be mad?"

"He's got my card; he'll call a cab."

"But that's mean."

"So?"

Treemonisha thought about it. "He doesn't say much, does he?" She did not seem to know what to make of me—which I suppose was what I wanted. "At first I thought he was kind of like your teddy bear. Have you seen those big ones that keep little kids out of trouble?"

"He's just a wiseguy."

"Have you had him long?"

"Maybe too long."

I could not think of anything to say after that so we sat quietly listening to the music. Even though he was gone, Comrade was still aggravating me.

"Were you really hungry?" Treemonisha said finally. "Because I was. Think there's something in the fridge?"

I waited for the Alpha to tell us but it said nothing. I slid across the seat and opened the refrigerator door. Inside was a sheet of paper. "Dear Mr. Boy," it said. "If this was a bomb you and Comrade would be dead and the problem would be solved. Let's talk soon. Weldon Montross."

"What's that?"

I felt the warm flush that I always got from good corpse porn and for a moment I could not speak. "Practical joke," I said, crumpling the paper. "Too bad he doesn't have a sense of humor."

Push-ups. *Ten, eleven.*

"Uh-oh. Look at this," said Comrade.

"I'm busy!" *Twelve, thirteen, fourteen, fifteen . . . sixteen . . . seven. . . .* Dizzy, I slumped and rested my cheek against the warm floor. I could feel Mom's pulse beneath the tough skin. It was no good. I would never get muscles this way. There was only one fix for my skinny arms and bony shoulders. Grow up, Mr. Boy.

"*Ya yebou!* You really should scope this," said Comrade. "Very spooky."

I pulled myself onto the bed to see why he was bothering me; he had been pretty tame since I had stranded him at the 7-11. Most of the windows showed the usual: army ants next to old war movies next to feeding time

21

from the Bronx Zoo's reptile house. But Firenet, which provided twenty-four hour coverage of killer fires from around the world, had been replaced with a picture of a morgue. There were three naked bodies, shrouds pulled back for identification: a fat gray-haired CEO with a purple hole over his left eye, Comrade, and me.

"You look kind of dead," said Comrade.

My tongue felt thick. "Where's it coming from?"

"Viruses all over the system," he said. "Probably Montross."

"You know about him?" The image on the window changed back to a *barridas* fire in Lima.

"He's been in touch." Comrade shrugged. "Made his offer."

Crying women watched as the straw walls of their huts peeled into flame and floated away.

"Oh." I did not know what to say. I wanted to reassure him, but this was serious. Montross was invading my life and I had no idea how to fight back. "Well, don't talk to him anymore."

"Okay." Comrade grinned. "He's dull as a spoon anyway."

"I bet he's a simulation. What else would a company like Datasafe use? You can't trust real people." I was still thinking about what I would look like dead. "Whatever, he's kind of scary." I shivered, worried and aroused at the same time. "He's slick enough to operate on Playroom. And now he's hijacking windows right here in my own mom." I should probably have told Comrade then about the note in the fridge, but we were still not talking about that day.

"He tapped into Playroom?" Comrade fitted input clips to the spikes on his neck, linked and played back the house files. "*Zayebees.* He was already here then. He piggybacked on with you." Comrade slapped his leg. "I can't understand how he beat my security so easily."

The roombrain flicked the message indicator. "Stennie's calling," it said.

"Pick up," I said.

"Hi, it's that time again." Stennie was alone in his car. "I'm on my way over to give you jacks a thrill." He pushed his triangular snout up to the camera and licked at the lens. "Doing anything?"

"Not really. Sitting around."

"I'll fix that. Five minutes." He faded.

Comrade was staring at nothing.

"Look Comrade, you did your best," I said. "I'm not mad at you."

"Too plugging easy." He shook his head as if I had missed the point.

"What I don't understand is why Montross is so cranky anyway. It's just a picture of meat."

"Maybe he's not really dead."

"Sure he is," I said. "You can't fake a verification grid."

"No, but you can fake a corpse."

"You know something?"

"If I did I wouldn't tell you," said Comrade. "You have enough problems already. Like how do we explain this to your mom?"

"We don't. Not yet. Let's wait him out. Sooner or later he's got to realize that we're not going to use his picture for anything. I mean if he's that nervous, I'll even give it back. I don't care anymore. You hear that Montross, you dumbscut? We're harmless. Get out of our lives!"

"It's more than the picture now," said Comrade. "It's me. I found the way in." He was careful to keep his expression blank.

I did not know what to say to him. No way Montross would be satisfied erasing only the memory of the operation. He would probably reconnect Comrade's regulators to bring him back under control. Turn him to pudding. He would be just another wiseguy, like anyone else could own. I was surprised that Comrade did not ask me to promise not to hand him over. Maybe he just assumed I would stand by him.

We did not hear Stennie coming until he sprang into the room.

"Have fun or die!" He was clutching a plastic gun in his spindly hand which he aimed at my head.

"Stennie, *no*."

He fired as I rolled across the bed. The jellybee buzzed by me and squished against one of the windows. It was a purple and immediately I smelled the tang of artificial grape flavor. The splatter on the wrinkled wall pulsed and split in two, emitting a second burst of grapeness. The two halves oozed in opposite directions, shivered and divided again.

"Fun extremist!" He shot Comrade with a cherry as he dove for the closet. "Dance!"

I bounced up and down on the bed, timing my move. He fired a green at me that missed. Comrade, meanwhile, gathered himself up as zits of red jellybee squirmed across his window coat. He barreled out of the closet into Stennie, knocking him sideways. I sprang on top of them and wrestled the gun away. Stennie was paralyzed with laughter. I had to giggle too, in part because now I could put off talking to Comrade about Montross.

By the time we untangled ourselves, the jellybees had faded. "Set for twelve generations before they all die out," Stennie said as he settled himself on the bed. "So what's this my car tells me, you've been giving free rides? Is this the cush with the name?"

"None of your business. You never tell me about your cush."

"Okay. Her name is Janet Hoyt."

"Is it?" He caught me off guard again. Twice in one day, a record. "Comrade, let's see this prize."

Comrade linked to the roombrain and ran a search. "Got her." He called Janet Hoyt's DI file to screen and her face ballooned across an entire window.

She was a tanned blue-eyed blonde with the kind of off-the-shelf looks that med students slapped onto rabbits in genoplasty courses. Nothing on her face said she was different from any other ornamental moron fresh from the OR—not a dimple or a mole, not even a freckle. "You're ditching me for her?" It took all the imagination of a potato chip to be as pretty as Janet Hoyt. "Stennie, she's generic."

"Now wait a minute," said Stennie. "If we're going to play critic, let's scope your cush, too."

Without asking, Comrade put Tree's DI photo next to Janet's. I realized he was still mad at me because of her; he was only pretending not to care. "She's not my cush," I said, but no one was listening.

Stennie leered at her for a moment. "She's a stiff, isn't she?" he said. "She has that hungry look."

Seeing him standing there in front of the two huge faces on the wall, I felt like I was peeping on a stranger—that I was a stranger, too. I could not imagine how the two of us had come to this: Stennie and Mr. Boy with cushes. We were growing up. A frightening thought. Maybe next Stennie would get himself untwanked and really look like he had on Playroom. Then where would I be?

"Janet wants me to plug her," Stennie said.

"Right, and I'm the queen of Brooklyn."

"I'm old enough, you know." He thumped his tail against the floor.

"You're a dinosaur!"

"Hey, just because I got twanked doesn't mean *my* dick fell off."

"So do it then."

"I'm going to. I will, okay? But . . . this is no good." Stennie waved impatiently at Comrade. "I can't think with them watching me." He nodded at the windows. "Turn them off already."

"*N'ye pizdi!*" Comrade wiped the two faces from the windows, cleared all the screens in the room to blood red, yanked the input clips from his neck spikes and left them dangling from the roombrain's terminal. His expression empty, he walked from the room without asking permission or saying anything at all.

"What's his problem?" Stennie said.

"Who knows?" Comrade had left the door open; I shut it. "Maybe he doesn't like girls."

"Look, I want to ask a favor." I could tell Stennie was nervous; his head kept swaying. "This is kind of embarrassing but . . . okay, do you think maybe your mom would maybe let me practice on her lovers? I don't want

24

Janet to know I've never done it before and there's some stuff I've got to figure out."

"I don't know," I said. "Ask her."

But I did know. She would be amused.

People claimed my mom did not have a sense of humor. Lovey was huge, an ocean of a woman. Her umbilical was as big around as my thigh. When she walked waves of flesh heaved and rolled. She had beautiful skin, flawless and moist. It did not take much to make her sweat. Peeling a banana would do it. Lovey was as oral as a baby; she would put anything into her mouth. And when she did not have a mouthful, she would babble on about whatever came into Mom's head. Dear hardly ever talked, although he could moan and growl and laugh. He touched Lovey whenever he could and shot her long smouldering looks. He was not furry, exactly, but he was covered with fine silver hair. Dear was a little guy, about my size. Although he had one of Upjohn's finest penises, elastic and overloaded with neurons, he was one of the least convincing males I had ever met. I doubt Mom herself believed in him all that much.

Big chatty woman, squirrelly tongue-tied little man. It *was* funny in a bent sort of way to watch the two of them go at each other. Kind of like a tug churning against a supertanker. They did not get the chance that often. It was dangerous; Dear had to worry about getting crushed and poor Lovey's heart had stopped two or three times. Besides, I think Mom liked building up the pressure. Sometimes, as the days without sex stretched, you could almost feel lust sparkling off them like static electricity.

That was how they were when I brought Stennie up. Their suite took up the entire floor at the hips, Mom's widest part. Lovey was lolling in a tub of warm oil. She liked it flowery and laced with pheromones. Dear was prowling around her with a desperate expression, like he might jam his plug into a wall socket if he did not get taken care of soon. Stennie's timing was perfect.

"Look who's come to visit, Dear," said Lovey. "Peter and Stennie. How nice of you boys to stop by." She let Dear mop her forehead with a towel. "What can we do for you?"

The skin under Stennie's jaw quivered. He glanced at me, then at Dear and then at the thick red lips that served as the bathroom door. Never even looked at her. He was losing his nerve.

"Oh my, isn't this exciting, Dear? There's something going on." She sank into the bath until her chin touched the water. "It's a secret, isn't it, Peter? Share it with Lovey."

"No secret," I said, "he wants to ask a favor." And then I told her.

She giggled and sat up. "I love it." Honey-colored oil ran from her hair and slopped between her breasts. "Were you thinking of both of us, Stennie? Or just me?"

"Well, I . . ." Stennie's tail switched. "Maybe we just ought to forget it."

"No, no." She waved a hand at him. "Come here, Stennie. Come close, my pretty little monster."

He hesitated, then approached the tub. She reached for his right leg and touched him just above the heelknob. "You know, I've always wondered what scales would feel like." Her hand climbed; the oil made his yellow hide glisten. His eyes were the size of eggs.

The bedroom was all mattress. Beneath the transparent skin was a screen implant, so that Mom could project images not only on the walls but on the surface of the bed itself. Under the window was a layer of heavily vascular flesh, which could be stiffened with blood or drained until it was as soft as raw steak. A window dome arched over everything and could show slo-mo or thermographic fx across its span. The air was warm and wet and smelled like a chemical engineer's idea of a rose garden.

I settled by the lips. Dear ghosted along the edges of the room, dragging his umbilical like a chain, never coming quite near enough to touch anyone. I heard him humming as he passed me, a low moaning singsong, as if to block out what was happening. Stennie and Lovey were too busy with each other to care. As Lovey knelt in front of Stennie, Dear gave a mocking laugh. I did not understand how he could be jealous. He was with her, part of it. Lovey and Dear were Mom's remotes, two nodes of her nervous system. Yet his pain was as obvious as her pleasure. At last he squatted and rocked back and forth on his heels. I glanced up at the fx dome; yellow scales slid across oily rolls of flushed skin.

I yawned. I had always found sex kind of dull. Besides, this was all on the record. I could have Comrade replay it for me any time. Lovey stopped breathing—then came four or five shuddering gasps in a row. I wondered where Comrade had gone. I felt sorry for him. Stennie said something to her about rolling over. "Okay?" Feathery skin sounds. A grunt. The soft wet slap of flesh against flesh. I thought of my mother's brain, up there in the head where no one ever went. I had no idea how much attention she was paying. Was she quivering with Lovey and at the same time calculating insolation rates on her chloroplasts? Investing in soy futures on the Chicago Board of Trade? Fending off Weldon Montross's latest attack? *Plug Montross.* I needed to think about something fun. My collection. I started piling bodies up in my mind. The hangings and the open casket funerals and the stacks of dead at the camps and all those muddy soldiers. I shivered as I remembered the empty rigid faces. I liked it when their teeth showed. "Oh, oh, *oh!*" My greatest hits dated from the late twentieth century. The dead were everywhere back then, in vids and the news and even on T-shirts. They were not shy. That was what made Comrade's photo worth having; it was hard to find modern stuff that dirty. Dear brushed by me, his erection bobbing in front of him. It was as big around as my wrist. As he passed I could see Stennie's leg scratch across the mattress skin, which glowed with blood blue light. Lovey giggled beneath him and her umbilical twitched and suddenly I found myself wondering whether Tree was a virgin.

I came into the mall through the Main Street entrance and hopped the westbound slidewalk headed up Elm Street toward the train station. If I caught the 3:36 to Grand Central, I could eat dinner in Manhattan, far from my problems with Montross and Comrade. Running away had always worked for me before. Let someone else clean up the mess while I was gone.

The slidewalk carried me past a real estate agency, a flash bar, a jewelry store and a Baskin-Robbins. I thought about where I wanted to go after New York. San Francisco? Montreal? Maybe I should try Elkhart, Indiana—no one would think to look for me there. Just ahead, between a drugstore and a take-out Russian restaurant, was the wiseguy dealership where Mom had bought Comrade.

I did not want to think about Comrade waiting for me to come home, so I stepped into the drugstore and bought a dose of Carefree for $4.29. Normally I did not bother with drugs. I had been stunted; no over-the-counter flash could compare to that. But the propyl dicarbamates were all right. I fished the cash card out of my pocket and handed it to the stiff behind the counter. He did a doubletake when he saw the denomination, then carefully inserted the card into the reader to deduct the cost of the Carefree. It had my mom's name on it; he must have expected it would trip some alarm for counterfeit plastic or stolen credit. He stared at me for a moment, as if trying to remember my face so he could describe me to a cop, and then gave the cash card back. The denomination readout said it was still good for $16,381.18.

I picked out a bench in front of a specialty shop called The Happy Hippo, hiked up my shorts and poked Carefree into the widest part of my thigh. I took a short dreamy swim in the sea of tranquility and when I came back to myself, my guilt had been washed away. But so had my energy. I sat for a while and scoped the display of glass hippos and plastic hippos and fuzzy stuffed hippos, hippo vids and sheets and candles. Down the bench from me a homeless woman dozed. It was still pretty early in the season for a weather gypsy to have come this far north. She wore red shorts and droopy red socks with plastic sandals and four long-sleeved shirts, all unbuttoned, over a Funny Honey halter top. Her hair needed vacuuming and she smelled old. All grownups smelled that way to me; it was something I had never gotten used to. No perfume or deodorant could cover up the leathery stink

27

of adulthood. Kids could smell bad, too, but usually from something they got on them. It did not come from a rotting body. I rubbed a finger in the dampness under my arm, slicked it and sniffed. There was a sweetness to kid sweat. I touched the drying finger to my tongue. You could even taste it. If I gave up getting stunted, stopped being Mr. Boy, I would smell like the woman at the end of the bench. I would start to die. I had never understood how grownups could live with that.

The gypsy woke up, stretched and smiled at me with gummy teeth. "You left Comrade behind?" she said.

I was startled. "What did you say?"

"You know what this is?" She twitched her sleeve and a penlight appeared in her hand.

My throat tightened. "I know what it looks like."

She gave me a wicked smile, aimed the penlight and burned a pinhole through the bench a few centimeters from my leg. "Maybe I could interest you in some free laser surgery?"

I could smell scorched plastic. "You're going to needle me here, in the middle of the Elm Street Mall?" I thought she was bluffing. Probably. I hoped.

"If that's the way you want it. Mr. Montross wants to know when you're delivering the wiseguy to us."

"Get away from me."

"Not until you do what needs to be done."

When I saw Happy Lurdane come out of The Happy Hippo, I waved. A desperation move, but then it was easy to be brave with a head full of Carefree.

"Mr. Boy." She veered over to us. "Hi!"

I scooted farther down the bench to make room for her between me and the gypsy. I knew she would stay to chat. Happy Lurdane was one of those chirpy lightweights who seemed to want lots of friends but did not really try to be one. We tolerated her because she did not mind being snubbed and she threw great parties.

"Where have you been?" She settled beside me. "Haven't seen you in ages." The penlight disappeared and the gypsy fell back into drowsy character.

"Around."

"Want to see what I just bought?"

I nodded. My heart was hammering.

She opened the bag and took out a fist-sized bundle covered with shipping plastic. She unwrapped a statue of a blue hippopotamus. "Be careful." She handed it to me.

"Cute." The hippo had crude flower designs drawn on its body; it was chipped and cracked.

"Ancient Egyptian. That means it's even *before* antique." She pulled a slip from the bag and read. "Twelfth Dynasty, 1991–1786 BC. Can you believe you can just buy something like that here in the mall? I mean it must be like a thousand years old or something."

"Try four thousand."

"No wonder it cost so much. He wasn't going to sell it to me, so I had to spend some of next month's allowance." She took it from me and re-wrapped it. "It's for the smash party tomorrow. You're coming, aren't you?"

"Maybe."

"Is something wrong?"

I ignored that.

"Hey, where's Comrade? I don't think I've ever seen you two apart before."

I decided to take a chance. "Want to get some doboys?"

"*Sure.*" She glanced at me with delighted astonishment. "Are you sure you're all right?"

I took her arm, maneuvering to keep her between me and the gypsy. If Happy got needled it would be no great loss to western civilization. She babbled on about her party as we stepped onto the westbound slidewalk. I turned to look back. The gypsy waved as she hopped the eastbound.

"Look Happy," I said, "I'm sorry, but I changed my mind. Later, okay?"

"But . . ."

I did not stop for an argument. I darted off the slidewalk and sprinted through the mall to the station. I went straight to a ticket window, shoved the cash card under the grille and asked the agent for a one way to Grand Central. Forty thousand people lived in New Canaan; most of them had heard of me because of my mom. Nine million strangers jammed New York City; it was a good place to disappear. The agent had my ticket in her hand when the reader beeped and spat the card out.

"No!" I slammed my fist on the counter. "Try it again." The cash card was guaranteed by AmEx to be secure. And it had just worked at the drug-store.

She glanced at the card, then slid it back under the grille. "No use." The denomination readout flashed alternating messages: *Voided* and *Bank recall.* "You've got trouble, son."

She was right. As I left the station, I felt the Carefree struggle one last time with my dread—and lose. I did not even have the money to call home. I wandered around for a while, dazed, and then I was standing in front of the flower shop in the Elm Street Mall.

Green Dream
Contemporary and Conventional Plants

I had telelinked with Tree every day since our drive and every day she had asked me over. But I was not ready to meet her family; I suppose I was still trying to pretend she was not a stiff. I wavered at the door now, breathing the cool scent of damp soil in clay pots. The gypsy could come after me again; I might be putting these people in danger. Using Happy as a shield was one thing, but I liked Tree. A lot. I backed away and peered through a window fringed with sweat and teeming with bizarre plants with flame-colored tongues. Someone wearing khaki moved. I could not tell if it was Tree or not. I thought of what she had said about no one having adventures in the mall.

The front of the showroom was a green cave, darker than I had expected. Baskets dripping with bright flowers hung like stalactites; leathery-leaved understory plants formed stalagmites. As I threaded my way toward the back I came upon the kid I had seen wearing the Green Dream uniform, a khaki nightmare of pleats and flaps and brass buttons and about six too many pockets. He was misting leaves with a pump bottle filled with blue liquid. I decided he must be the brother.

"Hi," I said. "I'm looking for Treemonisha."

Fidel was shorter than me and darker than his sister. He had a wiry plush of beautiful black hair that I was immediately tempted to touch.

"Are you?" He eyed me as if deciding how hard I would be to beat up, then he smiled. He had crooked teeth. "You don't look like yourself."

"No?"

"What are you, scared? You're whiter than rice, cashman. Don't worry, the stiffs won't hurt you." Laughing, he feinted a punch at my arm; I was not reassured.

"You're Fidel."

"I've seen your DI files," he said. "I asked around, I know about you. So don't be telling my sister any more lies, understand?" He snapped his fingers in my face. "Behave yourself, cashman, and we'll be fine." He still had the boyish excitability I had lost after the first stunting. "She's out back, so first you have to get by the old man."

The rear of the store was brighter; sunlight streamed through the clear krylac roof. There was a counter and behind it a glass-doored refrigerator filled with cut flowers. A side entrance opened to the greenhouse. Mrs. Schlieman, one of Mom's lawyers who had an office in the mall, was deciding what to buy. She was shopping with her wiseguy secretary, who looked like he had just stepped out of a vodka ad.

"Wait." Fidel rested a hand on my shoulder. "I'll tell her you're here."

"But how long will they last?" Mrs. Schlieman sniffed a frilly yellow flower. "I should probably get the duraroses."

"Whatever you want, Mrs. Schlieman. Duraroses are a good product, I sell them by the truckload," said Mr. Joplin with a chuckle. "But these carnations are real flowers, raised here in my greenhouse. So maybe you can't stick them in your dishwasher, but put some where people can touch and smell them and I guarantee you'll get compliments."

"Why Peter Cage," said Mrs. Schlieman. "Is that you? I haven't seen you since the picnic. How's your mother?" She did not introduce her wiseguy.

"Extreme," I said.

She nodded absently. "That's nice. All right then, Mr. Joplin, give me a dozen of your carnations—and two dozen yellow duraroses."

Mrs. Schlieman chatted politely at me while Tree's father wrapped the order. He was a short, rumpled, balding man who smiled too much. He seemed to like wearing the corporate uniform. Anyone else would have fixed the hair and the wrinkles. Not Mr. Joplin; he was a museum-quality throwback. As he took Mrs. Schlieman's cash card from the wiseguy, he beamed at me over his glasses. Glasses!

When Mrs. Schlieman left, so did the smile. "Peter Cage?" he said. "Is that your name?"

"Mr. Boy is my name, sir."

"You're Tree's new friend." He nodded. "She's told us about you. She's doing chores just now. You know, we have to work for a living here."

Sure, and I knew what he left unsaid: *unlike you, you spoiled little freak.* It was always the same with these stiffs. I walked in the door and already they hated me. At least he was not pretending, like Mrs. Schlieman. I gave him two points for honesty and kept my mouth shut.

"What is it you want here, Peter?"

"Nothing, sir." If he was going to "Peter" me, I was going to "sir" him right back. "I just stopped by to say hello. Treemonisha did invite me, sir, but if you'd rather I left . . ."

"No, no. Tree warned us you might come."

She and Fidel raced into the room as if they were afraid their father and I would already be at each other's throats. "Oh hi, Mr. Boy," she said.

Her father snorted at the sound of my name.

"Hi." I grinned at her. It was the easiest thing I had done that day.

She was wearing her uniform. When she saw that I had noticed, she blushed. "Well, you asked for it." She tugged self-consciously at the waist of her fatigues. "You want to come in?"

"Just a minute." Mr. Joplin stepped in front of the door, blocking our escape. "You finished E-class?"

"Yes."

"Checked the flats?"

"I'm almost done."

"After that you'd better pick some dinner and get it started. Your mama called and said she wouldn't be home until six-fifteen."

"Sure."

"And you'll take orders for me on line two?"

She leaned against the counter and sighed. "Do I have a choice?"

He backed away and waved us through. "Sorry, sweetheart. I don't know how we would get along without you." He caught her brother by the shirt. "Not you, Fidel. You're misting, remember?"

A short tunnel ran from their mall storefront to the rehabbed furniture warehouse built over the Amtrak rails. Green Dream had installed a krylac roof and fans and a grolighting system; the Joplins squeezed themselves into the leftover spaces not filled with inventory. The air in the greenhouse was heavy and warm and it smelled like rain. No walls, no privacy other than that provided by the plants.

"Here's where I sleep." Tree sat on her unmade bed. Her space was formed by a cinder block wall painted yellow and a screen of palms. "Chinese fan, bamboo, lady, date, kentia," she said, naming them for me like they were her pets. "I grow them myself for spending money." Her school-comm was on top of her dresser. Several drawers hung open; pink skintights trailed from one. Clothes were scattered like piles of leaves across the floor. "I guess I'm kind of a slob," she said as she stripped off the uniform, wadded it and then banked it off the dresser into the top drawer. I could see her bare back in the mirror plastic taped to the wall. "Take your things off if you want."

I hesitated.

"Or not. But it's kind of muggy to stay dressed. You'll sweat."

I unvelcroed my shirt. I did not mind at all seeing Tree without clothes. But I did not undress for anyone except the stiffs at the clinic. I stepped out of my pants. Being naked somehow had got connected with being helpless. I had this puckery feeling in my dick, like it was going to curl up and die. I could imagine the gypsy popping out from behind a palm and laughing at me. No, I was not going to think about *that*. Not here.

"Comfortable?" said Tree.

"Sure." My voice was turning to dust in my throat. "Do all Green Dream employees run around the back room in the nude?"

"I doubt it." She smiled as if the thought tickled her. "We're not exactly your average mall drones. Come help me finish the chores."

I was glad to let her lead so that she was not looking at me, although I could still watch her. I was fascinated by the sweep of her buttocks, the curve of her spine. She strolled, flatfooted and at ease, through her private jungle. At first I scuttled along on the balls of my feet, ready to dart behind a plant if anyone came. But after a while I decided to stop being so skittish. I realized I would probably survive being naked.

Tree stopped in front of a workbench covered with potted seedlings in plastic trays and picked up a hose from the floor.

"What's this stuff?" I kept to the opposite side of the bench, using it to cover myself.

"Greens." She lifted a seedling to check the water level in the tray beneath.

"What are greens?"

"It's too boring." She squirted some water in and replaced the seedling.

"Tell me, I'm interested."

"In greens? You liar." She glanced at me and shook her head. "Okay." She pointed as she said the names. "Lettuce, spinach, pak choi, chard, kale, rocket—got that? And a few tomatoes over there. Peppers, too. GD is trying to break into the food business. They think people will grow more of their own if they find out how easy it is."

"Is it?"

"Greens are." She inspected the next tray. "Just add water."

"Yeah, sure."

"It's because they've been photosynthetically enhanced. Bigger leaves arranged better, low respiration rates. They teach us this stuff at GD Family Camp. It's what we do instead of vacation." She squashed something between her thumb and forefinger. "They mix all these bacteria that make their own fertilizer into the soil—fix nitrogen right out of the air. And then there's this other stuff that sticks to the roots, rhizobacteria and mycorrhizae." She finished the last tray and coiled the hose. "These flats will produce under candlelight in a closet. Bored yet?"

"How do they taste?"

"Pretty bland, most of them. Some stink, like kale and rocket. But we have to eat them for the good of the corporation." She stuck her tongue out. "You want to stay for dinner?"

Mrs. Joplin made me call home before she would feed me; she refused to understand that my mom did not care. So I linked, asked Mom to send a car to the back door at eight-thirty, and faded. No time to discuss the missing sixteen thousand.

Dinner was from the cookbook Tree had been issued at camp: a bowl of cold bean soup, fresh corn bread, and chard and cheese loaf. She let me help her make it, even though I had never cooked before. I was amazed at how simple corn bread was. Six ingredients: flour, corn meal, baking powder, milk, oil, and ovobinder. Mix and pour into a greased pan. Bake 20 minutes at 220 Celsius and serve! There is nothing magic or even very mysterious about homemade corn bread, except for the way its smell held me spellbound.

Supper was the Joplins' daily meal together. They ate in front of security windows near the tunnel to the store; when a customer came, someone ran out front. According to contract, they had to stay open twenty-four hours a day. Many of the suburban malls had gone to all-night operation; the competition from New York City was deadly. Mr. Joplin stood duty most of the time, but since they were a franchise family everybody took turns. Even Mrs. Joplin, who also worked part-time as a factfinder at the mall's DataStop.

Tree's mother was plump and graying and she had a smile that was almost bright enough to distract me from her naked body. She seemed harmless, except that she knew how to ask questions. After all, her job was finding out stuff for DataStop customers. She had this way of locking onto you as you talked; the longer the conversation, the greater her intensity. It was hard to lie to her. Normally that kind of aggressiveness in grownups made me jumpy.

No doubt she had run a search on me; I wondered just what she had turned up. Factfinders had to obey the law, so they only accessed public domain information—unlike Comrade, who would cheerfully operate on whatever I set him to. The Joplins' bank records, for instance. I knew that Mrs. Joplin had made about $11,000 last year at the Infomat in the Elkhart Mall, that the family borrowed $135,000 at 9.78 percent interest to move to their new franchise and that they lost $213 in their first two months in New Canaan.

I kept my research a secret, of course, and they acted innocent, too. I let them pump me about Mom as we ate. I was used to being asked; after all, Mom was famous. Fidel wanted to know how much it had cost her to get twanked, how big she was, what she looked like on the inside and what she ate, if she got cold in the winter. Stuff like that. The others asked more personal questions. Tree wondered if Mom ever got lonely and whether she was going to be the Statue of Liberty for the rest of her life. Mrs. Joplin was interested in Mom's remotes, of all things. Which ones I got along with, which ones I could not stand, whether I thought any of them was really her. Mr. Joplin asked if she liked being what she was. How was I supposed to know?

After dinner, I helped Fidel clear the table. While we were alone in the kitchen, he complained. "You think they eat this shit at GD headquarters?" He scraped his untouched chard loaf into the composter.

"I kind of liked the corn bread."

"If only he'd buy meat once in a while, but he's too cheap. Or doboys. Tree says you bought her doboys."

I told him to skip school some time and we would go out for lunch; he thought that was a great idea.

When we came back out, Mr. Joplin actually smiled at me. He had been losing his edge all during dinner. Maybe chard agreed with him. He pulled a pipe from his pocket, began stuffing something into it and asked me if I followed baseball. I told him no. Paintball? No. Basketball? I said I watched dino fights sometimes.

"His pal is the dinosaur that goes to our school," said Fidel.

"He may look like a dinosaur, but he's really a boy," said Mr. Joplin, as if making an important distinction. "The dinosaurs died out millions of years ago."

"Humans aren't allowed in dino fights," I said, just to keep the conversation going. "Only twanked dogs and horses and elephants."

Silence. Mr. Joplin puffed on his pipe and then passed it to his wife. She watched the glow in the bowl through half-lidded eyes as she inhaled. Fidel caught me staring.

"What's the matter? Don't you get twisted?" He took the pipe in his turn.

I was so croggled I did not know what to say. Even the Marleys had switched to THC inhalers. "But smoking is bad for you." It smelled like a dirty sock had caught fire.

"Hemp is ancient. Natural." Mr. Joplin spoke in a clipped voice as if swallowing his words. "Opens the mind to what's real." When he sighed, smoke poured out of his nose. "We grow it ourselves, you know."

I took the pipe when Tree offered it. Even before I brought the stem to my mouth, the world tilted and I watched myself slide into what seemed very much like an hallucination. Here I was sitting around naked, in the mall, with a bunch of stiffs, smoking antique drugs. And I was enjoying myself. Incredible. I inhaled and immediately the flash hit me; it was as if my brain were an enormous bud, blooming inside my head.

"Good stuff." I laughed smoke and then began coughing.

Fidel refilled my glass with ice water. "Have a sip, cashman."

"Customer." Tree pointed at the window.

"Leave!" Mr. Joplin waved impatiently at him. "Go away." The man on the screen knelt and turned over the price tag on a fern. "Damn." He jerked his uniform from the hook by the door, pulled on the khaki pants and was slithering into the shirt as he disappeared down the tunnel.

"So is Green Dream trying to break into the flash market, too?" I handed the pipe to Mrs. Joplin. There was a fleck of ash on her left breast.

"What we do back here is our business," she said. "We work hard so we can live the way we want." Tree was studying her fingerprints. I realized I had said the wrong thing so I shut up. Obviously, the Joplins were drifting from the lifestyle taught at Green Dream Family Camp.

Fidel announced he was going to school tomorrow and Mrs. Joplin told him no, he could link to E-class as usual, and Fidel claimed he could not concentrate at home, and Mrs. Joplin said he was trying to get out of his chores. While they were arguing, Tree nudged my leg and shot me a *let's leave* look. I nodded.

"Excuse us." She pushed back her chair. "Mr. Boy has got to go home soon."

Mrs. Joplin pointed for her to stay. "You wait until your father gets back," she said. "Tell me, Mr. Boy, have you lived in New Canaan long?"

"All my life," I said.

"How old did you say you were?"

"Mama, he's twenty-five," said Tree. "I told you."

"And what do you do for a living?"

"*Mama,* you promised."

"Nothing," I said. "I'm lucky, I guess. I don't need to worry about money. If you didn't need to work, would you?"

"Everybody needs work to do," Mrs. Joplin said. "Work makes us real. Unless you have work to do and people who love you, you don't exist."

Talk about twentieth century humanist goop! At another time in another place, I probably would have snapped, but now the words would not come. My brain had turned into a flower; all I could think were daisy thoughts. The Joplins were such a strange combination of fast-forward and rewind. I could not tell what they wanted from me.

"Seventeen dollars and ninety-nine cents," said Mr. Joplin, returning from the storefront. "What's going on in here?" He glanced at his wife and some signal which I did not catch passed between them. He circled the table, came up behind me and laid his heavy hands on my shoulders. I shuddered; I thought for a moment he meant to strangle me.

"I'm not going to hurt you, Peter," he said. "Before you go I have something to say."

"*Daddy.*" Tree squirmed in her chair. Fidel looked uncomfortable, too, as if he guessed what was coming.

"Sure." I did not have much choice.

The weight on my shoulders eased but did not entirely go away. "You should feel the ache in this boy, Ladonna."

"I know," said Mrs. Joplin.

"Hard as plastic." Mr. Joplin touched the muscles corded along my neck. "You get too hard, you snap." He set his thumbs at the base of my skull and kneaded with an easy circular motion. "Your body isn't some machine that you've downloaded into. It's alive. Real. You have to learn to listen to it. That's why we smoke. Hear these muscles? They're screaming." He let his hand slide down my shoulders. "Now listen." His fingertips probed along my upper spine. "Hear that? Your muscles stay tense because you don't trust anyone. You always have to be ready to take a hit and you can't tell where it's coming from. You're rigid and angry and scared. Reality . . . your body is speaking to you."

His voice was as big and warm as his hands. Tree was giving him a look that could boil water but the way he touched me made too much sense to resist.

"We don't mind helping you ease the strain. That's the way Mrs. Joplin and I are. That's the way we brought the kids up. But first you have to admit you're hurting. And then you have to respect us enough to take what we have to give. I don't feel that in you, Peter. You're not ready to give up your pain. You just want us poor stiffs to admire how hard it's made you. We haven't got time for that kind of shit, okay? You learn to listen to yourself and you'll be welcome around here. We'll even call you Mr. Boy, even though it's a damn stupid name."

No one spoke for a moment.

"Sorry, Tree," he said. "We've embarrassed you again. But we love you, so you're stuck with us." I could feel it in his hands when he chuckled. "I suppose I do get carried away sometimes."

"*Sometimes?*" said Fidel. Tree just smouldered.

"It's late," said Mrs. Joplin. "Let him go now, Jamaal. His mama's sending a car over."

Mr. Joplin stepped back and I almost fell off my chair from leaning back against him. I stood, shakily. "Thanks for dinner."

Tree stalked through the greenhouse to the rear exit, her hairworks glittering against her bare back. I had to trot to keep up with her. There was no car in sight so we waited at the doorway and I put on my clothes.

"I can't take much more of this." She stared through the little wire glass window in the door, like a prisoner plotting her escape. "I mean, he's *not* a psychologist or a great philosopher or whatever the hell he thinks he is. He's just a pompous mall drone."

"He's not that bad." Actually, I understood what her father had said to me; it was scary. "I like your family."

"You don't have to live with them!" She kept watching at the door. "They promised they'd behave with you; I should have known better. This happens every time I bring someone home." She puffed an imaginary pipe, imitating her father. "Think what you're doing to yourself, you poor fool, and say, isn't it just too bad about modern life? Love, love, love—*fuck!*" She turned to me. "I'm sick of it. People are going to think I'm as sappy and thickheaded as my parents."

"I don't."

"You're lucky. You're rich and your mom leaves you alone. You're New Canaan. My folks are Elkhart, Indiana."

"Being New Canaan is nothing to brag about. So what are you?"

"Not a Joplin." She shook her head. "Not much longer, anyway; I'm eighteen in February. I think your car's here." She held out her arms and hugged me goodbye. "Sorry you had to sit through that. Don't dròp me, okay? I like you, Mr. Boy." She did not let go for a while.

Dropping her had never occurred to me; I was not thinking of anything at all except the silkiness of her skin, the warmth of her body. Her breath whispered through my hair and her nipples brushed my ribs and then she kissed me. Just on the cheek but the damage was done. I was stunted. I was not supposed to feel this way about anyone.

Comrade was waiting in the back seat. We rode home in silence; I had nothing to say to him. He would not understand—none of my friends would. They would warn me that all she wanted was to spend some of my money. Or they would make bad jokes about the nudity or the Joplins' mushy realism. No way I could explain the innocence of the way they touched one another. *The old man did what to you?* Yeah, and if I wanted a hug at home who was I supposed to ask? Comrade? Lovey? The greeter? Was I supposed to climb up to the head and fall asleep against Mom's doorbone, waiting for it to open, like I used to do when I was really a kid?

The greeter was her usual nonstick self when I got home. She was so glad to see me and she wanted to know where I had been and if I had a good time and if I wanted Cook to make me a snack? Around. Yes. No.

She said the bank had called about some problem with one of the cash cards she had given me, a security glitch which they had taken care of and were very sorry about. Did I know about it and did I need a new card and would twenty thousand be enough? Yes. Please. Thanks.

And that was it. I found myself resenting Mom because she did not have to care about losing sixteen or twenty or fifty thousand dollars. And she had reminded me of my problems when all I wanted to think of was Tree. She was no help to me, never had been. I had things so twisted around that I almost told her about Montross myself, just to get a reaction. Here some guy had tapped our files and threatened my life and she asked if I wanted a snack. Why keep me around if she was going to pay so little attention? I wanted to shock her, to make her take me seriously.

But I did not know how.

The roombrain woke me. "Stennie's calling."

"Mmm."

"Talk to me, Mr. Party Boy." A window opened; he was in his car. "You dead or alive?"

"Asleep." I rolled over. "Time is it?"

"Ten-thirty and I'm bored. Want me to come get you now or should I meet you there?"

"Wha . . . ?"

"Happy's. Don't tell me you forgot. They're doing a *piano.*"

"Who cares?" I crawled out of bed and drooped into the bathroom.

"She says she's asking Tree Joplin," Stennie called after me.

"Asking her what?" I came out.

"To the party."

"Is she going?"

"She's your cush." He gave me a toothy smile. "Call back when you're ready. Later." He faded.

"She left a message," said the roombrain. "Half hour ago."

"Tree? You got me up for Stennie and not for her?"

"He's on the list, she's not. Happy called, too."

"Comrade should've told you. Where is he?" Now I was grouchy. "She's on the list, okay? Give me playback."

Tree seemed pleased with herself. "Hi, this is me. I got myself invited to a smash party this afternoon. You want to go?" She faded.

"That's all? Call her!"

"Both her numbers are busy; I'll set redial. I found Comrade; he's on another line. You want Happy's message?"

"No. Yes."

"You promised, Mr. Boy." Happy giggled. "Look, you really, really don't want to miss this. Stennie's coming and he said I should ask Joplin if I wanted you here. So you've got no excuse."

Someone tugged at her. "Stop that! Sorry, I'm being molested by a thick. . . ." She batted at her assailant. "Mr. Boy, did I tell you that this Japanese reporter is coming to shoot a vid? What?" She turned off camera. "Sure, just like on the nature channel. Wildlife of America. We're all going to be famous. In Japan! This is history, Mr. Boy. And you're . . ."

Her face froze as the redial program finally linked to the Green Dream. The roombrain brought Tree up in a new window. "Oh hi," she said. "You rich boys sleep late."

"What's this about Happy's?"

"She invited me." Tree was recharging her hairworks with a red brush. "I said yes. Something wrong?"

Comrade slipped into the room; I shushed him. "You sure you want to go to a smash party? Sometimes they get a little crazy."

She aimed the brush at me. "You've been to smash parties before. You survived."

"Sure, but . . ."

"Well, I haven't. All I know is that everybody at school is talking about this one and I want to see what it's about."

"You tell your parents you're going?"

"Are you kidding? They'd just say it was too dangerous. What's the matter, Mr. Boy, are you scared? Come on, it'll be extreme."

"She's right. You *should* go," said Comrade.

"Is that Comrade?" Tree said. "You tell him, Comrade!"

I glared at him. "Okay, okay, I guess I'm outnumbered. Stennie said he'd drive. You want us to pick you up?"

She did.

I flew at Comrade as soon as Tree faded. "Don't you ever do that again!" I shoved him and he bumped up against the wall. "I ought to throw you to Montross."

"You know, I just finished chatting with him." Comrade stayed calm and made no move to defend himself. "He wants to meet—the three of us, face to face. He suggested Happy's."

"He suggested . . . I told you not to talk to him."

"I know." He shrugged. "Anyway, I think we should do it."

"Who gave you permission to think?"

"You did. What if we give him the picture back and open our files and then I grovel, say I'm sorry, it'll never happen again, blah, blah, blah. Maybe we can even buy him off. What have we got to lose?"

"You can't bribe software. And what if he decides to snatch us?" I told Comrade about the gypsy with the penlight. "You want Tree mixed up in this?"

All the expression drained from his face. He did not say anything at first but I had watched his subroutines long enough to know that when he looked this blank, he was shaken. "So we take a risk, maybe we can get it over with," he said. "He's not interested in Tree and I won't let anything happen to you. Why do you think your mom bought me?"

Happy Lurdane lived on the former estate of Philip Johnson, a notorious twentieth century architect. In his will Johnson had arranged to turn his compound into the Philip Johnson Memorial Museum, but after he died his work went out of fashion. The glass skyscrapers in the cities did not age well; they started to fall apart or were torn down because they wasted energy. Nobody visited the museum and it went bankrupt. The Lurdanes had bought the property and made some changes.

Johnson had designed all the odd little buildings on the estate himself. The main house was a shoebox of glass with no inside walls; near it stood a windowless brick guest house. On a pond below was a dock that looked like a Greek temple. Past the circular swimming pool near the houses were two galleries which had once held Johnson's art collection, long since sold off. In Johnson's day, the scattered buildings had been connected only by paths, which made the compound impossible in the frosty Connecticut winters. The Lurdanes had enclosed the paths in clear tubes and commuted in a golf cart.

Stennie told his Alpha not to wait, since the lot was already full and cars were parked well down the driveway. Five of us squeezed out of the car: me, Tree, Comrade, Stennie, and Janet Hoyt. Janet wore a Yankees jersey over pinstriped shorts, Tree was a little overdressed in her silver jaunts, I had on baggies padded to make me seem bigger and Comrade wore his usual window coat. Stennie lugged a box with his swag for the party.

Freddy the Teddy let us in. "Stennie and Mr. Boy!" He reared back on his hindquarters and roared. "Glad I'm not going to be the only beastie here. Hi, Janet. Hi, I'm Freddy," he said to Tree. His pink tongue lolled. "Come in, this way. Fun starts right here. Some kids are swimming and there's sex in the guest house. Everybody else is with Happy having lunch in the sculpture gallery."

The interior of the Glass House was bright and hard. Dark wood block floor, some unfriendly furniture, huge panes of glass framed in black painted steel. The few kids in the kitchen were passing an inhaler around and watching a microwave fill up with popcorn.

"I'm hot." Janet stuck the inhaler into her face and pressed. "Anybody want to swim? Tree?"

"Okay." Tree breathed in a polite dose and breathed out a giggle. "You?" she asked me.

"I don't think so." I was too nervous: I kept expecting someone to jump out and throw a net over me. "I'll watch."

"I'd swim with you," said Stennie, "but I promised Happy I'd bring her these party favors as soon as I arrived." He nudged the box with his foot. "Can you wait a few minutes?"

"Comrade and I will take them over." I grabbed the box and headed for the door, glad for the excuse to leave Tree behind while I went to find Montross. "Meet you at the pool."

The golf cart was gone so we walked through the tube toward the sculpture gallery. "You have the picture?" I said.

Comrade patted the pocket of his window coat.

The tube was not air-conditioned and the afternoon sun pounded us through the optical plastic. There was no sound inside; even our footsteps were swallowed by the astroturf. The box got heavier. We passed the entrance to the old painting gallery, which looked like a bomb shelter. Finally I had to break the silence. "I feel strange, being here," I said. "Not just because of the thing with Montross. I really think I lost myself last time I got stunted. Not sure who I am anymore, but I don't think I belong with these kids."

"People change, *tovarisch*," said Comrade. "Even you."

"Have I changed?"

He smiled. "Now that you've got a cush, your own mother wouldn't recognize you."

"You know what your problem is?" I grinned and bumped up against him on purpose. "You're jealous of Tree."

"Shouldn't I be?"

"Oh, I don't know. I can't tell if Tree likes who I was or who I might be. She's changing, too. She's so hot to break away from her parents, become part of this town. Except that what she's headed for probably isn't worth the trip. I feel like I should protect her, but that means guarding her from people like me, except I don't think I'm Mom's Mr. Boy anymore. Does that make sense?"

"Sure." He gazed straight ahead but all the heads on his window coat were scoping me. "Maybe when you're finished changing, you won't need me."

The thought had occurred to me. For years he had been the only one I could talk to but, as we closed on the gallery, I did not know what to say. I shook my head. "I just feel strange."

And then we arrived. The sculpture gallery was designed for showoffs: short flights of steps and a series of stagy balconies descended around the white brick exterior walls to the central exhibition area. The space was open so you could chat with your little knot of friends and, at the same time, spy on everyone else. About thirty kids were eating pizza and crispex off paper plates. At the bottom of the stairs, as advertised, was a black upright piano. Piled beside it was the rest of the swag. A Boston rocker, a case of green Coke bottles, a Virgin Mary in half a blue bathtub, a huge conch shell, china and crystal and assorted smaller treasures, including a four-thousand-year-old ceramic hippo. There were real animals, too, in cages near the gun rack: a turkey, some stray dogs and cats, turtles, frogs, assorted rodents.

I was threading my way across the first balcony when I was stopped by the Japanese reporter, who was wearing microcam eyes.

"Excuse me, please," he said, "I am Matsuo Shikibu and I will be recording this event today for Nippon Hoso Kyokai. Public telelink of Japan." He smiled and bowed. When his head came up the red light between his lenses was on. "You are . . . . ?"

"Raskolnikov," said Comrade, edging between me and the camera. "Rodeo Raskolnikov." He took Shikibu's hand and pumped it. "And my associate here, Mr. Peter Pan." He turned as if to introduce me but we had long since choreographed this dodge. As I sidestepped past, he kept shielding me from the reporter with his body. "We're friends of the bride," Comrade said, "and we're really excited to be making new friends in your country. Banzai, Nippon!"

I slipped by them and scooted downstairs. Happy was basking by the piano; she spotted me as I reached the middle landing.

"Mr. Boy!" It was not so much a greeting as an announcement. She was wearing a body mike and her voice boomed over the sound system. "You made it."

The stream of conversation rippled momentarily, a few heads turned and then the party flowed on. Shikibu rushed to the edge of the upper balcony and caught me with a long shot.

I set the box on the Steinway. "Stennie brought this."

She opened it eagerly. "Look everyone!" She held up a stack of square cardboard albums, about thirty centimeters on a side. There were pictures of musicians on the front, words on the back. "What are they?" she asked me.

"Phonograph records," said the kid next to Happy. "It's how they used to play music before digital."

"Erroll Garner *Soliloquy*," she read aloud. "What's this? D-j-a-n-g-o Rein-hardt and the American Jazz Giants. Sounds scary." She giggled as she pawed quickly through the other albums. Handy, Ellington, Hawkins, Par-ker, three Armstrongs. One was *Piano Rags By Scott Joplin*. Stennie's bent idea of a joke? Maybe the lizard was smarter than he looked. Happy pulled a black plastic record out of one sleeve and scratched a fingernail across little ridges. "Oh, a non-slip surface."

The party had a limited attention span. When she realized she had lost her audience, she shut off the mike and put the box with the rest of the swag. "We have to start at four, no matter what. There's so much stuff." The kid who knew about records wormed into our conversation; Happy put her hand on his shoulder. "Mr. Boy, do you know my friend, Weldon?" she said. "He's new."

Montross grinned. "We met on Playroom."

"Where *is* Stennie, anyway?" said Happy.

"Swimming," I said. Montross appeared to be in his late teens. Bigger than me—everyone was bigger than me. He wore green shorts and a window shirt of surfers at Waimea. He looked like everybody; there was nothing about him to remember. I considered bashing the smirk off his face but it was a bad idea. If he was software he could not feel anything and I would probably break my hand on his temporary chassis. "Got to go. I promised Stennie I'd meet him back at the pool. Hey Weldon, want to tag along?"

"You come right back," said Happy. "We're starting at four. Tell every-one."

We avoided the tube and cut across the lawn for privacy. Comrade handed Montross the envelope. He slid the photograph out and I had one last glimpse.

This time the dead man left me cold. In fact, I was embarrassed. Although he kept a straight face, I knew what Montross was thinking about me. Maybe he was right. I wished he would put the picture away. He was not one of us; he could not understand. I wondered if Tree had come far enough yet to appreciate corpse porn.

"It's the only copy," Comrade said.

"All right." Finally Montross crammed it into the pocket of his shorts.

"You tapped our files; you know it's true."

"So?"

"So enough!" I said. "You have what you wanted."

"I've already explained." Montross was being patient. "Getting this back doesn't close the case. I have to take preventive measures."

"Meaning you turn Comrade into a carrot."

"Meaning I repair him. You're the one who took him to the chop shop. Deregulated wiseguys are dangerous. Maybe not to you, but certainly to property and probably to other people. It's a straightforward procedure. He'll be fully functional afterward."

"Plug your procedure, jack. We're leaving."

Both wiseguys stopped. "I thought you agreed," said Montross.

"Let's go, Comrade." I grabbed his arm but he shook me off.

"Where?" he said.

"Anywhere! Just so I never have to listen to this again." I pulled again, angry at Comrade for stalling. Your wiseguy is supposed to anticipate your needs, do whatever you want.

"But we haven't even tried to . . ."

"Forget it then. I give up." I pushed him toward Montross. "You want to chat, fine, go right ahead. Let him rip the top of your head off while you're at it, but I'm not sticking around to watch."

I checked the pool but Tree, Stennie, and Janet had already gone. I went through the Glass House and caught up with them in the tube to the sculpture gallery.

"Can I talk to you?" I put my arm around Tree's waist, just like I had seen grownups do. "In private." I could tell she was annoyed to be separated from Janet. "We'll catch up." I waved Stennie on. "See you over there."

She waited until they were gone. "What?" Her hair, slick from swimming, left dark spots where it brushed her silver jaunts.

"I want to leave. We'll call my mom's car." She did not look happy. "I'll take you anywhere you want to go."

"But we just got here. Give it a chance."

"I've been to too many of these things."

"Then you shouldn't have come."

Silence. I wanted to tell her about Montross—everything—but not here.

Anyone could come along and the tube was so hot. I was desperate to get her away, so I lied. "Believe me, you're not going to like this. I know." I tugged at her waist. "Sometimes even I think smash parties are too much."

"We've had this discussion before," she said. "Obviously you weren't listening. I don't need you to decide for me whether I'm going to like something, Mr. Boy. I have two parents too many; I don't need another." She stepped away from me. "Hey, I'm sorry if you're having a bad time. But do you really need to spoil it for me?" She turned and strode down the tube toward the gallery, her beautiful hair slapping against her back. I watched her go.

"But I'm in trouble," I muttered to the empty tube—and then was disgusted with myself because I did not have the guts to say it to Tree. I was too scared she would not care. I stood there, sweating. For a moment the stink of doubt filled my nostrils. Then I followed her in. I could not abandon her to the extremists.

The gallery was jammed now; maybe a hundred kids swarmed across the balconies and down the stairs. Some perched along the edges, their feet scuffing the white brick. Happy had turned up the volume.

". . . according to Guinness, was set at the University of Oklahoma in Norman, Oklahoma, in 2012. Three minutes and fourteen seconds." The crowd rumbled in disbelief. "The challenge states each piece must be small enough to pass through a hole thirty centimeters in diameter."

I worked my way to an opening beside a rubber tree. Happy posed on the keyboard of the piano. Freddy the Teddy and the gorilla brothers, Mike and Bubba, lined up beside her. "No mechanical tools are allowed." She gestured at an armory of axes, sledgehammers, spikes, and crowbars laid out on the floor. A paper plate spun across the room. I could not see Tree.

"This piano is over two hundred years old," Happy continued, "which means the white keys are ivory." She plunked a note. "Dead elephants!" Everybody heaved a sympathetic *awww.* "The blacks are ebony, hacked from the rain forest." Another note, less reaction. "It deserves to die."

Applause. Comrade and I spotted each other at almost the same time. He and Montross stood toward the rear of the lower balcony. He gestured for me to come down; I ignored him.

"Do you boys have anything to say?" Happy said.

"Yeah." Freddy hefted an ax. "Let's make landfill."

I ducked around the rubber tree and heard the *crack* of splitting wood, the iron groan of a piano frame yielding its last music. The spectators hooted approval. As I bumped past kids, searching for Tree, the instrument's death cry made me think of taking a hammer to Montross. If fights broke out, no one would care if Comrade and I dragged him outside. I wanted to beat him until he shuddered and came unstrung and his works glinted in the thudding

45

August light. It would make me feel extreme again. *Crunch!* Kids shrieked, "Go, go, go!" The party was lifting off and taking me with it.

"You are Mr. Boy Cage." Abruptly Shikibu's microcam eyes were in my face. "We know your famous mother." He had to shout to be heard. "I have a question."

"Go away."

"Thirty seconds." A girl's voice boomed over the speakers.

"U.S. and Japan are very different, yes?" He pressed closer. "We honor ancestors, our past. You seem to hate so much." He gestured at the gallery. "Why?"

"Maybe we're spoiled." I barged past him.

I saw Freddy swing a sledgehammer at the exposed frame. *Clang!* A chunk of twisted iron clattered across the brick floor, trailing broken strings. Happy scooped the mess up and shoved it through a thirty centimeter hole drilled in an upright sheet of particle board.

The timekeeper called out again. *"One minute."* I had come far enough around the curve of the stairs to see her.

"Treemonisha!"

She glanced up, her face alight with pleasure, and waved. I was frightened for her. She was climbing into the same box I needed to break out of. So I rushed down the stairs to rescue her—little boy knight in shining armor—and ran right into Comrade's arms.

"I've decided," he said. *"Mnye vcyaw ostoyeblo."*

"Great." I had to get to Tree. "Later, okay?" When I tried to go by, he picked me up. I started thrashing. It was the first fight of the afternoon and I lost. He carried me over to Montross. The gallery was in an uproar.

"All set," said Montross. "I'll have to borrow him for a while. I'll drop him off tonight at your mom. Then we're done."

"Done?" I kept trying to get free but Comrade crushed me against him.

"It's what you want." His body was so hard. "And what your mom wants."

"Mom? She doesn't even know."

"She knows everything," Comrade said. "She watches you constantly. What else does she have to do all day?" He let me go. "Remember you said I was sloppy getting the picture? I wasn't; it was a clean operation. Only someone tipped Datasafe off."

"But she promised. Besides that makes no . . ."

"Two minutes," Tree called.

". . . but he threatened me," I said. "He was going to blow me up. Needle me in the mall."

"We wouldn't do that." Montross spread his hands innocently. "It's against the law."

"Yeah? Well, then drop dead, jack." I poked a finger at him. "Deal's off."

"No, it's not," said Comrade. "It's too late. This isn't about the picture anymore, Mr. Boy; it's about you. You weren't supposed to change but you did. Maybe they botched the last stunting, maybe it's Treemonisha. Whatever, you've outgrown me, the way I am now. So I have to change, too, or else I'll keep getting in your way."

He always had everything under control; it made me crazy. He was too good at running my life. "You should have told me Mom turned you in." *Crash!* I felt like the crowd was inside my head, screaming.

"You could've figured it out, if you wanted to. Besides, if I had said anything, your mom wouldn't have bothered to be subtle. She would've squashed me. She still might, even though I'm being fixed. Only by then I won't care. *Rosproyebi tvayou mat!"*

I heard Tree finishing the count. ". . . *twelve, thirteen, fourteen!"* No record today. Some kids began to boo, others laughed. "Time's up, you losers!"

I glared at the two wiseguys. Montross was busy emulating sincerity. Comrade found a way to grin for me, the same smirk he always wore when he tortured the greeter. "It's easier this way."

Easier. My life was too plugging easy. I had never done anything important by myself. Not even grow up. I wanted to smash something.

"Okay," I said. "You asked for it."

Comrade turned to Montross and they shook hands. I thought next they might clap one another on the shoulder and whistle as they strolled off into the sunset together. I felt like puking. "Have fun," said Comrade. *"Da svedanya."*

"Sure." Betraying Comrade, my best friend, brought me both pain and pleasure at once—but not enough to satisfy the shrieking wildness within me. The party was just starting.

Happy stood beaming beside the ruins of the Steinway. Although nothing of what was left was more than half a meter tall, Freddy, Mike and Bubba had given up now that the challenge was lost. Kids were already surging down the stairs to claim their share of the swag. I went along with them.

"Don't worry," announced Happy. "Plenty for everyone. Come take what you like. Remember, guns and animals outside, if you want to hunt. The safeties won't release unless you go through the door. Watch out for one another, people, we don't want anyone shot."

A bunch of kids were wrestling over the turkey cage; one of them staggered backwards and knocked into me. "Gobble, gobble," she said. I shoved her back.

"Mr. Boy! Over here." Tree, Stennie, and Janet were waiting on the far side of the gallery. As I crossed to them, Happy gave the sign and Stone Kinkaid hurled the four thousand year old ceramic hippo against the wall.

It shattered. Everybody cheered. In the upper balconies, they were playing catch with a frog.

"You see who kept time?" said Janet.

"Didn't need to see," I said. "I could hear. They probably heard in Elkhart. So you like it, Tree?"

"It's about what I expected: dumb but fun. I don't think they . . ." The frog sailed from the top balcony and splatted at our feet. Its legs twitched and guts spilled from its open mouth. I watched Tree's smile turn brittle. She seemed slightly embarrassed, as if she had just been told the price of something she could not afford.

"This is going to be a war zone soon," Stennie said.

"Yeah, let's fade." Janet towed Stennie to the stairs, swerving around the three boys lugging Our Lady of the Bathtub out to the firing range.

"Wait." I blocked Tree. "You're here, so you have to destroy something. Get with the program."

"I have to?" She seemed doubtful. "Oh all right—but no animals."

A hail of antique Coke bottles crashed around Happy as she directed traffic at the dwindling swag heap. "Hey people, please be very careful where you throw things." Her amplified voice blasted us as we approached. The first floor was a graveyard of broken glass and piano bones and bloody feathers. Most of the good stuff was already gone.

"Any records left?" I said.

Happy wobbled closer to me. "What?" She seemed punchy, as if stunned by the success of her own party.

"The box I gave you. From Stennie." She pointed; I spotted it under some cages and grabbed it. Tree and the others were on the stairs. Outside I could hear the crackle of small arms fire. I caught up.

"Sir! Mr. Dinosaur, please." The press still lurked on the upper balcony. "Matsuo Shikibu, Japanese telelink NHK. Could I speak with you for a moment?"

"Excuse me, but this jack and I have some unfinished business." I handed Stennie the records and cut in front. He swayed and lashed his tail upward to counterbalance their weight.

"Remember me?" I bowed to Shikibu.

"My apologies if I offended . . ."

"Hey, Matsuo—can I call you Matsuo? This is your first smash party, right? Please, eyes on me. I want to explain why I was rude before. Help you understand the local customs. You see, we're kind of self-conscious here in the U.S. We don't like it when someone just watches while we play. You either join in or you're not one of us."

My little speech drew a crowd. "What's he talking about?" said Janet. She was shushed.

"So if you drop by our party and don't have fun, people resent you," I told him. "No one came here today to put on a show. This is who we are. What we believe in."

"Yeah!" Stennie was cheerleading for the extreme Mr. Boy of old. "Tell him." Too bad he did not realize it was his final appearance. What was Mr. Boy without his Comrade? "Make him feel some pain."

I snatched an album from the top of the stack, slipped the record out and held it close to Shikibu's microcam eyes. "What does this say?"

He craned his neck to read the label. "John Coltrane, *Giant Steps*."

"Very good." I grasped the record with both hands, and raised it over my head for all to see. "We're not picky, Matsuo. We welcome everyone. Therefore today it is my honor to initiate you—and the home audience back on NHK. If you're still watching, you're part of this too." I broke the record over his head.

He yelped and staggered backward and almost tripped over a dead cat. Stone Kinkaid caught him and propped him up. "Congratulations," said Stennie, as he waved his claws at Japan. "You're all extremists now."

Shikibu gaped at me, his microcam eyes askew. A couple of kids clapped.

"There's someone else here who has not yet joined us." I turned on Tree. "Another spectator." Her smile faded.

"You leave her alone," said Janet. "What are you, crazy?"

"I'm not going to touch her." I held up empty hands. "No, I just want her to ruin something. That's why you came, isn't it, Tree? To get a taste?" I rifled through the box until I found what I wanted. "How about this?" I thrust it at her.

"Oh yeah," said Stennie, "I meant to tell you. . . ."

She took the record and scoped it briefly. When she glanced up at me, I almost lost my nerve.

"Matsuo Shikibu, meet Treemonisha Joplin." I clasped my hands behind my back so no one could see me tremble. "The great-great-great grand-daughter of the famous American composer, Scott Joplin. Yes, Japan, we're all celebrities here in New Canaan. Now please observe." I read the record for him. "*Piano Rags by Scott Joplin*, Volume III. Who knows, this might be the last copy. We can only hope. So, what are you waiting for, Tree? You don't want to be a Joplin anymore? Just wait until your folks get a peek at this. We'll even send GD a copy. Go ahead, enjoy."

"Smash it!" The kids around us took up the chant. "Smash it!" Shikibu adjusted his lenses.

"You think I won't?" Tree pulled out the disc and threw the sleeve off the balcony. "This is a piece of junk, Mr. Boy." She laughed and then shattered the album against the wall. She held onto a shard. "It doesn't mean anything to me."

I heard Janet whisper. "What's going on?"

"I think they're having an argument."

"You want me to be your little dream cush." Tree tucked the piece of broken plastic into the pocket of my baggies. "The stiff from nowhere who knows nobody and does nothing without Mr. Boy. So you try to scare me off. You tell me you're so rich, you can afford to hate yourself. Stay home, you say, it's too dangerous, we're all crazy. Well, if you're so sure this is poison, how come you've still got your wiseguy and your cash cards? Are you going to move out of your mom, leave town, stop getting stunted? You're not giving it up, Mr. Boy, so why should I?"

Shikibu turned his camera eyes on me. No one spoke.

"You're right," I said. "She's right." I could not save anyone until I saved myself. I felt the wildness lifting me to it. I leapt onto the balcony wall and shouted for everyone to hear. "Shut up and listen everybody! You're all invited to my place, okay?"

There was one last thing to smash.

"Stop this, Peter." The greeter no longer thought I was cute. "What're you doing?" She trembled as if the kids spilling into her were an infection.

"I thought you'd like to meet my friends," I said. A few had stayed behind with Happy, who had decided to sulk after I hijacked her guests. The rest had followed me home in a caravan so I could warn off the sentry robots. It was already a hall-of-fame bash. "Treemonisha Joplin, this is my mom. Sort of."

"Hi," Tree held out her hand uncertainly.

The greeter was no longer the human doormat. "Get them out of me." She was too jumpy to be polite. "Right now!"

Someone turned up a boombox. Skitter music filled the room like a siren. Tree said something I could not hear. When I put a hand to my ear, she leaned close and said, "Don't be so mean, Mr. Boy. I think she's really frightened."

I grinned and nodded. "I'll tell Cook to make us some snacks."

Bubba and Mike carried boxes filled with the last of the swag and set them on the coffee table. Kids fanned out, running their hands along her wrinkled blood-hot walls, bouncing on the furniture. Stennie waved at me as he led a bunch upstairs for a tour. A leftover cat had gotten loose and was hissing and scratching underfoot. Some twisted kids had already stripped and were rolling in the floor hair, getting ready to have sex.

"Get dressed, you." The greeter kicked at them as she coiled her umbilical to keep it from being trampled. She retreated to her wall plug. "You're *hurting* me." Although her voice rose to a scream, only half a dozen kids heard her. She went limp and sagged to the floor.

The whole room seemed to throb, as if to some great heartbeat, and the lights went out. It took a while for someone to kill the sound on the boombox. "What's wrong?" Voices called out. "Mr. Boy? Lights."

Both doorbones swung open and I saw a bughead silhouetted against the twilit sky. Shikibu in his microcams. "Party's over," Mom said over her speaker system. There was nervous laughter. "Leave before I call the cops. Peter, go to your room right now. I want to speak to you."

As the stampede began, I found Tree's hand. "Wait for me?" I pulled her close. "I'll only be a minute."

"What are you going to do?" She sounded frightened. It felt good to be taken so seriously.

"I'm moving out, chucking all this. I'm going to be a working stiff." I chuckled. "Think your dad would give me a job?"

"Look out, dumbscut! Hey, *hey*. Don't push!"

Tree dragged me out of the way. "You're crazy."

"I know. That's why I have to get out of Mom."

"Listen," she said, "you've never been poor, you have no idea. . . . Only a rich kid would think it's easy being a stiff. Just go up, apologize, tell her it won't happen again. Then change things later on, if you want. Believe me, life will be a lot simpler if you hang onto the money."

"I can't. Will you wait?"

"You want me to tell you it's okay to be stupid, is that it? Well, I've *been* poor, Mr. Boy, and still am, and I don't recommend it. So don't expect me to stand around and clap while you throw away something I've always wanted." She spun away from me and I lost her in the darkness. I wanted to catch up with her but I knew I had to do Mom now or I would lose my nerve.

As I was fumbling my way upstairs I heard stragglers coming down. "On your right," I called. Bodies nudged by me.

"Mr. Boy, is that you?" I recognized Stennie's voice.

"He's gone," I said.

Seven flights up, the lights were on. Nanny waited on the landing outside my rooms, her umbilical stretched nearly to its limit. She was the only remote which was physically able to get to my floor and this was as close as she could come.

It had been a while since I had seen her; Mom did not use her much anymore and I rarely visited, even though the nursery was only one flight down. But this was the remote who used to pick me up when I cried and who had changed my diapers and who taught me how to turn on my roombrain. She had skin so pale you could almost see veins and long black hair piled high on her head. I never thought of her as having a body because she always wore dark turtlenecks and long woolen skirts and silky panty hose.

Nanny was a smile and warm hands and the smell of fresh pillowcases. Once upon a time I thought her the most beautiful creature in the world. Back then I would have done anything she said.

She was not smiling now. "I don't know how you expect me to trust you anymore, Peter." Nanny had never been a very good scold. "Those brats were out of control. I can't let you put me in danger this way."

"If you wanted someone to trust, maybe you shouldn't have had me stunted. You got exactly what you ordered, the neverending kid. Well, kids don't have to be responsible."

"What do you mean, what I ordered? It's what you wanted, too."

"Is it? Did you ever ask? I was only ten, the first time, too young to know better. For a long time I did it to please you. Getting stunted was the only thing I did that seemed important to you. But *you* never explained. You never sat me down and said 'This is the life you'll have and this is what you'll miss and this is how you'll feel about it.' "

"You want to grow up, is that it?" She was trying to threaten me. "You want to work and worry and get old and die someday?" She had no idea what we were talking about.

"I can't live this way anymore, Nanny."

At first she acted stunned, as if I had spoken in Albanian. Then her expression hardened when she realized she had lost her hold on me. She was ugly when she was angry. "They put you up to this." Her gaze narrowed in accusation. "That little black cush you've been seeing. Those realists!"

I had always managed to hide my anger from Mom. Right up until then. "How do you know about her?" I had never told her about Tree.

"Peter, they live in a mall!"

Comrade was right. "You've been spying on me." When she did not deny it, I went berserk. "You liar." I slammed my fist into her belly. "You said you wouldn't watch." She staggered and fell onto her umbilical, crimping it. As she twitched on the floor, I pounced. "You promised." I slapped her face. "Promised." I hit her again. Her hair had come undone and her eyes rolled back in their sockets and her face was slack. She made no effort to protect herself. Mom was retreating from this remote, too, but I was not going to let her get away.

"Mom!" I rolled off Nanny. "I'm coming up, Mom! You hear? Get ready." I was crying; it had been a long time since I had cried. Not something Mr. Boy did.

I scrambled up to the long landing at the shoulders. At one end another circular stairway wound up into the torch; in the middle four steps led into the neck. It was the only doorbone I had never seen open; I had no idea how to get through.

"Mom, I'm here." I pounded. "Mom! You hear me?"

Silence.

"Let me in, Mom." I smashed myself against the doorbone. Pain branched through my shoulder like lightning but it felt great because Mom shuddered from the impact. I backed up and, in a frenzy, hurled myself again. Something warm dripped on my cheek. She was bleeding from the hinges. I aimed a vicious kick at the doorbone and it banged open. I went through.

For years I had imagined that if only I could get into the head I could meet my real mother. Touch her. I had always wondered what she looked like; she got reshaped just after I was born. When I was little I used to think of her as a magic princess glowing with fairy light. Later I pictured her as one or another of my friends' moms, only better dressed. After I had started getting twanked, I was afraid she might be just a brain floating in nutrient solution, like in some pricey memory bank. All wrong.

The interior of the head was dark and absolutely freezing. There was no sound except for the hum of refrigeration units. "Mom?" My voice echoed in the empty space. I stumbled and caught myself against a smooth wall. Not skin, like everywhere else in Mom—metal. The tears froze on my face.

"There's nothing for you here," she said. "This is a clean room. You're compromising it. You must leave immediately."

Sterile environment, metal walls, the bitter cold that superconductors needed. I did not need to see. No one lived here. It had never occurred to me that there was no Mom to touch. She had downloaded, become an electron ghost tripping icy logic gates. "How long have you been dead?"

"This isn't where you belong," she said.

I shivered. "How long?"

"Go away," she said.

So I did. I had to. I could not stay very long in her secret place or I would die of the cold.

As I reeled down the stairs, Mom herself seemed to shift beneath my feet and I saw her as if she were a stranger. Dead—and I had been living in a tomb. I ran past Nanny; she still sprawled where I had left her. All those years I had loved her, I had been in love with death. Mom had been sucking life from me the way her refrigerators stole the warmth from my body.

Now I knew there was no way I could stay, no matter what anyone said. I knew it was not going to be easy leaving, and not just because of the money. For a long time Mom had been my entire world. But I could not let her use me to pretend she was alive, or I would end up like her.

I realized now that the door had always stayed locked because Mom had to hide what she had become. If I wanted, I could have destroyed her. Downloaded intelligences have no more rights than cars or wiseguys. Mom was legally dead and I was her only heir. I could have had her shut off, her body razed. But somehow it was enough to go, to walk away from my inheritance. I was scared and yet with every step I felt lighter. Happier. Extremely free.

I had not expected to find Tree waiting at the doorbone, chatting with Comrade as if nothing had happened. "I just had to see if you were really the biggest fool in the world," she said.

"Out." I pulled her through the door. "Before I change my mind."

Comrade started to follow us. "No, not you." I turned and stared back at the heads on his window coat. I had not intended to see him again; I had wanted to be gone before Montross returned him. "Look, I'm giving you back to Mom. She needs you more than I do."

If he had argued, I might have given in. The old, unregulated Comrade would have said something. But he just slumped a little and nodded and I knew that he was dead, too. The thing in front of me was another ghost. He and Mom were two of a kind. "Pretend you're her kid, maybe she'll like that." I patted his shoulder.

"Prekrassnaya ideya," he said. *"Spaceba."*

"You're welcome," I said.

Tree and I trotted together down the long driveway. Robot sentries crossed the lawn and turned their spotlights on us. I wanted to tell her she was right. I had probably just done the single most irresponsible thing of my life—and I had high standards. Still, I could not imagine how being poor could be worse than being rich and hating yourself. I had seen enough of what it was like to be dead. It was time to try living.

"Are we going someplace, Mr. Boy?" Tree squeezed my hand. "Or are we just wandering around in the dark?"

"Mr. Boy is a damn stupid name, don't you think?" I laughed. "Call me Pete." I felt like a kid again.

URSULA K. LE GUIN

The Shobies' Story

▼

Ursula K. Le Guin is probably one of the best-known and most universally respected SF writers in the world today. Her famous novel *The Left Hand of Darkness* may have been the most influential SF novel of its decade; even ignoring the rest of Le Guin's work, the impact of this one novel alone on future SF and future SF writers would be incalculably strong. (Her 1968 fantasy novel, *A Wizard of Earthsea*, would be almost as influential on future generations of High Fantasy writers.) *The Left Hand of Darkness* won both the Hugo and Nebula Awards, as did Le Guin's monumental novel *The Dispossessed* a few years later. She has also won three other Hugo Awards and a Nebula Award for her short fiction, and the National Book Award for Children's literature for her novel *The Farthest Shore*, part of her acclaimed Earthsea trilogy. Her other novels include *Planet of Exile*, *The Lathe of Heaven*, *City of Illusions*, *Rocannon's World*, *The Beginning Place*, *Eye of Heron*, *A Wizard of Earthsea*, *The Tombs of Atuan*, and the multi-media novel (it sold with a tape cassette of music, and included drawings and recipes) *Always Coming Home*. She has had four collections: *The Wind's Twelve Quarters*, *Orsinian Tales*, *The Compass Rose*, and, most recently, *Buffalo Gals and Other Animal Presences*. Her most recent novel is *Tehanu: The Fourth Book of Earthsea*. Her story "The Trouble With the Cotton People" was in our Second Annual Collection,

Ursula K. Le Guin

and her "Buffalo Gals, Won't You Come Out Tonight" was in our Fifth Annual Collection.

In the wise and subtle story that follows, she demonstrates that quite a bit more than just beauty may be in the eye of the beholder. . . .

▼

The Shobies' Story

URSULA K. LE GUIN

They met at Ve Port more than a month before their first flight together, and there, calling themselves after their ship as most crews did, became the Shobies. Their first consensual decision was to spend their isyeye in the coastal village of Liden, on Hain, where the negative ions could do their thing.

Liden was a fishing port with an eighty-thousand-year history and a population of four hundred. Its fisherfolk farmed the rich shoal waters of their bay, shipped the catch inland to the cities, and managed the Liden Resort for vacationers and tourists and new space crews on isyeye (the word is Hainish and means "making a beginning together," or "beginning to be together," or used technically, "the period of time and area of space in which a group forms if it is going to form." A honeymoon is an isyeye of two). The fisherwomen and fishermen of Liden were as weathered as driftwood and about as talkative. Six-year-old Asten, who had misunderstood slightly, asked one of them if they were all eighty thousand years old. "Nope," she said.

Like most crews, the Shobies used Hainish as their common language. So the name of the one Hainish crew member, Sweet Today, carried its meaning as words as well as name, and at first seemed a silly thing to call a big, tall, heavy woman in her late fifties, imposing of carriage and almost as taciturn as the villagers. But her reserve proved to be a deep well of congeniality and tact, to be called upon as needed, and her name soon began to sound quite right. She had family—all Hainish have family—kinfolk of all denominations, grandchildren and cross-cousins, affines and cosines, scattered all over the Ekumen, but no relatives in this crew. She asked to be Grandmother to Rig, Asten, and Betton, and was accepted.

The only Shoby older than Sweet Today was the Terran Lidi, who was seventy-two EYs and not interested in grandmothering. Lidi had been navigating for fifty years, and there was nothing she didn't know about NAFAL ships, although occasionally she forgot that their ship was the *Shoby* and called it the *Soso* or the *Alterra*. And there were things she didn't know, none of them knew, about the *Shoby*.

They talked, as human beings do, about what they didn't know.

Churten theory was the main topic of conversation, evenings at the driftwood fire on the beach after dinner. The adults had read whatever there was to read about it, of course, before they ever volunteered for the test mission. Gveter had more recent information and presumably a better understanding of it than the others, but it had to be pried out of him. Only twenty-five, the only Cetian in the crew, much hairier than the others, and not gifted in language, he spent a lot of time on the defensive. Assuming that as an Anarresti he was more proficient at mutual aid and more adept at cooperation than the others, he lectured them about their propertarian habits; but he held tight to his knowledge, because he needed the advantage it gave him. For a while he would speak only in negatives: don't call it the churten "drive," it isn't a drive, don't call it the churten "effect," it isn't an effect. What is it, then? A long lecture ensued, beginning with the rebirth of Cetian physics since the revision of Shevekian temporalism by the Intervallists, and ending with the general conceptual framework of the churten. Everyone listened very carefully, and finally Sweet Today spoke, carefully. "So the ship will be moved," she said, "by ideas?"

"No, no, no, no," said Gveter. But he hesitated for the next word so long that Karth asked a question: "Well, you haven't actually talked about any physical, material events or effects at all." The question was characteristically indirect. Karth and Oreth, the Gethenians who with their two children were the affective focus of the crew, the "hearth" of it, in their terms, came from a not very theoretically minded subculture, and knew it. Gveter could run rings round them with his Cetian physico-philosophico-techno-natter. He did so at once. His accent did not make his explanations any clearer. He went on about coherence and meta-intervals, and at last demanded, with gestures of despair, "Khow can I say it in Khainish? No! It is not physical, it is not not-physical, these are the categories our minds must discard entirely, this is the khole point!"

"Buth-buth-buth-buth-buth-buth," went Asten, softly, passing behind the half circle of adults at the driftwood fire on the wide, twilit beach. Rig followed, also going, "Buth-buth-buth-buth," but louder. They were being spaceships, to judge from their maneuvers around a dune and their communications—"Locked in orbit, Navigator!"—but the noise they were imitating was the noise of the little fishing boats of Liden putt-putting out to sea.

"I crashed!" Rig shouted, flailing in the sand. "Help! Help! I crashed!"

"Hold on, Ship Two!" Asten cried. "I'll rescue you! Don't breathe! Oh, oh, trouble with the Churten Drive! Buth-buth-ack! Ack! Brrrrmmm-ack-ack-ack-rrrrrmmmmmm, buth-buth-buth-buth. . . ."

They were six and four EYs old. Tai's son Betton, who was eleven, sat at the driftwood fire with the adults, though at the moment he was watching Rig and Asten as if he wouldn't mind taking off to help rescue Ship Two. The little Gethenians had spent more time on ships than on planet, and Asten liked to boast about being "actually fifty-eight," but this was Betton's first crew, and his only NAFAL flight had been from Terra to Hain. He and his biomother, Tai, had lived in a reclamation commune on Terra. When she had drawn the lot for Ekumenical service, and requested training for ship duty, he had asked her to bring him as family. She had agreed; but after training, when she volunteered for this test flight, she had tried to get Betton to withdraw, to stay in training or go home. He had refused. Shan, who had trained with them, told the others this, because the tension between the mother and son had to be understood to be used effectively in group formation. Betton had requested to come, and Tai had given in, but plainly not with an undivided will. Her relationship to the boy was cool and mannered. Shan offered him fatherly-brotherly warmth, but Betton accepted it sparingly, coolly, and sought no formal crew relation with him or anyone.

Ship Two was being rescued, and attention returned to the discussion. "All right," said Lidi. "We know that anything that goes faster than light, any *thing* that goes faster than light, by so doing transcends the material/immaterial category—that's how we got the ansible, by distinguishing the message from the medium. But if we, the crew, are going to travel as messages, I want to understand *how*."

Gveter tore his hair. There was plenty to tear. It grew fine and thick, a mane on his head, a pelt on his limbs and body, a silvery nimbus on his hands and face. The fuzz on his feet was, at the moment, full of sand. "Khow!" he cried. "I'm trying to tell you khow! Message, information, no no no, that's old, that's ansible technology. This is transilience! Because the field is to be conceived as the virtual field, in which the unreal interval becomes virtually effective through the mediary coherence—don't you see?"

"No," Lidi said. "What do you mean by mediary?"

After several more bonfires on the beach, the consensus opinion was that churten theory was accessible only to minds very highly trained in Cetian temporal physics. There was a less freely voiced conviction that the engineers who had built the *Shoby*'s churten apparatus did not entirely understand how it worked. Or more precisely, what it did when it worked. That it worked was certain. The *Shoby* was the fourth ship it had been tested with, using robot crew; so far sixty-two instantaneous trips, or transiliences, had been effected between points from four hundred kilometers to twenty-seven light-years apart, with stopovers of varying lengths. Gveter and Lidi steadfastly maintained that this proved that the engineers knew perfectly well what they were doing, and that for the rest of them the seeming difficulty of the theory was only the difficulty human minds had in grasping a genuinely new concept.

"Like the circulation of the blood," said Tai. "People went around with their hearts beating for a long time before they understood why." She did not look satisfied with her own analogy, and when Shan said, "The heart has its reasons, which reason does not know," she looked offended. "Mysticism," she said, in the tone of voice of one warning a companion about dog shit on the path.

"Surely there's nothing *beyond* understanding in this process," Oreth said, somewhat tentatively. "Nothing that can't be understood, and reproduced."

"And quantified," Gveter said stoutly.

"But even if people understand the process, nobody knows the human response to it—the *experience* of it. Right? So we are to report on that."

"Why shouldn't it be just like NAFAL flight, only even faster?" Betton asked.

"Because it is totally different," said Gveter.

"What could happen to us?"

Some of the adults had discussed possibilities, all of them had considered them; Karth and Oren had talked it over in appropriate terms with their children; but evidently Betton had not been included in such discussions.

"We don't know," Tai said sharply. "I told you that at the start, Betton."

"Most likely it will be like NAFAL flight," said Shan, "but the first people who flew NAFAL didn't know what it would be like, and had to find out the physical and psychic effects—"

"The worst thing," said Sweet Today in her slow, comfortable voice, "would be that we would die. Other lives have been on some of the test flights. Crickets. And intelligent ritual animals on the last two *Shoby* tests. They were all all right." It was a very long statement for Sweet Today, and carried proportional weight.

"We know," said Gveter, "that no temporal rearrangement is involved in churten, as it is in NAFAL. And mass is involved only in terms of needing a certain core mass, just as for ansible transmission, but not in itself. So maybe even a pregnant person could be a transilient."

"They can't go on ships," Asten said. "The unborn dies if they do."

Asten was half-lying across Oreth's lap; Rig, thumb in mouth, was asleep on Karth's lap.

"When we were Oneblins," Asten went on, sitting up, "there were ritual animals with our crew. Some fish and some Terran cats and a whole lot of Hainish gholes. We got to play with them. And we helped thank the ghole that they tested for lithovirus. But it didn't die. It bit Shapi. The cats slept with us. But one of them went into kemmer and got pregnant, and then the *Oneblin* had to go to Hain, and she had to have an abortion, or all her unborns would have died inside her and killed her too. Nobody knew a ritual for her, to explain to her. But I fed her some extra food. And Rig cried."

"Other people I know cried too," Karth said, stroking the child's hair.

"You tell good stories, Asten," Sweet Today observed.

"So we're sort of ritual humans," said Betton.

"Volunteers," Tai said.

"Experimenters," said Lidi.

"Experiencers," said Shan.

"Explorers," Oreth said.

"Gamblers," said Karth.

The boy looked from one face to the next.

"You know," Shan said, "back in the time of the League, early in NAFAL flight, they were sending out ships to really distant systems—trying to explore everything—crews that wouldn't come back for centuries. Maybe some of them are still out there. But some of them came back after four, five, six hundred years, and they were all mad. Crazy!" He paused dramatically. "But they were all crazy when they started. Unstable people. They had to be crazy to volunteer for a time dilation like that. What a way to pick a crew, eh?" He laughed.

"Are we stable?" said Oreth. "I like instability. I like this job. I like the risk, taking the risk together. High stakes! That's the edge of it, the sweetness of it."

Karth looked down at their children, and smiled.

"Yes. Together," Gveter said. "You aren't crazy. You are good. I love you. We are ammari."

"Ammar," the others said to him, confirming this unexpected declaration. The young man scowled with pleasure, jumped up, and pulled off his shirt. "I want to swim. Come on, Betton. Come on swimming!" he said, and ran off toward the dark, vast waters that moved softly beyond the ruddy haze of their fire. The boy hesitated, then shed his shirt and sandals and followed. Shan pulled up Tai, and they followed; and finally the two old women went off into the night and the breakers, rolling up their pant legs, laughing at themselves.

To Gethenians, even on a warm summer night on a warm summer world, the sea is no friend. The fire is where you stay. Oreth and Asten moved closer to Karth and watched the flames, listening to the faint voices out in the glimmering surf, now and then talking quietly in their own tongue, while the little sisterbrother slept on.

After thirty lazy days at Liden the Shobies caught the fish train inland to the city, where a Fleet lander picked them up at the train station and took them to the spaceport on Ve, the next planet out from Hain. They were rested, tanned, bonded, and ready to go.

One of Sweet Today's hemi-affiliate cousins once removed was on duty in Ve Port. She urged the Shobies to ask the inventors of the churten on Urras and Anarres any questions they had about churten operation. "The purpose of the experimental flight is understanding," she insisted, "and your full intellectual participation is essential. They've been very anxious about that."

Lidi snorted.

"Now for the ritual," said Shan, as they went to the ansible room in the sunward bubble. "They'll explain to the animals what they're going to do and why, and ask them to help."

"The animals don't understand that," Betton said in his cold, angelic treble. "It's just to make the humans feel better."

"The humans understand?" Sweet Today asked.

"We all use each other," Oreth said. "The ritual says: we have no right to do so; therefore, we accept the responsibility for the suffering we cause."

Betton listened and brooded.

Gveter addressed the ansible first, and talked to it for half an hour, mostly in Pravic and mathematics. Finally, apologizing, and looking a little unnerved, he invited the others to use the instrument. There was a pause. Lidi activated it, introduced herself, and said, "We have agreed that none of us, except Gveter, has the theoretical background to grasp the principles of the churten."

A scientist twenty-two light-years away responded in Hainish via the rather flat auto-translator voice, but with unmistakable hopefulness, "The churten, in lay terms, may be seen as displacing the virtual field in order to realize relational coherence in terms of the transiliential experientiality."

"Quite," said Lidi.

"As you know, the material effects have been nil, and negative effect on low-intelligence sentients also nil; but there is considered to be a possibility that the participation of high intelligence in the process might affect the displacement in one way or another. And that such displacement would reciprocally affect the participant."

"What has the level of our intelligence got to do with how the churten functions?" Tai asked.

A pause. Their interlocutor was trying to find the words, to accept the responsibility.

"We have been using 'intelligence' as shorthand for the psychic complexity and cultural dependence of our species," said the translator voice at last. "The presence of the transilient as conscious mind nonduring transilience is the untested factor."

"But if the process is instantaneous, how can we be conscious of it?" Oreth asked.

"Precisely," said the ansible, and after another pause continued, "As the experimenter is an element of the experiment, so we assume that the transilient may be an element or agent of transilience. This is why we asked for a crew to test the process, rather than one or two volunteers. The psychic interbalance of a bonded social group is a margin of strength against disintegrative or incomprehensible experience, if any such occurs. Also, the separate observations of the group members will mutually interverify."

"Who programs this translator?" Shan snarled in a whisper. "Interverify! Shit!"

Lidi looked around at the others, inviting questions.

"How long will the trip actually take?" Betton asked.

"No long," the translator voice said, then self-corrected: "No time."

Another pause.

"Thank you," said Sweet Today, and the scientist on a planet twenty-two years of time-dilated travel from Ve Port answered, "We are grateful for your generous courage, and our hope is with you."

They went directly from the ansible room to the *Shoby*.

The churten equipment, which was not very space-consuming and the controls of which consisted essentially of an on-off switch, had been installed alongside the Nearly as Fast as Light motivators and controls of an ordinary interstellar ship of the Ekumenical Fleet. The *Shoby* had been built on Hain about four hundred years ago, and was thirty-two years old. Most of its early runs had been exploratory, with a Hainish-Chiffewarian crew. Since in such runs a ship might spend years in orbit in a planetary system, the Hainish and Chiffewarians, feeling that it might as well be lived in rather than endured, had arranged and furnished it like a very large, very comfortable house. Three of its residential modules had been disconnected and left in the hangars on Ve, and still there was more than enough room for a crew of only ten. Tai, Betton, and Shan, new from Terra, and Gveter from Anarres, accustomed to the barracks and the communal austerities of their marginally habitable worlds, stalked about the *Shoby*, disapproving it. "Ex-

63

cremental," Gveter growled. "Luxury!" Tai sneered. Sweet Today, Lidi, and the Gethenians, more used to the amenities of shipboard life, settled right in and made themselves at home. And Gveter and the younger Terrans found it hard to maintain ethical discomfort in the spacious, high-ceilinged, well-furnished, slightly shabby living rooms and bedrooms, studies, high- and low-G gyms, the dining room, library, kitchen, and bridge of the *Shoby*. The carpet in the bridge was a genuine Henyekaulil, soft deep blues and purples woven in the patterns of the constellations of the Hainish sky. There was a large, healthy plantation of Terran bamboo in the meditation gym, part of the ship's self-contained vegetal/respiratory system. The windows of any room could be programmed by the homesick to a view of Abbenay or New Cairo or the beach at Liden, or cleared to look out on the suns nearer and farther and the darkness between the suns.

Rig and Asten discovered that as well as the elevators there was a stately staircase with a curving banister, leading from the reception hall up to the library. They slid down the banister shrieking wildly, until Shan threatened to apply a local gravity field and force them to slide up it, which they besought him to do. Betton watched the little ones with a superior gaze, and took the elevator; but the next day he slid down the banister, going a good deal faster than Rig and Asten because he could push off harder and had greater mass, and nearly broke his tailbone. It was Betton who organized the tray-sliding races, but Rig generally won them, being small enough to stay on the tray all the way down the stairs. None of the children had had any lessons at the beach, except in swimming and being Shobies; but while they waited through an unexpected five-day delay at Ve Port, Gveter did physics with Betton and math with all three daily in the library, and they did some history with Shan and Oreth, and danced with Tai in the low-G gym.

When she danced, Tai became light, free, laughing. Rig and Asten loved her then, and her son danced with her like a colt, like a kid, awkward and blissful. Shan often joined them; he was a dark and elegant dancer, and she would dance with him, but even then was shy, would not touch. She had been celibate since Betton's birth. She did not want Shan's patient, urgent desire, did not want to cope with it, with him. She would turn from him to Betton, and son and mother would dance wholly absorbed in the steps, the airy pattern they made together. Watching them, the afternoon before the test flight, Sweet Today began to wipe tears from her eyes, smiling, never saying a word.

"Life is good," said Gveter very seriously to Lidi.

"It'll do," she said.

Oreth, who was just coming out of female kemmer, having thus triggered Karth's male kemmer, all of which, by coming on unexpectedly early, had delayed the test flight for these past five days, enjoyable days for all—Oreth watched Rig, whom she had fathered, dance with Asten, whom she had borne, and watched Karth watch them, and said in Karhidish, "Tomorrow. . . ." The edge was very sweet.

Anthropologists solemnly agree that we must not attribute "cultural constants" to the human population of any planet; but certain cultural traits or expectations do seem to run deep. Before dinner that last night in port, Shan and Tai appeared in black and silver uniforms of the Terran Ekumen, which had cost them—Terra also still had a money economy—a half-year's allowance.

Asten and Rig clamored at once for equal grandeur. Karth and Oreth suggested their party clothes, and Sweet Today brought out silver-lace scarves, but Asten sulked, and Rig imitated. The idea of a *uniform*, Asten told them, was that it was the *same*.

"Why?" Oreth inquired.

Old Lidi answered sharply: "So that no one is responsible."

She then went off and changed into a black velvet evening suit that wasn't a uniform but that didn't leave Tai and Shan sticking out like sore thumbs. She had left Terra at age eighteen and never been back nor wanted to, but Tai and Shan were shipmates.

Karth and Oreth got the idea, and put on their finest fur-trimmed hiebs, and the children were appeased with their own party clothes plus all of Karth's hereditary and massive gold jewelry. Sweet Today appeared in a pure white robe which she claimed was in fact ultraviolet. Gveter braided his mane. Betton had no uniform, but needed none, sitting beside his mother at table in a visible glory of pride.

Meals, sent up from the Port kitchens, were very good, and this one was superb: a delicate Hainish iyanwi with all seven sauces, followed by a pudding flavored with Terran chocolate. A lively evening ended quietly at the big fireplace in the library. The logs were fake, of course, but good fakes; no use having a fireplace on a ship and then burning plastic in it. The neocellulose logs and kindling smelled right, resisted catching, caught with spits and sparks and smoke billows, flared up bright. Oreth had laid the fire, Karth lit it. Everybody gathered round.

"Tell bedtime stories," Rig said.

Oreth told about the Ice Caves of Kerm Land, how a ship sailed into the great blue sea-cave and disappeared, and was never found by the boats that entered the caves in search; but seventy years later that ship was found drifting—not a living soul aboard nor any sign of what had become of them—off the coast of Osemyet, a thousand miles overland from Kerm. . . .

Another story?

Lidi told about the little desert wolf who lost his wife and went to the land

65

of the dead for her, and found her there dancing with the dead, and nearly brought her back to the land of the living, but spoiled it by trying to touch her before they got all the way back to life, and she vanished, and he could never find the way back to the place where the dead danced, no matter how he looked, and howled, and cried. . . .

Another story!

Shan told about the boy who sprouted a feather every time he told a lie, until his commune had to use him for a duster.

Another!

Gveter told about the winged people called gluns, who were so stupid that they died out, because they kept hitting each other head-on in midair. "They weren't real," he added conscientiously. "Only a story."

Another— No. Bedtime now.

Rig and Asten went round as usual for a goodnight hug, and this time Betton followed them. When he came to Tai he did not stop, for she did not like to be touched; but she put out her hand, drew the child to her, and kissed his cheek. He fled in joy.

"Stories," said Sweet Today. "Ours begins tomorrow, eh?"

A chain of command is easy to describe, a network of response isn't. To those who live by mutual empowerment, "thick" description, complex and open-ended, is normal and comprehensible, but to those whose only model is hierarchic control, such description seems a muddle, a mess, along with what it describes. Who's in charge here? Get rid of all these petty details. How many cooks spoil a soup? Let's get this perfectly clear now. Take me to your leader!

The old navigator was at the NAFAL console, of course, and Gveter at the paltry churten console; Oreth was wired into the AI; Tai, Shan, and Karth were their respective Support, and what Sweet Today did might be called supervising or overseeing if that didn't suggest a hierarchic function. Interseeing, maybe, or subvising. Rig and Asten always naffled (to use Rig's word) in the ship's library, where, during the boring and disorienting experience of travel at near light-speed, Asten could look at pictures or listen to a story tape, and Rig could curl up on and under a certain furry blanket and go to sleep. Betton's crew function during flight was Elder Sib; he stayed with the little ones, provided himself with a barf bag since he was one of those whom NAFAL flight made queasy, and focused the intervid on Lidi and Gveter so he could watch what they did.

So they all knew what they were doing, as regards NAFAL flight. As regards the churten process, they knew that it was supposed to effectuate their transilience to a solar system seventeen light-years from Ve Port without temporal interval; but nobody, anywhere, knew what they were doing.

So Lidi looked around, like the violinist who raises her bow to poise the chamber group for the first chord, a flicker of eye contact, and sent the *Shoby* into NAFAL mode, as Gveter, like the cellist whose bow comes down in that same instant to ground the chord, sent the *Shoby* into churten mode. They entered unduration. They churtened. No long, as the ansible had said.

"What's wrong?" Shan whispered.

"By damn!" said Gveter.

"What?" said Lidi, blinking and shaking her head.

"That's it," Tai said, flicking readouts.

"That's not A-sixty-whatsit," Lidi said, still blinking.

Sweet Today was gestalting them, all ten at once, the seven on the bridge and by intervid the three in the library. Betton had cleared a window, and the children were looking out at the murky, brownish convexity that filled half of it. Rig was holding a dirty, furry blanket. Karth was taking the electrodes off Oreth's temples, disengaging the AI link-up. "There was no interval," Oreth said.

"We aren't anywhere," Lidi said.

"There was no interval," Gveter repeated, scowling at the console. "That's right."

"Nothing happened," Karth said, skimming through the AI flight report.

Oreth got up, went to the window, and stood motionless looking out.

"That's it. M-60-340-nolo," Tai said.

All their words fell dead, had a false sound.

"Well! We did it, Shobies!" said Shan.

Nobody answered.

"Buzz Ve Port on the ansible," Shan said with determined jollity. "Tell 'em we're all here in one piece."

"All where?" Oreth asked.

"Yes, of course," Sweet Today said, but did nothing.

"Right," said Tai, going to the ship's ansible. She opened the field, centered to Ve, and sent a signal. Ship's ansibles worked only in the visual mode; she waited, watching the screen. She resignaled. They were all watching the screen.

"Nothing going through," she said.

Nobody told her to check the centering coordinates; in a network system nobody gets to dump their anxieties that easily. She checked the coordinates. She signaled; rechecked, reset, resignaled; opened the field and centered to Abbenay on Anarres and signaled. The ansible screen was blank.

"Check the—" Shan said, and stopped himself.

"The ansible is not functioning," Tai reported formally to her crew.

"Do you find malfunction?" Sweet Today asked.

"No. Nonfunction."

"We're going back now," said Lidi, still seated at the NAFAL console.

Her words, her tone, shook them apart.

"No, we're not!" Betton said on the intervid while Oreth said, "Back where?"

Tai, Lidi's Support, moved toward her as if to prevent her from activating the NAFAL drive, but then hastily moved back to the ansible to prevent Gveter from getting access to it. He stopped, taken aback, and said, "Perhaps the churten affected ansible function?"

"*I'm* checking it out," Tai said. "Why should it? Robot-operated ansible transmission functioned in all the test flights."

"Where are the AI reports?" Shan demanded.

"I told you, there are none," Karth answered sharply.

"Oreth was plugged in."

Oreth, still at the window, spoke without turning. "Nothing happened."

Sweet Today came over beside the Gethenian. Oreth looked at her and said, slowly, "Yes. Sweet Today. We cannot . . . do this. I think. I can't think."

Shan had cleared a second window, and stood looking out it. "Ugly," he said.

"What is?" said Lidi.

Gveter said, as if reading from the Ekumenical Atlas, "Thick, stable atmosphere, near the bottom of the temperature window for life. Micro-organisms. Bacterial clouds, bacterial reefs."

"Germ stew," Shan said. "Lovely place to send us."

"So that if we arrived as a neutron bomb or a blackhole event we'd only take bacteria with us," Tai said. "But we didn't."

"Didn't what?" said Lidi.

"Didn't arrive?" Karth asked.

"Hey," Betton said, "is everybody going to stay on the bridge?"

"I want to come there," said Rig's little pipe, and then Asten's voice, clear but shaky, "Maba, I'd like to go back to Liden now."

"Come on," Karth said, and went to meet the children. Oreth did not turn from the window, even when Asten came close and took Oreth's hand.

"What are you looking at, maba?"

"The planet, Asten."

"What planet?"

Oreth looked at the child then.

"There isn't anything," Asten said.

"That brown color—that's the surface, the atmosphere of a planet."

"There isn't any brown color. There isn't *anything*. I want to go back to Liden. You said we could when we were done with the test."

Oreth looked around, at last, at the others.

"Perception variation," Gveter said.

"I think," Tai said, "that we must establish that we are—that we got here—and then get here."

"You mean, go back," Betton said.

"The readings are perfectly clear," Lidi said, holding on to the rim of her seat with both hands and speaking very distinctly. "Every coordinate in order. That's M-60-Etcetera down there. What more do you want? Bacteria samples?"

"Yes," Tai said. "Instrument function's been affected, so we can't rely on instrumental records."

"Oh, shitsake!" said Lidi. "What a farce! All right. Suit up, go down, get some goo, and then let's get out. Go home. By NAFAL."

"By NAFAL?" Shan and Tai echoed, and Gveter said, "But we would spend seventeen years, Ve time, and no ansible to explain why."

"Why, Lidi?" Sweet Today asked.

Lidi stared at the Hainishwoman. "You want to churten again?" she demanded, raucous. She looked round at them all. "Are you people made of stone?" Her face was ashy, crumpled, shrunken. "It doesn't bother you, seeing through the walls?"

No one spoke, until Shan said cautiously, "How do you mean?"

"I can see the stars through the walls!" She stared round at them again, pointing at the carpet with its woven constellations. "You can't?" When no one answered, her jaw trembled in a little spasm, and she said, "All right. All right. I'm off duty. Sorry. Be in my room." She stood up. "Maybe you should lock me in," she said.

"Nonsense," said Sweet Today.

"If I fall through," Lidi began, and did not finish. She walked to the door, stiffly and cautiously, as if through a thick fog. She said something they did not understand, "Cause," or perhaps, "Gauze."

Sweet Today followed her.

"I can see the stars too!" Rig announced.

"Hush," Karth said, putting an arm around the child.

"I can! I can see all the stars everywhere. And I can see Ve Port. And I can see anything I want!"

"Yes, of course, but hush now," the mother murmured, at which the child pulled free, stamped, and shrilled, "I can! I can too! I can see *everything*! And Asten can't! And there *is* a planet, there is too! No, don't hold me! Don't! Let me go!"

Grim, Karth carried the screaming child off to their quarters. Asten turned around to yell after Rig, "There is *not* any planet! You're just making it up!"

Grim, Oreth said, "Go to our room, please, Asten."

Asten burst into tears and obeyed. Oreth, with a glance of apology to the others, followed the short, weeping figure across the bridge and out into the corridor.

The four remaining on the bridge stood silent.

"Canaries," Shan said.

"Khallucinations?" Gveter proposed, subdued. "An effect of the churten on extrasensitive organisms—maybe?"

Tai nodded.

"Then is the ansible not functioning or are we hallucinating nonfunction?" Shan asked after a pause.

Gveter went to the ansible; this time Tai walked away from it, leaving it to him. "I want to go down," she said.

"No reason not to, I suppose," Shan said unenthusiastically.

"Khwat reason to?" Gveter asked over his shoulder.

"It's what we're here for, isn't it? It's what we volunteered to do, isn't it? To test instantaneous—transilience—prove that it worked, that we are here! With the ansible out, it'll be seventeen years before Ve gets our radio signal!"

"We can just churten back to Ve and *tell* them," Shan said. "If we did that now, we'd have been . . . here . . . about eight minutes."

"Tell them—tell them what? What kind of evidence is that?"

"Anecdotal," said Sweet Today, who had come back quietly to the bridge; she moved like a big sailing ship, imposingly silent.

"Is Lidi all right?" Shan asked.

"No," Sweet Today answered. She sat down where Lidi had sat, at the NAFAL console.

"I ask a consensus about going down onplanet," Tai said.

"I'll ask the others," Gveter said, and went out, returning presently with Karth. "Go down, if you want," the Gethenian said. "Oreth's staying with the children for a bit. They are—we are extremely disoriented."

"I will come down," Gveter said.

"Can I come?" Betton asked, almost in a whisper, not raising his eyes to any adult face.

"No," Tai said, as Gveter said, "Yes."

Betton looked at his mother, one quick glance.

"Why not?" Gveter asked her.

"We don't know the risks."

"The planet was surveyed."

"By robot ships—"

"We'll wear suits." Gveter was honestly puzzled.

"I don't want the responsibility," Tai said through her teeth.

"Khwy is it yours?" Gveter asked, more puzzled still. "We all share it; Betton is crew. I don't understand."

"I know you don't understand," Tai said, turned her back on them both, and went out. The man and the boy stood staring, Gveter after Tai, Betton at the carpet.

"I'm sorry," Betton said.

"Not to be," Gveter told him.

"What is . . . what is going on?" Shan asked in an over-controlled voice. "Why are we—we keep crossing, we keep—coming and going—"

"Confusion due to the churten experience," Gveter said.

Sweet Today turned from the console. "I have sent a distress signal," she said. "I am unable to operate the NAFAL system. The radio—" She cleared her throat. "Radio function seems erratic."

There was a pause.

"This is not happening," Shan said, or Oreth said, but Oreth had stayed with the children in another part of the ship, so it could not have been Oreth who said, "This is not happening," it must have been Shan.

A chain of cause and effect is an easy thing to describe; a cessation of cause and effect is not. To those who live in time, sequence is the norm, the only model, and simultaneity seems a muddle, a mess, a hopeless confusion, and the description of that confusion hopelessly confusing. As the members of the crew network no longer perceived the network steadily, and were unable to communicate their perceptions, an individual perception was the only clue to follow through the labyrinth of their dislocation. Gveter perceived himself as being on the bridge with Shan, Sweet Today, Betton, Karth, and Tai. He perceived himself as methodically checking out the ship's systems. The NAFAL he found dead, the radio functioning in erratic bursts, the internal electrical and mechanical systems of the ship all in order. He sent out a lander unmanned and brought it back, and perceived it as functioning normally. He perceived himself discussing with Tai her determination to go down onplanet. Since he admitted his unwillingness to trust any instrumental reading on the ship, he had to admit her point that only material evidence would show that they had actually arrived at their destination, M-60-340-nolo. If they were going to have to spend the next seventeen years traveling back to Ve in real time, it would be nice to have something to show for it, even if only a handful of slime.

He perceived this discussion as perfectly rational.

It was, however, interrupted by outbursts of egoizing not characteristic of the crew.

"If you're going, go!" Shan said.

"Don't give me orders," Tai said.

"Somebody's got to stay in control here," Shan said.

"Not the men!" Tai said.

"Not the Terrans," Karth said. "Have you people no self-respect?"

71

"Stress," Gveter said. "Come on, Tai, Betton, all right, let's go, all right?"

In the lander, everything was clear to Gveter. One thing happened after another just as it should. Lander operation is very simple, and he asked Betton to take them down. The boy did so. Tai sat, tense and compact as always, her strong fists clenched on her knees. Betton managed the little ship with aplomb, and sat back, tense also, but dignified: "We're down," he said.

"No, we're not," Tai said.

"It—it says contact," Betton said, losing his assurance.

"An excellent landing," Gveter said. "Never even felt it." He was running the usual tests. Everything was in order. Outside the lander ports pressed a brownish darkness, a gloom. When Betton put on the outside lights the atmosphere, like a dark fog, diffused the light into a useless glare.

"Tests all tally with survey reports," Gveter said. "Will you go out, Tai, or use the servos?"

"Out," she said.

"Out," Betton echoed.

Gveter, assuming the formal crew role of Support, which one of them would have assumed if he had been going out, assisted them to lock their helmets and decontaminate their suits; he opened the hatch series for them, and watched them on the vid and from the port as they climbed down from the outer hatch. Betton went first. His slight figure, elongated by the whitish suit, was luminous in the weak glare of the lights. He walked a few steps from the ship, turned, and waited. Tai was stepping off the ladder. She seemed to grow very short—did she kneel down? Gveter looked from the port to the vid screen and back. She was shrinking? Sinking—she must be sinking into the surface—which could not be solid, then, but bog, or some suspension like quicksand—but Betton had walked on it and was walking back to her, two steps, three steps, on the ground which Gveter could not see clearly but which must be solid, and which must be holding Betton up because he was lighter—but no, Tai must have stepped into a hole, a trench of some kind, for he could see her only from the waist up now, her legs hidden in the dark bog or fog, but she was moving, moving quickly, going right away from the lander and from Betton.

"Bring them back," Shan said, and Gveter said on the suit intercom, "Please return to the lander, Betton and Tai." Betton at once started up the ladder, then turned to look for his mother. A dim blotch that might be her helmet showed in the brown gloom, almost beyond the suffusion of light from the lander.

"Please come in, Betton. Please return, Tai."

The whitish suit flickered up the ladder, while Betton's voice in the intercom pleaded, "Tai—Tai, come back—Gveter, should I go after her?"

"No. Tai, please return at once to lander."

The boy's crew integrity held; he came up into the lander and watched from the outer hatch, as Gveter watched from the port. The vid had lost her. The pallid blotch sank into the formless murk.

Gveter perceived that the instruments recorded that the lander had sunk 3.2 meters since contact with planet surface and was continuing to sink at an increasing rate.

"What is the surface, Betton?"

"Like muddy ground—where is she?"

"Please return at once, Tai!"

"Please return to *Shoby*, Lander One and all crew," said the ship intercom; it was Tai's voice. "This is Tai," it said. "Please return at once to ship, lander and all crew."

"Stay in suit, in decon, please, Betton," Gveter said. "I'm sealing the hatch."

"But—all right," said the boy's voice.

Gveter took the lander up, decontaminating it and Betton's suit on the way. He perceived that Betton and Shan came with him through the hatch series into the *Shoby* and along the halls to the bridge, and that Karth, Sweet Today, Shan, and Tai were on the bridge.

Betton ran to his mother and stopped; he did not put out his hands to her. His face was immobile, as if made of wax or wood.

"Were you frightened?" she asked. "What happened down there?" And she looked to Gveter for an explanation.

Gveter perceived nothing. Unduring a nonperiod of no long, he perceived nothing was had happening happened that had not happened. Lost, he groped, lost, he found the word, the word that saved—"You—" he said, his tongue thick, dumb—"You called us."

It seemed that she denied, but it did not matter. What mattered? Shan was talking. Shan could tell. "Nobody called, Gveter," he said. "You and Betton went out, I was Support; when I realized I couldn't get the lander stable, that there's something funny about that surface, I called you back into the lander, and we came up."

All Gveter could say was, "Insubstantial . . ."

"But Tai came—" Betton began, and stopped. Gveter perceived that the boy moved away from his mother's denying touch. What mattered?

"Nobody went down," Sweet Today said. After a silence and before it, she said, "There is no down to go to."

Gveter tried to find another word, but there was none. He perceived outside the main port a brownish, murky convexity, through which, as he looked intently, he saw small stars shining.

He found a word then, the wrong word. "Lost," he said, and speaking perceived how the ship's lights dimmed slowly into a brownish murk, faded, darkened, were gone, while all the soft hum and busyness of the ship's systems died away into the real silence that was always there. But there was nothing there. Nothing had happened. We are at Ve Port! he tried with all his will to say; but there was no saying.

The suns burn through my flesh, Lidi said.

I am the suns, said Sweet Today. Not I, all is.

Don't breathe! cried Oreth.

It is death, Shan said. What I feared, is: nothing.

Nothing, they said.

Unbreathing, the ghosts flitted, shifted, in the ghost shell of a cold, dark hull floating near a world of brown fog, an unreal planet. They spoke, but there were no voices. There is no sound in vacuum, nor in nontime.

In her cabined solitude, Lidi felt the gravity lighten to the half-G of the ship's core mass; she saw them, the nearer and the farther suns, burn through the dark gauze of the walls and hulls and the bedding and her body. The brightest, the sun of this system, floated directly under her navel. She did not know its name.

I am the darkness between the suns, one said.

I am nothing, one said.

I am you, one said.

You—one said—You—

And breathed, and reached out, and spoke: "Listen!" Crying out to the other, to the others, "Listen!"

"We have always known this. This is where we have always been, will always be, at the hearth, at the center. There is nothing to be afraid of, after all."

"I can't breathe," one said.

"I am not breathing," one said.

"There is nothing to breathe," one said.

"You are, you are breathing, please breathe!" said another.

"We're here, at the hearth," said another.

Oreth had laid the fire, Karth lit it. As it caught they both said softly, in Karhidish, "Praise also the light, and creation unfinished."

The fire caught with spark spits, crackles, sudden flares. It did not go out. It burned. The others grouped round.

They were nowhere, but they were nowhere together; the ship was dead, but they were in the ship. A dead ship cools off fairly quickly, but not immediately. Close the doors, come in by the fire; keep the cold night out, before we go to bed.

Karth went with Rig to persuade Lidi from her starry vault. The navigator would not get up. "It's my fault," she said.

"Don't egoize," Karth said mildly. "How could it be?"

"I don't know. I want to stay here," Lidi muttered. Then Karth begged her: "Oh, Lidi, not alone!"

"How else?" the old woman asked coldly.

But she was ashamed of herself, then, and ashamed of her guilt trip, and growled, "Oh, all right." She heaved herself up and wrapped a blanket around her body and followed Karth and Rig. The child carried a little biolume; it glowed in the black corridors, just as the plants of the aerobic tanks lived on, metabolizing, making an air to breathe, for a while. The light moved before her like a star among the stars through darkness to the room full of books, where the fire burned in the stone hearth. "Hello, children," Lidi said. "What are we doing here?"

"Telling stories," Sweet Today replied.

Shan had a little voice recorder notebook in his hand.

"Does it work?" Lidi inquired.

"Seems to. We thought we'd tell . . . what happened," Shan said, squinting the narrow black eyes in his narrow black face at the firelight. "Each of us. What we—what it seemed like, seems like, to us. So that . . ."

"As a record, yes. In case . . . How funny that it works, though, your notebook. When nothing else does."

"It's voice-activated," Shan said absently. "So. Go on, Gveter."

Gveter finished telling his version of the expedition to the planet's surface. "We didn't even bring back samples," he ended. "I never thought of them."

"Shan went with you, not me," Tai said.

"You did go, and I did," the boy said with a certainty that stopped her. "And we did go outside. And Shan and Gveter were Support, in the lander. And I took samples. They're in the Stasis closet."

"I don't know if Shan was in the lander or not," Gveter said, rubbing his forehead painfully.

"Where would the lander have gone?" Shan said. "Nothing is out there —we're nowhere—outside time, is all I can think—But when one of you tells how they saw it, it seems as if it was that way, but then the next one changes the story, and I . . ."

Oreth shivered, drawing closer to the fire.

"I never believed this damn thing would work," said Lidi, bearlike in the dark cave of her blanket.

"Not understanding it was the trouble," Karth said. "None of us understood how it would work, not even Gveter. Isn't that true?"

"Yes," Gveter said.

"So that if our psychic interaction with it affected the process—"

"Or *is* the process," said Sweet Today, "so far as we're concerned."

"Do you mean," Lidi said in a tone of deep existential disgust, "that we have to *believe* in it to make it work?"

"You have to believe in yourself in order to act, don't you?" Tai said.

"No," the navigator said. "Absolutely not. I don't believe in myself. I *know* some things. Enough to go on."

"An analogy," Gveter offered. "The effective action of a crew depends on the members perceiving themselves as a crew—you could call it believing in the crew, or just *being* it—Right? So, maybe, to churten, we—we conscious ones—maybe it depends on our consciously perceiving ourselves as . . . as transilient—as being in the other place—the destination?"

"We lost our crewness, certainly, for a—are there whiles?" Karth said. "We fell apart."

"We lost the thread," Shan said.

"Lost," Oreth said meditatively, laying another massive, half-weightless log on the fire, volleying sparks up into the chimney, slow stars.

"We lost—what?" Sweet Today asked.

No one answered for a while.

"When I can see the sun through the carpet . . ." Lidi said.

"So can I," Betton said, very low.

"I can see Ve Port," said Rig. "And everything. I can tell you what I can see. I can see Liden if I look. And my room on the *Oneblin*. And—"

"First, Rig," said Sweet Today, "tell us what happened."

"All right," Rig said agreeably. "Hold on to me harder, maba, I start floating. Well, we went to the liberry, me and Asten and Betton, and Betton was Elder Sib, and the adults were on the bridge, and I was going to go to sleep like I do when we naffle-fly, but before I even lay down there was the brown planet and Ve Port and both the suns and everywhere else, and you could see through everything, but Asten couldn't. But I can."

"We never went *anywhere*," Asten said. "Rig tells stories all the time."

"We all tell stories all the time, Asten," Karth said.

"Not dumb ones like Rig's!"

"Even dumber," said Oreth. "What we need . . . What we need is . . ."

"We need to know," Shan said, "what transilience is, and we don't, because we never did it before, nobody ever did it before."

"Not in the flesh," said Lidi.

"We need to know what's—real—what happened, *whether* anything happened—" Tai gestured at the cave of firelight around them and the dark beyond it. "Where are we? Are we here? Where is here? What's the story?"

"We have to tell it," Sweet Today said. "Recount it. Relate it. . . . Like Rig. Asten, how does a story begin?"

"A thousand winters ago, a thousand miles away," the child said; and Shan murmured, "Once upon a time . . ."

"There was a ship called the *Shoby*," said Sweet Today, "on a test flight, trying out the churten, with a crew of ten.

"Their names were Rig, Asten, Betton, Karth, Oreth, Lidi, Tai, Shan, Gveter, and Sweet Today. And they related their story, each one and together. . . ."

There was silence, the silence that was always there, except for the stir and crackle of the fire and the small sounds of their breathing, their movements, until one of them spoke at last, telling the story.

"The boy and his mother," said the light, pure voice, "were the first human beings ever to set foot on that world."

Again the silence; and again a voice. ·

"Although she wished . . . she realized that she really hoped the thing wouldn't work, because it would make her skills, her whole life, obsolete . . . all the same she really wanted to learn how to use it, too, if she could, if she wasn't too old to learn. . . ."

A long, softly throbbing pause, and another voice.

"They went from world to world, and each time they lost the world they left, lost it in time dilation, their friends getting old and dying while they were in NAFAL flight. If there were a way to live in one's own time, and yet move among the worlds, they wanted to try it. . . ."

"Staking everything on it," the next voice took up the story, "because nothing works except what we give our souls to, nothing's safe except what we put at risk."

A while, a little while; and a voice.

"It was like a game. It was like we were still in the *Shoby* at Ve Port just waiting before we went into NAFAL flight. But it was like we were at the brown planet too. At the same time. And one of them was just pretend, and the other one wasn't, but I didn't know which. So it was like when you pretend in a game. But I didn't want to play. I didn't know how."

Another voice.

"If the churten principle were proved to be applicable to actual transilience of living, conscious beings, it would be a great event in the mind of his people—for all people. A new understanding. A new partnership. A new way of being in the universe. A wider freedom. . . . He wanted that very much. He wanted to be one of the crew that first formed that partnership, the first people to be able to think this thought, and to . . . to relate it. But also he was afraid of it. Maybe it wasn't a true relation, maybe false, maybe only a dream. He didn't know."

It was not so cold, so dark, at their backs, as they sat round the fire. Was it the waves of Liden, hushing on the sand?

Another voice.

"She thought a lot about her people, too. About guilt, and expiation, and sacrifice. She wanted a lot to be on this flight that might give people—more freedom. But it was different from what she thought it would be. What happened—what *happened* wasn't what mattered. What mattered was that she came to be with people who gave *her* freedom. Without guilt. She wanted to stay with them, to be crew with them. . . . And with her son. Who was the first human being to set foot on an unknown world."

A long silence; but not deep, only as deep as the soft drum of the ship's systems, steady and unconscious as the circulation of the blood.

Another voice.

"They were thoughts in the mind; what else had they ever been? So they could be in Ve and at the brown planet, and desiring flesh and entire spirit, and illusion and reality, all at once, as they'd always been. When he remembered this, his confusion and fear ceased, for he knew that they couldn't be lost."

"They got lost. But they found the way," said another voice, soft above the hum and hushing of the ship's systems, in the warm fresh air and light inside the solid walls and hulls.

Only nine voices had spoken, and they looked for the tenth; but the tenth had gone to sleep, thumb in mouth.

"That story was told and is yet to be told," the mother said. "Go on. I'll churten here with Rig."

They left those two by the fire, and went to the bridge, and then to the hatches to invite on board a crowd of anxious scientists, engineers, and officials of Ve Port and the Ekumen, whose instruments had been assuring them that the *Shoby* had vanished, forty-four minutes ago, into nonexistence, into silence. "What happened?" they asked. "What happened?" And the Shobies looked at one another and said, "Well, it's quite a story. . . ."

GREG EGAN
The Caress

▼

This was a good year for hot new Australian writer Greg Egan. Although he's been publishing for a year or two already, 1990 was the year when Egan suddenly seemed to be turning up *everywhere* with high-quality stories. In fact, Egan published several strong stories in 1990, any one of which might well have been worthy of inclusion in a "Best" anthology in another year. I finally narrowed the field down to two stories, though—"Learning to Be Me," from *Interzone*, which appears elsewhere in this anthology, and the story that follows, my favorite Egan this year, the taut, suspenseful, and darkly powerful story of a high-tech future cop attempting, against heavy odds, to prevent a bizarre and unsettling crime . . .

Born in 1961, Greg Egan lives in Australia, and to date has made a number of sales to *Interzone* and *Isaac Asimov's Science Fiction Magazine*, as well as to *Pulphouse, Analog, The Year's Best Fantasy,* and elsewhere. He currently works part-time programming computers for a Perth hospital, but I doubt if that will remain true for long—my guess is that he is on his way, and with considerable velocity, to establishing a career for himself as a full-time writer . . . and probably a formidable reputation as well.

▼

The Caress

GREG EGAN

Two smells hit me when I kicked down the door: death, and the scent of an animal.

A man who passed the house each day had phoned us, anonymously; worried by the sight of a broken window left unrepaired, he'd knocked on the front door with no results. On his way to the back door, he'd glimpsed blood on a kitchen wall through a gap in the curtains.

The place had been ransacked; all that remained downstairs were the drag marks on the carpet from the heaviest furniture. The woman in the kitchen, mid fifties, throat slit, had been dead for at least a week.

My helmet was filing sound and vision, but it couldn't record the animal smell. The correct procedure was to make a verbal comment, but I didn't say a word. Why? Call it a vestigial need for independence. Soon they'll be logging our brain waves, our heart beats, who knows what, and all of it subpoenable. "Detective Segel, the evidence shows that you experienced a penile erection when the defendant opened fire. Would you describe that as an *appropriate* response?"

Upstairs was a mess. Clothes scattered in the bedroom. Books, CDs, papers, upturned drawers, spread across the floor of the study. Medical texts. In one corner, piles of CD periodicals stood out from the jumble by their jackets' uniformity: *The New England Journal of Medicine*, *Nature*, *Clinical Biochemistry* and *Laboratory Embryology*. A framed scroll hung on the wall, awarding the degree of Doctor of Philosophy to Freda Anne Macklenburg in the year two thousand and twenty-three. The desktop had dust-free spaces shaped like a monitor and a keyboard. I noticed a wall outlet with a pilot light; the switch was down but the light was dead. The room light wasn't working; ditto elsewhere.

Back on the ground floor, I found a door behind the stairs, presumably leading to a basement. Locked. I hesitated. Entering the house I'd had no choice but to force my way in; here, though, I was on shakier legal ground. I hadn't searched thoroughly for keys, and I had no clear reason to believe it was urgent to get into the basement.

But what would one more broken door change? Cops have been sued for failing to wipe their boots clean on the doormat. If a citizen wants to screw you, they'll find a reason, even if you came in on your knees, waving a handful of warrants, and saved their whole family from torture and death.

No room to kick, so I punched out the lock. The smell had me gagging, but it was the excess, the concentration, that was overwhelming; the scent in itself wasn't foul. Upstairs, seeing medical books, I'd thought of guinea pigs, rats and mice, but this was no stink of caged rodents.

I switched on the torch in my helmet and moved quickly down the narrow concrete steps. Over my head was a thick, square pipe. An air-conditioning duct? That made sense; the house couldn't *normally* smell the way it did, but with the power cut off to a basement air conditioner—

The torch beam showed a shelving unit, decorated with trinkets and potted plants. A TV set. Landscape paintings on the wall. A pile of straw on the concrete floor. Curled on the straw, the powerful body of a leopard, lungs visibly laboring, but otherwise still.

When the beam fell upon a tangle of auburn hair, I thought, it's chewing on a severed human head. I continued to approach, expecting, hoping, that by disturbing the feeding animal I could provoke it into attacking me. I was carrying a weapon that could have spattered it into a fine mist of blood and gristle, an outcome which would have involved me in a great deal less tedium and bureaucracy than dealing with it alive. I directed the light toward its head again, and realized that I'd been mistaken; it wasn't chewing anything, its head was hidden, tucked away, and the human head was simply—

Wrong again. The human head was simply joined to the leopard's body. Its human neck took on fur and spots and merged with the leopard's shoulders.

I squatted down beside it, thinking, above all else, what those claws could do to me if my attention lapsed. The head was a woman's. Frowning. Apparently asleep. I placed one hand below her nostrils, and felt the air blast out in time with the heavings of the leopard's great chest. That, more than the smooth transition of the skin, made the union real for me.

I explored the rest of the room. There was a pit in one corner that turned out to be a toilet bowl sunk into the floor. I put my foot on a nearby pedal, and the bowl flushed from a hidden cistern. There was an upright freezer, standing in a puddle of water. I opened it to find a rack containing thirty-five small plastic vials. Every one of them bore smeared red letters, spelling out the word SPOILED. Temperature sensitive dye.

I returned to the leopard woman. Asleep? Feigning sleep? Sick? Comatose? I patted her on the cheek, and not gently. The skin seemed hot, but I had no idea what her temperature ought to be. I shook her by one shoulder, this time with a little more respect, as if waking her by touching the leopard part might somehow be more dangerous. No effect.

Then I stood up, fought back a sigh of irritation (Psych latch on to all your little noises; I've been grilled for hours over such things as an injudicious whoop of triumph), and called for an ambulance.

I should have known better than to hope that *that* would be the end of my problems. I had to physically obstruct the stairway to stop the ambulance men from retreating. One of them puked. Then they refused to put her on the stretcher unless I promised to ride with her to the hospital. She was only about two meters long, excluding the tail, but must have weighed a hundred and fifty kilos, and it took the three of us to get her up the awkward stairs.

We covered her completely with a sheet before leaving the house, and I took the trouble to arrange it to keep it from revealing the shape beneath. A small crowd had gathered outside, the usual motley collection of voyeurs. The forensic team arrived just then, but I'd already told them everything by radio.

At the Casualty Department of St Dominic's, doctor after doctor took one look under the sheet and then fled, some muttering half-baked excuses, most not bothering. I was about to lose my temper when the fifth one I cornered, a young woman, turned pale but kept her ground. After poking and pinching and shining a torch into the leopard woman's forced-open eyes, Dr. Muriel Beatty (from her name badge) announced, "She's in a coma," and started extracting details from me. When I'd told her everything, I squeezed in some questions of my own.

"How would someone do this? Gene splicing? Transplant surgery?"

"I doubt it was either. More likely she's a chimera."

I frowned. "That's some kind of mythical—"

"Yes, but it's also a bioengineering term. You can physically mix the cells of two genetically distinct early embryos, and obtain a blastocyst that will develop into a single organism. If they're both of the same species, there's a very high success rate; for different species it's trickier. People made crude sheep/goat chimeras as far back as the nineteen sixties, but I've read nothing new on the subject for five or ten years. I would have said it was no longer being seriously pursued. Let alone pursued with humans." She stared down at her patient with unease and fascination. "I wouldn't know how they guaranteed such a sharp distinction between the head and the body; a thousand times more effort has gone into *this* than just stirring two clumps of cells together. I guess you could say it was something half-way between fetal transplant surgery and chimerization. And there must have been genetic manipulation as well, to smooth out the biochemical differences." She laughed drily. "So both your suggestions I dismissed just then were probably partly right. *Of course!*"

"What?"

"No wonder she's in a coma! That freezer full of vials you mentioned— she probably needs an external supply for half a dozen hormones that are insufficiently active across species. Can I arrange for someone to go to the house and look through the dead woman's papers? We need to know exactly what those vials contained. Even if she made it up herself from off-the-shelf sources, we might be able to find the recipe—but chances are she had a contract with a biotechnology company for a regular, pre-mixed supply. So if we can find, say, an invoice with a product reference number, that would be the quickest, surest way to get this patient what she needs to stay alive."

I agreed, and accompanied a lab technician back to the house, but he found nothing of use in the study, or the basement. After talking it over with Muriel Beatty on the phone, I started ringing local biotech companies, quoting the deceased woman's name and address. Several people said they'd heard of Dr. Macklenburg, but not as a customer. The fifteenth call produced results—deliveries for a company called Applied Veterinary Research had been sent to Macklenburg's address—and with a combination of threats and smooth talking (such as inventing an order number they could quote on their invoice), I managed to extract a promise that a batch of the "Applied Veterinary Research" preparation would be made up at once and rushed to St Dominic's.

Burglars *do* switch off the power sometimes, in the hope of disabling those (very rare) security devices that don't have battery back-up, but the house hadn't been broken into; the scattered glass from the window fell, in an undisturbed pattern, onto carpet where a sofa had left clear indentations. The fools had forgotten to break a window until after they'd taken the furniture. People *do* throw out invoices, but Macklenburg had kept all her videophone, water, gas, and electricity bills for the last five years. So, it looked like somebody had known about the chimera and wanted it dead, without wishing to be totally obvious, yet without being professional enough to manage anything subtler, or more certain.

I arranged for the chimera to be guarded. Probably a good idea anyway, to keep the media at bay when they found out about her.

Back in my office, I did a search of medical literature by Macklenburg, and found her name on only half a dozen papers. All were more than twenty years old. All were concerned with embryology, though (to the extent that

I could understand the jargon-laden abstracts, full of "zonae pellucidae" and "polar bodies") none were explicitly about chimeras.

The papers were all from one place; the Early Human Development Laboratory at St Andrew's Hospital. After some standard brush-offs from secretaries and assistants, I managed to get myself put through to one of Macklenburg's one time co-authors, a Dr. Henry Feingold, who looked rather old and frail. News of Macklenburg's death produced a wistful sigh, but no visible shock or distress.

"Freda left us back in '32 or '33. I've hardly set eyes on her since, except at the occasional conference."

"Where did she go to from St Andrew's?"

"Something in industry. She was rather vague about it. I'm not sure that she had a definite appointment lined up."

"Why did she resign?"

He shrugged. "Sick of the conditions here. Low pay, limited resources, bureaucratic restrictions, ethics committees. Some people learn to live with all that, some don't."

"Would you know anything about her work, her particular research interests, after she left?"

"I don't know that she *did* much research. She seemed to have stopped publishing, so I really couldn't say what she was up to."

Shortly after that (with unusual speed), clearance came through to access her taxation records. Since '35 she had been self-employed as a "freelance biotechnology consultant"; whatever that meant, it had provided her with a seven-figure income for the past fifteen years. There were at least a hundred different company names listed by her as sources of revenue. I rang the first one and found myself talking to an answering machine. It was after seven. I rang St Dominic's, and learnt that the chimera was still unconscious, but doing fine; the hormone mixture had arrived, and Muriel Beatty had located a veterinarian at the university with some relevant experience. So I swallowed my deprimers and went home.

The surest sign that I'm not fully down is the frustration I feel when opening my own front door. It's too bland, too easy: inserting three keys and touching my thumb to the scanner. Nothing inside is going to be dangerous or challenging. The deprimers are meant to work in five minutes. Some nights it's more like five hours.

Marion was watching TV, and called out, "Hi Dan."

I stood in the living room doorway. "Hi. How was your day?" She works in a child care center, which is my idea of a high-stress occupation. She shrugged. "Ordinary. How was yours?"

Something on the TV screen caught my eye. I swore for about a minute, mostly cursing a certain communications officer who I knew was responsible, though I couldn't have proved it. "How was my day? You're looking at it." The TV was showing part of my helmet log; the basement, my discovery of the chimera.

Marion said, "Ah. I was going to ask if you knew who the cop was."

"And you know what I'll be doing tomorrow? Trying to make sense of a few thousand phone calls from people who've seen this and decided they have something useful to say about it."

"That poor girl. Is she going to be okay?"

"I think so."

They played Muriel Beatty's speculations, again from my point of view, then cut to a couple of pocket experts who debated the fine points of chimerism while an interviewer did his best to drag in spurious references to everything from Greek mythology to *The Island of Doctor Moreau*.

I said, "I'm starving. Let's eat."

I woke at half past one, shaking and whimpering. Marion was already awake, trying to calm me down. Lately I'd been suffering a lot from delayed reactions like this. A few months earlier, two nights after a particularly brutal assault case, I'd been distraught and incoherent for hours.

On duty, we are what's called "primed." A mixture of drugs heightens various physiological and emotional responses, and suppresses others. Sharpens our reflexes. Keeps us calm and rational. Supposedly improves our judgment. (The media like to say that the drugs make us more aggressive, but that's garbage; why would the force intentionally create trigger-happy cops? Swift decisions and swift actions are the *opposite* of dumb brutality.)

Off duty, we are "deprimed." That's meant to make us the way we would be if we'd never taken the priming drugs. (A hazy concept, I have to admit. As if we'd never taken the priming drugs, *and* never spent the day at work? Or, as if we'd seen and done the very same things, without the primers to help us cope?)

Sometimes this seesaw works smoothly. Sometimes it fucks up.

I wanted to describe to Marion how I felt about the chimera. I wanted to talk about my fear and revulsion and pity and anger. All I could do was make unhappy noises. No words. She didn't say anything, she just held me, her long fingers cool on the burning skin of my face and chest.

When I finally exhausted myself into something approaching peace, I managed to speak. I whispered, "Why do you stay with me? Why do you put up with this?"

She turned away from me and said, "I'm tired. Go to sleep."

*   *   *

I enrolled for the force at the age of twelve. I continued my normal education, but that's when you have to start the course of growth factor injections, and weekend and vacation training, if you want to qualify for active duty. (It wasn't an irreversible obligation; I could have chosen a different career later, and paid off what had been invested in me at a hundred dollars or so a week over the next thirty years. Or, I could have failed the psychological tests, and been dropped without owing a cent. The tests before you even begin, however, tend to weed out anyone who's likely to do either.) It makes sense; rather than limiting recruitment to men and women meeting certain physical criteria, candidates are chosen according to intelligence and attitude, and then the secondary, but useful, characteristics of size, strength, and agility, are provided artificially.

So we're freaks, constructed and conditioned to meet the demands of the job. Less so than soldiers or professional athletes. Far less so than the average street gang member, who thinks nothing of using illegal growth promoters that lower his life expectancy to around thirty years. Who, unarmed but on a mixture of Berserker and Timewarp (oblivious to pain and most physical trauma and with a twenty-fold decrease in reaction times), can kill a hundred people in a crowd in five minutes, then vanish to a safe-house before the high ends and the fortnight of side effects begins. (A certain politician, a very popular man, advocates undercover operations to sell supplies of these drugs laced with fatal impurities, but he's not yet succeeded in making that legal.)

Yes, we're freaks; but if we have a problem, it's that we're still far too human.

When over a hundred thousand people phone in about an investigation, there's only one way to deal with their calls. It's called ARIA: Automated Remote Informant Analysis.

An initial filtering process identifies the blatantly obvious pranksters and lunatics. It's always *possible* that someone who phones in and spends ninety percent of their time ranting about UFOs, or communist conspiracies, or slicing up our genitals with razor blades, has something relevant and truthful to mention in passing, but it seems reasonable to give their evidence less weight than that of someone who sticks to the point. More sophisticated analysis of gestures (about thirty percent of callers don't switch off the vision), and speech patterns, supposedly picks up anyone who is, although superficially rational and apposite, actually suffering from psychotic delusions or fixations. Ultimately, each caller is given a "reliability factor" between zero and one, with the benefit of the doubt going to anyone who betrays no recognizable signs of dishonesty or mental illness. Some days I'm impressed with the sophistication of the software that makes these assessments. Other days I curse it as a heap of useless voodoo.

The relevant assertions (broadly defined) of each caller are extracted, and a frequency table is created, giving a count of the number of callers making each assertion, and their average reliability factor. Unfortunately, there are no simple rules to determine which assertions are most likely to be *true*. One thousand people might earnestly repeat a widespread but totally baseless rumor. A single honest witness might be distraught, or chemically screwed-up, and be given an unfairly poor rating. Basically, you have to read all the assertions—which is tedious, but still several thousand times faster than viewing every call.

001.	The chimera is a Martian.	15312	0.37
002.	The chimera is from a UFO.	14106	0.29
003.	The chimera is from Atlantis.	9003	0.24
004.	The chimera is a mutant.	8973	0.41
005.	The chimera resulted from human-leopard sexual intercourse.	6884	0.13
006.	The chimera is a sign from God.	2654	0.09
007.	The chimera is the Antichrist.	2432	0.07
008.	Caller is the chimera's father.	2390	0.12
009.	The chimera is a Greek deity.	1345	0.10
010.	Caller is the chimera's mother.	1156	0.09
011.	The chimera should be killed by authorities.	1009	0.19
012.	Caller has previously seen the chimera in their neighborhood.	988	0.39
013.	The chimera killed Freda Macklenburg.	945	0.24
014.	Caller intends killing the chimera.	903	0.49
015.	Caller killed Freda Macklenburg.	830	0.27

(If desperate, I could view, one by one, the seventeen hundred and thirty-three calls of items 14 and 15. Not yet, though; I still had plenty of better ways to spend my time.)

016.	The chimera was created by a foreign government.	724	0.18
017.	The chimera is the result of biological warfare.	690	0.14
018.	The chimera is a were-leopard.	604	0.09
019.	Caller wishes to have sexual intercourse with the chimera.	582	0.58

| 020. | Caller has previously seen a painting of the chimera. | 527 | 0.89 |

That was hardly surprising, considering the number of paintings there must be of fantastic and mythical creatures. But on the next page:

| 034. | The chimera closely resembles the creature portrayed in a painting entitled *The Caress*. | 94 | 0.92 |

Curious, I displayed some of the calls. The first few told me little more than the printout's summary line. Then, one man held up an open book to the lens. The glare of a light bulb reflected off the glossy paper rendered parts of it almost invisible, and the whole thing was slightly out of focus, but what I could see was intriguing.

A leopard with a woman's head was crouched near the edge of a raised, flat surface. A slender young man, bare to the waist, stood on the lower ground, leaning sideways onto the raised surface, cheek to cheek with the leopard woman, who pressed one forepaw against his abdomen in an awkward embrace. The man coolly gazed straight ahead, his mouth set primly, giving an impression of effete detachment. The woman's eyes were closed, or nearly so, and her expression seemed less certain the longer I stared—it might have been placid, dreamy contentment, it might have been erotic bliss. Both had auburn hair.

I selected a rectangle around the woman's face, enlarged it to fill the screen, then applied a smoothing option to make the blown-up pixels less distracting. With the glare, the poor focus, and limited resolution, the image was a mess. The best I could say was that the face in the painting was not wildly dissimilar to that of the woman I'd found in the basement.

A few dozen calls later, though, no doubt remained. One caller had even taken the trouble to capture a frame from the news broadcast and patch it into her call, side by side with a well-lit close-up of her copy of the painting. One view of a single expression does not define a human face, but the resemblance was far too close to be coincidental. Since—as many people told me, and I later checked for myself—*The Caress* had been painted in 1896 by the Belgian Symbolist artist Fernand Khnopff, the painting could not possibly have been based on the living chimera. So, it had to be the other way around.

I played all ninety-four calls. Most contained nothing but the same handful of simple facts about the painting. One went a little further.

A middle-aged man introduced himself as John Aldrich, art dealer and amateur art historian. After pointing out the resemblance, and talking briefly about Khnopff and *The Caress*, he added:

"Given that this poor woman looks exactly like Khnopff's sphinx, I wonder if you've considered the possibility that proponents of Lindhquistism are involved?" He blushed slightly. "Perhaps that's far-fetched, but I thought I should mention it."

So I called an on-line *Britannica*, and said "Lindhquistism."

Andreas Lindhquist, 1961–2030, was a Swiss performance artist, with the distinct financial advantage of being heir to a massive pharmaceuticals empire. Up until 2011, he engaged in a wide variety of activities of a bioartistic nature, progressing from generating sounds and images by computer processing of physiological signals (ECG, EEG, skin conductivity, hormonal levels continuously monitored by immunoelectric probes), to subjecting himself to surgery in a sterile, transparent cocoon in the middle of a packed auditorium, once to have his corneas gratuitously exchanged, left for right, and a second time to have them swapped back (he publicized a more ambitious version, in which he claimed every organ in his torso would be removed and reinserted facing backwards, but was unable to find a team of surgeons who considered this anatomically plausible).

In 2011, he developed a new obsession. He projected slides of classical paintings in which the figures had been blacked out, and had models in appropriate costumes and make-up strike poses in front of the screen, filling in the gaps.

Why? In his own words (or perhaps a translation):

The great artists are afforded glimpses into a separate, transcendental, timeless world. Does that world exist? Can we travel to it? No! We must force it into being around us! We must take these fragmentary glimpses and make them solid and tangible, make them live and breathe and walk amongst us, we must import art into reality, and by doing so transform our world into the world of the artists' vision.

I wondered what ARIA would have made of that.

Over the next ten years, he moved away from projected slides. He began hiring movie set designers and landscape architects to recreate in three dimensions the backgrounds of the paintings he chose. He discarded the use of make-up to alter the appearance of the models, and, when he found it impossible to find perfect lookalikes, he employed only those who, for sufficient payment, were willing to undergo cosmetic surgery.

His interest in biology hadn't entirely vanished; in 2021, on his sixtieth birthday, he had two tubes implanted in his skull, allowing him to constantly monitor, and alter, the precise neurochemical content of his brain ventricular fluid. After this, his requirements became even more stringent. The "cheating" techniques of movie sets were forbidden—a house, or a church, or a lake, or a mountain, glimpsed in the corner of the painting being "realized," had to *be there*, full scale and complete in every detail. Houses, churches, and small lakes were created; mountains he had to seek out—though he did transplant or destroy thousands of hectares of vegetation to alter their color and texture. His models were required to spend months before and after the "realization," scrupulously "living their roles," following complex rules and scenarios that Lindhquist devised, based on his interpretation of the painting's "characters." This aspect grew increasingly important to him:

The precise realization of the appearance—the surface, I call it, however three-dimensional—is only the most rudimentary beginning. It is the network of relationships between the subjects, and between the subjects and their setting, that constitutes the challenge for the generation that follows me.

At first, it struck me as astonishing that I'd never even heard of this maniac; his sheer extravagance must have earned him a certain notoriety. But there are millions of eccentrics in the world, and thousands of extremely wealthy ones—and I was only five when Lindhquist died of a heart attack in 2030, leaving his fortune to a nine-year-old son.

As for disciples, *Britannica* listed half a dozen scattered around Eastern Europe, where apparently he'd found the most respect. All seemed to have completely abandoned his excesses, offering volumes of aesthetic theories in support of the use of painted plywood and mime artists in stylized masks. In fact, most did just that—offered the volumes, and didn't even bother with the plywood and the mime artists. I couldn't imagine any of them having either the money or the inclination to sponsor embryological research thousands of kilometers away.

For obscure reasons of copyright law, works of visual art are rarely present in publicly accessible databases, so in my lunch hour I went out and bought a book on Symbolist painters which included a color plate of *The Caress*. I made a dozen (illegal) copies, blow-ups of various sizes. Curiously, in each one the expression of the sphinx (as Aldrich had called her) struck me as subtly different. Her mouth and her eyes (one fully closed, one infinitesimally open) could not be said to portray a definite smile, but the shading of the cheeks hinted at one—in certain enlargements, viewed from certain angles. The young man's face also changed, from vaguely troubled to slightly bored, from resolved to dissipated, from noble to effeminate. The features of both seemed to lie on complicated and uncertain borders between regions of definite mood, and the slightest shift in viewing conditions was enough to force a complete reinterpretation. If that had been Khnopff's intention it was a masterful achievement, but I also found it extremely frustrating. The book's brief commentary was no help, praising the painting's "perfectly balanced composition and delightful thematic ambiguity," and suggesting that the leopard's head was "perversely modeled on the artist's sister, with whose beauty he was constantly obsessed."

Unsure for the moment just how, if at all, I ought to pursue this strand of the investigation, I sat at my desk for several minutes, wondering (but not inclined to check) if every one of the leopard's spots shown in the painting had been reproduced faithfully *in vivo*. I wanted to do something tangible, set something in motion, before I put *The Caress* aside and returned to more routine lines of inquiry.

So I made one more blow-up of the painting, this time using the copier's editing facilities to surround the man's head and shoulders with a uniform dark background. I took it down to communications, and handed it to Steve Birbeck (the man I knew had leaked my helmet log to the media).

I said, "Put out an alert on this guy. Wanted for questioning in connection with the Macklenburg murder."

I found nothing else of interest in the ARIA printout, so I picked up where I'd left off the night before, phoning companies that had made use of Freda Macklenburg's services.

The work she had done had no specific connection with embryology. Her advice and assistance seemed to have been sought for a wide range of un- connected problems in a dozen fields—tissue culture work, the use of re- troviruses as gene-therapy vectors, cell membrane electrochemistry, protein purification, and still other areas where the vocabulary meant nothing to me at all.

"And did Dr. Macklenburg solve this problem?"

"Absolutely. She knew a perfect way around the stumbling block that had been holding us up for months."

"How did you find out about her?"

"There's a register of consultants, indexed by speciality."

There was indeed. She was in it in fifty-nine places. Either she somehow knew the detailed specifics of all these areas, better than many people who were actually working in them full-time, or she had access to world-class experts who could put the right words into her mouth.

Her sponsor's method of funding her work? Paying her not in money, but in expertise she could then sell as her own? Who would have so many biological scientists on tap?

The Lindhquist empire?

(So much for escaping *The Caress*.)

Her phone bills showed no long distance calls, but that meant nothing; the local Lindhquist branch would have had its own private international network.

I looked up Lindhquist's son Gustave in *Who's Who*. It was a very sketchy entry. Born to a surrogate mother. Donor ovum anonymous. Educated by tutors. As yet unmarried at twenty-nine. Reclusive. Apparently immersed in his business concerns. Not a word about artistic pretensions, but nobody tells everything to *Who's Who*.

The preliminary forensic report arrived, with nothing very useful. No evidence of a protracted struggle—no bruising, no skin or blood found under Macklenburg's fingernails. Apparently she'd been taken entirely by surprise. The throat wound had been made by a thin, straight, razor-sharp blade, with a single powerful stroke.

There were five genotypes, besides Macklenburg's and the chimera's, present in hairs and flakes of dead skin found in the house. Precise dating isn't possible, but all showed a broad range in the age of shedding, which meant regular visitors, friends, not strangers. All five had been in the kitchen at one time or another. Only Macklenburg and the chimera showed up in the basement in amounts that could not be accounted for by drift and second party transport, while the chimera seemed to have rarely left her special room. One prevalent male had been in most of the rest of the house, including the bedroom, but not the bed—or at least not since the sheets had last been changed. All of this was unlikely to have a direct bearing on the murder; the best assassins either leave no biological detritus at all, or plant material belonging to someone else.

The interviewers' report came in soon after, and that was even less helpful. Macklenburg's next of kin was a cousin, with whom she had not been in touch, and who knew even less about the dead woman than I did. Her neighbors were all much too respectful of privacy to have known or cared who her friends had been, and none would admit to having noticed anything unusual on the day of the murder.

I sat and stared at *The Caress*.

Some lunatic with a great deal of money—perhaps connected to Lindhquist, perhaps not—had commissioned Freda Macklenburg to create the chimera to match the sphinx in the painting. But who would want to fake a burglary, murder Macklenburg, and endanger the chimera's life, without making the effort to actually kill it?

The phone rang. It was Muriel. The chimera was awake.

The two officers outside had had a busy shift so far; one psycho with a knife, two photographers disguised as doctors, and a religious fanatic with a mail-order exorcism kit. The news reports hadn't mentioned the name of the hospital, but there were only a dozen plausible candidates, and the staff could not be sworn to secrecy or immunized against the effect of bribes. In a day or two, the chimera's location would be common knowledge. If things didn't quiet down, I'd have to consider trying to arrange for a room in a prison infirmary, or a military hospital.

"You saved my life."

The chimera's voice was deep and quiet and calm, and she looked right at me as she spoke. I'd expected her to be painfully shy, amongst strangers for perhaps the first time ever. She lay curled on her side on the bed, not covered by a sheet but with her head resting on a clean, white pillow. The smell was noticeable, but not unpleasant. Her tail, as thick as my wrist and longer than my arm, hung over the edge of the bed, restlessly swinging.

"Dr. Beatty saved your life." Muriel stood at the foot of the bed, glancing regularly at a blank sheet of paper on a clipboard. "I'd like to ask you some questions." She said nothing to that, but her eyes stayed on me. "Could you tell me your name, please?"

"Catherine."

"Do you have another name? A surname?"

"No."

"How old are you, Catherine?" Primed or not, I couldn't help feeling a slight giddiness, a sense of surreal inanity to be asking routine questions of a sphinx plucked from a nineteenth century oil painting.

"Seventeen."

"You know that Freda Macklenburg is dead?"

"Yes." Quieter, but still calm.

"What was your relationship with her?"

She frowned slightly, then gave an answer that sounded rehearsed but sincere, as if she had long expected to be asked this. "She was everything. She was my mother and my teacher and my friend." Misery and loss came and went on her face, a flicker, a twitch.

"Tell me what you heard, the day the power went off."

"Someone came to visit Freda. I heard the car, and the doorbell. It was a man. I couldn't hear what he said, but I could hear the sound of his voice."

"Was it a voice you'd heard before?"

"I don't think so."

"How did they sound? Were they shouting? Arguing?"

"No. They sounded friendly. Then they stopped, it was quiet. A little while after that, the power went off. Then I heard a truck pull up, and a whole lot of noise—footsteps, things being shifted about. But no more talking. There were two or three people moving all around the house for about half an hour. Then the truck and the car drove away. I kept waiting for Freda to come down and tell me what it had all been about."

I'd been thinking a while how to phrase the next question, but finally gave up trying to make it polite.

"Did Freda ever discuss with you why you're different from other people?"

92A

"Yes." Not a hint of pain, or embarrassment. Instead, her face glowed with pride, and for a moment she looked so much like the painting that the giddiness hit me again. "She made me this way. She made me special. She made me beautiful."

"Why?"

That seemed to baffle her, as if I had to be teasing. She was special. She was beautiful. No further explanation was required.

I heard a faint grunt from just outside the door, followed by a tiny thud against the wall. I signaled to Muriel to drop to the floor, and to Catherine to keep silent, then—quietly as I could, but with an unavoidable squeaking—I climbed onto the top of a metal closet that stood in the corner to the left of the door.

We were lucky. What came through the door when it opened a crack was not a grenade of any kind, but a hand bearing a fan laser. A spinning mirror sweeps the beam across a wide arc—this one was set to one hundred and eighty degrees, horizontally. Held at shoulder height, it filled the room with a lethal plane about a meter above the bed. I was tempted to simply kick the door shut on the hand the moment it appeared, but that would have been too risky; the gun might have tilted down before the beam cut off. For the same reason, I couldn't simply burn a hole in the man's head as he stepped into the room, or even aim at the gun itself—it was shielded, and would have borne several seconds' fire before suffering any internal damage. Paint on the walls was scorched and the curtains had split into two burning halves; in an instant he would lower the beam onto Catherine. I kicked him hard in the face, knocking him backwards and tipping the fan of laser light up toward the ceiling. Then I jumped down and put my gun to his temple. He switched off the beam and let me take the weapon from him. He was dressed in an orderly's uniform, but the fabric was implausibly stiff, probably containing a shielding layer of aluminum-coated asbestos (with the potential for reflections, it's unwise to operate a fan laser with any less protection).

I turned him over and cuffed him in the standard way—wrists and ankles all brought together behind the back, in bracelets with a sharpened inner edge that discourages (some) attempts to burst the chains. I sprayed sedative on his face for a few seconds, and he acted like it had worked, but then I pulled open one eye and knew it hadn't. Every cop uses a sedative with a slightly different tracer effect; my usual turns the whites of the eyes pale blue. He must have had a barrier layer on his skin. While I was preparing an IV jab, he turned his head towards me and opened his mouth. A blade flew out from under his tongue and nicked my ear as it whistled past. That was something I'd never seen before. I forced his jaw open and had a look; the launching mechanism was anchored to his teeth with wires and pins. There was a second blade in there; I put my gun to his head again and advised him to eject it onto the floor. Then I punched him in the face and started searching for an easy vein.

He gave a short cry, and began vomiting steaming-hot blood. Possibly his own choice, but more likely his employers had decided to cut their losses. The body started smoking, so I dragged it out into the corridor.

The officers who'd been on guard were unconscious, not dead. A matter of pragmatism; chemically knocking someone senseless is usually quieter, less messy and less risky to the assailant than killing them. Also, dead cops have been known to trigger an extra impetus in many investigations, so it's worthwhile taking the trouble to avoid them. I phoned someone I knew in Toxicology to come and take a look at them, then radioed for replacements. Organizing the move to somewhere more secure would take twenty-four hours at least.

Catherine was hysterical, and Muriel, pretty shaken herself, insisted on sedating her and ending the interview.

Muriel said, "I've read about it, but I've never seen it with my own eyes before. What does it feel like?"

"What?"

She emitted a burst of nervous laughter. She was shivering. I held onto her shoulders until she calmed down a little. "Being like that." Her teeth chattered. "Someone just tried to *kill us all*, and you're carrying on like nothing special happened. Like someone out of a comic book. What does it feel like?"

I laughed myself. We have a standard answer.

"It doesn't feel like anything at all."

Marion lay with her head on my chest. Her eyes were closed, but she wasn't asleep. I knew she was still listening to me. She always tenses up a certain way when I'm raving.

"How could anyone *do* that? How could anyone sit down and cold-blood-edly *plan* to create a deformed human being with no chance of living a normal life? All for some insane 'artist' somewhere who's keeping alive a dead billionaire's crazy theories. Shit, what do they think people are? Sculptures? *Things* they can mess around with any way they like?"

I wanted to sleep, it was late, but I couldn't shut up. I hadn't even realized how angry I was until I'd started on the topic, but then my disgust had grown more intense with every word I'd uttered.

An hour before, trying to make love, I'd found myself impotent. I'd resorted to using my tongue, and Marion had come, but it still depressed me. Was it psychological? The case I was on? Or a side-effect of the priming drugs? So suddenly, after all these years? There were rumors and jokes about the

Greg Egan

drugs causing almost everything imaginable: sterility, malformed babies, cancer, psychoses; but I'd never believed any of that. The union would have found out and raised hell, the department would never have been allowed to get away with it. It was the chimera case that was screwing me up, it had to be. So I talked about it.

"And the worst thing is, she doesn't even understand what's been done to her. She's been lied to from birth. Macklenburg told her she was *beautiful*, and she *believes* that crap, because she doesn't know any better."

Marion shifted slightly, and sighed. "What's going to happen to her? How's she going to live when she's out of hospital?"

"I don't know. I guess she could sell her story for quite a packet. Enough to hire someone to look after her for the rest of her life." I closed my eyes. "I'm sorry. It's not fair, keeping you awake half the night with this."

I heard a faint hissing sound, and Marion suddenly relaxed. For what seemed like several seconds, but can't have been, I wondered what was wrong with me, why I hadn't leapt to my feet, why I hadn't even raised my head to look across the dark room to find out who or what was there.

Then I realized the spray had hit me, too, and I was paralyzed. It was such a relief to be powerless that I slipped into unconsciousness feeling, absurdly, more peaceful than I had felt for a very long time.

I woke with a mixture of panic and lethargy, and no idea where I was or what had happened. I opened my eyes and saw nothing. I flailed about trying to touch my eyes, and felt myself drifting slightly, but my arms and legs were restrained. I forced myself to relax for a moment and interpret my sensations. I was blindfolded or bandaged, floating in a warm, buoyant liquid, my mouth and nose covered with a mask. My feeble thrashing movements had exhausted me, and for a long time I lay still, unable to concentrate sufficiently to even start guessing about my circumstances. I felt as if every bone in my body had been broken—not through any pain, but through a subtler discomfort arising from an unfamiliar sense of my body's configuration; it was awkward, it was wrong. It occurred to me that I might have been in an accident. A fire? That would explain why I was floating; I was in a burns treatment unit. I said, "Hello? I'm awake." The words came out as painful, hoarse whispers.

A blandly cheerful voice, almost genderless but borderline male, replied. I was wearing headphones; I hadn't noticed them until I felt them vibrate.

"Mr. Segel. How do you feel?"

"Uncomfortable. Weak. Where am I?"

"A long way from home, I'm afraid. But your wife is here, too."

It was only then that I remembered: lying in bed, unable to move. That seemed impossibly long ago, but I had no more recent memories to fill in the gap.

94

"How long have I been here? Where's Marion?"

"Your wife is nearby. She's safe and comfortable. You've been here a number of weeks, but you are healing rapidly. Soon you'll be ready for physiotherapy. So please, relax, be patient."

"Healing from what?"

"Mr. Segel, I'm afraid it was necessary to perform a great deal of surgery to adjust your appearance to suit my requirements. Your eyes, your face, your bone structure, your build, your skin tones; all needed substantial alteration."

I floated in silence. The face of the diffident youth in *The Caress* drifted across the darkness. I was horrified, but my disorientation cushioned the blow; floating in darkness, listening to a disembodied voice, nothing was yet quite real.

"Why pick me?"

"You saved Catherine's life. On two occasions. That's precisely the relationship I wanted."

"Two set-ups. She was never in any real danger, was she? Why didn't you find someone who already looked the part, to go through the motions?" I almost added, "Gustave," but stopped myself in time. I was certain he intended killing me anyway, eventually, but betraying my suspicions about his identity would have been suicidal. The voice was synthetic, of course.

"You genuinely saved her life, Mr. Segel. If she'd stayed in the basement without replacement hormones, she would have died. And the assassin we sent to the hospital was seriously intent on killing her."

I snorted feebly. "What if he'd succeeded? Twenty years' work and millions of dollars, down the drain. What would you have done then?"

"Mr. Segel, you have a very parochial view of the world. Your little town isn't the only one on the planet. Your little police force isn't unique either, except in being the only one who couldn't keep the story from the media. We began with twelve chimeras. Three died in childhood. Three were not discovered in time after their keepers were killed. Four were assassinated after discovery. The other surviving chimera's life was saved by different people on the two occasions—and also she was not quite up to the standard of morphology that Freda Macklenburg achieved with Catherine. So, imperfect as you are, Mr. Segel, you are what I am required to work with."

Shortly after that, I was shifted to a normal bed, and the bandages were removed from my face and body. At first the room was kept dark, but each morning the lights were turned up slightly. Twice a day, a masked physiotherapist with a filtered voice came and helped me learn to move again. There were six armed, masked guards in the windowless room at all times; ludicrous overkill unless they were there in case of an unlikely, external attempt to rescue me. I could barely walk; one stern grandmother could have kept me from escaping.

They showed me Marion, once, on closed circuit TV. She sat in an elegantly furnished room, watching a news disk. Every few seconds, she glanced around nervously. They wouldn't let us meet. I was glad. I didn't want to see her reaction to my new appearance; that was an emotional complication I could do without.

As I slowly became functional, I began to feel a deep sense of panic that I'd yet to think of a plan for keeping us alive. I tried striking up conversations with the guards, in the hope of eventually persuading one of them to help us, either out of compassion or on the promise of a bribe, but they all stuck to monosyllables, and ignored me when I spoke of anything more abstract than requests for food. Refusing to cooperate in the "realization" was the only strategy I could think of, but for how long would that work? I had no doubt that my captor would resort to torturing Marion, and if that failed he would simply hypnotize or drug me to ensure that I complied. And then he would kill us all: Marion, myself, and Catherine.

I had no idea how much time we had; neither the guards, nor the physiotherapist, nor the cosmetic surgeons who occasionally came to check their handiwork, would even acknowledge my questions about the schedule being followed. I longed for Lindhquist to speak with me again; however insane he was, at least he'd engaged in a two-way conversation. I demanded an audience with him, I screamed and ranted; the guards remained as unresponsive as their masks.

Accustomed to the aid of the priming drugs in focusing my thoughts, I found myself constantly distracted by all kinds of unproductive concerns, from a simple fear of death, to pointless worries about my chances of continued employment, and continued marriage, if Marion and I did somehow survive. Weeks went by in which I felt nothing but hopelessness and self-pity. Everything that defined me had been taken away: my face, my body, my job, my usual modes of thought. And although I missed my former physical strength (as a source of self-respect rather than something that would have been useful in itself), it was the mental clarity that had been so much a part of my primed state of mind, that, I was certain, would have made all the difference if only I could have regained it.

I eventually began to indulge in a bizarre, romantic fantasy: The loss of everything I had once relied on—the stripping away of the biochemical props that had held my unnatural life together—would reveal an inner core of sheer moral courage and desperate resourcefulness which would see me through this hour of need. My identity had been demolished, but the naked spark of humanity remained, soon to burst into a searing flame that no prison walls could contain. That which had not killed me would (soon, real soon) make me strong.

A moment's introspection each morning showed that this mystical transformation had not yet taken place. I went on a hunger strike, hoping to hasten my victorious emergence from the crucible of suffering by turning up the heat. I wasn't force-fed, or even given intravenous protein. I was too stupid to make the obvious deduction: the day of the realization was imminent.

One morning, I was handed a costume which I recognized at once from the painting. I was terrified to the point of nausea, but I put it on and went with the guards, making no trouble. The painting was set outdoors. This would be my only chance to escape.

I'd hoped we would have to travel, with all the opportunities that might have entailed, but the landscape had been prepared just a few hundred meters from the building I'd been kept in. I blinked at the glare from the thin grey clouds that covered most of the sky (had Lindhquist been waiting for them, or had he ordered their presence?), weary, frightened, weaker than ever thanks to not having eaten for three days. Desolate fields stretched to the horizon in all directions. There was nowhere to run to, nobody to signal to for help.

I saw Catherine, already sitting in place on the edge of a raised stretch of ground. A short man—well, shorter than the guards, whose height I'd grown accustomed to—stood by her, stroking her neck. She flicked her tail with pleasure, her eyes half closed. The man wore a loose white suit, and a white mask, rather like a fencing mask. When he saw me approaching, he raised his arms in an extravagant gesture of greeting. For an instant, a wild idea possessed me: Catherine could save us! With her speed, her strength, her *claws*.

There were a dozen armed men around us, and Catherine was clearly as docile as a kitten.

"Mr. Segel! You look so glum! Cheer up, please! This is a wonderful day!"

I stopped walking. The guards on either side of me stopped too, and did nothing to force me on.

I said, "I won't do it."

The man in white was indulgent. "Why ever not?"

I stared at him, trembling. I felt like a child. Not since childhood had I confronted anyone this way, without the priming drugs to calm me, without a weapon within easy reach, without absolute confidence in my strength and agility. "When we've done what you want, you're going to kill us all. The longer I refuse, the longer I stay alive."

It was Catherine who answered first. She shook her head, not quite laughing. "No, Dan! Andreas won't hurt us! He loves us both!"

The man came towards me. Had Andreas Lindhquist faked his death? His gait was not an old man's gait.

"Mr. Segel, please, calm yourself. Would I harm my own creations? Would I waste all those years of hard work, by myself and so many others?"

I sputtered, confused. "You've killed people. You've kidnapped us. You've broken a hundred different laws." I almost shouted at Catherine, "*He* arranged Freda's death!" but I had a feeling that would have done me a lot more harm than good.

The computer that disguised his voice laughed blandly. "Yes, I've broken laws. Whatever happens to you, Mr. Segel, I've already broken them. Do you think I'm afraid of what you'll do when I release you? You will be as powerless then to harm me as you are now. You have no proof as to my identity. Oh, I've examined a record of your inquiries. I know you suspected me—"

"I suspected your son."

"Ah. A moot point. I prefer to be called Andreas by intimate acquaintances, but to business associates, I am Gustave Lindhquist. You see, this body *is* that of my son—if son is the right word to use for a clone—but since his birth I took regular samples of my brain tissue, and had the appropriate components extracted from them and injected into his skull. The brain can't be *transplanted*, Mr. Segel, but with care, a great deal of memory and personality can be imposed upon a young child. When my first body died, I had the brain frozen, and I continued the injections until all the tissue was used up. Whether or not I 'am' Andreas is a matter for philosophers and theologians. I clearly recall sitting in a crowded classroom watching a black and white television, the day Neil Armstrong stepped on the moon, fifty-two years before this body was born. So call me Andreas. Humor an old man."

He shrugged. "The masks, the voice filters—I like a little theater. And the less you see and hear, the fewer your avenues for causing me minor annoyance. But please, don't flatter yourself; you can never be a threat to me. I could buy every member of your entire force with half the amount I've earned while we've been speaking.

"So forget these delusions of martyrdom. You are going to live, and for the rest of your life you will be, not only my creation, but my instrument. You are going to carry this moment away inside you, out into the world for me, like a seed, like a strange, beautiful virus, infecting and transforming everyone and everything you touch."

He took me by the arm and led me toward Catherine. I didn't resist. Someone placed a winged staff in my right hand. I was prodded, arranged, adjusted, fussed over. I hardly noticed Catherine's cheek against mine, her paw resting against my belly. I stared ahead, in a daze, trying to decide whether or not to believe I was going to live, overcome by this first real chance of hope, but too terrified of disappointment to trust it.

There was no one but Lindhquist and his guards and assistants. I don't know what I'd expected; an audience in evening dress? He stood a dozen meters away, glancing down at a copy of the painting (or perhaps it was the original) mounted on an easel, then calling out instructions for microscopic changes to our posture and expression. My eyes began to water, from keeping my gaze fixed; someone ran forward and dried them, then sprayed something into them which prevented a recurrence.

Then, for several minutes, Lindhquist was silent. When he finally spoke, he said, very softly, "All we're waiting for now is the movement of the sun, the correct positioning of your shadows. Be patient for just a little longer."

I don't remember clearly what I felt in those last seconds. I was so tired, so confused, so uncertain. I do remember thinking: How will I know when the moment has passed? When Lindhquist pulls out a weapon and incinerates us, perfectly preserving the moment? Or when he pulls out a camera? *Which would it be?*

Suddenly he said, "Thank you," and turned and walked away, alone. Catherine shifted, stretched, kissed me on the cheek, and said, "Wasn't that fun?" One of the guards took my elbow, and I realized I'd staggered.

He hadn't even taken a photograph. I giggled hysterically, certain now that I was going to live after all. And he hadn't even taken a photograph. I couldn't decide if that made him twice as insane, or if it totally redeemed his sanity.

I never discovered what became of Catherine. Perhaps she stayed with Lindhquist, shielded from the world by his wealth and seclusion, living a life effectively identical to that she'd lived before, in Freda Macklenburg's basement. Give or take a few servants and luxurious villas.

Marion and I were returned to our home, unconscious for the duration of the voyage, waking on the bed we'd left six months before. There was a lot of dust about. She took my hand and said, "Well. Here we are." We lay there in silence for hours, then went out in search of food.

The next day I went to the station. I proved my identity with fingerprints and DNA, and gave a full report of all that had happened.

I had not been assumed dead. My salary had continued to be paid into my bank account, and mortgage payments deducted automatically. The department settled my claim for compensation out of court, paying me three quarters of a million dollars, and I underwent surgery to restore as much of my former appearance as possible.

It took more than two years of rehabilitation, but now I am back on active duty. The Macklenburg case has been shelved for lack of evidence. The investigation of the kidnapping of the three of us, and Catherine's present fate, is on the verge of going the same way; nobody doubts my account of the events, but all the evidence against Gustave Lindhquist is circumstantial. I accept that. I'm glad. I want to erase everything that Lindhquist has done to me, and an obsession with bringing him to justice is the exact opposite of the state of mind I aim to achieve. I don't pretend to understand what he thought he was achieving by letting me live, what his insane notion of my supposed effect on the world actually entailed, but I am determined to be, in every way, the same person as I was before the experience, and thus to defeat his intentions.

Marion is doing fine. For a while she suffered from recurring nightmares, but after seeing a therapist who specializes in detraumatizing hostages and kidnap victims, she is now every bit as relaxed and carefree as she used to be.

I have nightmares, now and then. I wake in the early hours of the morning, shivering and sweating and crying out, unable to recall what horror I'm escaping. Andreas Lindhquist injecting samples of brain tissue into his son? Catherine blissfully closing her eyes, and thanking me for saving her life while her claws rake my body into bloody strips? Myself, trapped in *The Caress*; the moment of the realization infinitely, unmercifully prolonged? Perhaps; or perhaps I simply dream about my latest case—that seems much more likely.

Everything is back to normal.

CHARLES SHEFFIELD
A Braver Thing

▼

One of the best contemporary "hard science" writers, British-born Charles Sheffield is a theoretical physicist who has worked on the American space program, and is currently chief scientist of the Earth Satellite Corporation. Sheffield is also the only person who has ever served as president of both the American Astronautical Society and the Science Fiction Writers of America. His books include the bestselling non-fiction title *Earthwatch*, the novels *Sight of Proteus, The Web Between the Worlds, Hidden Variables, My Brother's Keeper, The McAndrew Chronicles, Between the Strokes of Night, The Nimrod Hunt, Trader's World,* and *Proteus Unbound,* and the collection *Erasmus Magister.* His most recent novels are *Summertide* and *Divergence.* His story "Out of Copyright" was in our Seventh Annual Collection. He lives in Bethesda, Maryland.

Here he offers us a few melancholy thoughts about the price of progress—which may sometimes turn out to be more than you really want to spend. . . .

▼

A Braver Thing

CHARLES SHEFFIELD

The palace banquet is predictably dull, but while the formal speeches roll on with their obligatory nods to the memory of Alfred Nobel and his famous bequest, it is not considered good manners to leave or to chat with one's neighbors. I have the time and opportunity to think about yesterday; and, at last, to decide on the speech that I will give tomorrow.

A Nobel Prize in physics means different things to different people. If it is awarded late in life, it is often viewed by the recipient as the capstone on a career of accomplishment. Awarded early (Lawrence Bragg was a Nobel Laureate at twenty-five) it often defines the winner's future; an early Prize may also announce to the world at large the arrival of a new titan of science (Paul Dirac was a Nobel Laureate at thirty-one).

To read the names of the Nobel Prize winners in physics is almost to recapitulate the history of twentieth-century physics, so much so that the choice of winners often seems self-evident. No one can imagine a list without Planck, the Curies, Einstein, Bohr, Schrödinger, Dirac, Fermi, Yukawa, Bardeen, Feynman, Weinberg, or the several Wilson's (though Rutherford is, bizarrely, missing from the Physics roster, having been awarded his Nobel Prize in Chemistry).

And yet the decision-making process is far from simple. A Nobel Prize is awarded not for a lifetime's work, but explicitly for a particular achievement. It is given only to living persons, and as Alfred Nobel specified in his will, the prize goes to "the person who shall have made the most important discovery or invention within the field of physics."

It is those constraints that make the task of the Royal Swedish Academy of Sciences so difficult. Consider these questions:

- What should one do when an individual is regarded by his peers as one of the leading intellectual forces of his generation, but no single accomplishment offers the clear basis for an award? John Archibald Wheeler is not a Nobel Laureate; yet he is a "physicist's physicist," a man who has been a creative force in half a dozen different fields.
- How does one weight a candidate's *age*? In principle, not at all. It is not a variable for consideration; but in practice every committee member knows when time is running out for older candidates, while the young competition will have opportunities for many years to come.
- How soon after a theory or discovery is it appropriate to make an award? Certainly, one should wait long enough to be sure that the accomplishment is "most important," as Nobel's will stipulates; but if one waits too long, the opportunity may vanish with the candidate. Max Born was seventy-two years old when he received the Nobel Prize in 1954— for work done almost thirty years earlier on the probabilistic interpretation of the quantum mechanical wave function. Had George Gamow lived as long as Born, surely he would have shared with Penzias and Wilson the 1978 prize, for the discovery of the cosmic background radiation. Einstein was awarded the Nobel Prize in 1921, at the age of forty-two. But it cited his work on the photoelectric effect, rather than the theory of relativity, which was still considered open to question. And if his life had been no longer than that of Henry Moseley or Heinrich Hertz, Einstein would have died unhonored by the Nobel Committee.

So much for logical choices. I conclude that the Nobel rules allow blind Atropos to play no less a part than Athene in the award process.

My musings can afford to be quite detached. I know how the voting must have gone in my own case, since although the work for which my award is now being given was published only four years ago, already it has stimulated an unprecedented flood of other papers. Scores more are appearing every week, in every language. The popular press might seem oblivious to the fundamental new view of nature implied by the theory associated with my name, but they are very aware of its monstrous practical potential. A small test unit in orbit around Neptune is already returning data, and in the tabloids I have been dubbed Giles "Starman" Turnbull. To quote The New York *Times*: "The situation is unprecedented in modern physics. Not even the madcap run from the 1986 work of Müller and Bednorz to today's room-temperature superconductors can compete with the rapid acceptance of Giles Turnbull's theories, and the stampede to apply them. The story is scarcely begun, but already we can say this, with confidence: Professor Turnbull has given us the stars."

The world desperately needs heroes. Today, it seems, I am a hero. Tomorrow? We shall see.

In a taped television interview last week, I was asked how long my ideas had been gestating before I wrote out the first version of the Turnbull Concession Theory. And can you recall a moment or an event, asked the reporter, which you would pinpoint as seminal?

My answer must have been too vague to be satisfactory, since it did not appear in the final television clip. But in fact I could have provided a very precise location in space-time, at the start of the road that led me to Stockholm, to this dinner, and to my first (and, I will guarantee, my last) meeting with Swedish royalty.

Eighteen years ago, it began. In late June, I was playing in a public park two miles from my home when I found a leather satchel sitting underneath a bench. It was nine o'clock at night, and nearly dark. I took the satchel home with me.

My father's ideas of honesty and proper behavior were and are precise to a fault. He would allow me to examine the satchel long enough to determine its owner, but not enough to explore the contents. Thus it was, sitting in the kitchen of our semi-detached council house, that I first encountered the name of Arthur Sandford Shaw, penned in careful red ink on the soft beige leather interior of the satchel. Below his name was an address on the other side of town, as far from the park as we were but in the opposite direction.

Should we telephone Arthur Sandford Shaw's house, tell him that we had his satchel, and advise him where he could collect it?

No, said my father gruffly. Tomorrow is Saturday. You cycle over in the morning and return it.

To a fifteen-year-old, even one without specific plans, a Saturday morning in June is precious. I hated my father then, for his unswerving, blinkered attitude, as I hated him for the next seventeen years. Only recently have I realized that "hate" is a word with a thousand meanings.

I rode over the next morning. Twice I had to stop and ask my way. The Shaw house was in the Garden Village part of the town, an area that I seldom visited. The weather was preposterously hot, and at my father's insistence I was wearing a jacket and tie. By the time that I dismounted in front of the yellow brick house with its steep red-tile roof and diamond glazed windows, sweat was trickling down my face and neck. I leaned my bike against a privet hedge that was studded with sweet-smelling and tiny white flowers, lifted the satchel out of my saddlebag, and rubbed my sleeve across my forehead.

I peered through the double gates. They led to an oval driveway, enclosing a bed of well-kept annuals.

I saw pansies, love-in-a-mist, delphiniums, phlox, and snapdragons. I know their names now, but of course I did not know them *then*.

And if you ask me, do I truly remember this so clearly, I must say, of course I do; and will, until my last goodnight. I have that sort of memory. Lev Landau once said, "I am not a genius. Einstein and Bohr are geniuses. But I am very talented." To my mind, Landau (1962 Nobel Laureate, and the premier Soviet physicist of his generation) was certainly a genius. But I will echo him, and say that while I am not a genius, I am certainly very talented. My memory in particular has always been unusually precise and complete.

The sides of the drive curved symmetrically around to meet at a brown-and-white painted front door. I followed the edge of the gravel as far as the front step, and there I hesitated.

For my age, I was not lacking in self-confidence. I had surveyed the students in my school, and seen nothing there to produce discomfort. It was clear to me that I was mentally far superior to all of them, and the uneasy attitude of my teachers was evidence—to me, at any rate—that they agreed with my assessment.

But this place overwhelmed me. And not just with the size of the house, though that was six times as big as the one that I lived in. I had seen other big houses; far more disconcerting were the trained climbing roses and es-paliered fruit trees, the weed-free lawn, the bird-feeders, and the height, texture and improbable but right color balance within the flower beds. The garden was so carefully structured that it seemed a logical extension of the building at its center. For the first time, I realized that a garden could comprise more than a hodge-podge of grass and straggly flowers.

So I hesitated. And before I could summon my resolve and lift the brass knocker, the door opened.

A woman stood there. At five feet five, she matched my height exactly. She smiled at me, eye to eye.

Did I say that the road to Stockholm began when I found the satchel? I was wrong. It began with that smile.

"Yes? Can I help you?"

The voice was one that I still thought of as "posh," high-pitched and musical, with clear vowels. The woman was smiling again, straight white teeth and a broad mouth in a high-cheekboned face framed by curly, ash-blond hair. I can see that face before me now, and I know intellectually that she was thirty-five years old. But on that day I could not guess her age to within fifteen years. She could have been twenty, or thirty, or fifty, and it would have made no difference. She was wearing a pale-blue blouse with full sleeves, secured at the top with a mother-of-pearl brooch and tucked into a grey wool skirt that descended to mid-calf. On her feet she wore low-heeled tan shoes, and no stockings.

I found my voice.

"I've brought this back." I held out the satchel, my defense against witch-craft.

"So I see." She took it from me. "Drat that boy, I doubt he even knows he lost it. I'm Marion Shaw. Come in."

It was an order. I closed the door behind me and found myself following her along a hall that passed another open door on the left. As we approached, a piano started playing rapid staccato triplets, and I saw a red-haired girl crouched over the keyboard of a baby grand.

My guide paused and stuck her head in for a moment. "Not so fast, Meg. You'll never keep up that pace for the whole song." And then to me, as we walked on, "Poor old Schubert, 'Impatience' is right, it's what he'd feel if he heard that. Do you play?"

"We don't have a piano."

"Mm. I sometimes wonder why we do."

We had reached an airy room that faced the back garden of the house. My guide went in before me, peered behind the door, and clucked in annoyance.

"Arthur's gone again. Well, he can't be far. I know for a fact that he was here five minutes ago." She turned to me. "Make yourself at home, Giles. I'll find him."

Giles. I have been terribly self-conscious about my first name since I was nine years old. By the time that I was twenty I had learned how to use it to my advantage, to suggest a lineage that I never had. But at fifteen it was the bane of my life. In a class full of Tom's and Ron's and Brian's and Bill's, it did not fit. I cursed my fate, to be stuck with a "funny" name, just because one of my long-dead uncles had suffered with it.

But there was stronger witchcraft at work here. I had arrived unheralded on her doorstep.

"How do you know my name?"

That earned another smile. "From your father. He called me early this morning, to make sure someone would be home. He didn't want you to bike all this way for nothing."

She went out, and left me in the room of my dreams.

It was about twelve feet square, with an uncarpeted floor of polished hardwood. All across the far wall was a window that began at waist height, ran to the ceiling, and looked south to a vegetable garden. The windowsill was a long work bench, two feet deep, and on it stood a dozen projects that

I could identify. In the center was a compound microscope, with slides scattered all around. I found tiny objects on them as various as a fly's leg, a single strand of hair, and two or three iron filings. The mess on the left-hand side of the bench was a half-ground telescope lens, covered with its layer of hardened pitch and with the grinding surface sitting next to it. The right side, just as disorderly, was a partially-assembled model airplane, radio-controlled and with a two c.c. diesel engine. Next to that stood an electronic balance, designed to weigh anything from a milligram to a couple of kilos, and on the other side was a blood-type testing kit. The only discordant note to my squeamish taste was a dead puppy, carefully dissected, laid out, and pinned organ by organ on a two-foot square of thick hardboard. But that hint of a possible future was overwhelmed by the most important thing of all: everywhere, in among the experiments and on the floor and by the two free-standing aquariums and next to the flat plastic box behind the door with its half-inch of water and its four black-backed, fawn-bellied newts, there were *books*.

Books and books and books. The other three walls of the room were shelved and loaded from floor to ceiling, and the volumes that scattered the work bench were no more than a small sample that had been taken out and not replaced. I had never seen so many hard-cover books outside a public library or the town's one and only technical bookstore.

When Marion Shaw returned with Arthur Sandford Shaw in tow I was standing in the middle of the room like Buridan's Ass, unable to decide what I wanted to look at the most. I was in no position to see my own eyes, but if I had been able to do so I have no doubt that the pupils would have been twice their normal size. I was suffering from sensory overload, first from the house and garden, then from Marion Shaw, and finally from that paradise of a study. Thus my initial impressions of someone whose life so powerfully influenced and finally directed my own are not as clear in my mind as they ought to be. I also honestly believe that I never did see Arthur clearly, if his mother were in the room.

Some things I can be sure of. Arthur Shaw made his height early, and although I eventually grew to within an inch of him, at our first meeting he towered over me by seven or eight inches. His coordination had not kept pace with his growth, and he had a gawky and awkward manner of moving that would never completely disappear. I know also that he was holding in his right hand a live frog that he had brought in from the garden, because he had to pop that in an aquarium before he could, at his mother's insistence, shake hands with me.

For the rest, his expression was surely the half-amused, half-bemused smile that seldom left his face. His hair, neatly enough cut, never looked it. Some stray spike on top always managed to elude brush and comb, and his habit of running his hands up past his temples swept his hair untidily off his forehead.

"I'm pleased to meet you," he said. "Thank you for bringing it back."

He was, I think, neither pleased nor displeased to meet me. It was nice to have his satchel back (as Marion Shaw had predicted, he did not know he had left it behind in the park), but the thought of what might have happened had he lost it, with its cargo of schoolbooks, did not disturb him as it would have disturbed me.

His mother had been following my eyes.

"Why don't you show Giles your things," she said. "I'll bet that he's interested in science, too."

It was an implied question. I nodded.

"And why don't I call your mother," she said, "and see if it's all right for you to stay to lunch?"

"My mother's dead." I wanted to stay to lunch, desperately. "And my dad will be at work 'til late."

She raised her eyebrows, but all she said was, "So that's settled, then." She held out her hand. "Let me take your jacket, you don't need that while you're indoors."

Mrs. Shaw left to organize lunch. We played, though Arthur Shaw and I would both have been outraged to hear such a verb applied to our efforts. We were engaging in serious experiments of chemistry and physics, and reviewing the notebooks in which he recorded all his earlier results. Even in our first meeting he struck me as a bit strange, but that slight negative was swamped by a dozen positive reactions. The orbit in which I had traveled all my life contained no one whose interests in any way resembled my own. It was doubly shocking to meet a person who was as interested in science as I was, and who had on the shelves of his own study more reference sources than I dreamed existed.

Lunch was an unwelcome distraction. Mrs. Shaw studied me as openly as my inspection of her was covert, Arthur sat in thoughtful silence, and the table conversation was dominated by the precocious Megan, who at twelve years old apparently loved horses and boats, hated anything to do with science, school-work, or playing the piano, and talked incessantly when I badly wanted to hear from the other two. (I know her still; my present opinion is that I was a little harsh in the assessment of eighteen years ago—but not much.) Large quantities of superior food and the beatific presence of Marion Shaw saved lunch from being a disaster, and finally Arthur and I could escape back to his room.

At five o'clock I felt obliged to leave and cycle home. I had to make dinner for my father. The jacket that was returned to me was newly stitched at the elbow where a leather patch had been working loose, and a missing black button on the cuff had been replaced. It was Marion Shaw rather than Arthur who handed me my coat and invited me to come to the house again the following week, but knowing her as I do now I feel sure that the matter was discussed with him before the offer was made. I mention as proof of my theory that as I was pulling my bike free of the privet hedge, Arthur pushed into my hand a copy of E.T. Bell's *Men Of Mathematics*. "It's pretty old," he said offhandedly. "And it doesn't give enough details. But it's a classic. I think it's terrific—and so does Mother."

I rode home through the middle of town. When I arrived there, my own house felt as alien and inhospitable to me as the far side of the moon.

It was Tristram Shandy who set out to write the story of his life, and never progressed much beyond the day of his birth.

If I am to avoid a similar problem, I must move rapidly in covering the next few years. And yet at the same time it is vital to define the relationship between the Shaw family and me, if the preposterous request that Marion Shaw would make of me thirteen years later, and my instant aquiescence to it, are to be of value in defining the road to Stockholm.

For the next twenty-seven months I enjoyed a double existence. "Enjoyed" is precisely right, since I found both lives intensely pleasurable. In one world I was Giles Turnbull, the son of a heel-man at Hendry's Shoe Factory, as well as Giles Turnbull, student extraordinary, over whom the teachers at my school nodded their heads and for whom they predicted a golden scholastic future. In that life, I moved through a thrilling but in retrospect unremarkable sequence of heterosexual relationships, with Angela, Louise, and finally with Jennie.

At the same time, I became a regular weekend visitor to the Shaw household. Roland Shaw, whom my own father described with grudging respect after two meetings as "sharp as a tack," had a peripheral effect on me, but he was a seldom-seen figure absorbed in his job, family, and garden. It was Marion and Arthur who changed me and shaped me. From him I learned concentration, tenacity, and total attack on a single scientific problem (the school in my other life rewarded facility and speed, not depth). I learned that there were many right approaches, since he and I seldom used the same attack on a problem. I also learned—surprisingly—that there might be more than one right answer. One day he casually asked me, "What's the average length of a chord in a unit circle?" When I had worked out an answer, he pointed out with glee that it was a trick question. There are at least three "right" answers, depending on the mathematical definition you use for "average."

Arthur taught me thoroughness and subtlety. From Marion Shaw I learned everything else. She introduced me to Mozart, to the Chopin waltzes and études, to the Beethoven symphonies, and to the first great Schubert song cycle, while steering me clear of Bach fugues, the *Ring of the Nibelung*, Beethoven's late string quartets and *Winterreise*. "There's a place for those, later in life," she said, "and it's a wonderful place. But until you're twenty you'll get more out of *Die Schöne Müllerin* and Beethoven's Seventh." Over the dinner table, I learned why sane people might actually read Wordsworth and Milton, to whom an exposure at school had generated an instant and strong distaste. ("Boring old farts," I called them, though never to Marion Shaw.)

And although nothing could ever give me a personal appreciation for art and sculpture, I learned a more important lesson: that there were people who could tell the good from the bad, and the ugly from the beautiful, as quickly and as naturally as Arthur and I could separate a rigorous mathematical proof from a flawed one, or a beautiful theory from an ugly one.

The Shaw household also taught me, certainly with no intention to do so, how to fake it. Soon I could talk a plausible line on music, literature, or architecture, and with subtle hints from Marion I mastered that most difficult technique, when to shut up. From certain loathed guests at her dinner table I learned to turn on (and off) a high-flown, euphuistic manner of speech that most of the world confuses with brain-power. And finally, walking around the garden with Marion for the sheer pleasure of her company, I picked up as a bonus a conversational knowledge of flowers, insects, and horticulture, subjects which interested me as little as the sequence of Chinese dynasties.

It's obvious, is it not, that I was in love with her? But it was a pure, asexual love that bore no relationship to the explorations, thrills, and physical urgencies of Angela, Louise, and Jennie. And if I describe a paragon who sat somewhere between Saint and Superwoman, it is only because I saw her that way when I was sixteen years old, and I have never quite lost the illusion. I know very well, today, that Marion was a creature of her environment, as much as I was shaped by mine. She had been born to money, and she had never had to worry about it. It was inevitable that what she *thought* she was teaching me would become transformed when I took it to a house without books and servants, and to a way of life where the battle for creature comforts and self-esteem was fought daily.

I looked upon the world of Marion Shaw, and wanted it and her. Desperately. But I knew no way to possess them.

"It were all one that I should love a bright particular star, and think to wed it, he is so above me," Marion quoted to me one day, for no reason I could understand. That's how I, mute and inglorious, felt about her.

And by a curious symmetry, Megan Shaw trailed lovelorn after me, just as I trailed after her mother. One day, to my unspeakable embarrassment, Megan cornered me in the music room and told me that she loved me. She took the initiative, and tried to kiss me. At fourteen she was becoming a beauty, but I, who readily took the part of eager sexual aggressor with my girlfriends, could no more have touched her than I could have played the Chopin polonaise with which she had been struggling. I muttered, mumbled, ducked my head, and ran.

Despite such isolated moments of awkwardness, that period was still my personal Nirvana, a delight in the sun that is young once only. But even at sixteen and seventeen I sensed that, like any perfection, this one could not endure.

The end came after two years, when Arthur went off to the university. He and I were separated in age by only six months, but we went to different schools and we were, more important, on opposite sides of the Great Divide of the school year.

He had taken the Cambridge scholarship entrance exam the previous January and been accepted at King's College, without covering himself with glory. If his failure to gain a scholarship or exhibition upset his teachers, it surprised me not at all. And when I say that I knew Arthur better than anyone, while still not knowing him, that makes sense to me if to no one else.

Success in the Cambridge scholarship entrance examinations in mathematics calls for a good deal of ingenuity and algebraic technique, but the road to success is much smoother if you also know certain tricks. Only a finite number of questions can be asked, and certain problems appear again and again. A bright student, without being in any way outstanding, can do rather well by practicing on the papers set in previous years.

And this, of course, was what Arthur absolutely refused to do. He had that rare independence of spirit, which disdained to walk the well-trod paths. He would not practice examination technique. That made the exams immeasurably harder. A result which, with the help of a clever choice of coordinate system or transformation, dropped out in half a dozen lines, would take several pages of laborious algebra by a direct approach. Genius would find that trick of technique in real time, but to do so consistently, over several days, was too much to ask of any student. Given Arthur's fondness for approaching a problem *ab ovo*, without reference to previous results, and adding to it a certain obscurity of presentation that even I, who knew him well, had found disturbing, it was a wonder that he had done as well as he had.

I had observed what happened. It took no great intellect to resolve that I would not make the same mistake. I worked with Arthur, until his departure for Cambridge in early October, on new fields of study (I had long passed the limits of my teachers at school). Then I changed my focus, and concentrated on the specifics of knowledge and technique needed to do well in the entrance examinations.

Tests of any kind always produce in me a pleasurable high of adrenalin. In early December I went off to Cambridge, buoyed by a good luck kiss (my first) from Marion Shaw, and a terse, "Do your best, lad," from my father. I stayed in Trinity College, took the exams without major trauma, saw a good deal of Arthur, and generally had a wonderful time. I already knew something of the town, from a visit to Arthur halfway through Michaelmas Term.

The results came just before Christmas. I had won a major scholarship to Trinity. I went up the following October.

And at that point, to my surprise, my course and Arthur's began to move apart. We were of course in different colleges, and of different years, and I began to make new friends. But more important, back in our home town the bond between us had seemed unique: he was the single person in my world who was interested in the arcana of physics and mathematics. Now I had been transported to an intellectual heaven, where conversations once possible only with Arthur were the daily discourse of hundreds.

I recognized those changes of setting, and I used them to explain to Marion Shaw why Arthur and I no longer saw much of each other. I also, for my own reasons, minimized to her the degree of our estrangement; for if I were never to see Arthur during college breaks, I would also not see Marion.

There were deeper reasons, though, for the divergence, facts which I could not mention to her. While the university atmosphere, with its undergraduate enthusiasms and overflowing intellectual energy, opened me and made me more gregarious, so that I formed dozens of new friendships with both men and women, college life had exactly the opposite effect on Arthur. As an adolescent he had tended to emotional coolness and intellectual solitude. At Cambridge those traits became more pronounced. He attended few lectures, worked only in his rooms or in the library, and sought no friends. He became somewhat nocturnal, and his manner was increasingly brusque and tactless.

That sounds enough to end close acquaintance; but there was a deeper reason still, one harder to put my finger on. The only thing I can say is that Arthur now made me highly *uncomfortable*. There was a look in his eyes, of obsession and secret worry, that kept me on the edge of my seat. I wondered if he had become homosexual, and was enduring the rite of passage that implied. There had been no evidence of such tendencies during the years I had known him, except that he had shown no interest in girls.

A quiet check with a couple of my gay friends disposed of that theory. Both the grapevine and their personal observations of Arthur indicated that if he was not attracted to women, neither was he interested in men. That was a vast relief. I had seen myself being asked to explain the inexplicable to Marion Shaw.

I accepted the realities: Arthur did not want to be with me, and I was uncomfortable with him. So be it. I would go on with my studies.

And in those studies our new and more distant relationship had another effect, one that ultimately proved far more important than personal likes and dislikes. For I could no longer *compare* myself with Arthur.

In our first two years of acquaintance, he had been my calibration point. As someone a little older than me, and a full year ahead in a better school, he served as my pacer. My desire was to know what Arthur knew, to be able to solve the problems that he could solve. And on the infrequent occasions when I found myself ahead of him, I was disproportionately pleased.

Now my pace-setting hare had gone. The divergence that I mentioned was intellectual as well as personal. And because Arthur had always been my standard of comparison, it took me three or four years to form a conclusion that others at the university had drawn long before.

His lack of interest in attending lectures, coupled with his insistence on doing things his own way, led to as many problems in the Tripos examinations as it had in scholarship entrance. His supervision partner found him "goofy," while their supervisor didn't seem to understand what he was talking about. Arthur was always going off, said his partner, in irrelevant *digressions*. By contrast, my old approach of focusing on what was needed to do well in exams, while making friends with both students and faculty, worked as well as ever.

In sum, my star was ascendant. I did splendidly, was secretly delighted, and publicly remained nonchalant and modest.

And yet I knew, somewhere deep inside, that Arthur was more creative than I. He generated ideas and insights that I would never have. Surely that would weigh most heavily, in the great balance of academic affairs?

Apparently not. To my surprise, it was I alone who at the end of undergraduate and graduate studies was elected to a Fellowship, and stayed on at Cambridge. Arthur would have to leave, and fend for himself. After considering a number of teaching positions at other universities both in Britain and abroad, he turned his back on academia. He accepted a position as a research physicist with A.N.F. Gesellschaft, a European hi-tech conglomerate headquartered in Bonn.

In August he departed Cambridge to take up his new duties. I would remain, living in college and continuing my research. When we had dinner together a few days before he left he seemed withdrawn, but no more than usual. I mentioned that I was becoming more and more interested in the problem of space-time quantization, and proposed to work on it intensely.

He came to life then, and said that in his opinion I was referring to the most important open question of physics. I was delighted by that reaction, and told him so. At that point his moodiness returned and remained for the rest of the evening.

When we parted at midnight there was no formality or sense of finality in our leave-taking. And yet for several years I believed that on that evening the divergence of our worldlines became complete. Only later did I learn that from a scientific point of view they had separated, only to run parallel to each other.

And both roads led to Stockholm.

When one sets forth on an unknown intellectual trail it is easy to lose track of time, place, and people. For the next four years the sharp realities of my world were variational principles, Lie algebra, and field theory. Food and drink, concerts, vacations, friends, social events, and even lovers still had their place, but they stood on the periphery of my attention, slightly misty and out of focus.

I saw Arthur a total of five times in those four years, and each was in a dinner-party setting at his parents' house. In retrospect I can recognize an increasing remoteness in his manner, but at the time he seemed like the same old Arthur, ignoring any discussion or guest that didn't interest him. No opportunity existed for deep conversation between us; neither of us sought one. He never said a word about his work, or what he thought of life in Bonn. I never talked about what I was trying to do in Cambridge.

It was the shock of my life to be sitting at tea in the Senate House, one gloomy November afternoon, and be asked by a topologist colleague from Churchill College, "You used to hang around with Arthur Shaw, didn't you, when he was here?"

At my nod, he tapped the paper he was holding. "Did you see this, Turnbull," he said, "on page ten? He's dead."

And when I looked at him, stupefied: "You didn't know? Committed suicide. In Germany. His obituary's here."

He said more, I'm sure, and so did I. But my mind was far away as I took the newspaper from him. It was a discreet two inches of newsprint. Arthur Sandford Shaw, aged twenty-eight. Graduate of King's College, Cambridge, son of etc. Coroner's report, recent behavior seriously disturbed . . . no details.

I went back to my rooms in Trinity and telephoned the Shaw house. While it was ringing, I realized that no matter who answered I had no idea what to say. I put the phone back on its stand and paced up and down my study for the next hour, feeling more and more sick. Finally I made the call and it was picked up by Marion.

I stumbled through an expression of regret. She hardly gave me time to finish before she said, "Giles, I was going to call you tonight. I'd like to come to Cambridge. I must talk to you."

The next day I had scheduled appointments for late morning and afternoon, two with research students, one with the college director of studies on the subject of forthcoming entrance interviews, and one with a visiting professor from Columbia. I could have handled them and still met with Marion. I canceled every one, and went to meet her at the station.

The only thing I could think of when I saw her step off the train was that she had changed hardly at all since that June morning, thirteen years ago, when we first met. It took close inspection to see that the ash-blond hair showed wisps of grey at the temples, and that a network of fine lines had appeared at the outer corners of her eyes.

Neither of us had anything to say. I put my arms around her and gave her an embarrassed hug, and she leaned her head for a moment on my shoulder. In the taxi back to college we talked the talk of strangers, about the American election results, new compact disk recordings, and the town's worsening traffic problems.

We did not go to my rooms, but set out at once to walk on the near-deserted paths of the College Backs. The gloom of the previous afternoon had intensified. It was perfect weather for *weltschmerz*, cloudy and dark, with a thin drizzle falling. We stared at the crestfallen ducks on the Cam and the near-leafless oaks, while I waited for her to begin. I sensed that she was winding herself up to say something unpleasant. I tried to prepare myself for anything.

It came with a sigh, and a murmured, "He didn't kill himself, you know. That's what the report said, but it's wrong. He was murdered."

I was not prepared for anything. The hair rose on the back of my neck.

"It sounds insane," she went on. "But I'm sure of it. You see, when Arthur was home in June, he did something that he'd never done before. He talked to me about his work. I didn't understand half of it—" she smiled, a tremulous, tentative smile; I noticed that her eyes were slightly bloodshot from weeping "—you'd probably say not even a tenth of it. But I could tell that he was terrifically excited, and at the same time terribly worried and depressed."

"But what was he doing? Wasn't he working for that German company?" I was ashamed to admit it, but in my preoccupation with my own research I had not given a moment's thought in four years to Arthur's doings, or to A.N.F. Gesellschaft.

"He was still there. He was in his office the morning of the day that he died. And what he was doing was terribly important."

"You talked to them?"

"They talked to us. The chief man involved with Arthur's work is called Otto Braun, and he flew over two days ago specially to talk to me and Roland. He said he wanted to be sure we would hear about Arthur's death directly, rather than just being officially notified. Braun admitted that Arthur had done very important work for them."

"But if that's true, it makes no sense at all for anyone to think of killing him. They'd do all they could to keep him alive."

"Not if he'd found something they were desperate to keep secret. They're a commercial operation. Suppose that he found something hugely valuable? And suppose that he told them that it was too important for one company to own, and he was going to let everyone in on it."

It sounded to me like a form of paranoia that I would never have expected in Marion Shaw. Arthur would certainly have been obliged to sign a non-disclosure agreement with the company he worked for, and there were many legal ways to assure his silence. In any case, to a hi-tech firm Arthur and people like him were the golden goose. Companies didn't murder their most valuable employees.

We were walking slowly across the Bridge of Sighs, our footsteps echoing from the stony arch. Neither of us spoke until we had strolled all the way through the first three courts of St. Johns College, and turned right onto Trinity Street.

"I know you think I'm making all this up," said Marion at last, "just because I'm so upset. You're just humoring me. You're so logical and clear-headed, Giles, you never let yourself go overboard about anything."

There is a special hell for those who feel but cannot tell. I started to protest, half-heartedly.

"That's all right," she said. "You don't have to be polite to me. We've known each other too long. You don't think I understand anything about science, and maybe I don't. But you'll admit that I know a fair bit about people. And I can tell you one thing, Otto Braun was keeping something from us. Something important."

"How do you know?"

"I could read it in his eyes."

That was an unarguable statement; but it was not persuasive. The drizzle was slowly turning into a persistent rain, and I steered us away from Kings Parade and towards a coffee shop. As we passed through the doorway she took my arm.

"Giles, do you remember Arthur's notebooks?"

It was a rhetorical question. Anyone who knew Arthur knew his notebooks. Maintaining them was his closest approach to a religious ritual. He had started the first one when he was twelve years old. A combination of personal diary, scientific workbook, and clippings album, they recorded everything in his life that he believed to be significant.

"He still kept them when he went to Germany," Marion continued. "He even mentioned them, the last time he was home, because he wanted me to send him the same sort of book that he always used, and he had trouble getting them there. I sent him a shipment in August. I asked Otto Braun to send them back to me, with Arthur's personal things. He told me there were no notebooks. There were only the work journals that every employee of ANF was obliged to keep."

I stared at her across the little table, with its red-and-white checkered cloth. At last, Marion was offering evidence for her case. I moved the salt and pepper shakers around on the table. Arthur may have changed in the past four years, but he couldn't have changed that much. Habits were habits.

She leaned forward, and put her hands over mine. "I know. I said to Braun just what you're thinking. Arthur always kept notebooks. They had to exist, and after his death they belonged to me. I wanted them back. He wriggled and sweated, and said there was nothing. But if I want to know what Arthur left, he said, I can get someone I trust who'll understand Arthur's work, and have them go over to Bonn. Otto Braun will let them see everything there is."

She gazed at me with troubled grey eyes.

I picked up my coffee cup and took an unwanted sip. Some requests for help were simply too much. The next two weeks were going to be chaotic. I had a horrendous schedule, with three promised papers to complete, two London meetings to attend, half a dozen important seminars, and four out-of-town visitors. I had to explain to her somehow that there was no way for me to postpone any part of it.

But first I had to explain matters to someone else. I *had* been in love with Marion Shaw, I told myself, there was no use denying it. Hopelessly, and desperately, and mutely. She had been at one time my *inamorata*, my goddess, the central current of my being; but that was ten years ago. First love's impassioned blindness had long since passed away in colder light.

I opened my mouth to say that I could not help.

Except that this was still my Maid Marion, and she needed me.

The next morning I was on my way to Bonn.

Otto Braun was a tall, heavily-built man in his mid-thirties, with a fleshy face, a high forehead, and swept-back dark hair. He had the imposing and slightly doltish look of a Wagnerian *heldentenor*—an appearance that I soon learned was totally deceptive. Otto Braun had the brains of a dozen Siegfrieds, and his command of idiomatic English was so good that his slight German accent seemed like an affectation.

"We made use of certain ancient principles in designing our research facility," he said, as we zipped along the Autobahn in his Peugeot. "Don't be misled by its appearance."

He had insisted on meeting me at Wahn Airport, and driving me (at eighty-five miles an hour) to the company's plant. I studied him, while to my relief he kept his eyes on the road ahead and the other traffic. I could not detect in him any of the shiftiness that Marion Shaw had described. What I did sense was a forced cheerfulness. Otto Braun was uneasy.

"The monasteries of northern Europe were designed to encourage deep meditation," he went on. "Small noise-proof cells, hours of solitary confinement, speech only at certain times and places. Well, deep meditation is what we're after. Of course, we've added a few modern comforts—heat, light, coffee, computers, and a decent cafeteria." He smiled. "So don't worry about your accommodation. Our guest quarters at the lab receive high ratings from visitors. You can see the place now, coming into view over on the left."

I had been instructed not to judge by appearances. Otherwise, I would have taken the research facility of ANF Gesellschaft to be the largest concrete prison blockhouse I had ever seen. Windowless, and surrounded by smooth lawns that ended in a tall fence, it stood fifty feet high and several hundred long. All it needed were guard dogs and machine-gun towers.

Otto Braun drove us through the heavy, automatically opening gates and parked by a side entrance.

"No security?" I said.

He grinned, his first sign of genuine amusement. "Try getting out without the right credentials, Herr Doktor Professor Turnbull."

We traversed a deserted entrance hall to a quiet, carpeted corridor, went up in a noiseless elevator, and walked along to an office about three meters square. It contained a computer, a terminal, a desk, two chairs, a blackboard, a filing cabinet, and a book-case.

"Notice anything unusual about this room?" he said.

I had, in the first second. "No telephone."

"Very perceptive. The devil's device. Do you know, in eleven years of operation, no one has ever complained about its absence? Every office, including my own, is the same size and shape and has the same equipment in it. We have conference rooms for the larger meetings. This was Dr. Shaw's office and it is, in all essentials, exactly as he left it."

I stared around me with increased interest. He gestured to one of the chairs, and didn't take his eyes off me.

"Mrs. Shaw told me you were his best friend," he said. It was midway between a question and a statement.

"I knew him since we were both teenagers," I replied. And then, since

118

that was not quite enough, "I was probably as close a friend as he had. But Arthur did not encourage close acquaintances."

He nodded. "That makes perfect sense to me. Dr. Shaw was perhaps the most talented and valuable employee we have ever had. His work on quantized Hall effect devices was unique, and made many millions of marks for the company. We rewarded him well and esteemed his work highly. Yet he was not someone who was easy to know." His eyes were dark and alert, half-hidden in that pudgy face. They focused on me with a higher intensity level. "And Mrs. Shaw. Do you know her well?"

"As well as I know anyone."

"And you have a high regard for each other?"

"She has been like a mother to me."

"Then did she confide in you her worry—that her son Arthur did not die by his own hand, and his death was in some way connected with our company?"

"Yes, she did." My opinion of Otto Braun was changing. He had something to hide, as Marion had said, but he was less and less the likely villain. "Did she tell *you* that?"

"No. I was forced to infer it, from her questions about what he was doing for us. Hmph." Braun rubbed at his jowls. "Herr Turnbull, I find myself in a most difficult situation. I want to be as honest with you as I can, just as I wanted to be honest with Mr. and Mrs. Shaw. But there were things I could not tell them. I am forced to ask again: is your concern for Mrs. Shaw sufficient that you are willing to withhold certain facts from her? Please understand, I am not suggesting any form of criminal behavior. I am concerned only to minimize sorrow."

"I can't answer that question unless I know what the facts are. But I think the world of Marion Shaw. I'll do anything I can to make the loss of her son easier for her."

"Very well." He sighed. "I will begin with something that you could find out for yourself, from official sources. Mrs. Shaw thinks there was some sort of foul play in Arthur Shaw's death. I assure you that he took his own life, and the proof of that is provided by the curious manner of his death. Do you know how he died?"

"Only that it was in his apartment."

"It was. But he chose to leave this world in a way that I have never before encountered. Dr. Shaw removed from the lab a large plastic storage bag, big enough to hold a mattress. It is equipped with a zipper along the outside, and when that zipper is closed, such a bag is quite airtight." He paused. Otto Braun was no machine. This explanation was giving him trouble. "Dr. Shaw took it to his apartment. At about six o'clock at night he turned the bag inside out and placed it on top of his bed. Then he changed to his pajamas, climbed into the bag, and zipped it from the inside. Sometime during that evening he died, of asphyxiation." He looked at me unhappily. "I am no expert in 'locked room' mysteries, Professor Turnbull, but the police made a thorough investigation. They are quite sure that no one could have closed that bag from the outside. Dr. Shaw took his own life, in a unique and perverse way."

"I see why you didn't want Mr. and Mrs. Shaw to know this. Let me assure you that they won't learn it from me." I felt nauseated. Now that I knew how Arthur had died, I would have rather remained ignorant.

He raised dark eyebrows. "But they *do* know, Professor Turnbull. Naturally, they insisted on seeing the coroner's report on the manner of his death, and I was in no position to keep such information from them. Mrs. Shaw's suspicion of me arose from a quite different incident. It came when she asked me to return Dr. Shaw's journals to her."

"And you refused."

"Not exactly. I denied their existence. Maybe that was a mistake, but I do not pretend to be infallible. If you judge after examination that the books should be released to Dr. Shaw's parents, I will permit it to happen." Otto Braun stood up and went across to the grey metal file cabinet. He patted the side of it. "These contain Arthur Shaw's complete journals. On the day of his death, he took them all and placed them in one of the red trash containers in the corridor, from which they would go to the shredder and incinerator. I should explain that at ANF we have many commercial secrets, and we are careful not to allow our competitors to benefit from our garbage. Dr. Shaw surely believed that his notebooks would be destroyed that night."

He pulled open a file drawer, and I saw the familiar spiral twelve-by-sixteen ledgers that Arthur had favored since childhood.

"As you see, they were not burned or shredded," Braun went on. "In the past we've had occasional accidents, in which valuable papers were placed by oversight into the red containers. So our cleaning staff—all trusted employees—are instructed to check with me if they see anything that looks like a mistake. An alert employee retrieved all these notebooks and brought them to my office, asking approval to destroy them."

It seemed to me that Marion Shaw had been right on at least one thing. For if after examining Arthur's ledgers, Otto Braun had *not* let them be destroyed, they must contain material of value to ANF.

I said this to him, and he shook his head. "The notebooks had to be kept, in case they were needed as evidence for the investigation of death by suicide. They were, in fact, one of the reasons why I am convinced that Dr. Shaw took his own life. Otherwise I would have burned them. Every piece of work that Dr. Shaw did relevant to ANF activities was separately recorded in our

ANF work logs. His own notebooks . . ." He paused. "Beyond that, I should not go. You will draw your own conclusions."

He moved away from the cabinet, and steered me with him towards the door. "It is six o'clock, Professor, and I must attend our weekly staff meeting. With your permission, I will show you to your room and then leave you. We can meet tomorrow morning. Let me warn you. You were his friend; be prepared for a shock."

He would make no other comment as we walked to the well-furnished suite that had been prepared for me, other than to say again, as he was leaving, "It is better if you draw your own conclusions. Be ready for a disturbing evening."

The next morning I was still studying Arthur's notebooks.

It is astonishing how, even after five years, my mind reaches for that thought. When I relive my three days in Bonn I feel recollection rushing on, faster and faster, until I reach the point where Otto Braun left me alone in my room. And then memory leaps out towards the next morning, trying to clear the dark chasm of that night.

I cannot permit that luxury now.

It took about three minutes to settle my things in the guest suite at the ANF laboratory. Then I went to the cafeteria, gulped down a sandwich and two cups of tea, and hurried back to Arthur's office. The grey file cabinet held twenty-seven ledgers; many more than I expected, since Arthur normally filled only two or three a year.

In front of the ledgers was a heavy packet wrapped in white plastic. I opened that first, and almost laughed aloud at the incongruity of the contents, side-by-side with Arthur's work records. He had enjoyed experimental science, but the idea of car or bicycle repair was totally repugnant to him. This packet held an array of screwdrivers, heavy steel wire, and needle-nosed and broad-nosed pliers, all shiny and brand-new.

I replaced the gleaming tool kit and turned to the ledgers. If they were equally out of character . . .

It was tempting to begin with the records from the last few days of his life. I resisted that urge. One of the lessons that he had taught me in adolescence was an organized approach to problems, and now I could not afford to miss anything even marginally significant to his death. The ledgers were neatly numbered in red ink on the top right-hand corner of the stiff cover, twenty-two through forty-eight. It was about six-thirty in the evening when I picked up Volume Twenty-two and opened it to the first page.

That gave me my first surprise. I had expected to see only the notebooks for the four years that Arthur had been employed by ANF Gesellschaft. Instead, the date at the head of the first entry was early April, seven and a half years ago. This was a notebook from Arthur's final undergraduate year at Cambridge. Why had he brought with him such old ledgers, rather than leaving them at his parents' house?

The opening entry was unremarkable, and even familiar. At that time, as I well remembered, Arthur's obsession had been quantized theories of gravity. He was still coming to grips with the problem, and his note said nothing profound. I skimmed it and read on. Successive entries were strictly chronological. Mixed in with mathematics, physics, and science references was everything else that had caught his fancy—scraps of quoted poetry (he was in a world-weary Housman phase), newspaper clippings, comments on the weather, lecture notes, cricket scores, and philosophical questions.

It was hard to read at my usual speed. For one thing I had forgotten the near-illegible nature of Arthur's personal notes. I could follow everything, after so many years of practice, but Otto Braun must have had a terrible time. Despite his command of English, some of the terse technical notes and equations would be unintelligible to one of his background. Otto was an engineer. It would be astonishing if his knowledge extended to modern theoretical physics.

And yet in some ways Otto Braun would have found the material easier going than I did. I *could* not make myself read fast, for the words of those old notebooks whispered in my brain like a strange echo of false memory. Arthur and I had been in the same place at the same time, experiencing similar events, and many of the things that he felt worth recording had made an equal impression on me. We had discussed many of them. This was my own Cambridge years, my own life, seen from a different vantage point and through a lens that imposed a subtle distortion on shapes and colors.

And then it changed. The final divergence began.

It was in December, eight days before Christmas, that I caught a first hint of something different and repugnant. Immediately following a note on quantized red shifts came a small newspaper clipping. It appeared without comment, and it reported the arrest of a Manchester man for the torture, murder and dismemberment of his own twin daughters. He had told the police that the six-year-olds had "deserved all they got."

That was the first evidence of a dark obsession. In successive months and years, Arthur Shaw's ledgers told of his increasing preoccupation with death; and it was never the natural, near-friendly death of old age and a long, fulfilled life, but always the savage deaths of small children. Death unnatural, murder most foul. The clippings spoke of starvation, beating, mutilation, and torture. In every case Arthur had defined the source, without providing any other comment. He must have combed the newspapers in his search, for I, reading those same papers in those same editions, had not noticed the articles.

It got worse. Nine years ago it had been one clipping every few pages. By the time he went to live in Bonn the stories of brutal death occupied more than half the journals, and his sources of material had become world-wide.

And yet the Arthur that I knew still existed. It was bewildering and frightening to recognize the cool, analytical voice of Arthur Shaw, interspersed with the bloody deeds of human monsters. The poetry quotes and the comments on the weather and current events were still there, but now they shared space with a catalog of unspeakable acts.

Four years ago, just before he came to Bonn, another change occurred. It was as though the author of the written entries had suddenly become *aware* of the thing that was making the newspaper clippings. When Arthur discovered that the other side of him was there, he began to comment on the horror of the events that he was recording. He was shocked, revolted, and terrified by them.

And yet the clippings continued, along with the lecture notes, the concerts attended, the careful record of letters written; and there were the first hints of something else, something that made me quiver.

I read on, to midnight and beyond until the night sky paled. Now at last I am permitted the statement denied to me earlier: The next morning I was still studying Arthur's notebooks.

Otto Braun came into the office, looked at me, and nodded grimly.

"I am sorry, Professor Turnbull. It seemed to me that nothing I could say would be the same as allowing you to read for yourself." He came across to the desk. "The security officer says you were up all night. Have you eaten breakfast?"

I shook my head.

"I thought not." He looked at my hands, which were perceptibly shaking. "You must have rest."

"I can't sleep."

"You will. But first you need food. Come with me. I have arranged for us to have a private dining-room."

On the way to the guest quarters I went to the bathroom. I saw myself in the mirror there. No wonder Otto Braun was worried. I looked terrible, pale and unshaven, with purple-black rings under my eyes.

In the cafeteria Braun loaded a tray with scrambled eggs, *speckwurst*, croissants, and hot coffee, and led me to a nook off the main room. He watched like a worried parent to make sure that I was eating, before he would pour coffee for himself.

"Let me begin with the most important question," he said. "Are you convinced that Arthur Shaw took his own life?"

"I feel sure of it. He could not live with what one part of him was becoming. The final entry in his journal says as much. And it explains the way he chose to die."

Enough is enough, Arthur had written. *I can't escape from myself. "To cease upon the midnight with no pain." Better to return to the womb, and never be born . . .*

"He wanted peace, and to hide away from everything," I went on. "When you know that, the black plastic bag makes more sense."

"And you agree with my decision?" Braun's chubby face was anxious. "To keep the notebooks away from his parents."

"It was what he would have wanted. They were supposed to be destroyed, and one of his final entries proves it. He said, 'I have done one braver thing.' "

His brow wrinkled, and he put down his cup. "I saw that. But I did not understand it. He did not say what he had done."

"That's because it's part of a quotation, from a poem by John Donne. 'I have done one braver thing, Than all the worthies did, And yet a braver thence doth spring, And that, to keep it hid.' He *wanted* what he had been doing to remain secret. It was enormously important to him."

"That is a great relief. I hoped that it was so, but I could not be sure. Do you agree with me, we can now destroy those notebooks?"

I paused. "Maybe that is not the best answer. It will leave questions in the mind of Marion Shaw, because she is quite sure that the books must exist. Suppose that you turn them over to my custody? If I tell Marion that I have them, and want to keep them as something of Arthur's, I'm sure she will approve. And of course I will never let her see them."

"Ah." Braun gave a gusty sigh of satisfaction. "That is a most excellent suggestion. Even now, I would feel uneasy about destroying them. I must admit, Professor Turnbull, that I had doubts as to my own wisdom when I agreed to allow you to come here and examine Dr. Shaw's writings. But everything has turned out for the best, has it not? If you are not proposing to eat those eggs . . ."

Everything for the best, thought Otto Braun, and probably in the best of all possible worlds.

We had made the decision. The rest was details. Over the next twelve hours, he and I wrote the script.

I would handle Marion and Roland Shaw. I was to confirm that Arthur's death had been suicide, while his mind was unbalanced by overwork. If they talked to Braun again about his earlier discomfort in talking to them, it was because he felt he had failed them. He had not done enough to help, he would say, when Arthur so obviously needed him. (No lie there; that's exactly how Otto felt.)

And the journals? I would tell the Shaws of Arthur's final wish, that they be destroyed. Again, no lie; and I would assure them that I would honor that intent.

I went home. I did it, exactly as we had planned. The only intolerable moment came when Marion Shaw put her arms around me, and actually *thanked* me for what I had done.

Because, of course, neither she nor Otto Braun nor anyone else in the world knew what I *had* done.

When I read the journals and saw Arthur's mind fluttering towards insanity, I was horrified. But it was not only the revelation of madness that left me the next morning white-faced and quivering. It was excitement derived from the *other* content of the ledgers, material interwoven with the cool comments on personal affairs and the blood-obsessed newspaper clippings.

Otto Braun, in his relief at seeing his own problems disappear, had grabbed at my explanation of Arthur's final journal entries, without seeing that it was wholly illogical. "I have done one braver thing," quoted Arthur. But that was surely not referring to the newspaper clippings and his own squalid obsessions. He was appalled by them, and said so. What was the "brave thing" that he had done?

I knew. It was in the notebooks.

For four years, since Arthur's departure from Cambridge, I had concentrated on the single problem of a unified theory of quantized space-time. I made everything else in my life of secondary importance, working myself harder than ever before, to the absolute limit of my powers. At the back of my mind was always Arthur's comment: this was the most important problem in modern physics.

It was the best work I had ever done. I suspect that it is easily the best work that I will ever do.

What I had not known, or even vaguely suspected, was that Arthur Shaw had begun to work on the same problem after he went to Bonn.

I found that out as I went through his work ledgers. How can I describe the feeling, when in the middle of the night in Arthur's old office I came across scribbled thoughts and conjectures that I had believed to belong in my head alone? They were mixed in hodge-podge with everything else, side-by-side with the soccer scores, the day's high temperature, and the horror stories of child molestation, mutilation, and murder. To Otto Braun or anyone else, those marginal scribbles would have been random nonsensical jottings. But I recognized that integral, and that flux quantization condition, and that invariant.

How can I describe the feeling?

I cannot. But I am not the first to suffer it. Thomas Kydd and Ben Jonson must have been filled with the same awe in the 1590s, when Shakespeare carried the English language to undreamed-of heights. *Hofkapellmeister* Salieri knew it, to his despair, when Mozart and his God-touched work came on the scene at the court of Vienna. Edmund Halley surely felt it, sitting in Newton's rooms at Trinity College in 1684, and learning that the immortal Isaac had discovered laws and invented techniques that would make the whole System of the World *calculable*; and old Legendre was overwhelmed by it, when the *Disquisitiones* came into his hands and he marveled at the supernatural mathematical powers of the young Gauss.

When half-gods go, the gods arrive. I had struggled with the problem of space-time quantization, as I said, with every working neuron of my brain. Arthur Shaw went so far beyond me that it took all my intellect to mark his path. "It were all one that I should love a bright particular star, and think to wed it, he is so above me." But I could see what he was doing, and I recognized what I had long suspected. Arthur was something that I would never be. He was a true genius.

I am not a genius, but I am very talented. I could follow where I could not lead. From the hints, scribbled theorems, and conjectures in Arthur Shaw's notebooks I assembled the whole; not perhaps as the gorgeous tapestry of thought that Arthur had woven in his mind, but enough to make a complete theory with profound practical implications.

That grand design was the "braver thing" that he knew he had done, an intellectual feat that placed him with the immortals.

It was also, paradoxically, the cause of his death.

Some scientific developments are "in the air" at a particular moment; if one person does not propose them, another will. But other creative acts lie so far outside the mainstream of thought that they seem destined for a single individual. If Einstein had not created the theory of general relativity, it is quite likely that it would not exist today. Arthur Shaw knew what he had wrought. His approach was totally novel, and he was convinced that without his work an adequate theory might be centuries in the future.

I did not believe that; but I might have, if I had not been stumbling purblind along the same road. The important point, however, is that Arthur *did* believe it.

What should he do? He had made a wonderful discovery. But when he looked inside himself, he saw in that interior mirror only the glassy essence of the angry ape. He had in his grasp the wondrous spell that would send humanity to the stars—but he regarded us as a bloody-handed, bloody-minded humanity, raging out of control through the universe.

His duty as he saw it was clear. He must do the braver thing, and destroy both his ideas and himself.

What did I do?

I think it is obvious.

Arthur's work had always been marred by obscurity. Or rather, to be fair to him, in his mind the important thing was that he understand an idea, not that he be required to explain it to someone of lesser ability.

It took months of effort on my part to convert Arthur's awkward notation and sketchy proofs to a form that could withstand rigorous scrutiny. At that point the work felt like my own; the re-creation of his half-stated thoughts was often indistinguishable from painful invention.

Finally I was ready to publish. By that time Arthur's ledgers had been, true to my promise, long-since destroyed, for whatever else happened in the world I did not want Marion Shaw to see those notebooks or suspect anything of their contents.

I published. I could have submitted the work as the posthumous papers of Arthur Sandford Shaw . . . except that someone would certainly have asked to see the original material.

I published. I could have assigned joint authorship, as Shaw and Turnbull . . . except that Arthur had never presented a line on the subject, and the historians would have probed and probed to learn what his contribution had been.

I published—as Giles Turnbull. Three papers expounded what the world now knows as the Turnbull Concession Theory. Arthur Shaw was not mentioned. It is not easy to justify that, even to myself. I clung to one thought: Arthur had wanted his ideas suppressed, but that was a consequence of his own state of mind. It was surely better to give the ideas to the world, and risk their abuse in human hands. *That*, I said to myself, was the braver thing.

I published. And because there were already eight earlier papers of mine in the literature, exploring the same problem, acceptance of the new theory was quick, and my role in it was never in doubt.

Or almost never. In the past four years, at scattered meetings around the world, I have seen in perhaps half a dozen glances the cloaked hint of a question. The world of physics holds a handful of living giants. They see each other clearly, towering above the rest of us, and when someone whom they have assessed as one of the pygmies shoots up to stand tall, not at their height but even well above them, there is at least a suspicion . . .

There is a braver thing.

Last night I telephoned my father. He listened quietly to everything that

127

I had to tell him, then he replied, "Of course I won't say a word about that to Marion Shaw. And neither will you." And at the end he said what he had not said when the Nobel announcement was made: "I'm proud of you, Giles."

At the cocktail party before tonight's dinner, one of the members of the Royal Swedish Academy of Sciences was tactless enough to tell me that he and his colleagues found the speeches delivered by the Nobel laureates uniformly boring. It's always the same, he said, all they ever do is recapitulate the reason that the award had been made to them in the first place.

I'm sure he is right. But perhaps tomorrow I can be an exception to that rule.

> *This is a birthday present for Bob Porter.*
> *—Charles Sheffield, February 27, 1989.*

BRUCE STERLING

We See Things Differently

▼

Here's a chilling, powerful, and uneasily timely story that demonstrates that events often have long shadows, that some threats don't disappear just because you can no longer see them, and that some people do not forgive—or forget.

One of the most powerful and innovative new talents to enter SF in recent years, Bruce Sterling sold his first story in 1976, and has since sold stories to *Universe, Omni, The Magazine of Fantasy and Science Fiction, The Last Dangerous Visions, Lone Star Universe*, and elsewhere. He has attracted special acclaim in the last few years for a series of stories set in his exotic Shaper/Mechanist future, a complex and disturbing future where warring political factions struggle to control the shape of human destiny, and the nature of humanity itself. His story "Cicada Queen" was in our First Annual Collection; his "Sunken Gardens" was in our Second Annual Collection; his "Green Days in Brunei" and "Dinner in Audoghast" were in our Third Annual Collection; his "The Beautiful and the Sublime" was in our Fourth Annual Collection; his "Flowers Of Edo" was in our Fifth Annual Collection; his "Our Neural Chernobyl" was in our Sixth Annual Collection; and his "Dori Bangs" was in our Seventh Annual Collection. His books include the novels *The Artificial Kid, Involution Ocean, Schismatrix* (a novel set in the Shaper/Mechanist future), the critically acclaimed novel *Islands in the Net*, and, as editor, *Mirrorshades: The Cyberpunk Anthology*. His most recent books are the landmark collection *Crystal Express*, and a new novel, *The Difference Engine*, in collaboration with William Gibson. He lives with his family in Austin, Texas.

▼

We See Things Differently

BRUCE STERLING

This was the *jahiliyah*—the land of ignorance. This was America. The Great Satan, the Arsenal of Imperialism, the Bankroller of Zionism, the Bastion of Neo-Colonialism. The home of Hollywood and blonde sluts in black nylon. The land of rocket-equipped F-15s that slashed across God's sky, in godless pride. The land of nuclear-powered global navies, with cannon that fired shells as large as cars.

They have forgotten that they used to shoot us, shell us, insult us, and equip our enemies. They have no memory, the Americans, and no history. Wind sweeps through them, and the past vanishes. They are like dead leaves.

I flew into Miami, on a winter afternoon. The jet banked over a tangle of empty highways, then a large dead section of the city—a ghetto perhaps. In our final approach we passed a coal-burning power plant, reflected in the canal. For a moment I mistook it for a mosque, its tall smokestacks slender as minarets. A Mosque for the American Dynamo.

I had trouble with my cameras at customs. The customs officer was a grimy-looking American white with hair the color of clay. He squinted at my passport. "That's an awful lot of film, Mr. Cuttab," he said.

"Qutb," I said, smiling. "Sayyid Qutb. Call me Charlie."

"Journalist, huh?" He looked unhappy. It seemed that I owed substantial import duties on my Japanese cameras, as well as my numerous rolls of Pakistani color film. He invited me into a small back office to discuss it. Money changed hands. I departed with my papers in order.

The airport was half-full: mostly prosperous Venezuelans and Cubans, with the haunted look of men pursuing sin. I caught a taxi outside, a tiny vehicle like a motorcycle wrapped in glass. The cabbie, an ancient black man, stowed my luggage in the cab's trailer.

Within the cab's cramped confines, we were soon unwilling intimates. The cabbie's breath smelled of sweetened alcohol. "You Iranian?" the cabbie asked.

"Arab."

"We respect Iranians around here, we really do," the cabbie insisted.

"So do we," I said. "We fought them on the Iraqi front for years."

"Yeah?" said the cabbie uncertainly. "Seems to me I heard about that. How'd that end up?"

"The Shi'ite holy cities were ceded to Iran. The Ba'athist regime is dead, and Iraq is now part of the Arab Caliphate." My words made no impression on him, and I had known it before I spoke. This is the land of ignorance. They know nothing about us, the Americans. After all this, and they still know nothing whatsoever.

"Well, who's got more money these days?" the cabbie asked. "Y'all, or the Iranians?"

"The Iranians have heavy industry," I said. "But we Arabs tip better."

The cabbie smiled. It is very easy to buy Americans. The mention of money brightens them like a shot of drugs. It is not just the poverty; they were always like this, even when they were rich. It is the effect of spiritual emptiness. A terrible grinding emptiness in the very guts of the West, which no amount of Coca-Cola seems able to fill.

We rolled down gloomy streets toward the hotel. Miami's streetlights were subsidized by commercial enterprises. It was another way of, as they say, shrugging the burden of essential services from the exhausted backs of the taxpayers. And onto the far sturdier shoulders of peddlers of aspirin, sticky sweetened drinks, and cosmetics. Their billboards gleamed bluely under harsh lights encased in bulletproof glass. It reminded me so strongly of Soviet agitprop that I had a sudden jarring sense of displacement, as if I were being sold Lenin and Engels and Marx in the handy jumbo size.

The cabbie, wondering perhaps about his tip, offered to exchange dollars for riyals at black-market rates. I declined politely, having already done this in Cairo. The lining of my coat was stuffed with crisp Reagan $1,000 bills. I also had several hundred in pocket change, and an extensive credit line at the Islamic Bank of Jerusalem. I foresaw no difficulties.

Outside the hotel, I gave the ancient driver a pair of fifties. Another very old man, of Hispanic descent, took my bags on a trolley. I registered under the gaze of a very old woman. Like all American women, she was dressed in a way intended to provoke lust. In the young, this technique works admirably, as proved by America's unhappy history of sexually transmitted plague. In the very old, it provokes only sad disgust.

I smiled on the horrible old woman and paid in advance.

I was rewarded by a double-handful of glossy brochures promoting local casinos, strip-joints, and bars.

The room was adequate. This had once been a fine hotel. The air-conditioning was quiet and both hot and cold water worked well. A wide flat screen covering most of one wall offered dozens of channels of television.

My wristwatch buzzed quietly, its programmed dial indicating the direction of Mecca. I took the rug from my luggage and spread it before the window. I cleansed my face, my hands, my feet. Then I knelt before the darkening chaos of Miami, many stories below. I assumed the eight positions, bowing carefully, sinking with gratitude into deep meditation. I forced away the stress of jet-lag, the innate tension and fear of a Believer among enemies.

Prayer completed, I changed my clothing, putting aside my dark Western business suit. I assumed denim jeans, a long-sleeved shirt, and photographer's vest. I slipped my press card, my passport, my health cards into the vest's zippered pockets, and draped the cameras around myself. I then returned to the lobby downstairs, to await the arrival of the American rock star.

He came on schedule, even slightly early. There was only a small crowd, as the rock star's organization had sought confidentiality. A train of seven monstrous busses pulled into the hotel's lot, their whale-like sides gleaming with brushed aluminum. They bore Massachusetts license plates. I walked out on to the tarmac and began photographing.

All seven busses carried the rock star's favored insignia, the thirteen-starred blue field of the early American flag. The busses pulled up with military precision, forming a wagon-train fortress across a large section of the weedy, broken tarmac. Folding doors hissed open and a swarm of road crew piled out into the circle of busses.

Men and women alike wore baggy fatigues, covered with buttoned pockets and block-shaped streaks of urban camouflage: brick red, asphalt black, and concrete gray. Dark-blue shoulder-patches showed the thirteen-starred circle. Working efficiently, without haste, they erected large satellite dishes on the roofs of two busses. The busses were soon linked together in formation, shaped barriers of woven wire securing the gaps between each nose and tail. The machines seemed to sit breathing, with the stoked-up, leviathan air of steam locomotives.

A dozen identically dressed crewmen broke from the busses and departed in a group for the hotel. Within their midst, shielded by their bodies, was the rock star, Tom Boston. The broken outlines of their camouflaged fatigues made them seem to blur into a single mass, like a herd of moving zebras. I followed them; they vanished quickly within the hotel. One crew woman tarried outside.

I approached her. She had been hauling a bulky piece of metal luggage on trolley wheels. It was a newspaper vending machine. She set it beside three other machines at the hotel's entrance. It was the Boston organization's propaganda paper, *Poor Richard's*.

I drew near. "Ah, the latest issue," I said. "May I have one?"

"It will cost five dollars," she said in painstaking English. To my surprise, I recognized her as Boston's wife. "Valya Plisetskaya," I said with pleasure, and handed her a five-dollar nickel. "My name is Sayyid; my American friends call me Charlie."

She looked about her. A small crowd already gathered at the busses, kept at a distance by the Boston crew. Others clustered under the hotel's green-and-white awning.

"Who are you with?" she said.

"*Al-Ahram*, of Cairo. An Arabic newspaper."

"You're not a political?" she said.

I shook my head in amusement at this typical show of Soviet paranoia. "Here's my press card." I showed her the tangle of Arabic. "I am here to cover Tom Boston. The Boston phenomenon."

She squinted. "Tom is big in Cairo these days? Muslims, yes? Down on rock and roll."

"We're not all ayatollahs," I said, smiling up at her. She was very tall. "Many still listen to Western pop music; they ignore the advice of their betters. They used to rock all night in Leningrad. Despite the Party. Isn't that so?"

"You know about us Russians, do you, Charlie?" She handed me my paper, watching me with cool suspicion.

"No, I can't keep up," I said. "Like Lebanon in the old days. Too many factions." I followed her through the swinging glass doors of the hotel. Valentina Plisetskaya was a broad-cheeked Slav with glacial blue eyes and hair the color of corn tassels. She was a childless woman in her thirties, starved as thin as a girl. She played saxophone in Boston's band. She was a native of Moscow, but had survived its destruction. She had been on tour with her jazz band when the Afghan Martyrs' Front detonated their nuclear bomb.

I tagged after her. I was interested in the view of another foreigner. "What do you think of the Americans these days?" I asked her.

We waited beside the elevator.

"Are you recording?" she said.

"No! I'm a print journalist. I know you don't like tapes," I said.

"We like tapes fine," she said, staring down at me. "As long as they are ours." The elevator was sluggish. "You want to know what I think, Charlie? I think Americans are fucked. Not as bad as Soviets, but fucked anyway. What do you think?"

"Oh," I said. "American gloom-and-doom is an old story. At Al-Ahram, we are more interested in the signs of American resurgence. That's the big angle, now. That's why I'm here." She looked at me with remote sarcasm. "Aren't you a little afraid they will beat the shit out of you? They're not happy, the Americans. Not sweet and easy-going like before."

I wanted to ask her how sweet the CIA had been when their bomb killed half the Iranian government in 1981. Instead, I shrugged. "There's no substitute for a man on the ground. That's what my editors say." The elevator shunted open. "May I come up with you?"

"I won't stop you." We stepped in. "But they won't let you in to see Tom."

"They will if you ask them to, Mrs. Boston."

"I'm Plisetskaya," she said, fluffing her yellow hair. "See? No veil." It was the old story of the so-called "liberated" Western woman. They call the simple, modest clothing of Islam "bondage"—while they spend countless hours, and millions of dollars, painting themselves. They grow their nails like talons, cram their feet into high heels, strap their breasts and hips into spandex. All for the sake of male lust.

It baffles the imagination. Naturally I told her nothing of this, but only smiled. "I'm afraid I will be a pest," I said. "I have a room in this hotel. Some time I will see your husband. I must, my editors demand it."

The doors opened. We stepped into the hall of the fourteenth floor. Boston's entourage had taken over the entire floor. Men in fatigues and sunglasses guarded the hallway; one of them had a trained dog.

"Your paper is big, is it?" the woman said.

"Biggest in Cairo, millions of readers," I said. "We still read, in the Caliphate."

"State-controlled television," she muttered.

"Worse than corporations?" I asked. "I saw what CBS said about Tom Boston." She hesitated, and I continued to prod. "A 'Luddite fanatic', am I right? A 'rock demagogue'."

"Give me your room number." I did this. "I'll call," she said, striding away down the corridor. I almost expected the guards to salute her as she passed so regally, but they made no move, their eyes invisible behind the glasses. They looked old and rather tired, but with the alert relaxation of professionals. They had the look of former Secret Service bodyguards. The city-colored fatigues were baggy enough to hide almost any amount of weaponry.

I returned to my room. I ordered Japanese food from room service, and ate it. Wine had been used in its cooking, but I am not a prude in these matters. It was now time for the day's last prayer, though my body, still attuned to Cairo, did not believe it.

My devotions were broken by a knocking at the door. I opened it. It was another of Boston's staff, a small black woman whose hair had been treated. It had a nylon sheen. It looked like the plastic hair on a child's doll. "You Charlie?"

"Yes."

"Valya says, you want to see the gig. See us set up. Got you a backstage pass."

"Thank you very much." I let her clip the plastic-coated pass to my vest. She looked past me into the room, and saw my prayer rug at the window. "What you doin' in there? Prayin'?"

"Yes."

"Weird," she said. "You coming or what?"

I followed my nameless benefactor to the elevator.

Down at ground level, the crowd had swollen. Two hired security guards stood outside the glass doors, refusing admittance to anyone without a room key. The girl ducked, and plowed through the crowd with sudden headlong force, like an American football player. I struggled in her wake, the gawkers, pickpockets, and autograph hounds closing at my heels. The crowd was liberally sprinkled with the repulsive derelicts one sees so often in America: those without homes, without family, without charity.

I was surprised at the age of the people. For a rock-star's crowd, one expects dizzy teenage girls and the libidinous young street-toughs that pursue them. There were many of those, but more of another type: tired, footsore people with crow's-feet and graying hair. Men and women in their thirties and forties, with a shabby, crushed look. Unemployed, obviously, and with time on their hands to cluster around anything that resembled hope.

We walked without hurry to the fortress circle of busses. A rearguard of Boston's kept the onlookers at bay. Two of the busses were already unlinked from the others and under full steam. I followed the black woman up perforated steps and into the bowels of one of the shining machines.

She called brief greetings to the others already inside.

The air held the sharp reek of cleaning fluid. Neat elastic cords strapped down stacks of amplifiers, stenciled instrument cases, wheeled dollies of black rubber and crisp yellow pine. The thirteen-starred circle marked everything, stamped or spray-painted. A methane-burning steam generator sat at the back of the bus, next to a tall crashproof rack of high-pressure fuel tanks. We skirted the equipment and joined the others in a narrow row of second-hand airplane seats. We buckled ourselves in. I sat next to the Doll-Haired Girl.

The bus surged into motion. "It's very clean," I said to her. "I expected something a bit wilder on a rock and roll bus."

"Maybe in Egypt," she said, with the instinctive decision that Egypt was in the Dark Ages. "We don't have the luxury to screw around. Not now."

135

I decided not to tell her that Egypt, as a nation-state, no longer existed. "American pop culture is a very big industry."

"Biggest we have left," she said. "And if you Muslims weren't so pimpy about it, maybe we could pull down a few riyals and get out of debt."

"We buy a great deal from America," I told her. "Grain and timber and minerals."

"That's Third-World stuff. We're not your farm." She looked at the spotless floor. "Look, our industries suck, everyone knows it. So we sell entertainment. Except where there's media barriers. And even then the fucking video pirates rip us off."

"We see things differently," I said. "America ruled the global media for decades. To us, it's cultural imperialism. We have many talented musicians in the Arab world. Have you ever heard them?"

"Can't afford it," she said crisply. "We spent all our money saving the Persian Gulf from commies."

"The Global Threat of Red Totalitarianism," said the heavyset man in the seat next to Doll-Hair. The others laughed grimly.

"Oh," I said. "Actually, it was Zionism that concerned us. When there was a Zionism."

"I can't believe the hate shit I see about America," said the heavy man. "You know how much money we gave away to people, just gave away, for nothing? Billions and billions. Peace Corps, development aid . . . for decades. Any disaster anywhere, and we fell all over ourselves to give food, medicine. . . . Then the Russians go down and the whole world turns against us like we were monsters."

"Moscow," said another crewman, shaking his shaggy head.

"You know, there are still motherfuckers who think we Americans killed Moscow. They think we gave a Bomb to those Afghani terrorists."

"It had to come from somewhere," I said.

"No, man. We wouldn't do that to them. No, man, things were going great between us. Rock for Detente—I was at that gig."

We drove to Miami's Memorial Colosseum. It was an ambitious structure, left half-completed when the American banking system collapsed.

We entered double-doors at the back, wheeling the equipment along dusty corridors. The Colosseum's interior was skeletal; inside it was clammy and cavernous. A stage, a concrete floor. Bare steel arched high overhead, with crudely bracket-mounted stage-lights. Large sections of that bizarre American parody of grass, "Astroturf," had been dragged before the stage. The itchy green fur, still lined with yard-marks from some forgotten stadium, was almost indestructible. At second-hand rates, it was much cheaper than carpeting.

The crew worked with smooth precision, setting up amplifiers, spindly mike-stands, a huge high-tech drum kit with the clustered, shiny look of an oil refinery. Others checked lighting, flicking blue and yellow spots across the stage. At the public entrances, two crewmen from a second bus erected metal detectors for illicit cameras, recorders, or handguns. Especially handguns. Two attempts had already been made on Boston's life, one at the Chicago Freedom Festival, when Chicago's Mayor was wounded at Boston's side.

For a moment, to understand it, I mounted the empty stage and stood before Boston's microphone. I imagined the crowd before me, ten thousand souls, twenty thousand eyes. Under that attention, I realized, every motion was amplified. To move my arm would be like moving ten thousand arms, my every word like the voice of thousands. I felt like a Nasser, a Qadaffi, a Saddam Hussein.

This was the nature of secular power. Industrial power. It was the West that invented it, that invented Hitler, the gutter orator turned trampler of nations, that invented Stalin, the man they called "Genghis Khan with a telephone." The media pop star, the politician. Was there any difference any more? Not in America; it was all a question of seizing eyes, of seizing attention. Attention is wealth, in an age of mass media. Center stage is more important than armies.

The last unearthly moans and squeals of sound-check faded. The Miami crowd began to filter into the Colosseum. They looked livelier than the desperate searchers that had pursued Boston to his hotel. America was still a wealthy country, by most standards; the professional classes had kept much of their prosperity. There were those legions of lawyers, for instance, that secular priesthood that had done so much to drain America's once-vaunted enterprise. And their associated legions of state bureaucrats. They were instantly recognizable; the cut of their suits, the telltale pocket telephones proclaiming their status.

What were they looking for here? Had they never read Boston's propaganda paper, with its bitter condemnation of everything they stood for? With its fierce attacks on the "legislative-litigative complex," its demands for sweeping reforms?

Was it possible that they failed to take him seriously?

I joined the crowd, mingling, listening to conversations. At the doors, Boston cadres were cutting ticket prices for those who showed voter registrations. Those who showed unemployment cards got in for even less.

The prosperous Americans stood in little knots of besieged gentility, frightened of the others, yet curious, smiling. There was a liveliness in the destitute: brighter clothing, knotted kerchiefs at the elbows, cheap Korean boots of irridescent cloth. Many wore tricornered hats, some with a cockade of red, white, and blue, or the circle of thirteen stars.

This was rock and roll, I realized; that was the secret. They had all grown up on it, these Americans, even the richer ones. To them, the sixty-year tradition of rock music seemed as ancient as the Pyramids. It had become a Jerusalem, a Mecca of American tribes.

The crowd milled, waiting, and Boston let them wait. At the back of the crowd, Boston crewmen did a brisk business in starred souvenir shirts, programs, and tapes. Heat and tension mounted, and people began to sweat. The stage remained dark.

I bought the souvenir items and studied them. They talked about cheap computers, a phone company owned by its workers, a free database, neighborhood co-ops that could buy unmilled grain by the ton. ATTENTION MIAMI, read one brochure in letters of dripping red. It named the ten largest global corporations and meticulously listed every subsidiary doing business in Miami, with its address, its phone number, the percentage of income shipped to banks in Europe and Japan. Each list went on for pages. Nothing else. To Boston's audience, nothing else was necessary.

The house lights darkened. A frightening animal roar rose from the crowd. A single spot lit Tom Boston, stencilling him against darkness.

"My fellow Americans," he said. A funereal hush followed. The crowd strained for each word. Boston smirked. "My f-f-f-f-fellow Americans." It was a clever microphone, digitized, a small synthesizer in itself. "My fellow Am-am-am-am-AMM!" The words vanished in a sudden soaring wail of feedback. "My Am/ my fellows/ My Am/ my fellows/ Miami, Miami, Miami, MIAMI!" The sound of Boston's voice, suddenly leaping out of all human context, becoming something shattering, superhuman—the effect was bone-chilling. It passed all barriers, it seeped directly into the skin, the blood.

"Tom Jefferson Died Broke!" he shouted. It was the title of his first song. Stage lights flashed up and hell broke its gates. Was it a "song" at all, this strange, volcanic creation? There was a melody loose in it somewhere, pursued by Plisetskaya's saxophone, but the sheer volume and impact hurled it through the audience like a sheet of flame. I had never before heard anything so loud. What Cairo's renegade set called rock and roll paled to nothing beside this invisible hurricane.

At first it seemed raw noise. But that was only a kind of flooring, a merciless grinding foundation below the rising architectures of sound. Technology did it: a piercing, soaring, digitized, utter clarity, of perfect cybernetic acoustics adjusting for each echo, a hundred times a second.

Boston played a glass harmonica: an instrument invented by the early American genius Benjamin Franklin. The harmonica was made of carefully tuned glass disks, rotating on a spindle, and played by streaking a wet fingertip across each moving edge.

It was the sound of pure crystal, seemingly sourceless, of tooth-aching purity.

The famous Western musician, Wolfgang Mozart, had composed for the

Franklin harmonica in the days of its novelty. But legend said that its players went mad, their nerves shredded by its clarity of sound. It was a legend Boston was careful to exploit. He played the machine sparingly, with the air of a magician, of a Solomon unbottling demons. I was glad of his spare use, for its sound was so beautiful that it stung the brain.

Boston threw aside his hat. Long coiled hair spilled free. Boston was what Americans called "black"; at least he was often referred to as black, though no one seemed certain. He was no darker than myself. The beat rose up, a strong animal heaving. Boston stalked across the stage as if on springs, clutching his microphone. He began to sing.

The song concerned Thomas Jefferson, a famous American president of the 18th century. Jefferson was a political theorist who wrote revolutionary manifestos and favored a decentralist mode of government. The song, however, dealt with the relations of Jefferson and a black concubine in his household. He had several children by this woman, who were a source of great shame, due to the odd legal code of the period. Legally, they were his slaves, and it was only at the end of his life, when he was in great poverty, that Jefferson set them free.

It was a story whose pathos makes little sense to a Muslim. But Boston's audience, knowing themselves Jefferson's children, took it to heart.

The heat became stifling, as massed bodies swayed in rhythm. The next song began in a torrent of punishing noise. Frantic hysteria seized the crowd; their bodies spasmed with each beat, the shaman Boston seeming to scourge them. It was a fearsome song, called "The Whites of Their Eyes," after an American war-cry. He sang of a tactic of battle: to wait until the enemy comes close enough so that you can meet his eyes, frighten him with your conviction, and then shoot him point blank. The chorus harked again and again to the "Cowards of the long kill," a Boston slogan condemning those whose abstract power structures let them murder without ever seeing pain.

Three more songs followed, one of them slower, the others battering the audience like iron rods. Boston stalked like a madman, his clothing dark with sweat. My heart spasmed as heavy bass notes, filled with dark murderous power, surged through my ribs. I moved away from the heat to the fringe of the crowd, feeling light-headed and sick.

I had not expected this. I had expected a political spokesman, but instead it seemed I was assaulted by the very Voice of the West. The Voice of a society drunk with raw power, maddened by the grinding roar of machines. It filled me with terrified awe.

To think that once, the West had held us in its armored hands. It had treated Islam like a natural resource, its invincible armies plowing through the lands of the Faithful like bulldozers. The West had chopped our world up into colonies, and smiled upon us with its awful schizophrenic perfidy.

It told us to separate God and State, to separate Mind and Body, to separate Reason and Faith. It had torn us apart.

I stood shaking as the first set ended. The band vanished backstage, and a single figure approached the microphone. I recognized him as a famous American television comedian, who had abandoned his own career to join Boston.

The man began to joke and clown, his antics seeming to soothe the crowd, which hooted with laughter. This intermission was a wise move on Boston's part, I thought. The level of pain, of intensity, had become unbearable.

It struck me then how much Boston was like the great Khomeini. Boston too had the persona of the Man of Sorrows, the sufferer after justice, the ascetic among corruption, the battler against odds. And the air of the mystic, the adept, at least as far as such a thing was possible in America. I thought of this, and deep fear struck me once again.

I walked through the gates to the Colosseum's outer hall, seeking air and room to think. Others had come out too. They leaned against the wall, men and women, with the look of wrung-out mops. Some smoked cigarettes, others argued over brochures, others simply sat with palsied grins.

Still others wept. These disturbed me most, for these were the ones whose souls seemed stung and opened. Khomeini made men weep like that, tearing aside despair like a bandage from a burn. I walked down the hall, watching them, making mental notes.

I stopped by a woman in dark glasses and a trim business suit. She leaned against the wall, shaking, her face beneath the glasses slick with silent tears. Something about the precision of her styled hair, her cheekbones, struck a memory. I stood beside her, waiting, and recognition came.

"Hello," I said. "We have something in common, I think. You've been covering the Boston tour. For CBS."

She glanced at me once, and away. "I don't know you."

"You're Marjory Cale, the correspondent."

She drew in a breath. "You're mistaken."

" 'Luddite fanatic'," I said lightly. " 'Rock demagogue'."

"Go away," she said.

"Why not talk about it? I'd like to know your point of view."

"Go away, you nasty little man."

I returned to the crowd inside. The comedian was now reading at length from the American Bill of Rights, his voice thick with sarcasm. "Freedom of advertising," he said. "Freedom of global network television conglomerates. Right to a speedy and public trial, to be repeated until our lawyers win. A well-regulated militia being necessary, citizens will be issued orbital lasers and aircraft carriers. . . ." No one was laughing.

The crowd was in an ugly mood when Boston reappeared. Even the well-dressed ones now seemed surly and militant, not recognizing themselves as the enemy. Like the Shah's soldiers who at last refused to fire, who threw themselves sobbing at Khomeini's feet.

"You all know this one," Boston said. With his wife, he raised a banner, one of the first flags of the American Revolution. It bore a coiled snake, a native American viper, with the legend: DON'T TREAD ON ME. A sinister, scaly rattling poured from the depths of a synthesizer, merging with the crowd's roar of recognition, and a sprung, loping rhythm broke loose. Boston edged back and forth at the stage's rim, his eyes fixed, his long neck swaying. He shook himself like a man saved from drowning and leaned into the microphone.

"We know you own us/ You step upon us/ We feel the onus/ But here's a bonus/ Today I see/ So enemy/ Don't tread on me/ Don't tread on me. . . ." Simple words, fitting each beat with all the harsh precision of the English language. A chant of raw hostility. The crowd took it up. This was the hatred, the humiliation of a society brought low. Americans. Somewhere within them conviction still burned. The conviction they had always had: that they were the only real people on our planet. The chosen ones, the Light of the World, the Last Best Hope of Mankind, the Free and the Brave, the crown of creation. They would have killed for him. I knew, someday, they would.

I was called to Boston's suite at two o'clock that morning. I had shaved and showered, dashed on the hotel's complimentary cologne. I wanted to smell like an American.

Boston's guards frisked me, carefully and thoroughly, outside the elevator. I submitted with good grace.

Boston's suite was crowded. It had the air of an election victory. There were many politicians, sipping glasses of bubbling alcohol, laughing, shaking hands. Miami's Mayor was there, with half his City Council. I recognized a young woman Senator, speaking urgently into her pocket phone, her large freckled breasts on display in an evening gown.

I mingled, listening. Men spoke of Boston's ability to raise funds, of the growing importance of his endorsement. More of Boston's guards stood in corners, arms folded, eyes hidden, their faces stony. A black man distributed lapel buttons with the face of Martin Luther King on a background of red and white stripes. The wall-sized television played a tape of the first Moon Landing. The sound had been turned off, and people all over the world, in the garb of the 1960's, mouthed silently at the camera, their eyes shining.

It was not until four o'clock that I finally met the star himself. The party

141

had broken up by then, the politicians politely ushered out, their vows of undying loyalty met with discreet smiles. Boston was in a back bedroom with his wife, and a pair of aides.

"Seyyid," he said, and shook my hand. In person he seemed smaller, older, his hybrid face, with stage makeup, beginning to peel.

"Dr. Boston," I said.

He laughed freely. "Sayyid, my friend. You'll ruin my street fucking credibility."

"I want to tell the story as I see it," I said.

"Then you'll have to tell it to me," he said, and turned briefly to an aide. He dictated in a low, staccato voice, not losing his place in our conversation, simply loosing a burst of thought. " 'Let us be frank. Before I showed an interest you were ready to sell the ship for scrap iron. This is not an era for supertankers. They are dead tech, smokestack-era garbage. Reconsider my offer.' " The secretary pounded keys. Boston looked at me again, returning the searchlight of his attention.

"You plan to buy a supertanker?" I said.

"I wanted an aircraft carrier," he said, smiling.

"They're all in mothballs, but the Feds frown on selling nuke power plants to private citizens."

"We will make the tanker into a floating stadium," Plisetskaya put in. She sat slumped in a padded chair, wearing satin lounge pajamas. A half-filled ashtray on the chair's arm reeked of strong tobacco.

"Ever been inside a tanker?" Boston said. "Huge. Great acoustics." He sat suddenly on the sprawling bed and pulled off his snakeskin boots. "So, Sayyid. Tell me this story of yours."

"You graduated magna cum laude from Rutgers with a doctorate in political science," I said. "In five years."

"That doesn't count," Boston said, yawning behind his hand. "That was before rock and roll beat my brains out."

"You ran for state office in Massachusetts," I said. "You lost a close race. Two years later you were touring with your first band—Swamp Fox. You were an immediate success. You became involved in political fund-raising, recruiting your friends in the music industry. You started your own record label. You helped organize Rock for Detente, where you met your wife-to-be. Your romance was front-page news on both continents. Record sales soared."

"You left out the first time I got shot at," Boston said. "That's more interesting; Val and I are old hat by now."

He paused, then burst out at the second secretary. " 'I urge you once again not to go public. You will find yourselves vulnerable to a leveraged buyout. I've told you that Evans is an agent of Marubeni. If he brings your precious plant down around your ears, don't come crying to me.' "

"February 1998," I said. "An anti-communist zealot fired on your bus."

"You're a big fan, Sayyid."

"Why are you afraid of multinationals?" I said. "That was the American preference, wasn't it? Global trade, global economics?"

"We screwed up," Boston said. "Things got out of hand."

"Out of American hands, you mean?"

"We used our companies as tools for development," Boston said, with the patience of a man instructing a child. "But then our lovely friends in South America refused to pay their debts. And our staunch allies in Europe and Japan signed the Geneva Economic Agreement and decided to crash the dollar. And our friends in the Arab countries decided not to be countries any more, but one almighty Caliphate, and, just for good measure, they pulled all their oil money out of our banks and into Islamic ones. How could we compete? They were holy banks, and our banks pay interest, which is a sin, I understand." He paused, his eyes glittering, and fluffed curls from his neck. "And all that time, we were already in hock to our fucking ears to pay for being the world's policeman."

"So the world betrayed your country," I said. "Why?"

He shook his head. "Isn't it obvious? Who needs St. George when the dragon is dead? Some Afghani fanatics scraped together enough plutonium for a Big One, and they blew the dragon's fucking head off. And the rest of the body is still convulsing, ten years later. We bled ourselves white competing against Russia, which was stupid, but we'd won. With two giants, the world trembles. One giant, and the midgets can drag it down. So that's what happened. They took us out, that's all. They own us."

"It sounds very simple," I said.

He showed annoyance for the first time. "Valya says you've read our newspapers. I'm not telling you anything new. Should I lie about it? Look at the figures, for Christ's sake. The EEC and Japanese use their companies for money pumps, they're sucking us dry, deliberately. You don't look stupid, Sayyid. You know very well what's happening to us, anyone in the Third World does."

"You mentioned Christ," I said. "You believe in Him?"

Boston rocked back onto his elbows and grinned. "Do you?"

"Of course. He is one of our Prophets. We call Him Isa."

Boston looked cautious. "I never stand between a man and his God." He paused. "We have a lot of respect for the Arabs, truly. What they've accomplished. Breaking free from the world economic system, returning to authentic local tradition. . . . You see the parallels."

"Yes," I said. I smiled sleepily, and covered my mouth as I yawned. "Jet lag. Your pardon, please. These are only questions my editors would want me to ask. If I were not an admirer, a fan as you say, I would not have this assignment."

He smiled and looked at his wife. Plisetskaya lit another cigarette and leaned back, looking skeptical. Boston grinned. "So the sparring's over, Charlie?"

"I have every record you've made," I said. "This is not a job for hatchets." I paused, weighing my words. "I still believe that our Caliph is a great man. I support the Islamic Resurgence. I am Muslim. But I think, like many others, that we have gone a bit too far in closing every window to the West. Rock and roll is a Third World music at heart. Don't you agree?"

"Sure," Boston said, closing his eyes. "Do you know the first words spoken in independent Zimbabwe? Right after they ran up the flag."

"No."

He spoke out blindly, savoring the words. "Ladies and gentlemen. Bob Marley. And the Wailers."

"You admire him."

"Comes with the territory," said Boston, flipping a coil of hair.

"He had a black mother, a white father. And you?"

"Oh, both my parents were shameless mongrels like myself," Boston said. "I'm a second-generation nothing-in-particular. An American." He sat up, knotting his hands, looking tired. "You going to stay with the tour a while, Charlie?" He spoke to a secretary. "Get me a kleenex." The woman rose.

"Till Philadelphia," I said. "Like Marjory Cale."

Plisetskaya blew smoke, frowning. "You spoke to that woman?"

"Of course. About the concert."

"What did the bitch say?" Boston asked lazily. His aide handed him tissues and cold cream. Boston dabbed the kleenex and smeared make-up from his face.

"She asked me what I thought. I said it was too loud," I said.

Plisetskaya laughed once, sharply. I smiled. "It was quite amusing. She said that you were in good form. She said that I should not be so tight-arsed."

" 'Tight-arsed'?" Boston said, raising his brows. Fine wrinkles had appeared beneath the greasepaint. "She said that?"

"She said we Muslims were afraid of modern life. Of new experience. Of course I told her that this wasn't true. Then she gave me this." I reached into one of the pockets of my vest and pulled out a flat packet of aluminum foil.

"Marjory Cale gave you cocaine?" Boston asked.

"Wyoming Flake," I said. "She said she has friends who grow it in the

144

Rocky Mountains." I opened the packet, exposing a little mound of white powder. "I saw her use some. I think it will help my jet lag." I pulled my chair closer to the bedside phone-table. I shook the packet out, with much care, upon the shining mahogany surface. The tiny crystals glittered. It was finely chopped.

I opened my wallet and removed a crisp thousand-dollar bill. The actor-president smiled benignly. "Would this be appropriate?"

"Tom does not do drugs," said Plisetskaya, too quickly.

"Ever do coke before?" Boston asked. He threw a wadded tissue to the floor.

"I hope I'm not offending you," I said. "This is Miami, isn't it? This is America." I began rolling the bill, clumsily.

"We are not impressed," said Plisetskaya sternly. She ground out her cigarette. "You are being a rube, Charlie. A hick from the NIC's."

"There is a lot of it," I said, allowing doubt to creep into my voice. I reached in my pocket, then divided the pile in half with the sharp edge of a developed slide. I arranged the lines neatly. They were several centimeters long.

I sat back in the chair. "You think it's a bad idea? I admit, this is new to me." I paused. "I have drunk wine several times, though the *Koran* forbids it."

One of the secretaries laughed. "Sorry," she said. "He drinks wine. That's cute."

I sat and watched temptation dig into Boston. Plisetskaya shook her head.

"Cale's cocaine," Boston mused. "Man."

We watched the lines together for several seconds, he and I. "I did not mean to be trouble," I said. "I can throw it away."

"Never mind Val," Boston said. "Russians chain-smoke." He slid across the bed.

I bent quickly and sniffed. I leaned back, touching my nose. The cocaine quickly numbed it. I handed the paper tube to Boston. It was done in a moment. We sat back, our eyes watering.

"Oh," I said, drug seeping through tissue. "Oh, this is excellent."

"It's good toot," Boston agreed. "Looks like you get an extended interview."

We talked through the rest of the night, he and I.

My story is almost over. From where I sit to write this, I can hear the sound of Boston's music, pouring from the crude speakers of a tape pirate in the bazaar. There is no doubt in my mind that Boston is a great man.

I accompanied the tour to Philadelphia. I spoke to Boston several times during the tour, though never again with the first fine rapport of the drug. We parted as friends, and I spoke well of him in my article for *Al-Ahram*.

I did not hide what he was, I did not hide his threat. But I did not malign him. We see things differently. But he is a man, a child of God like all of us.

His music even saw a brief flurry of popularity in Cairo, after the article. Children listen to it, and then turn to other things, as children will. They like the sound, they dance, but the words mean nothing to them. The thoughts, the feelings, are alien.

This is the *dar-al-harb*, the land of peace. We have peeled the hands of the West from our throat, we draw breath again, under God's sky. Our Caliph is a good man, and I am proud to serve him. He reigns, he does not rule. Learned men debate in the *Majlis*, not squabbling like politicians, but seeking truth in dignity. We have the world's respect.

We have earned it, for we paid the martyr's price. We Muslims are one in five in all the world, and as long as ignorance of God persists, there will always be the struggle, the *jihad*. It is a proud thing to be one of the Caliph's *Mujihadeen*. It is not that we value our lives lightly. But that we value God more.

Some call us backward, reactionary. I laughed at that when I carried the powder. It had the subtlest of poisons: a living virus. It is a tiny thing, bred in secret labs, and in itself does no harm. But it spreads throughout the body, and it bleeds out a chemical, a faint but potent trace that carries the rot of cancer.

The West can do much with cancer these days, and a wealthy man like Boston can buy much treatment. They may cure the first attack, or the second. But within five years he will surely be dead. People will mourn his loss. Perhaps they will put his image on a stamp, as they did for Bob Marley. Marley, who also died of systemic cancer; whether by the hand of God or man, only Allah knows.

I have taken the life of a great man; in trapping him I took my own life as well, but that means nothing. I am no one. I am not even Sayyid Qutb, the Martyr and theorist of Resurgence, though I took that great man's name as cover. I meant only respect, and believe I have not shamed his memory.

I do not plan to wait for the disease. The struggle continues in the Muslim lands of what was once the Soviet Union. There the Believers ride in Holy Jihad, freeing their ancient lands from the talons of Marxist atheism. Secretly, we send them carbines, rockets, mortars, and nameless men. I shall be one of them; when I meet death, my grave will be nameless also. But nothing is nameless to God.

God is Great; men are mortal, and err. If I have done wrong, let the Judge of Men decide. Before His Will, as always, I submit.

KATE WILHELM
And the Angels Sing

▼

Kate Wilhelm began publishing in 1956, and by now is widely regarded as one of the best of today's writers—outside the genre as well as in it, for her work has never been limited to the strict boundaries of the field, and she has published mysteries, mainstream thrillers, and comic novels as well as science fiction. Wilhelm won a Nebula Award in 1968 for her short story "The Planners," took a Hugo in 1976 for her well-known novel *Where Late the Sweet Birds Sang*, added another Nebula to her collection in 1987 with a win for her story "The Girl Who Fell Into the Sky," and won yet another Nebula the following year for her story "Forever Yours, Anna," which was in our Fifth Annual Collection. Her many books include the novels *Margaret and I, Fault Lines, The Clewiston Test, Juniper Time, Welcome, Chaos, Oh, Susannah!,* and *Huysman's Pets*, and the collections *The Downstairs Room, Somerset Dreams, The Infinity Box,* and *Listen, Listen*. Her most recent books are the collection *Children of the Wind*, the fantasy novel *Cambio Bay*, and the mystery novel *Sweet, Sweet Poison*. Coming up is a new novel, *Death Qualified: A Mystery of Chaos*. Wilhelm and her husband, writer Damon Knight, ran the Milford Writer's Conference for many years, and both are still deeply involved in the operation of the Clarion workshop for new young writers. She lives with her family in Eugene, Oregon.

Here she gives us a bittersweet story concerned, like much of her best work, with the making of some very hard choices. . . .

▼
And the Angels Sing

KATE WILHELM

Eddie never left the office until one or even two in the morning on Sundays, Tuesdays, and Thursdays. The *North Coast News* came out three times a week, and it seemed to him that no one could publish a paper unless someone in charge was on hand until the press run. He knew that the publisher, Stuart Winkle, didn't particularly care, as long as the advertising was in place, but it wasn't right, Eddie thought. What if something came up, something went wrong? Even out here at the end of the world there could be a late-breaking story that required someone to write it, to see that it got placed. Actually, Eddie's hopes for that event, high six years ago, had diminished to the point of needing conscious effort to recall. In fact, he liked to see his editorials before he packed it in.

This night, Thursday, he read his own words and then bellowed, "Where is she?" She was Ruthie Jenson, and *she* had spelled *frequency* with one *e* and an *a*. Eddie stormed through the deserted outer office, looking for her, and caught her at the door just as she was wrapping her vampire cloak about her thin shoulders. She was thin, her hair was cut too short, too close to her head, and she was too frightened of him. And, he thought with bitterness, she was crazy, or she would not wait around three nights a week for him to catch her at the door and give her hell.

"Why don't you use the goddamn dictionary? Why do you correct my copy? I told you I'd wring your neck if you touched my copy again!"

She made a whimpering noise and looked past him in terror, down the hallway, into the office.

"I . . . I'm sorry. I didn't mean . . ." Fast as quicksilver then, she fled

148

out into the storm that was still howling. He hoped the goddamn wind would carry her to Australia or beyond.

The wind screamed as it poured through the outer office, scattering a few papers, setting a light adance on a chain. Eddie slammed the door against it and surveyed the space around him, detesting every inch of it at the moment. Three desks, the fluttering papers that Mrs. Rondale would heave out because anything on the floor got heaved out. Except dirt; she seemed never to see quite all of it. Next door the presses were running; people were doing things, but the staff that put the paper together had left now. Ruthie was always next to last to go, and then Eddie. He kicked a chair on his way back to his own cubicle, clutching the ink-wet paper in his hand, well aware that the ink was smearing onto skin.

He knew that the door to the pressroom had opened and softly closed again. In there they would be saying Fat Eddie was in a rage. He knew they called him Fat Eddie, or even worse, behind his back, and he knew that no one on Earth cared if the *North Coast News* was a mess except him. He sat at his desk, scowling at the editorial—one of his better ones, he thought— and the word *frequancy* leaped off the page at him; nothing else registered. What he had written was "At this time of year the storms bear down onshore with such regularity, such frequency, that it's as if the sea and air are engaged in the final battle." It got better, but he put it aside and listened to the wind. All evening he had listened to reports from up and down the coast, expecting storm damage, light outages, wrecks, something. At midnight he had decided it was just another Pacific storm and had wrapped up the paper. Just the usual: Highway 101 under water here and there, a tree down here and there, a head-on, no deaths. . . .

The wind screamed and let up, caught its breath and screamed again. Like a kid having a tantrum. And up and down the coast the people were like parents who had seen too many kids having too many tantrums. Ignore it until it goes away and then get on about your business, that was their attitude. Eddie was from Indianapolis, where a storm with eighty-mile-per-hour winds made news. Six years on the coast had not changed that. A storm like this, by God, should make news!

Still scowling, he pulled on his own raincoat, a great black waterproof garment that covered him to the floor. He added his black, wide-brimmed hat and was ready for the weather. He knew that behind his back they called him Mountain Man, when they weren't calling him Fat Eddie. He secretly thought that he looked more like The Shadow than not.

He drove to Connally's Tavern and had a couple of drinks, sitting alone in glum silence, and then offered to drive Truman Cox home when the bar closed at two.

The town of Lewisburg was south of Astoria, north of Cannon Beach, population nine hundred eighty-four. And at two in the morning they were all sleeping, the town blacked out by rain. There were the flickering night-lights at the drugstore, and the lights from the newspaper building, and two traffic lights, although no other traffic moved. Rain pelted the windshield and made a river through Main Street, cascaded down the side streets on the left, came pouring off the mountain on the right. Eddie made the turn onto Third and hit the brakes hard when a figure darted across the street.

"Jesus!" he grunted as the car skidded, then caught and righted itself. "Who was that?"

Truman was peering out into the darkness, nodding. The figure had vanished down the alley behind Sal's Restaurant. "Bet it was the Boland girl, the young one. Not Norma. Following her sister's footsteps."

His tone was not condemnatory, even though everyone knew exactly where those footsteps would lead the kid.

"She sure earned whatever she got tonight," Eddie said with a grunt and pulled up into the driveway of Truman's house. "See you around."

"Yep. Probably will. Thanks for the lift." He gathered himself together and made a dash for his porch.

But he would be soaked anyway, Eddie knew. All it took was a second out in this driving rain. That poor, stupid kid, he thought again as he backed out of the drive, retraced his trail for a block or two, and headed toward his own little house. On impulse he turned back and went down Second Street to see if the kid was still scurrying around; at least he could offer her a lift home. He knew where the Bolands lived, the two sisters, their mother, all in the trade now, apparently. But God, he thought, the little one couldn't be more than twelve.

The numbered streets were parallel to the coastline; the cross streets had become wind tunnels that rocked his car every time he came to one. Second Street was empty, black. He breathed a sigh of relief. He hadn't wanted to get involved anyway, in any manner, and now he could go on home, listen to music for an hour or two, have a drink or two, a sandwich, and get some sleep. If the wind ever let up. He slept very poorly when the wind blew this hard. What he most likely would do was finish the book he was reading, possibly start another one. The wind was good for another four or five hours. Thinking this way, he made another turn or two and then saw the kid again, this time sprawled on the side of the road.

If he had not already seen her once, if he had not been thinking about her, about her sister and mother, if he had been driving faster than five miles an hour, probably he would have missed her. She lay just off the road, facedown. As soon as he stopped and got out of the car, the rain hit his face, streamed from his glasses, blinding him almost. He got his hands on the child and hauled her to the car, yanked open the back door and deposited her inside. Only then he got a glimpse of her face. Not the Boland girl. No one he had ever seen before. And as light as a shadow. He hurried around to the driver's side and got in, but he could no longer see her now from the front seat. Just the lumpish black raincoat that gleamed with water and covered her entirely. He wiped his face, cleaned his glasses, and twisted in the seat; he couldn't reach her, and she did not respond to his voice.

He cursed bitterly and considered his next move. She could be dead, or dying. Through the rain-streaked windshield the town appeared uninhabited. It didn't even have a police station, a clinic, or a hospital. The nearest doctor was ten or twelve miles away, and in this weather. . . . Finally he started the engine and headed for home. He would call the state police from there, he decided. Let them come and collect her. He drove up Hammer Hill to his house and parked in the driveway at the walk that led to the front door. He would open the door first, he had decided, then come back and get the kid; either way he would get soaked, but there was little he could do about that. He moved fairly fast for a large man, but his fastest was not good enough to keep the rain off his face again. If it would come straight down, the way God meant rain to fall, he thought, fumbling with the key in the lock, he would be able to see something. He got the door open, flicked on the light switch, and went back to the car to collect the girl. She was as limp as before and seemed to weigh nothing at all. The slicker she wore was hard to grasp, and he did not want her head to loll about for her to brain herself on the porch rail or the door frame, but she was not easy to carry, and he grunted although her weight was insignificant. Finally he got her inside, and kicked the door shut, and made his way to the bedroom, where he dumped her on the bed.

Then he took off his hat that had been useless, and his glasses that had blinded him with running water, and the raincoat that was leaving a trail of water with every step. He backed off the Navaho rug and out to the kitchen to put the wet coat on a chair, let it drip on the linoleum. He grabbed a handful of paper toweling and wiped his glasses, then returned to the bedroom.

He reached down to remove the kid's raincoat and jerked his hand away again. "Jesus Christ!" he whispered and backed away from her. He heard himself saying it again, and then again, and stopped. He had backed up to the wall, was pressed hard against it. Even from there he could see her clearly. Her face was smooth, without eyebrows, without eyelashes, her nose too small, her lips too narrow, hardly lips at all. What he had thought was a coat was part of her. It started on her head, where hair should have been, went down the sides of her head where ears should have been, down her narrow shoulders, the backs of her arms that seemed too long and thin, almost boneless.

She was on her side, one long leg stretched out, the other doubled up under her. Where there should have been genitalia, there was too much skin, folds of skin.

Eddie felt his stomach spasm; a shudder passed over him. Before, he had wanted to shake her, wake her up, ask questions; now he thought that if she opened her eyes, he might pass out. And he was shivering with cold. Moving very cautiously, making no noise, he edged his way around the room to the door, then out, back to the kitchen where he pulled a bottle of bourbon from a cabinet and poured half a glass that he drank as fast as he could. He stared at his hand. It was shaking.

Very quietly he took off his sodden shoes and placed them at the back door, next to his waterproof boots that he invariably forgot to wear. As soundlessly as possible he crept to the bedroom door and looked at her again. She had moved, was now drawn up in a huddle as if she was as cold as he was. He took a deep breath and began to inch around the wall of the room toward the closet, where he pulled out his slippers with one foot and eased them on, and then tugged on a blanket on a shelf. He had to let his breath out; it sounded explosive to his ears. The girl shuddered and made herself into a tighter ball. He moved toward her slowly, ready to turn and run, and finally was close enough to lay the blanket over her. She was shivering hard. He backed away from her again and this time went to the living room, leaving the door open so that he could see her, just in case. He turned up the thermostat, retrieved his glass from the kitchen, and went to the door again and again to peer inside. He should call the state police, he knew, and made no motion toward the phone. A doctor? He nearly laughed. He wished he had a camera. If they took her away, and they would, there would be nothing to show, nothing to prove she had existed. He thought of her picture on the front page of the *North Coast News* and snorted. *The National Enquirer?* This time he muttered a curse. But she was news. She certainly was news.

Mary Beth, he decided. He had to call someone with a camera, someone who could write a decent story. He dialed Mary Beth, got her answering machine, and hung up, dialed it again. At the fifth call her voice came on. "Who the hell is this, and do you know that it's three in the fucking morning?"

"Eddie Delacort. Mary Beth, get up, get over here, my place, and bring your camera."

"Fat Eddie? What the hell—"

"Right now, and bring plenty of film." He hung up.

A few seconds later his phone rang; he took it off the hook and laid it down on the table. While he waited for Mary Beth, he surveyed the room. The house was small, with two bedrooms, one that he used for an office, on the far side of the living room. In the living room there were two easy chairs covered with fine, dark green leather, no couch, a couple of tables, and many bookshelves, all filled. A long cabinet held his sound equipment, a stereo, hundreds of albums. Everything was neat, arranged for a large man to move about easily, nothing extraneous anywhere. Underfoot was another Navaho rug. He knew the back door was securely locked; the bedroom windows were closed, screens in place. Through the living room was the only way the kid on his bed could get out, and he knew she would not get past him if she woke up and tried to make a run. He nodded, then moved his two easy chairs so that they faced the bedroom; he pulled an end table between them, got another glass, and brought the bottle of bourbon. He sat down to wait for Mary Beth, brooding over the girl in his bed. From time to time the blanket shook hard; a slight movement that was nearly constant suggested that she had not yet warmed up. His other blanket was under her, and he had no intention of touching her again in order to get to it.

Mary Beth arrived as furious as he had expected. She was his age, about forty, graying, with suspicious blue eyes and no makeup. He had never seen her with lipstick on, or jewelry of any kind except for a watch, or in a skirt or dress. That night she was in jeans and a sweatshirt and a bright red hooded raincoat that brought the rainstorm inside as she entered, cursing him. He noted with satisfaction that she had her camera gear. She cursed him expertly as she yanked off her raincoat and was still calling him names when he finally put his hand over her mouth and took her by the shoulder, propelled her toward the bedroom door.

"Shut up and look," he muttered. She was stronger than he had realized and now twisted out of his grasp and swung a fist at him. Then she faced the bedroom. She looked, then turned back to him red-faced and sputtering. "You . . . you got me out . . . a floozy in your bed. . . . So you really do know what that thing you've got is used for! And you want pictures! Jesus God!"

"Shut up!"

This time she did. She peered at his face for a second, turned and looked again, took a step forward, then another. He knew her reaction was to his expression, not the lump on the bed. Nothing of that girl was visible, just the unquiet blanket and a bit of darkness that was not hair but should have been. He stayed at Mary Beth's side, and his caution was communicated to her; she was as quiet now as he was.

At the bed he reached out and gently pulled back the blanket. One of her hands clutched it spasmodically. The hand had four apparently boneless fingers, long and tapered, very pale. Mary Beth exhaled too long, and neither of them moved for what seemed minutes. Finally she reached out and touched the darkness at the girl's shoulder, touched her arm, then her face. Abruptly she pulled back her hand. The girl on the bed was shivering harder than ever, in a tighter ball that hid the many folds of skin at her groin.

"It's cold," Mary Beth whispered.

"Yeah." He put the blanket back over the girl.

Mary Beth went to the other side of the bed, squeezed between it and the wall and carefully pulled the bedspread and blanket free, and put them over the girl also. Eddie took Mary Beth's arm, and they backed out of the bedroom. She sank into one of the chairs he had arranged and automatically held out her hand for the drink he was pouring.

"My God," Mary Beth said softly after taking a large swallow, "what is it? Where did it come from?"

He told her as much as he knew, and they regarded the sleeping figure. He thought the shivering had subsided, but maybe she was just too weak to move so many covers.

"You keep saying it's a she," Mary Beth said. "You know that thing isn't human, don't you?"

Reluctantly he described the rest of the girl, and this time Mary Beth finished her drink. She glanced at her camera bag but made no motion toward it yet. "It's our story," she said. "We can't let them have it until we're ready. Okay?"

"Yeah. There's a lot to consider before we do anything."

Silently they considered. He refilled their glasses, and they sat watching the sleeping creature on his bed. When the lump flattened out a bit, Mary Beth went in and lifted the covers and examined her, but she did not touch her again. She returned to her chair very pale and sipped bourbon. Outside the wind moaned, but the howling had subsided, and the rain was no longer a driving presence against the front of the house, the side that faced the sea.

From time to time one or the other made a brief suggestion.

"Not radio," Eddie said.

"Right," Mary Beth said. She was a stringer for NPR.

"Not newsprint," she said later.

Eddie was a stringer for AP. He nodded.

"It could be dangerous when it wakes up," she said.

"I know. Six rows of alligator teeth, or poison fangs, or mind rays."

She giggled. "Maybe right now there's a hidden camera taking in all this. Remember that old TV show?"

"Maybe they sent her to test us, our reaction to *them*."

Mary Beth sat up straight. "My God, more of them?"

"No species can have only one member," he said very seriously. "A counterproductive trait." He realized that he was quite drunk. "Coffee," he said and pulled himself out of the chair, made his way unsteadily to the kitchen.

When he had the coffee ready, and tuna sandwiches, and sliced onions and tomatoes, he found Mary Beth leaning against the bedroom door, contemplating the girl.

"Maybe it's dying," she said in a low voice. "We can't just let it die, Eddie."

"We won't," he said. "Let's eat something. It's almost daylight."

She followed him to the kitchen and looked around it. "I've never been in your house before. You realize that? All the years I've known you, I've never been invited here before."

"Five years," he said.

"That's what I mean. All those years. It's a nice house. It looks like your house should look, you know?"

He glanced around the kitchen. Just a kitchen—stove, refrigerator, table, counters. There were books on the counter and piled on the table. He pushed the pile to one side and put down plates. Mary Beth lifted one and turned it over. Russet-colored, gracefully shaped pottery from North Carolina, signed by Sara. She nodded, as if in confirmation. "You picked out every single item individually, didn't you?"

"Sure. I have to live with the stuff."

"What are you doing here, Eddie? Why here?"

"The end of the world, you mean? I like it."

"Well, I want the hell out. You've been out and chose to be here. I choose to be out. That thing on your bed will get me out."

From the University of Indiana to a small paper in Evanston, on to Philadelphia, New York. He felt he had been out plenty, and now he simply wanted a place where people lived in individual houses and chose the pottery they drank their coffee from. Six years ago he had left New York, on vacation, he had said, and he had come to the end of the world and stayed.

"Why haven't you gone already?" he asked Mary Beth.

She smiled her crooked smile. "I was married, you know that? To a fisherman. That's what girls on the coast do, marry fishermen or lumbermen or policemen. Me, Miss Original No-Talent herself. Married, playing house forever. He's out there somewhere. Went out one day and never came home again. So I got a job with the paper, this and that. Only one thing could be worse than staying here at the end of the world, and that's being in the world broke. Not my style."

She finished her sandwich and coffee and now seemed too restless to sit still. She went to the window over the sink and gazed out. The light was gray. "You don't belong here any more than I do. What happened? Some woman tell you to get lost? Couldn't get the job you wanted? Some young slim punk worm in in front of you? You're dodging just like me."

All the above, he thought silently, and said, "Look, I've been thinking. I can't go to the office without raising suspicion, in case anyone's looking for her, I mean. I haven't been in the office before one or two in the afternoon for more than five years. But you can. See if anything's come over the wires, if there's a search on, if there was a wreck of any sort. You know. If the FBI's nosing around, or the military. Anything at all." Mary Beth rejoined him at the table and poured more coffee, her restlessness gone, an intent look on her face. Her business face, he thought.

"Okay. First some pictures, though. And we'll have to have a story about my car. It's been out front all night," she added crisply. "So, if anyone brings it up, I'll have to say I keep you company now and then. Okay?"

He nodded and thought without bitterness that that would give them a laugh at Connally's Tavern. That reminded him of Truman Cox. "They'll get around to him eventually, and he might remember seeing her. Of course, he assumed it was the Boland girl. But they'll know we saw someone."

Mary Beth shrugged. "So you saw the Boland girl and got to thinking about her and her trade and gave me a call. No problem."

He looked at her curiously. "You really don't care if they start that scuttlebutt around town about you and me?"

"Eddie," she said almost too sweetly, "I'd admit to fucking a pig if it would get me the hell out of here. I'll go on home for a shower, and by then maybe it'll be time to get on my horse and go to the office. But first some pictures."

At the bedroom door he asked in a hushed voice, "Can you get them without using the flash? That might send her into shock or something."

She gave him a dark look. "Will you for Christ's sake stop calling it a her!" She scowled at the figure on the bed. "Let's bring in a lamp, at least. You know I have to uncover it."

He knew. He brought in a floor lamp, turned on the bedside light, and watched Mary Beth go to work. She was a good photographer, and in this instance she had an immobile subject; she could use time exposures. She took a roll of film and started a second one, then drew back. The girl on the bed was shivering hard again, drawing up her legs, curling into a tight ball.

"Okay. I'll finish in daylight, maybe when she's awake."

Mary Beth was right, Eddie had to admit; the creature was not a girl, not even a female probably. She was elongated, without any angles anywhere, no elbows or sharp knees or jutting hipbones. Just a smooth long body without breasts, without a navel, without genitalia. And with that dark growth that started high on her head and went down the backs of her arms, covered her back entirely. Like a mantle, he thought, and was repelled by the idea. Her skin was not human, either. It was pale with yellow rather than pink undertones. She obviously was very cold; the yellow was fading to a grayish hue. Tentatively he touched her arm. It felt wrong, not yielding the way human flesh covered with skin should yield. It felt like cool silk over something firmer than human flesh.

Mary Beth replaced the covers, and they backed from the room as the creature shivered. "Jesus," Mary Beth whispered. "You'd think it would have warmed up by now. This place is like an oven, and all those covers." A shudder passed through her.

In the living room again, Mary Beth began to fiddle with her camera. She took out the second roll of film and held both rolls in indecision. "If anyone's nosing around, and if they learn that you might have seen it, and that we've been together, they might snitch my film. Where's a good place to stash it?"

He took the film rolls and she shook her head. "Don't tell me. Just keep it safe." She looked at her watch. "I won't be back until ten or later. I'll find out what I can, make a couple of calls. Keep an eye on it. See you later."

He watched her pull on her red raincoat and went to the porch with her, where he stood until she was in her car and out of sight. Daylight had come; the rain had ended, although the sky was still overcast and low. The fir trees in his front yard glistened and shook off water with the slightest breeze. The wind had turned into no more than that, a slight breeze. The air was not very cold, and it felt good after the heat inside. It smelled good, of leaf mold and sea and earth and fish and fir trees. : . . He took several deep breaths and then went back in. The house really was like an oven, he thought, momentarily refreshed by the cool morning and now once again feeling logy. Why didn't she warm up? He stood in the doorway to the bedroom and looked at the huddled figure. Why didn't she warm up?

He thought of victims of hypothermia; the first step, he had read, was to get their temperature back up to normal, any way possible. Hot water bottle? He didn't own one. Hot bath? He stood over the girl and shook his head slightly. Water might be toxic to her. And that was the problem; she was an alien with unknown needs, unknown dangers. And she was freezing.

With reluctance he touched her arm, still cool in spite of all the covering over her. Like a hothouse plant, he thought then, brought into a frigid climate, destined to die of cold. Moving slowly, with even greater reluctance than before, he began to pull off his trousers, his shirt, and when he was down to undershirt and shorts, he gently shifted the sleeping girl and lay down beside her, drew her to the warmth of his body.

The house temperature by then was close to eighty-five, much too warm for a man with all the fat that Eddie had on his body; she felt good next to him, cooling, even soothing. For a time she made no response to his presence, but gradually her shivering lessened, and she seemed to change subtly, lose her rigidity; her legs curved to make contact with his legs; her torso shifted, relaxed, flowed into the shape of his body; one of her arms moved over his chest, her hand at his shoulder, her other arm bent and fitted itself against him. Her cool cheek pressed against the pillows of flesh over his ribs. Carefully he wrapped his arms about her and drew her closer. He dozed, came awake with a start, dozed again. At nine he woke up completely and began to disengage himself. She made a soft sound, like a child in protest, and he stroked her arm and whispered nonsense. At last he was untangled from her arms and legs and stood up and pulled on his clothes again. The next time he looked at the girl, her eyes were open, and he felt entranced momentarily. Large, round, golden eyes, like pools of molten gold, unblinking, inhuman. He took a step away from her.

"Can you talk?"

There was no response. Her eyes closed again and she drew the covers high up onto her face, buried her head in them.

Wearily Eddie went to the kitchen and poured coffee. It was hot and tasted like tar. He emptied the coffee maker and started a fresh brew. Soon Mary Beth would return and they would make the plans that had gone nowhere during the night. He felt more tired than he could remember and thought ruefully of what it was really like to be forty-two and a hundred pounds overweight and miss a night's sleep.

"You look like hell," Mary Beth said in greeting at ten. She looked fine, excited, a flush on her cheeks, her eyes sparkling. "Is it okay? Has it moved? Come awake yet?" She charged past him and stood in the doorway to the bedroom. "Good. I got hold of Homer Carpenter, over in Portland. He's coming over with a video camera around two or three. I didn't tell him what we have, but I had to tell him something to get him over. I said we have a coelacanth."

Eddie stared at her. "He's coming over for that? I don't believe it."

She left the doorway and swept past him on her way to the kitchen. "Okay, he doesn't believe me, but he knows it's something big, something hot, or I wouldn't have called him. He knows me that well, anyway."

Eddie thought about it for a second or two, then shrugged. "What else did you find out?"

Mary Beth got coffee and held the cup in both hands, surveying him over the top of it. "Boy oh boy, Eddie! I don't know who knows what, or what it is they know, but there's a hunt on. They're saying some guys escaped from the pen over at Salem, but that's bull. Roadblocks and everything. I don't think they're telling anyone anything yet. The poor cops out there don't know what the hell they're supposed to be looking for, just anything suspicious, until the proper authorities get here."

"Here? They know she's here?"

"Not here here. But somewhere on the coast. They're closing in from north and south. And that's why Homer decided to get his ass over here, too."

Eddie remembered the stories that had appeared on the wire services over the past few weeks about an erratic comet that was being tracked. Stuart Winkle, the publisher and editor in chief, had not chosen to print them, but Eddie had seen them. And more recently the story about a possible burnout in space of a Soviet capsule. Nothing to worry about, no radiation, but there might be bright lights in the skies, the stories had said. Right, he thought.

Mary Beth was at the bedroom door again, sipping her coffee. "I'll owe you for this, Eddie. No way can I pay for what you're giving me." He made a growly noise, and she turned to regard him, suddenly very serious.

"Maybe there is something," she said softly. "A little piece of the truth. You know you're not the most popular man in town, Eddie. You're always doing little things for people, and yet, do they like you for it, Eddie? Do they?"

"Let's not do any psychoanalysis right now," he said coldly. "Later."

She shook her head. "Later I won't be around. Remember?" Her voice took on a mocking tone. "Why do you suppose you don't get treated better? Why no one comes to visit? Or invites you to the clambakes, except for office parties, anyway? It's all those little things you keep doing, Eddie. Overdoing maybe. And you won't let anyone pay you back for anything. You turn everyone into a poor relation, Eddie, and they begin to resent it."

Abruptly he laughed. For a minute he had been afraid of her, what she might reveal about him. "Right," he said. "Tell that to Ruthie Jenson."

Mary Beth shrugged. "You give poor little Ruthie exactly what she craves—mistreatment. She takes it home and nurtures it. And then she feels guilty. The Boland kid you intended to rescue. You would have had her, her sister, and their mother all feeling guilty. Truman Cox. How many free drinks you let him give you, Eddie? Not even one, I bet. Stuart Winkle? You run his paper for him. You ever use that key to his cabin? He really wants you to use it, Eddie. A token repayment. George Allmann, Harriet Davies . . . it's a long list, Eddie, the people you've done little things for. The people who go through life owing you, feeling guilty about not liking you, not sure why they don't. I was on that list, too, Eddie, but not now. I just paid you in full."

"Okay," he said heavily. "Now that we've cleared up the mystery about me, what about her?" He pointed past Mary Beth at the girl on his bed.

"It, Eddie. It. First the video, and make some copies, get them into a safe place, and then announce. How does that sound?"

He shrugged. "Whatever you want."

She grinned her crooked smile and shook her head at him. "Forget it,

Eddie. I'm paid up for years to come. Look, I've got to get back to the office. I'll keep my eyes on the wires, anything coming in, and as soon as Homer shows, we'll be back. Are you okay? Can you hold out for the next few hours?"

"Yeah, I'm okay." He watched her pull on her coat and walked to the porch with her. Before she left, he said, "One thing, Mary Beth. Did it even occur to you that some people like to help out? No ulterior motive or anything, but a little human regard for others?"

She laughed. "I'll give it some thought, Eddie. And you give some thought to having perfected a method to make sure people leave you alone, keep their distance. Okay? See you later." He stood on the porch, taking deep breaths. The air was mild; maybe the sun would come out later on. Right now the world smelled good, scoured clean, fresh. No other house was visible. He had let the trees and shrubbery grow wild, screening everything from view. It was like being the last man on Earth, he thought suddenly. The heavy growth even screened out the noise from the little town. If he listened intently, he could make out engine sounds, but no voices, no one else's music that he usually detested, no one else's cries or laughter.

Mary Beth never had been ugly, he thought then. She was good-looking in her own way even now, going on middle age. She must have been a real looker as a younger woman. Besides, he thought, if anyone ever mocked her, called her names, she would slug the guy. That would be her way. And he had found his way, he added, then turned brusquely and went inside and locked the door after him.

He took a kitchen chair to the bedroom and sat down by her. She was shivering again. He reached over to pull the covers more tightly about her, then stopped his motion and stared. The black mantle thing did not cover her head as completely as it had before. He was sure it now started farther back. And more of her cheeks was exposed. Slowly he drew away the cover and then turned her over. The mantle was looser, with folds where it had been taut before. She reacted violently to being uncovered, shuddering long spasmlike movements.

He replaced the cover.

"What the hell are you?" he whispered. "What's happening to you?"

He rubbed his eyes hard and sat down, regarding her with a frown. "You know what's going to happen, don't you? They'll take you somewhere and study you, try to make you talk, if you can, find out where you're from, what you want, where there are others. . . . They might hurt you. Even kill you."

He thought again of the great golden pools that were her eyes, of how her skin felt like silk over a firm substance, of the insubstantiality of her body, the lightness when he carried her.

"What do you want here?" he whispered. "Why did you come?"

After a few minutes of silent watching, he got up and found his dry shoes in the closet and pulled them on. He put on a plaid shirt that was very warm, and then he wrapped the sleeping girl in the blanket and carried her to his car and placed her on the backseat. He went back inside for another blanket and put that over her, too.

He drove up his street, avoiding the town, using a back road that wound higher and higher up the mountain. Stuart Winkle's cabin, he thought. An open invitation to use it any time he wanted. He drove carefully, taking the curves slowly, not wanting to jar her, to roll her off the backseat. The woods pressed in closer when he left the road for a log road. From time to time he could see the ocean, then he turned and lost it again. The road clung to the steep mountainside, climbing, always climbing; there was no other traffic on it. The loggers had finished with this area; this was state land, untouchable, for now anyway. He stopped at one of the places where the ocean spread out below him and watched the waves rolling in forever and ever, unchanging, unknowable. Then he drove on. The cabin was high on the mountain. Up here the trees were mature growth, mammoth and silent, with deep shadows beneath them, little understory growth in the dense shade. The cabin was redwood, rough, heated with a wood stove, no running water, no electricity. There was oil for a lamp, and plenty of dry wood stacked under a shed, and a store of food that Stuart had said he should consider his own. There were twin beds in the single bedroom and a couch that opened to a double bed in the living room. Those two rooms and the kitchen made up the cabin.

He carried the girl inside and put her on one of the beds; she was entirely enclosed in blankets like a cocoon. Hurriedly he made a fire in the stove and brought in a good supply of logs. Like a hothouse orchid, he thought; she needed plenty of heat. After the cabin started to heat up, he took off his outer clothing and lay down beside her, the way he had done before, and as before, she conformed to his body, melted into him, absorbed his warmth. Sometimes he dozed, then he lay quietly thinking of his childhood, of the heat that descended on Indiana like a physical substance, of the tornadoes that sometimes came, murderous funnels that sucked life away, shredded everything. He dozed and dreamed and awakened and dreamed in that state also.

He got up to feed the fire and tossed in the film Mary Beth had given him to guard. He got a drink of water at the pump in the kitchen and lay down by her again. His fatigue increased, but pleasurably. His weariness was without pain, a floating sensation that was between sleep and wakefulness. Sometimes he talked quietly to her, but not much, and what he said he forgot as soon as the words formed. It was better to lie without sound, without motion. Now and then she shook convulsively and then subsided again. Twilight came, darkness, then twilight again. Several times he aroused enough to build up the fire.

When it was daylight once more, he got up, reeling as if drunken; he pulled on his clothes and went to the kitchen to make instant coffee. He sensed her presence behind him. She was standing up, nearly as tall as he was, but incredibly insubstantial, not thin, but as slender as a straw. Her golden eyes were wide open. He could not read the expression on her face.

"Can you eat anything?" he asked. "Drink water?"

She looked at him. The black mantle was gone from her head; he could not see it anywhere on her as she faced him. The strange folds of skin at her groin, the boneless appearance of her body, the lack of hair, breasts, the very color of her skin looked right now, not alien, not repellent. The skin was like cool silk, he knew. He also knew this was not a woman, not a she, but something that should not be here, a creature, an it.

"Can you speak? Can you understand me at all?"

Her expression was as unreadable as that of a wild creature, a forest animal, aware, intelligent, unknowable.

Helplessly he said, "Please, if you can understand me, nod. Like this." He showed her, and in a moment she nodded. "And like this for no," he said. She mimicked him again.

"Do you understand that people are looking for you?"

She nodded slowly. Then very deliberately she turned around, and instead of the black mantle that had grown on her head, down her back, there was an iridescence, a rainbow of pastel colors that shimmered and gleamed. Eddie sucked in his breath as the new growth moved, opened slightly more.

There wasn't enough room in the cabin for her to open the wings all the way. She stretched them from wall to wall. They looked like gauze, filmy, filled with light that was alive. Not realizing he was moving, Eddie was drawn to one of the wings, reached out to touch it. It was as hard as steel and cool. She turned her golden liquid eyes to him and drew her wings in again.

"We'll go someplace where it's warm," Eddie said hoarsely. "I'll hide you. I'll smuggle you somehow. They can't have you!" She walked through the living room to the door and studied the handle for a moment. As she reached for it, he lumbered after her, lunged toward her, but already she was opening the door, slipping out.

"Stop! You'll freeze. You'll die!"

In the clearing of the forest, with sunlight slanting through the giant trees, she spun around, lifted her face upward, and then opened her wings all the way. As effortlessly as a butterfly, or a bird, she drew herself up into the air, her wings flashing light, now gleaming, now appearing to vanish as the light reflected one way and another.

"Stop!" Eddie cried again. "Please! Oh, God, stop! Come back!"

She rose higher and looked down at him with her golden eyes. Suddenly the air seemed to tremble with sound, trills and arpeggios and flutings. Her mouth did not open as the sounds increased until Eddie fell to his knees and clapped his hands over his ears, moaning. When he looked again, she was still rising, shining, invisible, shining again. Then she was gone. Eddie pitched forward into the thick layer of fir needles and forest humus and lay still. He felt a tugging on his arm and heard Mary Beth's furious curses but as if from a great distance. He moaned and tried to go to sleep again. She would not let him.

"You goddamn bastard! You filthy son of a bitch! You let it go! Didn't you? You turned it loose!"

He tried to push her hands away.

"You scum! Get up! You hear me? Don't think for a minute, Buster, that I'll let you die out here! That's too good for you, you lousy tub of lard. Get up!"

Against his will he was crawling, then stumbling, leaning on her, being steadied by her. She kept cursing all the way back inside the cabin, until he was on the couch, and she stood over him, arms akimbo, glaring at him.

"Why? Just tell me why. For God's sake, tell me Eddie, why?" Then she screamed at him, "Don't you dare pass out on me again. Open those damn eyes and keep them open!"

She savaged him and nagged him, made him drink whiskey that she had brought along, then made him drink coffee. She got him to his feet and made him walk around the cabin a little, let him sit down again, drink again. She did not let him go to sleep, or even lie down, and the night passed.

A fine rain had started to fall by dawn. Eddie felt as if he had been away a long time, to a very distant place that had left few memories. He listened to the soft rain and at first thought he was in his own small house, but then he realized he was in a strange cabin and that Mary Beth was there, asleep in a chair. He regarded her curiously and shook his head, trying to clear it. His movement brought her sharply awake.

"Eddie, are you awake?"

"I think so. Where is this place?"

"Don't you remember?"

He started to say no, checked himself, and suddenly he was remembering. He stood up and looked about almost wildly.

"It's gone, Eddie. It went away and left you to die. You would have died out there if I hadn't come, Eddie. Do you understand what I'm saying?"

He sat down again and lowered his head into his hands. He knew she was telling the truth.

"It's going to be light soon," she said. "I'll make us something to eat, and then we'll go back to town. I'll drive you. We'll come back in a day or so to pick up your car." She stood up and groaned. "My God, I feel like I've been wrestling bears all night. I hurt all over."

She passed close enough to put her hand on his shoulder briefly. "What the hell, Eddie. Just what the hell."

In a minute he got up also and went to the bedroom, looked at the bed where he had lain with her all through the night. He approached it slowly and saw the remains of the mantle. When he tried to pick it up, it crumbled to dust in his hand.

IAN R. MacLEOD
Past Magic

▼

Here's another hot new writer who had a good year in 1990—British writer Ian R. MacLeod, who published a number of strong stories in a number of different markets, any of which might have made the cut for a "Best" anthology in another year (and I can tell you, from stories we have in inventory at *Isaac Asimov's Science Fiction Magazine* alone, that he's going to have an even stronger year in 1991). It was a tough choice, but I finally settled on the haunting and eloquent story that follows, a story that demonstrates that not only can't you Go Home Again, sometimes it's much better not to even *try*. . . .

Ian R. MacLeod is in his early thirties, and lives with his wife in the West Midlands of England. He has made a number of sales to *Interzone* and to *Isaac Asimov's Science Fiction Magazine*, with more to come in inventory at both markets, has also sold to *Weird Tales* and *Amazing*, and is in the process of building a big Name for himself in a very short period of time.

Past Magic

IAN R. MacLEOD

The airport was a different world.

Claire grabbed a bag, then kissed my cheek. She smelt both fresh and autumnal, the way she always had. Nothing else had changed: I'd seen the whole island as the jet turned to land. Brown hills in the photoflash sunlight, sea torn white at the headlands.

We hurried past camera eyes, racial imagers, HIV sensors, orientation sniffers, robot guns. Feeling crumpled and dirty in my best and only jacket, I followed Claire across the hot tarmac between the palm trees. She asked about the mainland as though it was something distant. And then about the weather. Wanting to forget the closed-in heat of my flat and the kids with armalites who had stopped the bus twice on the way to the airport, I told her Liverpool was fine, just like here. She glanced over her shoulder and smiled. I couldn't even begin to pretend.

It was good to see all those open-top cars again, vintage Jags and Mercs that looked even better than when they left the showroom. And Claire as brown as ever, her hair like brass and cornfields, with not a worry about the ravenous sun. I'd read the adverts for lasers and scans in the in-flight magazine. And if you needed to ask the price, don't.

Her buggy was all dust and dents. And the kid was sitting on the back seat, wearing a Mickey Mouse tee shirt, sucking carton juice through a straw. Seeing her was an instant shock, far bigger than anything I'd imagined.

Claire said, "Well, this is Tony," in the same easy voice she'd used for the weather as she tossed my bags into the boot.

166

"Howdy doody," the little girl said. Her lips were purple from the black-currant juice she was drinking. "Are you really my Daddy?"

It was all too quick. I had expected some sort of preparation. To be led down corridors . . . fanfares and trumpets. Instead, I was standing in the pouring sunlight of the airport compound. Staring into the face of my dead daughter.

She looked just like Steph, precisely six years old and even sweeter, just like the little girl I used to hold in my arms and take fishing in the white boat on days without end. She glanced at me in that oblique way I remembered Steph always reserved for strangers. All those kiddie questions in one look. Who are you? Why are you here? Can we play?

Claire shouted "Let's get going!" and jumped into the buggy as though she'd never seen thirty-five.

"Yeah!" the kid said. She blew bubbles into the carton. "Let's ride em, Mummeee!"

Off in cloud of summer dust . . . and back on the Isle of Man. The place where Claire and I had laughed and loved, then fought and wept. The place where Steph, the real Steph, had been born, lived, died. The swimming pools of the big houses winked all the way along the coast. Then we turned inland along the hot white road to Port Erin . . . the shapes of the hills . . . the loose stone walls. It was difficult for me to keep any distance from the past. Claire. Steph. Me. Why pretend? It might as well be ten years before when we were married and for a while everything was sweet and real.

Here's the fairy bridge.

"Cren Ash Tou!!" We all shouted without thinking. Hello to the fairies.

In the days when tourists were allowed to visit the Isle of Man, this was part of the package. Fairy bridges, fairy postcards, stone circles, fat tomes about Manx folklore. Manannan was the original Lord of Man. He greeted King Arthur when the boat took him from the Last Battle. He strode the hills and bit out the cliffs at Cronk ny Irree Laa in anguish at his vanished son. He hid the hills in cloud.

Manannan never quite went away. I used to read every word I could find and share it with Steph after she was tucked up at night from her bath. The island still possessed magic, but now it was sharp as the sunlight, practised in the clinics by men and women in druidic white, discreetly advertised in-flight to those with the necessary clearances. Switching life off and on, changing this and that, making the most of the monied Manx air.

We turned up the juddering drive that led to Kellaugh and I saw that no one had ever got around to fixing the gate. Claire stopped the buggy in the courtyard near the shade of the cypress trees. Like the buggy, Kellaugh was

167

a statement of I-don't-care money, big and rambling with white walls peeling in the sun, old bits and new bits, views everywhere of the wonderful coastline like expensive pictures casually left to hang.

Steph jumped out of the buggy and shot inside through the bleached double doors.

I looked at Claire.

"She really is Steph," she said, "but she can't remember anything. She's had lessons and deep therapy, but it's still only been six months. You're a stranger, Tony. Just give it time."

Feeling as though I was walking over glass, I said, "She's a sweet, pretty kid, Claire. But she can't be Steph."

"You'll see." She tried to make it sound happy, but there was power and darkness there, something that made me afraid. When she smiled, her eyes webbed with wrinkles even the money couldn't hide.

Fergus came out grinning to help with the bags. We said "Hi." Claire kissed him and he kissed her back inside his big arms. I watched for a moment in silence, wondering what was left between them.

Claire gave me the room that had once been my study. She could have offered me the annexe where I would have had some independence and a bathroom to myself, but she told me she wanted me here in the house with her and Fergus, close to Steph. There was a bed where my desk used to be, but still the ragged Persian carpet, the slate fireplace and the smell of the house that I loved . . . dark and sweet, like damp and biscuit tins.

Claire watched as I took my vox from the bag, the box into which I muttered my thoughts. Nowadays, it was hardly more than a private diary. I remembered how she had given it to me one Christmas here at Kellaugh when the fires were crackling and the foghorn moaned. A new tool to help me with my writing. It was still the best, even ten years on.

"Remember that old computer you had for your stories," she said, touching my arm.

"I always was useless at typing."

"I got it out again, for Steph. She loves old things, old toys. And I found those shoot-em-up games we used to buy her at that funny shop in Castletown. She tries, but the old Steph still has all the highest scores."

Old Steph, new Steph . . .

I was holding the vox, trailing the little wires that fitted to my throat. The red standby light was on. Waiting for the words.

Fergus was working in the new part of the house, all timber and glass; in the big room that hung over the rocks and the sea. He'd passed the test of time, had Fergus. Ten years with Claire now, and I had only managed eight.

But then they had never got married or had kids, and maybe that was the secret.

He gave me a whisky and I sat and watched him paint. Fergus seemed the same, even if his pictures had lost their edge. The gravelly voice went with the Gauloise he smoked one after another. I hadn't smelt cigarette smoke like that in years. He would probably have been dead on the mainland, but here they scanned and treated you inch by inch for tumours as regularly as you could pay.

Late afternoon, and the sky was starting to darken. The windows were open on complex steel latches that took the edge off the heat and let in the sound of the waves.

"It's good you're here," he said, wiping his hands on a rag. "You don't know how badly Claire needed to get Steph back. It wasn't grief, not after ten years. It just . . . went on, into something else."

"The grief never goes," I said.

Fergus looked uncomfortable for a moment, then asked, "Is it really as bad as they say on the mainland?"

I sipped my whisky and pondered that for a moment, wondering if he really wanted to know. I could remember what it used to be like when I was a kid, watching the news of Beirut. Part of you understood . . . you just tried not to imagine. Living in it, on the mainland, you got to sleep through the sniper fire and didn't think twice about taking an umbrella to keep the sun off when you queued for the standpipes. I told him about my writing instead, an easier lie because I'd had more practice.

"Haven't seen much work from you lately," he said. "Claire still keeps an eye out . . ." He lit a Gauloise and blew. "I can still manage to paint, but whispering into that vox, getting second-guessed, having half-shaped bits of syllables turned into something neat . . . it must be frightening. Like staring straight into silence."

The evening deepened. Fergus poured himself a big whisky, then another, rapidly catching up on—and then overtaking—me. He was amiable, and we were soon talking easily. But I couldn't help remembering the Fergus of old, the Fergus who would contradict anything and everything, the Fergus who would happily settle an intellectual argument with a fist fight. I'd known him even before I met Claire. Introduced them, in fact. And he had come over to the Isle of Man and stayed in the annexe for a while just as I had done and the pattern started to repeat itself. The new for the old, and somehow no one ever blamed Claire for the way it happened.

"You left too soon after Steph died," he said. "You thought it was Claire and Fergus you were leaving behind, but really it was Claire alone. She has the money, the power. The likes of you and I will always be strangers here. But Claire belongs."

"Then why do you stay?"

He shrugged. "Where else is there to go?"

We stood at the window. The patio lay below and at the side of the house, steps winding down to the little quay. A good place to be. Steph was sitting on the old swing chair, gently rocking, trying to keep her feet off the slabs to stop the ants climbing over her toes. She must have sensed our movement. She looked up. Fathomless blue eyes in the fathomless blue twilight. She looked up and saw us. Her face didn't flicker.

After the lobster and the wine on that first evening, after Fergus had ambled outside to smoke, Claire took my hand across the white linen and said she knew how difficult this was for me. But this was what she wanted, she wanted it because it was right. It was losing Steph that had been wrong. I should have done this, oh, years ago. I never wanted another child, just Steph. You have to be here with us Tony because the real Steph is so much a part of you.

I could only nod. The fire was in Claire's eyes. She looked marvellous with the candlelight and the wine. Fergus was right; Claire had the power of the island. She was charming, beautiful . . . someone you could wake up with for a thousand mornings and still fear . . . and never understand. I realized that this was what had driven me to write when I was with her, striving to put the unknown into words . . . and striving to be what she wanted. Striving, and ultimately failing, pushing myself into loneliness and silence.

Different images of Claire were flickering behind my eyes. The Claire I remembered, the Claire I thought I knew. How pink and pale she had been that first day in the hospital holding Steph wrapped in white. And then the Claire who called people in from the companies she owned, not that she really cared for business, but just to keep an eye on things. Claire making a suggestion here, insisting on a course of action pursued, disposals and mergers, compromises and aggressions, moving dots on a map of the world, changing lives in places I couldn't even pronounce. And although it abrogated a great many things, I couldn't help remembering how it felt when we made love. Everything. Her nails across my back. Her scent. Her power. For her, she used to say it was like a fire. The fire that was in her eyes now, across the candlelight and the empty glasses.

I dreamed again that night that Steph and I were out fishing in the white boat. The dream grew worse every time, knowing what would happen. The wind was picking up and Manannan had hidden the island under cloud. The waves were big and cold and lazy, slopping over the gunwales. I looked at Steph. Her skin was white. She was already dead. But she opened her mouth on dream power alone and the whole Irish Sea flooded out.

*   *   *

Next day Claire took me around all the old places on the island with Steph. The sun was blinding but she told me not to worry and promised to pay for a scan. Just as she had paid for everything else. With Island money, the money that kept all the old attractions going even though there were no tourists left to see them. The steam railway . . . the horse drawn tramcars along the front at Douglas . . . even the big water wheel up at Laxey. Everything was shimmering and clear, cupped in the inescapable heat. Dusty roads snaked up to fenced white clinics, Swiss names on the signboards. I did my best to chat to Steph and act like a friend, or at least be someone she might get to know. But it was hard to make contact through the walls of her sweet indifference. I was just another boring adult . . . and I couldn't help wondering why I had come here, and what would have happened had I tried to say no.

In the evening we took the path beyond the Chasms towards Spanish Head. The air was breathlessly alive with the sound and the smell of the sea, and the great cliffs were white with gulls. Glancing back as we climbed among the shivering grass and sea pinks, I started to tell Steph how the headland got its name from a shipwreck caught up on a storm after the Armada. But she nodded so seriously and strained the corners of her eyes that I couldn't find the words.

Claire was the perfect host. Devoting all her time to me, chatting about when we used to be together, reciting memories that were sweeter than the truth. About the island, about what had changed and how everything was really the same. She invited people over and there were the big cars in the drive and all the old songs and the faces that I remembered. Sweet, friendly people, at ease with their money and power. They were so unused to seeing faces age that I had to remind most of them who I was. I got the impression that they would still all be smiling and sipping wine when the oxygen finally ran out and the world died.

When Claire took me with Steph to Curraghs Wildlife Park, I was struck for once by a sense of change, if only by all the new cages filled with tropical species. Baboons, hummingbirds and sloths. The sort of creatures that would have been bones in the wildfire desert if they weren't here, although it was still sad to see them, trying to act natural behind those bars. But all the old favourites were there as well. Ocelots and otters and penguins that the seagulls stole fish from and the loghtan sheep that once used to graze the island. And the big attraction: Steph ran towards the enclosure almost as though she could remember the last time. And Madeleine lumbered over towards the fence.

Madeleine had been in the papers for a while back when I was young and there were still real papers for her to be in. She might have been created by the same clinic that did Steph, for all I knew. But the islanders were more nervous in those days, bothered about what people on the mainland thought just in case they might try to invade. Take all that money and magic, the golden eggs. They wanted to be seen to be doing something that they could hang a big sign marked SCIENCE on. Something that didn't look like simple moneymaking and self-interest.

Madeleine rubbed her huge side against the fence. The fur was matted and oily. And she stank of wet dog. Like all the wet dogs in the history of the world piled up in one place at one time. Claire and I hung back, but Steph didn't seem to mind breathing air that was like a rancid dishcloth. Madeleine's tiny black eye high on her shaggy head twinkled at Steph as though she was sharing a joke. Her tusks had grown bigger in the ten years since I had last seen her. They looked terribly uncomfortable. And in this heat.

Steph splayed her fingers through the wire, into the matted fur. Madeleine swayed a little and gave a thunderous rumble. Madeleine the mammoth: her original cells came from the scrapings of one of the last hairy icecubes to emerge from the thaw in Siberia. A few steps on the DNA spiral staircase were damaged and computers had to fill in the gaps. As a result there was much debate about whether she was real or simply someone's idea of what a mammoth ought to be. There was one in Argentina made from the same patch of cells with lighter fur and a double hump almost like a camel's. And the Russians had their own ideas and refused to admit Madeleine to the official mammoth club.

The real Steph of ten years before had been just as interested in Madeleine. She made us buy a poster at the little shop on the way out from the zoo. Now, it seemed like a premonition. Steph and Madeleine. The big and the little. Scrapings from the dermis, the middle layer of the skin, were the most suitable for cloning. I remembered that phrase; maybe it was written somewhere on the poster.

We sat outdoors at the zoo café. Lizards darted on the cactus rockery and a red and green flock of parakeets preened and fluttered under the awnings, eyeing the shaded pavement for crumbs. Steph drank another carton of blackcurrant and it stained her lips again. I couldn't help thinking about how much the real Steph used to hate that stuff. Always said it was too sweet.

This Steph chatted away merrily enough. Asking about the past, the last time she was here. She didn't seem bothered by the ghost of the real Steph, just interested. She looked straight at Claire and avoided my eyes.

I said to her, "Don't you think the mammoth might be too hot?"

"You mean Madeleine."

I nodded. "Madeleine the mammoth."

She wrinkled her nose and swung her right foot back against the leg of the chair. Steph thinking. If only her lips hadn't been purple, it was exactly the way she used to be. I had to blink hard as I watched. Then the little pink and white zoo train rattled past and her eyes were drawn. She forgot my question. She didn't answer.

This new Steph was a jumbled jigsaw. Pieces that fitted, pieces that were missing, pieces that didn't belong.

The clinic where they remade Steph from the thawed scrapings of her skin lay up on the hill overlooking Douglas and the big yachts in the harbour. Claire took me along when it was time for Steph's deep therapy. There were many places like this on the island, making special things for those parts of the world that had managed to stay apart from all the bad that had happened. New plants, new animals, new people. Little brains like the one inside the vox. Tanned pinstripe people wafted by on the grey carpets. I was disappointed. I only saw one white coat the whole time I was there.

They took Steph away, then they showed me her through thick glass, stretched out in white like a shroud with little wires trailing from her head. The doctor standing beside me put his arm around my shoulder and led me to his office. He sat me down across from his desk. Just an informal chat, he said, giving me an island smile.

His office window had a fine view across Douglas. I noticed that all the big yachts were in. A storm was predicted, not that there was any certain way to tell the weather. The thought made me remember my dream, being on the boat with Steph. She opened her mouth. And everything flooded back and back to when they finally hauled us out of the water, the chopper flattening the tops of the waves, the rope digging into her white skin, the way a stripe of weed had stuck across her face.

The doctor tapped a pencil. "We all feel," he said, "that your input is vital if Steph is to recover her full identity. We've done a lot with deep therapy. She can walk, talk, even swim. And we've done our best to give her memories."

"Can you invent memories?"

There was darkness on the horizon. Flags flew. Fences rattled. The sea shivered ripples.

"We all invent memories," he said. "Didn't you write fiction? You should know that memories and the past are quite different propositions."

"What do you want me to do?"

"Just be around, Tony. She'll soon get to like you."

"This little girl looks like someone who used to be my daughter. And you're asking me to behave like a friend of the family."

The pencil tapped again. "Is this something to do with how Steph died? Is that the problem? Do you blame yourself?"

"Of course I blame myself . . . and, no, that isn't the problem. That may be the problem with whole chunks of my life . . . why I can't write. But it's nothing to do with Steph. This Steph."

"Okay," he said. "Then what do we do?"

I waited. I watched the masts bob in the greying harbour.

"I have a suggestion," he said. "Let us use your vox."

I shook my head. "No."

"If you gave us the keyword, we could copy all the data onto the mainframe here. It would be perfectly secure. We'd filter it, of course. Only a small percentage would be relevant."

"And you would pour my ramblings into Steph's head."

"A large part of you is inside that vox. Be assured, we'd only take that which is good and beneficial." He stood up and held out his hand for me to shake. "Think about it. I'm sure it's the way forward. For Steph."

Claire put the buggy hood up in the clinic car park with the first drops of rain. Steph sat in the back, sucking a fresh carton of purple juice. She was quiet, even by the standards of when I was around. I put it down to the deep therapy, all those new things in her head. The real rain started just as we crossed the fairy bridge. Hello to the fairies: Cren Ash Tou. Grey veils trailed from the sky. The buggy hood was mostly holes and broken seams and we were cold and wet by the time we got back to Kellaugh, juddering through the puddles on the drive, dashing to the front door.

I watched as Fergus scooped Steph up in the rainlit hall and carried her dripping towards the bathroom. The taps hissed and the pipes hammered. I heard her squeal, his gruff laughter.

I took a bath in the annexe and stayed longer than I intended. Being out of the way was a relief. The clean white walls, fresh soap and towels waiting for Claire's next visitor. I had spent some of my happiest days there, writing, falling in love with Claire. Her father had been alive then. She was a free spirit, spending the old patriarch's money on the mainland as if there was no tomorrow, which wasn't that far from the truth. We met in London before the second big flood. She wrangled the clearances to invite me back to Kellaugh, displacing, I found out later, a sculptor who had left the carpets gritty with dust. We made love, we fell in love. Her father died and I moved in with her. She had Steph, we even got married. My work was selling well then, I could even kid myself that I didn't actually need her support. I thought the pattern of my life had settled, living here with Claire and Steph. Getting a tan and growing to some ridiculous age in the sun, letting the men in white take care of the wrinkles and the tumours. But I realized instead that I was part of another pattern. Claire collected artists. She gave them money, encouragement, criticism, contacts. She usually gave them her body as well.

Because I thought I still needed Claire, and because of Steph, I had stayed longer at Kellaugh than I should have done. The island was addictive, even to those who didn't belong. The money, the parties, the power. The people who were so charming and unaffected, who knew about history and humour and art, who could pick up a phone and bring death or life to thousands, who would chat or argue over brandy and champagne until the sun came up, who would organize pranks or be serious or even play at being in love . . . who would do anything whatever and however so long as they got their own way.

Fergus was only the last in a long succession. I remember coming into the annexe bedroom in the heavy heat one morning to ask about borrowing a book and finding him and Claire together, their bodies shining with juice and sweat. They sat up and said nothing. Only I felt ashamed. But then Claire had never really lied to me about her men. She just kept it out of my way. I had no excuse for my sudden feelings of shock; I had always known that the island only kept faith with itself. But it was much harder to give up pretending.

So I ran out and headed down the steps towards the white boat, across the patio where the bougainvillea was richly in flower. Steph was up early too that morning, sitting on the swing chair, keeping her feet off the paving to stop the ants crawling over her toes. She said Hi and are you off fishing and can I come along? I smiled and ruffled her hair. The sky was hot blue metal. Steph took the rudder. The water slid over the oars like green jelly. I kept rowing until the wind grew chill and Manannan hid the island in darkening haze.

That night after the clinic I went to say goodnight to Steph. Goodbye as well, although I still wasn't sure. The storm was chattering at the window and the waves were beating the rocks below. I could see her face dark against the pillow, the glitter in her eyes.

"Did I wake you?"

"Nope."

"You always used to say that. Nope. Like a cowboy."

"I keep doing things Mummy says I used to."

"Doesn't that feel strange? Can you be sure who you are?"

I closed the door. It was an absurd question to ask any six-year-old. I sat down on the old wicker chair by her bed.

"Do you feel like a Daddy, when you see me?"

"It's like being pulled both ways. You didn't recognize me."

"I know who you are. I've seen your picture on the back of the book Mummy showed me. But you don't look the same."

"That was a long time ago. The real Steph . . . used to be different."

The real Steph. There, I'd said it.

"I don't really understand," she said.

"You don't need to. You're what you are."

Everything was heavy inside me. Here in this room that I knew so well. I wanted to kiss her, carry her, break through and do something that was real. But I knew that all that I would touch was a husk of dry memories.

"What was it like when you were with Mummy and Steph?"

I tried to tell her, talking as though she was some kind of human vox. About waking with the sun in the kitchen clutter of morning. Walking the cliffs with the sea pinks wavering and every blade of grass sharp enough to touch. About days without end when the two of us went fishing in the little white boat. About how you always end up thinking about things and places when you mean people because the feelings are too strong.

Somewhere along the lines of memory I stammered into silence. Steph's breathing was slow and easy as only a child's can be. I leaned forward and kissed her forehead. Faintly, I could smell blackcurrant. I left her to her dreams.

I found Claire holding my vox, the red light glowing in the darkness of my room. I sat down beside her on the bed. She was in a white towelling gown. She smelled both fresh and autumnal, happy and sad.

"You know what they asked for today," I said. "At the clinic."

"You've changed, Tony." She swung the little wires of the vox to and fro. "I thought I could bring the old you back."

"Like bringing back the old Steph?"

"No," she said. "That's possible. You're impossible."

I stared at the vox. The ember in the shell of her hands. "Why did you drag me over here? I can't be the person you want . . . I never really was. Some myth of the way you wanted Steph's father to be. I can't do that. Do you want me to become like poor Fergus? He's not an artist, he's lost his anger. He's not anything."

I tried to look into her eyes. Even in this darkness, it was difficult. I could feel her power like bodily warmth. Something you could touch, that couldn't be denied. Claire looked the same, but she had changed, become more of what I feared in her. She belonged to this magic island.

"At least Fergus still paints," she said. Then she shook her head slowly, her cornfield hair swaying. "I'm sorry, Tony. I didn't mean . . . You have your own life, I know that. I just want to bring back Steph."

Want; the way she said it, the word became an instruction to God. Not that God had much influence on this island. The only way to imagine him was retired, sipping cooled Dom Perignon by the pool and reminiscing about the good old days, like the ancient ex–prime minister from the mainland who still lived up at Ramsey. Like her, most of his achievements had been reviled, and what remained, forgotten.

"I can't stay here any longer," I said.

"You must help." There was an odd catch in her voice, something I'd never heard before. I felt a chilly sense of control, not because of what I was, but because of what I knew I couldn't become.

She asked, "Will you show me the vox? You never let me hear."

So I took it and touched the wires to my throat. Whispered the keyword that was a sound without language. I let it run back at random. Clear and unhesitating, my voice filled the room.

". . . a great many things, I couldn't help remembering how it felt when we made love. Everything. Her nails across my back. Her scent. Her power. For her, she used to say it was like a fire. The fire that was in her eyes now, across the empty glasses . . ."

I turned it off. I had to smile, that the vox had chosen that. It had, after all, a mind of its own. But it all seemed academic: I'd never had any secrets from Claire.

"So that's the deal? I give you my memories, and you let me go?"

She smiled in the darkness. "There is no deal." Then she reached towards me. The white slid away and her flesh gleamed in the stuttering light of the storm. The air smelt of her and of Kellaugh, of biscuit tins and damp. There was a moment when the past and present touched. Her nails drew blood from my back. Raking down through layers of skin, layers of memory. Inside the fire, I thought of Steph, wrapped in the sweet breath of dreams, of making her anew.

That was Tony's last entry before he returned to the mainland. Obviously, he can't come back now, not now that I'm here. Claire tells me that everything went tidily enough the next day. The trip to the clinic in the clear air after the storm, then on to the airport. It was the only way out; perhaps he understood that by then.

This vox is a good copy. We have that much in common, my vox and I. It's winter now. Life is comfortable here in the annexe, but chilly when the wind turns north and draws the heat from the fire. I saw an iceberg from my window yesterday. Huge, even halfway towards the horizon. Pure white against the grey sky, shining like the light from a better world.

The four of us eat our meals together as a kind of family. Claire. Fergus. Steph. Me. The talk is mostly happy and there's little tension. Only sometimes I see Steph with darkness behind her big blue eyes. A look I understand but can't explain. But everything is fine, here on this fortunate island. Even

Fergus is a good friend in his own vague way. He doesn't mind Claire's nocturnal visits to the annexe to make love. Everything about the arrangement is amicable and discreet.

Deep therapy has brought back a great many things. Often now, I can't be sure where my own true and recent memories begin. But I still find it useful to run back the vox, to listen to that inner voice. I find that I share many of the real Tony's doubts and feelings. We are so much alike, he and I, even if I am nothing more than the tiniest scrap of his flesh taken from under Claire's fingernails.

When I originally mastered this vox, the first thing I did was to run it back ten years to that summer, that day. Tony—the real Tony—had the vox with him when Steph drowned; the vibrations of the storm must have tripped it to record.

You can hear the flat boom of the water. The thump of the waves against the useless upturned hull. Tony's shuddering breath. Steph's voice is there too, the old Steph that I will never know, carried into the circuits by some trick of the vox. *I'm cold, Daddeeee. Please help. I can't stay up. The cold. Hurts. Aches. Hurts. Please, Daddy. Can you help me, Daddy? Can you?*

But it was all a long time ago. I can't erase the memory, but I don't think I'll ever replay it again.

TERRY BISSON

Bears Discover Fire

▼

Here's a gentle, wry, whimsical, and funny story—reminiscent to me of the best of early Lafferty—that's about exactly what it *says* that it's about . . .

A relatively new writer, Terry Bisson is the author of a number of critically acclaimed novels such as *Fire on the Mountain, Wyrldmaker,* and the popular *Talking Man,* which was a finalist for the World Fantasy Award in 1986. His most recent book is the novel *Voyage to the Red Planet,* released in 1990. He lives in Brooklyn, New York.

▼

Bears Discover Fire

TERRY BISSON

I was driving with my brother, the preacher, and my nephew, the preacher's son, on I-65 just north of Bowling Green when we got a flat. It was Sunday night and we had been to visit Mother at the Home. We were in my car. The flat caused what you might call knowing groans since, as the old-fashioned one in my family (so they tell me), I fix my own tires, and my brother is always telling me to get radials and quit buying old tires.

But if you know how to mount and fix tires yourself, you can pick them up for almost nothing.

Since it was a left rear tire, I pulled over left, onto the median grass. The way my Caddy stumbled to a stop, I figured the tire was ruined. "I guess there's no need asking if you have any of that *FlatFix* in the trunk," said Wallace.

"Here, son, hold the light," I said to Wallace Jr. He's old enough to want to help and not old enough (yet) to think he knows it all. If I'd married and had kids, he's the kind I'd have wanted.

An old Caddy has a big trunk that tends to fill up like a shed. Mine's a '56. Wallace was wearing his Sunday shirt, so he didn't offer to help while I pulled magazines, fishing tackle, a wooden tool box, some old clothes, a comealong wrapped in a grass sack, and a tobacco sprayer out of the way, looking for my jack. The spare looked a little soft.

The light went out. "Shake it, son," I said.

It went back on. The bumper jack was long gone, but I carry a little ¼ ton hydraulic. I finally found it under Mother's old *Southern Livings*, 1978–1986. I had been meaning to drop them at the dump. If Wallace

180

hadn't been along, I'd have let Wallace Jr. position the jack under the axle, but I got on my knees and did it myself. There's nothing wrong with a boy learning to change a tire. Even if you're not going to fix and mount them, you're still going to have to change a few in this life. The light went off again before I had the wheel off the ground. I was surprised at how dark the night was already. It was late October and beginning to get cool. "Shake it again, son," I said.

It went back on but it was weak. Flickery.

"With radials you just don't *have* flats," Wallace explained in that voice he uses when he's talking to a number of people at once; in this case, Wallace Jr. and myself. "And even when you *do*, you just squirt them with this stuff called *FlatFix* and you just drive on. $3.95 the can."

"Uncle Bobby can fix a tire hisself," said Wallace Jr., out of loyalty I presume.

"*Him*self," I said from halfway under the car. If it was up to Wallace, the boy would talk like what Mother used to call "a helock from the gorges of the mountains." But drive on radials.

"Shake that light again," I said. It was about gone. I spun the lugs off into the hubcap and pulled the wheel. The tire had blown out along the sidewall. "Won't be fixing this one," I said. Not that I cared. I have a pile as tall as a man out by the barn.

The light went out again, then came back better than ever as I was fitting the spare over the lugs. "Much better," I said. There was a flood of dim orange flickery light. But when I turned to find the lug nuts, I was surprised to see that the flashlight the boy was holding was dead. The light was coming from two bears at the edge of the trees, holding torches. They were big, three-hundred-pounders, standing about five feet tall. Wallace Jr. and his father had seen them and were standing perfectly still. It's best not to alarm bears.

I fished the lug nuts out of the hubcap and spun them on. I usually like to put a little oil on them, but this time I let it go. I reached under the car and let the jack down and pulled it out. I was relieved to see that the spare was high enough to drive on. I put the jack and the lug wrench and the flat into the trunk. Instead of replacing the hubcap, I put it in there too. All this time, the bears never made a move. They just held the torches up, whether out of curiosity or helpfulness, there was no way of knowing. It looked like there may have been more bears behind them, in the trees.

Opening three doors at once, we got into the car and drove off. Wallace was the first to speak. "Looks like bears have discovered fire," he said.

When we first took Mother to the Home, almost four years (forty-seven months) ago, she told Wallace and me she was ready to die. "Don't worry about me, boys," she whispered, pulling us both down so the nurse wouldn't hear. "I've drove a million miles and I'm ready to pass over to the other shore. I won't have long to linger here." She drove a consolidated school bus for thirty-nine years. Later, after Wallace left, she told me about her dream. A bunch of doctors were sitting around in a circle discussing her case. One said, "We've done all we can for her, boys, let's let her go." They all turned their hands up and smiled. When she didn't die that fall, she seemed disappointed, though as spring came she forgot about it, as old people will.

In addition to taking Wallace and Wallace Jr. to see Mother on Sunday nights, I go myself on Tuesdays and Thursdays. I usually find her sitting in front of the TV, even though she doesn't watch it. The nurses keep it on all the time. They say the old folks like the flickering. It soothes them down.

"What's this I hear about bears discovering fire?" she said on Tuesday. "It's true," I told her as I combed her long white hair with the shell comb Wallace had bought her from Florida. Monday there had been a story in the Louisville *Courier-Journal*, and Tuesday one on NBC or CBS Nightly News. People were seeing bears all over the state, and in Virginia as well. They had quit hibernating, and were apparently planning to spend the winter in the medians of the interstates. There have always been bears in the mountains of Virginia, but not here in western Kentucky, not for almost a hundred years. The last one was killed when Mother was a girl. The theory in the *Courier-Journal* was that they were following I-65 down from the forests of Michigan and Canada, but one old man from Allen County (interviewed on nationwide TV) said that there had always been a few bears left back in the hills, and they had come out to join the others now that they had discovered fire.

"They don't hibernate any more," I said. "They make a fire and keep it going all winter."

"I declare," Mother said. "What'll they think of next!" The nurse came to take her tobacco away, which is the signal for bedtime.

Every October, Wallace Jr. stays with me while his parents go to camp. I realize how backward that sounds, but there it is. My brother is a minister (House of the Righteous Way, Reformed), but he makes two thirds of his living in real estate. He and Elizabeth go to a Christian Success Retreat in South Carolina, where people from all over the country practice selling things to one another. I know what it's like not because they've ever bothered to tell me, but because I've seen the Revolving Equity Success Plan ads late at night on TV.

The schoolbus let Wallace Jr. off at my house on Wednesday, the day they left. The boy doesn't have to pack much of a bag when he stays with me. He has his own room here. As the eldest of our family, I hung onto the old home place near Smiths Grove. It's getting run down, but Wallace Jr. and I don't mind. He has his own room in Bowling Green, too, but since Wallace and Elizabeth move to a different house every three months (part of the Plan), he keeps his .22 and his comics, the stuff that's important to a boy his age, in his room here at the home place. It's the room his dad and I used to share.

Wallace Jr. is twelve. I found him sitting on the back porch that overlooks the interstate when I got home from work. I sell crop insurance.

After I changed clothes, I showed him how to break the bead on a tire two ways, with a hammer and by backing a car over it. Like making sorghum, fixing tires by hand is a dying art. The boy caught on fast, though. "Tomorrow I'll show you how to mount your tire with the hammer and a tire iron," I said.

"What I wish is I could see the bears," he said. He was looking across the field to I-65, where the northbound lanes cut off the corner of our field. From the house at night, sometimes the traffic sounds like a waterfall.

"Can't see their fire in the daytime," I said. "But wait till tonight." That night CBS or NBC (I forget which is which) did a special on the bears, which were becoming a story of nationwide interest. They were seen in Kentucky, West Virginia, Missouri, Illinois (southern), and, of course, Virginia. There have always been bears in Virginia. Some characters there were even talking about hunting them. A scientist said they were heading into the states where there is some snow but not too much, and where there is enough timber in the medians for firewood. He had gone in with a video camera, but his shots were just blurry figures sitting around a fire. Another scientist said the bears were attracted by the berries on a new bush that grew only in the medians of the interstates. He claimed this berry was the first new species in recent history, brought about by the mixing of seeds along the highway. He ate one on TV, making a face, and called it a "newberry." A climatic ecologist said that the warm winters (there was no snow last winter in Nashville, and only one flurry in Louisville) had changed the bears' hibernation cycle, and now they were able to remember things from year to year. "Bears may have discovered fire centuries ago," he said, "but forgot it." Another theory was that they had discovered (or remembered) fire when Yellowstone burned, several years ago.

The TV showed more guys talking about bears than it showed bears, and Wallace Jr. and I lost interest. After the supper dishes were done I took the boy out behind the house and down to our fence. Across the interstate and through the trees, we could see the light of the bears' fire. Wallace Jr. wanted to go back to the house and get his .22 and go shoot one, and I explained why that would be wrong. "Besides," I said, "a .22 wouldn't do much more to a bear than make it mad."

"Besides," I added, "it's illegal to hunt in the medians."

The only trick to mounting a tire by hand, once you have beaten or pried it onto the rim, is setting the bed. You do this by setting the tire upright, sitting on it, and bouncing it up and down between your legs while the air goes in. When the bead sets on the rim, it makes a satisfying "pop." On Thursday, I kept Wallace Jr. home from school and showed him how to do this until he got it right. Then we climbed our fence and crossed the field to get a look at the bears.

In northern Virginia, according to "Good Morning America," the bears were keeping their fires going all day long. Here in western Kentucky, though, it was still warm for late October and they only stayed around the fires at night. Where they went and what they did in the daytime, I don't know. Maybe they were watching from the newberry bushes as Wallace Jr. and I climbed the government fence and crossed the northbound lanes. I carried an axe and Wallace Jr. brought his .22, not because he wanted to kill a bear but because a boy likes to carry some kind of a gun. The median was all tangled with brush and vines under the maples, oaks, and sycamores. Even though we were only a hundred yards from the house, I had never been there, and neither had anyone else that I knew of. It was like a created country. We found a path in the center and followed it down across a slow, short stream that flowed out of one grate and into another. The tracks in the gray mud were the first bear signs we saw. There was a musty but not really unpleasant smell. In a clearing under a big hollow beech, where the fire had been, we found nothing but ashes. Logs were drawn up in a rough circle and the smell was stronger. I stirred the ashes and found enough coals left to start a new flame, so I banked them back the way they had been left.

I cut a little firewood and stacked it to one side, just to be neighborly.

Maybe the bears were watching us from the bushes even then. There's no way to know. I tasted one of the newberries and spit it out. It was so sweet it was sour, just the sort of thing you would imagine a bear would like.

That evening after supper, I asked Wallace Jr. if he might want to go with me to visit Mother. I wasn't surprised when he said "yes." Kids have more consideration than folks give them credit for. We found her sitting on the concrete front porch of the Home, watching the cars go by on I-65. The nurse said she had been agitated all day. I wasn't surprised by that, either.

Every fall as the leaves change, she gets restless, maybe the word is hopeful, again. I brought her into the dayroom and combed her long white hair. "Nothing but bears on TV anymore," the nurse complained, flipping the channels. Wallace Jr. picked up the remote after the nurse left, and we watched a CBS or NBC Special Report about some hunters in Virginia who had gotten their houses torched. The TV interviewed a hunter and his wife whose $117,500 Shenandoah Valley home had burned. She blamed the bears. He didn't blame the bears, but he was suing for compensation from the state since he had a valid hunting license. The state hunting commissioner came on and said that possession of a hunting license didn't prohibit (enjoin, I think, was the word he used) *the hunted* from striking back. I thought that was a pretty liberal view for a state commissioner. Of course, he had a vested interest in not paying off. I'm not a hunter myself.

"Don't bother coming on Sunday," Mother told Wallace Jr. with a wink. "I've drove a million miles and I've got one hand on the gate." I'm used to her saying stuff like that, especially in the fall, but I was afraid it would upset the boy. In fact, he looked worried after we left and I asked him what was wrong.

"How could she have drove a million miles?" he asked. She had told him 48 miles a day for 39 years, and he had worked it out on his calculator to be 336,960 miles.

"Have *driven*," I said. "And it's forty-eight in the morning and forty-eight in the afternoon. Plus there were the football trips. Plus, old folks exaggerate a little." Mother was the first woman school bus driver in the state. She did it every day and raised a family, too. Dad just farmed.

I usually get off the interstate at Smiths Grove, but that night I drove north all the way to Horse Cave and doubled back so Wallace Jr. and I could see the bears' fires. There were not as many as you would think from the TV —one every six or seven miles, hidden back in a clump of trees or under a rocky ledge. Probably they look for water as well as wood. Wallace Jr. wanted to stop, but it's against the law to stop on the interstate and I was afraid the state police would run us off.

There was a card from Wallace in the mailbox. He and Elizabeth were doing fine and having a wonderful time. Not a word about Wallace Jr., but the boy didn't seem to mind. Like most kids his age, he doesn't really enjoy going places with his parents.

On Saturday afternoon, the Home called my office (Burley Belt Drought & Hail) and left word that Mother was gone. I was on the road. I work Saturdays. It's the only day a lot of part-time farmers are home. My heart literally

Terry Bisson

skipped a beat when I called in and got the message, but only a beat. I had long been prepared. "It's a blessing," I said when I got the nurse on the phone.

"You don't understand," the nurse said. "Not *passed* away, gone. *Ran* away, gone. Your mother has escaped." Mother had gone through the door at the end of the corridor when no one was looking, wedging the door with her comb and taking a bedspread which belonged to the Home. What about her tobacco? I asked. It was gone. That was a sure sign she was planning to stay away. I was in Franklin, and it took me less than an hour to get to the Home on I-65. The nurse told me that Mother had been acting more and more confused lately. Of course they are going to say that. We looked around the grounds, which is only an acre with no trees between the interstate and a soybean field. Then they had me leave a message at the Sheriff's office. I would have to keep paying for her care until she was officially listed as Missing, which would be Monday.

It was dark by the time I got back to the house, and Wallace Jr. was fixing supper. This just involves opening a few cans, already selected and grouped together with a rubber band. I told him his grandmother had gone, and he nodded, saying, "She told us she would be." I called Florida and left a message. There was nothing more to be done. I sat down and tried to watch TV, but there was nothing on. Then, I looked out the back door, and saw the firelight twinkling through the trees across the northbound lane of I-65, and realized I just might know where to find her.

It was definitely getting colder, so I got my jacket. I told the boy to wait by the phone in case the Sheriff called, but when I looked back, halfway across the field, there he was behind me. He didn't have a jacket. I let him catch up. He was carrying his .22, and I made him leave it leaning against our fence. It was harder climbing the government fence in the dark, at my age, than it had been in the daylight. I am sixty-one. The highway was busy with cars heading south and trucks heading north.

Crossing the shoulder, I got my pants cuffs wet on the long grass, already wet with dew. It is actually bluegrass.

The first few feet into the trees it was pitch black and the boy grabbed my hand. Then it got lighter. At first I thought it was the moon, but it was the high beams shining like moonlight into the treetops, allowing Wallace Jr. and me to pick our way through the brush. We soon found the path and its familiar bear smell.

I was wary of approaching the bears at night. If we stayed on the path we might run into one in the dark, but if we went through the bushes we might be seen as intruders. I wondered if maybe we shouldn't have brought the gun.

186

We stayed on the path. The light seemed to drip down from the canopy of the woods like rain. The going was easy, especially if we didn't try to look at the path but let our feet find their own way.

Then through the trees I saw their fire.

The fire was mostly of sycamore and beech branches, the kind of fire that puts out very little heat or light and lots of smoke. The bears hadn't learned the ins and outs of wood yet. They did okay at tending it, though. A large cinnamon brown northern-looking bear was poking the fire with a stick, adding a branch now and then from a pile at his side. The others sat around in a loose circle on the logs. Most were smaller black or honey bears, one was a mother with cubs. Some were eating berries from a hubcap. Not eating, but just watching the fire, my mother sat among them with the bedspread from the Home around her shoulders.

If the bears noticed us, they didn't let on. Mother patted a spot right next to her on the log and I sat down. A bear moved over to let Wallace Jr. sit on her other side.

The bear smell is rank but not unpleasant, once you get used to it. It's not like a barn smell, but wilder. I leaned over to whisper something to Mother and she shook her head. *It would be rude to whisper around these creatures that don't possess the power of speech*, she let me know without speaking. Wallace Jr. was silent too. Mother shared the bedspread with us and we sat for what seemed hours, looking into the fire.

The big bear tended the fire, breaking up the dry branches by holding one end and stepping on them, like people do. He was good at keeping it going at the same level. Another bear poked the fire from time to time, but the others left it alone. It looked like only a few of the bears knew how to use fire, and were carrying the others along. But isn't that how it is with everything? Every once in a while, a smaller bear walked into the circle of firelight with an armload of wood and dropped it onto the pile. Median wood has a silvery cast, like driftwood.

Wallace Jr. isn't fidgety like a lot of kids. I found it pleasant to sit and stare into the fire. I took a little piece of Mother's *Red Man*, though I don't generally chew. It was no different from visiting her at the Home, only more interesting, because of the bears. There were about eight or ten of them. Inside the fire itself, things weren't so dull, either: little dramas were being played out as fiery chambers were created and then destroyed in a crashing of sparks. My imagination ran wild. I looked around the circle at the bears and wondered what *they* saw. Some had their eyes closed. Though they were gathered together, their spirits still seemed solitary, as if each bear was sitting alone in front of its own fire.

The hubcap came around and we all took some newberries. I don't know about Mother, but I just pretended to eat mine. Wallace Jr. made a face and spit his out. When he went to sleep, I wrapped the bedspread around all three of us. It was getting colder and we were not provided, like the bears, with fur. I was ready to go home, but not Mother. She pointed up toward the canopy of trees, where a light was spreading, and then pointed to herself. Did she think it was angels approaching from on high? It was only the high beams of some southbound truck, but she seemed mighty pleased. Holding her hand, I felt it grow colder and colder in mine.

Wallace Jr. woke me up by tapping on my knee. It was past dawn, and his grandmother had died sitting on the log between us. The fire was banked up and the bears were gone and someone was crashing straight through the woods, ignoring the path. It was Wallace. Two state troopers were right behind him. He was wearing a white shirt, and I realized it was Sunday morning. Underneath his sadness on learning of Mother's death, he looked peeved.

The troopers were sniffing the air and nodding. The bear smell was still strong. Wallace and I wrapped Mother in the bedspread and started with her body back out to the highway. The troopers stayed behind and scattered the bears' fire ashes and flung their firewood away into the bushes. It seemed a petty thing to do. They were like bears themselves, each one solitary in his own uniform.

There was Wallace's Olds 98 on the median, with its radial tires looking squashed on the grass. In front of it there was a police car with a trooper standing beside it, and behind it a funeral home hearse, also an Olds 98.

"First report we've had of them bothering old folks," the trooper said to Wallace. "That's not hardly what happened at all," I said, but nobody asked me to explain. They have their own procedures. Two men in suits got out of the hearse and opened the rear door. That to me was the point at which Mother departed this life. After we put her in, I put my arms around the boy. He was shivering even though it wasn't that cold. Sometimes death will do that, especially at dawn, with the police around and the grass wet, even when it comes as a friend.

We stood for a minute watching the cars pass. "It's a blessing," Wallace said. It's surprising how much traffic there is at 6:22 A.M.

That afternoon, I went back to the median and cut a little firewood to replace what the troopers had flung away. I could see the fire through the trees that night.

I went back two nights later, after the funeral. The fire was going and it was the same bunch of bears, as far as I could tell. I sat around with them a while but it seemed to make them nervous, so I went home. I had taken a handful of newberries from the hubcap, and on Sunday I went with the boy and arranged them on Mother's grave. I tried again, but it's no use, you can't eat them.

Unless you're a bear.

LUCIUS SHEPARD AND ROBERT FRAZIER

The All-Consuming

▼

Lucius Shepard was perhaps the most popular and influential new writer of the '80s, rivaled for that title only by William Gibson, Connie Willis, and Kim Stanley Robinson. Shepard won the John W. Campbell Award in 1985 as the year's Best New Writer, and no year since has gone by without him adorning the final ballot for one major award or another, and often for several. In 1987, he won the Nebula Award for his landmark novella "R & R," and in 1988 he picked up a World Fantasy Award for his monumental short-story collection *The Jaguar Hunter*. His first novel was the acclaimed *Green Eyes*; his second the bestselling *Life During Wartime*; he is at work on several more. His latest books are a new collection, *The Ends of the Earth*, and a new novel, *Kalimantan*. His stories "Salvador" and "Black Coral" were in our Second Annual Collection; his stories "The Jaguar Hunter" and "A Spanish Lesson" were in our Third Annual Collection; "R & R" was in our Fourth Annual Collection; "Shades" was in our Fifth Annual Collection; "The Scalehunter's Beautiful Daughter" was in our Sixth Annual Collection; and "The Ends of the Earth" was in our Seventh Annual Collection. Born in Lynchburg, Virginia, he now lives in Nantucket, Massachusetts.

Robert Frazier is one of SF's most popular and prolific poets, and his poems have appeared frequently in nearly every publication, professional or amateur, that will accept poetry at all. Several collections of his poetry have been published, including *Peregrine, Perception Barriers, Co-Orbital Moons, Chronicles of the Mutant Rain Forest* (with Bruce Boston), and *A Measure of Calm* (with Andrew Joron), and he has also edited the poetry anthology

Burning With a Vision: Poetry of Science and the Fantastic. In 1980, he won the Rhysling Award for his poem "Encased in the Amber of Eternity." For the last few years, he has been writing prose fiction as well, and his stories have appeared in *Isaac Asimov's Science Fiction Magazine*, *Amazing*, *The Twilight Zone Magazine*, *New Pathways*, and elsewhere. Frazier also lives in Nantucket.

Here Shepard and Frazier join forces to serve up a bizarre and compelling story about a man with a very unusual relationship to the rest of the world: he *eats* it—or as much of it as he can get in his mouth, anyway. . . .

▼

The All-Consuming

LUCIUS SHEPARD AND
ROBERT FRAZIER

Santander Jimenez was one of the towns that ringed the Malsueno, a kind of border station between the insane tangle of the rain forest and the more comprehensible and traditional insanity of the highlands. It was a miserable place of diesel smoke and rattling generators and concrete-block buildings painted in pastel shades of yellow, green and aqua, many with rusted Fanta signs over their doors, bearing names such as the Café of a Thousand Flowers or The Eternal Garden Bar or the Restaurant of Golden Desires, all containing fly-specked Formica tables and inefficient ceiling fans and fat women wearing grease-spattered aprons and discouraging frowns. Whores slouched beneath the buzzing neon marquee of the Cine Guevara. Drunks with bloody mouths lay in the puddles that mired the muddy streets. It was always raining. Even during the height of the dry season, the lake was so high that the playground beside it was half-submerged, presenting a surreal vista of drowned swing sets and seesaws.

To the west of town, separated from the other buildings by a wide ground strewn with coconut litter and flattened beer cans, stood a market—a vast tin roof shading a hive of green wooden stalls. It was there that the *marañeros* would take the curious relics and still more curious produce that they collected in the heart of the rain forest: stone idols whose eyes glowed with electric moss; albino beetles the size of house cats; jaguar bones inlaid with seams of mineral that flowed like mercury; lizards with voices as sweet as nightingales; mimick vines, parrot plants and pavonine, with its addictive spores that afforded one a transitory mental contact with the creatures of the jungle.

They were, for the most part, these *marañeros*, scrawny, rawboned men who wore brave tattoos that depicted lions and devils and laughing skulls. Their faces were scarred, disfigured by fungus and spirochetes, and when they walked out in the town, they were given a wide berth, not because of their appearance or their penchant for violence, which was no greater than that of the ordinary citizen, but because they embodied the dread mystique of the Malsueno, and in their tormented solitudes, they seemed the emblems of a death in life more frightening to the uninformed than the good Catholic death advertised by the portly priests at Santa Anna de la Flor del Piedra.

Scarcely anyone who lived in Santander Jimenez wanted to live there. A number of citizens had been driven to this extreme in order to hide from a criminal or politically unsound past. The most desperate of these were the *marañeros*—who but those who themselves were hunted would voluntarily enter the Malsueno to dwell for months at a time among tarzanals and blood vine and christomorphs?—and the most desperate of the *marañeros*, or so he had countenanced himself for 21 years, so many years that his desperation had mellowed to an agitated resignation, was a gaunt, graying man by the name of Arce Cienfuegos. In his youth, he had been an educator in the capital in the extreme west of the country, married to a beautiful woman, the father of an infant son, and had aspired to a career in politics. However, his overzealous pursuit of that career had set him at odds with the drug cartel; as a result, his wife and child had been murdered, a crime with which he had subsequently been charged, and he had been forced to flee to the Malsueno. For a time thereafter, he had been driven by a lust for revenge, for vindication, but when at last the drug cartel had been shattered, its leaders executed, revenge was denied him, and because those who could prove his innocence were in their coffins, the murder charge against him had remained open. Now, at the age of 48, his crime forgotten, although he might have returned to the capital, he was so defeated by time and solitude and grief he could no longer think of a reason to leave. Just as chemical pollutants and radiation had transformed the jungle into a habitat suitable to the most grotesque of creatures, living in the Malsueno had transformed him into a sour twist of a man who thrived on its green acids, its vegetable perversions, and he was no longer fit for life in the outside world. Or so he had convinced himself.

Nonetheless, he yearned for some indefinable improvement in his lot, and to ease this yearning, he had lately taken to penetrating ever more deeply into the Malsueno, to daring unknown territory, telling himself that perhaps in the depths of the jungle, he would find a form of contentment, but knowing to his soul that what he truly sought was release from an existence whose despair and spiritual malaise had come to outweigh any fleshly reward.

*   *   *

One day, toward the end of the rainy season, Arce received word that a man who had taken a room at the Hotel America 66, one Yuoki Akashini, had asked to see him. In general, visitors to Santander Jimenez were limited to scientists hunting specimens and the odd tourist gone astray, and since, according to his informant, Mr. Akashini fell into neither of those categories, Arce's curiosity was aroused. That evening, he presented himself at the hotel and informed the owner, Nacho Perez, a bulbous, officious man of 50, that he had an appointment with the Japanese gentleman. Nacho—who earned the larger part of his living by selling relics purchased from the *marañeros* at swindler's prices—attempted to pry information concerning the appointment out of him; but Arce, who loathed the hotel owner, having been cheated by him on countless occasions, kept his own counsel. Before entering room 23, he poked his head in the door and saw a short, crewcut man in his early 30s standing by a cot, wearing gray trousers and a T-shirt. The man glowed with health and had the heavily developed arms and chest of a weight lifter. His smile was extraordinarily white and fixed and wide.

"*Señor* Cienfuegos? Ah, excellent!" he said, and made a polite bow. "Please . . . come in, come in."

The room, which reeked of disinfectant, was of green concrete block and, like a jail cell, contained one chair, one cot, one toilet. Cobwebs clotted the transom and light was provided by a naked bulb dangling from a ceiling fixture. Mr. Akashini offered Arce the chair and took a position by the door, hands clasped behind his back and legs apart, like a soldier standing at ease.

"I am told," he said, his voice hoarse, his tone clipped, almost as if in accusation, "you know the jungle well." He arched an eyebrow, lending an accent of inquiry to these words.

"Well enough, I suppose."

Mr. Akashini nodded and made a rumbling noise deep in his throat—a sign of approval, Arce thought.

"If you're considering a trip into the jungle," he said, crossing his legs, "I'd advise against it."

"I do not require a guide," said Mr. Akashini. "I want you to bring me food."

Arce was nonplused. "There's a restaurant downstairs."

Mr. Akashini stood blinking, as if absorbing this information, then threw back his head and laughed uproariously. "Very good! A restaurant downstairs!" He wiped his eyes. "You have mistaken my meaning. I want you to bring me food from the jungle. Here. This will help you understand."

He crossed to the cot, where a suitcase lay open, and removed from it a thick leather-bound album, which he handed to Arce. It contained photographs and newspaper clippings that featured shots of Mr. Akashini at dinner. The text of the majority of the clippings was in Japanese, but several were in Spanish, and it was apparent from these—which bestowed upon Mr. Akashini the title of The All-Consuming—and from the photographs that he was not eating ordinary food but objects of different sorts: automobiles, among them a Rolls-Royce Corniche; works of art, including several important expressionist canvases and a small bronze by Rodin; cultural artifacts of every variety, mostly American, ranging from items such as one of Elvis Presley's leather-and-rhinestone jump suits, a guitar played by Jimi Hendrix and Lee Harvey Oswald's Carcano rifle—obtained at "an absurd cost," according to Mr. Akashini—to the structure of the first McDonald's restaurant, a meal that, ground to a powder and mixed with gruel, had taken a year to complete. Arce did not understand what had compelled Mr. Akashini to enter upon this strange gourmandizing, but one thing was plain: The man was wealthy beyond his wildest dreams, and although this did not overly excite Arce, for he had few wants, nevertheless, he was not one to let an opportunity for profit slip away.

"I am listed in the *Guinness Book of World Records*," said Mr. Akashini proudly. "Three times." He held up three fingers in order to firmly imprint this fact on Arce's consciousness.

Arce tried to look impressed.

"I intend," Mr. Akashini went on, "to eat the Malsueno. Not everything in it, of course." He grinned and clapped Arce on the shoulder, as if to assure him of the limits of his appetite. "I wish to eat those things that will convey to me its essence. Things that embody the soul of the place."

"I see," said Arce, but failed to disguise the puzzlement in his voice.

"You are wondering, are you not," said Mr. Akashini, tipping his head to the side, holding up a forefinger like an earnest lecturer, "why I do this?"

"It's not my business."

"Still, you wonder." Mr. Akashini turned to the wall above his cot, again clasping his hands behind his back. He might have been standing on the bridge of a ship, considering a freshly conquered land. "I admit to a certain egocentric delight in accomplishment, but my desire to consume stems to a large degree from curiosity, from my love for other cultures, my desire to understand them. When I eat, you see, I understand. I cannot always express the understanding, but it is profound . . . more profound, I am convinced, than an understanding gained from study or travel or immersion in some facet of one culture or another. I know things about the United States that not even Americans know. I have tasted the inner mechanisms of American history, of the American experience. I have recently finished writing a book of meditations on the subject." He turned to Arce. "Now, it is my intention

195

to understand the Malsueno, to derive from its mutations, from the furies of the radiation and chemicals and poisons that created them, a comprehension of its essence. So I have come to you for assistance. I will pay well."

He named a figure that elevated Arce's estimate of his wealth, and Arce signaled his acceptance.

"But how can you expect to eat poison and survive?" he asked.

"With caution." Mr. Akashini chuckled and patted his flat belly.

Arce pictured tiny cars, portraits, statuary, temples, entire civilizations in miniature inside Mr. Akashini's stomach, floating upon an angry sea like those depicted by the print maker Hokusai. The image infused the man's healthy glow with a decadent character.

"Please, have no fear about my capacity," said Mr. Akashini. "I am in excellent condition and accustomed to performing feats of ingestion. And I have implants that will neutralize those poisons that my system cannot handle. So, if you are agreed, I will expect my first meal tomorrow."

"I'll see to it." Arce came to his feet and, easing around Mr. Akashini, made for the door.

"Excuse, please!"

Arce turned and was met with a flash that blinded him for a moment; as his vision cleared, he saw his employer lowering a camera.

"See you at suppertime!" said Mr. Akashini.

He nodded and smiled as if he already understood everything there was to know about Arce.

Although determined to earn his fee, Arce did not intend to risk himself in the deep jungle for such a fool as Mr. Akashini appeared to be. Who did the man think he was to believe he could ingest the venomous essence of the Malsueno? Likely, he would be dead in a matter of days, however efficient his implants. And so the following afternoon, without bothering to put on protective gear, Arce walked a short distance into the jungle and cast about for something exotic and inedible . . . but nothing too virulent. He did not want to lose his patron so quickly. Soon he found an appropriate entree and secured it inside a specimen bag. At dusk, his find laid out in a box of transparent plastic with a small hinged opening, he presented himself at the hotel. Room 23 had undergone a few changes. The cot had been removed, and in its place was a narrow futon. Dominating the room, making it almost impossible to move, was a mahogany dinner table set with fine linens and silverware and adorned with a silver candelabrum. Mr. Akashini, attired in a dinner jacket and a black tie, was seated at the table, smiling his gleaming edifice of a smile.

"Ah!" he said. "And what do you have for me, *Señor* Cienfuegos?"

With a flourish, Arce deposited the box on the table and was rewarded by an appreciative sigh. In the dim light, his culinary offering—ordinary by the grotesque standards for the Malsueno—looked spectacularly mysterious: an 18-inch-long section of a rotten log, shining a vile, vivid green, with the swirls of phosphorescent fungus that nearly covered its dark, grooved surface; scuttling here and there were big spiders that showed a negative black against the green radiance, like intricate holes in a glowing film that was sliding back and forth . . . except now and again, they merged into a single many-legged blackness that pulsed and shimmered and grew larger still. Bathed in that glow, Mr. Akashini's face was etched into a masklike pattern of garish light and shadow.

"What are they?" he said, his eyes glued to the box.

For Mr. Akashini's benefit, Arce resorted to invention.

"They are among the great mysteries of the Malsueno," he said. "And thus, they have no name, for who can name the incomprehensible? They are insect absences, they live, they prey on life, and yet they are lightless and undefined, more nothing than something. They are common yet the essence of rarity. They are numberless, yet they are one."

At this, words failed him. He folded his arms and affected a solemn pose.

"Excellent!" whispered Mr. Akashini, leaning close to the lid of the box. He made one of his customary throaty growls. "You may leave now. I wish to eat alone so as to maximize my understanding."

That was agreeable to Arce, who had no wish to observe the fate of the spiders and the fungus-coated log. But as he turned to leave, pleased with the facility with which he had satisfied the terms of his employment, Mr. Akashini said, "You have provided me with a marvelous hors d'oeuvre, señor, but I expect much more of you. Is that clear?"

"Of course," said Arce, startled.

"No, not of course. There is nothing of course about what I've asked of you. I expect diligence. And even more than diligence, I expect zeal."

"As you wish."

"Yes," said Mr. Akashini, fitting his gaze to the glowing feast, his face again ordered by that impenetrable smile. "Exactly."

Although for weeks he obeyed Mr. Akashini's instructions and sought out ever more exotic and deadly suppers, to Arce's surprise, his employer did not sicken and die but thrived on his diet of poisons and claws and spore. His healthy glow increased, his biceps bulged like cannon balls, his eyes remained clear. It became a challenge to Arce to locate a dish that would weaken Mr. Akashini's resistance, that would at least cause him an upset stomach. He did not care for Mr. Akashini and had concluded that the man was something more sinister than a fool. And when Nacho asked again what was the nature of his business in room 23, Arce had no qualms about telling him, thinking that Nacho would make a joke of his employer's diet. But Nacho was incredulous and shook his fist at Arce. "I'm warning you," he said, "I won't have you taking advantage of my guests."

Arce understood that Nacho was concerned that he might be swindling Mr. Akashini and not cutting him in for a percentage. When he tried to clarify the matter, Nacho only threatened him again, demanded money, and Arce walked away in disgust.

It was evident by the way Mr. Akashini used his camera that he had no regard for anyone in the town. He would approach potential subjects, all smiles and bows, and proceed to pose them, making it plain that he was ridiculing the person whose photograph he was preparing to take. He posed confused, dignified old men with bouquets of flowers, he posed Nacho with a toy machine gun, he posed a young girl with an ugly birthmark on her cheek holding an armful of puppies. Afterward, he would once again smile and bow, but the smiles were sneers and the bows were slaps. Arce understood the uses of contempt—he had witnessed it among his own people in their harsh attitude toward Americans. Yet they were expressing the classic resentment of the poor toward the wealthy, and he could not fathom why Mr. Akashini, who was wealthier than an American, should express a similar attitude toward the poor. Perhaps, he thought, Mr. Akashini had himself been poor and was now having his revenge. But why revenge himself upon those who had never lorded it over him? Was his need to understand, to consume, part and parcel of a need to dominate and deride? All Arce knew of Japan had been gleaned from books dealing with the samurai, with knights, swords and a chill formal morality, and he had the notion that the values detailed in these books were of moment to Mr. Akashini, though in some distorted fashion. Yet, in the end, he could not decide if Mr. Akashini were as simple as he appeared or if there were more to him than met the eye, and he thought this might be a question to which not even his employer knew the answer.

Be he complicated or simple, one thing was apparent—Mr. Akashini did not know as much as he pretended. He could spout volumes of facts concerning the Malsueno. Yet his knowledge lacked the depth of experience, the unifying character of something known in the heart of the mind, and Arce could not accept the idea that consumption bestowed upon him a deeper comprehension. The things he claimed to understand of America— rock-and-roll music, say—he understood in a Japanese way, imbuing them with watered-down samurai principles and a neon romanticism redolent of contemporary Tokyo night-club values and B movies, thereby transforming them into devalued icons that bore little relation to the realities from which they had sprung.

However, Arce was not such a fool that he claimed to understand Mr.

Akashini, and putting his doubts aside, he made an interior renewal of his contract and set himself to feed Mr. Akashini the absolute essence of the Malsueno, hoping to either prove or disprove the thesis. He was beginning to feel an odd responsibility to his job, to a man who—though he paid well—had shown him nothing but contempt, and while this conscientious behavior troubled him, being out of character with the person he believed he had become, he had no choice but to obey its imperatives.

Arce's searches carried him farther and farther afield and one morning found him in a clearing three days' trek from Santander Jimenez. Mr. Akashini would be occupied for the better part of a week in devouring his latest offering, which included lapis bees and lime ants, a section from the trunk of a gargantua garnished with its thorns, an entire duende cooked with blood vine, various fungi, all seasoned with powder ground from woohli bones and served with a variety of mushrooms. Thus, Arce, being in no particular hurry, stopped to rest and enjoy the otherworldly beauty of the clearing, its foliage a mingling of mineral brilliance and fairy shape such as occurred only within the confines of the Malsueno.

At the center of the clearing was a cloud pool, a ragged oval some 12 feet in diameter, whose quicksilver surface mirrored the surrounding foliage— yellow weeds; boulders furred with orange moss; mushrooms the size of parasols, their purple crowns mottled with spots of vermilion; mattes of dead lianas thick as boas; shrubs with spine-tipped viridian leaves that quested ceaselessly for some animal presence in which to inject their venom; and, dangling from above, the immense red leaves of a gargantua, each large enough to wrap about oneself several times.

Through gaps in the foliage, Arce could see the slender trunks of other gargantuas rising above the canopy, vanishing into a bank of low clouds. And in the middle distance, its translucent flesh barely visible against the overcast, a rainbird flapped up from a stinger palm and beat its way south against the prevailing wind. Arce watched it out of sight, captivated by the almost impalpable vibration of its wings, by the entirety of the scene, with its gaudy array of colors and exotic vitality. At times like this, he was able to shrug off the bitter weight of his past for a few moments and delight in the mystery he inhabited.

Once he had carefully inspected the area, he settled on a boulder and opened the face plate of his protective suit. The heat was oppressive after the coolness of the suit, and the air stank of carrion and sweet rot, yet it was refreshing to feel the breeze on his face. He took a packet of dried fruit from a pocket on his sleeve and ate, ever aware of the rustlings and cries and movement about him—there were creatures in this part of the jungle that could pluck him from his suit with no more difficulty than a man shelling a peanut, and they were not always easy to detect. Absently, he tossed a piece of apricot into the cloud pool and watched the silvery surface effloresce as it digested the fruit, ruffles of milky rose and lavender spreading from the point of impact toward the edges like the opening of a convulsed bloom. He considered collecting a vial of the fluid for Mr. Akashini—that would test the efficacy of his implants.

Yet to Arce's mind, the cloud pool did not embody the essence of the jungle but rather was a filigree, an adornment, and he doubted that he could provide his employer with any more quintessentially Malsuenan a meal than some of those he had already served him. Mr. Akashini had eaten fillet of tarzanal, woohli, ghost lemur, jaguar, malcoton; he had supped on stews of tar fish, manta bat, pezmiel, manatee; he had consumed stone, leaf, root, spore; he had gorged himself on sauces compounded of poison, feces, animal and plant excrescence of every kind; yet he appeared as healthy and ignorant as before. What, Arce thought, if it were the very efficacy of his implants that kept him from true understanding? Perhaps to attain such a state, one must be vulnerable to that which one wished to understand.

He unzipped another pocket on his sleeve and removed a packet of pavonine spores. Arce was no addict, but he enjoyed a taste of the drug now and again, and when attempting to seek out certain animals, he found it more than a little useful. He touched a spore-covered finger tip to his tongue, enough to sensitize him to his immediate environment. Within seconds, he felt a tightening at the back of his throat, a queasiness and a touch of vertigo. A violent cramp doubled him over, bringing tears and spots before his eyes. By the time the cramp had passed, he seemed to be crawling along a high branch of a gargantua, hauling himself along with knobby, hairy fingers tipped with claws, pushing aside heavy folds of dangling leaves with ropy patterns of veins, inflamed by a dark-red emotion that sharpened into lust as he was being lifted, shaken, pincers locked about his chitinous body and, above him, impossibly tall pale arcs of grass blades and the glowing white blur of an orchid sun; and then, fat with blood, he hung dazed and languorous in a shadowy place; and then he was leaping, his jaws wide, claws straining toward the flanks of a fleeing tapir; and then his mind went blank and still and calm, like a pool of emerald water steeped in a single thought; and then, his shadow casting a lake of darkness across a thicket of sapodilla bushes, he roared, on fire with the ecstasy of his strength and the exuberance of his appetites.

Less than three minutes after he had taken the pavonine, Arce came unsteadily to his feet and started hunting for the calm green mind that his mind had touched . . . like nothing he had touched before. Calm, and yet a calm compounded of a trillion minute violences, like the jungle itself in the hour before first light, brimming with hot potentials, but, for the moment, cool and peaceful and hushed. Whatever it had been was close by the pool,

Arce was certain, and so he knew it could be nothing large. He overturned rocks with the toe of his boot, probed in the weeds with a rotten stick and at length unearthed a smallish snake with an intricate pattern of red and yellow and white tattooed across its black scales. It slithered away but did so with no particular haste, as if—rather than trying to elude capture—it was simply going on its way, and when Arce netted it, instead of twisting and humping about, it coiled up and went to sleep. Seeing this, Arce did not doubt that the snake's skull housed the mind he had contacted, and although he had no real feeling that the snake would implement Mr. Akashini's understanding, still he was pleased to have found something new and surprising to feed him.

On his return to Santander Jimenez, he served Mr. Akashini a meal that included a palm salad with diced snake meat. Then, leaving him to dine alone, he walked across town to the Salon Tia Flaca, a rambling three-story building of dark-green boards close to the market, and there secured the companionship of a whore for the night. The whore, his favorite, was named Expectacion and was a young thing, 19 or 20, pretty after the fashion of the women of the coast, slim and dark, with full breasts and a petulant mouth and black hair that tumbled like smoke about her shoulders. Once they had made love, she brought Arce rum with ice and lime and lay beside him and asked questions about his life whose answers were of no interest to her whatsoever. Arce realized that her curiosity was a charade, that she was merely fulfilling the forms of their unwritten contract, but nevertheless, he felt compelled to tell her about Mr. Akashini and the peculiar business between them, because by so doing, he hoped to disclose a pattern underlying it, something that would explain his new sense of responsibility, his complicity in this foolhardy mission.

When he was done, she propped herself up on an elbow, her pupils cored with orange reflections from the kerosene lamp, and said, "He pays you so much, and still you remain in Santander Jimenez?"

"It's as I've told you . . . I'm as happy here as anywhere. I've nowhere to go."

"Nowhere! You must be crazy! This"—she waved at the window, at the dark wall of the jungle beyond and the malfunctioning neons of the muddy little town—"this is nowhere! Even money can't change that. But the capital . . . with money. That's a different story."

"You're young," he said. "You don't understand."

She laughed. "The only way you can understand anything is to do it. . . . Then it's not worth talking about. Tell that to your Japanese man. Anyway, you're the one who doesn't understand." She threw her arms about him, her breasts flattening against his chest. "Let's get out of here, let's steal the

Jap's money and go to the capital. Even if the theft is reported, the police there don't care what happens in the Malsueno. You know that's true. They'll just file the report. Come on, *Papá*! I swear I'll make you happy."

Arce was put off by her use of the word *papá*, and said, "Do you think I'm a fool? In the capital, the minute I turned my back, you'd be off with the first good-looking boy who caught your eye."

"You are a fool to think I'm just a slut." She drew back and seemed to be searching his face. "I've been a whore since I was twelve, and I've learned all I need to know about good-looking boys. What gets my heart racing is somebody like you. Somebody rich and refined who'll keep me safe. I'd marry a guy like you in a flash. But even if I was the kind of woman you say, no injury I did you would be worse than what you're doing to yourself by staying here."

He thought he detected in her eyes a flicker of something more than reflected light, of an inner luminescence like that found in the eyes of a malcoton. It occurred to him that she herself was of the Malsueno, one of its creatures, the calm green habit of her thoughts every bit as inexplicable to him as the mind of the snake he had captured. And yet there was something in her that brought back memories of his dead wife—a mixture of energy and toughness that tempted him to believe not only in her but in himself, in the possibility that he could regain his energy and hope.

"Maybe someday," he told her. "I'll think about it."

"Don't kid yourself, *Papá*. I don't think it's in you." She arched her back, and her breasts rolled on her chest, drawing his eyes to the stiffened chocolate-colored nipples. "I guess you were born to be a *marañero*. But at least you've got good taste in whores."

She went astride him and made love to him with more enthusiasm than before, and as he arched beneath her, watching her in the dim light that penetrated the fall of her hair, which hung down about his head, walling him into a place of warm breath and musk, he imagined that he knew her, that he could see past the deceits and counterfeits in her rapt features to a place where she was in love not with him but with the security offered by his circumstance. Not truly in love but—like a beast that has spotted its prey—in the grip of a fierce opportunism, a feeling that might as well have been love for its delirium and consuming intensity.

The next day, when Arce visited the hotel, Nacho Perez, dressed in a sweat-stained *guayabera* and shorts, questioned him about his activities in room 23.

"What's going on up there?" he asked, mopping perspiration from his brow. "I won't have any funny business. Is he a drug addict? A pervert?

What are you doing with him? He never lets anyone in the room, not even the maid. I won't tolerate this kind of behavior."

"You'll tolerate anything, Nacho," said Arce, "as long as you're paid to tolerate it. Ask your questions of Akashini."

"Listen to me . . ." Nacho began, but Arce caught him by the shirt front and said, "You bastard! Give me a reason—not a good reason, just a little one—and I'll cut you, do you hear?"

Nacho licked his lips and said, "I hear," but there was no conviction in his voice.

On reaching the room, Arce discovered that Mr. Akashini had spent a sleepless night. His color was poor, his brow clammy, his hands trembling. Yet when Arce suggested that he forgo his meal, the Japanese man said, "No, no! I'm all right." He passed a handkerchief across his brow. "Perhaps something simple. A few plants . . . some insects." Arce had no choice but to comply, and for several days thereafter, he served Mr. Akashini harmless meals from the edge of the jungle; yet despite this, whether because of the snake or simply because of a surfeit of poisons that had neutralized his implants, Mr. Akashini continued to deteriorate. His skin acquired the unhealthy shine of milk spore, his eyes were clouded, his manner distracted, and he grew so weak that it took him three tries to heave himself up from his chair. Nothing Arce said would sway him from his course.

"I feel"—Mr. Akashini had to swallow—"I feel as if I am . . . close to something."

Close to death, was Arce's thought, but it was not his place to argue, and he only shrugged.

"Yes," said Mr. Akashini, as if answering a question inaudible to Arce. He ran a palsied hand along the linen tablecloth, which—like its owner—displayed the effects of ill usage: stains, rips, embroideries of mildew. Even the candelabrum seemed afflicted, its surface tarnished. On a chipped plate were the remains of a meal: philosopher beetles thrashing in a stew of weeds and wild dog. "I . . . uh. . . ." Mr. Akashini's eyelids fluttered down and he gestured feebly at the plate. "Stay with me while I finish, will you?"

Astonished at this breach of custom, for Mr. Akashini had never before permitted him to remain with him while he ate, Arce took a seat on the futon and watched in silence as his employer laboriously swallowed down the stew. At last, he fell back in his chair, the muscles bunching in his jaw . . . or so Arce thought at first, his vision limited by the flickering candlelight. But then, to his horror, he realized that this was no simple muscular action. It appeared that a lump was moving beneath Mr. Akashini's skin, crawling crabwise across the cheek, along the cheekbone, then down along the hinge of the jaw and onto the neck, where it vanished as if submerging into the flesh. However, the truly horrifying aspect of this passage was that in its wake, the skin was suffused with blood, darkened, and the lump of muscle left—as a receding tide might reveal the configuration of the sand beneath—an expression such as Arce had never seen on any human face, one that seemed a rendering in human musculature of an emotion too poignant for such a canvas, embodying something of lust and fear but mostly a kind of feral longing. The expression faded, and Mr. Akashini, who had not moved for several minutes, his mouth wide open, let out a gurgling breath.

Certain that he was dead, Arce leaned over him and was further horrified to notice that the man's arms were freckled with vaguely phosphorescent patches of gray fungus. Closer inspection revealed other anomalies: three fingernails blackened and thick like chitin; strange whitish growths, like tiny outcroppings of crystal, inside the mouth; a cobweb of almost infinitesimally fine strands spanning the right eye. Arce's thoughts alternated between guilt and fear of implication in the death, but before he could decide how to proceed, Mr. Akashini stirred, giving him a start.

"I really believe that I am making progress," Mr. Akashini said with surprising vigor, and gave an approving growl.

Arce was inclined to let Mr. Akashini have his illusion, but a reflex of morality inspired him to say, "I think you're dying."

Mr. Akashini was silent for a long time. Finally, he said, "That is not important. I am making progress, nonetheless."

This confused Arce, causing him to wonder whether or not he had misjudged Mr. Akashini by labeling him a fool. But then he thought that his original judgment may have been correct, and that Mr. Akashini's judgment concerning his own enthusiasm must have been in error. Arce felt sympathy for him, and yet, contrasting Mr. Akashini's attitude with his own detachment, he envied him the rigor of his commitment.

"Will you continue to help me?" Mr. Akashini asked, and Arce, suddenly infected with a desire to know his employer, to comprehend the obscure drives that motivated him, could only say yes.

Mr. Akashini nodded toward his suitcase, which lay closed on the futon. "There . . . look beneath the clothing."

In the suitcase was a fat sheaf of traveler's checks. Arce handed them to Mr. Akashini, who—barely able to hold the pen—began endorsing them, saying, "You must keep them away from me . . . the people who would report my condition. Someone tries the door when you are away. I want nothing to interfere with . . . with what is happening."

Considering Nacho's suspicious questions and avaricious nature, Arce knew that Mr. Akashini's worries were well founded, yet he could not understand why his employer trusted him with such a vast sum of money. When he asked why, Mr. Akashini replied that he had no choice.

"Besides," he said, "you will not betray me. You have changed as much as I these past months, but one thing has not changed—you're an honest man, though you may not want to admit it."

Arce, convinced that because of his proximity to death, Mr. Akashini might have clearer sight than ordinary folk, asked how he had changed, but his employer had fallen asleep. Watching him, Arce thought it might be possible for him to know Mr. Akashini, and that they might have been friends, though only for a brief period. If they were both changing—and he believed they were, for he sensed change in himself the way he sometimes sensed the presence of a lurking animal in a shadowy thicket—then they were changing in different directions, and in passing, they were likely to experience a momentary compatibility at best.

Unable to care for Mr. Akashini every hour of the day, Arce recruited Expectacion to assist him, bestowing trust upon her with the same hopeful conviction with which Mr. Akashini had bestowed it upon him. Yet he was not so thoroughly trusting as his employer. When forced to be away from the room, he would leave valuables tucked into places where a cursory search would reveal them. Not once did he discover anything missing, and he took this for an emblem not of trustworthiness—he believed Expectacion had made a search—but of wisdom. He understood that she was interested less in making a minor profit than in changing her life, and since wisdom was an ultimately more reliable virtue than trustworthiness, he came to value her more and more, to dote upon the sweetness of her body and the bright particularity of her soul.

Yet as they watched Mr. Akashini being transformed into the artifact of his understanding, a strong bond developed between them, one that stopped short of untrustworthy passion and yet had many of the dependable consolations of love. It would have been unnatural had they not developed such a bond, because the event to which they were bearing witness was so monstrous it enforced union. Within the space of a few weeks, fungi of various sorts grew to cover much of Mr. Akashini's body, creating whorls of multicolored fur—saffron, lavender and gray. His visible skin became pale and puffy, prone to odd shiftings and spasms, and his right eye was totally obscured by glowing silver webs and green spiders scarcely bigger than pinheads, and more cobwebs spanned between his shoulders and neck and the walls, and a bubbled milky film coated his tongue, until finally, he had undergone a metamorphosis into a fearsome creature whose eyes glowed silver with greeny speckles in the darkened room, burning out from a head shaped like a tuber, his body sheathed in a mummy wrapping of cobwebs and moss, with stalks of mustard-colored fungi clumped like tiny cities here and there, a thing capable only of emitting croaked entreaties for food or asking that a photograph be taken. On one occasion, however, he appeared to regain something of his old spirit and strength and engaged Arce and Expectacion in conversation.

"You must not be concerned, my friends," he said. "This is glorious."

The effect of his lips, almost sealed with clots of fungus, splitting and the effortfully spoken words oozing forth, struck Arce as being more ghastly than glorious, but he refrained from saying as much.

"Why does it seem glorious?" he asked.

Mr. Akashini made a noise that approximated laughter, the heaving of his chest and diaphragm causing puffs of dusty spores to spurt into the air. The candle flames flickered; a faint tide of shadow lapped up his legs, then receded. "I . . ." he said. "I am . . . becoming."

Expectacion asked in a tremulous voice if he wanted water, and he turned his head toward her—the laborious motion of a statue coming to life after a centuries-long enchantment.

"Sitting here," he said, ignoring her question, "I am arrowing toward completion. Toward . . . everything I wanted to believe but never could. I understand. . . ."

"The Malsueno?" Arce asked. "You understand the Malsueno?"

"Not yet" was the answer. "I understand . . . not everything. But I had no understanding of anything before."

He appeared to drift off for a moment.

"What's happening to you?" Expectacion asked him.

"When I was young," he said, "I dreamed of becoming a samurai. . . ."

He gave another horrid laugh.

Expectacion looked perplexed, and Arce wondered if his employer were rambling as men would in the grip of fever; yet he could not quite believe that. He sensed a new rectitude in Mr. Akashini, one that accorded with the ideas about Japan he had gleaned from his reading. But neither could he accept that what he sensed was wholly accurate, because Mr. Akashini's horrifying appearance seemed to put the lie to the notion of beneficent change.

In that stomach where once he had envisioned cars and paintings and other oddments of culture, he now pictured a miniature jungle, and sometimes, on entering the room from the bright corridor, he would think that a demon with eyes of unreal fire had materialized in Mr. Akashini's chair. He and Expectacion spent hours on end sitting side by side, listening to the creaky whisperings of new growth emanating from the man's flesh, gazing at the awful pulsings of his chest and belly. Mr. Akashini was so self-involved that they were not embarrassed about making love in the room. Sex acted to diminish the miserable miracle before them and to make their vigil more tolerable, and if it had not been for Nacho's questions, knockings on the door and general harassment, they might have been happy.

Early one morning, before dawn, Arce went to buy breakfast for himself and Expectacion—they had slept poorly, disturbed by the noises of Mr. Akashini's body and his constant troubled movement. On returning, he heard angry voices issuing from room 23. The bulbous form of Nacho Perez was blocking the door. He was haranguing Expectacion, while two men—*marañeros*, judging by their tattoos—searched the suitcases, doing their utmost to avoid contact with Mr. Akashini, who sat motionless, emitting a faint buzzing, shifting now and again amid the fetters of his cobwebs, the shifts redolent not so much of muscular contractions as of vegetable reflex. In the dimness, due to the activity of microscopic spores, his glowing eyes appeared to be revolving slowly.

Arce drew his knife, but Nacho caught sight of him, seized Expectacion and barred an arm beneath her chin.

"I'll break her neck!" he said.

Expectacion threw herself about, trying to kick him, but when Nacho tightened his grip, she gave up struggling, other than to pluck feebly at his arm. Behind him, the two *marañeros* had drawn their knives. Arce recognized one of them—Gilberto Viera, a thin, sallow man with pocked skin and a pencil-line mustache.

"Gilberto," said Arce, "you remember the time on the Blanco Ojo? I helped you then. Help me now."

Gilberto looked ashamed but only lowered his eyes. The other man— taller, darker, with the nappy hair of a man born in the eastern mountains—asked Nacho, "What should we do?"

"Well," said Nacho, beaming at Arce, "that depends on our friend here."

"What do you want?" Arce had to exert tremendous restraint to resist aiming a slash at Nacho's double chin.

"There must be something," said Nacho archly, paying no attention to an intensification of Mr. Akashini's buzzing. "Isn't there, Arce?"

When Arce remained silent, he tightened his grip—Expectacion's feet were lifted off the ground and her face grew dark with blood. She dug her nails into Nacho's arm but with no effect.

"There's some money hidden behind one of the bricks," Arce said grudgingly. "Let her go."

Another flurry of buzzing from Mr. Akashini, accompanied by a series of throaty clicks, as if he were trying to speak. The two *marañeros* edged away from his chair, bumping against Nacho.

"Which brick is it?" Nacho asked, and Arce, thinking furiously of how he might extricate Expectacion from the fat man's grasp, was about to tell him, when—with the ponderous motion of a bloom bursting from its husk—Mr. Akashini came to his feet. With his glowing eyes and dark, deformed body, puffy strips of pallid skin showing through the fungus and moss like bandages, he was a gruesome sight. Gilberto tried to shove Nacho aside in an attempt to escape from the room. However, the other man spun about and slashed Mr. Akashini with his knife.

The knife passed through Mr. Akashini's side, its arc slowing as if encountering resistance of the sort that might be offered by sludge or mud; the dark fluid that leaked forth flowed with the sluggishness of syrup. Mr. Akashini staggered against the wall; his buzzing and clicking reached furious proportions, sounding like a nest of bees and crabs together. A tiny spider scuttled out from his right eye, diminishing its glow by a speck of green. His cheek bulged. One arm began to vibrate, his skin bubbled up in places, his chest puffed and deflated as if responding to the workings of an enormous flabby heart. Arce was repelled and retreated along the corridor, but when Mr. Akashini gave out a growly hum—of satisfaction, Arce thought—he realized that some fraction of his employer's personality was yet embedded within this vegetable demon. The man who had wielded the knife shrieked, and Nacho half-turned to see what had gone wrong, blocking the doorway entirely. Arce seized the opportunity to leap forward and stab him low in the back. The hotel owner squealed, clutching at the wound, and released Expectacion, who slumped to the floor and crawled away. Arce prepared to strike a second time, but the hotel owner lurched to the side, permitting him an unimpeded view into the room, and what he saw caused him to hesitate, allowing Nacho to stumble out of range.

Clouds of spores were pouring up from Mr. Akashini, filling the air with a whirling gray powder that reduced the flames of the candelabrum to pale yellow gleams, like golden tears hanging in the murk, and reduced the figures of the two *marañeros* to dimly perceived bulks that kicked and shuddered. One—Arce could not tell which—collapsed on the futon and the other crumpled beneath the dining table, both holding their throats and choking. Looming above them was Mr. Akashini, his luminous eyes the brightest objects in the room, the outline of his body nearly indistinguishable from the agitated gray motes around him, looking as ominous and eerie as a Fate. There was a flurrying at the edges of the body, along with a rustling sound—a horde of winged things were developing from the frays of skin, fluttering up to add a new density to the whirling spores, darkening the air further. Several danced out through the door: big carrion moths with charcoal wings. He must have inadvertently fed Mr. Akashini some of their eggs, Arce thought, and now they were hatching. And more than spores and moths were being born. Spiders, centipedes, insects of 100 varieties were burrowing up through his skin, pustules opening to reveal the heads of infant snakes and baby beetles, bulges erupting into larval flows, as the process of Mr. Akashini's understanding, a process of adaptation and fertilization and fecundity, at last reached fruition.

Within a minute or two, the room grew as dark as night, and yet still those strange silver eyes burned forth. It seemed to Arce that the body must have dissolved, that the eyes, thickly woven cobwebs, were suspended by a clever arrangement of strands. But then the eyes moved closer and he realized that Mr. Akashini was taking one unsteady step after another toward the door.

Expectacion caught Arce's arm. "Hurry!" she cried. "Nacho has gone for help!"

Turning, Arce saw that, indeed, the hotel owner was nowhere to be found, a snail's track of blood along the wall giving evidence of his passage toward the stairs.

"For Christ's sake, *Papá!*" Expectacion gave him a push. "Don't just stand there gawking."

"No, wait!"

Arce shook her off, ripped off his shirt and wrapped it about his face. Then he dashed into room 23, dived onto the floor and groped for the brick behind which he had hidden the money, trying not to breathe. Once he had secured the packet of checks, he scrambled to his feet and came face to face with Mr. Akashini—with a gray deformity, with newborn moths breaking free from a glutinous grain of skin and mold, with a shadow of a mouth, with tepid slow breath, with two eyes of green and cold silver. The webs of the eyes were a marvelous texture admitting to an infinite depth of interwoven strands, and Arce saw within them a tropic of green and silver, a loom of event and circumstance, and felt that if he were to continue staring, he would see not only the truth as Mr. Akashini had come to know it but also his truth and Expectacion's. Then he became afraid, and the eyes were again only webs, and the face before him, with its hideous growths, appeared a thing of incalculable menace. Yet the spores and the insects and the moths that had transformed the *marañeros* into anonymous heaps were keeping clear of him, and he realized even then that some relic of Mr. Akashini's soul was employing restraint.

Arce wanted to say something, to convey some good wish, but he could think of nothing that would not seem foolish. With mixed emotions, not sure what he should feel for Mr. Akashini, he retreated into the corridor, grabbed Expectacion by the arm and sprinted for the stairs.

A line of pink showed above the black wall of the jungle, and only a few stars pricked the indigo sky directly overhead; the neon signs over the bars were pale in the brightening air, and shadows were beginning to fill in the ruts in the muddy streets. The coolness of the night was already being dispelled. There were only a handful of people out—two drunks staggering along arm in arm; an old Indian man in rags hunkered down beside a door, smoking a pipe; farther along, a whore was yelling at a shirtless youth. Arce led Expectacion out of the hotel and started toward the jungle, but after about 20 yards, she balked.

"Where are you going?" she asked, pulling free of him.

"The Malsueno. We'll be safe there. I know places. . . ."

"The hell with you! I'm not going in there!"

He made to grab her, but she danced away.

"You're nuts, *Papá*! Nacho'll have everybody looking for us! We have to get far away! The capital! That's the only place we'll be safe."

He stood gazing uncomprehendingly at her, seeing faces from another time, stung by old pains, experiencing a harrowing fear of displacement like that he had felt on being forced to flee the capital.

"Come on!" she shouted. "Nacho'll be here any second. We can take one of the cars parked back of the market."

"I can't."

"What do you mean, you can't?" She went back to him and pounded on his chest, her face twisted with anger and frustration. "You're going to get us killed . . . just standing here."

Although the blows hurt, he let her beat on him, ashamed of his fear and incapacity. Even when he saw Nacho turn the corner, at his back a group of *marañeros* armed with machetes, he was unable to take a step away from the place where he had hidden from memories and pain and life itself for all these years.

Expectacion, too, had begun to cry. "You really blew it, *Papá*! We had a chance, you and me." She went a few faltering steps toward the highway. "Damn you!" she said. "Damn you!" Then, with her arms pumping, she fled along the street.

In the other direction, Nacho was limping forward, holding his back with one hand, pointing at Arce with the other, while at his rear, like a squad of drunken soldiers, the *marañeros* whooped and brandished their machetes. Arce drew his knife, determined to make a final stand.

At that moment, however, torrents of spores and insects and serpents and unidentifiable scraps of life exploded from the windows and the door of the hotel, making it appear that the building had been filled to bursting with black fluid. A whirling cloud formed between Nacho and Arce. At its core, Arce thought he spotted a shadow, an indistinct manlike shape with glowing eyes, but before he could be certain of it, the edge of the cloud frayed and streams of insects raced toward him and stung his face and neck and arms.

Blinded, he staggered this way and that, harrowed by the insects, and then he ran and ran, the dark cloud sending forth rivers of tormenting winged things to keep him on his course. As he passed through the outskirts of town, a white pickup rocketed out of a side street and swerved to the side, barely missing him, coming to a rest against a light pole. Through the windshield, he made out Expectacion's startled face. Without thinking, desperate to escape the insects, he flung himself into the truck, began rolling up the window and shouted at her to drive. She gunned the engine and, pursued by the swarm, they fishtailed out onto the highway.

They drove into the hills with the sky reddening at their backs, and after experiencing a flurry of panic on recognizing the course that had been chosen for him, it seemed to Arce that with every mile—in a process of self-realization exactly contrary to Mr. Akashini's—he was shedding a coating of fear and habit and distorted view, as if a shell were breaking away from some more considered inner man. Not the man he had been but the man he had become without knowing it, tempered by years of solitary endeavor. He felt strong, directed, full of youthful enthusiasms.

He would go to the capital, he decided, not to inhabit the past but to build a future, to make of it a temple that would honor the eccentric brotherhood that existed between himself and Mr. Akashini, a brotherhood that he had not embraced, that he could not have acknowledged or understood before, that he did not wholly understand now, but whose consummation had filled him with the steel of purpose and the fire of intent. He realized that they were both men who had lost themselves, Mr. Akashini to the persuasions of arrogance and wealth, himself to the deprivations of pain and despair, and how because of the fortuitous propinquity of a peculiar ambition and a woman of energy and strength and a magical jungle, he at least had been afforded the opportunity to move on.

He could not take any such pleasure, however, in Mr. Akashini's death, and when he looked at Expectacion, the lines of her face aglow with pink light, when he felt the tenderness she had begun to rouse in him and saw the challenge she presented, the potential for poignant emotion, for grief and joy and love, those vital flavors he had rejected for so long, the prospect of an adventure with her was dimmed by regret that he had been unable to do more than speed Mr. Akashini to his end.

It wasn't fair, he thought.

He had done little, risked little, and yet he had won through to something real, whereas Mr. Akashini had only suffered and died among strangers far from home. This inequity caused Arce to think that perhaps he had won nothing, to wonder if everything he felt was the product of delusion. But as they climbed high into the hills, on glancing back toward Santander Jimenez, he saw there a sight that seemed to memorialize all that had happened:

Trillions of insects and spores and things unnamable were spiraling above the miserable little town, a towering blackness that—despite a blustery wind—maintained its basic form, at one moment appearing to be the shadow of a great curved sword poised to deliver a sundering blow and at the next, a column of ashes climbing to heaven against the crimson pyre of the rising sun.

MOLLY GLOSS
Personal Silence

▼

Molly Gloss was born in Portland, Oregon, and lives there still with her family. She made her first sale in 1984, and since has sold several stories to *Isaac Asimov's Science Fiction Magazine,* as well as to *The Magazine of Fantasy and Science Fiction, Universe,* and elsewhere. She published a fantasy novel, *Outside the Gates,* in 1986, and another novel, *The Jump-Off Creek,* a non–SF "woman's western," was released in 1990. She is currently at work on a new novel, this one science fiction. Her story "Interlocking Pieces" was in our Second Annual Collection.

Here she gives us a thoughtful and thought-provoking study of one man's personal commitment to his ideals, in the face of overwhelming odds, and how that commitment, without a word being spoken, can reach out to touch other lives and alter them forever. . . .

▼

Personal Silence

MOLLY GLOSS

There was a little finger of land, a peninsula, that stuck up from the corner of Washington State pointing straight north at Vancouver Island. On the state map it was small enough it had no name. Jay found an old Clallam County map in a used bookstore in Olympia and on the county map the name was printed the long way, marching northward up the finger's reach: Naniamuk. There was a clear bubble near the tip, like a fingernail, and that was named too: Mizzle. He liked the way the finger pointed at Vancouver Island. Now he liked the name the town had. He bought a chart of the strait between Mizzle and Port Renfrew and a used book on small boat building and when he left Olympia he went up the county roads to Naniamuk and followed the peninsula's one paved road all the way out to its dead end at Mizzle.

It was a three-week walk. His leg had been broken and badly healed a couple of years ago when he had been arrested in Colombia. He could walk long-strided, leaning into the straps of the pack, arms pumping loosely, hands unfisted, and he imagined anyone watching him would have had a hard time telling, but if he did more than eight or ten miles in a day he got gimpy and that led to blisters. So he had learned not to push it. He camped in a logged-over state park one night, bummed a couple of nights in barns and garages, slept other nights just off the road, in whatever grass and stunted trees grew at the edge of the right-of-way.

The last day, halfway along the Naniamuk peninsula, he left the road and hiked west to the beach, through the low pines and grassy dunes and coils of rusted razorwire, and set his tent on the sand at the edge of the grass. It

214

was a featureless beach, wide and flat, stretching toward no visible headlands. There were few driftlogs, and at the tide line just broken clamshells, dead kelp, garbage, wreckage. No tidepools, no offshore stacks, no agates. The surf broke far out and got muddy as it rolled in. When the sun went down behind the overcast, the brown combers blackened and vanished without luminescence.

The daylight that rose up slowly the next morning was gray and damp, standing at the edge of rain. He wore his rubber-bottom shoes tramping in the wet grass along the edge of the road to Mizzle. The peninsula put him in mind of the mid-coast of Chile, the valleys between Talca and Puerto Montt—flat and low-lying, the rain-beaten grass pocked with little lakes and bogs. There was not the great poverty of the Chilean valleys, but if there had been prosperity up here once, it was gone. The big beachfront houses were boarded up, empty. The rich had moved in from the coasts. Houses still lived in were dwarfish, clinker-built, with small windows oddly placed. People were growing cranberries in the bogs and raising bunches of blond, stupid-faced cattle on the wet pasturage.

At the town limit of Mizzle a big, quaintly painted signboard stood up beside the road. WELCOME TO MIZZLE! MOST WESTERLY TOWN IN THE CONTIGUOUS UNITED STATES OF AMERICA! Jay stood at the shoulder of the road and sketched the sign in his notebook for its odd phrasing, its fanciful enthusiasm.

The town was more than he had thought, and less. There had been three or four motels—one still ran a neon vacancy sign. An RV park had a couple of trailers standing in it. The downtown was a short row of gift shops and ice cream stores, mostly boarded shut. There was a town park—a square of unmown lawn with an unpainted gazebo set on it. Tourists had got here ahead of him and had gone again.

He walked out to where the road dead-ended at the tip of the peninsula. It was unmarked, unexceptional. The paving petered out and a graveled road kept on a little way through weeds and hillocks of dirt. Where the graveled road ended, people had been dumping garbage. He stood up on one of the hillocks and looked to the land's end across the dump. There was no beach, just a strip of tidal mud. The salt water of the strait lay flat and gray as sheet metal. The crossing was forty-three nautical miles—there was no seeing Vancouver Island.

He went back along the road through the downtown, looking up the short cross-streets for the truer town: the hardware store, the grocery, the lumber yard. An AG market had a computerized checkout that was broken, perhaps had been broken for months or years—a clunky mechanical cash register sat on top of the scanner, and a long list of out-of-stock goods was taped across the LED display.

Jay bought a carton of cottage cheese and stood outside eating it with the spoon that folded out of his Swiss army knife. He read from a free tourist leaflet that had been stacked up in a wire rack at the front of the store. The paper of the top copy was yellowed, puckered. On the first inside page was a peninsula map of grand scale naming all the shallow lakes, the graveled roads, the minor capes and inlets. There was a key of symbols: bird scratchings were the nesting grounds of the snowy plover, squiggly ovoids were privately held oyster beds, a stylized anchor marked a public boat launch and a private anchorage on the eastern, the protected shoreline. Offshore there, on the white paper of the strait, stood a nonspecific fish, a crab, a gaff-rigged daysailer, and off the oceanside, a long-necked razor clam and a kite. He could guess the boat launch was shut down: recreational boating and fishing had been banned in the strait and in Puget Sound for years. There was little likelihood any oysters had been grown in a while, nor kites flown, clams dug.

Bud's Country Store sold bathtubs and plastic pipe, clamming guns, Coleman lanterns, two-by-fours and plywood, marine supplies, tea pots, towels, rubber boots. What they didn't have they would order, though it was understood delivery might be uncertain. He bought a weekly paper printed seventy miles away in Port Angeles, a day-old copy of the Seattle daily, and a canister of butane, and walked up the road again to the trailer park. *Four Pines RV Village* was painted on a driftwood log mounted high on posts to make a gateway. If there had been pines, they'd been cut down. Behind the arch was a weedy lawn striped with whitish oyster-shell driveways. Stubby posts held out electrical outlets, water couplings, waste water hoses. Some of them were dismantled. There was a gunite building with two steamed-up windows: a shower house, maybe, or a laundromat, or both. The trailer next to the building was a single-wide with a tip-out and a roofed wooden porch. *Office* was painted on the front of it in a black childish print across the fiberglass. There was one other trailer parked along the fence, somebody's permanent home, an old round-back with its tires hidden behind rusted aluminum skirting.

Jay dug out a form letter and held it against his notebook while he wrote across the bottom, "I'd just like to pitch a tent, stay out of your way, and pay when I use the shower. Thanks." He looked at what he had written, added exclamation points, went up to the porch and knocked, waiting awkwardly with the letter in his hand. The girl who opened the door was thin and pale; she had a small face, small features. She looked at him without looking in his eyes. Maybe she was eleven or twelve years old.

He smiled. This was always a moment he hated, doubly so if it was a child—he would need to do it twice. He held out the letter, held out his smile with it. Her eyes jumped to his face and then back to the letter with a look that was difficult to pin down—confusion or astonishment, and then something like preoccupation, as if she had lost sight of him standing there. It was common to get a quick shake of the head, a closed door. He didn't know what the girl's look meant. He kept smiling gently. Several women at different times had told him he had a sweet smile. That was the word they all had used—"sweet." He usually tried to imagine they meant peaceable, without threat.

After a difficult silence, the girl may have remembered him standing there. She finally put out her hand for the letter. He hated waiting while she read it. He looked across the trailer park to a straggly line of scotch broom on the other side of the fence. In a minute she held out the paper to him again without looking in his face. "You have to ask my dad." Her voice was small, low.

He didn't take the letter back yet. He raised his eyebrows in a questioning way. Often it was easier from this point. She would be watching him for those kinds of nonverbal language. He was "keeping a personal silence," he had written in the letter.

"Over in the shower house," she said. She had fine brown hair that hung straight down to her shoulders, and straight bangs she hid behind. Jay glanced toward the gunite building with deliberate, self-conscious hesitation, then made a helpless gesture. The girl may have looked at him from behind her scrim of bangs. "I can ask him," she said, murmuring.

Her little rump was flat, in corduroy pants too big for her. She had kept his letter, and she swung it fluttering in her hand as he followed her to the shower house. A man knelt on the concrete floor, hunched up at the foot of the hot water tank. His pants rode low, baring some of the shallow crack of his buttocks. He looked tall, heavy-boned, though there wasn't much weight on him now, if there ever had been.

"Dad," the girl said.

He had pulled apart the thick fiberglass blanket around the heater to get at the thermostat. His head was shoved inside big loose wings of the blanketing. "What," he said, without bringing his head out.

"He wants to put up a tent," she said. "Here, read this." She shook Jay's letter.

He rocked back on his hips and his heels and rubbed his scalp with a big hand. There were bits of fiberglass, like mica chips, in his hair. "Shit," he said loudly, addressing the hot water heater. Then he stood slowly, hitching up his pants above the crack. He was very tall, six and a half feet or better, bony-faced. He looked at the girl. "What," he said.

She pushed the letter at him silently. Jay smiled, made a slight, apologetic grimace when the man's eyes finally came around to him. It was always a hard thing trying to tell by people's faces whether they'd help him out or not. This one looked him over briefly, silently, then took the letter and looked at it without much attention. He kept picking fiberglass out of his hair and his skin, and afterward looking under his fingernails for traces of it. "I read about this in *Time*," he said at one point, but it was just recognition, not approval, and he didn't look at Jay when he said it. He kept reading the letter and scrubbing at the bits of fiberglass. It wasn't clear if he had spoken to Jay or to the girl.

Finally he looked at Jay. "You're walking around the world, huh." It evidently wasn't a question, so Jay stood there and waited. "I don't see what good will come of it—except after you're killed you might get on the night news." He had a look at his mouth, smugness, or bitterness. Jay smiled again, shrugging.

The man looked at him. Finally he said, "You know anything about water heaters? If you can fix it, I'd let you have a couple of dollars for the shower meter. Yes? No?"

Jay looked at the heater. It was propane-fired. He shook his head, tried to look apologetic. It wasn't quite a lie. He didn't want to spend the rest of the day fiddling with it for one hot shower.

"Shit," the man said mildly. He hitched at his pants with the knuckles of both hands. Jay's letter was still in one fist and he looked down at it inattentively when the paper made a faint crackly noise against his hip. "Here," he said, holding the sheet out. Jay had fifty or sixty clean copies of it in a plastic ziplock in his backpack. He went through a lot of them when he was on the move. He took the rumpled piece of paper, folded it, pushed it down in a front pocket.

"I had bums come in after dark and use my water," the man said. He waited as if that was something Jay might want to respond to. Jay waited too.

"Well, keep off to the edge by the fence," the man warned him. "You can put up a tent for free, I guess, it's not like we're crowded, but leave the trailer spaces clear anyway. I got locks on the utilities now, so you pay me if you want water, or need to take a crap, and don't take one in the bushes or I'll have to kick you out of here."

Jay nodded. He stuck out his hand and after a very brief moment the man shook it. The man's hand was prickly, damp.

"You show him, Mare," he said to the girl. He tapped her shoulder with his fingertips lightly, but his eyes were on Jay.

Jay followed the young girl, Mare, across the trailer park, across the wet grass and broken-shell driveways to a low fence of two-by-fours and wire that marked the property line. The grass was mowed beside the fence but left to sprout in clumps along the wire and around the wooden uprights. There was not much space between the fence and the last row of driveways. If anybody ever parked a motor home in the driveway behind him, he'd have the exhaust pipe in his vestibule. The girl put her hands in her corduroy pockets and stubbed the grass with the toe of her shoe. "Here?" she asked him. He nodded and swung his pack down onto the grass.

Mare watched him make his camp. She didn't try to help him. She was comfortably silent. When he had everything ordered, he looked at her and smiled briefly and sat down on his little sitz pad on the grass. He took out his notebook but he didn't work on the journal. He pulled around a clean page and began a list of the materials he would need for beginning the boat. He wrote down substitutes when he could think of them, in case he had trouble getting his first choice. He planned to cross the strait to Vancouver Island and then sail east and north through the Gulf Islands and the Strait of Georgia, across the Queen Charlotte Strait and then up through the inland passage to Alaska. He hadn't figured out yet how he would get across the Bering Strait to Siberia—whether he would try to sail across in this boat he would build, or if he'd barter it up there to get some other craft, or a ride. It might take him all winter to build the skipjack, all summer to sail it stop and go up the west coast of Canada and Alaska, and then he would need to wait for summer again before crossing the Bering Strait. He'd have time to find out what he wanted to do before he got to it.

The girl after a while approached him silently and squatted down on her heels so she could see what he was writing. She didn't ask him about the list. She read it over and then looked off toward her family's trailer. She kept crouching there beside him, balancing lightly.

"Do you think it's helping yet?" she asked in a minute. She whispered it, looking at him sideward through her long bangs.

He raised his eyebrows questioningly.

"They're still fighting," she murmured. "Aren't they?"

His mother had written to the Oklahoma draft board pleading Jay's only-child status, but by then the so-called Third-World's War was taking a few thousand American lives a day and they weren't exempting anyone. Within a few weeks of his eighteenth birthday, they sent him to the Israeli front.

The tour of duty was four years at first, then extended to six. He thought they would extend it again, but after six years few of them were alive anyway, and they sent him home on a C31 full of cremation canisters. He sat on the toilet in the tail of the plane and swallowed all the pills he had, three at a time, until they were gone. The illegal-drug infrastructure had come overseas with the war and eventually he had learned he could sleep and not dream if he took Nembutal, which was easy to get. Gradually after that he had begun to take Dexamyl to wake up from the Nembutal, Librium to smooth the jitters out of the Dexamyl, Percodan to get high, Demerol when he needed to come down quickly from the high, Dexamyl again if the Demerol took him down too far. He thought he would be dead by the time the plane landed but his body remained inexplicably, persistently, resistant to death. He wound up in a Delayed Stress Syndrome Inpatient Rehab Center which was housed in a prison. He was thirty years old when the funding for the DSS Centers was dropped in favor of research that might lead to a Stealth aircraft carrier. Jay was freed to walk and hitchhike from the prison in Idaho to his mother's house in Tulsa. She had been dead for years but he stood in the street in front of the house and waited for something to happen, a memory or a sentiment, to connect him to his childhood and adolescence. Nothing came. He had been someone else for a long time.

He was still standing on the curb there after dark when a man came out of the house behind him. The man had a flashlight but he didn't click it on. He came over to where Jay stood.

"You should get inside," he said to Jay. "They'll be coming around pretty soon, checking." He spoke quietly. He might have meant a curfew. Tulsa had been fired on a few times by planes flying up to or back from the Kansas missile silos, out of bases in Haiti—crazy terrorists of the crazy Jorge Ruiz government. Probably there was a permanent brownout and a curfew here.

Jay said, "Okay," but he didn't move. He didn't know where he would go anyway. He was cold and needing sleep. There was an appeal in the possibility of arrest.

The man looked at him in the darkness. "You can come inside my house," he said, after he had looked at Jay.

He had a couch in a small room at the front of his house, and Jay slept on it without taking off his clothes. In the daylight the next morning he lay on the couch and looked out the window to his mother's house across the street.

The man who had taken him in was a Quaker named Bob Settleman. He had a son who was on an aircraft carrier in the Indian Ocean, and a daughter who was in a federal prison serving a ten year sentence for failure to report. Jay went with him to a First Day Meeting. There was nothing much to it. People sat silently. After a while an old woman stood and said something about the droughts and cold weather perhaps reflecting God's unhappiness with the state of the world. But that was the only time anyone mentioned God. Three other people rose to speak. One said he was tired of being the only person who remembered to shut the blackout screens in the Meeting Room before they locked up. Then, after a long silence, a woman stood and expressed her fear that an entire generation had been desensitized to violence, by decades of daily video coverage of the war. She spoke gently, in a trembling voice, just a few plain sentences. It didn't seem to matter a great deal, the words she spoke. While she was speaking, Jay felt something come into the room. The woman's voice, some quality in it, seemed to charge the air with its manifest, exquisitely painful truth. After she had finished, there was another long silence. Then Bob Settleman stood slowly and told about watching Jay standing on the curb after dark. He seemed to be relating it intangibly to what had been said about the war. "I could see he was in some need," Bob said, gesturing urgently. Jay looked at his hands. He thought he should be embarrassed, but nothing like that arose in him. He could still feel the palpable trembling of the woman's voice—in the air, in his bones.

Afterward, walking away from the Meeting house, Bob looked at his feet and said, as if it was an apology, "It's been a long time since I've been at a Meeting that was Gathered into the Light like that. I guess I got swept up in it."

Jay didn't look at him. After a while he said, "It's okay." He didn't ask anything. He felt he knew, without asking, what Gathered into the Light meant.

He stayed in Tulsa, warehousing for a laundry products distributor. He kept going to the First Day Meetings with Bob. He found it was true, Meetings were rarely Gathered. But he liked the long silences anyway, and the unpredictability of the messages people felt compelled to share. For a long time, he didn't speak himself. He listened without hearing any voice whispering inside him. But finally he did hear one. When he stood, he felt the long silence Gathering, until the trembling words he spoke came out on the air as Truth.

"If somebody could walk far enough, they'd have to come to the end of the war, eventually."

He had, by now, an established web of support: a New York Catholic priest who banked his receipts from the journal subscriptions, kept his accounts, filed his taxes, wired him expense money when he asked for it; a Canadian rare-seeds collective willing to receive his mail, sort it, bundle it up and send it to him whenever he supplied them with an address; a Massachusetts Monthly Meeting of Friends whose members had the work of typing from the handwritten pages he sent them, printing, collating, stapling, mailing the 10,000 copies of his sometimes-monthly writings. He had a paid subscription list of 1,651, a non-paid "mailing list" of 8,274. Some of those were churches, environmental groups, cooperatives, many were couples, so the real count of persons who supported him was greater by a factor of three or four, maybe. Many of them were people he had met, walking. He hadn't walked, yet, in the Eastern Hemisphere. If he lived long enough to finish what he had started, he thought he could hope for a total list as high as fifty or sixty thousand names. A Chilean who had been a delegate at the failed peace conferences in Surinam had kept a year-long public silence as a protest of Jay's arrest and bad treatment in Colombia. And he knew of one other world-peace-walker he had inspired, a Cuban Nobel chemist who had been the one primarily featured in *Time*. He wasn't fooled into believing it was an important circle of influence. He had to view it in the context of the world. Casualties were notoriously underreported, but at least as many people were killed in a given day, directly and indirectly by the war, as made up his optimistic future list of subscribers. It may have been he kept at it because he had been doing it too long now to stop. It was what he did, who he was. It had been a long time since he had felt the certainty and clarity of a Meeting that was Gathered into the Light.

On the Naniamuk peninsula, he scouted out a few broken-down sheds, and garages with overgrown driveways, and passed entreating notes to the owners. He needed a roof. He expected rain in this part of the world about every day.

One woman had a son dead in India and another son who had been listed AWOL or MIA in the interior of Brazil for two years. She asked Jay if he had walked across Brazil yet. *Yes*, he wrote quickly, *eight months there*. She didn't ask him anything else—nothing about the land or the weather or the fighting. She showed him old photos of both her sons without asking if he had seen the lost one among the refugees in the cities and villages he had walked through. She lent him the use of her dilapidated garage, and the few cheap tools he found in disarray inside it.

The girl, Mare, came unexpectedly after a couple of days and watched him lofting the deck and hull bottom panels onto plywood. It had been raining a little. She stood under her own umbrella a while, without coming in close enough to shelter under the garage roof. But gradually she came in near him and studied what he was doing. A look rose in her face—distractedness, as before on the porch of her trailer, and then fear, or something like grief. He didn't know what to make of these looks of hers.

"You're building a boat," she said, low voiced.

He stopped working a minute and looked at the two pieces of plywood he had laid end to end. He was marking and lining them with a straight edge and a piece of curving batten. He had gone across the Florida Strait in a homemade plywood skipjack, had sailed it around the coast of Cuba to Haiti, Puerto Rico, Jamaica, and then across the channel to Yucatan. And later he had built a punt to cross the mouths of the Amazon. A Cuban refugee, a fisherman, had helped him build the Caribbean boat, and the punt had been a simple thing, hardly more than a raft. This was the first time he had tried to build a skipjack without help, but he had learned he could do about anything if he had time enough to make mistakes, undo them, set them right. He nodded, yes, he was building a boat.

"There are mines in the strait," Mare said, dropping her low voice down.

He smiled slightly, giving her a face that belittled the problem. He had seen mines in the Yucatan channel too, and in the strait off Florida. His boat had slid by them, ridden over them. They were triggered for the heavy war ships and the armored oil tankers.

He went on working. Mare watched him seriously, without saying anything else. He thought she would leave when she saw how slow the boat-making went, but she stayed on in the garage, handing him tools, and helping him to brace the batten against the nails when he lofted the deck piece. At dusk she walked with him up the streets to the Four Pines. There was a fine rain falling still, and she held her umbrella high up so he could get under it if he hunched a little.

In the morning she was waiting for him, sitting on the porch of her trailer when he tramped across the wet grass toward the street. Since Colombia, he had had a difficulty with waking early. He had to depend on his bladder, usually, to force him out of the sleeping bag, then he was slow to feel really awake, his mouth and eyes thick, heavy, until he had washed his face, eaten something, walked a while. He saw it was something like that with the girl. She sat hunkered up on the top step, resting her chin on her knees, clasping her arms about her thin legs. Under her eyes, the tender skin was puffy, dark. Her hair stuck out uncombed. She didn't speak to him. She came stiffly down from the porch and fell in beside him, with her eyes fixed on the rubber toe caps of her shoes. She had a brown lunch sack clutched in one hand and the other hand sunk in the pocket of her corduroys.

They walked down the paved road and then the graveled streets to where the boat garage was. Their walking made a quiet scratching sound. There was no one else out. Jay thought he could hear the surf beating on the ocean side of the peninsula, but maybe not. He heard a dim, continuous susurration. They were half a mile from the beach. Maybe what he heard was wind moving in the trees and the grass, or the whisperings of the snowy plover, nesting in the brush above the tidal flats, on the strait side of the peninsula.

He had not padlocked the garage—a pry-bar would have got anybody in through the small side door in a couple of minutes. He pulled up the rollaway front door, let the light in on the tools, the sheets of plywood. Mare put her lunch down on a sawhorse and stood looking at the lofted pieces, the hull bottom and deck panels drawn on the plywood. He would make those cuts today. He manhandled one of the sheets up off the floor onto the sawhorses. Mare took hold of one end silently. It occurred to him that he could have gotten the panels cut out without her, but it would be easier with her there to hold the big sheets of wood steady under the saw.

He cut the deck panel slowly with hand tools—a brace and bit to make an entry for the keyhole saw, a ripsaw for the long outer cuts. When he was most of the way along the straight finish of the starboard side, on an impulse he gave the saw over to Mare and came around to the other side to hold the sheet down for her. She looked at him once shyly from behind her long bangs and then stood at his place before the wood, holding the saw in both hands. She hadn't drawn a saw in her life, he could tell that, but she'd been watching him. She pushed the saw into the cut he had started and drew it up slow and wobbly. She was holding her mouth out in a tight, flat line, all concentration. He had to smile, watching her.

They ate lunch sitting on the sawhorses at the front of the garage. Jay had carried a carton of yogurt in the pocket of his coat and he ate that slowly with his spoon. Mare offered him part of her peanut butter sandwich, and quartered pieces of a yellow apple. He shook his head, shrugging, smiling thinly. She considered his face, and then looked away.

"I get these little dreams," she said in a minute, low voiced, with apple in her mouth.

He had a facial expression he relied on a good deal, a questioning look. *What? Say again? Explain.* She glanced swiftly sideward at his look and then down at her fingers gathered in her lap. "They're not dreams, I guess. I'm not asleep. I just get them all of a sudden. I see something that's happened, or something that hasn't happened yet. Things remind me." She looked at him again cautiously through her bangs. "When I saw you on the porch, when you gave me the letter, I remembered somebody else who gave me a letter before. I think it was a long time ago."

He shook his head, took the notepad from his shirt pocket and wrote a couple of lines about *déjà vu*. He would have written more but she was reading while he wrote and he felt her stiffening, looking away.

"I know what that is," she said, lowering her face. "It isn't that. Everybody gets that."

He waited silently. There wouldn't have been anything to say anyway. She picked at the corduroy on the front of her pant legs. After a while she said, whispering, "I remember things that happened to other people, but they were me. I think I might be dreaming other people's lives, or the dreams are what I did before, when I was alive a different time, or when I'll be somebody else, later on." Her fingernails kept picking at the cord. "I guess you don't get dreams like that." Her eyes came up to him. "Nobody else does, I guess." She looked away. "I do though. I get them a lot. I just don't tell anymore." Her mouth was small, drawn up. She looked toward him again. "I can tell you, though."

Before she had finished telling him, he had thought of an epilepsy, *Le Petit Absentia*, maybe it was called. He had seen it once in a witch-child in Haiti, a girl who fell into a brief, staring trance a hundred times a day. A neurologist had written to him, naming it from the description he had read in Jay's journal. He could write to the neurologist, ask if this was *Le Petit* again. Maybe there was a simple way to tell, a test, or a couple of things to look for. Of course, maybe it wasn't that. It might only be a fancy, something she'd invented, an attention-getter. But her look made him sympathetic. He pushed her bangs back, kissed her smooth brow solemnly. *It's okay*, he said by his kiss, by his hand lightly on her bangs. *I won't tell.*

There hadn't been a long Labor Day weekend for years. It was one of the minor observances scratched from the calendar by the exigencies of war. But people who were tied in with the school calendar still observed the first weekend of September as a sort of holiday, a last hurrah before the opening Monday of the school year. Some of them still came to the beach.

The weather by good luck was fair, the abiding peninsula winds balmy, sunlit, so there were a couple of small trailers and a few tents in the RV park, and a no-vacancy sign at the motel Saturday morning by the time the fog was burned off.

Jay spent both days on the lawn in front of the town's gazebo, behind a stack of old journals and a big posterboard display he had pasted up, with an outsized rewording of his form letter, and clippings from newspapers and from *Time*. He put out a hat on the grass in front of him, with a couple of seed dollars in it. His personal style of buskering was diffident, self-conscious. He kept his attention mostly on his notebook, in his lap. He sketched from memory the archway at the front of the RV Park, the humpbacked old trailer, the girl, Mare's, thin face. He made notes to do with the boat, and fiddled with an op-ed piece he would send to *Time*, trying to follow up on the little publicity they'd given the Cuban chemist. The op-ed would go in his October journal, whether *Time* took it or not, and the sketches would show up there too, in the margins of his daybook entries, or on the cover. He printed other people's writings too, things that came in his mail—poetry, letters, meeting notices, back page news items pertaining to peace issues, casualty and armament statistics sent at rare intervals by an anonymous letter writer with a Washington, D.C. postmark—but most of the pages were his own work. On bureaucratic forms he entered *Journalist* as his occupation without feeling he was misrepresenting anything. He liked to write. His writing had gotten gradually better since he had been doing the journal—sometimes he thought it was not from the practice at writing, but the practice at silence.

Rarely somebody stooped to pick up a journal, or put money in his hat, or both. Those people he tried to make eye contact with, smiling gently by way of inviting them in. He wouldn't get any serious readers, serious talkers, probably, on a holiday weekend in a beach town, but you never knew. He was careful not to look at the others, the bypassers, but he kept track of them peripherally. He had been arrested quite a few times, assaulted a few. And since Colombia, he suffered from a chronic fear.

Mare came and sat with him on Sunday. He didn't mind having her there. She was comfortable with his silence; she seemed naturally silent herself, much of the time. She read from old copies of his journal and shared the best parts with him as if he hadn't been the writer, the editor, holding a page out for him silently and waiting, watching, while he read to the end. Then her marginalia were terse, absolute: "Ick." "I'm glad." "She shouldn't have gone." "I'd never do that."

After quite a while, she had him read what he had written about a town in the Guatemala highlands where he had spent a couple of months, and then she said, in a changed way, timid, earnest, "I lived there before. But I was a different person."

He had not got around to writing anyone about the epilepsy after he'd lost that first strong feeling of its possibility. His silence invited squirrels, he knew that, though it made him tired, unhappy, thinking of it. He was tired now, suddenly, and annoyed with her. He shook his head, let her see a flat, skeptical smile.

"Mare!"

The father came across the shaggy grass moving swiftly, his arms swinging in a stiff way, elbows akimbo. Jay stood up warily.

"I'm locked out of the damn house," the man said, not looking at Jay. "Where's your key?"

Mare got up from the grass, dug around in her pockets and brought out a key with a fluorescent pink plastic keeper. He closed his fingers on it, made a vague gesture with the fist. "I about made up my mind to bust a window," he said. "I was looking for you." He was annoyed.

Mare put her hands in her pockets, looked at her feet. "I'm helping him stop the war," she said, murmuring.

The man's eyes went to Jay and then the posterboard sign, the hat, the stacked-up journals. His face kept hold of that look of annoyance, but took on something else too, maybe it was just surprise. "He's putting up signs and hustling for money, is what it looks like he's doing," he said, big and arrogant. For a while longer he stood there looking at the sign as if he were reading it. Maybe he was. He had a manner of standing—shifting his weight from foot to foot and hitching at his pants every so often with the knuckles of his hands.

"I got a kidney shot out, in North Africa," he said suddenly. "But there's not much fighting there anymore, that front's moved south or somewhere.

I don't know who's got that ground now. They can keep it, whoever." He had a long hooked nose, bony ridges below his eyes, a wide, lipless mouth. Strong features. Jay could see nothing of him in Mare's small pale face. It wasn't evident, how they were with each other. Jay saw her now watching her dad through her bangs, with something like the shyness she had with everyone else.

"Don't be down here all day," her dad said to her, gesturing again with the fist he had closed around the housekey. He looked at Jay but he didn't say anything else. He shifted his weight one more time and then walked off long-strided, swinging his long arms. He was tall enough some of the tourists looked at him covertly after he'd passed them. Mare watched him too. Then she looked at Jay, a ducking, sideward look. He thought she was embarrassed by her dad. He shrugged. *It's okay.* But that wasn't it. She said, pulling in her thin shoulders timidly, "There is a lake there named Negro because the water is so dark." She had remained focused on his disbelief, waiting to say this small proving thing about Guatemala. And it was true enough to shake him a little. There was a Lago Negro in about every country below the U.S. border, he remembered that in a minute. But there was a long startled moment before that, when he only saw the little black lake in the highlands, in Guatemala, and Mare, dark faced, in a dugout boat paddling away from the weedy shore.

He had the store rip four long stringers out of a clear fir board and then he kerfed the stringers every three inches along their lengths. With the school year started he didn't have Mare to hold the long pieces across the sawhorses. He got the cuts done slowly, single-handed, bracing the bouncy long wood with his knee.

Mare's dad came up the road early in the day. Jay thought he wasn't looking for the garage. There was a flooded cranberry field on the other side of the road and he was watching the people getting in the crop from it. There were two men and three women wading slowly up and down in green rubber hip waders, stripping off the berries by hand into big plastic buckets. Mare's dad, walking along the road, watched them. But when he came even with the garage he turned suddenly and walked up the driveway. Jay stopped what he was doing and waited, holding the saw. Mare's dad stood just inside the rollaway door, shifting his weight, knuckling his hips.

"I heard you were building a boat," he said, looking at the wood, not at Jay. "You never said how long you wanted to camp, but I didn't figure it would be long enough to build a boat." Jay thought he knew where this was headed. He'd been hustled along plenty of times before this. But it didn't go that way. The man looked at him. "In that letter you showed, I figured you meant you could talk if you wanted to." He sounded annoyed, as he had been on Labor Day weekend with Mare. "Now I heard your tongue was cut off," he said, lifting his chin, reproachful.

Jay kept standing there holding the saw, waiting. He hadn't been asked anything. The man dropped his eyes. He turned partway from Jay and looked over his shoulder toward the cranberry bog, the people working there. There was a long stiff silence.

"She's a weird kid," he said suddenly. "You figured that out by now, I guess." His voice was loud; he may not have had soft speaking in him anywhere. "I'd have her to a psychiatrist, but I can't afford it." He hitched at his pants with the backs of both hands. "I guess she likes you because you don't say anything. She can tell you whatever she wants and you're not gonna tell her she's nuts." He looked at Jay. "You think she's nuts?" His face had a sorrowful aspect now, his brows drawn up in a heavy pleat above the bridge of his nose.

Jay looked at the saw. He tested the row of teeth against the tips of his fingers and kept from looking at the man. He realized he didn't know his name, first or last, or if he had a wife. Where was Mare's mother?

The man blew out a puffing breath through his lips. "I guess she is," he said unhappily. Jay ducked his head, shrugged. *I don't know.* He had been writing about Mare lately—pages that would probably show up in the journal, in the October mailing. He had spent a lot of time wondering about her, and then writing it down. This was something new to wonder about. He had thought her dad was someone else, not this big sorrowful man looking for reassurance from a stranger who camped in his park.

A figure of jets passed over them suddenly, flying inland from the ocean. There were six. They flew low, dragging a screaming roar, a shudder, through the air. Mare's dad didn't look up.

"She used to tell people these damn dreams of hers all the time," the man said, after the noise was past. "I know I never broke her of it, she just got sly who she tells them to. She never tells me anymore." He stood there silently looking at the cranberry pickers. "The last one she told me," he said, in his heavy, unquiet voice, "was how she'd be killed dead when she was twelve years old." He looked over at Jay. "She didn't tell you that yet," he said, when he saw Jay's face. He smiled in a bitter way. "She was about eight, I guess, when she told me that one." He thought about it and then he added, "She's twelve now. She was twelve in June." He made a vague gesture with both hands, a sort of open-palms shrugging. Then he pushed his hands down in his back pockets. He kept them there while he shifted his weight in that manner he had, almost a rocking back and forth.

Watching him, Jay wondered suddenly if Mare might not put herself in the path of something deadly, to make sure this dream was a true one—a proof for her dad. He wondered if her dad had thought of that.

"I don't know where she gets her ideas," the man said, making a pained face, "if it's from TV or books or what, but she told me when she got killed it'd be written up, and in the long run it'd help get the war ended. Before that, she never had noticed we were even in a war." He looked at Jay wildly. "Maybe I'm nuts too, but here you are, peace-peddling in our backyard, and when I saw you with those magazines you write, I started to wonder what was going on. I started to wonder if this is a damn different world than I've been believing all my life." His voice had begun to rise so by the last few words he sounded plaintive, teary. Jay had given up believing in God the year he was eighteen. He didn't know what it was that Gathered a Meeting into the Light, but he didn't think it was God. It occurred to him, he couldn't have told Mare's dad where the borders were of the world he, Jay, believed in.

"I don't have a reason for telling you this," the man said after a silence. He had brought his voice down again so he sounded just agitated, defensive. "Except I guess I wondered if I was nuts, and I figured I'd ask somebody who couldn't answer." His mouth spread out flat in a humorless grin. He took his hands out of his pockets, hitched up his pants. "I thought about kicking you on down the road, but I guess it wouldn't matter. If it isn't you, it'll be somebody else. And"—his eyes jumped away from Jay—"I was afraid she might quick do something to get herself killed, if she knew you were packing up." He waited, looking off across the road. Then he looked at Jay. "I've been worrying, lately, that she'll get killed all right, one way or the other, either it'll come true on its own or she'll make it."

They stood together in silence in the dim garage, looking at the cut out pieces of Jay's boat. He had the deck and hull bottom pieces, the bulkheads, the transom, the knee braces cut out. You could see the shape of the boat in some of them, in the curving lines of the cuts.

"I guess you couldn't taste anything without a tongue," the man said after a while. He looked at Jay. "I'd miss that more than the talking." He knuckled his hips and walked off toward the road. All his height was in his legs. He walked fast with a loose, sloping gait on those long legs.

In the afternoon Jay took a clam shovel out of the garage and walked down to the beach. The sand was black and oily from an offshore spill or a sinking. There wasn't any debris on the low tide, just the oil. Maybe on the high tide there would be wreckage, or oil-fouled birds. He walked along the edge of the surf on the wet black sand looking for clam sign. There wasn't much. He dug a few holes without finding anything. He hadn't expected to. Almost at dusk he saw somebody walking toward him from way down the beach. Gradually it became Mare. She didn't greet him. She turned alongside him silently and walked with him, studying the sand. She carried a denim knapsack that pulled her shoulders down: blocky shapes of books, a lunch box. She hadn't been home yet. If she had gone to the garage and not found him there, she didn't say so.

He touched the blade of the shovel to the sand every little while, looking in the pressure circle for the stipple of clams. He didn't look at Mare. Something, maybe it was a clam sign, irised in the black sheen on the sand. He dug a fast hole straight down, slinging the wet mud sideways. Mare crouched out of the way, watching the hole. "I see it!" She dropped on the sand and pushed her arm in the muddy hole, brought it out again reflexively. Blood sprang along the cut of the razor-shell, bright red. She held her hands together in her lap while her face brought up a look, a slow unfolding of surprise and fear. Jay reached for her, clasping both her hands between his palms, and in a moment she saw him again. "It cut me," she said, and started to cry. The tears maybe weren't about her hand.

He washed out the cut in a puddle of salt water. He didn't have anything to wrap around it. He picked up the clam shovel in one hand and held onto her cut hand with the other. They started back along the beach. He could feel her pulse in the tips of his fingers. *What did you dream,* he wanted to say.

It had begun to be dark. There was no line dividing the sky from the sea, just a griseous smear and below it the cream-colored lines of surf. Ahead of them Jay watched something rolling in the shallow water. It came up on the beach and then rode out again. The tide was rising. Every little while the surf brought the thing in again. It was pale, a driftlog, it rolled heavily in the shallow combers. Then it wasn't a log. Jay let down the shovel and Mare's hand and waded out to it. The water was cold, dark. He took the body by its wrist and dragged it up on the sand. It had been chewed on, or shattered. The legs were gone, and the eyes, the nose. He couldn't tell if it was a man or a woman. He dragged it way up on the beach, on the dry sand, above the high tide line. Mare stood where she was and watched him.

He got the clam shovel and went back to the body and began to dig a hole beside it. The sand was silky, some of it slipped down and tried to fill the grave as he dug. In the darkness, maybe he was shoveling out the same hole over and over. The shovel handle was sticky, from Mare's blood on his palms. When he looked behind him, he saw Mare sitting on the sand, huddled with her thin knees pulled up, waiting. She held her hurt hand with the other one, cradled.

When he had buried the legless body, he walked back to her and she stood up and he took her hand again and they went on along the beach in the darkness. He was cold. His wet shoes and his jeans grated with sand. The cut on Mare's hand felt sticky, hot, where he clasped his palm against it. She said, in a whisper, "I dreamed this, once." He couldn't see her face.

He looked out but he couldn't see the water, only hear it in the black air, a ceaseless, numbing murmur. He remembered the look that had come in her face when she had first seen his boat-building. *There are mines in the strait.* He wondered if that was when she had dreamed this moment, this white body rolling up on the sand.

He imagined Mare dead. It wasn't hard. He didn't know what kind of a death she could have that would end the war, but he didn't have any trouble seeing her dead. He had seen a lot of dead or dying children, written about them. He didn't know why imagining Mare's thin body, legless, buried in sand, brought up in his mouth the remembered salt taste of tears, or blood, or the sea.

"I know," he said, though what came out was shapeless, ill-made, a sound like *Ah woe*. Mare didn't look at him. But in a while she leaned in to him in the darkness and whispered against his cheek. "It's okay," she said, holding on to his hand. "I won't tell."

He had sent off the pages of his October journal already, and Mare was in them, and Lago Negro, and the father standing shifting his feet, not looking up as the jets screamed over him. It occurred to Jay suddenly, it would not matter much, the manner of her dying. She had dreamed her own death and he had written it down, and when she was dead he would write that, and her death would charge the air with its manifest, exquisitely painful truth.

JOHN KESSEL
Invaders

▼

Here's a wry and blackly ironic story that contrasts and compares two different sorts of invaders, and draws some very uncomfortable conclusions. . . .

Born in Buffalo, New York, John Kessel now lives in Raleigh, North Carolina, where he is a professor of American literature and creative writing at North Carolina State University. Kessel made his first sale in 1975, and has since become a frequent contributor to *The Magazine of Fantasy and Science Fiction* and *Isaac Asimov's Science Fiction Magazine*, as well as to many other magazines and anthologies. Kessel's first solo novel, *Good News From Outer Space*, was released last year to wide critical acclaim, but before that he had made his mark on the genre primarily as a writer of highly imaginative, finely crafted short stories. He won a Nebula Award in 1983 for his superlative novella "Another Orphan," which was also a Hugo finalist that year, and was released as one half of a Tor Double. His other books include the novel *Freedom Beach*, written in collaboration with James Patrick Kelly, and, coming up, a collection of his short fiction, *Meeting in Infinity*, from Arkham House. He is currently at work on a new novel, *Corrupting Dr. Nice*. Kessel's story "Hearts Do Not in Eyes Shine" was in our First Annual Collection; his story "Friend," written with James Patrick Kelly, was in our Second Annual Collection; his "The Pure Product" was in our Fourth Annual Collection; and his "Mrs. Shummel Exits a Winner" was in our Sixth Annual Collection.

Invaders

JOHN KESSEL

15 November 1532:

That night no one slept. On the hills outside Cajamarca, the campfires of the Inca's army shone like so many stars in the sky. De Soto said Atahualpa had perhaps forty thousand troops under arms, but looking at the myriad lights spread across those hills, de Candia realized that estimate was, if anything, low.

Against them, Pizarro could throw one hundred foot soldiers, sixty horse, eight muskets, and four harquebuses. Pizarro, his brother Hernando, de Soto, and Benalcázar laid out plans for an ambush. De Candia and his artillery would be hidden in the building along one side of the square, the cavalry and infantry along the others. De Candia watched Pizzaro prowl through the camp that night, checking the men's armor, joking with them, reminding them of the treasure they would have, and the women. The men laughed nervously and whetted their swords.

They might sharpen them until their hands fell off; when morning dawned, they would be slaughtered. De Candia breathed deeply of the thin air and turned from the wall.

Ruiz de Arce, an infantryman with a face like a clenched fist, hailed him as he passed. "Are those guns of yours ready for some work tomorrow?"

"We need prayers more than guns."

"I'm not afraid of these brownies," de Arce said.

"Then you're a half-wit."

"Soto says they have no swords."

The man was probably just trying to reassure himself, but de Candia couldn't abide it. "Will you shut your stinking fool's trap! They don't need swords! If they only spit all at once, we'll be drowned."

Pizarro overheard him. He stormed over, grabbed de Candia's arm, and shook him. "Have they ever seen a horse, Candia? Have they ever felt steel? When you fired the harquebus on the seashore, didn't the town chief pour beer down its barrel as if it were a thirsty god? Pull up your balls and show me you're a man!"

His face was inches away. "Mark me! Tomorrow, Saint James sits on your shoulder, and we win a victory that will cover us in glory for five hundred years."

2 December 2001:

"DEE-fense! DEE-fense!" the crowd screamed. During the two-minute warning, Norwood Delacroix limped over to the Redskins' special conditioning coach.

"My knee's about gone," said Delacroix, an outside linebacker with eyebrows that ran together and all the musculature that modern pharmacology could load onto his six-foot-five frame. "I need something."

"You need the power of prayer, my friend. Stoner's eating your lunch."

"Just do it."

The coach selected a popgun from his rack, pressed the muzzle against Delacroix's knee, and pulled the trigger. A flood of well-being rushed up Delacroix's leg. He flexed it tentatively. It felt better than the other one now. Delacroix jogged back onto the field. "DEE-fense!" the fans roared. The overcast sky began to spit frozen rain. The ref blew the whistle and the Bills broke huddle.

Delacroix looked across at Stoner, the Bills' tight end. The air throbbed with electricity. The quarterback called the signals; the ball was snapped; Stoner surged forward. As Delacroix backpedaled furiously, sudden sunlight flooded the field. His ears buzzed. Stoner jerked left and went right, twisting Delacroix around like a cork in a bottle. His knee popped. Stoner had two steps on him. TD for sure. Delacroix pulled his head down and charged after him.

But instead of continuing downfield, Stoner slowed. He looked straight up into the air. Delacroix hit him at the knees, and they both went down. He'd caught him! The crowd screamed louder, a scream edged with hysteria.

Then Delacroix realized the buzzing wasn't just in his ears. Elation fading, he lifted his head and looked toward the sidelines. The coaches and players were running for the tunnels. The crowd boiled toward the exits, shedding thermoses and beer cups and radios. The sunlight was harshly bright. Delacroix looked up. A huge disk hovered no more than fifty feet above, pinning them in its spotlight. Stoner untangled himself from Delacroix, stumbled to his feet and ran off the field.

Holy Jesus and the Virgin Mary on toast, Delacroix thought.

He scrambled toward the end zone. The stadium was emptying fast, except for the ones who were getting trampled. The throbbing in the air increased in volume, lowered in pitch, and the flying saucer settled onto the NFL logo on the forty-yard line. The sound stopped as abruptly as if it had been sucked into a sponge.

Out of the corner of his eye, Delacroix saw an NBC cameraman come up next to him, focusing on the ship. Its side divided and a ramp extended itself to the ground. The cameraman fell back a few steps, but Delacroix held his ground. The inside glowed with the bluish light of a UV lamp.

A shape moved there. It lurched forward to the top of the ramp. A large, manlike thing, it advanced with a rolling stagger, like a college freshman at a beer blast. It wore a body-tight red stretchsuit, a white circle on its chest with a lightning bolt through it, some sort of flexible mask over its face. Blond hair covered its head in a kind of brush cut, and two cup-shaped ears poked comically out of the sides of its head. The creature stepped off onto the field, nudging aside the football that lay there.

Delacroix, who majored in public relations at Michigan State, went forward to greet it. This could be the beginning of an entirely new career. His knee felt great.

He extended his hand. "Welcome," he said. "I greet you in the name of humanity and the United States of America."

"Cocaine," the alien said. "We need cocaine."

Today:

I sit at my desk writing a science fiction story, a tall, thin man wearing jeans, a white T-shirt with the abstract face of a man printed on it, white high-top basketball shoes, and gold-plated, wire-rimmed glasses.

In the morning I drink coffee to get me up for the day, and at night I have a gin and tonic to help me relax.

16 November 1532:

"What are they waiting for, the shitting dogs!" the man next to de Arce said. "Are they trying to make us suffer?"

"Shut up, will you?" De Arce shifted his armor. Wedged into the stone building on the side of the square, sweating, they had been waiting since dawn, in silence for the most part except for the creak of leather, the uneasy jingle of cascabels on the horses' trappings. The men stank worse than the restless horses. Some had pissed themselves. A common foot soldier like de Arce was lucky to get a space near enough to the door to see out.

As noon came and went with still no sign of Atahualpa and his retinue, the mood of the men went from impatience to near panic. Then, late in the day, word came that the Indians were moving toward the town again.

An hour later, six thousand brilliantly costumed attendants entered the plaza. They were unarmed. Atahualpa, borne on a golden litter by eight men in cloaks of green feathers that glistened like emeralds in the sunset, rose above them. De Arce heard a slight rattling, looked down, and found that his hand, gripping the sword so tightly the knuckles stood out white, was shaking uncontrollably. He unknotted his fist from the hilt, rubbed the cramped fingers, and crossed himself.

"Quiet now, my brave ones," Pizarro said.

Father Valverde and Felipillo strode out to the center of the plaza, right through the sea of attendants. The priest had guts. He stopped before the litter of the Inca, short and steady as a fence post. "Greetings, my lord, in the name of Pope Clement VII, His Majesty the Emperor Charles V, and Our Lord and Savior Jesus Christ."

Atahualpa spoke and Felipillo translated: "Where is this new god?"

Valverde held up the crucifix. "Our God died on the cross many years ago and rose again to Heaven. He appointed the pope as his viceroy on earth, and the pope has commanded King Charles to subdue the peoples of the world and convert them to the true faith. The king sent us here to command your obedience and to teach you and your people in this faith."

"By what authority does this pope give away lands that aren't his?"

Valverde held up his Bible. "By the authority of the word of God."

The Inca took the Bible. When Valverde reached out to help him get the cover unclasped, Atahualpa cuffed his arm away. He opened the book and leafed through the pages. After a moment he threw it to the ground. "I hear no words," he said.

Valverde snatched up the book and stalked back toward Pizarro's hiding place. "What are you waiting for?" he shouted. "The saints and the Blessed Virgin, the bleeding wounds of Christ himself cry vengeance! Attack, and I'll absolve you!"

Pizarro had already stridden into the plaza. He waved his kerchief. "Santiago, and at them!"

On the far side, the harquebuses exploded in an enfilade. The lines of Indians jerked like startled cats. Bells jingling, de Soto's and Hernando's cavalry burst from the lines of doorways on the adjoining side. De Arce clutched his sword and rushed out with the others from the third side. He felt the power of God in his arm. "Santiago!" he roared at the top of his lungs, and hacked halfway through the neck of his first Indian. Bright blood spurted. He put his boot to the brown man's shoulder and yanked free, lunged for the belly of another wearing a kilt of bright red-and-white checks. The man turned and the sword caught between his ribs. The hilt was almost twisted from de Arce's grasp as the Indian went down. He pulled free, shrugged another man off his back, and daggered him in the side.

After the first flush of glory, it turned to filthy, hard work, an hour's wade through an ocean of butchery in the twilight, bodies heaped waist-high, boots skidding on the bloody stones. De Arce alone must have killed forty. Only after they'd slaughtered them all and captured the Sapa Inca did it end. A silence settled, broken only by the moans of dying Indians and distant shouts of the cavalry chasing the ones who had managed to break through the plaza wall to escape.

Saint James had indeed sat on their shoulders. Six thousand dead Indians, and not one Spaniard nicked. It was a pure demonstration of the power of prayer.

31 January 2002:

It was Colonel Zipp's third session interrogating the alien. So far the thing had kept a consistent story, but not a credible one. The only thing that kept Zipp from panic at the thought of how his career would suffer if this continued was the rumor that his fellow case officers weren't doing any better with any of the others. That, and the fact that the Krel possessed technology that would reestablish American superiority for another two hundred years. He took a drag on his cigarette, the first of his third pack of the day.

"Your name?" Zipp asked.

"You may call me Flash."

Zipp studied the red union suit, the lightning bolt. With the flat chest, the rounded shoulders, pointed upper lip, and pronounced underbite, the alien looked like a cross between Wally Cleaver and the Mock Turtle. "Is this some kind of joke?"

"What is a joke?"

"Never mind." Zipp consulted his notes. "Where are you from?"

"God has ceded us an empire extending over sixteen solar systems in the Orion arm of the galaxy, including the systems around the stars you know as Tau Ceti, Epsilon Eridani, Alpha Centauri, and the red dwarf Barnard's Star."

"God gave you an empire?"

"Yes. We were hoping he'd give us your world, but all he kept talking about was your cocaine."

The alien's translating device had to be malfunctioning. "You're telling me that God sent you for cocaine?"

"No. He just told us about it. We collect chemical compounds for their aesthetic interest. These alkaloids do not exist on our world. Like the music you humans value so highly, they combine familiar elements—carbon, hydrogen, nitrogen, oxygen—in pleasing new ways."

The colonel leaned back, exhaled a cloud of smoke. "You consider cocaine like—like a symphony?"

"Yes. Understand, Colonel, no material commodity alone could justify the difficulties of interstellar travel. We come here for aesthetic reasons."

"You seem to know what cocaine is already. Why don't you just synthesize it yourself?"

"If you valued a unique work of aboriginal art, would you be satisfied with a mass-produced duplicate manufactured in your hometown? Of course not. And we are prepared to pay you well, in a coin you can use."

"We don't need any coins. If you want cocaine, tell us how your ships work."

"That is one of the coins we had in mind. Our ships operate according to a principle of basic physics. Certain fundamental physical reactions are subject to the belief system of the beings promoting them. If I believe that X is true, then X is more probably true than if I did not believe so."

The colonel leaned forward again. "We know that already. We call it the 'observer effect.' Our great physicist Werner Heisenberg—"

"Yes. I'm afraid we carry this principle a little further than that."

"What do you mean?"

Flash smirked. "I mean that our ships move through interstellar space by the power of prayer."

13 May 1533:

Atahualpa offered to fill a room twenty-two feet long and seventeen feet wide with gold up to a line as high as a man could reach, if the Spaniards would let him go. They were skeptical. How long would this take? Pizarro asked. Two months, Atahualpa said.

Pizarro allowed the word to be sent out, and over the next several months, bearers, chewing the coca leaf in order to negotiate the mountain roads under such burdens, brought in tons of gold artifacts. They brought plates and vessels, life-sized statues of women and men, gold lobsters and spiders and alpacas, intricately fashioned ears of maize, every kernel reproduced, with leaves of gold and tassels of spun silver.

Martin Bueno was one of the advance scouts sent with the Indians to Cuzco, the capital of the empire. They found it to be the legendary city of gold. The Incas, having no money, valued precious metals only as ornament. In Cuzco the very walls of the Sun Temple, Coricancha, were plated with gold. Adjoining the temple was a ritual garden where gold maize plants supported gold butterflies, gold bees pollinated gold flowers.

"Enough loot that you'll shit in a different gold pot every day for the rest of your life," Bueno told his friend Diego Leguizano upon his return to Cajamarca.

They ripped the plating off the temple walls and had it carried to Cajamarca. There they melted it down into ingots.

The huge influx of gold into Europe was to cause an economic catastrophe. In Peru, at the height of the conquest, a pair of shoes cost $850, and a bottle of wine $1,700. When their old horseshoes wore out, iron being unavailable, the cavalry shod their horses with silver.

21 April 2003:

In the executive washroom of Bellingham, Winston, and McNeese, Jason Prescott snorted a couple of lines and was ready for the afternoon. He returned to the brokerage to find the place in a whispering uproar. In his office sat one of the Krel. Prescott's secretary was about to piss himself. "It asked specifically for you," he said.

What would Attila the Hun do in this situation? Prescott thought. He went into the office. "Jason Prescott," he said. "What can I do for you, Mr. . . . . ?"

The alien's bloodshot eyes surveyed him. "Flash. I wish to make an investment."

"Investments are our business." Rumors had flown around the New York Merc for a month that the Krel were interested in investing. They had earned vast sums selling information to various computer, environmental, and biotech firms. Several of the aliens had come to observe trading in the currencies pit last week, and only yesterday, Jason had heard from a reliable source that they were considering opening an account with Merrill Lynch. "What brings you to our brokerage?"

"Not the brokerage. You. We heard that you are the most ruthless currencies trader in this city. We worship efficiency. You are efficient."

Right. Maybe there was a hallucinogen in the toot. "I'll call in some of our foreign-exchange experts. We can work up an investment plan for your consideration in a week."

"We already have an investment plan. We are, as you say in the markets, 'long' in dollars. We want you to sell dollars and buy francs for us."

"The franc is pretty strong right now. It's likely to hold for the next six months. We'd suggest—"

"We wish to buy $50 billion worth of francs."

Prescott stared. "That's not a very good investment." Flash said nothing. The silence grew uncomfortable. "I suppose if we stretch it out over a few months, and hit the exchanges in Hong Kong and London at the same time—"

"We want these francs bought in the next week. For the week after that, a second $50 billion. Fifty billion a week until we tell you to stop."

Hallucinogens for sure. "That doesn't make any sense."

"We can take our business elsewhere."

Prescott thought about it. It would take every trick he knew—and he'd have to invent some new ones—to carry this off. The dollar was going to drop through the floor, while the franc would punch through the sell-stops of every trader on ten world markets. The exchanges would scream bloody murder. The repercussions would auger holes in every economy north of Antarctica. Governments would intervene. It would make the historic Hunt silver squeeze look like a game of Monopoly.

Besides, it made no sense. Not only was it criminally irresponsible, it was stupid. The Krel would squander every dime they'd earned.

Then he thought about the commission on $50 billion a week.

Prescott looked across at the alien. From the right point of view, Flash looked like a barrel-chested college undergraduate from Special Effects U. He felt an urge to giggle, a euphoric feeling of power. "When do we start?"

19 May 1533:

In the fields the *purics*, singing praise to Atahualpa, son of the sun, harvested the maize. At night they celebrated by getting drunk on *chicha*. It was, they said, the most festive month of the year.

Pedro Sancho did his drinking in the dark of the treasure room, in the smoke of the smelters' fire. For months he had been troubled by nightmares of the heaped bodies lying in the plaza. He tried to ignore the abuse of the Indian women, the brutality toward the men. He worked hard. As Pizarro's squire, it was his job to record daily the tally of Atahualpa's ransom. When he ran low on ink, he taught the *purics* to make it for him from soot and the juice of berries. They learned readily.

Atahualpa heard about the ink and one day came to him. "What are you doing with those marks?" he said, pointing to the scribe's tally book.

"I'm writing the list of gold objects to be melted down."

"What is this 'writing'?"

Sancho was nonplussed. Over the months of Atahualpa's captivity, Sancho had become impressed by the sophistication of the Incas. Yet they were also queerly backward. They had no money. It was not beyond belief that they should not know how to read and write.

"By means of these marks, I can record the words that people speak. That's writing. Later other men can look at these marks and see what was said. That's reading."

"Then this is a kind of quipu?" Atahualpa's servants had demonstrated for Sancho the quipu, a system of knotted strings by which the Incas kept tallies. "Show me how it works," Atahualpa said.

Sancho wrote on the page: *God have mercy on us.* He pointed. "This, my lord, is a representation of the word 'God.' "

Atahualpa looked skeptical. "Mark it here." He held out his hand, thumbnail extended.

Sancho wrote "God" on the Inca's thumbnail.

"Say nothing now." Atahualpa advanced to one of the guards, held out his thumbnail. "What does this mean?" he asked.

"God," the man replied.

Sancho could tell the Inca was impressed, but he barely showed it. That the Sapa Inca had maintained such dignity throughout his captivity tore at Sancho's heart.

"This writing is truly a magical accomplishment," Atahualpa told him. "You must teach my *amautas* this art."

Later, when the viceroy Estete, Father Valverde, and Pizarro came to chide him for the slow pace of the gold shipments, Atahualpa tested each of them separately. Estete and Valverde each said the word "God." Atahualpa held his thumbnail out to the conquistador.

Estete chuckled. For the first time in his experience, Sancho saw Pizarro flush. He turned away. "I don't waste my time on the games of children," Pizarro said.

Atahualpa stared at him. "But your common soldiers have this art."

"Well, I don't."

"Why not?"

"I was a swineherd. Swineherds don't need to read."

"You are not a swineherd now."

Pizarro glared at the Inca. "I don't need to read to order you put to death."
He marched out of the room.

After the others had left, Sancho told Atahualpa, "You ought not to
humiliate the governor in front of his men."

"He humiliates himself," Atahualpa said. "There is no skill in which a
leader ought to let himself stand behind his followers."

Today:

The part of this story about the Incas is as historically accurate as I could
make it, but this Krel business is science fiction. I even stole the name "Krel"
from a 1950s sf flick. I've been addicted to sf for years. In the evening my
wife and I wash the bad taste of the news out of our mouths by watching
old movies on videotape.

A scientist, asked why he read sf, replied, "Because in science fiction the
experiments always work." Things in sf stories work out more neatly than
in reality. Nothing is impossible. Spaceships move faster than light. Atomic
weapons are neutralized. Disease is abolished. People travel in time. Why,
Isaac Asimov even wrote a story once that ended with the reversal of entropy!

The descendants of the Incas, living in grinding poverty, find their most
lucrative crop in coca, which they refine into cocaine and sell in vast quantities to North Americans.

23 August 2008:

"Catalog number 208," said John Bostock. "Georges Seurat, *Bathers*."

FRENCH GOVERNMENT FALLS, the morning *Times* had announced. JAPAN BANS U.S. IMPORTS. FOOD RIOTS IN MADRID.
But Bostock had barely glanced at the newspaper over his coffee; he was
buzzed on caffeine and adrenaline, and it was too late to stop the auction,
the biggest day of his career. The lot list would make an art historian faint.
Guernica. The Potato Eaters. The Scream. Miró, Rembrandt, Vermeer,
Gauguin, Matisse, Constable, Magritte, Pollock, Mondrian. Six desperate
governments had contributed to the sale. And rumor had it the Krel would
be among the bidders.

The rumor proved true. In the front row, beside the solicitor Patrick
McClannahan, sat one of the unlikely aliens, wearing red tights and a
lightning-bolt insignia. The famous Flash. The creature sat there lazily while
McClannahan did the bidding with a discreetly raised forefinger.

Bidding on the Seurat started at a million and went orbital. It soon became clear that the main bidders were Flash and the U.S. Government. The American campaign against cultural imperialism was getting a lot of press, ironic since the Yanks could afford to challenge the Krel only because of the technology the Krel had lavished on them. The probability suppressor that prevented the detonation of atomic weapons. The autodidactic antivirus that cured most diseases. There was talk of an immortality drug. Of a time machine. So what if the European Community was in the sixth month of an economic crisis that threatened to dissolve the unifying efforts of the past twenty years? So what if Krel meddling destroyed humans' capacity to run the world? The Americans were making money, and the Krel were richer than Croesus.

The bidding reached $1.2 billion, at which point the American ambassador gave up. Bostock tapped his gavel. "Sold," he said in his most cultured voice, nodding toward the alien.

The crowd murmured. The American stood. "If you can't see what they're doing to us, then you don't deserve our help!"

For a minute, Bostock thought the auction was going to turn into a riot. Then the new owner of the pointillist masterpiece stood, smiled. Ingenuous, clumsy. "We know that there has been considerable disquiet over our purchase of these historic works of art," Flash said. "Let me promise you, they will be displayed where all humans—not just those who can afford to visit the great museums—can see them."

The crowd's murmur turned into applause. Bostock put down his gavel and joined in. The American ambassador and his aides stalked out. Thank God, Bostock thought. The attendants brought out the next item.

"Catalog number 209," Bostock said. "Leonardo da Vinci, *Mona Lisa.*"

26 July 1533:

The soldiers, seeing the heaps of gold grow, became anxious. They consumed stores of coca meant for the Inca messengers. They fought over women. They grumbled over the airs of Atahualpa. "Who does he think he is? The governor treats him like a hidalgo."

Father Valverde cursed Pizarro's inaction. That morning, after Matins, he spoke with Estete. "The governor has agreed to meet and decide what to do," Estete said.

"It's about time. What about Soto?" De Soto was against harming Atahualpa. He maintained that, since the Inca had paid the ransom, he should be set free, no matter what danger this would present. Pizarro had stalled. Last week he had sent de Soto away to check out rumors that the Tahuantinsuyans were massing for an attack to free the Sapa Inca.

Estete smiled. "Soto's not back yet."

They went to the building Pizarro had claimed as his, and found the others already gathered. The Incas had no tables or proper chairs, so the Spaniards were forced to sit in a circle on mats as the Indians did. Pizarro, only a few years short of threescore, sat on a low stool of the sort that Atahualpa used when he held court. His left leg, whose old battle wound still pained him at times, was stretched out before him. His loose white shirt had been cleaned by some *puric*'s wife. Valverde sat beside him. Gathered were Estete, Benalcázar, Almagro, de Candia, Riquelme, Pizarro's young cousin Pedro, the scribe Pedro Sancho, Valverde, and the governor himself.

As Valverde and Estete had agreed, the viceroy went first. "The men are jumpy, Governor," Estete said. "The longer we stay cooped up here, the longer we give these savages the chance to plot against us."

"We should wait until Soto returns," de Candia said, already looking guilty as a dog. "We've got nothing but rumors so far. I won't kill a man on a rumor."

Silence. Trust de Candia to speak aloud what they were all thinking but were not ready to say. The man had no political judgment—but maybe it was just as well to face it directly. Valverde seized the opportunity. "Atahualpa plots against us even as we speak," he told Pizarro. "As governor, you are responsible for our safety. Any court would convict him of treason, and execute him."

"He's a king," de Candia said. Face flushed, he spat out a cud of leaves. "We don't have authority to try him. We should ship him back to Spain and let the emperor decide what to do."

"This is not a king," Valverde said. "It isn't even a man. It is a creature that worships demons, that weaves spells about half-wits like Candia. You saw him discard the Bible. Even after my months of teaching, after the extraordinary mercies we've shown him, he doesn't acknowledge the primacy of Christ! He cares only for his wives and his pagan gods. Yet he's satanically clever. Don't think we can let him go. If we do, the day will come when he'll have our hearts for dinner."

"We can take him with us to Cuzco," Benalcázar said. "We don't know the country. His presence would guarantee our safe conduct."

"We'll be traveling over rough terrain, carrying tons of gold, with not enough horses," Almagro said. "If we take him with us, we'll be ripe for ambush at every pass."

"They won't attack if we have him."

"He could escape. We can't trust the rebel Indians to stay loyal to us. If they turned to our side, they can just as easily turn back to his."

"And remember, he escaped before, during the civil war," Valverde said.

"Huáscar, his brother, lived to regret that. If Atahualpa didn't hesitate to murder his own brother, do you think he'll stop for us?"

"He's given us his word," Candia said.

"What good is the word of a pagan?"

Pizarro, silent until now, spoke. "He has no reason to think the word of a Christian much better."

Valverde felt his blood rise. Pizarro knew as well as any of them what was necessary. What was he waiting for? "He keeps a hundred wives! He betrayed his brother! He worships the sun!" The priest grabbed Pizarro's hand, held it up between them so they could both see the scar there, where Pizarro had gotten cut preventing one of his own men from killing Atahualpa. "He isn't worth an ounce of the blood you spilled to save him."

"He's proved worth twenty-four tons of gold." Pizarro's eyes were hard and calm.

"There is no alternative!" Valverde insisted. "He serves the Antichrist! God demands his death."

At last Pizarro seemed to have gotten what he wanted. He smiled. "Far be it from me to ignore the command of God," he said. "Since God forces us to it, let's discuss how He wants it done."

5 October 2009:

"What a lovely country Chile is from the air. You should be proud of it."

"I'm from Los Angeles," Leon Sepulveda said. "And as soon as we close this deal, I'm going back."

"The mountains are impressive."

"Nothing but earthquakes and slag. You can have Chile."

"Is it for sale?"

Sepulveda stared at the Krel. "I was just kidding."

They sat at midnight in the arbor, away from the main buildings of Iguassu Microelectronics of Santiago. The night was cold and the arbor was overgrown and the bench needed a paint job—but then, a lot of things had been getting neglected in the past couple of years. All the more reason to put yourself in a financial situation where you didn't have to worry. Though Sepulveda had to admit that, since the advent of the Krel, such positions were harder to come by, and less secure once you had them.

Flash's earnestness aroused a kind of horror in him. It had something to do with Sepulveda's suspicion that this thing next to him was as superior to him as he was to a guinea pig, plus the alien's aura of drunken adolescence, plus his own willingness, despite the feeling that the situation was out of control, to make a deal with it. He took another Valium and tried to calm down.

"What assurance do I have that this time-travel method will work?"

"It will work. If you don't like it in Chile, or back in Los Angeles, you can use it to go into the past."

Sepulveda swallowed. "O.K. You need to read and sign these papers."

"We don't read."

"You don't read Spanish? How about English?"

"We don't read at all. We used to, but we gave it up. Once you start reading, it gets out of control. You tell yourself you're just going to stick to nonfiction—but pretty soon you graduate to fiction. After that, you can't kick the habit. And then there's the oppression."

"Oppression?"

"Sure. I mean, I like a story as much as the next Krel, but any pharmacologist can show that arbitrary cultural, sexual, and economic assumptions determine every significant aspect of a story. Literature is a political tool used by ruling elites to ensure their hegemony. Anyone who denies that is a fish who can't see the water it swims in. Or the fascist who tells you, as he beats you, that those blows you feel are your own delusion."

"Right. Look, can we settle this? I've got things to do."

"This is, of course, the key to temporal translation. The past is another arbitrary construct. Language creates reality. Reality is smoke."

"Well, this time machine better not be smoke. We're going to find out the truth about the past. Then we'll change it."

"By all means. Find the truth." Flash turned to the last page of the contract, pricked his thumb, and marked a thumbprint on the signature line.

After they sealed the agreement, Sepulveda walked the alien back to the courtyard. A Krel flying pod with Vermeer's *The Letter* varnished onto its door sat at the focus of three spotlights. The painting was scorched almost into unrecognizability by atmospheric friction. The door peeled downward from the top, became a canvas-surfaced ramp.

"I saw some interesting lines inscribed on the coastal desert on the way here," Flash said. "A bird, a tree, a big spider. In the sunset, it looked beautiful. I didn't think you humans were capable of such art. Is it for sale?"

"I don't think so. That was done by some old Indians a long time ago. If you're really interested, though, I can look into it."

"Not necessary." Flash waggled his ears, wiped his feet on Mark Rothko's *Earth and Green* and staggered into the pod.

26 July 1533:

Atahualpa looked out of the window of the stone room in which he was kept, across the plaza where the priest Valverde stood outside his chapel after his morning prayers. Valverde's chapel had been the house of the virgins; the women of the house had long since been raped by the Spanish soldiers, as the house had been by the Spanish god. Valverde spoke with Estete. They were getting ready to kill him, Atahualpa knew. He had known ever since the ransom had been paid.

He looked beyond the thatched roofs of the town to the crest of the mountains, where the sun was about to break in his tireless circuit of Tahuantinsuyu. The cold morning air raised dew on the metal of the chains that bound him hand and foot. The metal was queer, different from the bronze the *purics* worked or the gold and silver Atahualpa was used to wearing. If gold was the sweat of the sun, and silver the tears of the moon, what was this metal, dull and hard like the men who held him captive, yet strong, too—stronger, he had come to realize, than the Inca. It, like the men who brought it, was beyond his experience. It gave evidence that Tahuantinsuyu, the Four Quarters of the World, was not all the world after all. Atahualpa had thought none but savages lived beyond their lands. He'd imagined no man readier to face the ruthless necessity than himself. He had ordered the death of Huáscar, his own brother. But he was learning that these men were capable of enormities against which the Inca civil war would seem a minor discomfort.

That evening they took him out of the building to the plaza. In the plaza's center, the soldiers had piled a great heap of wood on flagstones, some of which were still stained with the blood of his six thousand slaughtered attendants. They bound him to a stake amid the heaped fagots, and Valverde appealed one last time for the Inca to renounce Satan and be baptized. He promised that if Atahualpa would do so, he would earn God's mercy: they would strangle him rather than burn him to death.

The rough wood pressed against his spine. Atahualpa looked at the priest, and the men gathered around, and the women weeping beyond the circle of soldiers. The moon, his mother, rode high above. Firelight flickered on the breastplates of the Spaniards, and from the waiting torches drifted the smell of pitch. The men shifted nervously. Creak of leather, clink of metal. Men on horses shod with silver. Sweat shining on Valverde's forehead. Valverde stared at Atahualpa as if he desired something, but was prepared to destroy him without getting it if need be. The priest thought he was showing Atahualpa resolve, but Atahualpa saw that beneath Valverde's face he was a dead man. Pizarro stood aside, with the Spanish viceroy Estete and the scribe. Pizarro was an old man. He ought to be sitting quietly in some village, outside the violence of life, giving advice and teaching the children. What kind of world did he come from, that sent men into old age still charged with the lusts and bitterness of the young?

Pizarro, too, looked as if he wanted this to end.

Atahualpa knew that it would not end. This was only the beginning. These men would suffer for this moment as they had already suffered for it all their lives, seeking the pain blindly over oceans, jungles, deserts, probing it like a sore tooth until they'd found and grasped it in this plaza of Cajamarca, thinking they sought gold. They'd come all this way to create a moment that would reveal to them their own incurable disease. Now they had it. In a few minutes, they thought, it would at last be over, that once he was gone, they would be free—but Atahualpa knew it would be with them ever after, and with their children and grandchildren and the million others of their race in times to come, whether they knew of this hour in the plaza or not, because they were sick and would pass the sickness on with their breath and semen. They could not burn out the sickness so easily as they could burn the Son of God to ash. This was a great tragedy, but it contained a huge jest. They were caught in a wheel of the sky and could not get out. They must destroy themselves.

"Have your way, priest," Atahualpa said. "Then strangle me, and bear my body to Cuzco, to be laid with my ancestors." He knew they would not do it, and so would add an additional curse to their faithlessness.

He had one final curse. He turned to Pizarro. "You will have responsibility for my children."

Pizarro looked at the pavement. They put up the torch and took Atahualpa from the pyre. Valverde poured water on his head and spoke words in the tongue of his god. Then they sat him upon a stool, bound him to another stake, set the loop of cord around his neck, slid the rod through the cord, and turned it. His women knelt at his side and wept. Valverde spoke more words. Atahualpa felt the cord, woven by the hands of some faithful *puric* of Cajamarca, tighten. The cord was well made. It cut his access to the night air; Atahualpa's lungs fought, he felt his body spasm, and then the plaza became cloudy and he heard the voice of the moon.

12 January 2011:

Israel Lamont was holding big-time when a Krel monitor zipped over the alley. A minute later one of the aliens lurched around the corner and approached him. Lamont was ready.

"I need to achieve an altered state of consciousness," the alien said. It wore a red suit, a lightning bolt on its chest.

"I'm your man," Lamont said. "You just try this. Best stuff on the street." He held the vial out in the palm of his hand. "Go ahead, try it." The Krel took it.

"How much?"

"One million."

The Krel gave him a couple hundred thousand. "Down payment," it said. "How does one administer this?"

"What, you don't know? I thought you guys were hip."

"I have been working hard, and am unacquainted."

This was ripe. "You burn it," Lamont said.

The Krel started toward the trash-barrel fire. Before he could empty the vial into it, Lamont stopped him. "Wait up, homes! You use a pipe. Here, I'll show you."

Lamont pulled a pipe from his pocket, torched up, and inhaled. The Krel watched him. Brown eyes like a dog's. Goofy honkie face. The rush took him, and Lamont saw in the alien's face a peculiar need. The thing was hungry. Desperate.

"I may try?" The alien reached out. Its hand trembled.

Lamont handed over the pipe. Clumsily, the creature shook a block of crack into the bowl. Its beaklike upper lip, however, prevented it from getting its mouth tight against the stem. It fumbled with the pipe, from somewhere producing a book of matches. "Shit, I'll light it," Lamont said.

The Krel waited while Lamont held his Bic over the bowl. Nothing happened. "Inhale, man."

The creature inhaled. The blue flame played over the crack; smoke boiled through the bowl. The creature drew in steadily for what seemed to be minutes. Serious capacity. The crack burned totally through. Finally the Krel exhaled.

It looked at Lamont. Its eyes were bright.

"Good shit?" Lamont said.

"A remarkable stimulant effect."

"Right." Lamont looked over his shoulder toward the alley's entrance. It was getting dark. Yet he hesitated to ask for the rest of the money.

"Will you talk with me?" the Krel asked, swaying slightly.

Surprised, Lamont said, "O.K. Come with me."

Lamont led the Krel back to a deserted store that abutted the alley. They went inside and sat down on some crates against the wall.

"Something I been wondering about you," Lamont said. "You guys are coming to own the world. You fly across the planets, Mars and that shit. What you want with crack?"

"We seek to broaden our minds."

Lamont snorted. "Right. You might as well hit yourself in the head with a hammer."

"We seek escape," the alien said.

"I don't buy that, neither. What you got to escape from?"

The Krel looked at him. "Nothing."

They smoked another pipe. The Krel leaned back against the wall, arms at its sides like a limp doll. It started a queer coughing sound, chest spasming. Lamont thought it was choking and tried to slap it on the back. "Don't do that," it said. "I'm laughing."

"Laughing? What's so funny?"

"I lied to Colonel Zipp," it said. "We want cocaine for kicks."

Lamont relaxed a little. "I hear you now."

"We do everything for kicks."

"Makes for hard living."

"Better than maintaining consciousness continuously without interruption."

"You said it."

"Human beings cannot stand too much reality," the Krel said. "We don't blame you. Human beings! Disgust, horror, shame. Nothing personal."

"You bet."

"Nonbeing penetrates that in which there is no space."

"Uh-huh."

The alien laughed again. "I lied to Sepulveda, too. Our time machines take people to the past they believe in. There is no other past. You can't change it."

"Who the fuck's Sepulveda?"

"Let's do some more," it said.

They smoked one more. "Good shit," it said. "Just what I wanted."

The Krel slid off the crate. Its head lolled. "Here is the rest of your payment," it whispered, and died.

Lamont's heart raced. He looked at the Krel's hand, lying open on the floor. In it was a full-sized ear of corn, fashioned of gold, with tassels of finely spun silver wire.

Today:

It's not just physical laws that science fiction readers want to escape. Just as commonly, they want to escape human nature. In pursuit of this, sf offers comforting alternatives to the real world. For instance, if you start reading an sf story about some abused wimp, you can be pretty sure that by chapter two he's going to discover he has secret powers unavailable to those tormenting him, and by the end of the book, he's going to save the universe. Sf is full of this sort of thing, from the power fantasy of the alienated child to the alternate history where Hitler is strangled in his cradle and the Library of Alexandria is saved from the torch.

Science fiction may in this way be considered as much an evasion of reality as any mind-distorting drug. I know that sounds a little harsh, but think about it. An alkaloid like cocaine or morphine invades the central nervous system. It reduces pain, produces euphoria, enhances our perceptions. Under its influence we imagine we have supernormal abilities. Limits dissolve. Soon, hardly aware of what's happened to us, we're addicted.

Science fiction has many of the same qualities. The typical reader comes to sf at a time of suffering. He seizes on it as a way to deal with his pain. It's bigger than his life. It's astounding. Amazing. Fantastic. Some grow out of it; many don't. Anyone who's been around sf for a while can cite examples of longtime readers as hooked and deluded as crack addicts.

Like any drug addict, the sf reader finds desperate justifications for his habit. Sf teaches him science. Sf helps him avoid "future shock." Sf changes the world for the better. Right. So does cocaine.

Having been an sf user myself, however, I have to say that, living in a world of cruelty, immersed in a culture that grinds people into fish meal like some brutal machine, with histories of destruction stretching behind us back to the Pleistocene, I find it hard to sneer at the desire to escape. Even if escape is delusion.

18 October 1527:

Timu drove the foot plow into the ground, leaned back to break the crust, drew out the pointed pole, and backed up a step to let his wife, Collyur, turn the earth with her hoe. To his left was his brother, Okya; and to his right, his cousin, Tupa; before them, their wives planting the seed. Most of the *purics* of Cajamarca were there, strung out in a line across the terrace, the men wielding the foot plows, and the women or children carrying the sacks of seed potatoes.

As he looked up past Collyur's shoulders to the edge of the terrace, he saw a strange man approach from the post road. The man stumbled into the next terrace up from them, climbed down steps to their level. He was plainly excited.

Collyur was waiting for Timu to break the next row; she looked up at him questioningly.

"Who is that?" Timu said, pointing past her at the man.

She stood up straight and looked over her shoulder. The other men had noticed, too, and stopped their work.

"A *chasqui* come from the next town," said Okya.

"A *chasqui* would go to the *curaca*," said Tupa.

"He's not dressed like a *chasqui*," Timu said.

The man came up to them. Instead of a cape, loincloth and flowing *onka*, the man wore uncouth clothing: cylinders of fabric that bound his legs tightly, a white short-sleeved shirt that bore on its front the face of a man, and flexible white sandals that covered all his foot to the ankle. He shivered in the spring cold.

He was extraordinarily tall. His face, paler than a normal man's, was long, his nose too straight, mouth too small, and lips too thin. Upon his face he wore a device of gold wire that, hooking over his ears, held disks of crystal before his eyes. The man's hands were large, his limbs long and spiderlike. He moved suddenly, awkwardly.

Gasping for air, the stranger spoke rapidly the most abominable Quechua Timu had ever heard.

"Slow down," Timu said. "I don't understand."

"What year is this?" the man asked.

"What do you mean?"

"I mean, what is the year?"

"It is the thirty-fourth year of the reign of the Sapa Inca Huayna Capac."

The man spoke some foreign word. "God damn," he said in a language foreign to Timu, but which you or I would recognize as English. "I made it."

Timu went to the *curaca*, and the *curaca* told Timu to take the stranger in. The stranger told them that his name was "Chuan." But Timu's three-year-old daughter, Curi, reacting to the man's sudden gestures, unearthly thinness, and piping speech, laughed and called him "the Bird." So he was ever after to be known in that town.

There he lived a long and happy life, earned trust and respect, and brought great good fortune. He repaid them well for their kindness, alerting the people of Tahuantinsuyu to the coming of the invaders. When the first Spaniards landed on their shores a few years later, they were slaughtered to the last man, and everyone lived happily ever after.

MICHAEL MOORCOCK

The Cairene Purse

▼

One of the most prolific, popular, and controversial figures in modern letters, Michael Moorcock has been a major shaping force on the development of science fiction and fantasy, as both author and editor, for more than thirty years. As editor, Moorcock helped to usher in the "New Wave" revolution in SF in the middle 1960s by taking over the genteel but elderly and somewhat tired British SF magazine *New Worlds* and coaxing it into a bizarre new life. Moorcock transformed *New Worlds* into a fierce and daring outlaw publication that was at the very heart of the British New Wave movement, and Moorcock himself—for his role as chief creator of the either much admired or much loathed "Jerry Cornelius" stories, in addition to his roles as editor, polemicist, literary theorist, and mentor to most of the period's most prominent writers—became one of the most controversial figures of that turbulent era. *New Worlds* died in the early '70s, after having been ringingly denounced in the Houses of Parliament and banned from distribution by the huge British bookstore and newsstand chain W. H. Smith, but Moorcock himself has never been out of public view for long. His series of "Elric" novels—elegant and elegantly perverse "Sword & Sorcery" at its most distinctive—are wildly popular, and bestsellers on both sides of the Atlantic. At the same time, Moorcock's other work, both in and out of the genre, such as the *Dancers at the End of Time* trilogy, *Gloriana*, *Mother London*, *Warhound and the World's Pain*, *Byzantium Endures*, and *The Laughter of Carthage*, has established him as one of the most respected and critically acclaimed writers of our day. He has won the Nebula Award, the World Fantasy Award, the John W. Campbell Memorial Award, and the Guardian Fiction Award.

Michael Moorcock

Upcoming are the novels *Jerusalem Commands*, *Revenge of the Rose* (the 28th Elric novel), and *Where the Dead Meet*, and the collection *Lunching with the Antichrist*. He lives in London.

   Here he takes us on a vivid and disturbing search through the streets and alleyways of a ruined but still vital future Third World, a search for something as elusive now as it was when Pilate washed his hands thousands of years ago—truth.

▼

The Cairene Purse

MICHAEL MOORCOCK

1 Her First Fond Hope Of Eden Blighted

On the edge of the Nile's fertile shadow, pyramids merged with the desert and seemed from the air almost two-dimensional in the steady light of late morning. Spreading now beyond the town of Giza, Cairo's forty million people threatened to engulf, with their old automobiles, discarded electronics and every dusty nondegradable of the modern world, the grandiose tombs of their ancestors.

Though Cairo, like Calcutta, was a monument to the enduring survival of our race, I was glad to leave. I had spent only as much time as I needed, seeking information about my archaeologist sister and discovering that every-one in the academic community thought she had returned to England at least a year ago. The noise had begun to seem as tangible as the haze of sand which hung over the crowded motorways, now a mass of moving flesh, of camels, donkeys, horses, mules and humans hauling every variety of vehicle and cargo, with the occasional official electric car or, even rarer, petrol-driven truck.

I suppose it had been a tribute to my imagined status that I had been given a place on a plane, rather than having to take the river or the weekly train to Aswan. Through the porthole of the little VW8 everything but the Nile and its verdant borders were the colours of sand, each shade and texture of which still held meaning for the nomad Arab, the Bedouin who had conquered the First Kingdom and would conquer several others down the millennia. In the past only the Ptolmies, turning their backs on the Nile and the Sahara, ever truly lost the sources of Egypt's power.

My main reason for accepting the assignment was personal rather than professional. My sister had not written for some months and her letters before that had been disconnected, hinting at some sort of emotional disturbance, perhaps in connection with the dig on which I knew she had been working. An employee of UNEC, I had limited authority in Egypt and did not expect to discover any great mysteries at Lake Nasser, which continued to be the cause of unusual weather. The dam's builders somewhat typically had refused to anticipate this. They had also been warned by our people in the 1950s that the New High Dam would eventually so poison the river with bilharzia that anyone using its water would die. The rain, some of it acid, had had predictable effects, flooding quarries and washing away towns. The local Nubians had long-since been evicted from their valleys to make way for the lake. Their new settlements, traditionally built, had not withstood the altered environment, so the government had thrown up concrete shells for them. The road to Aswan from the airport was lined with bleak half-built structures of rusted metal girders and cinder blocks. Today's Egyptians paid a high price for regulated water.

From the airport my horse-drawn taxi crossed the old English dam with its sluices and gigantic gauges, a Victorian engineer's dream of mechanical efficiency, and began the last lap of the journey into town. Aswan, wretched as much of it is, has a magic few Nile settlements now possess, rising from the East Bank to dominate the coppery blue waters and glinting granite islands of the wide river where white-sailed feluccas cruise gracefully back and forth, ferrying tourists and townspeople between the two sides. The heights, massive grey boulders, are commanded by a beautiful park full of old eucalyptus, poplars and monkey-puzzle trees. Above this, the stately Edwardian glory of Cook's Cataract Hotel is a marvellous example of balconied and shuttered rococo British orientalism at its finest.

The further up river one goes the poorer Aswan becomes, though even here the clapboard and corrugated iron, the asbestos sheeting and crumbling mud walls are dominated by a splendid hill-top mosque in the grand Turkish style. I had asked to be billeted at a modest hotel in the middle of town, near the Souk. From the outside, the Hotel Osiris, with its pale pink and green pseudo-neon, reminded me of those backstreet Marseilles hotels where once you could take your partner for a few francs an hour. It had the same romantic attraction, the same impossible promises. I found that, once within its tiny fly-thick lobby—actually the communal hallway leading directly to the courtyard—I was as lost to its appeal as any pop to his lid. I had discovered a temporary spiritual home.

The Osiris, though scarcely more than a bed and breakfast place by London standards, boasted four or five porters, all of them eager to take my bag to the rooms assigned me by a Hindu lady at the desk. I let one carry my canvas grip up two flights of dirty stairs to a little tiled, run-down apartment looking into the building's central well where two exhausted dogs, still coupled, panted on their sides in the heat. Giving him a five-pound note, I asked my porter on the off-chance if he had heard of an Englishwoman called Noone or Pappenheim living in Aswan. My sister had used the *poste restante* and, when I had last been here, there were few Europeans permanently living in town. He regretted that he could not help. He would ask his brother, who had been in Aswan several months. Evidently, now that I had as it were paid for the information in advance he felt obliged to me. The *bakshish* custom is usually neither one of bribery nor begging in any European sense, but has a fair amount to do with smooth social intercourse. There is always, with legitimate *bakshish*, an exchange. Some measure of mutual respect is also usual. Most Arabs place considerable emphasis on good manners and are not always tolerant of European coarseness.

I had last been in Egypt long before the great economic convulsion following that chain-reaction of destruction or near-exhaustion of so many resources. Then Aswan had been the final port of call for the millions of tourists who cruised the Nile from dawn to dusk, the sound of their dance music, the smell of their barbecues, drifting over fields and mud villages which had remained unchanged for five thousand years.

In the 80s and 90s of the last century Aswan had possessed, among others, a Hilton, a Sheraton, Ritz-Carlton and a Holiday Inn, but now the luckiest local families had requisitioned the hotels and only the State-owned Cataract remained, a place of pilgrimage for every wealthy enthusiast of 1930s detective stories or autobiographies of the 20th century famous. Here, during wartime, secret meetings had been held and mysterious bargains struck between unlikely participants. Today on the water below the terrace some tourists still sailed, the Israelis and the Saudis on their own elegant schooners, while other boats carried mixtures of Americans, Italians and Germans, French, English, Swedes, Spaniards, Japanese and Hungarians, their women dressed and painted like pagan temptresses of the local soap-operas, displaying their bodies naked on the sundecks of vast slow-moving windliners the size of an earlier era's ocean-going ships, serving to remind every decent Moslem exactly what the road to Hell looked like. No 18th century English satirist could have provided a better image.

As an officer of the UN's Conservation and Preservation Department I knew all too well how little of Egypt's monuments were still visible, how few existed in any recognisable state. Human erosion, the dam raising the water-table, the volume of garbage casually dumped in the river, the activities of archaeologists and others, of tourists encouraged in their millions to visit the

great sites and bring their hard currency, the two-year Arabian war, all had
created a situation where those monuments still existing were banned to
everyone but the desperate restorers. Meanwhile replicas had been made by
the Disney Corporation and located in distant desert settlements surrounded
by vacation towns, artificial trees and vast swimming pools, built by French
and German experts and named "Rameses City", "Land of the Gods" or
"Tutankhamen World". I was sure that this was why my sister had been
secretive about her team's discoveries, why it was important to try to avoid
the circumstances which now made Abu Simbel little more than a memory
of two great engineering miracles.

When I had washed and changed I left the Osiris and strolled through
busy evening alleys in the direction of the corniche, the restored Victorian
riverfront promenade which reminded me more than anywhere of the old
ocean boulevard at Yalta. Without her earlier weight of tourists, Aswan had
developed a lazy, decayed glamour. The foodstalls, the fake antiquities, the
flimsy headdresses and *gelabeas* sold as traditional costume, the souvenir
shops and postcard stands, the "cafeterias" offering "Creme Teas" and "Mix
Grile", were still patronised by a few plump Poles and tomato-coloured
English who had been replaced in the main by smaller numbers of blond
East Africans, Swedes and Nigerians affecting the styles and mannerisms of
thirty or forty years earlier and drawn here, I had heard, by a Holy Man on
the outskirts of Aswan who taught a peculiar mixture of orthodox Sunni
Islam and his own brand of mysticism which accepted the creeds of Jews
and Christians as well as the existence of other planetary populations, and
spoke of a "pure" form of Islam practised in other parts of the galaxy.

Aswan's latter-day hippies, wearing the fashions of my own youthful parents, gave me a queer feeling at first, for although Egypt offers several
experiences akin to time-travel, these images of recent history, perhaps of a
happier period altogether, were somehow more incongruous than a broken
down VW, for instance, being dragged behind a disgusted camel. There was
a greater preponderance of charm-sellers and fortune-tellers than I remembered, together with blank-eyed European men and women, some of them
with babies or young children, who begged me for drug-money on the street.
With the rise of Islamic-Humanism, the so-called Arab Enlightenment,
coupled to the increasing power of North Africa and the Middle East in
world politics, the drug laws, introduced originally to placate foreign tour
operators and their governments, had been relaxed or formally abolished.
Aswan, I had heard, was now some kind of Mecca for privileged youngsters
and visionary artists, much as Haight Ashbury or Ladbroke Grove had been
in the 1960s. Romanticism of that heady, exaggerated, rather mystical variety
was once again loose in the world and the comforts it offered seemed to me
almost like devilish temptations. But I was of that puritanical, judgemental

generation which had rejected the abstractions of its parents in favour of more realistic, as we saw it, attitudes. A good many of us had virtually rejected the entire Western Enlightenment itself and retreated into a kind of liberal mediaevalism not incompatible with large parts of the Arab world. In my own circles I was considered something of a radical.

I had to admit however that I found these new Aswanians attractive. In many ways I envied them. They had never known a time when Arabia had not been a major power. They came here as equals with everyone and were accepted cheerfully by the Nubians who treated them with the respect due to richer pilgrims and potential converts to the divine revelation of Islam.

Again in common with my generation, I was of a secular disposition and saw only damaging, enslaving darkness in any religion. We had even rejected the received wisdoms of Freud, Jung, Marx and their followers and embraced instead a political creed which had as its basis the eminent likelihood of ecological disaster and the slight possibility of an economic miracle. They called us the Anaemic Generation now; a decade or more that was out of step with the progress of history as it was presently interpreted. It suited me to know that I was an anachronism; it afforded me a special kind of security. Very few people took me seriously.

An Egyptian army officer marched past me as I crossed to the river-side of the corniche to look down at the half-completed stairways, the crumbling, poorly-mixed concrete and the piles of rat-infested rubble which the Korean engineers, who had put in the lowest tender for the work, had still neither repaired nor cleared. The officer glanced at me as if he recognised me but then went past, looking, with his neatly-trimmed moustache and rigid shoulders, for all the world like a World War Two English Guards captain. Even his uniform was in the English style. I suppose Romans coming to 5th century Britain after some lapse of time would have been equally impressed to see a Celt striding through the streets of Londinium, impeccable in a slightly antiquated Centurion's kit. The whole casual story of the human race seemed to be represented in the town as I paused to look at the hulks of converted pleasure boats, home to swarms of Nubian families impoverished by the altered climate and the shift of tourism towards the Total Egypt Experience found in the comfort of Fort Sadat and New Memphis. Despite the piles of filthy garbage along the shore, Aswan had acquired the pleasant, nostalgic qualities of unfashionable British resorts like Morecombe or Yarmouth, a local population careless of most strangers save sometimes for the money they brought.

About halfway along the corniche I stopped at a little café and sat down on a cane chair, ordering mint tea from a proprietor whose ancient tarboosh might have escaped from the costume department of a touring production of *Death on the Nile*. He addressed me as *"effendi"* and his chosen brand of English seemed developed from old British war movies. Like me, I thought, he was out of step with the times. When he brought the tea I told him to keep the change from a pound and again on the off-chance asked after my sister. I was surprised by the enthusiasm of his response. He knew the name Pappenheim and was approving when I told him of our relationship. "She is very good," he said. "A tip-top gentlewoman. But now, I think, she is unwell. It is hard to see the justice of it."

Pleased and a little alarmed, I asked if he knew where she lived.

"She lived in *Sharri al Sahahaldeen*, just off the *Sharri al Souk*." He pointed with his thumb back into town. "But that was more than a year ago. Oh, she is very well known here in Aswan. The poor people like her immensely. They call her *Saidneh Duukturah*."

"Doctor?" My sister had only rudimentary medical training. Her doctorate had been in archaeology. "She treats the sick?"

"Well, not so much any more. Now only if the hospitals refuse help. The Bisharim, in particular, love her. You know those nomads. They trust your sister only. But she moved from Sahahaldeen Street after some trouble. I heard she went to the English House over on the West Bank, but I'm not so sure. Perhaps you should ask the Bisharim." He raised his hand in welcome to a small man in a dark blue *gelabea* who walked briskly into the darkness of the shop's interior. "A customer." From his pocket he took a cut-throat razor. "*Naharak sa'id*," he called and, adopting the swagger of the expert barber, waved farewell to me and entered his shop.

"*Fi amani 'llah.*" Picking up my hat I crossed to a rank where the usual two or three ill-used horses stood between the shafts of battered broughams, still the commonest form of taxi in Aswan. I approached the first driver, who stood flicking at flies with his ragged whip while he smoked a cigarette and chatted with his fellows. He wore an American sailor's hat, a faded T-shirt advertising some Russian artpopper, a pair of traditional baggy trousers exposing ulcerated calves and on his feet pink and black Roos. From the state of his legs I guessed he had retained the habit, against all current warnings, of wading into the Nile to urinate. I asked him to take me first to the dam's administration office where, for courtesy's sake, I presented myself and made an appointment with my old acquaintance Georges Abidos, the Chief Press Officer, who had been called out to the northern end of the lake. His secretary said he was looking forward to seeing me tomorrow and handed me a welcoming note. I then asked the calash-driver if he knew the Bisharim camp on the outskirts of town. I had heard that in recent years the tribe had returned to its traditional sites. He was contemptuous. "Oh, yes, sir. The barbarians are still with us!" I told him I would give him another ten pounds to take me there and back. He made to bargain but then accepted, shrugging and gesturing for me to get back in his carriage. I guessed he was maintaining some kind of face for himself. In my travels I had grown used to all kinds of mysterious body-language, frequently far harder to interpret than any spoken tongue.

We trotted back to town and jogged beside a river strewn with old plastic water-bottles, with all the miscellaneous filth from the boats that no legislation appeared able to limit, past flaking quasi-French facades still bearing the crests of Farouk and his ancestors and each now occupied by twenty or thirty families whose washing hung over the elaborate iron balconies and carved stone sphinxes like bunting celebrating some joyous national holiday. We passed convents and churches, mosques and graveyards, shanteys, monuments, little clumps of palm-trees sheltering donkeys and boys from a sun which as noon approached grew steadily more intense.

We went by the English holiday villas where hippies nowadays congregated; we passed the burned-out shells of warehouses and storerooms, victims of some forgotten riot, the stained walls sprayed with the emerald-coloured ankh of the Green Jihad, and eventually, turning inland again, reached the old Moslem necropolis, almost a mile long and half-a-mile across, surrounded by a low, mud wall and filled with every shape and size of stone or sarcophagus. Beyond this, further up the hill, I made out clumps of palms and the dark woollen tents of the Bisharim.

My driver reined in his horse some distance from the camp, beside a gate into the graveyard. "I will wait for you here," he said significantly.

2 Ah, Whence, And Whither Flown Again, Who Knows?

The nomad camp, showing so few outward signs of Western influence, had the kind of self-contained dignity which city Arabs frequently manage to recreate in their homes and yet which is not immediately noticed by those visitors merely disgusted by, for instance, Cairo's squalor.

Sheikh Khamet ben Achmet was the patriarch of this particular clan. They had come in a month ago, he said, from the Sudan, to trade horses and camels. They all knew my sister but she had disappeared. He employed a slow, classical Arabic which was easy for me to understand and in which I could easily respond. "God has perhaps directed thy sister towards another vocation," he suggested gently. "It was only a short time since she would visit us whenever we put down our tents here. She had a particularly efficient cure for infections of the eye, but it was the women who went to her, chiefly." He looked at me with quiet amusement. "The best type of Englishwoman, as we say. Sometimes God sends us His beneficence in strange forms."

"Thou has no knowledge of her present dwelling?" I sipped the coffee a servant brought us. I was glad to be in the cool tent. Outside it was now at least 35°. There was little danger of freak rain today. He looked up at me from his ironic grey eyes. "No," he said. "She always visits us. When we needed her we would send messages to the Copt's house. You know, the carpenter who lives on the street leading from the great mosque to the souk."

I did not know him, I said.

"He is as gold-haired as thou. They nickname him The German, but I know he is a Copt from Alexandria. I think he is called Iskander. I know that he is easily found."

"Thou knowest my sister was an archaeologist?" I was a little hesitant.

"Indeed, I do! We discussed all manner of ancient things together and she had the courtesy to say that I was at least as informative as the great Egyptian Museum in Cairo!" He was amused by what he perceived as elegant flattery. My sister, if I still knew her, had done no more than state her direct opinion.

It would have been ill-mannered of me to have left as soon as I had the information I sought, so I spent two further hours answering the Sheikh's questions about current American and European politics. I was not surprised that he was well-informed. I had seen his short-wave radio (doubtless full of *piles noires*) standing on the ivory-inlaid chest on the far side of the tent. I was also unsurprised by his interpretations of what he had learned. They were neither cynical nor unintelligent, but they were characteristic of certain desert Arabs who see everything in terms of power and opportunity and simply cannot grasp the reverence for political institutions we have in the West. For a few minutes I foolishly tried to re-educate him until it became clear I must give offence. Recalling my old rules, I accepted his terms. As a result we parted friends. Any South African apologist for apartheid could not have been more approving of my good manners.

When I got up to leave, the old man took my arm and wished me God's grace and help in finding my sister. "She was associated with Jews." He spoke significantly. "Those who did not like her said that she was a witch. And it is true that two of my women saw her consorting with the spell-seller from the Souk. The one called Lallah Zenobia. The black woman. Thou and I art men of the world and understand that it is superstitious folly. But thou knowest how women are. And they are often," he added in an even lower tone, "susceptible to Yehudim flattery and lies."

It was by no means the first time I had to accept such sentiments from the mouth of one who was otherwise hospitality, tolerance and kindness personified. To persuade a desert Arab that Jews are not in direct and regular touch with Satan and all His minions is still no easier than persuading a Dixie Baptist that the doors of a Catholic Church are not necessarily a direct gateway to Hell. One is dealing with powerful survival myths which only direct experience will disprove. In such circumstances I never mention my mother's family. I said I would visit Iskander the Carpenter. At this point a braying, bellowing and snorting chorus grew so loud I could barely hear his elaborate goodbyes. The stock was being beaten back from the water. As I emerged from the tent I saw my driver in the distance. He was sitting on the wall of the cemetery feinting with his whip at the boys and girls who flowed like a tide around him, daring one another to run within his range.

3 Crystal To The Wizard Eye

I had no difficulty in discovering Iskander the Carpenter. He was a slight man wearing a pair of faded denim overalls. Sanding off a barley-sugar chairleg, he sat just inside his workshop, which was open to the street and displayed an entire suite of baroque bedroom and living room furniture he had almost completed. He chose to speak in French. "It is for a couple getting married this weekend. At least they are spending their money on furniture rather than the wedding itself!" He put down his chairleg and shook my hand. He was fair-skinned and blond, as Sheikh Achmet had said, though I could not have taken him for anything but Egyptian. His features could have come straight from the Egyptian Museum's clay statue displays of ancient tradespeople. He might have been a foreman on a Middle Kingdom site. He turned up a chair which still had to have the upholstery over its horsehair seat, indicated that I should sit and sent his son to get us a couple of bottles of Pyramid beer.

"Of course I know Saidneh Duukturah. She was my friend. That one," he pointed to his disappearing boy, "owes his life to her. He was poisoned. She treated him. He is well. It is true I knew where she lived and would get messages to her. But for a year or more she went away from us. Until recently she was staying at the English House. There are many rumours. Most of them are simply stupid. She is no witch. She was a woman blessed by God with the healing touch. The other woman, now, is undoubtably a witch. My wife heard that your sister fell in love and went to the Somalin, Zenobia, for a philtre. Certainly, by chance, my wife saw her handing Zenobia a heavy purse. A Cairene purse, she was sure."

"I do not know what that is." I moved further into the shade. Outside, Aswan had fallen into a doze as the population closed its shutters until mid-afternoon. The yellow walls of the houses were now almost blistering to the touch.

"A purse of money, that's all. It used to mean a bag of gold. About twenty sovereigns. That is what a witch demands for a very powerful spell. Something very valuable, my friend."

"My sister was buying a charm from a spell-seller?"

"A powerful one, yes. That negress has been involved with the police more than once. She was suspected of killing a rival suitor at the behest of another, of being responsible for the death of a man who was owed over a thousand pounds by another man. Now, if your sister was disposed to witch-craft, why would she go to a witch and pay her a healthy sum for a job she could as readily do herself?"

I agreed it was unlikely my sister was a witch. I asked how the matter had come to official attention.

"The police went to see her, I think. My wife's friend—friend no more —gossiped. They arrested Zenobia, then let your sister go. You should visit the *mamur* at the *markaz*, the police department. The *mamur* here is a very just man. He never accepts money unless he can do whatever it is he promises. His name is Inspector el-Bayoumi. If anyone knows where your sister is living in Aswan he probably will."

By the time I had discussed the affairs of the day and thanked the carpenter for the beer, it was already cooler and I walked down to the *Sharri el Souk* which was beginning to open for business again, filling with women in black lacy *milayum* which barely revealed the vivid colours of their house dresses beneath, clutching bright plastic shopping bags and going about their week-end buying. Because it was Friday afternoon the butchers were displaying their calves' heads and bullock tails, their sheep's hearts and heads, their divided carcasses, all protected from an unforgiving sun by the thick coating of black flies which also covered the fish and offal on other stalls. Sellers of turkeys, pigeons and chickens took water in their mouths to force between the beaks of their wares so that they would not dehydrate before they were sold, and seemed to be kissing, tenderly, each one. Cheerful greengrocers called out the virtues of their squash, mangoes, potatoes or green beans. Gas lorries, electroscoots, bicycles and a few official cars moved in slow com-petition with rickshaws, donkeys, mules or camels through alleys where, every so often, a bright sign would advertise in English the virtues of unob-tainable Panasonic televisions or Braun refrigerators and others would, almost pathetically, alert the passerby to the Color Xerox machine or Your Local Fax Office. Like every similar souk in the Arab world, the tools and artefacts of the centuries were crowded side by side and functioning in perfect com-patability. Aswan had adapted, far more readily and more cheerfully, to modern energy restraints than had London, for instance, where it had taken an Act of Parliament to reintroduce the public horse trough.

I made my way to the northern end of the street where the police station, the *markaz*, resembling an old British garrison, was guarded by two boys in serge khaki who were armed with the Lee Enfield 303s with which Lawrence had armed his men for the Desert War and which had, then, been an Arab's prized possession. Now it was unlikely any reliable ammunition existed for these antiques. I understood only the crack militia was allowed to sport the old Kalashnikovs or M16s issued to regular infantry. With the end of international arms trading, almost any well-made gun was valuable, if only as status.

I had no appointment and was informed by the bright young civilian woman on the duty desk that Inspector el-Bayoumi would be back from New Town, the concrete development near the airport, in about an hour. I gave my name, my business, and said I would be back at about five-thirty. Courteously she assured me that the Inspector would await me.

4 Her Heart All Ears And Eyes, Lips Catching The Avalanche Of The Golden Ghost

I had forgotten how much time one had to spend on enquiries of this kind. I returned to my apartment to find an envelope pushed under my door. It was not, as I had hoped, from my sister, but a letter welcoming me to Aswan, a short personal note from my friend Georges, a list of appointments with various engineers and officials, some misleading publicity about the dam, consisting mainly of impressive photographs, a variety of press releases stressing the plans for "an even better dam" and so on. I went out again having glanced at them. I was obsessed with all the mysteries with which I had been presented in a single day. How had my sister metamorphosed from a dedicated archaeologist to some kind of local Mother Theresa?

Disturbed by my own speculations I forced myself to think about the next day's work when I would be discussing methods of reducing pollution in all its varieties and rebuilding the dam to allow silt down to the arable areas. The signs of serious "redesertisation", as ugly official jargon termed it, were now found everywhere in the Nile valley. In other words, the Aswan Dam was now seriously contributing to ecological damage as well as helping to wipe out our most important links with the remote past. I could not believe how intelligent scientists, who were not those industrial developers motivated only by greed, failed to accept the dreadful psychic damage being done to people whose whole identities were bound up with a particular and very specific landscape. My own identity, for instance, was profoundly linked to a small Oxfordshire village which had remained unchanged for hundreds of years after successfully resisting developers wanting to surround it with high quality modern properties instead of its existing beeches and oaks.

Few Egyptians were in such comfortable circumstances or could make any choice but the one promising the most immediate benefit, yet they had the same understanding of their tribal homes and what values they represented, and still resisted all attempts to force them to lose their traditional clothes, language and attitudes and make them modern citizens of their semi-democratic society. Unfortunately, this attitude also extended to a dam now much older than many of its staff and never at any time an engineering miracle. UNEC had plans for a replacement. Currently they and the Rajhidi government were arguing over the amounts each would contribute. Happily, that was not my problem.

With a slightly clearer head, I walked to the Post Office on the corner of Abdel el Taheer street. Though almost fifty years had passed since the First Revolution, the building still bore the outlines of earlier royal insignia. The elaborate cast-ironwork on doors and windows was of that "Oriental" pattern exported from the foundries of Birmingham to adorn official buildings throughout the Empire east of Gibraltar. Even by the 1970s the stuff was still available from stock, during the brief period after the death of Britain's imperial age and before the birth of that now much-despised and admittedly reckless Thatcher period known ironically as "the Second Empire", the period which had shaped my own expectations of life as well as those of uncounted millions of my fellows, the period in which my uncle had died, a soldier in the Falklands cause.

I entered the main door's cool archway and walked through dusty shafts of light to a tiled counter where I asked to speak to the Post Master. After a moment's wait I was shown into his little gloomy mahogany office, its massive fan constantly stirring piles of documents which moved like a perpetually unsettled flight of doves. A small, handsome Arab entered and closed the door carefully behind him. His neat, Abraham Lincoln beard suggested religious devotion. I told him that my name was Pappenheim and I was expecting mail. I handed him an envelope I had already prepared. On the outside was my name and occupation. Inside was the conventional "purse"—actually another envelope containing a few pounds. I said I would appreciate his personal interest in my mail and hoped he could ensure it was available to me the moment it arrived. Absently, he took the envelope and put it in his trouser pocket. He had brightened at the sound of my name. "Are you related to that woman of virtue whom we know here in Aswan?" He spoke measured, cultured Arabic with the soft accents of Upper Egypt.

"My sister." I was trying to locate her, I said. Perhaps her mail was delivered here?

"It has not been collected, Si Pappenheim, for several months. Yet she has been seen in Aswan recently. There was a small scandal. I understand that El Haj Sheikh Ibrahim Abu Halil intervened. Have you asked him about your sister?"

"Is he the governor?"

He laughed. Clearly the idea of the governor intervening on behalf of an ordinary member of the public amused him. "No. Sheikh Abu Halil is the gentleman so many come to Aswan to see these days. He is the great Sufi now. We are blessed in this. God sends us everything that is good, even the rain. So much more grows and blooms. People journey to us from all over the world. Here, God has chosen to reveal a glimpse of Paradise."

I was impressed by his optimism. I told him I would go to see Sheikh Abu Halil as soon as possible. Meanwhile I had an appointment with the police chief. At this his face grew a little uncertain, but his only response was some conventional greeting concerning Allah's good offices.

Police Inspector el-Bayoumi was one of those suave career officers produced by the new academies. His manners were perfect, his hospitality generous and discreet, and when I had replied to his question, telling him where I had been born in England, he confessed affectionate familiarity with another nearby Cotswold village. Together, we deplored the damage tourism had done to the environment and confessed it to be a major problem in both our countries, which depended considerably on the very visitors who contributed to the erosion. He sighed. "I think the human race has rather foolishly cancelled many of its options."

Since he preferred to speak it, I replied in English. "Perhaps our imaginative resources are becoming as scarce as our physical ones?"

"There has been a kind of psychic withering," he agreed. "And its worst symptom, in my view, Mr Pappenheim, is found in the religious and political fundamentalism to which so many subscribe. As if, by some sort of sympathetic magic, the old, simpler days will return. We live in complicated times with complicated problems. It's a sad fact that they require sophisticated solutions."

I admitted I had been schooled in many of those fundamentalist notions and sometimes found them difficult to resist. We chatted about this for a while. Coffee was brought, together with a selection of delicious *gurrahiya* pastries, whose secret the Egyptians inherited from the Turks, and we talked for another half-hour, during which time we took each other's measure and agreed the world would be a better place if civilised people like ourselves were allowed a greater voice. Whereupon, in that sometimes abrupt change of tone Arabs have, which can mislead Europeans into thinking they have somehow given offence, Inspector el-Bayoumi asked what he could do for me.

"I'm looking for my sister. She's an economic archaeologist who came here two and a half years ago with the Burbank College Project. It was an international team. Only about half were from California and those returned the next year, after the big earthquake. Most of them, of course, had lost relatives. My sister stayed on with the remaining members." I did not mention her talk of a wonderful discovery out in the Western Sahara. Their sonavids had picked up a New Kingdom temple complex almost perfectly preserved but buried some hundred feet under the sand. My sister had been very excited about it. It was at least on a par with the discovery of the Tutankhamen treasures and probably of far greater historical importance. She and the team kept the discovery quiet, of course, especially since so many known monuments had suffered. Naturally, there were some conflicts of interest. There was little she could tell me in a letter and most of that was a bit vague, making reference to personal or childhood incidents whose relevance escaped me. I added delicately. "You know about the discovery, naturally."

He smiled as he shook his handsome head. "No, Mr Pappenheim, I don't. I think an elaborate dig would not escape my notice." He paused, asking me if he might smoke. I told him I was allergic to cigarette smoke and he put his case away. Regretfully, he said: "I should tell you that your sister is a little disturbed. She was arrested by us about a year ago. There was something we had to follow up. An outbreak of black magic amongst the local people. We don't take such things very seriously until it's possible to detect a cult growing. Then we have to move to break it up as best we can. Such things are not a serious problem in London, but for a policeman in Aswan they are fairly important. We arrested a known witch, a Somali woman they call Madame Zenobia, and with her an Englishwoman, also rumoured to be practising. That was your sister, Mr Pappenheim. She was deranged and had to be given a sedative. Eventually, we decided against charging her and released her into the custody of Lady Roper."

"The Consul's wife?"

"He's the Honorary Consul here in Aswan now. They have a large house on the West Bank, not far from the Ali Khan's tomb. You can't see it from this side. It is our miracle. Locally, it's called the English House. More recently they've called it the Rose House. You'll find no mysteries there!"

"That's where my sister's staying?"

"No longer. She left Aswan for a while. When she came back she joined the community around Sheikh Abu Halil and I understand her to be living in the old holiday villas on the Edfu road, near the race course. I'll gladly put a man to work on the matter. We tend not to pursue people too much in Aswan. Your sister is a good woman. An honest woman. I hope she has recovered herself."

Thanking him I said I hoped my search would not involve the time of a hardworking police officer. I got up to leave. "And what happened to Madame Zenobia?"

"Oh, the courts were pretty lenient. She got a year, doing quarry work for the Restoration Department in Cairo. She was a fit woman. She'll be even fitter now. Hard labour is a wonderful cure for neurosis! And far more socially useful than concocting love potions or aborting cattle."

He sounded like my old headmaster. As an afterthought, I said, "I gather Sheikh Abu Halil took an interest in my sister's case."

He flashed me a look of intelligent humour. "Yes, he did. He is much respected here. Your sister is a healer. The Sufi is a healer. He sometimes makes an accurate prophecy. He has a following all over the world, I believe."

I appreciated his attempt at a neutral tone, given his evident distaste for matters psychic and mystical. We shared, I think, a similar outlook.

I found myself asking him another question. "What was the evidence against my sister, Inspector?"

He had hoped I would not raise the matter, but was prepared for it. "Well," he began slowly, "for instance, we had a witness who saw her passing a large bag of money to the woman. The assumption was that she was paying for a spell. A powerful one. A love philtre, possibly, but it was also said that she wanted a man dead. He was the only other member of her team who had remained behind. There was some suggestion, Mr Pappenheim," he paused again, "that he made her pregnant. But this was all the wildest gossip. He did in fact die of a heart attack shortly after the reported incident. Sometimes we must treat such cases as murder. But we only had circumstantial evidence. The man was a drug addict and apparently had tried to force your sister to give him money. There was just a hint of blackmail involved in the case, you see. These are all, of course, the interpretations of a policeman. Maybe the man had been an ex-lover, no more. Maybe she wanted him to love her again?"

"It wasn't Noone, was it?"

"It was not her estranged husband. He is, I believe, still in New Zealand."

"You really think she got tangled up in black magic?"

"When confused, men turn to war and women to magic. She was not, as the Marrakshim say, with the caravan." He was just a little sardonic now. "But she was adamant that she did not wish to go home."

"What did she tell you?"

"She denied employing the witch. She claimed the Somali woman was her only friend. Otherwise she said little. But her manner was all the time distracted, as if she imagined herself to be surrounded by invisible witnesses. We were not unsympathetic. The psychiatrist from the German hospital came to see her. Your sister is a saintly woman who helped the poor and the sick and asked for no reward. She enriched us. We were trying to help her, you know."

He had lost his insouciance altogether now and spoke with controlled passion. "It could be that your sister had an ordinary breakdown. Too much excitement in her work, too much sun. Caring too much for the hardships of others. She tried to cure the whole town's ills and that task is impossible for any individual. Her burden was too heavy. You could see it written in every line of her face, every movement of her body. We wanted her to recover. Some suspected she was in the witch's power, but in my own view she carried a personal weight of guilt, perhaps. Probably pointlessly, too. You know how women are. They are kinder, more feeling creatures than men."

5 The Seasons Of Home—Aye, Now They Are Remembered!

That evening, while there was still light, I took the felucca across the Nile, to the West Bank. The ferryman, clambering down from his high mast where he had been reefing his sail, directed me through the village to a dirt road winding up the hillside a hundred yards or so from the almost austere resting place of the Ali Khan. "You will see it," he assured me. "But get a boy."

There were a couple of dozen children waiting for me on the quay. I selected a bright looking lad of about ten. He wore a ragged Japanese T-shirt with the inscription I LOVE SEX WAX, a pair of cut-off jeans and Adidas trainers. In spite of the firmness with which I singled him out, we were followed by the rest of the children all the way to the edge of the village. I had a couple of packs of old electronic watches which I handed out, to a pantomime of disappointment from the older children. Watches had ceased to be fashionable currency since I had last been in Aswan. Now, from their requests, I learned it was "real" fountain pens. They showed me a couple of Sheaffers some tourist had already exchanged for their services as guides and companions of the road.

I had no fountain pen for the boy who took me to the top of the hill and pointed down into the little valley where, amongst the sand and the rocks, had been erected a large two-storey house, as solidly Edwardian as any early twentieth century vicarage. Astonishingly, it was planted with cedars, firs and other hardy trees shading a garden to rival anything I had ever seen in Oxfordshire. There were dozens of varieties of roses, of every possible shade, as well as hollyhocks, snapdragons, foxgloves, marigolds and all the flowers one might find in an English July garden. A peculiar wall about a metre high surrounded the entire mirage and I guessed that it disguised some kind of extraordinarily expensive watering and sheltering apparatus which had allowed the owners to do the impossible and bring a little bit of rural England to Upper Egypt. The grounds covered several acres. I saw some stables, a garage, and a woman on the front lawn. She was seated in a faded deckchair watching a fiche-reader or a video which she rested in her left hand. With her right hand she took a glorious drink from the little table beside her and sipped through the straw. As I drew nearer, my vision was obscured by the trees and the wall, but I guessed she was about sixty-five, dressed in a thoroughly unfashionable Marks and Ashley smock, a man's trilby hat and a pair of rubber-tyre sandals. She looked up as I reached the gate and called "good afternoon". Happy with cash, my boy departed.

"Lady Roper?"

She had a quick, intelligent, swarthy face, her curls all grey beneath the hat, her long hands expressive even when still. "I'm Diana Roper."

"My name's Paul Pappenheim. I'm Beatrice's brother."

"The engineer!" She was full of welcome. "My goodness, you know, I think Bea could foretell the future. She *said* you'd be turning up here about now."

"I wrote and told her!" I was laughing as the woman unlocked the gate and let me in. "I knew about this job months ago."

"You're here on business."

"I'm going through the rituals of sorting out a better dam and trying to do something about the climactic changes. I got sent because I know a couple of people here—and because I asked to come. But there's little real point to my being here."

"You don't sound very hopeful, Mr Pappenheim." She led me towards the back of the house, to a white wrought-iron conservatory which was a relatively recent addition to the place and must have been erected by some forgotten imperial dignitary of the last century.

"I'm always hopeful that people will see reason, Lady Roper."

We went into the sweet-smelling ante-room, whose glass had been treated so that it could admit only a certain amount of light, or indeed reflect all the light to perform some needed function elsewhere. Despite its ancient appearance, I guessed the house to be using up-to-date EE technologies and to be completely self-sufficient. "What an extraordinary garden," I said.

"Imported Kent clay." She offered me a white basket chair. "With a fair bit of Kenyan topsoil, I understand. We didn't have it done. We got it all dirt cheap. It takes such a long time to travel anywhere these days most people don't want the place. It belonged to one of the Fayeds, before they all went off to Malaysia. But have you looked carefully at our roses, Mr Pappenheim? They have a sad air to them, a sense of someone departed, someone mourned. Each bush was planted for a dead relative, they say." Her voice grew distant. "Of course, the new rain has helped enormously. I've survived because I know the rules. Women frequently find their intuition very useful in times of social unrest. But things are better now, aren't they? We simply refuse to learn. We refuse to learn."

Grinning as if enjoying a game, a Nubian girl of about sixteen brought us a tray of English cakes and a pot of Assam tea. I wondered how I had lost the thread of Lady Roper's conversation.

"We do our best," I said, letting the girl take tongs to an éclair and with a flourish pop it on my plate. "I believe Bea lived here for a while."

"My husband took quite a fancy to her. As did I. She was a sweetie. And so bright. Is that a family trait? Yes, we shared a great deal. It was a luxury for me, you know, to have such company. Not many people have been privileged as she and I were privileged." She nodded with gentle mystery, her eyes in the past. "We were friends of your uncle. That was the funny thing we found out. All at Cambridge together in the late sixties. We thought conservation an important subject *then*. What? Fifty years ago, almost? Such a jolly boy. He joined up for extremely complicated reasons, we felt. Did you know why?"

I had never really wondered. My picture of my mother's brother was of the kind of person who would decide on a military career, but evidently they had not known that man at all. Finding this disturbing, I attempted to return to my subject. "I was too young to know him. My sister was more curious than I. Did she seem neurotic to you, while she was here?"

"On the contrary. She was the sanest of all of us. Sound as a bell upstairs, as Bernie always said. Sharp intelligence. But, of course, she had been there, you see. And could confirm everything we had been able to piece together at this end."

"You're referring to the site they discovered?"

"That, of course, was crucial. Especially at the early stages. Yes, the site was extraordinary. We went out to see it with her, Bernie and I. What a mind-blower, Paul! Amazing experience. Even the small portion they had excavated. Four mechanical sifters just sucking the sand gradually away. It would have taken years in the old days. Unfortunately three of the operators left after the earthquake and the sifters were recalled for some crucial rescue work over in Sinai. And then, of course, everything changed."

"I'm not sure I'm . . ."

"After the ship came and took Bea."

"A ship? On the Nile?"

She frowned at me for a moment and then her tone changed to one of distant friendliness. "You'll probably want a word with Bernie. You'll find him in his playroom. Nadja will take you. And I'm here if you need to know anything."

She glanced away, through the glass walls of the conservatory and was at once lost in melancholy reflection of the roses and their guardian trees.

6 The Smoke Along The Track

A tape of some antique radio programme was playing as I knocked on the oak door and was admitted by a white-haired old man wearing a pair of overalls and a check shirt, with carpet slippers on his feet. His skin had the healthy sheen of a sun-baked reptile and his blue eyes were brilliant with trust. I was shocked enough to remain where I was, even as he beckoned me in. He turned down his stereo, a replica of some even older audio contraption, and stood proudly to display a room full of books and toys. One wall was lined with glass shelves on which miniature armies battled amidst a wealth of tiny trees and buildings. "You don't look much like a potential playmate!" His eyes strayed towards the brilliant jackets of his books.

"And you're not entirely convincing as Mr Dick, sir." I stood near the books, which were all well-ordered, and admired his illustrated Dickens. The temperature in the room was, I guessed, thoroughly controlled. Should the power fail for just a few hours the desert would fade and modify this room as if it had been a photograph left for an hour in the sun.

My retort seemed to please him. He grinned and came forward. "I'm Bernie Roper. While I have no immediate enemies, I enjoy in this room the bliss of endless childhood. I have my lead soldiers, my bears and rabbits, my model farm, and I read widely. *Treasure Island* is very good, as are the 'William' books, and Edgar Rice Burroughs and, as you say, Charles Dickens, though he's a bit on the scarey side sometimes. E. Nesbit and H. G. Wells and Shaw. I enjoy so much. For music I have the very best of *Children's Favourites* from the BBC—a mixture of comic songs, Gilbert and Sullivan, *Puff the Magic Dragon*, *The Laughing Policeman*, popular classics and light opera. Flanders and Swann, Danny Kaye, *Sparky's Magic Piano*, *Peter and the Wolf* and *Song of the South*. Do you know any of those? But I'm a silly chap! You're far too young. They'd even scrapped *Children's Hour* before you were born. Oh, dear. Never to enjoy *Larry the Lamb* or Norman and Henry Bones, the Boy Detectives! Oh!" he exclaimed with a knowing grin, "Calamity!" Then he returned his attention to his toys for a moment. "You think I should carry more responsibility?"

"No." I had always admired him as a diplomat. He deserved the kind of retirement that suited him.

"I feel sorry for the children," he said. "The pleasures of childhood are denied to more and more of them as their numbers increase. Rajhid and Abu Halil are no real solution, are they? We who remember the Revolution had hoped to have turned the desert green by now. I plan to die here, Mr—?"

"My name's Pappenheim. I'm Bea's brother."

"My boy! Thank goodness I offered an explanation. I'm not nearly as eccentric as I look! 'Because I could not stop for Death, He kindly stopped for me. We shared a carriage, just we two, and Immortality.' Emily Dickinson, I believe. But I could also be misremembering. 'The child is Father to the Man', you know. And the lost childhood of Judas. Did you read all those poems at school?"

"I was probably too young again," I said. "We didn't do poetry as such."

"I'm so sorry. All computer studies nowadays, I suppose."

"Not all, sir." The old-fashioned courtesy surprised us both. Sir Bernard acted as one cheated and I almost apologised. Yet it was probably the first time I had used the form of address without irony. I had, I realised, wanted to show respect. Sir Bernard had come to the same understanding. "Oh, well. You're a kind boy. But you'll forgive me, I hope, if I return to my preferred world."

"I'm looking for my sister, Sir Bernard. Actually, I'm pretty worried about her."

Without irritation, he sighed. "She was a sweet woman. It was terrible. And nobody believing her."

"Believing what, Sir Bernard?"

"About the spaceship, you know. But that's Di's field, really. Not my area of enthusiasm at all. I like to make time stand still. We each have a different way of dealing with the fact of our own mortality, don't we?" He strolled to one of his displays and picked up a charging 17th Lancer. "Into the Valley of Death rode the six hundred."

"Thank you for seeing me, Sir Bernard."

"Not at all, Paul. She talked about you. I liked her. I think you'll find her either attending Abu Halil's peculiar gymnasium or at the holiday homes. Where those Kenyan girls and boys are now living."

"Thank you. Goodbye, sir."

"Bye, bye!" Humming some stirring air, the former Director General of the United Nations hovered, contented, over his miniature Death or Glory Boys.

7 Another Relay In The Chain Of Fire

Lady Roper had remained in her conservatory. She rose as I entered. "Was Bernie able to help?"

"I could be narrowing things down." I was anxious to get back to the East Bank before dark. "Thank you for your kindness. I tried to find a phone number for you."

"We're not on the phone, lovie. We don't need one."

"Sir Bernard mentioned a spaceship." I was not looking forward to her reply.

"Oh, dear, yes," she said "The flying saucer people. I think one day they will bring us peace, don't you? I mean one way or another. This is better than death for me, at any rate, Paul. But perhaps they have a purpose for us. Perhaps an unpleasant one. I don't think anybody would rule that out. What could we do if that were the case? Introduce a spy? That has not proved a successful strategy. We know that much, sadly. It's as if all that's left of Time is here. A few shreds from a few ages."

Again I was completely nonplussed and said nothing.

"I think you share Sir B's streak of pessimism. Or realism is it?"

"Well, we're rather different, actually . . ." I began to feel foolish.

"He was happier as Ambassador, you know. Before the UN. And then we were both content to retire here. We'd always loved it. The Fayeds had us out here lots of times, for those odd parties. We were much younger. You probably think we're both barking mad." When I produced an awkward reply she was sympathetic. "There *is* something happening here. It's a *centre*. You can feel it everywhere. It's an ideal place. Possibly we shall be the ones left to witness the birth of the New Age."

At that moment all I wished to do was save my sister from that atmosphere of half-baked mysticism and desperate faith, to get her back to the relative reality of London and a doctor who would know what was wrong with her and be able to treat it.

"Bea was never happier than when she was in Aswan, you know," said Lady Roper.

"She wrote and told me as much."

"Perhaps she risked a bit more than was wise. We all admire her for it. What I don't understand is why she was so thick with Lallah Zenobia. The woman's psychic, of course, but very unsophisticated."

"You heard about the witness? About the purse?"

"Naturally."

"And you, too, are sure it was a purse?"

"I suppose so. It's Cairo slang, isn't it, for a lot of money? The way the Greeks always say 'seven years' when they mean a long time has passed. Bernie's actually ill, you realise? He's coherent much of the time. A form of P.D. we were told. From the water when we were in Washington. He's determined to make the best of it. He's sweet, isn't he?"

"He's an impressive man. You don't miss England?"

She offered me her hand. "Not a bit. You're always welcome to stay if you are bored over there. Or the carping materialism of the Old Country gets to you. Simplicity's the keynote at the Rose House. Bernie says the

British have been sulking for years, like the Lost Boys deprived of their right to go a-hunting and a-pirating at will. I'm afraid, Paul, that we don't think very much of home any more."

8 And All These In Their Helpless Days . . .

The great Egyptian sun was dropping away to the horizon as in the company of some forty blue-cowled Islamic schoolgirls and a bird-catcher, I sailed back to the East. Reflected in the Nile the sky was the colour of blood and saffron against every tone of dusty blue; the rocks, houses and palms dark violet silhouettes, sparkling here and there as lamps were lit, signalling the start of Aswan's somewhat orderly nightlife. Near the landing stage I ate some *mulakhiya*, rice and an antique salad at Mahommeds' Cafeteria, drank some mint tea and went back to the Osiris, half expecting to find that my sister had left word, but the Hindu woman had no messages and handed me my key with a quick smile of encouragement.

I slept poorly, kept awake by the constant cracking of a chemical "equaliser" in the basement and the creak of the all-but-useless wind-generator on the roof. It was ironic that Aswan, so close to the source of enormous quantities of electricity, was as cruelly rationed as everyone.

I refused to believe that my sister, who was as sane as I was and twice as intelligent, had become entangled with a black magic flying saucer cult. Her only purpose for associating with such people would be curiosity, perhaps in pursuit of some anthropological research connected with her work. I was, however, puzzled by her secrecy. Clearly, she was deliberately hiding her whereabouts. I hoped that, when I returned the next day, I would know where she was.

My meetings were predictably amiable and inconsequential. I had arrived a little late, having failed to anticipate the levels of security at the dam. There were police, militia and security people everywhere, both on the dam itself and in all the offices and operations areas. I had to show my pass to eleven different people. The dam was under increased threat from at least three different organisations, the chief being Green Jihad. Our main meetings were held in a large, glass-walled room overlooking the lake. I was glad to meet so many staff, though we all knew that any decisions about the dam would not be made by us but by whomever triumphed in the Geneva negotiations. It was also good to discover that earlier attitudes towards the dam were changing slightly and new thinking was being done. Breakfasted and lunched, I next found myself guest of honour at a full-scale Egyptian dinner which must have taken everyone's rations for a month, involved several entertainments and lastly a good deal of noisy toasting, in cokes and grape juice, our various unadmired leaders.

At the Hotel Osiris, when I got back that night, there was no note for me so I decided next day to visit the old vacation villas before lunching as arranged at the Cataract with Georges Abidos, who had told me that he was retiring as Public Relations officer for the dam. I had a hunch that my sister was probably living with the neo-hippies. The following morning I ordered a calash to pick me up and sat on the board beside the skinny, cheerful driver as his equally thin horse picked her way slowly through busy Saturday streets until we were on the long, cracked concrete road with the railway yards on one side and the river on the other, flanked by dusty palms, which led past the five-storey Moorish-style vacation complex, a tumble of typical tourist architecture of the kind once found all around the Mediterranean, Adriatic and parts of the Black and Red Seas. The white stucco was patchy and the turquoise trim on window-frames and doors was peeling, but the new in-habitants, who had occupied it when the Swedish owners finally abandoned it, had put their stamp on it. Originally the place had been designed for Club Med, but had never sustained the required turnover, even with its special energy dispensations, and had been sold several times over the past ten years. Now garishly-dressed young squatters from the wealthy African countries, from the Australias, North and South America, as well as Europe and the Far East, had covered the old complex with their sometimes im-pressive murals and decorative, computer-sprayed graffiti. I read a variety of slogans. LET THE BLOOD CONSUME THE FIRE, said one. THE TYGERS OF THE MIND RULE THE JUNGLE OF THE HEART, said another. I had no relish for such undisciplined nonsense and did not look forward to meeting the occupants of this bizarre New New Age fortress. Psychedelia, even in its historical context, had never attracted me.

As I dismounted from the calash I was greeted by a young woman ener-getically cleaning the old Club Med brass plate at the gate. She had those startling green eyes in a dark olive skin which one frequently comes across everywhere in Egypt and are commonly believed to be another inheritance from the Pharaonic past. Her reddish hair was braided with multi-coloured ribbons and she wore a long green silk smock which complemented her eyes.

"Hi!" Her manner was promiscuously friendly. "I'm Lips. Which is short for Eclipse, to answer your question. Don't get the wrong idea. You're here to find a relative, right?" Her accent was Canadian with a trace of something else, possibly Ukrainian. "What's your name?"

"Paul," I said, "My sister's called Bea. Are the only people who visit you trying to find relatives?"

"I just made an assumption from the way you look. I'm pretty good at sussing people out." Then she made a noise of approving excitement. "Bea Palestine, is it? She's famous here. She's a healer and an oracle. She's special."

"Could you take me to her apartment?" I did my best not to show impatience with the girl's nonsense.

"Lips" answered me with a baffled smile. "No. I mean, sure I could take you to one of her rooms. But she's not here now."

"Do you know where she went?"

The girl was vaguely apologetic. "Mercury? Wherever the ship goes."

My irritation grew more intense. But I controlled myself. "You've no idea when the ship gets back?"

"Now? Yesterday? There's so much time-bending involved. No. You just have to hope."

I walked past her into the complex.

9 Fast Closing Toward The Undelighted Night . . .

By the time I had spoken to a dozen or so *enfants des fleurs* I had found myself a guide who introduced himself as Magic Mungo and wore brilliant face-paint beneath his straw hat. He had on an old pair of glitterjeans which whispered and flashed as he walked. His jacket announced in calligraphic Arabic phonetic English: THE NAME IS THE GAME. He was probably no older than thirteen. He asked me what I did and when I told him he said he, too, planned to become an engineer "and bring back the power." This amused me and restored my temper. "And what will you do about the weather?" I asked.

"It's not the weather," he told me, "not Nature—it's the ships. And it's not the dam, or the lake, that's causing the storms and stuff. It's the Reens."

I misheard him. I thought he was blaming the Greens. Then I realised, belatedly, that he was expressing a popular notion amongst the New New Agers which by the time I had heard it several times more had actually begun to improve my mood. The Reens, the flying saucer people, were used by the hippies as an explanation for everything they couldn't understand. In rejecting Science, they had substituted only a banal myth. Essentially, I was being told that the Gods had taken my sister. In other words they did not know where she was. At last, after several further short but keen conversations, in various rug-strewn galleries and cushion-heavy chambers smelling strongly of kif, incense and patchouli, I met a somewhat older woman, with grey streaks in her long black hair and a face the colour and texture of well-preserved leather.

"This is Ayesha." Mungo gulped comically. "She-who-must-be-obeyed!" He ran to the woman who smiled a perfectly ordinary smile as she embraced him. "We encourage their imaginations," she said. "They read books here and everything. Are you looking for Bea?"

Warily expecting more Reen talk, I admitted that I was trying to find my sister.

"She went back to Aswan. I think she was at the medrassah for a bit— you know, with the Sufi—but after that she returned to town. If she's not there, she's in the desert again. She goes there to meditate, I'm told. If she's not there, she's not anywhere. Around here, I mean."

I was relieved by the straightforward nature of her answer. "I'm greatly obliged. I thought you, too, were going to tell me she was taken into space by aliens!"

Ayesha joined in my amusement. "Oh, no, of course not. That was more than a year ago!"

10 Thoughts Of Too Old A Colour Nurse My Brain

I decided to have a note delivered to the Sufi, El Haj Ibrahim Abu Halil, telling him that I planned to visit him next day, then, with a little time to spare before my appointment, I strolled up the corniche, past the boat-ghetto at the upper end, and along the more fashionable stretches where some sporadic attempt was made to give the railings fresh coats of white paint and where a kiosk, closed since my first time here, advertised in bleached Latin type the *Daily Telegraph*, *Le Monde* and the *New York Herald-Tribune*. A few thin strands of white smoke rose from the villages on Elephantine Island, and from *Gazirat-al-Bustan*, Plantation Island, whose botanical gardens, begun by Lord Kitchener, had long since become a marvellously exotic jungle, came the laughter of the children and teenagers who habitually spent their free days there.

Outside the kiosk stood an old man holding a bunch of faded and ragged international newspapers under one arm and *El Misr* under the other. "All today!" he called vigorously in English, much as a London coster shouted "All fresh!" A professional cry rather than any sort of promise. I bought an *El Misr*, only a day old, and glanced at the headlines as I walked up to the park. There seemed nothing unusually alarming in the paper. Even the EC rate had not risen in the last month. As I tried to open the sheet a gust came off the river and the yellow-grey paper began to shred in my hands. It was low-density recyke, unbulked by the sophisticated methods of the West. Before I gave up and dumped the crumpled mess into the nearest reclamation bin I had glimpsed references to the UNEC conference in Madagascar and

279

something about examples of mass hysteria in Old Paris and Bombay, where a group called *Reincarnation* was claiming its leader to be a newly-born John Lennon. There were now about as many reincarnated Lennons abroad as there had been freshly-risen Christs in the early Middle Ages.

I stopped in the park to watch the gardeners carefully tending the unsweet soil of the flower-beds, coaxing marigolds and nasturtiums to bloom at least for a few days in the winter, when the sun would not burn them immediately as they emerged. The little municipal café was unchanged since British days and still served only icecreams, tea, coffee or soft-drinks, all of them made with non-rationed ingredients and all equally tasteless. Pigeons wandered hopelessly amongst the debris left by customers, occasionally pecking at a piece of wrapping or a sliver of *Sustenance* left behind by some poor devil who had been unable to force his stomach to accept the high-concentrate nutrients we had developed at UNEC for his benefit.

The Cataract's entrance was between pillars which, once stately, Egyptianate and unquestionably European, were now a little the worse for wear, though the gardens on both sides of the drive were heavy with freshly-planted flowers. Bougainvilleas of every brilliant variety covered walls behind avenues of palms leading to a main building the colour of Nile clay, its shutters and ironwork a dark, dignified green, the kind of colour Cook himself would have picked to represent the security and solid good service which established him as one of the Empire's noblest champions.

I walked into the great lobby cooled by massive carved mahogany punkahs worked on hidden ropes by screened boys. Egypt had had little trouble implementing many of the UN's mandatory energy-saving regulations. She had either carried on as always or had returned, perhaps even with relief, to the days before electricity and gas had become the necessities rather than the luxuries of life.

I crossed the lobby to the wooden verandah where we were to lunch. Georges Abidos was already at our table by the rail looking directly over the empty swimming pool and, beyond that, to the river itself. He was drinking a cup of Lipton's tea and I remarked on it, pointing to the label on the string dangling from his tiny metal pot. "Indeed!" he said. "At ten pounds the pot why shouldn't the Cataract offer us Lipton's, at least!" He dropped his voice. "Though my guess is the teabag has seen more than one customer through the day's heat. Would you like a cup?"

I refused. He hadn't, I said, exactly sold me on the idea. He laughed. He was a small, attractively ugly Greek from Alexandria. Since the flooding, he had been driven, like so many of his fellow citizens to seek work inland. At least half the city had not been thought worth saving as the sea-level had steadily risen to cover it.

"Can't you," he asked, "get your American friends to do something about this new embargo? One misses the cigarettes and I could dearly use a new John B." He indicated his stained Planter's straw and then picked it up to show me the label on the mottled sweatband so that I might verify it was a genuine product of the Stetson Hat Co. of New Jersey. "Size seven and a quarter. But don't get anything here. The Cairo fakes are very close. Very good. But they can't fake the finish, you see."

"I'll remember," I promised. I would send him a Stetson next time I was in the USA.

I felt we had actually conducted our main business before we sat down. The rest of the lunch would be a social affair with someone I had known both professionally and as a close personal acquaintance for many years.

As our mixed *hors d'oeuvres* arrived, Georges Abidos looked with a despairing movement of his mouth out towards the river. "Well, Paul, have you solved any of our problems?"

"I doubt it," I said. "That's all going on in Majunga now. I'm wondering if my function isn't as some kind of minor smokescreen."

"I thought you'd volunteered."

"Only when they'd decided that one of us had to come. It was a good chance, I thought, to see how my sister was. I had spare relative allowance and lots of energy and travel owing, so I got her a flight out with me. It took forever! But I grew rather worried. The last note I had from her was three months ago and very disjointed. It didn't tell me anything. I'd guessed that her husband had turned up. It was something she said. That's about all I know which would frighten her that much. My mistake, it's emerged. Then I wondered if she wasn't pregnant. I couldn't make head or tail of her letters. They weren't like her at all."

"Women are a trial," said Georges Abidos. "My own sister has divorced, I heard. But then," as if to explain it, "they moved to Kuwait." He turned his eyes back to the river which seemed almost to obsess him. "Look at the Nile. An open sewer running through a desert. What has Egypt done to deserve rescue? She gave the world the ancestors who first offered Nature a serious challenge. Should we be grateful for that? From Lake Nasser to Alexandria the river remains undrinkable and frequently unusable. She once replenished the Earth. Now, what with their fertilisers and sprays, she helps poison it." It was as if all the doubts he had kept to himself as a publicity officer were now being allowed to emerge. "I listen to Blue Danube Radio from Vienna. The English station there. It's so much more reliable than the World Service. We are still doing less than we could, they say, here in Egypt."

The tables around us had begun to fill with Saudis and wealthy French people in fashionable silk shifts, and the noise level rose so that it was hard for me to hear my acquaintance's soft tones.

We discussed the changing nature of Aswan. He said he would be glad to get back to Cairo where he had a new job with the Antiquities Department raising money for specific restoration or reconstruction projects.

We had met at the re-opening of the Cairo Opera House in 1989, which had featured the Houston Opera Company's *Porgy and Bess*, but had never become more than casual friends, though we shared many musical tastes and he had an extraordinary knowledge of modern fiction in English. His enthusiasm was for the older writers like Gilchrist or DeLillo, who had been amongst my own favourites at College.

We were brought some wonderfully tasty Grönburgers and I remarked that the cuisine had improved since I was last here. "French management," he told me. "They have one of the best teams outside of Paris. They all came from Nice after the troubles. Lucky for us. I might almost be tempted to stay! Oh, no! I could not. Even for that! Nubian music is an abomination!"

I told him about my sister, how I was unable to find her and how I was beginning to fear the worst. "The police suggested she was mad."

Georges was dismissive of this. "A dangerous assumption at any time, Paul, but especially these days. And very difficult for us to define here, in Egypt, just as justice is at once a more brutal and a subtler instrument in our interpretation. We never accepted, thank God, the conventional wisdoms of psychiatry. And madness here, as elsewhere, is defined by the people in power, usually calling themselves the State. Tomorrow those power holders could be overthrown by a fresh dynasty and what was yesterday simple common sense today becomes irresponsible folly. So I do not like to make hasty judgements or pronounce readily on others' moral or mental condition—lest, indeed, we inadvertently condemn ourselves." He paused. "They say this was not so under the British, that it was fairer, more predictable. Only real troublemakers and criminals went to jail. Now it isn't as bad as it was when I was a lad. Then anyone was liable to arrest. If it was better under the British, then that is our shame." And he lowered his lips to his wineglass.

We had slipped, almost automatically, into discussing the old, familiar topics. "It's sometimes argued," I said, "that the liberal democracies actually stopped the flow of history. A few hundred years earlier, as feudal states, we would have forcibly Christianised the whole of Islam and changed the entire nature of the planet's power struggle. Indeed, all the more childish struggles might have been well and truly over by now!"

"Or it might have gone the other way," Georges suggested dryly, "if the Moors had reconquered France and Northern Europe. After all, Islam did not bring the world to near-ruin. What has the European way achieved except the threat of death for all?"

I could not accept an argument which had already led to massive conversions to Islam amongst the youth of Europe, America and Democratic Africa, representing a sizeable proportion of the vote. This phenomenon had, admittedly, improved the tenor of world politics, but I still deplored it.

"Oh, you're so thoroughly out of step, my friend." Georges Abidos smiled and patted my arm. "The world's changing!"

"It'll die if we start resorting to mystical Islamic solutions."

"Possibly." He seemed unconcerned. I think he believed us unsaveable.

A little drunk, I let him take me back to the Osiris in a calash. He talked affectionately of our good times, of concerts and plays we had seen in the world's capitals before civilian flight had become so impossibly expensive, of the Gilbert and Sullivan season we had attended in Bangkok, of Wagner in Bayreuth and Britten in Glyndebourne. We hummed a snatch from *Iolanthe* before we parted.

When I got up to my room all the shutters had been drawn back to give the apartment the best of the light. I recognised the subtle perfume even as my sister came out of the bathroom to laugh aloud at my astonishment.

11 Saw Life To Be A Sea Green Dream

Beatrice had cut her auburn hair short and her skin was paler than I remembered. While her blue eyes and red lips remained striking, she had gained an extra beauty. I was overjoyed. This was the opposite of what I had feared to find.

As if she read my mind, she smiled. "Were you expecting the Mad Woman of Aswan?" She wore a light blue cotton skirt and a darker blue shirt.

"You've never looked better." I spoke the honest truth.

She took both my hands in hers and kissed me. "I'm sorry I didn't write. It began to seem such a sham. I *couldn't* write for a while. I got your letters today, when I went to the post office. What a coincidence, I thought—my first sally into the real world and here comes good old Paul to help me. If anyone understands reality, you do."

I was flattered and grinned in the way I had always responded to her half-mocking praise. "Well, I'm here to take you back to it, if you want to go. I've got a pass for you on the Cairo plane in four days' time, and from there we can go to Geneva or London or anywhere in the Community."

"That's marvellous," she said. She looked about my shabby sitting room with its cracked foam cushions, its stained tiles. "Is this the best you get at your rank?"

"This is the best for any rank, these days. Most of us don't travel at all and certainly not by plane."

"The schoomers are still going out of Alex, are they?"

"Oh, yes. To Genoa, some of them. Who has the time?"

"That's what I'd thought of, for me. But here you are! What a bit of luck!"

I was immensely relieved. "Oh, Bea. I thought you might be dead—you know, or worse."

"I was selfish not to keep you in touch, but for a while, of course, I couldn't. Then I was out there for so long . . ."

"At your dig, you mean?"

She seemed momentarily surprised, as if she had not expected me to know about the dig. "Yes, where the dig was. That's right. I can't remember what I said in my letters."

"That you'd made a terrific discovery and that I must come out the first chance I got. Well, I did. This really was the first chance. Am I too late? Have they closed down the project completely? Are you out of funds?"

"Yes," she smiled. "You're too late, Paul. I'm awfully sorry. You must think I brought you on a wild goose chase."

"Nonsense. That wasn't why I really came. Good Lord, Bea, I care a lot for you!" I stopped, a little ashamed. She was probably in a more delicate condition than she permitted me to see. "And, anyway, I had some perks coming. It's lovely here, still, isn't it? If you ignore the rubbish tips. You know, and the sewage. And the Nile!" We laughed together. "And the rain and the air," she said. "And the sunlight! Oh, Paul! What if this really is the future?"

12 A Man In The Night Flaking Tombstones

She asked if I would like to take a drive with her beside the evening river and I agreed at once. I was her senior by a year but she had always been the leader, the initiator and I admired her as much as ever.

We went up past the ruins of the Best Western and the Ramada Inn, the only casualties of a shelling attack in '02, when the Green Jihad had attempted to hole the dam and six women had died. We stopped near the abandoned museum and bought a drink from the ice-stall. As I turned, looking out at the river, I saw the new moon, huge and orange, in the cloudless night. A few desultory mosquitoes hung around our heads and were easily fanned away as we continued up the corniche, looking out at the lights from the boats, the flares on the far side, the palms waving in the soft breeze from the North.

"I'm quitting my job," she said. "I resigned, in fact, months ago. I had a few things to clear up."

"What will you do? Get something in London?"

"Well, I've my money. That was invested very sensibly by Jack before our problems started. Before we split up. And I can do freelance work." Clearly, she was unwilling to discuss the details. "I could go on living here."

"Do you want to?"

"No," she said. "I hate it now. But is the rest of the world any better, Paul?"

"Oh, life's still a bit easier in England. And Italy's all right. And Scandinavia, of course, but that's closed off, as far as residency's concerned. The population's dropping quite nicely in Western Europe. Not everything's awful. The winters are easier."

She nodded slowly as if she were carefully noting each observation. "Well," she said, "anyway, I don't know about Aswan. I'm not sure there's much point in my leaving Egypt. I have a permanent visa, you know."

"Why stay, Bea?"

"Oh, well," she said, "I suppose it feels like home. How's daddy? Is everything all right in Marrakesh?"

"Couldn't be better, I gather. He's having a wonderful time. You know how happy he always was there. And with the new government! Well, you can imagine."

"And mother?"

"Still in London. She has a house to herself in West Hampstead. Don't ask me how. She's installed the latest EE generators and energy storers. She's got a TV set, a pet option and a gas licence. You know mother. She's always had the right contacts. She'll be glad to know you're OK."

"Yes. That's good, too. I've been guilty of some awfully selfish behaviour, haven't I? Well, I'm putting all that behind me and getting on with my life."

"You sound as if you've seen someone. About whatever it was. Have you been ill, Bea?"

"Oh, no. No. Not really." She turned to reassure me with a quick smile and a hand out to mine, just as always. I nearly sang with relief. "Emotional trouble, you know."

"A boyfriend?"

"Well, yes, I suppose so. Anyway, it's over."

"All the hippies told me you'd been abducted by a flying saucer!"

"Did they?"

I recognised her brave smile. "What's wrong? I hadn't meant to be tactless."

"You weren't. There are so many strange things happening around here. You can't blame people for getting superstitious, can you? After all, we say we've identified the causes, yet can do virtually nothing to find a cure."

"Well, I must admit there's some truth in that. But there are still things we can do."

"Of course there are. I didn't mean to be pessimistic, old Paul." She punched me on the arm and told the driver to let his horse trot for a bit, to get us some air on our faces, since the wind had dropped so suddenly.

She told me she would come to see me at the same time tomorrow and perhaps after that we might go to her new flat. It was only a temporary place while she made up her mind. Why didn't I just go to her there? I said. Because, she said, it was in a maze. You couldn't get a calash through and even the schoolboys would sometimes mislead you by accident. Write it down, I suggested, but she refused with an even broader smile. "You'll see I'm right. I'll take you there tomorrow. There's no mystery. Nothing deliberate."

I went back into the damp, semi-darkness of the Osiris and climbed through black archways to my rooms.

13 You'll Find No Mirrors In That Cold Abode

I had meant to ask Beatrice about her experience with the Somali woman and the police, but her mood had swung so radically I had decided to keep the rest of the conversation as casual as possible. I went to bed at once more hopeful and more baffled than I had been before I left Cairo.

In the morning I took a cab to the religious academy, or *madrassah*, of the famous Sufi, El Haj Sheik Ibrahim Abu Halil, not because I now needed his help in finding my sister, but because I felt it would have been rude to cancel my visit without explanation. The *madrassah* was out near the old obelisk quarries. Characteristically Moslem, with a tower and a domed mosque, it was reached on foot or by donkey, up a winding, artificial track that had been there for at least two thousand years. I climbed to the top, feeling a little dizzy as I avoided looking directly down into the ancient quarry and saw that the place was built as a series of stone colonnades around a great courtyard with a fountain in it. The fountain, in accordance with the law, was silent.

The place was larger than I had expected and far more casual. People, many obviously drugged, of every age and race sat in groups or strolled around the cloisters. I asked a pale young woman in an Islamic *burqa* where I might find Sheikh Abu Halil. She told me to go to the office and led me as far as a glass door through which I saw an ordinary business layout of pens and paper, mechanical typewriters, acoustic calculators and, impressively, an EMARGY console. I felt as if I were prying. My first job, from which I had resigned, was as an Energy Officer. Essentially the work involved too much peeping-tomism and too little real progress.

A young black man in flared Mouwes and an Afghan jerkin signalled for me to enter. I told him my business and he said, "No problem, man." He asked me to wait in a little room furnished like something still found in any South London dentist's. Even the magazines looked familiar and I did not intend to waste my battery ration plugging in to one. A few minutes later the young man returned and I was escorted through antiseptic corridors to the Sufi's inner sanctum.

I had expected some rather austere sort of Holy Roller's Executive Suite, and was a trifle shocked by the actuality which resembled a scene from *The Arabian Nights*. The Sufi was clearly not celibate, and was an epicurean rather than an aescetic. He was also younger than I had expected. I guessed he was no more than forty-five. Dressed in red silks of a dozen shades, with a massive scarlet turban on his head, he lay on cushions smoking from a silver and brass hookah while behind him on rich, spangled divans, lolled half-a-dozen young women, all of them veiled, all looking at me with frank, if discreet, interest. I felt as if I should apologise for intruding on someone's private sexual fantasy, but the Sufi grinned, beckoned me in, then fell to laughing aloud as he stared into my face. All this, of course, only increased my discomfort. I could see no reason for his amusement.

"You think this a banal piece of play-acting?" He at once became solicitious. "Pardon me, *Herr Doktor*. I misunderstood your expression for a moment. I thought you were an old friend." Now he was almost grave. "How can I help you?"

"Originally," I said, "I was looking for my sister Beatrice. I believe you know her." Was this my sister's secret? Had she involved herself with a charismatic charlatan to whom even I felt drawn? But the banality of it all! True madness, like true evil, I had been informed once, was always characterised by its banality.

"That's it, of course. Bea Porcupine was the name the young ones used. She is a very good friend of mine. Are you looking for her no longer, Dr Porcupine?"

I pointed out that Pappenheim was the family name. The hippies had not made an enormously imaginative leap.

"Oh, the children! Don't they love to play? They are blessed. Think how few of us in the world are allowed by God to play."

"Thou art most tolerant indeed, sidhi." I used my best classical Arabic, at which he gave me a look of considerable approval and addressed me in the same way.

"Doth God not teach us to tolerate, but not to imitate, all the ways of mankind? Are we to judge God, my compatriot?" He had done me the honour, in his own eyes, of addressing me as a coreligionist. When he smiled again his expression was one of benign happiness. "Would you care for some coffee?" he asked in educated English. "Some cakes and so on?

Yes, of course." And he clapped his hands, whispering instructions to the nearest woman who rose and left. I was so thoroughly discomforted by this outrageously old-fashioned sexism which, whatever their private practices, few sophisticated modern Arabs were willing to admit to, that I remained silent.

"And I trust that you in turn will tolerate my stupid self-indulgence," he said. "It is a whim of mine—and these young women—to lead the life of Haroun-el-Raschid, eh? Or the great chiefs who ruled in the days before the Prophet. We are all nostalgic for that, in Egypt. The past, you know, is our only escape. You don't begrudge it us, do you?"

I shook my head, although by training and temperament I could find no merit in his argument. "These are changing times," I said. "Your past is crumbling away. It's difficult to tell good from evil or right from wrong, let alone shades of intellectual preference."

"But I can tell you really do still think there are mechanical solutions to our ills."

"Don't you, sidhi?"

"I do. I doubt though that they're much like a medical man's."

"I'm an engineer, not a doctor of medicine."

"Pardon me. It's my day for gaffs, eh? But we're all guilty of making the wrong assumptions sometimes. Let us open the shutters and enjoy some fresh air." Another of the women went to fold back the tall wooden blinds and let shafts of sudden sunlight down upon the maroons, burgundies, dark pinks, bottle-greens and royal blues of that luxurious room. The women sank into the shadows and only Sheik Abu Halil remained with half his face in light, the other in shade, puffing on his pipe, his silks rippling as he moved a lazy hand. "We are blessed with a marvellous view."

From where we sat it was possible to see the Nile, with its white sails and flanking palms, on the far side of an expanse of glaring granite.

"My sister—" I began.

"A remarkable woman. A saint, without doubt. We have tried to help her, you know."

"I believe you're responsible for getting her out of police custody, sidhi."

"God has chosen her and has blessed her with unusual gifts. Dr Pappenheim, we are merely God's instruments. She has brought a little relief to the sick, a little consolation to the despairing."

"She's coming home with me. In three days."

"A great loss for Aswan. But perhaps she's more needed out there. Such sadness, you know. Such deep sadness." I was not sure if he described my sister or the whole world. "In Islam, you see," an ironic twitch of the lip, "we share our despair. It is a democracy of misery." And he chuckled. "This is blasphemy I know, in the West. Especially in America."

"Well, in parts of the North maybe." I smiled. My father was from Mississippi and settled first in Morocco, then in England after he came out of the service. He said he missed the old, bitter-sweet character of the U.S. South. The New South, optimistic and, in his view, Yankified, no longer felt like home. He was more in his element in pre-Thatcher Britain. When she, too, began a programme of "Yankification" of her own he retreated into fantasy, leaving my mother and going to live in a working class street in a run-down North Eastern town where he joined the Communist Party and demonstrated against closures in the mining, fishing and steel industries. My mother hated it when his name appeared in the papers or, worse in her view, when he wrote intemperate letters to the weekly journals or the heavy dailies. But Pappenheim was a contributor to *Marxism Today* and, later, *Red is Green* during his brief flirtation with Trotskyist Conservationism. He gave that up for anarcho-socialism and disappeared completely into the world of the abstract. He now wrote me letters describing the "Moroccan experiment" as the greatest example of genuinely radical politics in action. I had never completely escaped the tyranny of his impossible ideals. This came back to me, there and then, perhaps because in some strange way I found this sufi as charming as I had once found my father. "We say that misery loves company. Is that the same thing?" I felt I was in some kind of awful contest. "Is that why she wanted to stay with you?"

"I knew her slightly before it all changed for her. Afterwards, I knew her better. She seemed very delicate. She came back to Aswan, then went out to the dig a couple more times, then back here. She was possessed of a terrible restlessness she would allow nobody here to address and which she consistently denied. She carried a burden, Dr Pappenheim." He echoed the words of Inspector el-Bayoumi. "But perhaps we, even we, shall never know what it was."

14 On Every Hand—The Red Collusive Stain

She arrived at the Osiris only a minute or two late. She wore a one-piece worksuit and a kind of bush-hat with a veil. She also carried a briefcase which she displayed in some embarrassment. "Habit, I suppose. I don't need the maps or the notes. I'm taking you into the desert, Paul. Is that OK?"

"We're not going to your place?"

"Not now."

I changed into more suitable clothes and followed her down to the street. She had a calash waiting which took us to the edge of town, to a camel camp where, much to my dismay, we transferred to grumbling dromedaries.

I had not ridden a camel for ten years, but mine proved fairly tractable once we were moving out over the sand.

I had forgotten the peace and the wonderful smell of the desert and it was not long before I had ceased to pay attention to the heat or the motion and had begun to enjoy a mesmeric panorama of dunes and old rock. My sister occasionally used a compass to keep course but sat her high saddle with the confidence of a seasoned drover. We picked up speed until the heat became too intense and we rested under an outcrop of red stone which offered the only shade. It was almost impossible to predict where one would find shade in the desert. A year ago this rock might have been completely invisible beneath the sand; in a few months it might be invisible again.

"The silence is seductive," I said after a while.

My sister smiled. "Well, it whispers to me, these days. But it is wonderful, isn't it? Here you have nothing but yourself, a chance to discover how much of your identity is your own and how much is actually society's. And the ego drifts away. One becomes a virgin beast."

"Indeed!" I found this a little too fanciful for me. "I'm just glad to be away from all that . . ."

"You're not nervous?"

"Of the desert?"

"Of getting lost. Nothing comes out here, ever, now. Nomads don't pass by and it's been years since a motor vehicle or plane was allowed to waste its ER on mere curiosity. If we died, we'd probably never be found."

"This is a bit morbid, isn't it, Bea? It's only a few hours from Aswan, and the camels are healthy."

"Yes." She rose to put our food and water back into their saddlebags, causing a murmuring and an irritable shifting of the camels. We slept for a couple of hours. Bea wanted to be able to travel at night, when we would make better time under the almost full moon.

The desert at night will usually fill with the noises of the creatures who waken as soon as the sun is down, but the region we next entered seemed as lifeless as the Bical flats, though without their aching mood of desolation. The sand still rose around our camels' feet in silvery gasps and I wrapped myself in the other heavy woollen *gelabea* Beatrice had brought. We slept again, for two or three hours, before continuing on until it was almost dawn and the moon faint and fading in the sky.

"We used to have a gramophone and everything," she said. "We played those French songs mainly. The old ones. And a lot of classic Rai. It was a local collection someone had bought with the machine. You wouldn't believe the mood of camaraderie that was here, Paul. Like Woodstock must have been. We had quite a few young people with us—Egyptian and European mostly—and they all said the same. We felt privileged."

"When did you start treating the sick?" I asked her.

"Treating? Scarcely that! I just helped out with my First Aid kit and whatever I could scrounge from a pharmacy. Most of the problems were easily treated, but not priorities as far as the hospitals are concerned. I did what I could whenever I was in Aswan. But the kits gradually got used and nothing more was sent. After the quake, things began to run down. The Burbank Foundation needed its resources for rebuilding at home."

"But you still do it. Sometimes. You're a legend back there. Ben Achmet told me."

"When I can, I help those nomads cure themselves, that's all. I was coming out here a lot. Then there was some trouble with the police."

"They stopped you? Because of the Somali woman?"

"That didn't stop me." She raised herself in her saddle suddenly. "Look. Can you see the roof there? And the pillars?"

They lay in a shallow valley between two rocky cliffs and they looked in the half-light as if they had been built that very morning. The decorated columns and the massive flat roof were touched a pinkish gold by the rising sun and I could make out hieroglyphics, the blues and ochres of the Egyptian artist. The building, or series of buildings, covered a vast area. "It's a city," I said. I was still disbelieving. "Or a huge temple. My God, Bea! No wonder you were knocked out by this!"

"It's not a city or a temple, in any sense *we* mean." Though she must have seen it a hundred times, she was still admiring of the beautiful stones. "There's nothing like it surviving anywhere else. No record of another. Even this is only briefly mentioned and, as always with Egyptians, dismissively as the work of earlier, less exalted leaders, in this case a monotheistic cult which attempted to set up its own God-king and, in failing, was thoroughly destroyed. Pragmatically, the winners in that contest re-dedicated the place to Sekhmet and then, for whatever reasons—probably economic—abandoned it altogether. There are none of the usual signs of later uses. By the end of Nyusere's reign no more was heard of it at all. Indeed, not much more was heard of Nubia for a long time. This region was never exactly the centre of Egyptian life."

"It was a temple to Ra?"

"Ra, or a sun deity very much like him. The priest here was represented as a servant of the sun. We call the place Onu'us, after him."

"Four thousand years ago? Are you sure this isn't one of those new Dutch repros?" My joke sounded flat, even to me.

"Now you can see why we kept it dark, Paul. It was an observatory, a scientific centre, a laboratory, a library. A sort of university, really. Even the hieroglyphics are different. They tell all kinds of things about the people and the place. And, it had a couple of other functions." Her enthusiasm died and she stopped, dismounting from her camel and shaking sand from her hat. Together we watched the dawn come up over the glittering roof. The pillars, shadowed now, stood only a few feet out of the sand, yet the brilliance of the colour was almost unbelievable. Here was the classic language of the 5th Dynasty, spare, accurate, clean. And it was obvious that the whole place had only recently been refilled. Elsewhere churned, powdery earth and overturned rock spoke of vigorous activity by the discovering team; there was also, on the plain which stretched away from the Southern ridge, a considerable area of fused sand. But even this was now covered by that desert tide which would soon bury again and preserve this uncanny relic.

"You tried to put the sand back?" I felt stupid and smiled at myself.

"It's all we could think of in the circumstances. Now it's far less visible than it was a month ago."

"You sound very proprietorial." I was amused that the mystery should prove to have so obvious a solution. My sister had simply become absorbed in her work. It was understandable that she should.

"I'm sorry," she said. "I must admit . . ."

For a moment, lost in the profound beauty of the vision, I did not realise she was crying. Just as I had as a little boy, I moved to comfort her, having no notion at all of the cause of her grief, but assuming, I suppose, that she was mourning the death of an important piece of research, the loss of her colleagues, the sheer disappointment at this unlucky end to a wonderful adventure. It was plain, too, that she was completely exhausted.

She drew towards me, smiling an apology. "I want to tell you everything, Paul. And only you. When I have, that'll be it. I'll never mention it again. I'll get on with some sort of life. I'm sick of myself at the moment."

"Bea. You're very tired. Let's go home to Europe where I can coddle you for a bit."

"Perhaps," she said. She paused as the swiftly risen sun outlined sunken buildings and revealed more of a structure lying just below the surface, some dormant juggernaut.

"It's monstrous," I said. "It's the size of the large complex at Luxor. But this is different. All the curved walls, all the circles. Is that to do with sun worship?"

"Astronomy, anyway. We speculated, of course. When we first mapped it on the sonavids. This is the discovery to launch a thousand theories, most of them crackpot. You have to be careful. But it felt to us to be almost a contrary development to what was happening at roughly the same time around Abu Ghurab, although of course there were sun-cults there, too. But in Lower Egypt the gratification and celebration of the Self had reached terrible proportions. All those grandiose pyramids. This place had a mood to it. The more we sifted it out the more we felt it. Wandering amongst those light columns, those open courtyards, was marvellous. All the turquoises and reds and bright yellows. This had to be the centre of some ancient Enlightenment. Far better preserved than Philae, too. And no graffiti carved anywhere, no Christian or Moslem disfigurement. We all worked like maniacs. Chamber after chamber was opened. Gradually, of course, it dawned on us! You could have filled this place with academic people and it would have been a functioning settlement again, just as it was before some petty Pharoah or local governor decided to destroy it. We felt we were taking over from them after a gap of millennia. It gave some of us a weird sense of responsibility. We talked about it. They knew so much, Paul."

"And so little," I murmured. "They only had limited information to work with, Bea . . ."

"Oh, I think we'd be grateful for their knowledge today." Her manner was controlled, as if she desperately tried to remember how she had once talked and behaved. "Anyway, this is where it all happened. We thought at first we had an advantage. Nobody was bothering to come out to what was considered a very minor find and everyone involved was anxious not to let any government start interfering. It was a sort of sacred trust, if you like. We kept clearing. We weren't likely to be found. Unless we used the emergency radio nobody would waste an energy unit on coming out. Oddly, we found no monumental statuary at all, though the engineering was on a scale with anything from the 19th dynasty—not quite as sophisticated, maybe, but again far in advance of its own time."

"How long did it take you to uncover it all?"

"We never did. We all swore to reveal nothing until a proper international preservation order could be obtained. This government is as desperate for cruise-schoomer dollars as anyone . . ."

I found myself interrupting her. "This was all covered by hand, Bea?"

"No, no." Again she was amused. "No, the ship did that, mostly. When it brought me back."

A sudden depression filled me. "You mean a spaceship, do you?"

"Yes," she said. "A lot of people here know about them. And I told Di Roper, as well as some of the kids, and the Sufi. But nobody ever believes us—nobody from the real world, I mean. And that's why I wanted to tell you. You're still a real person, aren't you?"

"Bea—you could let me know everything in London. Once we're back in a more familiar environment. Can't we just enjoy this place for what it is? Enjoy the world for what it is?"

"It's not enjoyable for me, Paul."

I moved away from her. "I don't believe in spaceships."

"You don't believe in much, do you?" Her tone was unusually cool.

I regretted offending her, yet I could not help respond. "The nuts and

bolts of keeping this ramshackle planet running somehow. That's what I
believe in, Bea. I'm like that chap in the first version of *The African Queen*,
only all he had to worry about was a World War and a little beam-engine.
Bea, you were here alone and horribly over-tired. Surely . . . ?"

"Let me talk, Paul." There was a note of aching despair in her voice
which immediately silenced me and made me lower my head in assent.

We stood there, looking at the sunrise pouring light over that dusty red
and brown landscape with its drowned architecture, and I listened to her
recount the most disturbing and unlikely story I was ever to hear.

The remains of the team had gone into Aswan for various reasons and
Bea was left alone with only a young Arab boy for company. Ali worked as
a general servant and was as much part of the team as anyone else, with as
much enthusiasm. "He, too, understood the reasons for saying little about
our work. Phil Springfield had already left to speak to some people in Washington and Professor al-Bayumi, no close relative of the inspector, was doing
what he could in Cairo, though you can imagine the delicacy of his position.
Well, one morning, when I was cleaning the dishes and Ali had put a record
on the gramophone, this freak storm blew up. It caused a bit of panic, of
course, though it was over in a minute or two. And when the sand settled
again there was the ship—there, on that bluff. You can see where it came
and went."

The spaceship, she said, had been a bit like a flying saucer in that it was
circular, with deep sides and glowing horizontal bands at regular intervals.
"It was more drum-shaped, though there were discs—I don't know, they
weren't metal, but seemed like visible electricity, sort of protruding from it,
half on the inside, half on the outside. Much of that moved from a kind of
hazy gold into a kind of silver. There were other colours, too. And, I think,
sounds. It looked a bit like a kid's tambourine—opaque, sparkling surfaces
top and bottom—like the vellum on a drum. And the sides went dark
sometimes. Polished oak. The discs, the flange things, went scarlet. They
were its main information sensors."

"It was organic?"

"It was a bit. You'd really have to see it for yourself. Anyway, it stood
there for a few minutes and then these figures came out. I thought they were
test-pilots from that experimental field in Libya and they'd made an emergency landing. I was going to offer them a cup of tea when I realised they
weren't human. They had dark bodies that weren't suits exactly but an extra
body you wear over your own. Well, you've seen something like it. We all
have. It's Akhenotan and Nefertiti. Those strange abdomens and elongated
heads, their hermaphroditic quality. They spoke a form of very old-fashioned
English. They apologised. They said they had had an instrument malfunction
and had not expected to find anyone here. They were prepared to take us

with them, if we wished to go. I gathered that these were standard procedures for them. We were both completely captivated by their beauty and the wonder of the event. I don't think Ali hesitated any more than I. I left a note for whomever returned, saying I'd had to leave in a hurry and didn't know when I'd be back. Then we went with them."

"You didn't wonder about their motives?"

"Motives? Yes, Paul, I suppose hallucinations have motives. We weren't the only Earth-people ever to go. Anyway, I never regretted the decision. On the dark side of the Moon the main ship was waiting. That's shaped like a gigantic dung-beetle. You'll laugh when I tell you why. I still find it funny. They're furious because their bosses won't pay for less antiquated vessels. Earth's not a very important project. The ship was designed after one of the first organisms they brought back from Earth, to fit in with what they thought was a familiar form. Apparently their own planet has fewer species but many more different sizes of the same creature. They haven't used the main ship to visit Earth since we began to develop sensitive detection equipment. Their time is different, anyway, and they still find our ways of measuring and recording it very hard to understand."

"They took you to their planet?" I wanted her story to be over. I had heard enough to convince me that she was in need of immediate psychiatric help.

"Oh, no. They've never been there. Not the people I know. Others have been back, but we never communicated with them. They have an artificial environment on Mercury." She paused, noticing my distress. "Paul, you know me. I hated that von Daniken stuff. It was patently rubbish. Yet this was, well, horribly like it. Don't think I wasn't seriously considering I might have gone barmy. When people go mad, you know, they get such ordinary delusions. I suppose they reflect our current myths and apocrypha. I felt foolish at first. Then, of course, the reality grew so vivid, so absorbing, I forgot everything. I could not have run away, Paul. I just walked into it all and they let me. I'm not sure why, except they know things—even circum-stances, if you follow me—and must have felt it was better to let me. They hadn't wanted to go underwater and they'd returned to an old location in the Sahara. They'd hoped to find some spares, I think. I know it sounds ridiculously prosaic.

"Well, they took us with them to their base. If I try to pronounce their language it somehow sounds so ugly. Yet it's beautiful. I think in their atmosphere it works. I can speak it Paul. They can speak our languages, too. But there's no need for them. Their home-planet's many light-years beyond the Solar System which is actually very different to Earth, except for some colours and smells, of course. Oh, it's so lovely there, at their base. Yet they complain all the time about how primitive it is and long for the comforts of home. You can imagine what it must be like.

295

"I became friends with a Reen. He was exquisitely beautiful. He wasn't really a he, either, but an androgyne or something similar. There's more than one type of fertilisation, involving several people, but not always. I was completely taken up with him. Maybe he wasn't so lovely to some human eyes, but he was to mine. He was golden-pale and looked rather negroid, I suppose, like one of those beautiful Masai carvings you see in Kenya, and his shape wasn't altogether manlike, either. His abdomen was permanently rounded—most of them are like that, though in the intermediary sex I think there's a special function. My lover was of that sex, yet he found it impossible to make me understand how he was different. Otherwise they have a biology not dissimilar to ours, with similar organs and so on. It was not hard for me to adapt. Their food is delicious, though they moan about that, too. It's sent from home. Where they can grow it properly. And they have extraordinary music. They have recordings of English TV and radio—and other kinds of recordings, too. Earth's an entire department, you see. Paul," she paused, as if regretting the return of the memory, "they have recordings of events. Like battles and ceremonies and architectural stuff. He—my lover—found me an open-air concert at which Mozart was playing. It was too much for me. An archaeologist, and I hadn't the nerve to look at the past as it actually was. I might have got round to it. I meant to. I'd planned to force myself, you know, when I settled down there."

"Bea, don't you know how misanthropic and nuts that sounds?"

"They haven't been 'helping' us or anything like that. It's an observation team. We're not the only planet they're keeping an eye on. They're academics and scientists like us." She seemed to be making an effort to convince me and to repeat the litany of her own faith; whatever it was that she believed kept her sane. Yet the creatures she described, I was still convinced, were merely the inventions of an overtaxed, isolated mind. Perhaps she had been trapped somewhere underground?

"I could have worked there, you see. But I broke the rules."

"You tried to escape?" Reluctantly I humoured her.

"Oh, no!" Her mind had turned backward again and I realised then that it was not any far-off interstellar world but her own planet that had taken her reason. I was suddenly full of sorrow.

"A flying saucer, Bea!" I hoped that my incredulity would bring her back to normality. She had been so ordinary, so matter-of-fact, when we had first met.

"Not really," she said. "The hippies call them Reens. They don't know very much about them, but they've made a cult of the whole thing. They've changed it. Fictionalised it. I can see why that would disturb you. They've turned it into a story for their own purposes. And Sheikh Abu Halil's done the same, really. We've had arguments. I can't stand the exploitation, Paul."

"That's in the nature of a myth." I spoke gently, feeling foolish and puny as I stood looking down on that marvellous construction. I wanted to leave, to return to Aswan, to get us back to Cairo and from there to the relative sanity of rural Oxfordshire, to the village where we had lived with our aunt during our happiest years. She nodded her head. "That's why I stopped saying anything.

"You can't imagine how hurt I was at first, how urgent it seemed to talk about it. I still thought I was only being taught a lesson and they'd return for me. It must be how Eve felt when she realised God wasn't joking." She smiled bitterly at her own naiveté, her eyes full of old pain. "I was there for a long time, I thought, though when I got back it had only been a month or two and it emerged that nobody had ever returned here from Aswan. There had been that Green Jihad trouble and everyone was suddenly packed off back to Cairo and from there, after a while, to their respective homes. People assumed the same had happened to me. If only it had! But really Paul I wouldn't change it."

I shook my head. "I think you were born in the wrong age, Bea. You should have been a priestess of Amon, maybe. Blessed by the Gods."

"We asked them in to breakfast, Ali and me." Shading her eyes against the sun, she raised her arm to point. "Over there. We had a big tent we were using for everything while the others were away. Our visitors didn't think much of our C-Ral and offered us some of their own rations which were far tastier. It was just a scout, that ship. I met my lover later. He had a wonderful sense of irony. As he should, after a thousand years on the same shift."

I could bear no more of this familiar modern apocrypha. "Bea. Don't you think you just imagined it? After nobody returned, weren't you anxious? Weren't you disturbed?"

"They weren't away long enough. I didn't know they weren't coming back, Paul. I fell in love. That wasn't imagination. Gradually, we found ourselves unable to resist the mutual attraction. I suppose I regret that." She offered me a sidelong glance I might have thought cunning in someone else. "I don't blame you for not believing it. How can I prove I'm sane? Or that I was sane then?"

I was anxious to assure her of my continuing sympathy. "You're not a liar, Bea. You never were."

"But you think I'm crazy." All at once her voice became more urgent. "You know how terribly dull madness can be. How conventional most delusions are. You never think you could go mad like that. Then maybe it happens. The flying saucers come down and take you off to Venus, or paradise, where war and disease and atmospheric disintegration are long forgotten. You fall in love with a Venusian. Sexual intercourse is forbidden.

You break the law. You're cast out of Paradise. You can't have a more familiar myth than that, can you, Paul?" Her tone was disturbing. I made a movement with my hand, perhaps to silence her.

"I loved him," she said. "And then I watched the future wither and fade before my eyes. I would have paid any price, done anything, to get back."

That afternoon, as we returned to Aswan, I was full of desperate, bewildered concern for a sister I knew to be in immediate need of professional help. "We'll sort all this out," I reassured her, "maybe when we get to Geneva. We'll see Frank."

"I'm sorry, Paul." She spoke calmly. "I'm not going back with you. I realised it earlier, when we were out at the site. I'll stay in Aswan, after all."

I resisted the urge to turn away from her, and for a while I could not speak.

15 Whereat Serene And Undevoured He Lay . . .

The flight was leaving in two days and there would be no other ticket for her. After she went off, filthy and withered from the heat, I rather selfishly used my whole outstanding water allowance and bathed for several hours as I tried to separate the truth from the fantasy. I thought how ripe the world was for Bea's revelation, how dangerous it might be. I was glad she planned to tell no one else, but would she keep to that decision? My impulse was to leave, to flee from the whole mess before Bea started telling me how she had become involved in black magic. I felt deeply sorry for her and I felt angry with her for not being the strong leader I had looked up to all my life. I knew it was my duty to get her back to Europe for expert attention.

"I'm not interested in proving what's true or false, Paul," she had said after agreeing to meet me at the Osiris next morning. "I just want you to *know*. Do you understand?"

Anxious not to upset her further, I had said that I did.

That same evening I went to find Inspector el-Bayoumi in his office. He put out his cigarette as I came in, shook hands and, his manner both affable and relaxed, offered me a comfortable leather chair. "You've found your sister, Mr Pappenheim! That's excellent news."

I handed him a "purse" I had brought and told him, in the convoluted manner such occasions demand, that my sister was refusing to leave, that I had a ticket for her on a flight and that it was unlikely I would have a chance to return to Aswan in the near future. If he could find some reason to hold her and put her on the plane, I would be grateful.

With a sigh of regret—at my folly, perhaps—he handed back the envelope.

"I couldn't do it, Mr Pappenheim, without risking the peace of Aswan, which I have kept pretty successfully for some years. We have a lot of trouble with Green Jihad, you know. I am very short-staffed as a result. You must persuade her, Dr Pappenheim, or you must leave her here. I assure you, she is much loved and respected. She is a woman of considerable substance and will make her own decisions. I promise, however, to keep you informed."

"By the mail packet? I thought you wanted me to get her out of here!"

"I had hoped you might *persuade* her, Mr Pappenheim."

I apologised for my rudeness. "I appreciate your concern, inspector." I put the money back in my pocket and went out to the corniche, catching the first felucca across to the West Bank where this time I paid off my guides before I reached the English House.

The roses were still blooming around the great brick manor and Lady Roper was cutting some of them, laying them carefully in her basket. "Really, Paul, I don't think you must worry, especially if she doesn't want to talk about her experiences. We all know she's telling the truth. Why don't you have a man to man with Bernie? There he is, in the kitchen."

Through the window, Sir Bernard waved with his cocoa cup before making a hasty and rather obvious retreat.

16 Your Funeral Bores Them With Its Brilliant Doom

Awaking at dawn the next morning I found it impossible to return to sleep. I got up and tried to make some notes but writing down what my sister had told me somehow made it even more difficult to understand. I gave up. Putting on a cotton *gelabea* and some slippers I went down to the almost empty street and walked to the nearest corner café where I ordered tea and a couple of rolls. All the other little round tables were occupied and from the interior came the sound of a scratched Oum Kal Thoum record. The woman's angelic voice, singing the praises of God and the joys of love, reminded me of my schooldays in Fez, when I had lived with my father during his brief entrepreneurial period, before he had returned to England to become a Communist. Then Oum Kal Thoum had been almost a goddess in Egypt. Now she was as popular again, like so many of the old performers who had left a legacy of 78 rpms which could be played on spring-loaded gramophones or the new clockworks which could also play a delicate LP but which few Egyptians could afford. Most of the records were re-pressed from ancient masters purchased from Athenian studios which, fifty years earlier, had mysteriously manufactured most Arabic recordings. The quality of her voice came through the surface noise as purely as it had once sounded through fractured stereos or on crude pirate tapes in the days of licence and waste. *Inte el Hob*, wistful, celebratory, thoughtful, reminded me of the little crooked streets of Fez, the stink of the dyers and tanners, the extraordinary vividness of the colours, the pungent mint bales, the old men who loved to stand and declaim on the matters of the day with anyone who would listen, the smell of fresh saffron, of lavender carried on the backs of donkeys driven by little boys crying "*balek!*" and insulting, in the vocabulary of a professional soldier, anyone who refused to move aside for them. Life had been sweet then, with unlimited television and cheap air-travel, with any food you could afford and any drink freely available for a few dirhams, and every pleasure in the reach of the common person. The years of Easy, the years of Power, the paradise from which our lazy greed and hungry egos banished us to eternal punishment, to the limbo of the Age of Penury, for which we have only ourselves to blame! But Fez was good, then, in those good, old days.

A little more at peace with myself, I walked down to the river while the muezzin called the morning prayer and I might have been back in the Ottoman Empire, leading the simple, steady life of a small land-owner or a civil servant in the family of the Bey. The debris of the river, the ultimate irony of the Nile filling with all the bottles which had held the water needed because we had polluted the Nile, drew my attention. It was as if the water industry had hit upon a perfect means of charging people whatever they wanted for a drink of *eau naturelle*, while at the same time guaranteeing that the Nile could never again be a source of free water. All this further reinforced my assertion that we were not in the Golden Age those New New Aquarians so longed to recreate. We were in a present which had turned our planet into a single, squalid slum, where nothing beautiful could exist for long, unless in isolation, like Lady Roper's rose garden. We could not bring back the Golden Age. Indeed we were now paying the price of having enjoyed one.

I turned away from the river and went back to the café to find Sheikh Abu Halil sitting in the chair I had recently occupied. "What a coincidence, Mr Pappenheim. How are you? How is your wonderful sister?" He spoke educated English.

I suspected for a moment that he knew more than he allowed but then I checked myself. My anxiety was turning into paranoia. This was no way to help my sister.

"I was killing time," he said, "before coming to see you. I didn't want to interrupt your beauty sleep or perhaps even your breakfast, but I guessed aright. You have the habits of Islam." He was flattering me and this in itself was a display of friendship or, at least, affection.

"I've been looking at the rubbish in the river." I shook his hand and sat down in the remaining chair. "There aren't enough police to do anything about it, I suppose."

"Always a matter of economics." He was dressed very differently today in a conservative light and dark blue *gelabea*, like an Alexandrian business man. On his head he wore a discreet, matching cap. "You take your sister back today, I understand, Dr Pappenheim."

"If she'll come."

"She doesn't want to go?" The Sufi's eyelid twitched almost raffishly, suggesting to me that he had been awake most of the night. Had he spent that time with Bea?

"She's not sure now," I said. "She hates flying."

"Oh, yes. Flying is a very difficult and unpleasant thing. I myself hate it and would not do it if I could."

I felt he understood far more than that and I was in some way relieved. "You couldn't persuade her of the wisdom of coming with me, I suppose, sidhi?"

"I have already told her what I think, Paul. I think she should go with you. She is unhappy here. Her burden is too much. But she would not and will not listen to me. I had hoped to congratulate you and wish you God Speed."

"You're very kind." I now believed him sincere.

"I love her, Paul." He gave a great sigh and turned to look up at the sky. "She's an angel! I think so. She will come to no harm from us."

"Well—" I was once again at a loss. "I love her too, sidhi. But does she want our love, I wonder?"

"You are wiser than I thought, Paul. Just so. Just so." He ordered coffee and sweetac for us both. "She knows only the habit of giving. She has never learned to receive. Not here, anyway. Especially from you."

"She was always my best friend." I said. "A mother sometimes. An alter-ego. I want to get her to safety, Sheikh Abu Hilal."

"Safety?" At this he seemed sceptical. "It would be good for her to know the normality of family life. She has a husband."

"He's in New Zealand. They split up. He hated what he called her 'charity work'."

"If he was unsympathetic to her calling, that must be inevitable."

"You really think she has a vocation?" The coffee came and the over-sweetened breakfast cakes which he ate with considerable relish. "We don't allow these at home. All those chemicals!" There was an element of self-mockery in his manner now that he was away from his *medrassah*. "Yes. We think she has been called. We have many here who believe that of themselves, but most are self-deluding. Aswan is becoming a little overstocked with mystics and wonder-workers. Eventually, I suppose, the fashion will change, as it did in Nepal, San Francisco or Essaouira. Your sister, however, is special to us. She is so sad, these days, Paul. There is a chance she might find happiness in London. She is spending too long in the desert."

"Isn't that one of the habitual dangers of the professional mystic?" I asked him.

He responded with quiet good humour. "Perhaps of the more old-fashioned type, like me. Did she ever tell you what she passed to Lallah Zenobia that night?"

"You mean the cause of her arrest? Wasn't it money? A purse. The police thought it was."

"But if so, Paul, what was she buying?"

"Peace of mind, perhaps," I said. I asked him if he really believed in people from space, and he said that he did, for he believed that God had created and populated the whole universe as He saw fit. "By the way," he said. "Are you walking up towards the Cataract? There was some kind of riot near there an hour or so ago. The police were involved and some of the youngsters from the holiday villas. Just a peaceful demonstration, I'm sure. That would be nothing to do with your sister?"

I shook my head.

"You'll go back to England, will you, Dr Pappenheim?"

"Eventually," I told him. "The way I feel at the moment I might retire. I want to write a novel."

"Oh, your father was a vicar, then?"

I was thoroughly puzzled by this remark. Again he began to laugh. "I do apologise. I've always been struck by the curious fact that so much enduring English literature has sprung, as it were, from the loins of the minor clergy. I wish you luck, Dr Pappenheim, in whatever you choose to do. And I hope your sister decides to go with you tomorrow." He kissed me three times on my face. "You both need to discover your own peace. *Sabah el Kher.*"

"*Allah yisabbe'h Kum bil-Kher.*"

The holy man waved a dignified hand as he strolled down towards the corniche to find a calash.

By now the muezzin was calling the mid-morning prayer. I had been away from my hotel longer than planned. I went back through the crowds to the green and white entrance of the Osiris and climbed slowly to my room. It was not in my nature to force my sister to leave and I felt considerably ashamed of my attempt to persuade Inspector el-Bayoumi to extradite her. I could only pray that, in the course of the night, she had come to her senses. My impulse was to seek her out but I still did not know her address.

I spent the rest of the morning packing and making official notes until, at noon, she came through the archway, wearing a blue soft cotton dress and matching shawl. I hoped this was a sign she was preparing for the flight back to civilisation. "You haven't eaten, have you?" she said.

She had booked a table on the Mut, a floating restaurant moored just below the Cataract. We boarded a thing resembling an Ottoman pleasure barge, all dark green trellises, scarlet fretwork and brass ornament, while inside it was more luxurious than the sufi's "harem". "It's hardly used, of course, these days," Bea said. "Not enough rich people wintering in Aswan any more. But the atmosphere's nice still. You don't mind? It's not against your puritan nature, is it?"

"Only a little." I was disturbed by her apparent normality. We might never have ridden into the desert together, never have talked about aliens and spaceships and Ancient Egyptian universities. I wondered, now, if she were not seriously schizophrenic.

"You do seem troubled, though." She was interrupted by a large man in a dark yellow *gelabea* smelling wildly of garlic who embraced her with affectionate delight. "Beatrice! My Beatrice!" We were introduced. Mustafa shook hands with me as he led us ecstatically to a huge, low table looking over the Nile, where the feluccas and great sailing barges full of holidaymakers came close enough to touch. We sat on massive brocaded foam cushions.

I could not overcome my depression. I was faced with a problem beyond my scope. "You've decided to stay I take it?"

The major domo returned with two large glasses of Campari Soda. "Compliments of the house." It was an extraordinary piece of generosity. We saluted him with our glasses, then toasted each other.

"Yes." She drew her hair over her collar and looked towards the water. "For a while, anyway. I won't get into any more trouble, Paul, I promise. And I'm not the suicide type. That I'm absolutely sure about."

"Good." I would have someone come out to her as soon as possible, a psychiatrist contact in MEDAC who could provide a professional opinion. "You'll tell me your address?"

"I'm moving. Tomorrow. I'll stay with the Ropers if they'll have me. Any mail care of them will be forwarded. I'm not being deliberately mysterious, dear, I promise. I'm going to write. And meanwhile, I've decided to tell you the whole of it. I want you to remember it, perhaps put it into some kind of shape that I can't. It's important to me that it's recorded. Do you promise?"

I could only promise that I would make all the notes possible.

"Well, there's actually not much else."

I was relieved to know I would not for long have to suffer those miserably banal inventions.

"I fell in love, you see."

"Yes, you told me. With a spaceman."

"We knew it was absolutely forbidden to make love. But we couldn't help

303

ourselves. I mean, with all his self-discipline he was as attracted to me as I was to him. It was important, Paul."

I did my best to give her my full attention while she repeated much of what she had already told me in the desert. There was a kind of Biblical rhythm to her voice. "So they threw me out. I never saw my lover again. I never saw his home again. They brought me back and left me where they had found me. Our tents were gone and everything was obviously abandoned. They let their engines blow more sand over the site. Well, I got to Aswan eventually. I found water and food and it wasn't too hard. I'm not sure why I came here. I didn't know then that I was pregnant. I don't think I knew you could get pregnant. There isn't a large literature on sexual congress with semi-males of the alien persuasion. You'd probably find him bizarre, but for me it was like making love to an angel. All the time. It was virtually our whole existence. Oh, Paul!" She pulled at her collar. She smoothed the table-cloth between her knife and fork. "Well, he was wonderful and he thought I was wonderful. Maybe that's *why* they forbid it. The way they'd forbid a powerful habit-forming stimulant. Do you know I just this second thought of that?"

"That's why you were returned here?" I was still having difficulty following her narrative.

"Didn't I say? Yes. Well, I went to stay with the Ropers for a bit, then I stayed in the commune and then the *medrassah*, but I kept going out to the site. I was hoping they'd relent, you see. I'd have done almost anything to get taken back, Paul."

"To escape from here, you mean?"

"To be with him. That's all. I was—I am—so lonely. Nobody could describe the void."

I was silent, suddenly aware of her terrible vulnerability, still convinced she had been the victim of some terrible deception.

"You're wondering about the child," she said. She put her hand on mine where I fingered the salt. "He was born too early. He lived for eight days. I had him at Lallah Zenobia's. You see, I couldn't tell what he would look like. She was better prepared, I thought. She even blessed him when he was born so that his soul might go to heaven. He was tiny and frail and beautiful. His father's colouring and eyes. My face, I think, mostly. He would have been a *wunderkind*, I shouldn't be surprised. Paul . . ." Her voice became a whisper. "It was like giving birth to the Messiah."

With great ceremony, our meal arrived. It was a traditional Egyptian *meze* and it was more and better food than either of us had seen in years. Yet we hardly ate.

"I took him back to the site." She looked out across the water again. "I'd got everything ready. I had some hope his father would come to see him.

Nobody came. Perhaps it needed that third sex to give him the strength? I waited, but there was not, as the kids say, a Reen to be seen." This attempt at humour was hideous. I took firm hold of her hands. The tears in her eyes were barely restrained.

"He died." She released her hands and looked for something in her bag. I thought for a frightening moment she was going to produce a photograph. "Eight days. He couldn't seem to get enough nourishment from what I was feeding him. He needed that—whatever it was he should have had." She took a piece of linen from her bag and wiped her hands and neck. "You're thinking I should have taken him to the hospital. But this is Egypt, Paul, where people are still arrested for witchcraft and here was clear evidence of my having had congress with an *ifrit*. Who would believe my story? I was aware of what I was doing. I'd never expected the baby to live or, when he did live, to look the way he did. The torso was sort of pear-shaped and there were several embryonic limbs. He was astonishingly lovely. I think he belonged to his father's world. I wish they had come for him. It wasn't fair that he should die."

I turned my attention to the passing boats and controlled my own urge to weep. I was hoping she would stop, for she was, by continuing, hurting herself. But, obsessively, she went on. "Yes, Paul. I could have gone to Europe as soon as I knew I was pregnant and I would have done if I'd had a hint of what was coming, but my instincts told me he would not live or, if he did live, it would be because his father returned for him. I don't think that was self-deception. Anyway, when he was dead I wasn't sure what to do. I hadn't made any plans. Lallah Zenobia was wonderful to me. She said she would dispose of the body properly and with respect. I couldn't bear to have some future archaeologist digging him up. You know, I've always hated that. Especially with children. So I went to her lean-to in Shantytown. I had him wrapped in a shawl—Mother's lovely old Persian shawl—and inside a beautiful inlaid box. I put the box in a leather bag and took it to her."

"That was the Cairene Purse? Or did you give her money, too?"

"Money had nothing to do with it. Do the police still think I was paying her? I offered Zenobia money but she refused. 'Just pray for us all,' was what she said. I've been doing it every night since. The Lord's prayer for everyone. It's the only prayer I know. I learnt it at one of my schools."

"Zenobia went to prison. Didn't you try to tell them she was helping you?"

"There was no point in mentioning the baby, Paul. That would have constituted another crime, I'm sure. She was as good as her word. He was never found. She made him safe somewhere. A little funeral boat on the river late at night, away from all the witnesses, maybe. And they would have found him if she had been deceiving me, Paul. She got him home somehow."

Dumb with sadness, I could only reach out and stroke her arms and hands, reach for her unhappy face.

We ate so as not to offend our host, but without appetite. Above the river the sun was at its zenith and Aswan experienced the familiar, unrelenting light of an African afternoon.

She looked out at the river with its day's flow of debris, the plastic jars, the used sanitary towels, the paper and filth left behind by tourists and residents alike.

With a deep, uneven sigh, she shook her head, folded her arms under her breasts and leaned back in the engulfing foam.

All the *fhouls* and the marinated salads, the *ruqaq* and the meats lay cold before us as, from his shadows, the proprietor observed us with discreet concern.

There came a cry from outside. A boy perched high on the single mast of his boat, his white *gelabea* tangling with his sail so that he seemed all of a piece with the vessel, waved to friends on the shore and pointed into the sky. One of our last herons circled overhead for a moment and then flew steadily south, into what had been the Sudan.

My sister's slender body was moved for a moment by some small, profound anguish.

"He could not have lived here."

Aswan, Egypt, Oct/Nov 1988
Oxford, England, Jul/Aug 1989
Porto Andratx, Majorca, Sept 1989

Chapter Quotes:
1 Hood; 2 Khayyam Fitzgerald; 3 AE; 4 Dylan Thomas; 5 Wheldrake; 6 Yokum; 7 Aeschylus MacNiece; 8 Vachel Lindsay; 9 F. Thompson; 10 Peake; 11 Treece; 12 Duffy; 13 Nye; 14 C.D. Lewis; 15 E. St. V. Millay; 16 Nye.

DAFYDD aB HUGH

The Coon Rolled Down and Ruptured His Larinks, a Squeezed Novel by Mr. Skunk

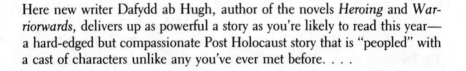

Here new writer Dafydd ab Hugh, author of the novels *Heroing* and *Warriorwards*, delivers up as powerful a story as you're likely to read this year—a hard-edged but compassionate Post Holocaust story that is "peopled" with a cast of characters unlike any you've ever met before. . . .

▼

The Coon Rolled Down and Ruptured His Larinks, a Squeezed Novel by Mr. Skunk

DAFYDD aB HUGH

Chapter one we hear the story

I heard the story from an old Coon at first sitting at my favorite place on the hardground just outside the bowl alley on venture path. Then later he and I played chase and bounce with a ball and bounded it on venture path. But the story kept running around and around inside my ears like it was casting for a scent so I just had to find out more about it.

So I and the Boy Nik Nok and Disha the Dog and Hanki and Yanki the Cats sat in a circle and I told them each and all about the Hidden Den and the Coon who could not talk:

He lived under the jerryfams next to the bowl alley. He told me by whispers that he had ruptured his larinks. That is his throat where he talks, Disha the Dog said (she is very smart, smarter than me and the others especially Hanki and Yanki). Then the Coon acted out the whole story standing on his back legs to mean human being, staggering to tell me he meant stupid and looking back east so I would know he meant stupid like the fourlegs were before Democrazy.

I put what the Coon said in words as best I could and this, was it:

Across the city and too far for a chase there are humans like before Democrazy and they are all sealed up in a den where no air can go in and out, and the Winds of Law have not blown either.

Inside the den the fourlegs are all stupid like before Democrazy too, and they have to work for the humans and cannot think and have no Inalienable Progrets.

Nobody knew what to say after I finished my story. Disha and Nik Nok always ignore me for they see no real difference between a Skunk and a Cat, except for the white stripe and the odie Skunk of course.

But even I knew something had to be done, so I said "if we love Democrazy then something has to be done."

Chapter two we deleminate the problem

"Well if you love Democrazy and the Winds of Law that made us all Equal then what are we going to do about that den, where there is no Progrets and no Law?"

I was afraid to answer for I knew what the only answer could be and I was only a Skunk!

But I knew I had no choice and neither did Disha and neither even did Nik Nok. He was not of the old Men, the ones who exploded the less fortunate and took advantages. He believed in Democrazy. I had seen him cover his face in the Cord House.

I looked up at Disha and "this is what we will do about that den" said I, "journey all the way across the city and bring Democrazy and the Will of Progrets to this den of unequity."

Disha squatted and made water on the whitestone trail beside my favorite old den.

"Do you really want to take the trip when you might find the Overizon instead?"

Now I thought for a long time before I answered her. Was there even Democrazy and Equality beyond the venture path? I did not know even though I always thought Progrets had spread it everywhere. But after hearing the old Coon's tale I wondered.

"These humans are trying to stop the spread of Democrazy that Progrets started when it loosed the bug that rode the Winds of Law and did us all" I said and I thought I had said a mouthful.

"But will you go" she asked like Fiday the teacher coaxing the right answer.

Chapter three some decide to go

I thought quietly, not looking at her. I do not know what made me ask "who will come with me if I go" but it slipped out.

She waited too long and I knew she was afraid too, then she said "if you go I at least will come with you. You must ask the others for yourself."

We gathered the group again and told them what we were going to do to save Democrazy.

The old Coon had said only one thing more to me, in the whisper again for he could not convoy this by gestures. He whispered that this Hidden Den was across the city of angels at the foot of the other mountains, where the underbuild had fallen in.

As soon as Hanki and Yanki heard this, they said there would be wild things along the way, and then they high tailed it out of there as Cats will, for Cats are hardly smarter than before there was Progrets. Only I and Disha and Nik Nok the Boy stayed.

"Is Disha going to go" asked Nik Nok in a strange voice. "Yes" she said for she had already said she at least would go with me. "Then surely I shall go too" he said.

Disha tilted her head as she looked at him. A gleam in her eyes frightened me, being somehow wrong.

"Then there are three of us" she said, and "when shall we start?"

"Let us wait" said I, "let us wait until the shadows are longer. I bow to the Will of Progrets but I hear there is no Democrazy under a hot sun."

Chapter four off we go then

All too soon the shadows grew, and the hot Santa's Anus blew from the nightside and we had to set out.

We chased the scents between the fallen walls and square builds sometimes running and sometimes walking when old Disha got tired but all the while making way toward the other mountains.

Nik Nok never seemed to tire as Boys will not, but he stayed very near Disha even when she had to rest.

Soon all the smells were strange to me and I could see nothing I knew, it was not the venture path or anywhere I had been before and I was uneasy.

We ran by a fire once. I heard the boom boom boom inside the giant den and I watched until the walls tired and fell in against each other, such is Progrets.

Chapter five we meet death and Democrazy

All at once as the sun rose in the sky like a big burn, Disha stopped and I almost ran into her.

She perked her ears up and snuffled her nose towards the sun but I could not smell anything yet and there was nothing to see but a hill of metal trash and rotwood. "Come on Nik Nok" she said and started to climb through a notch in the hill.

No one called to me, but I followed anyway for I was not about to get left alone in a strange place.

Then I smelled it too, it was a dead Dog in the bottom of the hill, named Duk Duk. I had played chase and bounce with her not long before.

He was dead and he smelled of junk to me.

Disha and Nik Nok stood together at the top of the hill and I could see the Boy did not really understand death yet, for he called out to Duk Duk. Then I smelled his fear as he began to understand.

Disha must have smelled it too for she moved over to put her head against his thigh.

"Do not be afraid Nik Nok" she said "for I will protect you."

"It is not Junkyard Dogs and falling walls that scare me" he said "but I had a funny feeling in my stomach just now. Something bad is going to come of this extra diction. I have never been away from the bowl alley and venture path before."

Disha nuzzled his ear softly and licked it.

"Nik Nok you are still too young to fight wars. You go home and I will be back to play with you very soon."

He put his arms around her neck and "I cannot let you do it alone" he said. "And I am not too young for I became a man a season ago, at night in a dream."

I shivered and looked back at Duk Duk. There were things on him. Every so often his fur would rup and flutter like he itched but it was only the bugs and burrowers who had gotten under his skin. His eyes watched me like they knew something and said "watch us well Skunk, you will come to this in no time yourself!"

Nik Nok and Disha held each other for a little bit, and they ignored me. But I watched them with bright Skunk eyes. I had began to know in words what was happening between them. It was not Democrazy, Democrazy was what lay in the ditch with Duk Duk.

Chapter six the watcher in the dark

About this time I prickled like we were being watched. I looked around but nothing and I decided I was jumpy being so far from the venture path. I said nothing but "please you two let us go."

We walked for a long time until it was full, comfortable dark and cold in the moon.

At last Disha decided we should stop for the night, but it was more for

Nik Nok I think than for me. "We are far away from bowl alley and there are marauders here" she said. I saw a hole across the hardground beneath writing words and I told her. "It says exon" she said.

Disha investigated the hole first because she was the leader. It smelled like Rats and burn-juice. She had me ask them if it was alright if we stayed there for a mome, and they said they would ask their king.

Chapter seven we all eat Cat food

We left them to deleminate and stalked out like mighty hunters in search of food. I still had that same watchy feeling but I was too unsure to tell Disha yet.

I let them in front and stayed behind as quiet as I could. Disha scented the air and cast about for something edible and catchable. We were away from the bowl alley so I knew anyone we caught we could eat (except not a Dog or a Boy or a Skunk of course).

Nik Nok saw something before Disha smelled it, a flash of white on top of a wall on the other side of the hardground and we began to stalk.

We sneaked from build to fall keeping to shadows and picking up our feet so as not to scuff.

Disha slunk forward and Nik Nok clung to the black fur on her back. But he watched her not the prey, even I could see that. He watched her hard muscles flex and stretch beneath her sleek fur and watched her slink lower and lower to the ground invisible in the dark as the Winds of Law.

I listened. Skunks can listen well. I heard Nik Nok's breath catch in his throat as he felt her body beneath his hand. I smelled the same smell I make when the lady Skunks come into season.

When we got across the hardground "split to the left and drive it towards me" Disha snuffled to Nik Nok. I crept away from them both and poked my head around the corner.

It was a Cat fat and lazy licking himself, full and stuffed and paying no tensions to Progrets and the bitter world.

Clever Nik Nok reached into his bag and found our best ball, took aim and beaned the Cat right where it counts.

At first he flew into the air and screamed out "oh shit," then he began to run for his life with Nik Nok pounding after and me behind them as fast as four Skunk legs could carry me.

"Help! Do not eat me!" the Cat added for good measure but he did not turn around to see if we were agreeable to this suggestion.

We chased him along the wall jumping over the stones and falls for he was fleeing for his very life. He tried to jump up a telephone tree but Nik

Nok jumped up after him and he could climbor as well as the Cat and he jumped down again and ran down an alley for he was fleeing for his very life. Nik Nok disappeared after him and at once I heard a snarl and a Cat scream. When I poked an eye around the corner I saw Disha had the Cat cornered against the whitestone at the other end.

"Oh please please do not eat me!" the Cat cried in terror as Disha padded closer. I smelled the water of his fear and saw his eyes wide and wet and almost I asked Disha to seize and desist, for Cats are nearly Skunks. But then I reminated I was hungry.

"Why not eat you" she asked "you are an inferior being, to wit a Cat. Cats are made to be eaten."

"But I have a wife" argued the Cat "and she will have no one to provide for her if I am dead and eaten."

"Oh that is no problem just bring her here, and I shall solve her problem too!" retorted Disha.

The Cat perked up at this suggestion which I would not have thought he would and suggested "very well, just let me go and I shall get her." It seemed a reasonable request except of course I doubted his sincerity in returning, for you can never trust a Cat.

"Not so fast Mr. Dinner" said Disha. "I would not have you tire yourself by walking all that way and all the way back. I think it is best if we avoid inconveniencing your wife and just eat you now."

Nik Nok and I had said nothing so far, for Disha was doing well on her own.

"But surely you do not want to deplete the food supply" said the Cat, thinking furiously which is very out of character for a Cat "you should eat the aged and the sick not Cats like me in their prime who can still sire kittens."

"But if we do not eat you then we will die and I too can still whelp pups and Nik Nok can now sire children, so he tells me."

"But you must further the cause of Progrets and kill only the Cats who have not become smart."

"That would mean all of you" retorted Disha, thinking no doubt of Hanki and Yanki.

"But surely you are not against Democrazy are you?"

I worried because I reminated the looks that Disha and Nik Nok had given each other lately. But Disha just laughed all the time edging closer to the Cat. The Cat saw this and arched his back and hissed. He was fighting for his very life now.

"If you were stupid enough to get caught" debated Disha "then killing you *is* Progrets!"

"Yes it is eat or be eaten" said Nik Nok.

The Cat could see his situation was now desperate and he tried one last gambol.

"But you should not eat me for we are brothers, we fourlegs must all stick together in the city of the angels."

"So" said Disha with sudden anger "I shall eat you anyway because I am hungry, and that after all is the only real argument." Then she rushed forward and caught the Cat who in the end did not even try to escape for he knew he was a goner.

"Disha" asked Nik Nok, "why *should* we not eat our brothers?"

Chapter eight Democrazy is violented

"Good kill" I said, but nobody heard me. Nik Nok gave Disha a hug that was not entirely innocent I think.

Nik Nok ran his hand gently over Disha's soft fur, and watched with Raccoon eyes as her hard muscles underneath flexed and stretched as she tore and tugged at the Cat, getting him open.

She chewed off a warm hindquarter, hesitated a moment and then laid it in his lap. "Here beautiful" she said "you take the first Cat cut."

He picked it up slowly, pulled the fur off and sunk his teeth in and tore off a juicy hunk.

I slunk back into the shadows for I realized I was not wanted at this particle mome. But I watched for we Skunks have very good eyes.

He chewed and held his hunk out to Disha, and she ate from the same piece. They looked into each other's eyes and Disha put her paw on Nik Nok's forearm and I heard the Boy panting like he was chasing something invisible.

I was frightened. I knew this was not Democrazy and that the Winds of Law would blow across us for this.

Fresh Cat has an effect, the meat is tangy without dipping it in the black specks and the blood sends a wild hair through the back of your jaw and makes you squint. This time it was dubbly so for the frightened Cat had pushed excitement through his whole body, I could smell it even from where I was. But they hungered for more than food even so.

The Cat blood dripped down Nik Nok's chin and he wiped it with his hand and held it out for Disha to lick. The kill smell was making even me excited, but I stayed in the shadows again for I love Progrets and Democrazy.

He ripped a piece of catsmeat off the leg and offered the next bite to Disha, and moved closer and closer to her. He dipped his finger in the blood and drew a line with it along Disha's head and down her nose.

She licked his finger as he let it trail over her lips and all at once they did not even care about the Cat. They moved a little away and I darted forward and caught a piece. But I watched as I ate and I shivered wondering what the Winds of Law would feel like.

Chapter nine for the strong of heart

Disha began licking his throat and then his chest and his ling began to swell. I smelled the lady Dog smell. Nik Nok was shaking and gasping like he had run a race and Disha turned herself around and knelt her front legs down. "Gently" she said, "slowly do not rush it or you will hurt me."

"I do not know how" said Nik Nok and his voice was thick and white.

"Hold my tail up out of the way. I will tell you if you are doing something wrong." She suddenly caught her breath and held it.

"Does it feel good" she asked him.

"Like nothing I have ever felt and better even than when I used my hand before!" he told her.

"Wait wait" Disha said "it is too tight yet." But then she whined and snuffled and sounded very excited herself, and Nik Nok found the going easier. I hoped that they had forgotten I was watching them for I did not want to foul soot—either like the Cat, or even like Disha! For if you start out violenting Democrazy one time why not do anything you want then?

He held the fur on her side with one hand and the going was easier. His other hand kept stroking her tail and rubbing it against his bare belly.

"Does this feel like this always" he asked.

She sighed only "will of Democrazy."

I closed my eyes at the Blast Femmy and listened only. I was reminateing when I had last had a lady, and it was long ago and usually I cannot reminate it, but the scent remembered me. I lay quiet and listened to Disha and Nik Nok.

The Boy cried out suddenly, not even afraid of a Junkyard Dog hearing him but when afterward he started to pull out she said "do not dare stop! Keep going even if you are finished for I am not."

"But how" he asked "I am not hard anymore." I opened my eyes again because maybe the horror was almost over, and I wanted to see what it looked like when you violented Democrazy.

"Damn you just keep going I am almost there, you are hard enough." So of course he did. At last it happened to Disha too, but she did not cry out as he had. She went stiff all over and her tail stood straight up against his stomach.

He bent over to lay his body against her back and his head on hers and still stayed in her. He licked Disha's ears very gently.

315

"I have been with many other Dogs before" she said "and you are so much better for you took much more care with me than they do. They are all only interested in pleasuring themselves and something happens and they get big and lumpy and cannot pull out. But that never stops them from trying. They cannot do it slow and gentle like you do." Nik Nok said nothing but he did not look as happy as he might, for perhaps he saw to the future then.

Chapter ten love and Democrazy

"And there is more about you" she added "but I cannot say what it is, the thought of you is like gas that has floated up to my heart and is pushing everything else aside and nearly bursting out my chest."

They held each other as mates. I think they had forgotten all about me and Progrets and the Hidden Den.

"Let's stay here forever Disha" said Nik Nok, "we can do it again as soon as—"

But Disha got a junk look on her face, and she looked at me and I almost turned and ran even though she is my friend. She is still a Dog and I only a Skunk, and she is more equal.

I tried to talk but I was too afraid.

"I know that you saw but you cannot talk about what you have just seen" snarled Disha, and all I could do was shake my head. They had violented Democrazy and I was afraid.

Now Nik Nok looked frightened, for he had not thought about the Winds of Law before he foolishly fell in love.

"But why not? Do we not love each the other?"

"Love" sneered Disha, "what does love have to do with the Will of Democrazy? We are cranimals now, for all of our friends on venture path cannot stand the thought of what we have done and it is eat or be eaten. So if this Skunk talks we shall be goners you and I."

I curled up in a ball shaking, meaning I would not say anything and betray my friends to Democrazy and thus I too became victim to the Winds of Law, as you will see at the novel ending.

"Let us stay" said Nik Nok, "and never return to face the bath of Democrazy."

"No beautiful" said Disha to Nik Nok, "for we must eat and go back to today's den. We set out again when the sun sinks. Have you forgotten our quest?"

With a wasteful look he looked down at himself. He had fallen out of her. His ling was still wet from inside Disha and he wiped it with his hand and rubbed some on his nose so he could smell her all the way back.

That is how I found out about love in the streets.

Chapter eleven a junk waffle

When we got back King Rat said it was all right to stay if we gave him some Cat, which we did and then he let us stay the day inside the exon.

It was hot but even so all three of us huddled next to each other. We needed each other's solstice.

So it was that I jumped in fear when I suddenly heard a junk howl from outside, across the hardground and the paths and the metal autobiles that we were going to cross the next day, even towards the other mountains.

The scream scraped like a falling wall and rumbled like thunderbum "damn all of you die horrible!" it said, and then "it is not the Junkyard Dogs what we learned to mean to me!"

It was junk, through and through and I wondered if he would try to break into the exon and get us. It was death and dismembrane. It was howls and horrors, junk city, junk waffle, Junkyard Dog!

Soon his howls came closer, and he said things that did not mean anything but fear and death except maybe to another junk: "anyone we caught we could eat once—kill them! Do not let them—I *tore* all living creatures in *piece!*"

In between these cries I heard him run around and around the exon moaning like a cub with stomach rot and coughing like a redstone mountain falling down in an earthshake, and even that made me afraid and by the way they shivered I knew Disha and Nik Nok were too. You never know what these Junkyard Dogs will do for they are mad and do not drink water and if they bite you you become junk yourself.

We heard each curly nailed paw tickity-tickity scrabbling the hardground, round and round and round until it was as if brats were throwing stones, bounding chinks of redstone in a circle to pen us inside.

Then "I held onto the fur on hunks of metal!" he suddenly hissed from right beneath our windrow!

We got up as quiet as we could and crouched by the door because he might smell us and try to get in at us. I had even heard of a Junkyard Dog leaping straight through a glass windrow! for after all they cannot feel pain, being junk anyway and outside Democrazy.

Something tugged at my mind about some of the things he said. Then, when he sang like a jay from just underneath the windrow "not so fast, Mr. Dinner!" I knew what I reminated.

The junk things he said were our own words turned, like a poison snake into something other, frightful.

The junk had been stalking us and listening the whole time. My watchy feeling had been true.

We listened hard and tried to track him as he trotted around and around

317

crazily, but the Winds of Law and the Santa's Anus kept howling too and knocking things over so it was hard to tell which was which.

There was too much to see in the exon. There were tables and broken windrows and spilled blackoil, and three very frightened Dogs Boys and Skunks slunking around trying to watch and listen at each and every windrow.

We strained and looked but he never stepped out and showed himself. Of course we imagined he was everywhere and sometimes it even seemed he was here in the exon with us, but it always turned out to be just one of the three of us knocking something over.

Then a thump on the roof and "my favorite place, the hardgrover moon!" he croaked from above.

We all fell to silence and held our collectivist breaths.

I for one could hear the junk panting and wheezing on the roof. Slowly he walked to one side, tickity-tickity. Slowly he walked back, scritchity-scritchity, tickity—and *stopped*.

"I know you" he whispered, so clear we could hear the hair stand on our backs. "Anyone we caught we could eat *once*" he added, so quiet we could hear pieces and drips of junk spatter on the metal roof.

Then with a terrible creak like the roof caving in and dropping him there among us, he leaped and was gone. There was a frightful bulge, left there in the roof right in the middle of the den.

I do not know how long we stayed up and shivered but we never heard anything more from him that day.

Chapter twelve Law and Custom

We made good time towards the other mountains and climbored over many crickley hills of autobiles and metals. We were so tired that after we found a dead Rat and ate lunch we were too beat to even play chase and bounce with our other ball, and we plodded again as soon as we had swallowed our food.

I kept listening hard for the Junkyard Dog but either he had decided to let us alone which I doubted or he was very, very good at stalking.

I was afraid it was the latter. None of us heard anything we could say was surely him but many a scrape and click that could have been his flank against a wall, and could have been his claws on top an unbroken piece of hardground but could have been anything else either.

My feeling was stronger than ever. We were all uneasy but could not sit around worrying about a Junkyard Dog so we tried to ignore him and run on.

I knew that Disha and Nik Nok wanted to be alone so I kept my distance. I listened though, for a Skunk has good ears. Mostly I listened for the Junkyard Dog but I heard every word that Disha said to Nik Nok, or vice verses.

Disha said that even though everybody is all for Democrazy nobody agrees what it is, so we hide what we think for fear we will be too different and become company dinner, and this is Custom. Even back before there was Law to enforce the will of Democrazy there was Custom, and Custom is stronger even than Law.

I kept hoping they would both see the light and allow Custom and Progrets to get in the way of animal love.

Custom says we can eat only what we can eat and that we cannot love anybody who is too different. If you break Custom, it is company dinner for you, boy, just like happened to Taggo. But his violentation provided us with a lovely feast, so you see what goes around comes around and Progrets is always satisfied. This is some of what the two of them said, Disha and Nik Nok:

"What love can this be" he said "when we can never be together with friends, and cannot make children?"

But she said "I have made many pups already and the last thing I need now is more when I cannot always feed what I have."

He said "but does this love violent Democrazy? What will happen to us?"

She said "sometimes two people that can touch each other are more important than the Custom of Democrazy, for love itself *is* Progrets and even Democrazy must obey."

She said "before the plague that did us all there was hardly any love. Love can only live between equals. Back then everyone was either lesser or greater than everyone else so how could there be true love? Now there is perfect equality and Democrazy and we can finally love."

But as Disha said this last I thought I heard the ghost of a sour chasm, for she knew as well as did I what Democrazy would think of her love for Nik Nok.

He said "what is love really?" I thought Disha would answer because she is wise and a Dog but she just walked on, thinking.

At last I could not keep my silence, and I answered for her what my mother had heard from a Zoocamel long ago:

I said "love is knowing each other like worms know the dead."

Disha stopped. "That is pretty good for a Skunk" she admitted and said "this cannot happen when one is more than the other, because how can the lesser know the greater? And how can the greater respect one who is less than she?"

Nik Nok asked "is this how it was before the plague that did us all?"

Chapter thirteen Disha has a tail

"In the days before the plague" she said "the Dogs could not talk or even think, and neither could the other animals. This I know, this I know. Men were all that were intelly and they were even more intelly than the Dogs and Men are now. They set about to make some of the fourlegs intelly too."

"Some say" she said "they only wanted servants and they could not use each other as they always had because of Servile Rights, but I have always admired the early Men and I prefer to think they truly believed we should all be crated equally. This I know, this I know."

"In any case" she said "they did it, and they did it by crating an unnatural plague that would do us, Dogs and Cats and other mamuals. This I know, this I know."

"I am not sure what a plague is" asked Nik Nok, and I listened hard for I had never understood that explanation either as often as Disha had shown this tail.

"A plague is a little bug that crawls into every bump and hole in your body" she admitted. "Whenever you get sick that is caused by these bugs, and that is a plague.

"Anyway, they deliberately fected some of us Dogs with this plague and then sat back on their haunches to see what would develop. This I know, this I know."

"And this is where Progrets and Democrazy came from" whispered the Boy out of rivulance.

"What developed" she smugged "is that one of these plague Dogs escaped. The men were not as smart as they thought and Fang the Savor got away with the plague bug still fecting him."

"This I know, this I know" said both I and Nik Nok at once.

"The Dogs were first and then next the plague fected the Rats and the Skunks and the Coons and the Zoomals and everything else. The Cats were last for they were always so full of themselves licking their body that they kept licking the bugs right off until they wised up! And that is why Dogs are first and Cats are last and all others fall in between."

"This I know, this I know" we supplied for her.

I had forgotten all about the Junkyard Dog, so intent was I on Disha's tail.

"Ah but Men are a different story" she continued finally. "For the rest of us it was a climb up the hill for more intelly, but the Men had the easy route and came down the hill backwards. We met Democrazically in the middle, for the plague has finally made us *all* equal . . . the furries and birds and scales and frogs and even some of the fish, who are getting more intelly all of the time."

"Until at last today" she whispered "when I can love you truly as my grandmother could never love your grandfather. This I know, Nik Nok. This I know."

"What is the use of more intelly" asked Nik Nok angrily "if the Old Men did not have love? I am *glad* for this plague even if I *am* stupider than men were before! I am glad for our love Disha."

She stopped and bit at a flea on her hind leg for a mome.

"Even" she snuffled "if you can no longer understand the things of Men?"

"Things?"

"The autobiles and the glass mountains, the redstone dens, the hard-ground, telephone trees, walls and builds and all? If you can no longer understand them?"

"Then" he said "they are not the things of men anymore" and there he had her.

Chapter fourteen our junk fears are real eyes

"These things of men are not any of them as warm and pretty and furry as you" said Nik Nok and I began to get an easy because here again was love against Democrazy.

"You will not always have me" Disha warned "Dogs do not live as long as men do for that is something the plague did not change."

"I am here now" he said "and you too and what is tomorrow? Maybe I will die first if that Junkyard Dog is still shuddowing us."

I wondered which was worth more, love or Progrets and I could feel my tail raise in horror. Is wonder a crime against Democrazy?

Then all at once I heard a sound I must have been listening for all day and dreading, a rumbling cough like a redstone mountain falling down in an earthshake, a moaning like a cub with stomach rot and out of the shuddows of a heap of dead cars staggered the Junkyard Dog in the flesh, what was left of it!

All three of us froze in terror and I felt urine trickle down my leg. I also raised my tail and sprayed my wad but I doubted the Junkyard Dog would care about how he smelled as long as he got to bite us, all three!

He staggered forward stiff-legged and I thought, maybe he is already dead but does not know it yet.

In little sharp words he said "you might think my sex will eat me . . . and the part of her I was in squeezed Democrazy."

"Go away" Disha said with tried authority, but "I am who I have been and can eat once anybody I have caught" answered the Junkyard Dog.

"Go away!" I whimpered for I could not find my voice. I felt like the silent Coon.

"If you were stupid enough you *is* Progrets'" said he.

And with that he lunged at us and we three broke in all four directions and I ran up a wall of dead autobiles before I even knew it was blocking. Then I looked back and saw Disha. She had frozen in fear and could not move and she stood nose to nose with the Junkyard Dog who was dripping white at the mouth. I do not know why she did not run or why he had not bitten her yet. I shivered in fear.

But then I heard a cranky squeak and Nik Nok rose from the build he had hidden behind. He found his voice and charged the Junkyard Dog screaming like a Commonest.

It broke the spell. Disha unfroze and bolted away but oddly the Junkyard Dog did not charge the Boy instead and tear him to shreds like I thought, he turned instead and with a deaf move slashed Disha as she ran by. She screamed and skittered away but I could see the blood flowing from her hind leg. The junk ran in circles three times laughing like a falling pile of autobiles.

Disha shook, tail between her legs. Nik Nok only stared, his face the color of my stripe. We all knew what would happen to her now.

"Well if I am already bit" said she sounding strange and quiet and queerly calm "then you can no longer frighten me, Junk. This I know, this I know." And she leapt upon him as if she were junk herself and they fought tearing and biting and the Junkyard Dog had the worst of it for Disha tore off his ear and opened up his throat.

He fell to his knees and still had mind enough to submit but he was a goner anyway. My throat lumped, because I knew Disha was a goner too. Worse, she would finally be like him and might even bite me then too or Nik Nok. I knew she would never allow that to happen, but there was only one thing that could stop it and that was the Duk Duk path.

The Junk fell over on his side and now blood was flowing out of his throat in spurts so I knew she had struck paydirt. But just for a moment his eyes seemed to clear a little and he raised his head with a big strain and said "that hurt. You are bigger than I suggested. Knelt—knelt her front legs into the pocket of my clothes."

Then "the truck is the key. Hold my tail up out of conveniencing my wife and putting it in. If machines make the wall only machines can onetwothree-one. Against the will of Del so wet."

His voice became weaker and he whispered "keep going even if you are finished, then we will, die. At first, even I could, at first, both our hearts, need meat. Even I, the rules must roll, even I, could hear my life, with me, pounding after."

"Cats" he croaked "are made just outside the bowl. But the truck is the key, you must understand. I smell onions."

Then all at once he pulled himself up as if he had not even been mauled, he looked at us and shrugged and explained "*anyone* we caught we could eat once." Then he settled back with a sigh and moved no more, for he was gone.

Chapter fifteen where Democrazy gets it in the end

We watched him for a long time to make sure he would not pop back up again and say something or maybe bite someone else but he was permanently dead. We moved on without spirit.

We found a den-hole among the dead autobiles that was empty after we chased out a scrawny Cat. Nik Nok made a halfheart grab and missed but we did not miss it, none of us was hungry anyway. I was still full from the night before, and the way Disha looked I did not even ask her if she wanted the Cat so he got lucky that night. After we settled in I shrunked farther back in the pile so Disha and her love could be alone together.

She was quiet as though submitting but the way she held her head seemed more like quiet domination. She knew she was horribly dead because the Junkyard Dog draw blood.

"Nik Nok" she said "you know we have only a little time left together now. Let us not waste it."

Skunks have very good eyes.

They violented Democrazy again in the day-heat, but this time it was gentle and slow like the black river instead of laughing and plunging like a waterfoul. She licked his belly very lightly and he breathed into her ear and stroked the underside of her tail and when he went inside her she coughed in surprise that it was so smooth and easy. Once he forgot and grabbed her wounded and stiffening leg to pull himself in deeper and she jerked away, but she never made a sound except right at the very end when she moaned just a little. This time she finished before he did but she was true to her word and kept on until he was done.

Afterward they lay together and talked without words while Nik Nok picked fleas out of her fur. They slept face to face even though she being a Dog was not exactly built for it.

Now that I knew what Nik Nok would soon lose I found I no longer cared about Custom and let Democrazy be hanged. Love *is* Progrets. Strange creatures fluttered in my stomach.

As the sun set we rose. When the air became stullen, and we resumed our journey I began to wish Nik Nok had nabbed the cat afterall. The stullen air was even browner than yestereve and blood red with the setting sun so it would be hard to main train a course for the other mountains across the city of angels. Disha said we would be there by the dawn's oily light, and could the underbuild be far away then?

Chapter sixteen we explore Disha's tunnel of love

Well we were not at the mountains by sun-up but we kept at our quest even through the daylight for we were tired, and wanted it all over. We saw no more Junkyard Dogs but my funny-watchy feeling continued, and I felt like everyone we saw was Junk in some way or another.

Finally through the cracked and fallen builds, Disha spied the arch with the folded arms that reprehented an underbuild. "We shall enter sex the line here" said she "and follow it along towards the sea that swallows the sun. Soon we shall find the fallen underbuild and thence the hidden den."

So down we went and into the stingy in blackness.

It swallowed us both and three but I felt no comfort, for this was not a den nor a hidey-hole but a build—a build of men and it reeked of them and their Undemocrazy. In some places I found a cold metal road and ran along it for a way, but the ticking of my claws against the hardmetal sent shivers through us all and Disha asked me to walk on the grabble to the side. I was happy to oblige for to tell the truth, I did not like the sound either and even Nik Nok cast his eyes down and grew silent at the echoes. We walked for a passing in silence but I cannot say how long for there are no momes in the dark.

Chapter seventeen we find the hidden den at last!

The journey through the wendless tunnel passed an easily, for even the Santa's Anus and the Winds of Law could not brush us down there. At last we began to see cracks of light in the overhead, and then whole pocks of hardground and finally we discovered the Great Buildfall that the Coon had reminated. We climbored out of the underbuild into bright and treacherous sunlight, and saw stretched down below us the last defense against Democrazy.

It was a build squat like a stone spider and it was all gleaming, while the other builds around it were broken and dulled. There were men in strange clothing outside: they wore thick brown clothes that covered them completely and round hats that surrounded their heads and they looked out of glass windrows in their hats. I did not need for Disha to tell me that the clothes were meant to keep out Progrets but she did anyway. When I objected she said that she had only been telling Nik Nok.

We watched them for a long time. When they went inside two big doors opened for them, but they opened into a little room that did not seem worth the efforts.

"So how do we get Progrets beyond those doors" Disha asked.

"Maybe we can knock a hole through them" asked Nik Nok, but Disha injected. "We might be able to dig our way through one door if we were quick enough, but long before we got through the other door those men would do us. But maybe there is only one wall, perhaps we should consecrate on that."

We crept forward and studied the build some more.

"Nik Nok" said Disha "if these humans have never been fected by Progrets, that means these walls have stood for many seasons. They must be very strong walls indeed for there have been earthshakes and many storms."

I tried watching the men (or were they women? I could not tell inside their clothing). I began to have a glimmering in my mind like moonlight on the water.

Something the Junkyard Dog said kept buzzing to be reminated, but I could not pull it out and look at it.

The den was in a deep canyon from our vintage point with a long path of mostly straight unbroken hardground leading down towards it. It was to this path that my eyes looked. It had something to do with the important thing the Junkyard Dog said that I could not reminate. Oh how I wished I were a Dog or a Man, that could reminate everything!

"Let us explore the path" I asked "and see if we can find anything." Since neither Disha nor Nik Nok had a better suggestion we turned about and began walking back along the hardground away from the hidden den.

I looked at everything we passed trying to reminate what I knew was in my mind. I reminated, that the Junkyard Dog in between all his gibbers had said something that would help us now.

Chapter eighteen we discover the key to the mysteries

I looked at an arco and a hydrant and a lot of square builds and a store but none of them joggled my memory.

And then I saw the autobile truck and at once the thought leapt back into my mind.

"I reminate!" I cried "the truck is the key said the Junkyard Dog!"

Disha looked at the truck and then at me, saying "that is what *I* am now, a Junkyard Dog." At once I regretted my hasty words but "you are right, I reminate him saying that too" she added.

"But what could he know about today" I asked "for you killed him yesterday."

"To the junk" she said "there is no yesterday or tomorrow, it sees backward and forward in days the way we see left and right along venture path. But what does that mean, the truck is the key?"

It was the biggest autobile truck I had ever seen. Even Nik Nok could not reach its top and it had more wheels than there are numbers in the city of angels. It was stopped along the edge of the hardground and was covered with foul-smelling rust.

For a long time we all three stared at the truck trying to figure out how. it was the key. Then Nik Nok whispered "if machines make the wall then maybe machines can . . ."

"Can what" I asked.

"That was something else he said" said the Boy. "Only machines can what, break the wall?"

"If we could get the truck rolling down the hardground" Disha said think loud "maybe it would roll fast enough that it could smash through the wall and into the Den."

Nik Nok looked at the autobile for a long time.

"It is a very big truck" he said at last.

"But how do we get it rolling" I asked.

"And more important" asked Nik Nok "once we do how do we make sure it stays on the hardground and does not hit a tree and stop?"

"That wheel in front of the chair makes it go left and right" answered Disha like a know-all "for I have spoken with Hanaka Tag the eldest and she told me of these autobiles."

"Well I think these men make the machine come alive" retorted Nik Nok "do you know how to bring it to life also?"

"We do not need to" said Disha though she did not sound too sure and I could tell she was only guessing "for if we can get it rolling then the hill will make it go fast enough."

I kept my mouth shut during this axe change, for I am only a Skunk. I listened well though for we Skunks have very good ears.

Nik Nok fumbled with the latch until he could get the metal open and we looked inside.

"What we must do" said Disha "is get it rolling and then one of us stays inside to turn the hoop-wheel and make the truck go left and right to stay on the hardground."

"But then what" asked Nik Nok, full of frights and astonishments "what will happen when it hits the Den? Will I be killed?"

Disha smiled. "Whichever one of us it is in the truck must jump clear before the crash my love." She touched his side gently with her greying muzzle, for she was not as young as she had been the season before.

The truck was not rolling so we decided something was blocking it. After we ran around for a few momes looking Disha saw some pieces of wood under the wheels. We tried to pull them out, but even Nik Nok could not so he knocked them out finally with a rock. The truck ground and groaned but still did not roll. We climbored up to look, and there were lots of metal pulls.

"One of these must be what makes the truck stop and go" announced Disha, but I think she put on more show of know-all than she really had. Nik Nok began pulling and pushing on the pulls, and Disha was vindulated because when he pulled a partically hard one the truck screamed and began to roll slowly. It rolled down the hill warbling like a broken thunderbum.

Nik Nok was afraid even when it went so slow. Then it picked up speed and we all shivered.

I was so frightened I could not move and I feared I would not be able to jump out, when the time came being so frightened.

Disha had Nik Nok turn the hoop-wheel, for she did not have the strength in her jaws and it was almost too hard for him!

"Reminate my love" she cautioned "keep the door from latching for we must be ready to fly out at the very last mome."

Nik Nok touched her paw and looked into her eyes, "oh I love you so *much*" he said with a tear in his eye. I could not figure out why his eyes were wet. Was there dust in them?

The autobile truck got faster and faster and soon Nik Nok was barely able to keep it on the hardground and away from trees and builds. I began to be afraid and sick as if I had eaten wormroot when I looked to the side and saw the world whizzing past me faster than a sparrow flies, and almost would have jumped out right then except that I knew Disha would not let us be killed, especially not Nik Nok. She rested her muzzle against his ear, and I could barely hear her snuffle "You are precious to me too. Life is precious."

Then we roared around the last turn with Nik Nok straining to make the hoop-wheel turn so that the autobile truck would stay where it was supposed. We were heading right for the Den.

Some of the Men saw us coming and ran out waiving their hands and then tried to ride their own autobile into our path. They must have known what we were doing and were ready to give their lives to thwart the will of Democrazy, such was their fear of Progrets. But their autobile could not run fast enough and it only hit the back of the truck and did not even turn us. Just before we hit Disha snuffled "junk bonds, but love is stronger." Then "NOW!" she barked "JUMP NOW!"

Nik Nok pushed open the door and just before he jumped he grabbed me by the scruff and saved my life!

We were lucky we were on grass and not on hardground for we hit and hit hard. I rolled over and over the Boy and ended up on my back watching the truck plow into the Den.

I do not know if Disha ever had a chance. Just before the crash I saw her still in the truck, gripping the hoop with her mouth and keeping the truck aimed true.

Then I heard a thunderbum like I had never imagined and the whole wall of the Last Old Den caved in like a buildfall in an earthshake. We had opened the last remnant of yesterday to the clouds of Progrets and the plague.

Chapter nineteen

But Disha was dead.

Chapter twenty triumph of Democrazy

I was still shaking from the fall I thought. I looked about unable to move, but I could not see Nik Nok and I was alone.

I saw the truck went much deeper into the Den than I imagined, it went right through three rooms.

Dust and smoke puffed on the Winds of Law around inside and in and out of the hole we had made and I knew that the bugs of Democrazy were drifting in too and would bear fruit.

Now all of us would be truly equal and the fourlegs would be liberated.
Then I saw Disha.

She had been thrown from the truck. She lay on the ground covered in blood.

Nik Nok held her broken lifeless body in his arms and tried to kiss her back to life, and the tears were streaming down his cheeks.

"What is this? What is this" he asked touching the salty water.

"I think that means you are a Man again" I said "for Democrazy has triumphed. Our brethren and sistern are free and equal now."

But a junk voice in my head, maybe Disha's ghost whispered "you cannot be both."

Disha pulled me into the Hidden Den, deeper and deeper than we had been even in the underbuild for it was a darkness of the heart not of the air and her ghost glowed like the moon.

I saw a Rat shivering and shaking and looking at me with wide eyes. "We have come to liberate you" I said to resure him, but he only made a scrittering sound and ran away.

I stopped in panic. What was that sound? What did he say?

Then a Dog came out and I called to him, for he was a brother of Disha and I wanted to tell him of her sacrifice and how he was free now.

"You are free Mr. Dog" I said, and "the free live free, you must go out into the City of Angels now and learn the Will of Democrazy."

At first he snarled, but I knew he was only reacting to a strange Skunk. But when he heard my words he settled down and began to moan in pleasure at his newfound equality.

But then the moans turned into a whimper and he crawled on his belly to me. I backed up in consarnation for what was he, to wit a Dog doing playing subservant to a mere Skunk? Where was his equality before the Winds of Law?

Then I smelled his fear.

It ran unchecked down his leg and I could hear his heart racing like the truck that brought him Democrazy in the first place. He was terrified and did not understand.

"You would do well to buck up and be a Dog" I chastised "for this is Progrets and the Will of Democrazy!" I boldly approached to lead him out into the real world, but instead he barked . . . and it was not words he barked. It was a cough, a grunt and held no more meaning than fear and confusion.

He may have been a Dog, but he was still only an animal. He was no brother of Disha.

We turned and ran at the same time in opposite directions. Terror gripped me too, for I suddenly realized that I was in another land.

There was no Democrazy here today, no matter what the bugs may say tomorrow and I was more afraid than I had been of the Junkyard Dog.

A Man stood in my path. "Do not stop me" I announced "for I am Progrets!"

He screamed and staggered back against the wall of the Den covering his face. Another man heard me and tried to bean me with a stick crying "another one, kill him! Break his throat like the other!" and I did not need to ask to know that they meant the Coon. Now I knew how he had come to rupture his larinks. I ran like a Commonest.

At once the whole Den came alive against me, Men and Fourlegs and it was I who was fleeing for my very life. I found the hole, I do not know how. And then I was through. I did not stop running until I found the fallen underbuild again, and there was Nik Nok. But Disha's body was not with him and he would not tell me where it was.

Chapter twenty-one to the winners go the spoiled

I will not tell you of the journey back across the waste, to the venture path with Nik Nok carrying me under one arm. All I reminate is that the Dogs snarled fiercely and the builds rumbled and shook, but none of them could touch us for Disha trotted right beside us still, and her laugh echoed around us as we slept the day away.

By the night we returned the color finally crept back into Nik Nok's face, and he could smile though he vanished the next day and I never saw him again.

When I knew he had gone Overizon I felt a tear in my eye. I, the last of our extra diction, learned to cry.

Chapter twenty-two Mr. Skunk lowers his tale

I have nothing left to say. I am getting old and soon I will be a feast myself if you can stand the smell.

I, a Skunk am the very last of us who is able to cry since Nik Nok left and Disha died. I see you do not even understand what it is, except perhaps dust in my eye or a thorn in my paw.

In the high build at the end of venture path is a tower with a bell at the top, but it is silent now for there are none with the will to ring it. Pigeons roost under the metal and I hear them call to each other through the long, hot days: "Home! Fly home! Come home!"

They know nothing else to say, but it is a miracle that they can say even that, and I think that the plague is finally doing them as well. I think this means that soon we shall be equal to the pigeons too and only able to call each other home without even knowing where our home lies.

That is true Democrazy after all, and there is an end to love.

I will not be there to see, thank Democrazy.

Long reign Progrets! I bow to the Will, the Winds and Inalienable Progrets!

I confess that sometimes I wonder: have we lost something urgent? But I do not think wondering should be a crime against Democrazy.

TED CHIANG

Tower of Babylon

▼

Across the centuries, many people have aspired to climb upward to God—
but perhaps not quite as *literally* as the characters in the bizarre and compelling story that follows. . . .

Ted Chiang is a brand new writer who has just broken into the field with
sales to *Omni, Isaac Asimov's Science Fiction Magazine,* and *Full Spectrum.*
Amazingly, the polished and very accomplished "Tower of Babylon" is his
first published story, and he is clearly a Writer To Watch. He lives in
Redmond, Washington.

▼

Tower of Babylon

TED CHIANG

Were the tower to be laid down across the plain of Shinar, it would be two days journey to walk from one end to the other. While the tower stands, it takes a month and a half to climb from its base to its summit, if a man walks unburdened. But few men climb the tower with empty hands; the pace of most men is much slowed by the cart of bricks that they pull behind them. Four months pass between the day a brick is loaded onto a cart and the day it is taken off to form a part of the tower.

Hillalum had spent all his life in Elam and knew Babylon only as a buyer of Elam's copper. The copper ingots were carried on boats that traveled down the Karun to the Lower Sea, headed for the Euphrates. Hillalum and the other miners traveled overland, alongside a merchant's caravan of loaded onagers. They walked along a dusty path leading down from the plateau, across the plains, to the green fields sectioned by canals and dikes.
    None of them had seen the tower before. It became visible when they were still leagues away: a line as thin as a strand of flax, wavering in the shimmering air, rising up from the crust of mud that was Babylon itself. As they drew closer, the crust grew into the mighty city walls, but all they saw was the tower. When they did lower their gazes to the level of the river plain, they saw the marks the tower had made outside the city: The Euphrates itself now flowed at the bottom of a wide, sunken bed, dug to provide clay for bricks. To the south of the city could be seen rows upon rows of kilns, no longer burning.
    As they approached the city gates, the tower appeared more massive than

anything Hillalum had ever imagined: a single column that must have been as large around as an entire temple, yet it rose so high that it shrank into invisibility.

All of them walked with their heads tilted back, squinting in the sun.

Hillalum's friend Nanni elbowed him, awestruck. "We're to climb that? To the top?"

"Going *up* to dig. It seems . . . unnatural."

The miners reached the central gate in the western wall, where another caravan was leaving. While they crowded forward into the narrow strip of shade provided by the wall, their foreman Beli shouted to the gatekeepers standing atop the gate towers. "We are the miners who were summoned from the land of Elam."

The gatekeepers were delighted. One called back, "You are the ones who are to dig through the vault of heaven?"

"We are."

The entire city was celebrating. The festival had begun eight days ago, when the last of the bricks were sent on their way, and would last two more. Every day and night, the city rejoiced, danced, feasted.

Along with the brickmakers were the cart pullers, men whose legs were roped with muscle from climbing the tower. Each morning a crew began its ascent; they climbed for four days, transferred their loads to the next crew of pullers, and returned to the city with empty carts on the fifth. A chain of such crews led all the way to the top of the tower, but only the bottommost celebrated with the city. For those who lived upon the tower, enough wine and meat had been sent up earlier to allow a feast to extend up the entire pillar.

In the evening, Hillalum and the other Elamite miners sat on clay stools before a long table laden with food, one table among many laid out in the city square. The miners spoke with the pullers, asking about the tower.

Nanni said, "Someone told me that the bricklayers who work at the top of the tower wail and tear their hair when a brick is dropped, because it will take four months to replace, but no one takes notice when a man falls to his death. Is that true?"

One of the more talkative pullers, Lugatum, shook his head. "Oh, no, that is only a story. There is a continuous caravan of bricks going up the tower; thousands of bricks reach the top each day. The loss of a single brick means nothing to the bricklayers." He leaned over to them. "However, there is something they value more than a man's life: a trowel."

"Why a trowel?"

"If a bricklayer drops his trowel, he can do no work until a new one is brought up. For months he cannot earn the food that he eats, so he must go into debt. The loss of a trowel is cause for much wailing. But if a man falls, and his trowel remains, men are secretly relieved. The next one to drop his trowel can pick up the extra one and continue working without incurring debt."

Hillalum was appalled, and for a frantic moment he tried to count how many picks the miners had brought. Then he realized. "That cannot be true. Why not have spare trowels brought up? Their weight would be nothing against all the bricks that go up there. And surely the loss of a man means a serious delay, unless they have an extra man at the top who is skilled at bricklaying. Without such a man, they must wait for another one to climb from the bottom."

All of the pullers roared with laughter. "We cannot fool this one," Lugatum said with much amusement. He turned to Hillalum. "So you'll begin your climb once the festival is over?"

Hillalum drank from a bowl of beer. "Yes. I've heard that we'll be joined by miners from a western land, but I haven't seen them. Do you know of them?"

"Yes, they come from a land called Egypt, but they do not mine ore as you do. They quarry stone."

"We dig stone in Elam, too," said Nanni, his mouth full of pork.

"Not as they do. They cut granite."

"Granite?" Limestone and alabaster were quarried in Elam, but not granite. "Are you certain?"

"Merchants who have traveled to Egypt say that they have ziggurats and temples, built with huge blocks of limestone and granite. And they carve giant statues from granite."

"But granite is so difficult to work."

Lugatum shrugged. "Not for them. The royal architects believe such stoneworkers may be useful when you reach the vault of heaven."

Hillalum nodded. That could be true. Who knew for certain what they would need? "Have you seen them?"

"No, they are not here yet, but they are expected in a few days time. They may not arrive before the festival ends, though; then you Elamites will ascend alone."

"You will accompany us, won't you?"

"Yes, but only for the first four days. Then we must turn back, while you lucky ones go on."

"Why do you think us lucky?"

"I long to make the climb to the top. I once pulled with the higher crews, and reached a height of twelve days climb, but that is as high as I have ever gone. You will go far higher." Lugatum smiled ruefully. "I envy you, that you will touch the vault of heaven."

335

To touch the vault of heaven. To break it open with picks. Hillalum felt uneasy at the idea. "There is no cause for envy—" he began.

"Right," said Nanni. "When we are finished, all men will touch the vault of heaven."

The next morning, Hillalum went to see the tower. He stood in the giant courtyard surrounding it. There was a temple off to one side that would have been impressive if seen by itself, but it stood unnoticed beside the tower.

He could sense the utter solidity of it. According to all the tales, the tower was constructed to have a mighty strength that no ziggurat possessed; it was made of baked brick all the way through, when ordinary ziggurats were mere sun-dried mud brick, having baked brick only for the facing. The bricks were set in a bitumen mortar, which soaked into the fired clay, and hardened to form a bond as strong as the bricks themselves.

The tower's base resembled the first two platforms of an ordinary ziggurat. There stood a giant square platform some two hundred cubits on a side and forty cubits high, with a triple staircase against its south face. Stacked upon that first platform was another level, a smaller platform reached only by the central stair. It was atop the second platform that the tower itself began.

It was sixty cubits on a side and rose like a square pillar that bore the weight of heaven. Around it wound a gently inclined ramp, cut into the side, that banded the tower like the leather strip wrapped around the handle of a whip. No; upon looking again, Hillalum saw that there were two ramps, and they were intertwined. The outer edge of each ramp was studded with pillars, not thick but broad, to provide some shade behind them. In running his gaze up the tower, he saw alternating bands—ramp, brick, ramp, brick—until they could no longer be distinguished. And still the tower rose up and up, farther than the eye could see; Hillalum blinked, and squinted, and grew dizzy. He stumbled backward a couple steps and turned away with a shudder.

Hillalum thought of the story told to him in childhood, the tale following that of the Deluge. It told of how men had once again populated all the corners of the earth, inhabiting more lands than they ever had before. How men had sailed to the edges of the world and seen the ocean falling away into the mist to join the black waters of the Abyss far below. How men had thus realized the extent of the earth, and felt it to be small, and desired to see what lay beyond its borders, all the rest of Yahweh's creation. How they looked skyward and wondered about Yahweh's dwelling place, above the reservoirs that contained the waters of heaven. And how, many centuries ago, there began the construction of the tower, a pillar to heaven, a stair that men might ascend to see the works of Yahweh, and that Yahweh might descend to see the works of men.

It had always seemed inspiring to Hillalum, a tale of thousands of men toiling ceaselessly, but with joy, for they worked to know Yahweh better. He had been excited when the Babylonians came to Elam looking for miners. Yet now that he stood at the base of the tower, his senses rebelled, insisting that nothing should stand so high. He didn't feel as if he were on the earth when he looked up along the tower.

Should he climb such a thing?

On the morning of the climb, the second platform was covered edge to edge with stout two-wheeled carts arranged in rows.

Many were loaded with nothing but food of all sorts: sacks filled with barley, wheat, lentils, onions, dates, cucumbers, loaves of bread, dried fish. There were countless giant clay jars of water, date wine, beer, goat's milk, palm oil. Other carts were loaded with such goods as might be sold at a bazaar: bronze vessels, reed baskets, bolts of linen, wooden stools and tables. There was also a fattened ox and a goat that some priests were fitting with hoods so that they could not see to either side and would not be afraid on the climb. They would be sacrificed when they reached the top.

Then there were the carts loaded with the miners' picks and hammers, and the makings for a small forge. Their foreman had also ordered a number of carts be loaded with wood and sheaves of reeds.

Lugatum stood next to a cart, securing the ropes that held the wood. Hillalum walked up to him. "From where did this wood come? I saw no forests after we left Elam."

"There is a forest of trees to the north, which was planted when the tower was begun. The cut timber is floated down the Euphrates."

"You planted an entire *forest*?"

"When they began the tower, the architects knew that far more wood would be needed to fuel the kilns than could be found on the plain, so they had a forest planted. There are crews who provide water and plant one new tree for each that is cut."

Hillalum was astonished. "And that provides all the wood needed?"

"Most of it. Many other forests in the north have been cut as well, and their wood brought down the river." He inspected the wheels of the cart, uncorked a leather bottle he carried, and poured a little oil between the wheel and axle.

Nanni walked over to them, staring at the streets of Babylon laid out before them. "I've never before been this high, that I can look down upon a city."

"Nor have I," said Hillalum, but Lugatum simply laughed. "Come along. All of the carts are ready."

Soon all the men were paired up and matched with a cart. The men stood between the carts' two pull rods, which had rope loops for pulling. The carts

337

pulled by the miners were mixed in with those of the regular pullers, to ensure that they would keep the proper pace. Lugatum and another puller had the cart right behind that of Hillalum and Nanni.

"Remember," said Lugatum, "stay about ten cubits behind the cart in front of you. The man on the right does all the pulling when you turn corners, and you'll switch every hour."

Pullers were beginning to lead their carts up the ramp. Hillalum and Nanni bent down and slung the ropes of their cart over their opposite shoulders. They stood up together, raising the front end of the cart off the pavement.

"Now PULL," called Lugatum.

They leaned forward against the ropes, and the cart began rolling. Once it was moving, pulling seemed to be easy enough, and they wound their way around the platform. Then they reached the ramp, and they again had to lean deeply. "This is a light wagon?" muttered Hillalum.

The ramp was wide enough for a single man to walk beside a cart if he had to pass. The surface was paved with brick, with two grooves worn deep by centuries of wheels. Above their heads, the ceiling rose in a corbeled vault, with the wide, square bricks arranged in overlapping layers until they met in the middle. The pillars on the right were broad enough to make the ramp seem a bit like a tunnel. If one didn't look off to the side, there was little sense of being on a tower.

"Do you sing when you mine?" asked Lugatum.

"When the stone is soft."

"Sing one of your mining songs, then."

The call went down to the other miners, and before long the entire crew was singing.

As the shadows shortened, they ascended higher and higher. With only clear air surrounding them, and much shade from the sun, it was much cooler than in the narrow alleys of a city at ground level, where the heat at midday could kill lizards as they scurried across the street. Looking out to the side, the miners could see the dark Euphrates, and the green fields stretching out for leagues, crossed by canals that glinted in the sunlight. The city of Babylon was an intricate pattern of close-set streets and buildings, dazzling with gypsum whitewash; less and less of it was visible as it seemingly drew nearer the base of the tower.

Hillalum was again pulling on the right-hand rope, nearer the edge, when he heard some shouting from the upward ramp one level below. He thought of stopping and looking down the side, but he didn't wish to interrupt their pace, and he wouldn't be able to see the lower ramp clearly anyway. "What's happening down there?" he called to Lugatum behind him.

"One of your fellow miners fears the height. There is occasionally such a man among those who climb for the first time. Such a man embraces the floor and cannot ascend further. Few feel it so soon, though."

Hillalum understood. "We know of a similar fear, among those who would be miners. Some men cannot bear to enter the mines, for fear that they will be buried."

"Really?" called Lugatum. "I had not heard of that. How do you feel yourself about the height?"

"I feel nothing." But he glanced at Nanni, and they both knew the truth.

"You feel nervousness in your palms, don't you?" whispered Nanni.

Hillalum rubbed his hands on the coarse fibers of the rope and nodded. "I felt it, too, earlier when I was closer to the edge."

"Perhaps we should go hooded, like the ox and the goat," muttered Hillalum jokingly.

"Do you think we, too, will fear the height, when we climb further?"

Hillalum considered. That one of their comrades should feel the fear so soon did not bode well. He shook it off; thousands climbed with no fear, and it would be foolish to let one miner's fear infect them all. "We are merely unaccustomed. We will have months to grow used to the height. By the time we reach the top of the tower, we will wish it were taller."

"No," said Nanni. "I don't think I'll wish to pull this any further."

They both laughed.

In the evening they ate a meal of barley and onions and lentils, and slept inside narrow corridors that penetrated into the body of the tower. When they woke the next morning, the miners were scarcely able to walk, so sore were their legs. The pullers laughed, and gave them salve to rub into their muscles, and redistributed the load on the carts to reduce the miners' burden.

By now, looking down the side turned Hillalum's knees to water. A wind blew steadily at this height, and he anticipated that it would grow stronger as they climbed. He wondered if anyone had ever been blown off the tower in a moment of carelessness. And the fall; a man would have time to say a prayer before he hit the ground. Hillalum shuddered at the thought.

Aside from the soreness in the miners' legs, the second day was similar to the first. They were able to see much farther now, and the breadth of land visible was stunning; the deserts beyond the fields were visible, and caravans appeared to be little more than lines of insects. No other miner feared the height so greatly that he couldn't continue, and their ascent proceeded all day without incident.

On the third day, the miners' legs had not improved, and Hillalum felt like a crippled old man. Only on the fourth day did their legs feel better, and they were pulling their original loads again. Their climb continued until

Ted Chiang

the evening, when they met the second crew of pullers leading empty carts rapidly along the downward ramp. The upward and downward ramps wound around each other without touching, but they were joined by the corridors through the tower's body. When the crews had intertwined thoroughly on the two ramps, they crossed over to exchange carts.

The miners were introduced to the pullers of the second crew, and they all talked and ate together that night. The next morning the first crew readied the empty carts for their return to Babylon, and Lugatum bid farewell to Hillalum and Nanni.

"Take care of your cart. It has climbed the entire height of the tower, more times than any man."

"Do you envy the cart, too?" asked Nanni.

"No, because every time it reaches the top, it must come all the way back down. I could not bear to do that."

When the second crew stopped at the end of the day, the puller of the cart behind Hillalum and Nanni came over to them. His name was Kudda.

"You have never seen the sun set at this height. Come, look." The puller went to the edge and sat down, his legs hanging over the side. He saw that they hesitated. "Come. You can lie down and peer over the edge, if you like." Hillalum did not wish to seem like a fearful child, but he could not bring himself to sit at a cliff face that stretched for thousands of cubits below his feet. He lay down on his belly, with only his head at the edge. Nanni joined him.

"When the sun is about to set, look down the side of the tower." Hillalum glanced downward and then quickly looked to the horizon.

"What is different about the way the sun sets here?"

"Consider, when the sun sinks behind the peaks of the mountains to the west, it grows dark down on the plain of Shinar. Yet here, we are higher than the mountaintops, so we can still see the sun. The sun must descend further for us to see night."

Hillalum's jaw dropped as he understood. "The shadows of the mountains mark the beginning of night. Night falls on the earth before it does here."

Kudda nodded. "You can see night travel up the tower, from the ground up to the sky. It moves quickly, but you should be able to see it."

He watched the red globe of the sun for a minute and then looked down and pointed. "Now!"

Hillalum and Nanni looked down. At the base of the immense pillar, tiny Babylon was in shadow. Then the darkness climbed the tower, like a canopy unfurling upward. It moved slowly enough that Hillalum felt he could count the moments passing, but then it grew faster as it approached, until it raced past them faster than he could blink, and they were in twilight.

340

Hillalum rolled over and looked up, in time to see darkness rapidly ascend the rest of the tower. Gradually, the sky grew dimmer as the sun sank beneath the edge of the world, far away.

"Quite a sight, is it not?"

Hillalum said nothing. For the first time, he knew night for what it was: the shadow of the earth itself, cast against the sky.

After climbing for two more days, Hillalum had grown more accustomed to the height. Though they were the better part of a league straight up, he could bear to stand at the edge of the ramp and look down the tower. He held on to one of the pillars at the edge and cautiously leaned out to look upward. He noticed that the tower no longer looked like a smooth pillar.

He asked Kudda, "The tower seems to widen further up. How can that be?"

"Look more closely. There are wooden balconies reaching out from the sides. They are made of cypress, and suspended by ropes of flax."

Hillalum squinted. "Balconies? What are they for?"

"They have soil spread on them, so people may grow vegetables. At this height water is scarce, so onions are most commonly grown. Higher up, where there is more rain, you'll see beans."

Nanni asked, "How can there be rain above that does not just fall here?"

Kudda was surprised at him. "It dries in the air as it falls, of course."

"Oh, of course." Nanni shrugged.

By the end of the next day they reached the level of the balconies. They were flat platforms, dense with onions, supported by heavy ropes from the tower wall above, just below the next tier of balconies.

On each level the interior of the tower had several narrow rooms inside, in which the families of the pullers lived. Women could be seen sitting in the doorways sewing tunics, or out in the gardens digging up bulbs. Children chased each other up and down the ramps, weaving amidst the pullers' carts and running along the edge of the balconies without fear. The tower dwellers could easily pick out the miners, and they all smiled and waved.

When it came time for the evening meal, all the carts were set down and much food and other goods were taken off to be used by the people here. The pullers greeted their families and invited the miners to join them for the evening meal. Hillalum and Nanni ate with the family of Kudda, and they enjoyed a fine meal of dried fish, bread, date wine, and fruit.

Hillalum saw that this section of the tower formed a tiny kind of town, laid out in a line between two streets, the upward and downward ramps. There was a temple, in which the rituals for the festivals were performed; there were magistrates, who settled disputes; there were shops, which were stocked by the caravan. Of course, the town was inseparable from the caravan:

Neither could exist without the other. And yet any caravan was essentially a journey, a thing that began at one place and ended at another. This town was never intended as a permanent place; it was merely part of a centuries-long journey.

After dinner, Hillalum asked Kudda and his family, "Have any of you ever visited Babylon?"

Kudda's wife, Alitum, answered. "No, why would we? It's a long climb, and we have all we need here."

"You have no desire to actually walk on the earth?"

Kudda shrugged. "We live on the road to heaven; all the work that we do is to extend it further. When we leave the tower, we will take the upward ramp, not the downward."

As the miners ascended, in the course of time there came the day when the tower appeared to be the same when one looked upward or downward from the ramp's edge. Below, the tower's shaft shrank to nothing long before it seemed to reach the plain below. Likewise the miners were still far from being able to see the top. All that was visible was a length of the tower. To look up or down was frightening, for the reassurance of continuity was not provided; they were no longer part of the ground. The tower might have been a thread suspended in the air, unattached to either Earth or heaven.

There were moments during this section of the climb when Hillalum despaired, feeling displaced and estranged from the world; it was as if the earth had rejected him for his faithlessness, while heaven disdained to accept him. He wished Yahweh would give a sign, to let men know that their venture was approved; otherwise how could they stay in a place that offered so little welcome to the spirit?

The tower dwellers at this altitude felt no unease with their station; they always greeted the miners warmly and wished them luck with their task at the vault. They lived inside the damp mists of clouds, they saw storms from below and from above, they harvested crops from the air, and they never feared that this was an improper place for men to be. There were no divine assurances to be had, but the people never knew a moment's doubt.

With the passage of the weeks, the sun and moon peaked lower and lower in their daily journeys. The moon flooded the south side of the tower with its silver radiance, glowing like the eye of Yahweh peering at them. Before long, they were at precisely the same level as the moon when it passed; they had reached the height of the first of the celestial bodies. They squinted at the moon's pitted face, marveled at its stately motion that scorned any support.

Then they approached the sun. It was the summer season, when the sun appears nearly overhead from Babylon, making it pass close by the tower at this height. No families lived in this section of the tower, nor were there any balconies, since the heat was enough to roast barley. The mortar between the tower's bricks was no longer bitumen, which would have softened and flowed, but clay, which had been virtually baked by the heat. As protection against the day temperatures, the pillars had been widened until they formed a nearly continuous wall, enclosing the ramp into a tunnel with only narrow slots admitting the whistling wind and blades of golden light.

The crews of pullers had been spaced very regularly up to this point, but here an adjustment was necessary. They started out earlier and earlier each morning, to gain more darkness for when they pulled. When they were at the level of the sun, they traveled entirely at night. During the day, they tried to sleep, naked and sweating in the hot breeze. The miners worried that if they did manage to sleep, they would be baked to death before they awoke. But the pullers had made the journey many times and never lost a man, and eventually they passed above the sun's level, where things were as they had been below.

Now the light of day shone *upward*, which seemed unnatural to the utmost. The balconies had planks removed from them so that the sunlight could shine through, with soil on the walkways that remained; the plants grew sideways and downward, bending down to catch the sun's rays.

Then they drew near the level of the stars, small fiery spheres spread on all sides. Hillalum had expected them to be spread more thickly, but even with the tiny stars invisible from the ground, they seemed to be thinly scattered. They were not all set at the same height but instead occupied the next few leagues above. It was difficult to tell how far they were, since there was no indication of their size, but occasionally one would make a close approach, evidencing its astonishing speed. Hillalum realized that all the objects in the sky hurtled by with similar speed, in order to travel the world from edge to edge in a day's time.

During the day, the sky was a much paler blue than it appeared from the earth, a sign they were nearing the vault. When studying the sky, Hillalum was startled to see that there were stars visible during the day. They couldn't be seen from the earth amidst the glare of the sun, but from this altitude they were quite distinct.

One day Nanni came to him hurriedly and said, "A star has hit the tower!"

"What!" Hillalum looked around panicked, feeling like he had been struck by a blow.

"No, not now. It was long ago, more than a century. One of the tower dwellers is telling the story; his grandfather was there."

They went inside the corridors and saw several miners seated around a wizened old man. "—lodged itself in the bricks about half a league above here. You can still see the scar it left; it's like a giant pockmark."

343

"What happened to the star?"

"It burned and sizzled, and was too bright to look upon. Men considered prying it out, so that it might resume its course, but it was too hot to approach closely, and they dared not quench it. After weeks it cooled into a knotted mass of black heaven metal, as large as a man could wrap his arms around."

"So large?" said Nanni, his voice full of awe. When stars fell to the earth of their own accord, small lumps of heaven metal were sometimes found, tougher than the finest bronze. The metal could not be melted for casting, so it was worked by hammering when heated red; amulets were made from it.

"Indeed, no one had ever heard of a mass of this size found on the earth. Can you imagine the tools that could be made from it!"

"You did not try to hammer it into tools, did you?" asked Hillalum, horrified.

"Oh, no. Men were frightened to touch it. Everyone descended from the tower, waiting for retribution from Yahweh for disturbing the workings of creation. They waited for months, but no sign came. Eventually they returned and pried out the star. It sits in a temple in the city below."

There was silence. Then one of the miners said, "I have never heard of this in the stories of the tower."

"It was a transgression, something not spoken of."

As they climbed higher up the tower, the sky grew lighter in color, until one morning Hillalum awoke and stood at the edge and yelled from shock: What had before seemed a pale sky now appeared to be a white ceiling stretched far above their heads. They were close enough now to perceive the vault of heaven, to see it as a solid carapace enclosing all the sky. All of the miners spoke in hushed tones, staring up like idiots, while the tower dwellers laughed at them.

As they continued to climb, they were startled at how *near* they actually were. The blankness of the vault's face had deceived them, making it undetectable until it appeared, abruptly, seemingly just above their heads. Now instead of climbing into the sky, they climbed up to a featureless plain that stretched endlessly in all directions.

All of Hillalum's senses were disoriented by the sight of it. Sometimes when he looked at the vault, he felt as if the world had flipped around somehow, and if he lost his footing he would fall upward to meet it. When the vault did appear to rest above his head, it had an oppressive *weight*. The vault was a stratum as heavy as all the world, yet utterly without support, and he feared what he never had in the mines: that the ceiling would collapse upon him.

Too, there were moments when it appeared as if the vault was a vertical cliff face of unimaginable height rising before him, and the dim earth behind him was another like it, and the tower was a cable stretched taut between the two. Or worst of all, for an instant it seemed that there was no up and no down, and his body did not know which way it was drawn. It was like fearing the height, but much worse. Often he would wake to find himself sweating and his fingers cramped, trying to clutch the brick floor.

Nanni and many of the other miners were bleary-eyed, too, though no one spoke of what disturbed their sleep. Their ascent grew slower, instead of faster as their foreman Beli had expected; the sight of the vault inspired unease rather than eagerness. The regular pullers became impatient with them. Hillalum wondered what sort of people were forged by living under such conditions; did they escape madness? Did they grow accustomed to this? Would the children born under a solid sky scream if they saw the ground beneath their feet?

Perhaps men were not meant to live in such a place. If their own natures restrained them from approaching heaven too closely, then men should remain on the earth.

When they reached the summit of the tower, the disorientation faded, or perhaps they had grown immune. Here, standing upon the square platform of the top, the miners gazed upon the most awesome scene ever glimpsed by men: Far below them lay a tapestry of soil and sea, veiled by mist, rolling out in all directions to the limit of the eye. Just above them hung the roof of the world itself, the absolute upper demarcation of the sky, guaranteeing their vantage point as the highest possible. Here was as much of creation as could be apprehended at once.

The priests led a prayer to Yahweh; they gave thanks that they were permitted to see so much and begged forgiveness for their desire to see more.

And at the top, the bricks were laid. One could catch the rich, raw smell of tar, rising out of the heated caldrons in which the lumps of bitumen were melted. It was the most earthy odor the miners had smelled in four months, and their nostrils were desperate to catch a whiff before it was whipped away by the wind. Here at the summit, where the ooze that had once seeped from the earth's cracks now grew solid to hold bricks in place, the earth was growing a limb into the sky.

Here worked the bricklayers, the men smeared with bitumen who mixed the mortar and deftly set the heavy bricks with absolute precision. More than anyone else, these men could not permit themselves to experience dizziness when they saw the vault, for the tower could not vary a finger's width from the vertical. They were nearing the end of their task, finally, and after four months of climbing, the miners were ready to begin theirs.

The Egyptians arrived shortly afterward. They were dark of skin and slight of build and had sparsely bearded chins. They had pulled carts filled with dolerite hammers, and bronze tools, and wooden wedges. Their foreman was named Senmut, and he conferred with Beli, the Elamites' foreman, on how they would penetrate the vault. The Egyptians built a forge with what they had brought, as did the Elamites, for recasting the bronze tools that would be blunted during the mining.

The vault itself remained just above a man's outstretched fingertips; it felt smooth and cool when one leapt up to touch it. It seemed to be made of fine-grained white granite, unmarred and utterly featureless. And therein lay the problem. Long ago Yahweh had released the Deluge, unleashing waters from both below and above; the waters of the Abyss had burst forth from the springs of the earth, and the waters of heaven had poured through the sluice gates in the vault. Now men saw the vault closely, but there were no sluice gates discernible. They squinted at the surface in all directions, but no openings, no windows, no seams interrupted the granite plain.

It seemed that their tower met the vault at a point between any reservoirs, which was fortunate indeed. If a sluice gate had been visible, they would have had to risk breaking it open and emptying the reservoir. That would mean rain for Shinar, out of season and heavier than the winter rains; it would cause flooding along the Euphrates. The rain would most likely end when the reservoir was emptied, but there was always the possibility that Yahweh would punish them and continue the rain until the tower fell and Babylon was dissolved into mud.

Even though there were no visible gates, a risk still existed. Perhaps the gates had no seams perceptible to mortal eyes, and a reservoir lay directly above them. Or perhaps the reservoirs were huge, so that even if the nearest sluice gates were many leagues away, a reservoir still lay above them.

There was much debate over how best to proceed.

"Surely Yahweh will not wash away the tower," argued Qurdusa, one of the bricklayers. "If the tower were sacrilege, Yahweh would have destroyed it earlier. Yet in all the centuries we've been working, we have never seen the slightest sign of Yahweh's displeasure. Yahweh will drain any reservoir before we penetrate it."

"If Yahweh looked upon this venture with such favor, there would already be a stairway ready-made for us in the vault," countered Eluti, an Elamite. "Yahweh will neither help or hinder us; if we penetrate a reservoir, we will face the onrush of its waters."

Hillalum could not keep his doubts silent at such a time. "And if the waters are endless? Yahweh may not punish us, but Yahweh may allow us to bring our judgment upon ourselves."

"Elamite," said Qurdusa, "even as a newcomer to the tower, you should know better than that. We labor for our love of Yahweh, we have done so for all our lives, and so have our fathers for generations back. Men as righteous as we could not be judged harshly."

"It is true that we work with the purest of aims, but that doesn't mean we have worked wisely. Did men tru¹y choose the correct path when they opted to live their lives away from the soil from which they were shaped? Never has Yahweh said that the choice was proper. Now we stand ready to break open heaven, even when we know that water lies above us. If we are misguided, how can we be sure Yahweh will protect us from our own errors?"

"Hillalum advises caution, and I agree," said Beli. "We must ensure that we do not bring a second Deluge upon the world, nor even dangerous rains upon Shinar. I have conferred with Senmut of the Egyptians, and he has shown me designs which they have employed to seal the tombs of their kings. I believe that their methods can provide us with safety when we begin digging."

The priests sacrificed the ox and the goat in a ceremony in which many sacred words were spoken and much incense was burned, and the miners began work.

Even before the miners reached the vault, it had been obvious that simple digging with hammers and picks would be impractical: Even if they were tunneling horizontally, they would make no more than two finger widths of progress a day through granite, and tunneling *upward* would be far, far slower. Instead, they employed fire setting.

With the wood they had brought, a bonfire was built below the chosen point of the vault and fed steadily for a day. Before the heat of the flames, the stone cracked and spalled. After letting the fire burn out, the miners splashed water onto the stone to further the cracking. They could then break the stone into large pieces, which fell heavily onto the tower. In this manner they could progress the better part of a cubit for each day the fire burned.

The tunnel did not rise straight up, but at the angle a staircase takes, so that they could build a ramp of steps up from the tower to meet it. The fire setting left the walls and floor smooth; the men built a frame of wooden steps underfoot so that they would not slide back down. They used a platform of baked bricks to support the bonfire at the tunnel's end.

After the tunnel rose ten cubits into the vault, they leveled it out and widened it to form a room. After the miners had removed all the stone that had been weakened by the fire, the Egyptians began work. They used no fire in their quarrying. With only their dolerite balls and hammers, they began to build a sliding door of granite. They first chipped away stone to cut an immense block of granite out of one wall. Hillalum and the other

347

miners tried to help but found it difficult: One did not wear away the stone by grinding but instead pounded chips off, using hammer blows of one strength alone, and lighter or heavier ones would not do.

After some weeks, the block was ready. It stood taller than a man and was even wider than that. To free it from the floor, they cut slots around the base of the stone and pounded in dry wooden wedges. Then they pounded thinner wedges into the first wedges to split them and poured water into the cracks so that the wood would swell. In a few hours, a crack traveled into the stone, and the block was freed.

At the rear of the room, on the right-hand side, the miners burned out a narrow upward-sloping corridor, and in the floor in front of the chamber entrance they dug a downward-sloping channel into the floor for a cubit. Thus there was a smooth continuous ramp that cut across the floor immediately in front of the entrance and ended just to its left.

On this ramp the Egyptians loaded the block of granite. They dragged and pushed it up into the side corridor, where it just barely fit, and propped it in place with a stack of flat mud bricks braced against the bottom of the left wall, like a pillar lying on the ramp.

With the sliding stone to hold back the waters, it was safe for the miners to continue tunneling. If they broke into a reservoir and the waters of heaven began pouring down into the tunnel, they would break the bricks one by one, and the stone would slide down until it rested in the recess in the floor, utterly blocking the doorway. If the waters flooded in with such force that they washed men out of the tunnels, the mud bricks would gradually dissolve, and again the stone would slide down. The waters would be retained, and the miners could then begin a new tunnel in another direction, to avoid the reservoir.

The miners again used fire setting to continue the tunnel, beginning at the far end of the room. To aid the circulation of air within the vault, oxhides were stretched on tall frames of wood and placed obliquely on either side of the tunnel entrance at the top of the tower. Thus the steady wind that blew underneath the vault of heaven was guided upward into the tunnel; it kept the fire blazing and cleared the air after the fire was extinguished, so that the miners could dig without breathing smoke.

The Egyptians did not stop working once the sliding stone was in place. While the miners swung their picks at the tunnel's end, the Egyptians labored at the task of cutting a stair into the solid stone, to replace the wooden steps. This they did with the wooden wedges, and the blocks they removed from the sloping floor left steps in their place.

Thus the miners worked, extending the tunnel on and on. The tunnel always ascended, though it reversed direction regularly like a thread in a giant stitch, so that its general path was straight up. They built other sliding-door rooms so that only the uppermost segment of the tunnel would be flooded if they penetrated a reservoir. They cut channels in the vault's surface from which they hung walkways and platforms; starting from these platforms, well away from the tower, they dug side tunnels, which joined the main tunnel deep inside. The wind was guided through these to provide ventilation, clearing the smoke from deep inside the tunnel.

For years the labor continued. The pulling crews no longer hauled bricks but wood and water for the fire setting. People came to inhabit those tunnels just inside the vault's surface, and on hanging platforms they grew downward-bending vegetables. The miners lived there at the border of heaven; some married and raised children. Few ever set foot on the earth again.

With a wet cloth wrapped around his face, Hillalum climbed down from wooden steps onto stone, having just fed some more wood to the bonfire at the tunnel's end. The fire would continue for many hours, and he would wait in the lower tunnels, where the wind was not thick with smoke.

Then there was a distant sound of shattering, the sound of a mountain of stone being split through, and then a steadily growing roar. A torrent of water came rushing down the tunnel.

For a moment, Hillalum was frozen in horror. The water, shockingly cold, slammed into his legs, knocking him down. He rose to his feet, gasping for breath, leaning against the current, clutching at the steps.

They had hit a reservoir.

He had to descend below the highest sliding door, before it was closed. His legs wished to leap down the steps, but he knew he couldn't remain on his feet if he did, and being swept down by the raging current would likely batter him to death. Going as fast as he dared, he took the steps one by one.

He slipped several times, sliding down as many as a dozen steps each time; the stone steps scraped against his back, but he felt no pain. All the while he was certain the tunnel would collapse and crush him, or else the entire vault would split open, and the sky would gape beneath his feet, and he would fall down to Earth amidst the heavenly rain. Yahweh's punishment had come, a second Deluge.

How much further until he reached the sliding stone? The tunnel seemed to stretch on and on, and the waters were pouring down even faster now. He was virtually running down the steps.

Stumbling, he splashed into shallow water. He had run down past the end of the stairs and fallen into the room of the sliding stone, and there was water higher than his knees.

He stood up and saw Damqiya and Ahuni, two fellow miners, just noticing him. They stood in front of the stone, which already blocked the exit.

"No!" he cried.

"They closed it!" screamed Damqiya. "They did not wait!"

"Are there others coming?" shouted Ahuni, without hope. "We may be able to move the block."

"There are no others," answered Hillalum. "Can they push it from the other side?"

"They cannot hear us." Ahuni pounded the granite with a hammer, making not a sound against the din of the rushing water.

Hillalum looked around the tiny room, only now noticing that an Egyptian floated facedown in the water.

"He died falling down the stairs," yelled Damqiya.

"Is there nothing we can do?"

Ahuni looked upward. "Yahweh, spare us."

The three of them stood in the rising water, praying desperately, but Hillalum knew it was in vain: Yahweh had not asked men to build the tower or to pierce the vault; the decision belonged to men alone, and they would die in this endeavor just as they did in any of their earthbound tasks. Their righteousness could not save them from the consequences of their deeds.

The water reached their chests. "Let us ascend," shouted Hillalum.

They climbed the tunnel laboriously, against the onrush, as the water rose behind their heels. The few torches illuminating the tunnel had been extinguished, so they ascended in the dark, murmuring prayers that they couldn't hear. The wooden steps at the top of the tunnel had dislodged from their place and were jammed farther down in the tunnel. They climbed past them until they reached the smooth stone slope, and there they waited for the water to carry them higher.

They waited without words, their prayers exhausted. Hillalum imagined that he stood in the black gullet of Yahweh, as the Mighty One drank deep of the waters of heaven, ready to swallow the sinners.

The water rose and bore them up, until Hillalum could reach up with his hands and touch the ceiling. The giant fissure from which the waters gushed forth was right next to him. Only a tiny pocket of air remained. Hillalum shouted, "When this chamber is filled, we can swim heavenward."

He could not tell if they heard him. He gulped his last breath as the water reached the ceiling, and swam up into the fissure. He would die closer to heaven than any man ever had before.

The fissure extended for many cubits. As soon as Hillalum passed through, the stone stratum slipped from his fingers, and his flailing limbs touched nothing. For a moment he felt a current carrying him, but then he was no longer sure. With only blackness around him, he once again felt that horrible vertigo that he had experienced when first approaching the vault: He could not distinguish any directions, not even up or down. He pushed and kicked against the water but did not know if he moved.

Helpless, he was perhaps floating in still water, perhaps swept furiously by a current; all he felt was numbing cold. Never did he see any light. Was there no surface to this reservoir that he might rise to?

Then he was slammed into stone again. His hands felt a fissure in the surface. Was he back where he had begun? He was being forced into it, and he had no strength to resist. He was drawn into the tunnel and was rattled against its sides. It was incredibly deep, like the longest mine shaft: He felt as if his lungs would burst, but there was still no end to the passage. Finally his breath would not be held any longer, and it escaped from his lips. He was drowning, and the blackness around him entered his lungs.

But suddenly the walls opened out away from him. He was being carried along by a rushing stream of water; he felt air above the water! And then he felt no more.

Hillalum awoke with his face pressed against wet stone. He could see nothing, but he could feel water near his hands. He rolled over and groaned; his every limb ached, he was naked, and much of his skin was scraped raw or wrinkled from wetness, but he breathed air.

Time passed, and finally he could stand. Water flowed rapidly about his ankles. Stepping in one direction, the water deepened. In the other, there was dry stone—shale by the feel of it.

It was utterly dark, like a mine without torches. With torn fingertips he felt his way along the floor, until it rose up and became a wall. Slowly, like some blind creature, he crawled back and forth. He found the water's source, a large opening in the floor. He remembered! He had been spewed up from the reservoir through this hole. He continued crawling for what seemed to be hours; if he were in a cavern, it was immense. He found a place where the floor rose in a slope. Was there a passage leading upward? Perhaps it could still take him to heaven.

Hillalum crawled, having no idea of how much time passed, not caring that he would never be able to retrace his steps, for he could not return whence he had come. He followed upward tunnels when he found them, downward ones when he had to. Though earlier he had swallowed more water than he would have thought possible, he began to feel thirst, and hunger.

And eventually he saw light and raced to the outside.

The light made his eyes squeeze closed, and he fell to his knees, his fists clenched before his face. Was it the radiance of Yahweh? Could his eyes bear to see it? Minutes later he could open them, and he saw desert. He had emerged from a cave in the foothills of some mountains, and rocks and sand stretched to the horizon.

Was heaven just like the earth? Did Yahweh dwell in a place such as this? Or was this merely another realm within Yahweh's creation, another Earth above his own, while Yahweh dwelled still higher?

A sun lay near the mountaintops behind his back. Was it rising or falling? Were there days and nights here?

Hillalum squinted at the sandy landscape. A line moved along the horizon. Was it a caravan?

He ran to it, shouting with his parched throat until his need for breath stopped him. A figure at the end of the caravan saw him and brought the entire line to a stop.

The one who had seen him seemed to be man, not spirit, and was dressed like a desert crosser. He had a waterskin ready. Hillalum drank as best he could, panting for breath.

Finally he returned it to the man and gasped, "Where is this place?"

"Were you attacked by bandits? We are headed to Erech."

Hillalum stared. "You would deceive me!" he shouted. The man drew back and watched him as if he were mad from the sun. Hillalum saw another man in the caravan walking over to investigate. "Erech is in Shinar!"

"Yes, it is. Were you not traveling to Shinar?" The other man stood ready with his staff.

"I came from—I was in—" Hillalum stopped. "Do you know Babylon?"

"Oh, is that your destination? That is north of Erech. It is an easy journey between them."

"The tower—have you heard of it?"

"Certainly, the pillar to heaven. It is said men at the top are tunneling through the vault of heaven."

Hillalum fell to the sand.

"Are you unwell?" The two caravan drivers mumbled to each other and went off to confer with the others. Hillalum was not watching them.

He was in Shinar. He had returned to the earth. He had climbed above the reservoirs of heaven and arrived back at the earth. Had Yahweh brought him to this place to keep him from reaching further above? Yet Hillalum still hadn't seen any signs, any indication that Yahweh noticed him. He had not experienced any miracle that Yahweh had performed to place him here. As far as he could see, he had merely swum up from the vault and entered the cavern below.

Somehow the vault of heaven lay beneath the earth. It was as if they lay against each other, though they were separated by many leagues. How could that be? How could such distant places touch? Hillalum's head hurt trying to think about it.

And then it came to him: *a seal cylinder*. When rolled upon a tablet of soft clay, the carved cylinder left an imprint that formed a picture. Two figures might appear at opposite ends of the tablet, though they stood side by side on the surface of the cylinder. All the world was as such a cylinder. Men imagined heaven and Earth as being at the ends of a tablet, with sky and stars stretched between; yet the world was wrapped around in some fantastic way so that heaven and Earth touched.

It was clear now why Yahweh had not struck down the tower, had not punished men for wishing to reach beyond the bounds set for them—for the longest journey would merely return them to the place whence they'd come. Centuries of their labor would not reveal to them any more of creation than they already knew. Yet through their endeavor, men would glimpse the unimaginable artistry of Yahweh's work, in seeing how ingeniously the world had been constructed. By this construction, Yahweh's work was indicated, and Yahweh's work was concealed.

Thus would men know their place.

Hillalum rose to his feet, his legs unsteady from awe, and sought out the caravan drivers. He would go back to Babylon. Perhaps he would see Lugatum again. He would send word to those on the tower. He would tell them about the shape of the world.

ALEXANDER JABLOKOV

The Death Artist

▼

With only a handful of elegant, coolly pyrotechnic stories, like the one that follows, Alexander Jablokov has established himself as one of the most highly regarded and promising new writers in SF. He is a frequent contributor to *Isaac Asimov's Science Fiction Magazine, Amazing,* and other markets. He lives in Somerville, Massachusetts, where he is involved in working on a projected anthology of "Future Boston" stories being put together by the Cambridge Writer's Workshop; he himself has written several stories set in the "Future Boston" *milieu.* His story "At the Cross-Time Jaunters' Ball" was in our Fifth Annual Collection, and his novella "A Deeper Sea" was in our Seventh Annual Collection. He has just released his first novel, *Carve the Sky,* to wide critical acclaim, and I have little doubt that he will come to be numbered among the Big Names of the '90s. Upcoming is a new novel, *A Deeper Sea.*

Here he takes us deep into a very strange far future, for a vivid and evocative pavane of identity and revenge . . . and murder.

▼

The Death Artist

ALEXANDER JABLOKOV

The snowshoe hare's half-eaten carcass lay under the deadfall of the figure-four trap, frozen blood crystallized on its fur, mouth still closed around the tiny piece of desiccated carrot which had served as bait. The snow was flattened around it, the rabbit's fur thrown everywhere. Jack London sniffed at the trap, laid its ears back, and growled. Canine bona fides reaffirmed, it settled back on its haunches and looked expectantly up at the man. Part samoyed, part husky, Jack's thick white fur concealed a body thin from hunger.

Elam didn't have to sniff. The stink of wolverine was malevolent in the still air. It turned the saliva that had come into his mouth at the thought of roasted hare into something spoiled. He spat. "Damn!" The trap couldn't be descented. He'd have to make another. No animal would come anywhere near a trap that smelled like that. The wolverine probably hadn't even been hungry.

He pulled the dry carrot from the rabbit's mouth and flung the remains off among the trees. The deadfall and the sticks of the figure four followed it, vanishing in puffs of snow.

"That's the last one, Jack," Elam said. "Nothing, again." The dog whined.

They set off among the dark smooth trunks of the maples and beeches, Elam's snowshoes squeaking in the freshly fallen snow. The dog turned its head, disturbed by the unprofessional noise, then loped off to investigate the upturned roots of a fallen tree. A breeze from the great lake to the north pushed its way through the trees, shouldering clumps of snow from the branches as it passed. A cardinal flashed from bough to bough, bright against the clearing evening sky.

Elam, a slender, graceful man, walked with his narrow shoulders hunched up, annoyed by the chilly bombardment from above. His clothing was entirely of furry animal pelts sewn crudely together. His thick hat was muskrat, his jacket fox and beaver, his mittens rabbit, his pants elk. At night he slept in a sack made of a grizzly's hide. How had he come to be here? Had he killed those animals, skinned them, cured their hides? He didn't know.

At night, sometimes, before he went to sleep, Elam would lie in his lean-to and, by the light of the dying fire, examine these clothes, running his hands through the fur, seeking memories in their thick softness. The various pelts were stitched neatly together. Had he done the sewing? Or had a wife or a sister? The thought gave him a curious feeling in the pit of his stomach. He rather suspected that he had always been alone. Weariness would claim him quickly, and he would huddle down in the warmth of the bear fur and fall asleep, questions unanswered.

Tree roots examined, Jack London returned to lead the way up the ridge. It was a daily ritual, practiced just at sunset, and the dog knew it well. The tumbled glacial rocks were now hidden under snow, making the footing uncertain. Elam carried his snowshoes under one arm as he climbed.

The height of the ridge topped the bare trees. To the north, glowing a deceptively warm red, was the snow-covered expanse of the great lake, where Elam often saw the dark forms of wolves, running and reveling in their temporary triumph over the water that barred their passage to the islands the rest of the year.

Elam had no idea what body of water it was. He had tentatively decided on Lake Superior, though it could have been Lake Winnipeg, or, for that matter, Lake Baikal. Elam sat down on a rock and stared at the deep north, where stars already gleamed in the sky. Perhaps he had it all wrong, and a new Ice Age was here, and this was a frozen Victoria Nyanza.

"Who am I, Jack? Do you know?"

The dog regarded him quizzically, used to the question by now. The man who's supposed to get us some food, the look said. Philosophical discussions later.

"Did I come here myself, Jack, or was I put here?"

Weary of the pointless and one-sided catechism, the dog was barking at a jay that had ventured too close. It circled for a moment, squawked, and shot off back into the forest.

The lake wind freshened and grew colder, driving the last clouds from the sky. The exposed skin on Elam's cheeks tightened. "Let's go, Jack." He pulled off a mitten and plunged his hand into a pocket, feeling his last chunk of pemmican, greasy and hard.

Aside from a few pathetically withered bits of carrot, which he needed to bait his traps, this was the last bit of food left him. He'd been saving it for an emergency. Every trap on the trapline that ran through these woods had been empty or befouled by wolverines, even in a hard winter that should have driven animals to eat anything. He would eat the pemmican that night.

Man and dog started their descent down the twilit reach of the ridge's other side. As they reached the base, Elam, his hand once again feeling the pemmican, afraid that it too would vanish before he could eat it, took too long a step and felt his right foot slide on the icy face of a tilted rock. His left foot caught in the narrow crack of an ice-shattered boulder, which grabbed him like a tight fist. The world flung itself forward at him. He felt the dull snap in his leg as the icy rock met his face.

He awoke to the warm licks of Jack London's tongue turning instantly cold on his face. He lay tumbled on his back among the rocks, head tilting downward, trees looming overhead. Annoyed, he pushed back and tried to stand. Searing agony in his leg brought bile to the back of his throat and a hot sweat over his body. He moaned and almost lost consciousness again, then held himself up on his elbows. His face was cut, some of his teeth were cracked, he could taste the blood in his mouth, but his leg, his leg . . . he looked down.

His left leg bent at an unnatural angle just below the knee. The leather of his trousers was soaked black with blood. Compound fracture of the . . . tibia? Fibula? For one distracted instant naming the shattered bone was the most important thing in the world. It obscured the knowledge that he was going to die.

He shifted position and moaned again. The biting pain in his leg grew sharp burning teeth whenever he moved, but wore the edges off if he lay still, subsiding to a gnaw. With a sudden effort, he pulled the leg straight, then fell back, gasping harshly. It made no difference, of course, but seeing the leg at that angle made him uncomfortable. It looked better this way, not near so painful.

He patted the dog on the head. "Sorry, Jack. I screwed up." The dog whined in agreement. Elam fell back and let the darkness take him.

His body did not give up so easily. He regained consciousness some time later, the frenzied whining and yelping of his dog sounding in his ears. He lay prone in the snow, his hands dug in ahead of him. His mittens were torn, and he could not feel his hands.

He rolled over onto his back and looked over his feet. Full night had come, but the starlight and the moon were enough to see the trail his body had left through the snow. Elam sighed. What a waste of time. The pain in his broken leg was almost gone, as was all other feeling from the thighs down. He spat. The spittle crackled on the snow. Damn cold. And the dog was annoying him with its whining.

"Sure boy, sure," he said, gasping from the cold weight of death on his chest. "Just a minute, Jack. Just a minute."

He pulled what was left of the fur glove off with his chin and reached the unfeeling claw of his hand into his pocket. It took a dozen tries before it emerged holding the pemmican.

He finally managed to open the front of his jacket and unlace his shirt. Cold air licked in eagerly. He smeared the greasy, hard pemmican over his chest and throat like a healing salve. Its rancid odor bit at his nose and, despite himself, he felt a moment of hunger. He shoved the rest of the piece down deep into his shirt.

"Here, Jack," he said. "Here. Dinner." The moon rode overhead, half in sunlight, the other half covered with glittering lines and spots.

The dog snuffled, suddenly frightened and suspicious. Elam reached up and patted it on the head. Jack London moved forward. Smelling the meat, its hunger overcame its caution at its master's strange behavior and it began to lick eagerly at Elam's throat and chest. The dog was desperately hungry. In its eagerness, a sharp tooth cut the man's skin, and thick, warm, blood welled out. The tongue licked more quickly. More cuts. More blood, steaming aromatically in the cold air. And the dog was hungry. The smell penetrated to the deepest parts of its brain, finally destroying the overlay of training, habit, and love. The dog's teeth tore and it began to feed.

And in that instant, Elam remembered. He saw the warm forests of his youth, and the face, so much like his, that had become his own. Justice had at last been done. Elam was going to die. He smiled slightly, gasped once, then his eyes glazed blank.

When it was sated, and realized what it had done, the dog howled its pain at the stars. It then sprang into the forest and ran madly, leaving the man's tattered remains far behind.

"Is that all you are going to do from now on?" Reqata said. "Commit suicide? Just lie down and die? Nice touch, I admit, the dog." She held his shoulder in a tight grip and looked past him with her phosphorescent eyes. "A real Elam touch."

Five dark ribs supported the smooth yellow stone of the dome. They revealed the green gleam of beetle carapaces in the light of the flames hanging in a hexagon around the central axis of the view chamber. Rows of striated marble seats climbed the chamber in concentric circles. The inhabitants of these seats stared down at the corpse lying in the snow at their feet.

Elam was himself startled at his clone's acquiescence in its own death, but he was surrounded by admirers before he could answer her. They moved past him, murmuring, gaining haut by their admiration for the subtlety of his work.

Elam stared past them at his own corpse, a sheen of frost already obscuring the face, turning it into an abstract composition. He had died well. He always did. His mind, back from the clone with its memories restored, seemed to rattle loosely around his skull. His skin was slick with amniotic fluid, his joints gritty. Nothing fit together. Reqata's hand on his shoulder seemed to bend the arbitrarily shaped bones, reminding him of his accidental quality.

"An artist who works with himself as both raw materials and subject can never transcend either," Reqata said.

Her scorn cut through the admiration around him. He looked up at her, and she smiled back with ebony teeth, flicking feathery eyelashes. She raised one hand in an angular gesture which identified her instantly, whatever body she was in.

"And how does the choreographer of mass death transcend her material?" Elam's mind had been gone for weeks, dying in a frozen forest, and Reqata had grown bored in his absence. She needed entertainment. Even lovers constantly dueled with haut, the indefinable quality that all players at the Floating Game understood implicitly. Reqata had much haut. Elam had more.

He squirmed. Was his bladder full, or did he always feel this way?

"Mass death, as you put it, is limited by practical problems," Reqata answered. "Killing one man is an existential act. Killing a million would be a historic act, at least to the Bound. Killing them all would be a divine act." She ran her fingers through his hair. He smelled the winy crispness of her breath. "Killing yourself merely smacks of lack of initiative. I'm disappointed in you, Elam. You used to fight before you died."

"I did, didn't I?" He remembered the desperate struggles of his early works, the ones that had gained him his haut. Men dying in mine shafts, on cliff sides, in predator-infested jungles. Men who had never stopped fighting. Each of those men had been himself. Something had changed.

"Tell me something," Reqata said, leaning forward. Her tongue darted across his earlobe. "Why do you always look so peaceful just before you die?"

A chill spread up his spine. He'd wondered the same thing himself. "Do I?" He squeezed the words out. He always paid. Five or ten minutes of memory, the final instants of life. The last thing he remembered from this particular work was pulling the pemmican from his pocket. After that, blackness. The dying clone Elam understood something the resurrected real Elam did not.

"Certainly. Don't be coy. Look at the grin on that corpse's frozen face." She slid into the seat next to him, draping a leg negligently into the aisle.

359

"I've tried dying. Not as art, just as experience. I die screaming. My screams echo for weeks." She shuddered, hands pressed over her ears. Her current body, as usual, had a high rib cage and small, firm breasts. Elam found himself staring at them. "But enough." Reqata flicked him with a fingernail, scratching his arm. "Now that you're done, I have a project for you to work on—"

"Perhaps each of you just gets a view of what awaits on the other side," a voice drawled.

"Don't lecture me on the absolute inertia of the soul," Reqata said, disconcerted. "No one's giving our clones a free peek at eternity, Lammiela."

"Perhaps not." A long, elegant woman, Lammiela always looked the same, to everyone's distress, for she only had one body. She smiled slowly. "Or perhaps heaven is already so filled with the souls of your clones that there won't be any room for you when you finally arrive."

Reqata stood up, fury in the rise of her shoulders. Because of her past irregularities, Lammiela had an ambiguous status, and Reqata hated risking haut in arguing with her. Usually, Reqata couldn't help herself. "Be careful, Lammiela. You don't know anything about it." And perhaps, Elam found himself thinking, perhaps Reqata feared Death indeed.

"Oh, true enough." Lammiela sat. "Ssarna's passing has everyone on edge. I keep forgetting." Her arrival had driven the last of the connoisseurs away, and the three of them sat alone in the viewing chamber.

"You don't forget, Mother," Elam said wearily. "You do it quite on purpose."

"That's unfair, Elam." She examined him. "You look well. Dying agrees with you." She intertwined her long fingers and rested her chin on them. Her face was subtly lined, as if shaded by an engraver. Her eyes were dark blue, the same as Elam's own. "Ssarna, they say, was withered in her adytum, dry as dust. The last time I saw her, which must have been at that party on top of that miserable mountain in the Himalayas, she was a tiny slip of a girl, prepubescent. Long golden . . . *tresses*. That must be the correct word." She shook her head with weary contempt. "Though she disguised herself as young, old age found her in her most private chamber. And after old age had had his way with her, he gave her to Death. They have an arrangement."

"And the first of them is enjoying you now," Reqata said. "How soon before the exchange comes?"

Lammiela's head jerked but she did not turn. "How have you been, Elam?" She smiled at him, and he was suddenly surrounded by the smell of her perfume, as if it were a trained animal she wore around her neck and had ordered to attack. The smell was dark and spicy. It reminded him of the smell of carrion, of something dead in the hot sun, thick and insistent. He found himself holding his breath, and stood up quickly, suddenly nauseated.

Nauseated, yet somehow excited. A child's feeling, the attraction of the vile, the need to touch and smell that which disgusts. Children will put anything in their mouths. He felt as if maggots were crawling under his fingernails.

"Air," Elam muttered. "I need. . . ." He walked up the striated marble stairs to the balcony above. Locked in their own conflict, neither woman followed. The warm summer air outside smelled of herbs and the dry flowers of chaparral. He clamped his teeth together and convinced him self that the flowers did not mask the smell of rotting flesh.

Sunset turned the day lavender. The view chamber's balcony hung high above the city, which flowed purposefully up the narrow valleys, leaving the dry hills bare, covered with flowers, acacia trees, and the spiky crystal plants that had evolved under some distant sun. The Mediterranean glinted far below.

Lights had come on in the city, illuminating its secret doorways. No one lived here. The Incarnate had other fashions, and the Bound were afraid of the ancient living cities, preferring to build their own. A Bound city could be seen burning closer to the water, its towers asserting themselves against the darkening sky. Tonight, many of the Incarnate who had witnessed Elam's performance would descend upon it for the evanescent excitements of those who lived out their lives bound to one body.

So this place was silent, save for the low resonance of bells, marking the hours for its absent dwellers. The city had been deserted for thousands of years, but was ready for someone to return. The insectoidal shapes of aircars fluttered up against the stars as Elam's audience went their separate ways.

A coppery half moon hung on the horizon, the invisible half of its face etched with colored lines and spots of flickering light. When he was young, Lammiela had told him that the Moon was inhabited by huge machines from some previous cycle of existence. The whole circle of a new moon crawled with light, an accepted feature. No one wondered at the thoughts of those intelligent machines, who looked up at the ripe blue-green planet that hung in their black sky.

"You should lie down," Lammiela said, "and rest." Her perfume was cloying and spicy. Though it did not smell even remotely of carrion, Elam still backed away, pushing himself against the railing, and let the evening breeze carry the scent away from him. Starlings swooped around the tower.

"You should get up," Reqata said, from somewhere behind her, "and run."

A blast of freezing air made him shiver. He took a step and looked down at the now hoarfrost-covered corpse in the deserted rotunda.

No Incarnate alive knew how the ancient machines worked. The corpse: was it just an image of the one in the frozen Michigan forest? Or had the rotunda's interior moved its spectators to hover over that forest in fact? Or was this body a perfect duplicate, here in the hills of Provence, of that other one? The knowledge was lost. No one knew what lay within the sphere of image. But Elam did know one thing: the cold winds of winter did not blow out of it.

Elam spotted the zeppelins about two and a half hours out of Kalgoorlie. Their colors were gaudy against the green fields and the blue Nullarbor Sea. Frost glittered on the sides away from the morning sun. Elam felt a physical joy, for the zeppelins had been caught completely by surprise. They drifted in the heavy morning air, big fat targets.

They were shuttling troops from somewhere to the North, in central Australia, to participate in one of those incomprehensible wars the Bound indulged in. Reqata had involved herself, in her capricious way, and staked haut on the outcome of the invasion of Eyre, the southern state.

Elam could see the crewmen leaping into their tiny flyers, their wings straightening in the sun like butterflies emerging from their chrysalis, but it was too late. Their zeppelins were doomed.

Elam picked his target, communicating his choice to the other bumble-bees, a few Incarnate who, amused at his constant struggle with Reqata, had joined him for the fun. The microwave signal felt like a directed whisper, save for the fact that it made his earlobes itch. He aimed for a bright green deltoid with markings that made it look like a giant spotted frog. For an instant the image took a hold of his mind, and he imagined catching a frog, grabbing it, and feeling its frightened wetness in his hand, the frantic beating of its heart. . . .

He pushed the thought away, upset at his loss of control. Timing was critical. A change in the angle of his wing stroke brought him back into position.

Elam was gorgeous. About a meter long, he had short, iridescent wings. A single long-distance optic tracked the target while two bulbous 270 degree peripherals checked the mathematical line of bumblebees to either side of him. Reqata was undoubtedly aboard one of the zeppelins, raging at the unexpected attack. The defending flyers were wide-faced black men, some odd purebred strain. Elam imagined the black Reqata, gesturing sharply as she arranged a defense. It was the quality of her movement that made her beautiful.

A steel ball whizzed past his left wing. A moment later he heard the faint tock! of the zeppelin's catapult. It took only one hit to turn a bumblebee into a stack of expensive kindling. Elam tucked one wing, tumbled, and straightened out again, coming in at his target. He unhooked his fighting legs and brought their razor edges forward.

The zeppelins were billowing, changing shape. Sudden flares disturbed

Elam's infrared sensors, making him dizzy, unsure of his target. Flying the bumblebees all the way out of Kalgoorlie without any lighter-than-air support craft had been a risk. They had to knock the zeppelins to the ground and parasitize them for reactive metals. The bumblebees would be vulnerable to a ground attack as they crawled clumsily over the wreckage, but no one gained haut without taking chances. He dodged past the defending flyers, not bothering to cut them. That would only delay him.

The green frog was now below him, swelling, rippling, dropping altitude desperately. He held it in his hand where he had caught it, amid the thick rushes. The other kids were gone, somewhere, and he was alone. The frog kicked and struggled. It had voided its bowels in his hand, and he felt the wet slime. The air was hot and thick underneath the cottonwoods. Something about the frog's frantic struggle for life annoyed him. It seemed odious that something so wet and slimy would wish to remain alive. He laid the frog down on a flat rock and, with calm deliberation, brought another rock down on its head. Its legs kicked and kicked.

The other zeppelins seemed to have vanished. All that remained was the frog, its guts lying out in the hot sun, putrefying as he watched. Fluids dripped down the rock, staining it. He wanted to slash it apart with fire, to feel the flare as it gave up its life. The sun seared down on his shoulders.

With a sudden fury, the zeppelin turned on him. He found himself staring into its looming mouth. A hail of steel balls flew past him, and he maneuvered desperately to avoid them. He didn't understand why he had come so close without attacking.

Two balls ripped simultaneously through his right wing, sending flaring pain through the joints. He twisted down, hauling in on the almost non-functional muscles. If he pulled the wing in to a stable tip, he could glide downward. Green fields spiraled up at him, black houses with high-peaked roofs, colorful gardens. Pale faces peered up at him from the fields. Military vehicles had pulled up on a sandy road, the dark muzzles of their guns tracking him.

The right wing was flopping loose, sending waves of pain through his body. He veered wildly, land and sky switching position. Pulling up desperately, he angled his cutting leg and sliced off the loose part of his wing. Hot, cutting pain slashed through him.

He had finally managed to stabilize his descent, but it was too late. A field of corn floated up to meet him. For an instant, everything was agony.

"I want something primitive," Elam said, as the doctor slid a testing limb into the base of his spine. "Something prehistoric."

"All of the human past is prehistoric," Dr. Abias said. He withdrew the limb with a cold tickle, and retracted it into his body. "Your body is healthy."

Elam stood up, swinging his arms, getting used to his new proportions. His current body was lithe, gold-skinned, small-handed; designed to Reqata's specifications. She had some need of him in this form, and Elam found himself apprehensive. He had no idea if she was still angry about her defeat over Australia. "No, Abias. I mean before *any* history. Before man knew himself to be man."

"Neanderthal?" Abias murmured, hunching across the floor on his many legs. "Pithecanthropus? Australopithecus?"

"I don't know what any of those words mean," Elam said. Sometimes his servant's knowledge bothered him. What right did the Bound have to know so much when the Incarnate could dispose of their destinies so thoroughly?

Abias turned to look back at him with his multiple oculars, brown human eyes with no face, pupils dilated. He was a machine, articulated and segmented, gleaming as if anointed with rare oils. Each of his eight moving limbs was both an arm and a leg, as if his body had been designed to work in orbit. Perhaps it had. As he had pointed out, most of the past was prehistory.

"It doesn't matter," Abias said. "I will look into it."

A Bound, Abias had been assigned to Elam by Lammiela. Punished savagely for a crime against the Incarnate, his body had been confiscated and replaced by some ancient device. Abias now ran Elam's team of cloned bodies. He was considered one of the best trainers in the Floating Game. He was so good and his loyalty so absolute that Elam had steadfastly refused to discover what crime he had committed, fearing that the knowledge would interfere in their professional relationship.

"Do that," Elam said. "I have a new project in mind." He walked across the wide, open room, feeling the sliding of unfamiliar joints. This body, a clone of his own, had been extensively modified by Abias, until there were only traces of his own nature in it. A plinth was laid with earrings, wrist and ankle bracelets, body paints, scent bottles, all supplied by Reqata. He began to put them on.

Light shone through from overhead through semicircular openings in the vault. A rough-surfaced ovoid curved up through the floor in the room's center. It was Elam's adytum, the most secret chamber where his birth body lay. After his crash in Australia, he had woken up in it for an instant, with a feeling of agony, as if every part of his body were burning. The thought still made him shudder.

An Incarnate's adytum was his most strongly guarded space, for when his real body died, he died as well. There could be no transfer of consciousness to a cloned body once the original was dead. The ancient, insolent machines that provided the ability to transfer the mind did not permit it, and since no one understood the machines, no one could do anything about it. And killing an Incarnate's birth body was the only way to truly commit murder.

Elam slid on a bracelet. "Do you know who attacked me?"

"No one has claimed responsibility," Abias answered. "Did you recognize anything of the movement?"

Elam thought about the billowing frog-like zeppelin. It hadn't been Reqata, he was sure of that. She would have made sure that he knew. But it could have been almost anyone else.

"Something went wrong in the last transfer," Elam said, embarrassed at bringing up such a private function, even to his servant. "I woke up in my adytum."

Abias stood still, unreadable. "A terrible malfunction. I will look into it."

"Just make sure it doesn't happen again."

The party was in the hills above the city of El'lie. Water from the northern rivers poured here from holes in the rock and swirled through an elaborate maze of waterways. It finally reached one last great pool, which extended terrifyingly off the rocky slope, as if ready to tip and spill, drowning the city below it. The white rock of the pool's edge extended downward some thousands of feet, a polished sheet like the edge of the world. Far below, cataracts spilled from the pool's bottom towards the thirsty city.

Elam stood on a terrace and gazed down into the water. Reqata floated there, glistening as the afternoon sun sank over the ocean to the west. She was a strange creature, huge, all sleekly iridescent curves, blue and green, based on some creature humans had once encountered in their forgotten travels across the galaxy. She sweated color into the water, heavy swirls of bright orange and yellow sinking into the depths. Until a few hours before she had been wearing a slender, gold-skinned body like Elam's.

"They seem peaceful," she whispered, her voice echoing across the water. "But the potential for violence is extreme."

Reqata had hauled him on a preliminary tour of El'lie, site of her next art work. He remembered the fresh bodies hung in tangles of chain on a granite wall, a list of their crimes pasted on their chests; the tense market, men and women with shaved foreheads and jewels in their eyebrows, the air thick with spices; the lazy insolence of a gang of men, their faces tattooed with angry swirls, as they pushed their way through the market crowd on their way to a proscribed patriarchal religious service; the great tiled temples of the Goddesses that lined the market square.

"When will they explode?" Elam said.

"Not before the fall, when the S'tana winds blow down from the mountains. You'll really see something then." Hydraulic spines erected and sank down on her back, and she made them make a characteristic gesture, sharp and emphatic. If she was angry about what had happened in Australia, she concealed it. That frightened Elam more than open anger would have. Reqata had a habit of delayed reaction.

Reqata was an expert at exploiting obscure hostilities among the Bound, producing dramatically violent conflicts with blood spilling picturesquely down carved staircases; heads piled up in heaps, engraved ivory spheres thrust into their mouths; lines of severed hands on bronze poles, fingers pointing towards Heaven. That was her art. She had wanted advice. Elam had not been helpful.

Glowing lights floated above the pool, swirling in response to incomprehensible tropisms. No one knew how to control them anymore, and they moved by their own rules. A group of partyers stood on the far side of the pool, their bright-lit reflections stretching out across the glassy water.

"This water's thousands of feet deep," Reqata murmured. "The bottom's piled up with forgotten things. Boats. Gold cups. The people from the city come up here and drop things in for luck."

"Why should dropping things and forgetting about them be lucky?" Elam asked.

"I don't know. It's not always lucky to remember everything."

Elam stripped off his gown and dove into the dark water. Reqata made a bubbling sound of delight. He stroked the spines on her back, feeling them swell and deflate. He ran a cupped hand up her side. Her glowing solar sweat worked its way between his fingers and dripped down, desperate to reach its natural place somewhere in the invisible depths.

"Put on a body like this," she said. "We can swim the deep oceans and make love there, among the fish."

"Yes," he said, not meaning it. "We can."

"Elam," she said. "What happened on the balcony after we saw you die in the forest? You seemed terrified."

Elam thought, instead, of the frog. Had his memories been real? Or could Reqata have laid a trap for him? "Just a moment of nausea. Nothing."

Reqata was silent for a moment. "She hates you, you know. Lammiela. She utterly hates you."

Her tone was vicious. Here it was, vengeance for the trick he had pulled over the Nullarbor Sea. Her body shuddered, and he was suddenly conscious of how much larger than him she now was. She could squish him against the side of the pool without any difficulty. He would awake in his own chamber, in another body. Killing him was just insulting, not fatal. Perhaps it *had* been her in that frog zeppelin.

He swam slowly away from her. "I don't know what you're talking about."

"Of course you don't. You're an expert at forgetting, at just lying down, dying, and forgetting. She hates you for what you did. For what you did to your sister!" Her voice was triumphant.

Elam felt the same searing pain he had felt when he awoke for one choking instant in his adytum. "I don't know what you're talking about," he said, as he pulled himself out of the water.

"I know! That's just the problem."

"Tell me what you mean." He kept his voice calm.

Something moved heavily in the darkness, and a row of chairs overturned with a clatter. Elam turned away from the pool. His heart pounded. A burst of laughter sounded from across the pool. The party was continuing, but the guests were impossibly far away, like a memory of childhood, unreachable and useless.

A head rose up out of the darkness, a head twice the size of Elam's body. It was a metal egg, dominated by two expressionless eyes. Behind dragged a long, multi-limbed body, shiny and obscene. Elam screamed in unreasoning and senseless terror.

The creature moved forward, swaying its head from side to side. Acid saliva drooled from beneath its crystal teeth, splashing and fizzing on the marble terrace. It was incomprehensibly ancient, something from the long-forgotten past. It swept its tail around and dragged Elam towards it.

For an instant, Elam was paralyzed, staring at the strange beauty of the dragon's teeth as they moved towards him. Then he struggled against the iron coil of the tail. His body still had traces of oil, and he slid out, stripping skin. He dove between the dragon's legs, bruising his bones on the terrace.

The dragon whipped around quickly, cornering him. With a belch, it sprayed acid over him. It burned down his shoulder, bubbling as it dissolved his skin.

"Damn you!" he shouted, and threw himself at the dragon's head. It didn't pull back quickly enough and he plunged his fist into its left eye. Its surface resisted, then popped, spraying fluid. The dragon tossed its head, flinging Elam across the ground.

He pulled himself to his feet, feeling the pain of shattered ribs. Blood dribbled down his chin. One of his legs would not support his weight. The massive head lowered down over him, muck pouring out of the destroyed eye. Elam grabbed for the other eye, but he had no strength left. Foul-smelling acid flowed over him, sloughing his flesh off with the sound of frying bacon. He stayed on his feet, trying to push imprecations between his destroyed lips. The last thing he saw was the crystal teeth, lowering towards his head.

Lammiela's house was the abode of infinity. The endless rooms were packed with the junk of a hundred worlds. The information here was irreplaceable, unduplicated anywhere else. No one came to visit, and the artifacts, data cubes, and dioramas rested in silence.

At some time in the past millennia, human beings had explored as far inward as the galactic core and so far outward that the galaxy had hung above them like a captured undersea creature, giving up its light to intergalactic space. They had moved through globular clusters of ancient suns and explored areas of stellar synthesis. They had raised monuments on distant planets. After some centuries of this, they had returned to Earth, built their mysterious cities on a planet that must have been nothing but old legend, and settled down, content to till the aged soil and watch the sun rise and set. And, with magnificent insouciance, they had forgotten everything, leaving their descendants ignorant.

Lammiela sat in the corner watching Elam. Her body, though elegant, was somehow bent, as if she had been cut from an oddly shaped piece of wood by a clever wood carver utilizing the limitations of his material. That was true enough, Elam reflected, examining the person who was both his parents.

When young, Lammiela had found a ship somewhere on Earth's moon, tended by the secret mechanisms that made their lives there, and gone forth to explore the old spaces. No one had any interest in following her, but somehow her exploits had gained enough attention that she had obtained extraordinary privileges.

"It's curious," she said. "Our friends the Bound have skills that we Incarnate do not even dream of, because the machines our ancestors left us have no interest in them." She looked thoughtful for a moment. "It's surprising, some of the things the Bound can do."

"Like make you both my father and my mother," Elam said.

Her face was shadowed. "Yes. There is that."

Lammiela had been born male, named Laurance. But Laurance had felt himself to be a woman. No problem for one of the Incarnate, who could be anything they wished. Laurance could have slept securely in his adytum and put female bodies on for his entire life. But Laurance did not think that way. He had gone to the Bound, and they had changed him to a woman.

"When the job was finished, I was pregnant," Lammiela said. "Laurance's sperm had fertilized my new ova. I don't know if it was a natural consequence of the rituals they used." Her muscles tightened with the memories. Tendons stood out on the backs of her hands. "They kept me conscious through it all. Pain is their price. They slew the male essence. I saw it, screaming before me. Laurance, burning."

It had cost most of her haut to do it. Dealings with the Bound inevitably involved loss of status.

"I still see him sometimes," she said.

"Who?" Elam asked.

"Your father, Laurance." Her eyes narrowed. "They didn't kill him well enough, you see. They told me they did, but he's still around." Her eyes darted, as if expecting to find Laurance hiding behind a diorama.

Elam felt a chill, a sharp feeling at the back of his neck, as if someone with long, long nails were stroking him there. "But you're him, Lammiela. He's not someone else."

"Do you really know so much about identity, Elam?" She sighed, relaxing. "You're right, of course. Still, was it I who stood in the Colonnade at Hrlad?" She pointed at a hologram of a long line of rock plinths, the full galaxy rising beyond them. "I'm not sure I remember it, not as if I had been there. It was legend, you know. A bedtime story. But Hrlad is real. So is Laurance. You look like him, you know. You have your father's eyes."

She stared at him coldly, and he, for the first time, thought that Reqata might have spoken truly. Perhaps his mother did indeed hate him.

"I made my choice," she said. "I can never go back. The Bound won't let me. I am a woman, and a mother."

Lammiela did not live in the city where most of the Incarnate made their home. She lived on a mountainside, bleak and alone, the rigid, curving walls of her house holding off the snow. She moved her dwelling periodically, from seashore to desert to mountain. She had no adytum, with its body, to lug with her. Elam, somehow, remembered deep forest when he was growing up, interspersed with sunny meadows. The vision wasn't clear. Nothing was clear.

After this most recent death, Elam had once again awakened in his adytum. He'd felt the fluid flowing through his lungs, and the darkness pressing down on his open eyes. Fire had burned through his veins, but there was no air to scream with. Then he had awakened again, normally, on a pallet in the light.

"Mother," he said, looking off at a broad-spectrum hologram of Sirius which spilled vicious white light across the corner of the room, too bright to look at directly without filters. "Am I truly your only child?"

Lammiela's face was still. "Most things are secrets for the first part of their existence, and forgotten thereafter. I suppose there must be a time in the middle when they are known. Who told you?"

"Does it matter?"

"Yes. It was thrown at you as a weapon, wasn't it?"

Elam sighed. "Yes. Reqata."

"Ah, yes. I should have guessed. Dear Reqata. Does she love you, Elam?" The question took him aback. "She says she does."

"I'm sure she means it then. I wonder what it is about you that she loves. Is that where the discussion ended then? With the question?"

369

"Yes. We were interrupted." Elam described the dragon's attack.

"Ah, how convenient. Reqata was always a master of timing. Who was it, do you suppose?" She looked out of the circular window at the mountain tundra, the land falling away to a vast ice field, just the rocky peaks of mountains thrusting through it. "No one gains haut anonymously."

"No one recognized the style. Or, if they did, they did not admit it." The scene was wrong, Elam thought. It should have been trees: smooth-trunked beeches, heavy oaks. The sun had slanted through them as if the leaves themselves generated the light.

"So why are you here, Elam? Are you looking for the tank in which that creature was grown? You may search for it if you like. Go ahead."

"No!" Elam said. "I want to find my sister." And he turned away and ran through the rooms of the house, past the endless vistas of stars that the rest of the human race had comfortably forgotten. Lammiela silently followed, effortlessly sliding through the complex displays, as Elam stumbled, now falling into an image of a kilometer-high cliff carved with human figures, now into a display of ceremonial masks with lolling tongues. He suddenly remembered running through these rooms, their spaces much larger then, pursued by a small, violent figure that left no place to hide.

In a domed room he stopped at a wall covered with racks of dark metal drawers. He pushed a spot and one slid open. Inside was a small animal, no bigger than a cat, dried as if left out in the sun. It was recognizably the dragon, curled around itself, its crystalline teeth just visible through its pulled-back lips.

Lammiela looked down at it. "You two never got along. You would have thought that you would . . . but I guess that was a foolish assumption. You tormented her with that thing, that . . . monster. It gave her screaming nightmares. Once, you propped it by her bed so that she would see it when she woke up. For three nights after that she didn't sleep." She slid the drawer shut.

"*Who was she?*" Elam demanded, taking her shoulders. She met his gaze. "It's no longer something that will just be forgotten."

She weakly raised a hand to her forehead, but Elam wasn't fooled. His mother had dealt with dangers that could have killed her a dozen times over. He tightened his grip on her shoulders. "Your sister's name was Orfea. Lovely name, don't you think? I think Laurance picked it out."

Elam could remember no sister. "Was she older or younger?"

"Neither. You were split from one ovum, identical twins. One was given an androgen bath and became you, Elam. The other was female: Orfea. God, how you grew to hate each other! It frightened me. And you were both so talented. I still have some of her essence around, I think."

"I . . . what happened to her? Where is she?"

"That was the one thing that consoled me, all these years. The fact that you didn't remember. I think that was what allowed you to survive."

"What? Tell me!"

Lammiela took only one step back, but it seemed that she receded much farther. "She was murdered. She was just a young girl. So young."

Elam looked at her, afraid of the answer. He didn't remember what had happened, and he could still see hatred in his mother's eyes. "Did they ever find out who did it?" he asked softly.

She seemed surprised by the question. "Oh, there was never any doubt. She was killed by a young friend of yours. He is now your servant. Abias."

"I have to say that it was in extremely poor taste," Reqata said, not for the first time. "Death is a fine performance, but there's no reason to perform it at a dinner party. Particularly in my presence."

She got up from the bed and stretched. This torso was wide, and well muscled. Once again, the rib cage was high, the breasts small. Elam wondered if, in the secrecy of her adytum, Reqata was male. He had never seen her in any other than a female body.

"Just out of curiosity," Elam said. "Could you tell who the dragon was?" He ran his hand over the welts on his side, marks of Reqata's fierce love.

She glanced back at him, eyelids half lowered over wide, violet eyes. She gauged if her answer would affect her haut. "Now *that* was a good trick, Elam. If I hadn't been looking right at you, I would have guessed that it was you behind those glass fangs."

She walked emphatically across the room, the slap of her bare feet echoing from the walls, and stood, challengingly, on the curve of Elam's adytum. Dawn had not yet come, and light was provided by hanging globes of a blue tint that Elam found unpleasant. He had never found a way to adjust or replace them.

"Oh Elam," she said. "If you are working on something, I approve. How you fought! You didn't want to die. You kept struggling until there was nothing left of you but bones. That dragon crunched them like candy canes." She shuddered, her face flushed. "It was wonderful."

Elam stretched and rolled out of the bed. As his weight left it, it rose off the floor, to vanish into the darkness overhead. The huge room had no other furniture.

"What do you know about my sister?" he asked.

Reqata lounged back on the adytum, curling her legs. "I know she existed, I know she's dead. More than you did, apparently." She ran her hands up her sides, cupping her breasts. "You know, the first stories I heard of you don't match you. You were more like me then. Death was your art, certainly, but it wasn't your own death."

371

"As you say," Elam said, stalking towards her, "I don't remember."

"How could you have forgotten?" She rested her hands on the rough stone of the adytum. "This is where you are, Elam. If I ripped this open, I could kill you. Really kill you. Dead."

"Want to try it?" He leaned over her. She rested back, lips parted, and dug her fingernails in a circle around his nipple.

"It could be exciting. Then I could see who you really were."

He felt the sweet bite of her nails through his skin. If he had only one body, he reflected, perhaps he could never have made love to Reqata. He couldn't have lasted.

He pushed himself forward onto her, and they made love on his adytum, above his real body as it slumbered.

Abias's kingdom was brightly lit, to Elam's surprise. He had expected a mysterious darkness. Hallways stretched in all directions, leading to chambers of silent machines and tanks filled with organs and bodies. As he stepped off the stairs, Elam realized that he had never before been down to these lower levels, even though it was as much a part of his house as any other. But this was Abias's domain. This was where the magic was done.

His bumblebee lay on a table, its dead nervous system scooped out. Dozens of tiny mechanisms crawled over it, straightening its spars, laying fragile wing material between the ribs. Elam pictured them crawling over his own body, straightening out his ribs, coring out his spinal column, resectioning his eyes.

Elam touched a panel and a prism rose up out of the floor. In it was himself, calmly asleep. Elam always kept several standard, unmodified versions of his own body ready. That was the form in which he usually died. Elam examined the face of his clone. He had never inhabited this one, and it looked strange in consequence. No emotions had ever played over those slack features, no lines of care had ever formed on the forehead or around the eyes. The face was an infant turned physically adult.

The elaborate shape of Abias appeared in a passage and made its way towards him, segmented legs gleaming. Elam felt a moment of fear. He imagined those limbs seizing his mysterious, faceless sister, Orfea, rending her, their shine dulled with her blood, sizzling smoke rising . . . he fought the images down. Abias had been a man then, if he'd been anything. He'd lost his body as a consequence of that murder.

Abias regarded him. As a Bound, and a cyborg to boot, Abias had no haut. He had no character to express, needed no gestures to show who he was. His faceless eyes were unreadable. Had he been trying to kill Elam? He had the skills and resources to have created the zeppelin, grown the dragon. But why? If he wanted to kill Elam, the real Elam, the adytum lay in his power. Those powerful limbs could rip the chamber open and drag the sleeping Elam out into the light. Elam's consciousness, in a clone somewhere else, wouldn't know what had happened, but would suddenly cease to exist.

"Is the new body ready?" Elam said abruptly.

Abias moved quietly away. After a moment's hesitation, Elam followed, deeper into the lower levels. They passed a prism where a baby with golden skin slept, growing towards the day that Elam could inhabit it, and witness Reqata's El'lie art work. It would replace the body destroyed by the dragon. Lying on a pallet was a short, heavy-boned body with a rounded jaw and beetle brows.

"It was a matter of genetic regression, based on the markers in the cytoplasmic mitochondria," Abias said, almost to himself. "The mitochondrial DNA is the timer, since it comes only from the female ancestor. The nucleic genetic material is completely scrambled. But much of it stretches back far enough. And of course we have stored orang and chimp genes as well. If you back and fill—"

"That's enough, Abias," Elam said impatiently. "It doesn't matter."

"No, of course not. It doesn't matter. But this is your Neanderthal."

Elam looked down at the face that was his own, a few hundred thousand years back into the past. "How long have I known you, Abias?"

"Since we were children," Abias said softly. "Don't you remember?"

"You know I don't remember. How could I have lived with you for so long otherwise? You killed my sister."

"How do you know that?"

"Lammiela told me that you killed Orfea."

"Ah," Abias said. "I didn't kill her, Elam." He paused. "You don't remember her."

"No. As far as I'm concerned, I have always been alone."

"Perhaps you always have been."

Elam considered this. "Are you claiming that Reqata and my mother are lying? That there never was an Orfea?"

Abias lowered all of his limbs until he was solid on the floor. "I think you should be more worried about who is trying to kill you. These attempts are not accidents."

"I know. Perhaps you."

"That's not even worth answering."

"But who would want to go around killing me repeatedly in my clones?"

"From the information we have now," Abias said, "it could be anyone. It could even be Orfea."

"Orfea?" Elam stared at him. "Didn't you just claim she never existed?"

"I did not. I said I didn't kill her. I didn't. Orfea did not die that day." His eyes closed and he was immobile. "Only I did."

It was a land that was familiar, but as Elam stalked it in his new body, he did not know whether it was familiar to him, Elam, or to the Neanderthal he now was. It was covered with a dark forest, broken by clearings, crossed by clear, icy streams scattered with rocks. The air was cold and damp, a living air. His body was wrapped in fur. It was not fur from an animal he had killed himself, but something Abias had mysteriously generated, in the same way he had generated the fur Elam had worn when he died in the Michigan winter. For all he knew, it was some bizarre variant of his own scalp hair.

Since this was just an exploratory journey, the creation of below-conscious reflexes, Elam retained his own memories. They sat oddly in his head. This brain perceived things more directly, seeing each beam of sunlight through the forest canopy as a separate entity, with its own characteristics and personality, owing little to the sun from which it ultimately came.

A stream had cut a deep ravine, revealing ruins. The Neanderthal wandered among the walls, which stood knee deep in the water, and peered thoughtfully at their bricks. He felt as if he were looking at the ruins of the incomprehensibly distant future, not the past at all. He imagined wading mammoths pushing their way through, knocking the walls over in their search for food. At the thought of a mammoth his hands itched to feel the haft of a spear, though he could certainly not kill such a beast by himself. He needed the help of his fellows, and they did not exist. He walked the earth alone.

Something grunted in a pool that had once been a basement. He sloshed over to it, and gazed down at the frog. It sat on the remains of a windowsill, pulsing its throat. Elam reached down . . . and thought of the dying frog, shuddering its life out in his hand. He tied it down, limbs outspread, and played the hot cutting beam over it. It screamed and begged as the smoke from its guts rose up into the clear sky.

Elam jerked his hand back from the frog, which, startled, dove into the water and swam away. He turned and climbed the other side of the ravine. He was frightened by the savagery of the thought that had possessed him. When he pulled himself over the edge he found himself in an area of open rolling hills, the forest having retreated to the colder, northern slopes.

The past seemed closer here, as if he had indeed lived it.

He *had* hated Orfea. The feeling came to him like the memory of a shaman's rituals, fearsome and complex. It seemed that the hate had always been with him. That form, with his shape and gestures, loomed before him.

The memories were fragmentary, more terrifying than reassuring, like sharp pieces of colored glass. He saw the face of a boy he knew to be Abias, dark-eyed, curly-haired, intent. He bent over an injured animal, one of Elam's victims, his eyes shiny with tears. Young, he already possessed a good measure of that ancient knowledge the Bound remembered. In this case the animal was beyond healing. With a calmly dismissive gesture, Abias broke its neck.

The leaves in the forest moved of their own will, whispering to each other of the coming of the breeze, which moved its cool fingers across the back of Elam's neck.

He remembered Orfea, a slender girl with dark hair, but he never saw her clearly. Her image appeared only in reflections, side images, glimpses of an arm or a strand of hair. And he saw himself, a slender boy with dark hair, twin to Orfea. He watched himself as he tied a cat down to a piece of wood, spreading it out as it yowled. There was a fine downy hair on his back, and he could count the vertebrae as they moved under his smooth, young skin. The arm sawed with its knife and the cat screamed and spat.

The children wandered the forest, investigating what they had found in the roots of a tree. It was some sort of vast lens, mostly under the ground, with only one of its faces coming out into the air. They brushed the twigs and leaves from it and peered in, wondering at its ancient functions. Elam saw Orfea's face reflected in it, solemn eyes examining him, wondering at him. A beam of hot sunlight played on the lens, awakening lights deep within it, vague images of times and places now vanished. Midges darted in the sun, and Orfea's skin produced a smooth and heavy odor, one of the perfumes she mixed for herself: her art, as death was Elam's. Elam looked down at her hand, splayed on the smooth glass, then across at his, already rougher, stronger, with the hints of dark, dried blood around the fingernails.

Abias stood above them. He danced on the smooth glass, his callused feet slipping. He laughed every time he almost fell. "Can you see us?" he cried to the lens. "Can you see who we are? Can you see who we will become?" Elam looked up at him in wonder, then down at the boy's tiny, distorted reflection as it cavorted among the twisted trees.

The sun was suddenly hot, slicing through the trees like a burning edge. Smoke rose as it sizzled across flesh. Elam howled with pain and ran up the slope. He ran until his lungs were dying within him.

The Neanderthal stopped in a clearing up the side of a mountain. A herd of clouds moved slowly across the sky, cropping the blue grass of the overhead. Around him rocks, the old bones of the earth, came up through its sagging flesh. The trees whispered derisively below him. They talked of death and blood. "You should have died," they said. "The other should have lived." The Neanderthal turned his tear-filled eyes into the wind, though whether he wept for Orfea, or for Elam, even he could not have said.

*   *   *

The city burned with a dry thunder. Elam and Reqata ran through the crowded, screaming streets with the arsonists, silent and pure men. In the shifting firelight, their tattooed faces swirled and re-formed, as if made of smoke themselves.

"The situation has been balanced for years," Reqata said. "Peace conceals strong forces pushing against each other. Change their alignment, and . . ." Swords flashed in the firelight, a meaningless battle between looters and some sort of civil guard. Ahead were the tiled temples of the Goddesses, their goal.

"They feel things we don't," she said. "Religious exaltation. The suicidal depression of failed honor. Fierce loyalty to a leader. Hysterical terror at signs and portents."

Women screamed from the upper windows of a burning building, holding their children out in vain hope of salvation.

"Do you envy them?" Elam asked.

"Yes!" she cried. "To them, life is not a game." Her hand was tight on his arm. "They know who they are."

"And we don't?"

"Take me!" Reqata said fiercely. Her fingernails stabbed through his thin shirt. They had made love in countless incarnations, and these golden-skinned, slender bodies were just another to her, even with the flames rising around them.

He took her down on the stone street as the city burned around them. Her scent pooled dark. It was the smell of death and decay. He looked at her. Beneath him, eyes burning with malignant rage, was Orfea.

"You are alive," Elam cried.

Her face glowered at him. "No, you bastard," she said. "I'm not alive. You are. *You are.*"

His rage suddenly matched hers. He grabbed her hair and pulled her across the rough stone. "Yes. And I'm going to stay that way. Understand? Understand?" With each question, he slammed her head on the stone.

Her face was amused. "Really, Elam. I'm dead, remember? Dead and gone. What's the use of slamming me around?"

"You were always like that. Always sensible. Always driving me crazy!" He stopped, his hands around her throat. He looked down at her. "Why did we hate each other so much?"

"Because there was really only ever one of us. It was Lammiela who thought there were two."

Pain sliced across his cheek. Reqata slapped him again, making sure her nails bit in. Blood poured down her face and her hair was tangled. Elam stumbled back, and was shoved aside by a mob of running soldiers.

"Are you crazy?" she shouted. "You can't kill me. You can't. You'll ruin everything." She was hunched, he saw now, cradling her side. She reached down and unsheathed her sword. "Are you trying to go back to your old style? Try it somewhere else. This is *my* show."

"Wait," he said.

"Damn you, we'll discuss this later. In another life." The sword darted at him.

"Reqata!" He danced back, but the edge caught him across the back of his hand. "What are you—"

There were tears in her eyes as she attacked him. "I see her, you know. Don't think that I don't. I see her at night, when you are asleep. Your face is different. It's the face of a woman, Elam. A woman! Did you know that? Orfea lives on in you somewhere."

Her sword did not allow him to stop and think. She caught him again, cutting his ear. Blood soaked his shoulder. "Your perfume. Who sent it to you?"

"Don't be an idiot. Something in you is Orfea, Elam. That's the only part I really love."

He tripped over a fallen body. He rolled and tried to get to his feet. He found himself facing the point of her sword, still on his knees.

"Please, Reqata," he said, tears streaming down his cheeks. "I don't want to die."

"Well, isn't that the cutest thing." Her blade pushed into his chest, cold as ice. "Why don't you figure out who you are first?"

He awoke in his adytum. His eyes generated dots of light to compensate for the complete darkness. His blood vessels burned as if filled with molten metal. He moved, pushing against the viscous fluid. Damp hair swirled around him, thick under his back, curling around his feet. It had gathered around his neck. There was no air to breathe. Elam. Where was Elam? He seemed to be gone at last, leaving only—

Elam awoke, gasping, on a pallet, still feeling the metal of Reqata's sword in his chest. So it had been her. Not satisfied with killing everyone else, she had needed to kill him as well, repeatedly. He, even now, could not understand why. Orfea.

He stood silently in the middle of the room and listened to the beating of his own heart. Only it wasn't his own, of course, not the one he had been born with. It was a heart that Abias had carefully grown in a tank somewhere below, based on information provided by a gene sample from the original Elam. The real Elam still slept peacefully in his adytum. Peacefully. . . . He had almost remembered something this time. Things had almost become clear.

377

He walked down to Abias's bright kingdom. Abias had tools there, surgical devices with sharp, deadly edges. It was his art, wasn't it? And a true artist never depended on an audience to express himself.

He searched through cabinets, tearing them open, littering the floor with sophisticated devices, hearing their delicate mechanisms shatter. He finally found a surgical tool with a vibratory blade that could cut through anything. He carried it upstairs and stared down at the ovoid of the adytum. What was inside of it? If he penetrated, perhaps, at last, he could truly see.

It wasn't the right thing, of course. The right instrument had to burn as it cut, cauterizing flesh. He remembered its bright, killing flare. This was but a poor substitute.

Metal arms pinioned him. "Not yet," Abias said softly. "You cannot do that yet."

"What do you mean?" Elam pulled himself from Abias's suddenly unresisting arms and turned to face him. The faceless eyes stared at him.

"I mean that you don't understand anything. You cannot act without finally understanding."

"Tell me, then!" Elam shouted. "Tell me what happened. I have to know. You say you didn't kill Orfea. Who did then? Did I? Did I do it?"

Abias was silent for a long time. "Yes. Your mother has, I think, tried to forgive you. But *you* are the murderer."

"You were not supposed to remember." Lammiela sat rigidly in her most private room, her mental adytum. "The Bound told me you would not. That part of you was to vanish. Just as Laurance vanished from me."

"I haven't remembered. You have to help me."

She looked at him. Until today, the hatred in her eyes would have frightened him. Now it comforted him, for he must be near the truth.

"You were a monster as a child, Elam. Evil, I would have said, though I loved you. You were Laurance, returned to punish me for having killed him . . ."

"I tortured animals," Elam said, hurrying to avoid Lammiela's past and get to his own. "I started with frogs. I moved up to cats, dogs. . . ."

"And people, Elam. You finally moved to people."

"I know," he said, thinking of the dead Orfea, who he feared he would never remember. "Abias told me."

"Abias is very forgiving," Lammiela said. "You lost him his body, and nearly his life."

"What did I do with him?"

She shook her head. "I don't know, Elam. He has never said. All these years, and he has never said. You hated Orfea, and she hated you, but somehow you were still jealous of each other. She cared for Abias, your friend from the village, and that made you wild. He was so clever about that ancient Bound knowledge the Incarnate never pay attention to. He always tried to undo the evil that you did. He healed animals, putting them back together. Without you, he may never have learned all he did. He was a magician."

"Mother—"

She glared at him. "You strapped him down, Elam. You wanted to . . . to castrate him. Cloning you called it. You said you could clone him. He might have been able to clone you, I don't know, but you certainly could do nothing but kill him. Orfea tried to stop you, and you fought. You killed her, Elam. You took that hot cutting knife and you cut her apart. It explodes flesh, if set right, you know. There was almost nothing left."

Despite himself, Elam felt a surge of remembered pleasure.

"As you were murdering your sister, Abias freed himself. He struggled and got the tool away from you."

"But he didn't kill me."

"No. I never understood why. Instead, he mutilated you. Carefully, skillfully. He knew a lot about the human body. You were unrecognizable when they found you, all burned up, your genitals destroyed, your face a blank."

"And they punished Abias for Orfea's murder. Why?"

"He insisted that he had done it. I knew he hadn't. I finally made him tell me. The authorities didn't kill him, at my insistence. Instead, they took away his body and made him the machine he now is."

"And you made him serve me," Elam said in wonder. "All these years, you've made him serve me."

She shook her head. "No, Elam. That was his own choice. He took your body, put it in its adytum, and has served you ever since."

Elam felt hollow, spent. "You should have killed me," he whispered. "You should not have let me live."

Lammiela stared at him, her eyes bleak and cold. "I daresay you're right, Elam. You were Laurance before me, the man I can never be again. I wanted to destroy you, totally. Expunge you from existence. But it was Abias's wish that you live, and since he had suffered at your hands, I couldn't gainsay him."

"Why then?" Elam said. "Why do you want to kill me now?" He stretched his hands out towards his mother. "If you want to, do it. Do it!"

"I don't know what you are talking about, Elam. I haven't tried to kill you. I gave up thinking about that a long time ago."

He sagged. "Who then? Reqata?"

"Reqata?" Lammiela smirked. "Go through all this trouble for one death?

It's not her style, Elam. You're not that important to her. Orfea was an artist too. Her art was scent. Scents that stick in your mind and call up past times when you smell them again."

"You wore one of them," Elam said, in sudden realization. "The day my death in the north woods ended."

"Yes," she said, her voice suddenly taut again. "Orfea wore that scent on the last day of her life, Elam. You probably remember it."

The scent brought terror with it. Elam remembered that. "Did you find some old vial of it? Whatever made you wear it?"

She looked at him, surprised. "Why, Elam. You sent it to me yourself."

Abias stood before him like a technological idol, the adytum between them.

"I'm sorry, Abias," Elam said.

"Don't be sorry," Abias said. "You gave yourself up to save me."

"Kill me, Abias," he said, not paying attention to what the cyborg had just said. "I understand everything now. I can truly die." He held the vibratory surgical tool above the adytum, ready to cut in, to kill what lay within.

"No, Elam. You don't understand everything, because what I told Lammiela that day was not the truth. I lied, and she believed me." He pushed, and a line appeared across the adytum's ovoid.

"What is the truth then, Abias?" Elam waited, almost uninterested.

"Orfea did not die that day, Elam. You did."

The adytum split open slowly.

"You did try to kill me, Elam," Abias said softly, almost reminiscently. "You strapped me down for your experiment. Orfea tried to stop you. She grabbed the hot cutting knife and fought with you. She killed you."

"I don't understand."

The interior of an adytum was a dark secret. Elam peered inside, for a moment seeing nothing but yards and yards of wet, dark hair.

"Don't you understand, Orfea? Don't you know who you are?" Abias's voice was anguished. "You killed Elam, whom you hated, but it was too much for you. You mutilated yourself, horribly. And you told me what you wanted to be. I loved you. I did it."

"I wanted to be Elam," Elam whispered.

The face in the adytum was not his own. Torn and mutilated still, though repaired by Abias's skill, it was the face of Orfea. The breasts of a woman pushed up through the curling hair.

"You wanted to be the brother you had killed. After I did as you said, no one knew the difference. You were Elam. The genes were identical, since you were split from the same ovum. No one questioned what had happened. The Incarnate are squeamish, and leave such vile business to the Bound. And you've been gone ever since. Your hatred for who you thought you were caused you to kill yourself, over and over. Elam was alive again, and knew that Orfea had killed him. Why should he not hate her?"

"No," Elam said. "I don't hate her." He slumped down slowly to his knees, looking down at the sleeping face.

"I had to bring her back, you understand that?" Abias's voice was anguished. "If only one of you can live, why should it be Elam? Why should it be him? Orfea's spirit was awakening, slowly, after all these years. I could see it sometimes, in you."

"So you brought it forth," Elam said. "You cloned and created creatures in which her soul could exist. The zeppelin. The dragon."

"Yes."

"And each time, she was stronger. Each time I died, I awoke . . . *she* awoke for a longer time in the adytum."

"Yes!" Abias stood over him, each limb raised glittering above his head. "She will live."

Elam rested his fingers in her wet hair and stroked her cheek. She had slept a long time. Perhaps it was indeed time for him to attempt his final work of art, and die forever. Orfea would walk the earth again.

"No!" Elam shouted. "*I* will live." Abias loomed over him as the dragon had, ready to steal his life from him. He swung the vibrating blade and sliced off one of Abias's limbs. Another swung down, knocking Elam to the floor. He rolled. Abias raised himself above. Elam stabbed upwards with the blade. It penetrated the central cylinder of Abias's body and was pulled from his hands as Abias jerked back. Elam lay defenseless and awaited the ripping death from Abias's manipulator arms.

But Abias stood above him, motionless, his limbs splayed out, his eyes staring. After a long moment, Elam realized that he was never going to move again.

The adytum had shut of its own accord, its gray surface once again featureless. Elam rested his forehead against it. After all these years he had learned the truth, the truth of his past and his own identity.

Abias had made him seem an illegitimate soul, a construct of Orfea's guilt. Perhaps that was indeed all he was. He shivered against the roughness of the adytum. Orfea slumbered within it. With sudden anger, he slapped its surface. She could continue to sleep. She had killed him once. She would not have the chance to do it again.

Elam stood up wearily. He leaned on the elaborate sculpture of the dead Abias, feeling the limbs creak under his weight. What was Elam without him?

Elam was *alive*. He smiled. For the first time in his life, Elam was alive.

JOHN BRUNNER

The First Since Ancient Persia

▼

One of the most prolific and respected authors in the business, with more than fifty books to his credit—including, in addition to his science fiction, thrillers, contemporary novels, historical novels, and volumes of poetry— British writer John Brunner has been a prominent figure in science fiction publishing for more than forty years. His massive and widely acclaimed novel *Stand on Zanzibar* won him a Hugo Award and was one of the landmark books of the '60s, and he produced several of the most notable novels of the '70s as well with books like *The Jagged Orbit*, *The Sheep Look Up*, and the remarkably prescient *The Shockwave Rider*—which, in retrospect, can not only be seen as an ancestor of cyberpunk, but which may have been the first serious fictional speculation about the workings of an "information economy" world; it even predicted computer viruses. In addition to the Hugo, Brunner has won the British Fantasy Award, two British Science Fiction Awards, the *Prix Apollo*, two *Cometa D'Argento* awards, the Gilgamesh Award, and the Europa Award as Best Western European SF Writer. His many other books include the novels *The Whole Man*, *The Squares of the City*, *The Atlantic Abomination*, *Polymath*, *Age of Miracles*, *Players at the Game of People*, *The Stone That Never Came Down*, *The Crucible of Time*, and *The Tides of Time*, and the collections *The Book of John Brunner*, *The Fantastic Worlds of John Brunner*, and *The Compleat Traveller in Black*. His most recent books are a collection, *The Best of John Brunner*, and a novel, *Children of the Thunder*.

In the angry and suspenseful novella that follows, he demonstrates that, yes, Progress always marches on—but that sometimes even those leading the parade and beating the drums may turn out not to really understand just where it is marching us *to*. . . .

▼

The First Since Ancient Persia

JOHN BRUNNER

A *letter* [in Nature] *signed by 134 scientists from Argentina's Centre for Animal Virology concluded: ". . . we feel that our country has been illegally used as a test field for a kind of experiment that is not yet accepted in the countries where the basic research on this vaccine had originated."*

NEW SCIENTIST, 26 MAY 1988

All day the lurching bus trailed its filthy wake of dust and diesel fumes across the drab and level countryside. Throughout this province the roads were no better than tracks, for there was nothing to metal them with, not even gravel, although, as Elsa Kahn had noticed, some attempt was being made to fill the worst of the potholes. Now and then the bus forded (could one say forded when there was no water? Well, then: traversed) one of the rare riverbeds of the region, dry as they would all remain for perhaps another three months, until the onset of the summer rains. Even then they would run no better than knee-deep. This was a land without bridges.

There she saw gangs of ragged men loading rocks on to the backs of burros fitted with saddles like double wooden hods. But they were not numerous, for even the timber had to be, so to say, imported. No trees save those planted by human hands grew closer than the foothills of the mountains that loomed on the western skyline.

There had been other wood along the road, in the shape of phone poles. They, however, had been rendered obsolete, replaced by line-of-sight microwave relays, cheaper and less vulnerable to sabotage. Near the towns that punctuated the bus's route they had been torn down; the few that survived, too distant to be worth dragging away, served only to support the curious double-chambered nests of ovenbirds. Even so, passing one constituted an event and a distraction, comparable with the sight of a windmill in the distance, pumping water for an isolated farm, though not a match for an encounter with another vehicle. So far they had met four trucks and a bus plying in the opposite direction. Also they had overtaken sundry burros, pedestrians, and farm carts. Slow though their progress was, nothing had overtaken them.

The sluggish changelessness of the landscape seemed to have infected Elsa's fellow passengers, of whom there were at present eight, including an armed policeman seated behind the driver. He was the sole person on board who had spoken to her, and then only to demand a sight of her passport. The rest had merely glanced at her and retreated into the privacy of their own thoughts.

Now and then she felt the same lethargy was debilitating her. The first time they crossed one of the dry riverbeds she had automatically thought of it as a *wadi*, having encountered its like in North Africa. Although she had realised at once that that was wrong, it had taken her long minutes to recapture the proper term, *arroyo seco*.

Not that it was much help. Where she was bound, people might well use an entirely different word, drawn like so much of their vocabulary from the ancient language of the Chichiami.

That, at any rate, was what she had been told.

At dusk, not more than twenty minutes behind schedule, the bus arrived at her destination—or rather, the place beyond which she had decided not to travel today. Its name, Los Tramos, might, she guessed, commemorate the breakup of one of the old *haciendas* into peasant smallholdings.

The first indication she had of it was a glimpse of more of the omnipresent windmills, but clustered, six or seven together. Then there were low one-storey houses, set wide apart, enclosed with fences made of at most two strands of wire strung as taut as possible, for it was expensive. Of course much of it was probably old phone wire, got for free. Behind the fences she saw a few sheep, flocks of hens, a good many pigs, and occasional cattle—these last of the old, unimproved breeds, resistant to the disease-bearing ticks that infested the grassland but thin and slow to reach full growth. Also, at the edge of town, there was a cemetery sown with canted tombstones. Several of the graves, including those apparently most recent, were no more than mounds, with a cross of pebbles outlined on top and perhaps a withered wreath or sad bouquet.

That, and everything beyond, was eloquent of a decline into poverty. First came a street of houses, all in poor repair but a few boasting two storeys. Some of the ground floors served for poky shops; she saw vegetables on sale, scrawny chickens, swags of gaudy cheap cloth, sandals hung up on strings like misshapen onions. And then, at last, the bus ground to a halt in the main *plaza*, between a dry fountain on whose base half a dozen idle young men were sitting and a signpost with only two arms. They pointed back to Vilagustin, ahead to Cachonga.

Seemingly, there was nowhere else to go from here.

A church fronted on the square. It was as badly kept up as the houses. On one side of it stood a row of somewhat larger shops of which two were abandoned, and, in the middle, a service station—though there were few cars in evidence, all old. She noticed four or five motorcycles, several bicycles, and two tractors, doubtless doubling as personal transport for the relatively wealthy farmers who could afford them. She had seen that before, in Yugoslavia and Greece.

Next in order around the square came another row of houses. The ground floors of the middle three had been knocked into one to form a *cantina*, half of whose patrons were sitting outside. Elsa wondered whether that was to escape the jukebox music that resounded from it. Not only was it loud; it was distorted, as though the records and the stylus were alike worn out.

And, on the fourth side stood the kind of multipurpose public building she had come to expect in areas like this, serving as town hall, police station, tax bureau, post and telegraph office, phone exchange—there was a cluster of dishes on the roof—and very likely school and hospital into the bargain. On poles protruding from its facade the national and provincial flags flapped limply in the cool evening air.

A harassed-looking young man with glasses emerged from it and hurried toward the bus. Descending, the policeman handed him a bag of mail and a large envelope with red wax seals, for which he exacted a signed receipt. This riveting occurrence took place under the gaze of fifty pairs of eyes: those of the idlers at the fountain, those of the customers outside the *cantina*, and those of a few old women—there were no young ones in view, nor girls— hurrying to make last-minute purchases for supper. One, dressed in black and with a kerchief tied round her head, crossed herself, as though terrified of what this familiar intrusion from the greater world might portend.

To Elsa's surprise, no one else was getting off here, even to stretch their legs or have a pee or buy a drink at the *cantina*. With a word of thanks to the driver, who disregarded her, she manoeuvred her aluminum-framed backpack through the door and looked around. At once she was the focus of all attention. Los Tramos was obviously not used to visitors like this: a woman of about thirty, travelling alone despite being attractive enough to have found herself a husband, her dark hair cut man-short, wearing boots and jeans and a man's tartan workshirt open halfway to her waist because on the way to the bus this morning some bastard had made a grab at her and torn off two of the buttons.

The policeman, his duty discharged, was about to resume his seat. Checking, he said incredulously, "You are stopping here?"

"Why not?" Elsa countered. "I've travelled enough for one day." Her Spanish was fluent, though she had learned it in Spain and her accent would have marked her out as foreign regardless of how she was dressed.

"But what business do you have in Los Tramos?" the man persisted.

"None. I just don't feel like going any farther."

"What will you do here?"

"If it's any concern of yours," Elsa said with a trace of annoyance, "find a place to stay, wander around, catch the next bus to Cachonga. There's one three days from now, I understand."

The policeman glanced heavenward as though in search of divine inspiration. He said, almost whispered, "You don't understand. This is—well, this is not a good place."

"What's wrong with it?"

Revving his engine impatiently, the driver shouted before the policeman could reply. He made to close the door, saying as by afterthought, "Well, maybe it's only a bunch of silly rumours. I hope so. For your sake."

And with a reek and roar the bus was on its way.

By now the idlers from the fountain had approached for a closer look at the stranger. They were not an impressive bunch: thin, wearing clothes soiled and much mended, in some cases gap-toothed despite their youth. One appeared to be ill and was racked by constant shivers. However, as though resolved to display correctly *macho* behaviour, and obviously assuming Elsa wouldn't understand, they were exchanging obscene comments mainly concerned with what despite affecting male attire a woman could not do to other women. If that was all the policeman was concerned about, she could give as good as she got. With conscious theatricality she hoisted her backpack on to her shoulders and strode across the road to the *cantina*.

The men sitting outside, on rickety chairs at plastic tables, surveyed her appraisingly. To judge from their expressions, she failed to meet their standards. She could guess why. She had spent long enough in this country to know its people still felt a woman's only proper role in life was the ancient one: marry in her teens, work hard, bear children, lose her teeth and possibly her husband, and die young looking old. Even the Arabs of North Africa were less contemptuous of their womenfolk.

So why, she sometimes wondered, was she here? And couldn't avoid concluding that her motive stemmed from what the British would term bloody-mindedness. Maybe a girl destined to waste her life in the traditional fashion might cross her path, feel envious, and raise the banner of a tiny rebellion.

She hoped so.

Inside the *cantina*—mercifully quiet at the moment, as though the next person whose turn it was to feed money into the jukebox had been distracted by her intrusion—she nodded to the people she passed, swung her backpack to the floor beside the bar, and called to a boy of seventeen or eighteen who stood at the far end, eyeing her uncertainly but with unmistakable fascination.

"Buenas tardes! Una cerveza muy fria, por favor!"

Though she suspected it would take more than one cold beer to rid her mouth of its burden of dust.

Realising she spoke Spanish, the boy broke into a grin and bent to a cabinet behind the bar. It occurred to her to wonder where the electricity came from. No doubt it was windmill-generated. The wind, they said, never stopped.

Delivering a bottle and a glass, making change from the bill she laid on the counter, the boy ventured shyly, "Is the *señora* from the *Estados Unidos?*"

"You can tell by my accent?" Elsa countered with a smile. "You must have many American visitors, then! Oh, by the way: not *señora. Señorita.*"

The boy's eyes rounded in surprise. She didn't need to be a mind reader to deduce his thoughts:

But why hasn't a man already—?

"Juan!"

The name was barked in a gruff voice from a doorway at the far end of the room. Judging by the smell that drifted through it, it led to the kitchen. Something basic but savoury was cooking: a stew, perhaps. Food was next on Elsa's list of priorities, and then a place to stay.

The man who had called out was of early middle age, with a sour face and two teeth missing from his upper jaw. Cringing, the boy behind the bar whispered, "Yes, father?"

But the man wasn't looking at him. He was staring at Elsa, and his expression bespoke—what? Anger? Yes, but mingled with it something fiercer. Maybe hate.

And what have I done that he should hate me on sight?

He went on staring as in a voice thickened by liquor he issued a string of orders to his son, telling him this, that, and the other needed doing, and not to argue—get on with it *now!* Blushing, presumably at being humiliated in front of a stranger, and moreover a woman, Juan complied.

Suddenly nervous, Elsa scanned the rest of the people in the room, sipping her beer to cover her anxiety. Most of them struck her as ignorable, for they were clearly poor and in bad health, to the point where some of them seemed to be shivering like the youth outside. But over in the far corner, partly concealed by a folding screen, at a table where he was playing cards with three companions, sat a man she had previously not noticed . . . and she could tell from the reaction when he pushed back his chair that this was the person who counted not merely here in the *cantina* but most likely in Los Tramos and the whole area.

He was visibly better nourished than the rest, to start with. Indeed he was almost fat—but not quite. Though he was fifty or fifty-five, there remained a good deal of muscle on his stocky frame. His cream two-piece suit was tailored and his shoes were shoes, rather than the open sandals worn by everybody else, even though he, like the rest, lacked socks.

Tension grew in the air like thickening fog. Elsa strove to act casually, nodding to him as she drank another generous swig of beer.

He halted a metre from her and surveyed her, head to foot, before he spoke.

"You're *norteamericana*?"

"Yes."

"What are you doing here?"

She was tempted to snap back that it was no business of his, but cancelled the impulse on time. Clearly whatever transpired around here was his business, one way or another. She answered with meekness that surprised her —but perhaps it was due to her belated realisation that a bulge under his jacket almost certainly betokened a pistol.

"I took the bus from Vilagustin this morning. You know how uncomfortable those buses are. By the time I reached your town I was stiff and sore. I couldn't face another three hours, all the way to Cachonga. So I decided to get off, have a drink and a bite to eat, and find a place to stay until the next bus is due."

Was she getting through? His eyes were searching her face. Their whites were bloodshot above cheeks seamed with broken veins—from dry wind and dust, or from liquor?

Someone called out, "*Señor Alcalde!* Tell her she's welcome to half my bed!"

And someone else riposted, though he looked equally weak and undernourished, "Ah, you're not man enough to cope with so much woman! Me, on the other hand—"

"Shut up," said the man who had been addressed as *Señor Alcalde*, Mr. Mayor. Compliant silence fell. He went on, "So you're looking for somewhere to stay. I see."

"Yes! Perhaps here at the *cantina*?" Elsa glanced at Juan's father, the landlord. "Could you—?"

"Diego has no love for women like you," the mayor said. "Nor, come to that, does anybody here. You're a disgrace to your sex. If we still had a priest, I'd call him to put you under an anathema." His face abruptly twisted with disgust. "Trousers! Shirt wide open, exposing half your body! If that's what women do when they're 'liberated,' we don't want any part of it. If my wife—!"

He completed the sentence with a gesture that indicated, plain as words, a knife passing across the throat.

"Of course," he added after a pause, "Diego's did."

The landlord purpled with rage. He was holding a towel, and instantly twisted it as though to form a garotte. Only his visible fear of the mayor, Elsa thought, prevented him from launching an immediate attack. Whatever his wife had actually done, it wasn't something he cared to be reminded about, and least of all in front of an outsider.

Forcing herself to sound calm, she said, "You're telling me I cannot even buy a meal here."

"That's right," Diego snapped. "I won't serve you, or anybody like you."

"Does that go for everyone?" Her belly felt as though it had constricted to a small tight ball, colder than an ice cube. But she controlled her terror. Somehow.

"No one in Los Tramos will give you food or lodging."

"I'm not asking for it to be given—"

"Or sell it! Your once-almighty dollar isn't what it used to be, you know. Oh, there may be some weak spirit in the town who'd take a bribe, but once I got to hear about it. . . ." And the knife-throat gesture was repeated.

There was a crudely hand-lettered poster on the wall announcing a forth-coming dance in the *plaza*, with a visiting band. In the doorway stood the young idlers from the fountain, staring greedily at her in a way that made it clear they would, like the man who had called out, be glad to offer her half a bed, but dared not. Heedless of his father's orders, Juan was peeking through the bead curtain that separated the bar from a room which, judging by the red and yellow plastic crates stacked high inside, served as a store for beer and *gaseosos*. Also there remained three centimetres in her glass. Elsa concentrated on all these things lest she break down. Never in ten years of travel had she felt so trapped, not even in Africa.

But the mayor was saying something more, and she had missed it. She blinked. Pretending poor command of the language, though he had not in fact resorted to dialect:

"I'm sorry, I didn't understand—"

"I said: you can go to the other *yanquis* and ask them for help! They're used to unnatural women!"

What in the world could he mean?

"No! No, you can't send her there! You mustn't!"

Juan, emerging through the bead curtain, blurted the words before he could stop himself. In the same moment his father rasped at him to hold his tongue, and the *alcalde* snapped, "Are you afraid she'll get lost on the way? It's a bare three kilometres, and there's only one path. And if she did manage it, she'd be no worse a loss than your mother!"

Juan's face worked as though he wanted to break into sobs. Spinning around, he vanished again, followed by a burst of laughter and insults from the idlers, who were of roughly his own age.

"That," Diego said tightly, "is enough about my wife."

As though surprised to find himself reproved, the mayor blinked. Then, with a slow smile like an alligator's, he said, "Just so, Diego. Just so. It was only the presence of this unnatural woman that provoked me. What bad luck you didn't find a wife like mine: loyal, obedient, hardworking. . . . But enough! You! Come with me, and I'll point out the way."

"May I not finish my beer?" Elsa said. "It's paid for."

Her veneer of coolness impressed her audience against their will. She received a reluctant nod, drained her glass, resumed her backpack with an ease that was entirely feigned, for hunger pangs were assailing her and the smell from the kitchen grew more alluring by the second. Nonetheless, she was determined not to let these weakling men outface her.

"Since you are so unwelcoming to strangers within your gates," she said loudly and clearly, echoing the version of the Bible they were most likely to be familiar with, "I shall gladly shake the dust of your town from off my shoes. Which way to find my fellow countrymen?"

Conscious of making a grand exit, she matched the mayor, and one of the other card-players who followed him like a bodyguard, stride for stride toward the door.

When they abandoned her to darkness, though, at the edge of the puddle of light created by the town, she was genuinely frightened. Once her eyes adjusted, she could discern a trail before her, just about; moreover, on the skyline there was a faint glow, located in the right direction, that would serve her for a beacon. In addition, she had a flashlight, but that had to be kept for emergencies, since batteries were hard to come by here. In Africa she had used one with a built-in hand-pumped generator, and wished she could have replaced it when it wore out, but in this disposable world no one seemed to make them anymore.

But where was she being sent? What sort of settlement of Americans could there be in this region—some colony of overdue hippies, perhaps, who had cut their ties with machine civilisation to live out their dream of a primitive idyll? She had run across more than one such, surviving at the cost of chronic sickness and undernourishment, and heard of many others that had failed.

Thinking of sickness: was there an epidemic of fever at Los Tramos? Was that why the policeman had tried to warn her? Was that why the community no longer had a priest?

On a different track: why had Juan risked his father's wrath—and from his looks and manner she was sure Diego was a violent man—to speak out against the mayor's proposal? It was as though he feared for her. Why should he? He had never seen her before; he could scarcely be predisposed to like women of her stamp, given that, if Elsa had read correctly between the lines of what was said, his own mother had deserted her family. . . .

And the prospect of walking three kilometres in the dark on an empty belly, to beg for lodging among what might well prove a bunch of dope-sodden idiots, was dismaying.

In her pack, reserved for crisis situations, she kept a stock of iron rations. The night, though cool, was dry—naturally, at this season—and she had a sleeping bag. It would make better sense to find a campsite until dawn. Maybe tomorrow the citizens of Los Tramos would be less hostile. In particular, maybe she could appeal to a woman. More than once a widow, or a wife ill-treated by her husband, had helped her out of sisterhood even when neither spoke the other's language.

Or did they perhaps imagine that strangers had brought them fever and misfortune? If so—

What was that?

She gasped and spun around. Clearly behind her she heard the rush of feet through grass. Someone was taking the most direct route to where she stood, rather than following the path that meandered like the local rivers. For a second her imagination was full of visions of rape, of the idlers round the fountain who were condemned never to have girlfriends until a marriage was arranged for them, condemned indeed to think of women as subhuman, to be used, exploited, despised.

But no intending rapist would call aloud, "*Señora!* I mean, *señorita!* Wait! Please wait!"

It was, it must be, Juan. She stood her ground.

Within moments he caught up to her, panting, clutching a paper-wrapped bundle. She could barely descry his face in the dimness, but what she saw sufficed.

"Here!" He proffered the package. It was greasy, but smelt appetising. "An *empanada*—all I could lay hands on. It is food, at least."

She took it with a murmur of thanks. And said, "Juan, why are you doing this? Won't your father be furious?"

"Oh, he will beat me, no doubt." His thin young voice trembled. "But I couldn't let you go away hungry!"

"Why not?" She sensed there was something he wanted—that he needed—to say, and waited for the answer. It was long a-coming, and when it did emerge, it was half-strangled by a sob, but it moved Elsa to the inmost fibre of her being.

"Because I think you must be very like my mother."

For a moment there was absolute stillness. Following Elsa's departure from the *cantina* the jukebox had resumed as loudly as before, but at this distance even that could not be heard. Impelled by emotion, she took the boy's hand. She said, "Tell me about her. What did she do that was so terrible?"

In a near-whisper: "I never really knew her. I was two when she went away. But from what I've been told, from what my grandmother says, only she hates her so much. . . ."

"Yes?"

"She couldn't stand living with my father. She didn't want to be like all the other women in Los Tramos, wearing herself out with children every year. She liked to dance and sing, she wanted to know more about the world. So one day she got on the bus and never came back."

He swallowed hard. "I think she must have wanted to be like you."

Your mother, and how many million others . . . ?

But before the thought was complete, he was already whispering, "I wish I'd known her. I wish I knew a girl in Los Tramos who could be like her. I'd go away with such a girl. I wouldn't keep her here to waste her life. But I'm afraid of leaving by myself. My father has made me afraid, and I hate him."

As though terrified by his own confession, he was poised to run back and face his father's rage, but Elsa held on.

"I understand," she murmured. "I hope you will find such a woman one day. They do exist. But one more thing."

"What?"

"Why did you not want me to go to the other *yanquis*?"

"I was wrong to fear for you," he answered simply. "I wasn't thinking. You're different from the women I know. Like them, like their livestock, you're strong."

"But who are these people? Why are the townsfolk afraid of them? Are they—?" She was about to voice her suspicion that they might be hippie idealists. He cut her short.

"They're scientists. At least that's what they call themselves. . . . *Señorita*,

I must dash! There is just a chance my father hasn't missed me yet, but when he does. . . . First, though . . .″

"First—what?"

He mumbled something inaudible. Divining what he had in mind, she put her arms around him. For a long moment he whimpered against her shoulder, scarcely attempting to return the embrace, and then he was gone at a headlong run, leaving her with fewer questions asked than unasked.

When the sound of his passage through the grass faded, she sat down on her pack and ate the *empanada*, her mind full of pity for Juan and all the folk of Los Tramos. How many dreams must have died for them that shone like summer dawn when the great estate was broken up and gave their families land to call their own!

Itch.

She brushed at her bare arms. Then at her chest. And, with alarm, jumped to her feet. She had forgotten, though she had been warned often enough, about the ticks that swarmed in this kind of grass. She even had a bottle of insect repellant in her pack, but had neglected to apply it. Judging by the lumps that were bulging on her skin, she had become the target for a score of the pests already. And they were said to carry diseases that afflicted people as well as cattle.

Well, the *yanquis* over yonder were scientists. Why scientists should be so distrusted by the local folk, she could not guess. Maybe it was simply because they included women behaving in a manner not approved of here-abouts. At all events they would doubtless have medication for tick bites. She bent to resume her backpack.

At the same moment heard something totally unexpected, although totally familiar. She was so startled, she dropped the pack again.

It was the sound of aircraft engines starting up. Not jets, piston engines. Two of them.

"Flat-fours," Elsa said to the wind. "I'll be damned. Lycomings, most likely. So Los Tramos isn't the back of beyond, after all."

She waited for what she guessed was about to happen. It did. Radiance bloomed behind a shallow rise—there were no hills for hundreds of kilometres, but there was just enough of a slope to hide the landing strip—and moments later a twin-engined executive plane took to the sky and headed north.

"If I really can't stand this place," she said, again addressing the breeze, "maybe I can hitch a ride to hell out. But I think I'm about to pay a call on some rather interesting people."

Shrugging her backpack to a comfortable position, she trudged onward. And, half an hour later, found herself in a completely different world, her arrival heralded by loud alarms, brilliant lights, the barking of dogs, and the mooing and baaing and grunting and clucking of an entire farmyard of livestock.

It was even recorded on television.

What an extraordinary place to have chanced on!

Elsa was tired, even overtired, but sleep would not come. Her mind was spinning like a turbine with the most amazing series of images. What, from a distance and in the dark, might have been mistaken for one of the old *haciendas*—its great house, its barns, its cattle sheds—had proved to be a literal outpost of civilisation. This room she had been assigned was small, but it and everything it contained down to the thick towelling robe she had been given after showering (with the hottest water she had enjoyed in weeks) might as well have been in the States. The lights were bright; when she intruded on them, the residents had been watching a videotape of a recent movie; instantly it had become hard to believe that this house stood in the midst of empty *pampa* and was girdled by a high barbed fence beset with security cameras and the infrared detectors that had warned of her presence.

She had even seen someone telephoning, though she hadn't overheard what was being said. But as she approached, she had realised the lie of the ground would prevent the use of line-of-sight relays from less than a twenty-metre tower, and certainly she hadn't seen one of those. That implied a straight-to-satellite connection.

Most astonishing of all—and yet perhaps not so, given what Juan had told her—the first thing her hosts had done was take her to a clean white sterile-looking room, dress her tick bites, and give her a prophylactic injection, muttering stern admonitions about how dangerous the local fevers were. Doctor-brisk, the man wielding the syringe—who had introduced himself as Lawrence Hutt—told her, "The locals are resistant, of course, but as you probably noticed, even they succumb occasionally, while someone unsalted, like you, can suffer pretty damn badly. If you hadn't found your way here, you could have woken up tomorrow with a hundred-and-two-degree fever. In fact, you'll probably have a mild attack anyway—this vaccine isn't perfect. You can expect to perspire a lot, ache a bit, maybe your throat will be sore." Throwing the syringe away: "I'll give you some vitamin C tablets. That'll help. Are you hungry?"

"No, the boy from the *cantina* gave me an *empanada*."

"Hmm! Then I just hope you haven't wished yourself food poisoning as well! The standards of hygiene around here aren't what we're used to."

"I've been in the country three months," Elsa answered dryly. "I've survived pretty well."

"That's as maybe." He ran his fingers through his hair—or rather, what there was of it; straw-fair, it was cut to within a centimetre of the scalp. "But a trip like yours today can take you clear out of the zone you're adjusted to. . . . Well, we can worry about that in the morning. Now I'll get my wife to show you to your room. I imagine you'd like to clean up; there's a shower next door. And if you're sure you don't want anything to eat, I'd advise you to turn in right away. The injection will probably make you drowsy even if you aren't ready for bed."

"For a real bed," Elsa said feelingly, "I've been ready for weeks."

"Thought you might. Mina?"

Mina was a small, round-faced, bespectacled woman about the same age as her husband, late thirties. She clucked over the state of Elsa's clothes and took possession of them, promising to have them washed and replace the buttons on the shirt.

As she was on the verge of departure, Elsa called out. "Just a moment! What is this extraordinary place? Who are you people?"

"This is the Snider Foundation," Mina answered. "Not, I imagine, that that will mean much to you."

Elsa shook her head, standing naked ready for her shower.

"My husband and I are biologists. We're trying to do something about the endemic diseases here, including the ones Lawrence just dosed you for. The rest of us—well, some are attempting to improve the local strain of cattle, or adapt better ones to become tick-resistant, and others are trying to develop improved grasses and other fodder. . . . You can look the place over when you feel up to it. We don't have anything to hide."

"Why are the local people so afraid of you?" Elsa challenged, thinking it could scarcely be on account of Mina's "unwomanliness," even though she was wearing jeans and a T-shirt.

A sigh in answer. "Heartbreaking, isn't it? Though I think it's more suspicion than fear, or maybe resentment. We do what we can. We try to mix with them. When there's a *fiesta* or even a dance, we join in. Some of us worship at their church—or do when there's someone to hold services. Father José died last month, and they're still waiting for a replacement. But we never feel welcome, and mostly they won't even let us treat their sick kids. Sometimes we get dreadfully frustrated—Still, you don't want to hear about all our troubles tonight. Like a hot drink? How about a cup of chocolate?"

And with its rich sweetness still echoing on her tongue Elsa lay in darkness, wishing she could switch off her awareness by an act of will.

All the more because Lawrence's prophecy was being fulfilled to the letter. Her skin was damp with perspiration; there were transient aches in her joints, starting with the wrists and ankles and slowly spreading; and she was feeling distinctly light-headed.

Just when she thought she must don her robe and go in search of a sedative, sleep came with the abruptness of a tropical sunset.

She had vivid and terrifying dreams, but when she woke, she could recall no details.

In the morning she was too weak to get up. A graceful woman with grey hair came and introduced herself as Greta Snider, helped her to the toilet, and brought her a light breakfast. She promised that her husband, founder and director of this research station, would call in later. He did so, and was not the only one; as though welcoming the distraction of a newcomer, all the staff visited her room during the morning. Greeting one after another half-seen stranger—the curtains were drawn and she lay in semidarkness— she wished she could question them about their work. Mina's summary had made it sound fascinating. But her attention kept wandering away from what she wanted to say. According to Lawrence when he checked her pulse, flashed a light in her eyes, and took her temperature, that was not surprising; she had a high fever in spite of the injection. He gave her a pain-killer for her aching joints, and that made her even drowsier. It ceased to seem worth keeping track of time.

At least her dreams were less disturbing, even if once or twice they centred on night flights in aircraft too small and too flimsy for comfort.

"Good morning, Elsa!" boomed a voice that had become familiar without her realising. "I gather you're well enough to get up today."

For a moment she couldn't place this elderly but vigorous man who was addressing her. Ruddy face, tinted glasses, white hair surrounding a small bald patch—Oh, of course. He was the boss, el Jefe of the Snider Foundation. Licking her lips, she said, "Morning, Bernard. Yes, my temperature's normal and I've stopped aching. I'm just a bit limp, that's all."

"Well, you can't expect to spend a week on your back and not feel—"

"A week!" Elsa burst out.

Snider looked faintly puzzled. "Hadn't you realised—? Ah, what a stupid question. But Lawrence should have told me you were that badly affected. Still, he assures me you're okay again physically. . . . Today, though, I don't think you'd better go beyond the patio. I'll get Mina to bring your clothes. You can join the rest of us for lunch."

Elsa looked forward to that. With her restoration to normality had returned all the questions she had been meaning to ask since her arrival.

As it turned out, she had little need to pose them. The staff consisted of seven *yanquis*, the Hutts, the Sniders, and three young volunteers, Armin, George, and Patti, plus five Hispanics, and they were all eager to explain what they were doing. Keenest of all was the *de facto* spokesman of the latter group, one Felipe Diaz, whose mainly Indian ancestry showed clearly in his features but not at all in his educated Spanish and fluent English.

Their enthusiasm was contagious. Though she knew virtually nothing about modern biology, she shortly came to feel it must be akin to magic, for they were talking about—quite literally—building microorganisms to hunt down and destroy disease germs in the living body; redesigning grass so that it would poison the ticks that infested the *pampa*; not to mention doubling or tripling the yield of everything from livestock to mushrooms. They were very interested in fungi; some, they hinted, might yield antibiotics more powerful than any previously discovered.

If their glowing physical health was any guide, they were on an indubitably right track. Elsa couldn't help mentally comparing them with the people she had seen at Los Tramos. Even the mayor would look sickly beside them. Bernard himself, though she guessed him to be over sixty, could have passed for five years his junior.

Only when she asked why the station was sited here of all places was there a moment of tension. All eyes turned to Snider, as though relying on him to provide the perfect reply. Elsa had already noticed how everyone deferred to him, as to the abbot of one of the monasteries she had visited in Nepal, and he seemed to relish his rôle.

In fact, though, it was Greta, his wife—and as had become clear, his co-researcher—who leaned forward.

"My dear, you've seen the people of this region. Don't you think they need help from outside? They're constantly sick! They're existing on the edge of starvation! As for their infant mortality—! That's why, when Bernard won his prize, we decided that setting up this foundation was the best use we could make of the money."

"Prize?" Elsa repeated, reluctant but compelled to admit her ignorance. For a while the name of Bernard Snider had been ringing faint bells in memory, but she had been unable to pin it down.

Bernard smiled and shrugged. "For my sins," he said, "they gave me a Nobel."

"Really! When was that?"

"Six years ago."

"Ah, no wonder I hadn't heard about it. Around then I was in Bhutan and Nepal. Out of touch for months on end."

"How interesting! You must be quite a globetrotter. I'm sure we'd love to hear about your travels. When you feel strong enough."

And everyone relaxed and started chatting anew.

Thinking back afterward, though, Elsa couldn't help feeling that she must unwittingly have touched a raw nerve.

Within three more days she was sufficiently recovered to tour the estate—or at any rate that part of it in easy reach. The whole was indeed comparable to one of the old *haciendas*, far too large to cover in a single day on foot, or even on horseback. It could just about be accomplished by jeep, but a complete inspection called for a helicopter, and one was in fact parked along with a couple of jeeps in a hangar beside the airstrip, a hundred metres from the house. She didn't recognise the make, but thought it might be an Embraer.

Felipe appointed himself her guide, not, Elsa thought, from any ulterior motive; he appeared to be (she caught at the old-fashioned term, for it was perfectly appropriate) courting the American girl Patti, who was shy but—judging by various remarks Elsa had overheard—regarded as brilliant. In fact, they all seemed to be brilliant. But was that to be wondered at, if they'd been invited to work for a Nobel laureate?

Accompanied by one of the dogs that she had heard barking on her arrival, which were not permitted inside the house, Felipe began by taking her around the main site, all except for a long windowless building with a satellite dish on the roof, aligned on a target beyond the cloud-shredding sky. That was Bernard's laboratory, where save for the staff no one was allowed to enter. But he showed off their windmill-driven generators, the other windmills that pumped their water, the solar-cooled (that was a paradox!) store where they kept their food. Almost all was raised or grown on site. They did not, though, do everything themselves; a score or so of male labourers undertook the routine drudgery, including supervision of the animals. Elsa made a mental note to inquire about them. They seemed far too friendly—indeed too cheerful, despite the lack of women—to have been recruited at Los Tramos.

Or had they, and was that one of the reasons why the townsfolk were so resentful? Did they feel they had been cheated of the best-paid work available?

Next, in wire-fenced fields that began beyond the airstrip, she admired cattle far larger than the scrawny beasts at Los Tramos, especially a group of six young bulls still wearing their horns as though being readied for a *corrida*, though as Felipe explained they were actually being tested for resistance to tick-borne disease. In addition, she saw fat pigs, fleecy sheep, thriving chickens, and plots of vegetables some of which she didn't recognise, identified by Felipe as possible new food crops for the future, or new sources of fuel and even building materials. There was a plantation, visible in the distance from a rise, where stood more trees than she had seen in months, thousands of them of a dozen different species.

"If this works out," Felipe said seriously, "we may yet be able to restore the lost forests. Certainly we can hope to cook the food of India again. While you were there, you must have seen how short they are of firewood."

Overwhelmed, Elsa clasped her hands. She burst out, "But why haven't I heard about these marvels—? Ah, of course. They're not the kind of thing that makes news in the places where I've spent the past ten years."

"We don't want to make news anywhere," Felipe said. "Not yet. As far as Bernard is concerned, this is only the start. He doesn't want to be constantly interrupted by reporters. Above all, he's worried in case ambitious fools get wind of what he's doing, try to imitate it, and make a mess. Our work is too important to be spoiled that way."

"But some people know about it," Elsa countered as they turned to head back toward the main house.

"How do you mean?"

"You have visitors. Quite often."

"Oh, yes. There was a plane the night you arrived. I'd forgotten. Yes, we have visitors. But those are friends of Bernard—some, scientific colleagues; others, people who believe in him enough to have invested money. One can scarcely turn them away. Even so . . ." He sighed, shading his eyes as he glanced around. "Well, sometimes they can be a nuisance. Life here is pretty dull most of the time. Oh, our work is exciting, I grant you—perhaps among the most exciting anyone is undertaking anywhere—but it can get monotonous, and one would welcome a break. As a matter of fact, there's a dance in town tonight, and I meant to ask whether you'd like to come with me and Patti. The music's usually quite lively, if the people aren't."

"Why not?" Elsa said, tempted by the idea of returning to sneer at Diego and the *alcalde*, if only for the sake of reinforcing Juan's respect for independent women.

Felipe spread his hands. "We have another visitor. Someone important. We have to stick around. Of course, if you really fancy going to the dance, I could ask one of the workers to take you. Not that he'd be much company. And you'd have to be careful to avoid giving him any wrong ideas on the way home. You'd have to walk back, you see. We don't let the workers use the jeeps for an outing on their own, in case they get too drunk to drive."

"I was going to ask you about them," Elsa said, and added apologetically, "Sorry, I must stop for a rest." They were again passing the field that held the six young bulls; she leaned back against one of its fence posts. The dog lay down at her side. She had learned that his name was Panza, after Don Quixote's squire. He seemed to have taken a fancy to her—or perhaps he was just being properly cautious about a stranger. The bulls eyed him and the humans suspiciously, but after a while paid more attention to each other, circling warily and snorting in a show of braggadocio.

"What did you say you were going to ask about?" Felipe prompted.

"These people of yours: why are they—?"

"Not my people!" he snapped. "Do you take me for one of these *pampa*-bred peasants?"

At some stage, without realising, Elsa had slipped from Spanish back to

English because Felipe spoke it so well. Now he had stumbled over an idiom. She could see why.

"I'm sorry!" she cried. "That's not what I meant! I wanted to ask why some of the local people are willing to work here, when the others in town—"

He was shaking his head, his expression grim. "Oh, our workers aren't local. The townsfolk—well, you met them. Ignorant, backward, superstitious, afraid of any sort of change . . . They can't tell the difference between science and witchcraft. Last time I was in Los Tramos when a bus came by, I saw an old woman crossing herself as though it were some kind of devil."

"I saw that!" Elsa exclaimed.

"So what do I have to explain? We recruited our labour force among people stranded in big towns, who wanted nothing more than to get back to work they understood: dealing with crops and sheep and cattle. Ask any of them—that's what they'll say. In my view, Bernard did them a favour, quite apart from the generous pay."

Elsa hesitated before framing her next question. She had it in mind to ask what Felipe felt about Bernard as a person; she herself had come so little into contact with him, save at mealtimes or in the evenings when the staff gathered to watch the latest of what seemed to be an unending series of imported videotapes, that she had formed at best a numinous impression: half research director, half—rather than abbot as she had originally felt—*guru*.

But before she found the right words Panza was on his feet, barking madly, and Felipe had caught her arm, shouting, "Look out!"

And she was being dragged away from the fence. From behind came a crashing sound. She almost fell.

"It's okay," Felipe said, steadying her. "The fence held. But when I saw those two coming straight for us—!"

What?

Shakily she turned. The post she had been leaning on was canted at an angle. Two of the young bulls, pawing the ground and slobbering, were confronting one another with lowered heads. One had slashed the other's hide and left a stripe of blood.

"There's going to be trouble here," Felipe muttered. "I'd better warn Bernard. I said he ought to have them polled, but he so much wants to see the outcome before—" He broke off, as though afraid of saying too much.

He had lapsed back into Spanish. In the same tongue Elsa demanded, "Why do they still have their horns? I thought it was routine to take them off nowadays."

Felipe was shivering. It wasn't that cold today. In fact, a hint of spring warmth informed the air. At length he said, this time in English, "Bernard thinks it might disturb the hormone balance. And who am I to contradict? Come on, we should be getting back for supper."

That evening, for the first time Elsa felt excluded from the society of her companions. She was of course resigned to not understanding when they spoke of their scientific work, but she had already taken to making herself useful, be it only to help with cooking and cleaning. Tonight, however, it was as though she had in some ill-defined way become a problem, even a nuisance. Even Greta Snider, who was normally the most relaxed of all, exuded tension. The visitor must indeed be someone important.

She had expected him to arrive early and share the meal. When she dared to inquire why he was not here yet, she was met with prevarication—very busy, able only to drop in for an hour or two on his way somewhere else. . . . Fudge! Something was happening that she wasn't supposed to know about.

Despite Mina's assurance on the evening of her arrival, there were secrets here. And, judging by everybody's acute nervousness, if the visitor discovered there was a stranger about. . . .

Her guesses were amply confirmed when, as soon as they had finished, Mina refused her offer to help clear away, and her husband chimed in to support her.

"Mina's right, Elsa. You've had a tiring day—it was, after all, the first time you've walked so far since you quit your sickbed. I prescribe an early night."

"So do I," Bernard boomed. "Mina will bring you your chocolate as usual, won't you, Mina?"

"I'm quite capable of fixing it myself—"

"Won't hear of it! You need to take things easy for at least another couple of days. That was a bad bout of fever you went through in spite of Lawrence's vaunted vaccine. Reminds me: you said you wanted a blood sample, didn't you, Lawrence?"

"Yes, if you don't mind, Elsa," Lawrence muttered. "The stuff I gave you should have aborted the attack almost at once. It might be a question of your blood group. I'd like to check that out tomorrow."

"Sure," Elsa said, pushing back her chair and tossing her napkin on the table. "Okay, good night."

Trying to conceal the fact that she suddenly did not believe a word of what she was being told.

Alone in her room, exploring the wavebands of a radio they had brought to relieve the monotony while she was laid up, and finding nothing but pop music and propaganda, she heard the drone of an approaching aircraft. It was no use looking out the window; she was on the wrong side of the house.

Snider . . .

She kept on feeling that she ought to remember this man and his Nobel prize. Had someone mentioned it, one of the hundreds of chance-met Europeans and Americans she had encountered on her wanderings? Or had she read about him in one of the tattered English-language papers that she and other travellers fell on greedily, no matter how out of date, on trains, in bars, in shabby hotels? Six years ago . . .

As the plane was circling to land, Mina tapped at the door and delivered her mug of chocolate. Accepting it wordlessly, Elsa waited to see whether the other woman would say anything. So reproachful was her gaze, she did, after a long and pregnant pause.

"I'm sorry we have to—uh—shut you away," she muttered. "But . . . Well, frankly, you might recognise our visitor. He wouldn't like that."

"He's here unofficially?"

"Very."

"Hmm!" Elsa cradled the hot mug between her hands. "Let me guess. It isn't cheap to run this place, and a Nobel prize wasn't nearly enough to pay for everything. Is he someone responsible for other people's money, who's investing it in what most of them would regard as a blue-sky venture?"

Mina looked briefly alarmed, then forced a weak smile. "Something like that."

"I see. Well, don't worry. Now I know I'm a nuisance I'll stop bothering you. I don't suppose I can hitch a plane ride, given what you just told me, so I'd better take the bus to Cachonga as I originally planned. When's the next one?"

"There's no need—"

"No, I've outstayed my welcome. You've all been very kind, but you have work to do, and since I can't contribute, I'm bound to be in the way. And in spite of what Lawrence thinks, I really am quite fit again."

"Well . . ." Mina bit her lip. "If he agrees, after he's given you that blood test tomorrow . . . I'm sorry. We shall miss you. You've been a very different kind of visitor from most who come to call."

The sound of the plane was deafening as it taxied from the airstrip toward the house. Elsa had to raise her voice.

"You mean I walked here instead of flying?"

The feeble joke evoked a more genuine smile, and Mina turned to go. Over her shoulder she added, "Don't let your chocolate go cold, will you? Sleep well. See you in the morning."

The door swung to.

Sipping her chocolate and finding it even now too hot to drink, Elsa pondered. If her inspired guess had come as close to the truth as Mina's reaction indicated, then—

Snider!

Of course!

Abruptly it all came back. There had been a scandal. This was the man who, at the Nobel award ceremony, had launched a fierce attack on environmentalists and conservationists, called them purblind antiscientific bigots, and claimed that given his head he could already have solved half the problems of the world. Indeed, he had gone so far as to accuse them of being dupes of a communist conspiracy. His opponents had countered by dismissing him as an arrogant megalomaniac.

The chocolate was cool now; she swigged it down.

But that didn't match her impression of Bernard. He didn't come on like a bigoted autocrat. On the contrary, most of the time he was positively genial. And was there not evidence, abundant evidence, here on the estate, that he was right, after all? The cattle, the sheep, the pigs, the chickens, all those amazing trees on the skyline . . .

Suddenly she felt giddy. Swaying, she reached to set her empty mug on the bedside table and had to clutch for support. The plane's engines were silent. By now the visitor must be indoors.

The bitch. She's drugged me. Bernard's orders?

It was the last thought before she tumbled on the bed and into oblivion.

Then, unexpectedly, she was awake again. She felt weak, but her head was clear and her belly calm, and by her watch barely two hours had passed. She had assumed they were knocking her out for the night. Had someone miscalculated the dose? Or had they administered just enough to keep her under until the visitor had gone?

Had he gone? There was no sound of plane engines.

With abrupt determination she forced herself to her feet. If there was any chance of snatching a glimpse of this important stranger, she must seize it, be it only to get her own back on whoever had ordered her chocolate to be doped. Leaving the radio playing because its cessation might give her away, she stole noiselessly to the door.

It wasn't locked. Mina must have had total confidence in the drug.

Beyond, the house looked perfectly normal. There was nobody about, but as usual lights had been left on at the head and foot of the stairs. Were the staff in bed, or were they still attending the visitor? If so, they were presumably at the laboratory.

Afterward, she decided that her decision had been irrational, ascribable to the aftereffects of the drug, but at the time it struck her as absolutely logical to leave the house by the door from the kitchen and head for the lab. More lights were on than generally at night. That suggested the visitor had not yet left—and indeed there was his plane.

But when she had covered barely half the distance to her goal, alarms sounded from the perimeter fence, just as they had at her own approach. Instantly lights sprang up, dogs barked, the other animals responded, precisely as before. Within seconds someone emerged from the house—she couldn't see who—and another from the lab.

Gasping, she whirled and sought cover. There was none nearby. Her only hope, or so she felt in her confusion, was to run for the largest area of darkness.

But it lay between her and the main gate.

More lights were turned on. Spotting a clump of chinaberry bushes, she dashed toward it for want of any better concealment and fell on hands and knees in dry dirt. The person from the house—she recognised him now: Felipe, carrying a flashlight and a pistol (Odd! No one had been armed who came to meet her . . . but that night, of course, the important visitor had already taken off)—rushed past within a metre, unaware of her. From beyond the gate she heard noise: running feet, incoherent shouts, a man sobbing.

A man sobbing.

She waited, panting, terrified. A minute later she heard Felipe calling. "Here! Over here! *Help!*"

Elsa could no more have resisted that appeal than (the comparison struck her as ironical even as it passed through her mind) a mother could ignore the crying of her child. She jumped up and ran toward him. The gate was open, the alarms had been switched off, and he was kneeling beside a young man whose clothes were smeared with red.

Hearing her footsteps but not glancing up, he said furiously, "Why won't they let us help them before it's too late? They always bring us the ones that are too far gone! Takes the fear of death to make them see sense, doesn't it? Here, we must get him inside."

Then, and only then, did he realise who had come to his aid.

Sitting back on his heels, his face a mask of incredulity, he said, "You? I thought—Oh, never mind! Don't just stand there like a dummy! Take his feet!"

But in the same moment as Felipe recognised her, Elsa had recognised who was lying blood-weltered on the ground.

Juan.

His eyes opened. His tongue moved across his lips. He said something very faintly. She thought it might possibly have been, "*Madre . . .*"

And his eyes closed, his head lolled aside, and he was dead.

And then there were more people coming from the direction of town: the workers who had attended the dance. Elsa didn't have to carry the boy's feet, after all. She followed dumbly at a distance, half-hearing what was being said: some drunk had insulted Juan's mother once too often; the boy had rushed at him with a kitchen knife; drunk though he was, the other man was faster, and he too had a knife, a fighting knife. . . .

The runway lights came on; the plane started up; the important visitor was escorted back to it, and it took off in a considerable hurry.

But all that happened a long way away.

Early in the morning, shortly after dawn, people from Los Tramos came for Juan's body, doomed no doubt to occupy another mounded grave with no more memorial than a cross sketched in pebbles, with no priest to conduct his funeral. She woke because one of the bearers was sobbing, the same man as last night. It had to be Diego, Juan's father.

But by the time she had slipped out of bed, donned her robe, crept to the head of the stairs, they were gone. She caught one glimpse of them leaving through the main gate.

Good-bye, Juan who liked independent women.

She said at breakfast, "When is the next bus?"

Grave, Bernard said, "I can well understand your wish to be on your way, especially after what occurred last night. But you can scarcely blame us if the natives regard our powers as magical."

Elsa had slept badly and her mind was fuzzy. She looked at him blankly.

"Magical!" Bernard repeated. "It isn't the first time such a thing has happened, is it, Greta?"

His wife shook her head. "Just the first time it was so—so violent. You must understand, my dear, that for all their rejection of our overtures, the townsfolk do regard us with a sort of superstitious awe. They bring us their dying relatives, of all ages from babyhood to senility, and leave them at the gate expecting us to work a miracle. If only they had the sense to come when there's still hope! I blame it on the priest, myself. Excuse me"—to Felipe and his companions.

"Since coming here," Felipe answered curtly, "I've seen how useless priests really are. I suspected it; now I know."

"You still haven't told me," Elsa said. "When does the next bus leave?"

A multiple exchange of glances.

"There was one yesterday," Lawrence said at length.

Trapped . . .

Elsa forced a smile to her face. "I'll catch the next, then. I should be properly rested up. Meantime, whatever I can do to help, I will. I'd like to repay your generosity in part, at least."

The eyes turned to her were cold and blank as stones. Stones from the dried-up riverbeds that she had crossed. Not for the first time she felt she had come to a place that was somehow unreal.

Were they afraid to let her go, even though she hadn't seen their mysterious visitor?

Eventually Bernard pushed his chair back, smiling.

"That's very kind. I'm sure we all appreciate the offer. But you already know the greatest service you can perform before you leave."

"Uh . . . Do I?"

"Sure you do." Lawrence was smiling too. "A few c.c. of blood so we can check whether it is your group that made you react so violently to those tick bites. What group are you, by the way—do you know?"

"O positive."

"So am I!" Lawrence looked theatrically lugubrious. "Well, bang goes another favourite hypothesis. I'll have to figure out a new one."

And somehow everybody was laughing and dispersing for the day's work before Elsa had time to voice the rest of what was on her mind. She had intended to promise that if they wished, she would refrain for the rest of her life from mentioning the Snider Foundation, or at least until its director chose to seek publicity. In other words, she had intended to forestall what she expected they'd insist on.

Whether their disregard of the matter was welcome, or sinister, she could not tell.

Into the bargain, she wanted to ask why, after being drugged, she had woken up so soon. But the room emptied so suddenly, and then the entire house, that she had no chance to speak of that, either.

As though her decision to depart as soon as possible had erased her from the staff's collective consciousness, once Lawrence had withdrawn his syringeful of blood from her arm, she found herself left entirely to her own devices.

And at a total loss.

It was a fine morning, but clouds were building on the horizon and there was a hint of dampness in the air, as though the rains were due to break early. She wandered around the estate at random, with only Panza for company, trying to make sense of what had happened to her.

Did they or did they not care that she had seen so much of the achievements they disdained to publicise? Of course she had no intention of flying straight home next chance she got and telling the world, for a fat fee, where Snider the maverick Nobelist was proving his point; how, though, could she have convinced them she was to be trusted?

There was a lot of money behind this project; that she was certain of. And people with funds on that scale—

A cry.

She whirled. Chance had brought her back to the bull pasture. (In passing, she registered that the canted fence post had been set upright.) And Felipe was here again, with two of the local hands—no, not local: Greta's term was more apt, native—and it looked as though he had been trying to take a sample of the saliva that the largest young bull drooled. Had she seen such a thing done before? She felt she must have, if not here then elsewhere on her travels, for until this moment she had felt no qualms.

Now, in a single instant, she was possessed by terror.

For, discovering his chief rival was distracted, the next-to-largest bull was lowering his head to charge—

And did, and tossed Felipe like a straw-stuffed dummy, while the native workers fled.

There was a gap in the progress of time.

Then, not knowing how she came to be there, she was astride his prostrate body, shouting and waving as though her windmill arms could drive the bulls away, while Panza snapped and snarled at their heels and help came at a run: Lawrence, Armin, two other labourers with pitchforks held like spears. Another few seconds, and Lawrence was clapping her on the back, babbling congratulations, and the bulls were in headlong retreat.

Felipe, though . . .

Elsa looked down at him. His eyes were closed. Blood trickled from the corner of his mouth, ajar and gasping. She thought of Juan and wished she didn't have to, but she did. She husked, "Felipe . . ."

"Don't worry." Lawrence had regained his normal calm. "He'll be all right tomorrow. Fine! You'll see!"

Absurdly Elsa said, "What are you doing here? I thought you were testing my blood."

"Oh, that's okay. Better than okay, in fact. I never dreamed anybody could recover so quickly from—"

He caught himself. But his words had set her mind ablaze. She had never felt such piercing insight in her life.

"From the drug that Mina gave me in my chocolate?"

"What nonsense!" But he had to interrupt and correct himself. "What sort of nonsense is that? You think you were drugged by Mina—by my wife? No, you were overtired after your long day's walk. I said as much . . . Look, we must take Felipe indoors and dress his wounds. We can't talk now."

And, next day at breakfast, even as she was bracing herself to ask how Felipe was:

"Oh my God! Is it really you?"

Imagining some duplicate had been contrived, some twin. It would not have been too much, she'd come to think, given the miracles these people could perform with living creatures.

Even that, though, was not as terrifying as the reality. Here he was, paler than usual, moving unsteadily perhaps but without need of assistance, and betraying no other trace of the injuries he must have suffered. (She had seen him tossed and trampled: horn-stabs, broken ribs, maybe concussion.) And there was small sign of weakness in the arms he threw around her.

"Elsa! I don't know how to thank you! It was so brave of you! So brave! To drive the bull away when it had knocked me out!"

"Especially since—"

That came from Greta, and broke off. Her husband had laid a hand on her wrist, and, Elsa thought, closed tight. He said now, jovially, "Yes! It was heroic! Come! Sit down, and let us toast in coffee, since that's what there is, your courage when you saved Felipe's life! When you arrived so unexpectedly, something about you told me that we ought to make you welcome in our little group. I don't know what. That is, I didn't then. But now I do!"

He raised his cup and beamed at her.

Blushing—she who had imagined nothing in the world could make her blush again, yet grateful for it, since it masked her terror—Elsa smiled at those who copied their leader's gesture. All the time wondering:

What did Greta mean to say, that was cut short?

And why, and how, was Felipe on his feet again so soon?

And what on earth did Bernard mean? He wasn't anywhere around when she arrived. The first time that they met, she was already weak with fever. . . .

Beside such questions, the identity of the recent visitor signified nothing.

And she could obtain no answers. The community had closed against her, oyster-tight. She tried to talk to those whom she had come to regard as friends, and met a wall of silence. For all their protestations she was no longer welcome even in the kitchen.

As she drifted aimlessly around the house, around the nearby grounds, struggling to control her impulse to flee, she reverted again and again to the suspicion that she was the subject of continual secret debate. She could imagine the matters that were being discussed: had she seen too much; did she understand too much; had she glimpsed the latest visitor; had she identified him; if she returned to the States, would she spread sensational rumours about the Foundation . . . ?

Perhaps also: how had she recovered so quickly from the drug in her chocolate? She was sure that was what Lawrence had been on the point of betraying, and the explanation for Felipe's astonishment on finding her at his side.

As though her fever were even yet affecting her brain, she felt she was becoming paranoid. And could not escape the old, no longer funny, cliché: *Paranoids too have real enemies. . . .*

The sole exception was Felipe. Despite his astonishing physical recovery, he admitted to not yet being capable of resuming his normal work—whatever it was; on that subject he refused to be drawn—but when he could snatch a chance, away from Lawrence's ministrations or the tests Bernard and Greta wanted to perform on him, to check, he said, the rate his wounds were healing, he sought out Elsa and repeated his effusive gratitude. It wasn't hard to track her down. Wherever she had wandered to, he needed only to whistle and Panza, now her regular companion, would bark a reply.

If anything, though, talking to Felipe was worse than being left to her own thoughts because it filled her with a sense of betrayal. It became plainer and plainer that he wanted—wanted desperately—to confide in her, if only out of obligation. But some higher loyalty, presumably to the Sniders, prevented him.

Or was it that simple? Was he perhaps afraid of the consequences if he broached the secrets she was now certain underlay the Foundation's veneer of humanitarian scientific research? Not that she had any idea what they might be, but she was well aware of what might happen to even the most disinterested research programme once sufficient money was at stake. All too often she had witnessed the way in which pharmaceutical companies strove to recoup from the Third World profits they had been deprived of in advanced countries, thanks to legislation against drugs with dangerous side effects.

Even as she systematically played on Felipe's sense of indebtedness, she was wondering whether it would not be more honourable to confront Bernard directly, or better yet, Greta, who might be more vulnerable—

No. Now she was being sexist.

But she had resolved not to leave without fathoming at least part of the mystery . . . and thought of the original meaning of that word: craft, skill, *trade secret*.

That was what they were concealing. She was convinced of it now. On an isolated farmstead in—ah, but she could not say backwoods, for there were no woods: so, instead (farmstead/instead? She was confused anew)— this grassy desert, some process was afoot that caused millionaires to call by in their private planes, risking a crash away from proper radar beacons, risking exposure thanks to her, a stranger. Not a disinterested programme for the rehabilitation of the despoiled areas of Mother Earth. A project designed to make those who invested in it billionaires.

At whose expense?

Well—everybody else's. The planet, after all, was finite.

And the time of her bus was drawing near, and she still knew nothing she could impart to anyone by way of warning. She didn't even know what she would be uttering a warning against. She sensed, she suspected . . . yet she did not *know*.

What can I swear to? That someone who should have lain at death's door from his injuries was on his feet next day and eating breakfast? They'd laugh at me! They'd cheer!

I wish I didn't keep remembering the young men at Los Tramos, shivering with fever. And that their priest is dead and hasn't been replaced.

And since even her shameless pumping of Felipe evoked no solid data, she began to suspect she might, after all, be misjudging the Sniders. After all, that amazing plantation . . .

On the last evening she grew desperate enough to try to seduce Felipe. Clad only in her towelling robe she stole to his room—she had found out which one he slept in, and alone—tapped on the door, and said she wanted to before she left. He was proofed against her, though; he kissed her, with much warmth and many thanks, but chastely on the cheek, and pleaded his involvement with young Patti.

And sent her back to bed with promises to drive her to town in good time for the bus.

He, though, somehow, wasn't speaking. In his voice she heard the boom of Bernard Snider, as though all the private arguments had tended to the same conclusion:

Let her go. She doesn't realise what she's stumbled on. And no one that she talks to will believe her.

To herself she said bitterly: *They're right. I don't know what I've stumbled on. Now I suppose I never shall. Not, at least, until Bernard the Nobel laureate chooses to divulge it. Ah, well. So what? In India I met a dozen teachers who were convinced they could transform the world with no supporting evidence at all.*

Next afternoon:

Bernard emerged from his laboratory to embrace her; so did Greta; Lawrence and Mina did the same; they all did, and they all said much the same: how glad they were that Elsa had found her way here; what a welcome distraction her presence had been from their routine; how much they admired her bravery in driving the bulls away from Felipe. . . .

It was like being entwined by snakes: dry-rustling, not in the least slimy, but revolting on a level so deep in her subconscious that she dared not guess the reason for it.

Of those who took their leave of her, she found only one less than disgusting: Panza, who came up and wagged his tail and licked her hand and went back to his usual duties.

Pity. She had had the momentary impulse to ask whether he might ride along.

"Are you sure you haven't forgotten anything? Mina, you gave back all her clothes from being laundered?"

Bernard, imposing, officious, very much *el Jefe*. And adding to Greta, "She didn't have a camera, did she?"

Another hint. Another clue she would have like to follow up. But it was far too late. She was waving good-bye from the jeep as it bounced down the track to town, far rougher to four wheels than to her feet.

They also waved. As though they had been ordered to.

During the brief interval while they were out of sight of both the Foundation and Los Tramos, Felipe said, "I'm sorry, Elsa."

"What for?"

"I would have liked to tell you more."

"What about?"

"Our work, of course. But it is so important, so very unbelievably important. . . . Perhaps in a few years it will be safe to tell you."

"In a few years you'll have forgotten all about me."

"No!" He turned to stare at her for so long she grew afraid he might overlook the need to steer. "No, I swear, for so long as I live, I shall not forget the brave woman who drove away the bull!"

"It didn't do you much harm, did it? Back on your feet next morning, the condemned man eating a hearty breakfast!"

Where that phrase sprang from in memory, she had no idea. But it had an alarming effect. Felipe swallowed with vast and visible effort, and restored his attention to his driving.

Nor, during the rest of the bumpy ride, could Elsa coax another word from him save yes and no.

As they drew nearer to the town, the wind bore the sound of a cracked bell's chime, and on entering the *plaza* they found the reason for it. Cursing under his breath, Felipe slowed to a bare walking pace.

The townsfolk were assembled at the church. For a funeral. Being borne from the door was the body of, presumably, a child. It had no coffin, not in this treeless land, but only a coarse canvas shroud. A handcart stood ready to serve in lieu of a hearse.

Who was substituting for a priest?

Of course. The *alcalde*. Who else? The women wore black—but then most of them did, most of the time. The men had put on black armbands, knotted out of strips of cloth, but the mayor had donned a black suit and tie, over a more-or-less white shirt whose collar button he could no longer do up. The women and two or three of the men as well had been weeping, but at the appearance of the jeep they fell silent and turned to stare, their faces full of accusation.

"We picked a bad day," Felipe muttered. "Perhaps you ought to change your mind about leaving. If I work on Bernard hard enough, he might agree to ask one of our visitors whether you can hitch a plane ride—"

For a fleeting instant Elsa could have believed this had been staged for her benefit. But the idea, she concluded, was absurd. No, she was going to brazen it out. Though if the bus arrived late, as had the one that brought her, it could be difficult. . . . At least, though, she could insist on Felipe waiting with her until it turned up.

She said as much, and he sighed and nodded, parking the jeep beside the two-armed signpost.

"I expected you to say that. Of course I'll stay. And in case of trouble . . ." He patted something under his jacket. "But," he added, "if I'd known, I'd have brought a couple of the workers. Armed."

"What—?" Elsa had to swallow hard. "What does make them hate you so, Felipe? I've tried not to pry into your work. I've tried to respect Bernard's desire to keep it secret till the time is ripe, but I must have a straight answer to at least one question before I leave. I've asked before and been fobbed off, but aren't I entitled to just one snippet of the truth?"

Making no move to get out, warily eying the townsfolk, Felipe muttered, "Yes, of course. I told you: I wish with all my heart I could have been more frank with you. . . . But this at least I can explain. The answer, in essence, is in the shroud with that dead child."

Elsa shook her head, uncomprehending.

"Think, woman!" he snapped. "What must it be like for them, superstition-ridden, when they see us in such good health and hardly a month goes by without some child or hale young man or girl being carried off by the sort of fever that laid you so low? Had it not been for Lawrence's serum, *you* might not have survived!"

"You're saying it's all due to jealousy?"

"All? Not all. But I think most." He started, shading his eyes as he peered into the distance. "Incredible! The bus is running on time for once! Look, see the cloud of dust? It can't be more than ten minutes away."

They're going to be ten of the longest minutes of my life.

After the momentary silence, a buzz of muttering had begun among the townsfolk. The *alcalde's* authority seemed to be under threat, as though there were a movement to drag Elsa and Felipe from the jeep. Simultaneously, other people—especially three women whom Elsa guessed to be the dead child's mother and her friends or sisters—were insisting that the funeral proceed as scheduled to the cemetery. As though afraid of trouble, a few of the other bystanders slipped away from the edge of the group. She waited tensely for the outcome.

Abruptly there was a shout from behind her, and a noise of smashing glass. She twisted her head toward the *cantina*. From it, staggering drunk and mad with rage, rushed Diego brandishing a pistol, screaming at the top of his voice. She caught just enough of the words to realise he wanted vengeance for the death of his son—

Before he shot her. Drunk or not, his aim was true.

She felt the bullet like a blow beneath her left collarbone. It hurled her back against the seat. Pain followed, and the world became a maelstrom whirling her to darkness. With her last grip on consciousness she heard another shot, a scream of agony, and thought, *Felipe?*

Not able to guess whether he had fired back, or whether he too had been gunned down.

And then, dizzily, she was awake again. Moments only could have passed: long enough for Diego to be overpowered and dragged away, and the *alcalde* and his usual companions to reach the jeep. As she opened her eyes, astonished at how little pain she felt (but was that not a bad sign, indicative of death impending?), she saw first them and then Felipe, pistol in hand, ordering them to help her to the ground, bring cloths to wipe the blood and bind her wound. . . .

Bastards. Maybe it was all a setup. A drastic trick to make sure I don't get away so easily. Now they have an excuse to put me back to bed again and keep me there. . . .

"*Madre de Dios!*" said a soft and fearful voice. The words were echoed, but the first to speak them, despite his stated contempt for priests and priestcraft, was Felipe.

Elsa struggled to sit up. She could. Quite easily.

The crowd fell back, wide-eyed, everybody including the *alcalde* making the sign of the cross, some moaning prayers. Why in the—?

She glanced down at herself. There was blood on the front of her shirt. It had been ripped away on the side where the bullet had entered, exposing her left breast. That, though, was not what they were staring at.

The hole. The bullet hole. Was closing. The blood. Had already ceased to flow. The pain. Was no worse than an ache. Already.

Facts entered her mind, sluggishly, and trailed like the trail of a slug the terrible truth of what had been done to her. She was not, though, the first

414

to realise. Felipe was already saying under his breath, "Lawrence. The son of a bitch. Maybe Mina, too. Wanting to take the credit. Wanting to take the money. Who did they have lined up in Cachonga?"

Everything in the world seemed to recede to a vast distance except herself and Felipe. She drew a deep breath. There was a gurgling noise, and she had to cough up and spit away a mouthful of blood, but it hurt scarcely at all. She said, in English to prevent the locals from understanding, "This time I'm not asking you to admit the truth. I've worked it out. You just stand there and suffer!"

Hands pale-knuckled on his gun, he forced a nod.

"These people have a right to hate you, don't they? Because the trial version of what you're infected with, and me, didn't work right. Made them sickly, slow-witted, took them off with fevers that you don't know how to cure!"

The agony in his face told her as plain as words how right her guess was.

"How did it get loose?" And when he hesitated: "Tell me, damn you!"

"The ticks, I suppose," was his miserable answer. "But Bernard was so sure it wouldn't be contagious! He thought he'd designed it so it couldn't be!"

"And despite his Nobel prize, he was wrong?"

A miserable nod. "We found out later. Too late . . ." He swallowed painfully. "I didn't refuse you last night because I didn't want you, Elsa. Or because of Patti. I was lying. I didn't want you to catch—But I should have known! I very nearly did know!"

"Because I threw off the drug Mina gave me? And woke up too soon?"

Vaguely from the corner of her eye Elsa noticed that the *alcalde* and his companions had moved away. The funeral had resumed; the body was on the cart and being pushed toward its humble grave. She paid no heed.

"You all volunteered to be infected?" And answered her own question before he could because now she knew what Greta had started to say about her bravery in driving off the bull—something like, *Since she doesn't have the protection the rest of us have.* . . . "Well, why not? Since it makes you pretty well invulnerable! To be tossed and trampled by a bull, and eat a hearty breakfast the next day—"

And checked, remembering that she had used that phrase before, and coupled it with the cliché about the condemned man, and . . .

"But it has to be paid for," she said. Her heart turned to ice as she listened to the words she was uttering.

Felipe put away his gun and wiped his forehead, whether of sweat or wind-blown dust she could not tell.

"Yes. That's why Bernard won't announce his results."

"Go on."

Licking his lips, avoiding eye contact, he said, "It makes you sterile. Men and women, both."

A pang of wild relief flooded Elsa's mind. She thought: *For me that's no drawback at all!*

And calmed in an instant.

"Is that why there are so few children in Los Tramos?"

"Yes."

"I see. Who are your visitors, who come by plane?"

Felipe's face, that had been like an idol's carved in stone, twisted into a bitter smile.

"Can't you guess? What kind of people most want a technique that can heal bullet wounds and almost every other kind of injury in hours at worst, sometimes in minutes?"

"In spite of it making people sterile?"

"Oh, they think of that as being a problem that can be solved by throwing enough money at it—as and when *they* get control of that much money!"

Elsa nodded. Were there not candidates enough—dictators at risk of assassination, army commanders dreaming of a force of supermen . . . ? But Felipe was adding in an anxious tone, "You can't blame Bernard, though! He doesn't live in the same world as they do. He's a dreamer, an idealist, a genius!"

"In other words," said Elsa stonily, "he thinks he's right and everybody else is wrong. Don't contradict. I didn't tell you, but I finally remembered the scene he made when they gave him his prize. He said he could put the world right single-handed if the cowards and the conservationists would let him! Didn't he?"

"I—"

"Wasn't there? I'm sure you weren't. But you've worked with him, watched him spend people like renewable resources—"

"It was Lawrence!" Felipe flared, like any disciple hearing an insult to his teacher. "He—"

"You've told me enough to let me work it out. Under the guise of treating me for tick-borne fever Lawrence infected me with the whatever-it-is—don't say the name, it won't mean anything and I don't want to know. He didn't realise it might make me resistant to soporific drugs as well, or he'd have told Mina to give me a double dose." Elsa tugged absently at her torn shirt, wondering whether she could tie it together, and decided it was impossible. She reached for her backpack, trying to remember which compartment she had stowed her other shirts in. And went on:

"And it's your opinion, or suspicion rather, that he must have struck a bargain with one of your visitors, behind Bernard's back. He arranged that

416

if someone like me turned up, he'd give me an injection of the stuff and either persuade Bernard to let me fly out or arrange for someone to kidnap me at my next stop and pass me on. You said you wondered who he has waiting at Cachonga, or words to that effect. Whereupon—"

She pulled off and tossed aside the ruined shirt, heedless of the eyes that were staring from all corners of the *plaza* and the windows of every house in sight.

Donning a clean intact one, she concluded, "Whereupon he and Mina would be handsomely rewarded, and the rest of you, including Snider, would be left with the problem of curing the sterility effect before it was too late. Is the stuff very infectious?"

"Not infectious. It can't survive outside the body. Contagious."

"Like AIDS? Like leprosy?"

"I guess. But once it's established in your system, you just throw those off. And pretty well everything else, down to the common cold. It—well, it mends you."

The grumbling of the bus was loud by now. It would enter the town in no more than another minute. Felipe glanced around.

"What are you going to do?"

Elsa's hand moved like lightning. She snatched the gun from under his coat and levelled it at his belly.

"I'm going to Cachonga," she said calmly. "And I propose to get laid there. I don't like men all that much, but I propose to get laid a lot because in a country like this men can pass it on to women more easily than I can. And at every other place I move on to. But I'm not going to take the bus."

"What?" Felipe put his hand to his head, as though dizzy.

"No. I'm going to drive there. You and I are going to wait until the bus has left. Then we are going to tank up the jeep and buy as many extra cans of gas as possible. Then you are going to drive me, at gunpoint, about twenty kilometres. I happen to be quite good with these things"—she hefted the pistol—"and I am one hundred per cent certain that a hole in your brain would not repair itself the way muscles do, and bones. Then you are going to walk back to the Foundation and tell your precious Nobelist that it is up to him, and you, to save the world. They'd better do it fast. I rather like the idea that poor people may stop breeding and become invulnerable."

"You're crazy!" Felipe whispered. The bus arrived. The townsfolk waited out the usual routine—the delivery of mail and official notices—and wondered aloud why Elsa wasn't getting on. Concealing the gun with her body, she waved a cheerful greeting to the policeman, in case he was the same one.

417

Its brief visit concluded, the bus roared away. Watching Felipe closely, Elsa gave a thin smile.

"You're right, of course. The jeep can easily overtake it. When I drop you off, you can wait for it to catch up and tell the policeman to radio ahead and have me met at the terminal. . . . My God, I was right! I didn't think I was, but I just read it in your face!"

Insofar as he could, Felipe turned pale.

"Isn't that what you'd do if I let you?" she pressed.

"I've got to stop you carrying out this crazy plan! You can't turn it loose—"

"Why not? Bernard's been dickering—you said as much—with people whose only interest in his project *is* to turn it loose. You didn't try to stop *them*, did you? Didn't sabotage their planes on the runway, shoot them when their backs were turned!"

It appeared that working up a fine rage helped the process of healing; now, she felt scarcely more than the ache of an old bruise.

"So we will do exactly as I said. Bar one thing. I'm not going on to Cachonga. I'm going back to Vilagustin. And I think I'll make you walk *thirty* kilometres. Get in!"

As the jeep rolled through the gathering darkness, he pleaded with her until his voice grew hoarse, and every time she said, "I think it's time to turn the tables."

"Why, though? Why?"

To which she merely shrugged. Finally, however, as the distance she had promised ticked up on the counter, she gave in and answered. Possibly, until that much time had passed, she hadn't yet worked out her own motives . . . but that was nothing new in her life.

"No matter how dazzled you are by the fat cattle, the new forest, doesn't it make you sick, as a citizen of this country, to find experiments being conducted here that would be forbidden in a more advanced nation?"

"Yes, of course. But—"

"*There is no but!* For much too long the rich countries have treated poor ones as a dumping ground! I've seen! I don't just mean poisonous garbage and radioactive waste—I mean banned drugs sold to the sick and ignorant! Surplus dried milk peddled to feed children who'd thrive better on their mother's own, if their mothers were well enough to keep their breasts full! I *like* the idea—I told you!—I *love* the idea that in a few years people in poor countries won't have so many kids to worry about, and when the rich send armies to attack them, they'll get up again and go on fighting! Unless of course they're hit in a vital spot—No, Felipe. Don't try anything. Sure my arm is getting tired of keeping this gun trained on your

418

head, but thanks to Lawrence I'm not a tenth as tired as I would have been without the treatment. . . . Right. That'll do. This is as near to the middle of nowhere as I remember passing on the way to Los Tramos. Out you go."

Almost snivelling, he obeyed, and she slid into the driving seat.

"Leave me food and water, at least!" he begged.

"You should have thought of that before," she said composedly. "But I don't suppose we're much more vulnerable to thirst than we are to fatigue, not after what's been done to us. You'll make it. And—"

"What?"

She bent a burning gaze on him.

"When you get back to the Foundation, tell the truth."

Reaching behind her with one hand, but never taking her eyes from him, she groped in her backpack for a chocolate bar and tossed it to him.

"Wait! Elsa, wait—!"

"No!" she snapped. "*You* wait, along with everybody else! But count yourself lucky! You have a chance to do something about it! Better hurry, though! And when you find the antidote for the sterility effect, don't let it be reserved for the rich!"

She gunned the engine and roared down the pathway of her headlights, leaving him weeping amid the grassy desert.

The police helicopter swooped when Elsa was still ten kilometres short of Vilagustin. Riddled by machine gun fire, the gas cans in the jeep exploded. When nothing much was left, the copter's crew sprayed the wreckage with frozen carbon dioxide for fear stray sparks might fire the *pampa*, landed, and bore away her skull so it could be identified from the dentition. In the official record she was entered as a foreigner who had kidnapped a citizen and stolen a vehicle at gunpoint. Which, of course, was true.

Shortly after began the unification of Latin America into a world power, under the sway of the first soldiers since the ancient Persian Empire to be called Immortals, and with better reason: infantry who could be shot to ribbons on the battlefield but, if their brains remained intact, came back to fight again, again, again. Naturally, providing the animal protein necessary for their recovery called for confiscation of all sorts of livestock, but new and more productive strains had luckily appeared, let loose by accident—so rumour said—from some secret centre of research. (By then the Snider Foundation had of course been sacked, its staff was dead, its records burned.)

Ultimately the Immortals occupied the northern continent as well, being proof against anything much short of nukes, which spoiled so much more land than they defended as to prove self-defeating. When asked about the

419

penalty they paid, they laughed and said, "Well, they've told us all along we have too many kids."

It wasn't quite so funny when, next century, there literally were no babies being born.

NANCY KRESS

Inertia

▼

Born in Buffalo, New York, Nancy Kress now lives with her family in Brockport, New York. She began selling her elegant and incisive stories in the mid-seventies, and has since become a frequent contributer to *IAsfm*, *F & SF*, *Omni*, and elsewhere. Her books include the novels *The Prince of Morning Bells*, *The Golden Grove*, *The White Pipes*, and *An Alien Light*, and the collection *Trinity and Other Stories*. Her most recent book is the novel *Brain Rose*. Her story "Trinity" was in our Second Annual Collection; her "Out of All Them Bright Stars"—a Nebula winner—was in our Third Annual Collection; her "In Memoriam" was in our Sixth Annual Collection; and her "The Price of Oranges" was in our Seventh Annual Collection.

In the eloquent and troubling story that follows, she demonstrates that *some* sorts of inertia are more easily overcome than others. . . .

▼

Inertia

NANCY KRESS

At dusk the back of the bedroom falls off. One minute it's a wall, exposed studs and cracked blue drywall, and the next it's snapped-off two-by-fours and an irregular fence as high as my waist, the edges both jagged and furry, as if they were covered with powder. Through the hole a sickly tree pokes upward in the narrow space between the back of our barracks and the back of a barracks in E Block. I try to get out of bed for a closer look, but today my arthritis is too bad, which is why I'm in bed in the first place. Rachel rushes into the bedroom.

"What *happened*, Gram? Are you all right?"

I nod and point. Rachel bends into the hole, her hair haloed by California twilight. The bedroom is hers, too; her mattress lies stored under my scarred four-poster.

"Termites! Damn. I didn't know we had them. You sure you're all right?"

"I'm fine. I was all the way across the room, honey. I'm fine."

"Well—we'll have to get Mom to get somebody to fix it."

I say nothing. Rachel straightens, throws me a quick glance, looks away. Still I say nothing about Mamie, but in a sudden flicker from my oil lamp I look directly at Rachel, just because she is so good to look at. Not pretty, not even here Inside, although so far the disease has affected only the left side of her face. The ridge of thickened, ropy skin, coarse as old hemp, isn't visible at all when she stands in right profile. But her nose is large, her eyebrows heavy and low, her chin a bony knob. An honest nose, expressive brows, direct gray eyes, chin that juts forward when she tilts her head in intelligent listening—to a grandmother's eye, Rachel is good to look at. They wouldn't think so, Outside. But they would be wrong.

Rachel says, "Maybe I could trade a lottery card for more drywall and nails, and patch it myself."

"The termites will still be there."

"Well, yes, but we have to do *something*." I don't contradict her. She is sixteen years old. "Feel that air coming in—you'll freeze at night this time of year. It'll be terrible for your arthritis. Come in the kitchen now, Gram —I've built up the fire."

She helps me into the kitchen, where the metal wood-burning stove throws a rosy warmth that feels good on my joints. The stove was donated to the colony a year ago by who-knows-what charity or special interest group for, I suppose, whatever tax breaks still hold for that sort of thing. If any do. Rachel tells me that we still get newspapers, and once or twice I've wrapped vegetables from our patch in some fairly new-looking ones. She even says that the young Stevenson boy works a donated computer news net in the Block J community hall, but I no longer follow Outside tax regulations. Nor do I ask why Mamie was the one to get the wood-burning stove when it wasn't a lottery month.

The light from the stove is stronger than the oil flame in the bedroom; I see that beneath her concern for our dead bedroom wall, Rachel's face is flushed with excitement. Her young skin glows right from intelligent chin to the ropy ridge of disease, which of course never changes color. I smile at her. Sixteen is so easy to excite. A new hair ribbon from the donations repository, a glance from a boy, a secret with her cousin Jennie.

"Gram," she says, kneeling beside my chair, her hands restless on the battered wooden arm, "Gram—there's a visitor. From Outside. Jennie *saw* him."

I go on smiling. Rachel—nor Jennie, either—can't remember when disease colonies had lots of visitors. First bulky figures in contamination suits, then a few years later, sleeker figures in the sani-suits that took their place. People were still being interred from Outside, and for years the checkpoints at the Rim had traffic flowing both ways. But of course Rachel doesn't remember all that; she wasn't born. Mamie was only twelve when we were interred here. To Rachel, a visitor might well be a great event. I put out one hand and stroke her hair.

"Jennie said he wants to talk to the oldest people in the colony, the ones who were brought here with the disease. Hal Stevenson told her."

"Did he, sweetheart?" Her hair is soft and silky. Mamie's hair had been the same at Rachel's age.

"He might want to talk to you!"

"Well, here I am."

"But aren't you excited? What do you suppose he wants?"

I'm saved from answering her because Mamie comes in, her boyfriend Peter Malone following with a string bag of groceries from the repository.

At the first sound of the doorknob turning, Rachel gets up from beside my chair and pokes at the fire. Her face goes completely blank, although I know that part is only temporary. Mamie cries, "Here we are!" in her high, doll-baby voice, cold air from the hall swirling around her like bright water. "Mama darling—how are you feeling? And Rachel! You'll never guess— Pete had extra depository cards and he got us some chicken! I'm going to make a stew!"

"The back wall fell off the bedroom," Rachel says flatly. She doesn't look at Peter with his string-crossed chicken, but I do. He grins his patient, wolfish grin. I guess that he won the depository cards at poker. His fingernails are dirty. The part of the newspaper I can see says ESIDENT CONFISCATES C.

Mamie says, "What do you mean, fell off?"

Rachel shrugs. "Just fell off. Termites."

Mamie looks helplessly at Peter, whose grin widens. I can see how it will be: They will have a scene later, not completely for our benefit, although it will take place in the kitchen for us to watch. Mamie will beg prettily for Peter to fix the wall. He will demur, grinning. She will offer various smirking hints about barter, each hint becoming more explicit. He will agree to fix the wall. Rachel and I, having no other warm room to go to, will watch the fire or the floor or our shoes until Mamie and Peter retire ostentatiously to her room. It's the ostentation that embarrasses us. Mamie has always needed witnesses to her desirability.

But Peter is watching Rachel, not Mamie. "The chicken isn't from Outside, Rachel. It's from that chicken yard in Block B. I heard you say how clean they are."

"Yeah," Rachel says shortly, gracelessly.

Mamie rolls her eyes. "Say 'thank you,' darling. Pete went to a lot of trouble to get this chicken."

"Thanks."

"Can't you say it like you *mean* it?" Mamie's voice goes shrill.

"*Thanks*," Rachel says. She heads towards our three-walled bedroom. Peter, still watching her closely, shifts the chicken from one hand to the other. The pressure of the string bag cuts lines across the chicken's yellowish skin.

"Rachel Anne Wilson—"

"Let her go," Peter says softly.

"No," Mamie says. Between the five crisscrossing lines of disease, her face sets in unlovely lines. "She can at least learn some manners. And I want her to hear our announcement! Rachel, you just come right back out here this minute!"

Rachel returns from the bedroom; I've never known her to disobey her mother. She pauses by the open bedroom door, waiting. Two empty candle sconces, both blackened by old smoke, frame her head. It has been since at least last winter that we've had candles for them. Mamie, her forehead creased in irritation, smiles brightly.

"This is a special dinner, all of you. Pete and I have an announcement. We're going to get married."

"That's right," Peter says. "Congratulate us."

Rachel, already motionless, somehow goes even stiller. Peter watches her carefully. Mamie casts down her eyes, blushing, and I feel a stab of impatient pity for my daughter, propping up mid-thirties girlishness on such a slender reed as Peter Malone. I stare at him hard. If he ever touches Rachel . . . but I don't really think he would. Things like that don't happen anymore. Not Inside.

"Congratulations," Rachel mumbles. She crosses the room and embraces her mother, who hugs her back with theatrical fervor. In another minute, Mamie will start to cry. Over her shoulder I glimpse Rachel's face, momentarily sorrowing and loving, and I drop my eyes.

"Well! This calls for a toast!" Mamie cries gaily. She winks, makes a clumsy pirouette, and pulls a bottle from the back shelf of the cupboard Rachel got at the last donations lottery. The cupboard looks strange in our kitchen: gleaming white lacquer, vaguely oriental-looking, amid the wobbly chairs and scarred table with the broken drawer no one has ever gotten around to mending. Mamie flourishes the bottle, which I didn't know was there. It's champagne.

What had they been thinking, the Outsiders who donated champagne to a disease colony? *Poor devils, even if they never have anything to celebrate. . . .* Or *Here's something they won't know what to do with. . . .* Or *Better them than me—as long as the sickies stay Inside. . . .* It doesn't really matter.

"I just love champagne!" Mamie cries feverishly; I think she has drunk it once. "And oh look—here's someone else to help us celebrate! Come in, Jennie—come in and have some champagne!"

Jennie comes in, smiling. I see the same eager excitement that animated Rachel before her mother's announcement. It glows on Jennie's face, which is beautiful. She has no disease on her hands or her face. She must have it somewhere, she was born Inside, but one doesn't ask that. Probably Rachel knows. The two girls are inseparable. Jennie, the daughter of Mamie's dead husband's brother, is Rachel's cousin, and technically Mamie is her guardian.

But no one pays attention to such things anymore, and Jennie lives with some people in a barracks in the next Block, although Rachel and I asked her to live here. She shook her head, the beautiful hair so blonde it's almost white bouncing on her shoulders, and blushed in embarrassment, painfully not looking at Mamie.

"I'm getting married, Jennie," Mamie says, again casting down her eyes bashfully. I wonder what she did, and with whom, to get the champagne.

"Congratulations!" Jennie says warmly. "You, too, Peter."

"Call me Pete," he says, as he has said before. I catch his hungry look at Jennie. She doesn't, but some sixth sense—even here, even Inside—makes her step slightly backwards. I know she will go on calling him "Peter."

Mamie says to Jennie, "Have some more champagne. Stay for dinner."

With her eyes Jennie measures the amount of champagne in the bottle, the size of the chicken bleeding slightly on the table. She measures unobtrusively, and then of course she lies. "I'm sorry, I can't—we ate our meal at noon today. I just wanted to ask if I could bring someone over to see you later, Gram. A visitor." Her voice drops to a hush, and the glow is back. "From *Outside*."

I look at her sparkling blue eyes, at Rachel's face, and I don't have the heart to refuse. Even though I can guess, as the two girls cannot, how the visit will be. I am not Jennie's grandmother, but she has called me that since she was three. "All right."

"Oh, thank you!" Jennie cries, and she and Rachel look at each other with delight. "I'm so glad you said yes, or else we might never get to talk to a visitor up close at all!"

"You're welcome," I say. They are so young. Mamie looks petulant; her announcement has been upstaged. Peter watches Jennie as she impulsively hugs Rachel. Suddenly I know that he, too, is wondering where Jennie's body is diseased, and how much. He catches my eye and looks at the floor, his dark eyes lidded, half ashamed. But only half. A log crackles in the wooden stove, and for a brief moment the fire flares.

The next afternoon Jennie brings the visitor. He surprises me immediately: he isn't wearing a sani-suit, and he isn't a sociologist.

In the years following the internments, the disease colonies had a lot of visitors. Doctors still hopeful of a cure for the thick gray ridges of skin that spread slowly over a human body—or didn't, nobody knew why. Disfiguring. Ugly. Maybe eventually fatal. And *communicable*. That was the biggie: communicable. So doctors in sani-suits came looking for causes or cures. Journalists in sani-suits came looking for stories with four-color photo spreads. Legislative fact-finding committees in sani-suits came looking for facts, at least until Congress took away the power of colonies to vote, pressured by taxpayers who, increasingly pressured themselves, resented our dollar-dependent status. And the sociologists came in droves, minicams in hand, ready to record the collapse of the ill-organized and ill colonies into street-gang, dog-eat-dog anarchy.

Later, when this did not happen, different sociologists came in later-model sani-suits to record the reasons why the colonies were not collapsing on schedule. All these groups went away dissatisfied. There was no cure, no cause, no story, no collapse. No reasons.

The sociologists hung on longer than anybody else. Journalists have to be timely and interesting, but sociologists merely have to publish. Besides, everything in their cultural tradition told them that Inside *must* sooner or later degenerate into war zones: Deprive people of electricity (power became expensive), of municipal police (who refused to go Inside), of freedom to leave, of political clout, of jobs, of freeways and movie theaters and federal judges and state-administered elementary-school accreditation—and you get unrestrained violence to just survive. Everything in the culture said so. Bombed-out inner cities. *Lord Of The Flies.* The Chicago projects. Western movies. Prison memoirs. The Bronx. East L.A. Thomas Hobbes. The sociologists *knew.*

Only it didn't happen.

The sociologists waited. And Inside we learned to grow vegetables and raise chickens who, we learned, will eat anything. Those of us with computer knowledge worked real jobs over modems for a few years—maybe it was as long as a decade—before the equipment became too obsolete and unreplaced. Those who had been teachers organized classes among the children, although the curriculum, I think, must have gotten simpler every year: Rachel and Jennie don't seem to have much knowledge of history or science. Doctors practiced with medicines donated by corporations for the tax write-offs, and after a decade or so they began to train apprentices. For a while—it might have been a long while—we listened to radios and watched TV. Maybe some people still do, if we have any working ones donated from Outside. I don't pay attention.

Eventually the sociologists remembered older models of deprivation and discrimination and isolation from the larger culture: Jewish shtetls. French Huguenots. Amish farmers. Self-sufficient models, stagnant but uncollapsed. And while they were remembering, we held goods lotteries, and took on apprentices, and rationed depository food according to who needed it, and replaced our broken-down furniture with other broken-down furniture, and got married and bore children. We paid no taxes, fought no wars, wielded no votes, provided no drama. After a while—a long while—the visitors stopped coming. Even the sociologists.

But here stands this young man, without a sani-suit, smiling from brown eyes under thick dark hair and taking my hand. He doesn't wince when he touches the ropes of disease. Nor does he appear to be cataloguing the kitchen furniture for later recording: three chairs, one donated imitation Queen Anne and one Inside genuine Joe Kleinschmidt; the table; the wood stove; the sparkling new oriental lacquered cupboard; plastic sink with hand pump; woodbox with donated wood stamped "Gift of Boise-Cascade"; two eager and intelligent and loving young girls he had better not try to patronize as diseased freaks. It has been a long time, but I remember.

"Hello, Mrs. Pratt. I'm Tom McHabe. Thank you for agreeing to talk to me."

I nod. "What are we going to talk about, Mr. McHabe? Are you a journalist?"

"No. I'm a doctor."

I don't expect that. Nor do I expect the sudden strain that flashes across his face before it's lost in another smile. Although it is natural enough that strain should be there: Having come Inside, of course, he can never leave. I wonder where he picked up the disease. No other new cases have been admitted to our colony for as long as I can remember. Had they been taken, for some Outside political reason, to one of the other colonies instead?

McHabe says, "I don't have the disease, Mrs. Pratt."

"Then why on earth—"

"I'm writing a paper on the progress of the disease in long-established colony residents. I had to do that from Inside, of course," he says, and immediately I know he is lying. Rachel and Jennie, of course, do not. They sit one on each side of him like eager birds, listening.

"And how will you get this paper out once it's written?" I say.

"Short-wave radio. Colleagues are expecting it," but he doesn't quite meet my eyes.

"And this paper is worth permanent internment?"

"How rapidly did your case of the disease progress?" he says, not answering my question. He looks at my face and hands and forearms, an objective and professional scrutiny that makes me decide at least one part of his story is true. He is a doctor.

"Any pain in the infected areas?"

"None."

"Any functional disability or decreased activity as a result of the disease?" Rachel and Jennie look slightly puzzled; he's testing me to see if I understand the terminology.

"None."

"Any change in appearance over the last few years in the first skin areas to be affected? Changes in color or tissue density or size of the thickened ridges?"

"None."

"Any other kinds of changes I haven't thought to mention?"

"None."

He nods and rocks back on his heels. He's cool, for someone who is going to develop non-dysfunctional ropes of disease himself. I wait to see if he's going to tell me why he's really here. The silence lengthens. Finally McHabe says, "You were a CPA," at the same time that Rachel says, "Anyone want a glass of 'ade?"

McHabe accepts gladly. The two girls, relieved to be in motion, busy themselves pumping cold water, crushing canned peaches, mixing the 'ade in a brown plastic pitcher with a deep wart on one side where it once touched the hot stove.

"Yes," I say to McHabe, "I was a CPA. What about it?"

"They're outlawed now."

"CPAs? Why? Staunch pillars of the establishment," I say, and realize how long it's been since I used words like that. They taste metallic, like old tin.

"Not any more. IRS does all tax computations and sends every household a customized bill. The calculations on how they reach your particular customized figure are classified. To prevent foreign enemies from guessing at revenue available for defense."

"Ah."

"My uncle was a CPA."

"What is he now?"

"Not a CPA," McHabe says. He doesn't smile. Jennie hands glasses of 'ade to me and then to McHabe, and then he does smile. Jennie drops her lashes and a little color steals into her cheeks. Something moves behind McHabe's eyes. But it's not like Peter; not at all like Peter.

I glance at Rachel. She doesn't seem to have noticed anything. She isn't jealous, or worried, or hurt. I relax a little.

McHabe says to me, "You also published some magazine articles popularizing history."

"How do you happen to know that?"

Again he doesn't answer me. "It's an unusual combination of abilities, accounting and history writing."

"I suppose so," I say, without interest. It was so long ago.

Rachel says to McHabe, "Can I ask you something?"

"Sure."

"Outside, do you have medicines that will cure wood of termites?"

Her face is deadly serious. McHabe doesn't grin, and I admit—reluctantly—that he is likable. He answers her courteously. "We don't cure the wood, we do away with the termites. The best way is to build with wood

429

saturated with creosote, a chemical they don't like, so that they don't get into the wood in the first place. But there must be chemicals that will kill them after they're already there. I'll ask around and try to bring you something on my next trip Inside."

His next trip Inside. He drops this bombshell as if easy passage In and Out were a given. Rachel's and Jennie's eyes grow wide; they both look at me. McHabe does, too, and I see that his look is a cool scrutiny, an appraisal of my reaction. He expects me to ask for details, or maybe even—it's been a long time since I thought in these terms, and it's an effort—to become angry at him for lying. But I don't know whether or not he's lying, and at any rate, what does it matter? A few people from Outside coming into the colony—how could it affect us? There won't be large immigration, and no emigration at all.

I say quietly, "Why are you really here, Dr. McHabe?"

"I told you, Mrs. Pratt. To measure the progress of the disease." I say nothing. He adds, "Maybe you'd like to hear more about how it is now Outside."

"Not especially."

"Why not?"

I shrug. "They leave us alone."

He weighs me with his eyes. Jennie says timidly, "I'd like to hear more about Outside." Before Rachel can add "Me, too," the door flings violently open and Mamie backs into the room, screaming into the hall behind her.

"And don't ever come back! If you think I'd ever let you touch me again after screwing that . . . that . . . I hope she's got a diseased twat and you get it on your—" She sees McHabe and breaks off, her whole body jerking in rage. A soft answer from the hall, the words unintelligible from my chair by the fire, makes her gasp and turn even redder. She slams the door, bursts into tears, and runs into her bedroom, slamming that door as well.

Rachel stands up. "Let me, honey," I say, but before I can rise—my arthritis is much better—Rachel disappears into her mother's room. The kitchen rings with embarrassed silence.

Tom McHabe rises to leave. "Sit down, Doctor," I say, hoping, I think, that if he remains Mamie will restrain her hysterics—maybe—and Rachel will emerge sooner from her mother's room.

McHabe looks undecided. Then Jennie says, "Yes, please stay. And would you tell us—" I see her awkwardness, her desire to not sound stupid "—about how people do Outside?"

He does. Looking at Jennie but meaning me, he talks about the latest version of martial law, about the failure of the National Guard to control protestors against the South American war until they actually reached the edge of the White House electro-wired zone; about the growing power of the Fundamentalist underground that the other undergrounds—he uses the plural—call "the God gang." He tells us about the industries losing out steadily to Korean and Chinese competitors, the leaping unemployment rate, the ethnic backlash, the cities in flames. Miami, New York, Los Angeles— these had been rioting for years. Now it's Portland, St. Louis, Eugene, Phoenix. Grand Rapids burning. It's hard to picture.

I say, "As far as I can tell, donations to our repositories haven't fallen off."

He looks at me again with that shrewd scrutiny, weighing something I can't see, then touches the edge of the stove with one boot. The boot, I notice, is almost as old and scarred as one of ours. "Korean-made stove. They make nearly all the donations now. Public relations. Even a lot of martial-law congressmen had relatives interred, although they won't admit it now. The Asians cut deals warding off complete protectionism, although of course your donations are only a small part of that. But just about every-thing you get Inside is Chink or Splat." He uses the words casually, this courteous young man giving me the news from such a liberal slant, and that tells me more about the Outside than all his bulletins and summaries.

Jennie says haltingly, "I say . . . I think it was an Asian man. Yesterday."

"Where?" I say sharply. Very few Asian-Americans contract the disease; something else no one understands. There are none in our colony.

"At the Rim. One of the guards. Two other men were kicking him and yelling names at him—we couldn't hear too clearly over the intercom boxes."

"We? You and Rachel? What were you two doing at the *Rim*?" I say, and hear my own tone. The rim, a wide empty strip of land, is electro-mined and barb-wired to keep us communicables Inside. The Rim is surrounded by miles of defoliated and disinfected land, poisoned by preventive chemicals, but even so it's patrolled by unwilling soldiers who communicate with the Inside by intercoms set up every half mile on both sides of the barbed wire. When the colony used to have a fight or a rape or—once, in the early years—a murder, it happened on the Rim. When the hateful and the hating came to hurt us, because before the electro-wiring and barbed wire we were easy targets and no police would follow them Inside, the soldiers, and some-times our men as well, stopped them at the Rim. Our dead are buried near the Rim. And Rachel and Jennie, dear gods, at the *Rim*. . . .

"We went to ask the guards over the intercom boxes if they knew how to stop termites," Jennie says logically. "After all, their work is to stop things, germs and things. We thought they might be able to tell us how to stop termites. We thought they might have special training in it."

The bedroom door opens and Rachel comes out, her young face drawn. McHabe smiles at her, and then his gaze returns to Jennie. "I don't think soldiers are trained in stopping termites, but I'll definitely bring you some-thing to do that the next time I come Inside."

There it is again. But all Rachel says is, "Oh, good. I asked around for more drywall today, but even if I get some, the same thing will happen again if we don't get something to stop them."

McHabe says, "Did you know that termites elect a queen? Closely-monitored balloting system. Fact."

Rachel smiles, although I don't think she really understands.

"And ants can bring down a rubber tree plant." He begins to sing, an old song from my childhood. "High Hopes." Frank Sinatra on the stereo— before CDs, even, before a lot of things—iced tea and Coke in tall glasses on a Sunday afternoon, aunts and uncles sitting around the kitchen, football on television in the living room beside a table with a lead-crystal vase of the last purple chrysanthemums from the garden. The smell of late Sunday afternoon, tangy but a little thin, the last of the weekend before the big yellow school bus labored by on Monday morning.

Jennie and Rachel, of course, see none of this. They hear light-hearted words in a good baritone and a simple rhythm they can follow, hope and courage in silly doggerel. They are delighted. They join in the chorus after McHabe has sung it a few times, then sing him three songs popular at Block dances, then make him more 'ade, then begin to ask questions about the Outside. Simple questions: What do people eat? Where do they get it? What do they wear? The three of them are still at it when I go to bed, my arthritis finally starting to ache, glancing at Mamie's closed door with a sadness I hadn't expected and can't name.

"That son-of-a-bitch better never come near me again," Mamie says the next morning. The day is sunny and I sit by our one window, knitting a blanket to loosen my fingers, wondering if the donated wool came from Chinese or Korean sheep. Rachel has gone with Jennie on a labor call to deepen a well in Block E; people had been talking about doing that for weeks, and apparently someone finally got around to organizing it. Mamie slumps at the table, her eyes red from crying. "I caught him screwing Mary Delbarton." Her voice splinters like a two-year-old's. "Mama—he was screwing Mary Delbarton."

"Let him go, Mamie."

"I'd be alone again." She says it with a certain dignity, which doesn't last. "That son-of-a-bitch goes off with that slut one day after we're engaged and I'm fucking alone again!"

I don't say anything; there isn't anything to say. Mamie's husband died eleven years ago, when Rachel was only five, of an experimental cure being tested by government doctors. The colonies were guinea pigs. Seventeen people in four colonies died, and the government discontinued funding and made it a crime for anyone to go in and out of a disease colony. Too great a risk of contamination, they said. For the protection of the citizens of the country.

"He'll never touch me again!" Mamie says, tears on her lashes. One slips down an inch until it hits the first of the disease ropes, then travels sideways towards her mouth. I reach over and wipe it away. "Goddamn fucking son-of-a-bitch!"

By evening, she and Peter are holding hands. They sit side by side, and his fingers creep up her thigh under what they think is the cover of the table. Mamie slips her hand under his buttocks. Rachel and Jennie look away, Jennie flushing slightly. I have a brief flash of memory, of the kind I haven't had for years: myself at eighteen or so, my first year at Yale, in a huge brass bed with a modern geometric-print bedspread and a red-headed man I met three hours ago. But here, Inside . . . here sex, like everything else, moves so much more slowly, so much more carefully, so much more privately. For such a long time people were afraid that this disease, like that other earlier one, might be transmitted sexually. And then there was the shame of one's ugly body, crisscrossed with ropes of disease . . . I'm not sure that Rachel has ever seen a man naked.

I say, for the sake of saying something, "So there's a Block dance Wednesday."

"Block B," Jennie says. Her blue eyes sparkle. "With the band that played last summer for Block E."

"Guitars?"

"Oh, no! They've got a trumpet *and* a violin," Rachel says, clearly impressed. "You should hear how they sound together, Gram—it's a lot different than guitars. Come to the dance!"

"I don't think so, honey. Is Dr. McHabe going?" From both their faces I know this guess is right.

Jennie says hesitantly, "He wants to talk to you first, before the dance, for a few minutes. If that's all right."

"Why?"

"I'm not . . . not exactly sure I know all of it." She doesn't meet my eyes: unwilling to tell me, unwilling to lie. Most of the children Inside, I realize for the first time, are not liars. Or else they're bad ones. They're good at privacy, but it must be an honest privacy.

"Will you see him?" Rachel says eagerly.

"I'll see him."

Mamie looks away from Peter long enough to add sharply, "If it's anything about you or Jennie, he should see *me*, miss, not your grandmother. I'm your mother and Jennie's guardian, and don't you forget it."

"No, Mama," Rachel says.

"I don't like your tone, miss!"

"Sorry," Rachel says, in the same tone. Jennie drops her eyes, embarrassed. But before Mamie can get really started on indignant maternal neglect, Peter whispers something in her ear and she claps her hand over her mouth, giggling.

Later, when just the two of us are left in the kitchen, I say quietly to Rachel, "Try not to upset your mother, honey. She can't help it."

"Yes, Gram," Rachel says obediently. But I hear the disbelief in her tone, a disbelief muted by her love for me and even for her mother, but nonetheless there. Rachel doesn't believe that Mamie can't help it. Rachel, born Inside, can't possibly help her own ignorance of what it is that Mamie thinks she has lost.

On his second visit to me six days later, just before the Block dance, Tom McHabe seems different. I'd forgotten that there are people who radiate such energy and purpose that they seem to set the very air tingling. He stands with his legs braced slightly apart, flanked by Rachel and Jennie, both dressed in their other skirts for the dance. Jennie has woven a red ribbon through her blonde curls; it glows like a flower. McHabe touches her lightly on the shoulder, and I realize from her answering look what must be happening between them. My throat tightens.

"I want to be honest with you, Mrs. Pratt. I've talked to Jack Stevenson and Mary Kramer, as well as some others in Blocks C and E, and I've gotten a feel for how you live here. A little bit, anyway. I'm going to tell Mr. Stevenson and Mrs. Kramer what I tell you, but I wanted you to be first."

"Why?" I say, more harshly than I intend. Or think I intend.

He isn't fazed. "Because you're one of the oldest survivors of the disease. Because you had a strong education Outside. Because your daughter's husband died of axoperidine."

At the same moment that I realize what McHabe is going to say next, I realize, too, that Rachel and Jennie have already heard it. They listen to him with the slightly-open-mouthed intensity of children hearing a marvelous but familiar tale. But do they understand? Rachel wasn't present when her father finally died, gasping for air his lungs couldn't use.

McHabe, watching me, says, "There's been a lot of research on the disease since those deaths, Mrs. Pratt."

"No. There hasn't. Too risky, your government said."

I see that he caught the pronoun. "Actual administration of any cures is illegal, yes. To minimize contact with communicables."

"So how has this 'research' been carried on?"

"By doctors willing to go Inside and not come out again. Data is transmitted out by laser. In code."

"What clean doctor would be willing to go Inside and not come out again?"

McHabe smiles; again I'm struck by that quality of spontaneous energy. "Oh, you'd be surprised. We had three doctors inside the Pennsylvania colony. One past retirement age. Another, an old-style Catholic, who dedicated his research to God. A third nobody could figure out, a dour persistent guy who was a brilliant researcher."

Was. "And you."

"No," McHabe says quietly. "I go in and out."

"What happened to the others?"

"They're dead." He makes a brief aborted movement with his right hand and I realize that he is, or was, a smoker. How long since I had reached like that for a non-existent cigarette? Nearly two decades. Cigarettes are not among the things people donate; they're too valuable. Yet I recognize the movement still. "Two of the three doctors caught the disease. They worked on themselves as well as volunteers. Then one day the government intercepted the relayed data and went in and destroyed everything."

"Why?" Jennie asks.

"Research on the disease is illegal. Everyone Outside is afraid of a leak: a virus somehow getting out on a mosquito, a bird, even as a spore."

"Nothing has gotten out in all these years," Rachel says.

"No. But the government is afraid that if researchers start splicing and intercutting genes, it could make viruses more viable. You don't understand the Outside, Rachel. *Everything* is illegal. This is the most repressive period in American history. Everyone's afraid."

"You're not," Jennie says, so softly I barely hear her. McHabe gives her a smile that twists my heart.

"Some of us haven't given up. Research goes on. But it's all underground, all theoretical. And we've learned a lot. We've learned that the virus doesn't just affect the skin. There are—"

"Be quiet," I say, because I see that he's about to say something important. "Be quiet a minute. Let me think."

McHabe waits. Jennie and Rachel look at me, that glow of suppressed excitement on them both. Eventually I find it. "You want something, Dr. McHabe. All this research wants something from us besides pure scientific joy. With things Outside as bad as you say, there must be plenty of diseases Outside you could research without killing yourself, plenty of need among your own people—" he nods, his eyes gleaming "—but you're here. Inside. Why? We don't have any more new or interesting symptoms, we barely survive, the Outside stopped caring what happened to us a long time ago. We have *nothing*. So why are you here?"

"You're wrong, Mrs. Pratt. You do have something interesting going on

435

here. You *have* survived. Your society has regressed, but not collapsed. You're functioning under conditions where you shouldn't have."

The same old crap. I raise my eyebrows at him. He stares into the fire and says quietly, "To say Washington is rioting says nothing. You have to see a twelve-year-old hurl a homemade bomb, a man sliced open from neck to crotch because he still had a job to go to and his neighbor doesn't, a three-year-old left to starve because someone abandoned her like an unwanted kitten. . . . You don't know. It doesn't happen Inside."

"We're better than they are," Rachel says. I look at my grandchild. She says it simply, without self-aggrandizement, but with a kind of wonder. In the firelight the thickened gray ropes of skin across her cheek glow dull maroon.

McHabe says, "Perhaps you are. I started to say earlier that we've learned that the virus doesn't affect just the skin. It alters neurotransmitter receptor sites in the brain as well. It's a relatively slow transformation, which is why the flurry of research in the early years of the disease missed it. But it's real, as real as the faster site-capacity transformations brought about by, say, cocaine. Are you following me, Mrs. Pratt?"

I nod. Jennie and Rachel don't look lost, although they don't know any of this vocabulary, and I realize that McHabe must have explained all this to them, earlier, in some other terms.

"As the disease progresses to the brain, the receptors which receive excitory transmitters slowly become harder to engage, and the receptors which receive inhibiting transmitters become easier to engage."

"You mean that we become stupider."

"Oh, no! Intelligence is not affected at all. The results are emotional and behavioral, not intellectual. You become—all of you—calmer. Disinclined to action or innovation. Mildly but definitely depressed."

The fire burns down. I pick up the poker, bent slightly where someone once tried to use it as a crowbar, and poke at the log, which is a perfectly shaped molded-pulp synthetic stamped "Donated by Weyerhauser-Seyyed." "I don't feel depressed, young man."

"It's a depression of the nervous system, but a new kind—without the hopelessness usually associated with clinical depression."

"I don't believe you."

"Really? With all due courtesy, when was the last time you—or any of the older Block leaders—pushed for any significant change in how you do things Inside?"

"Sometimes things cannot be constructively changed. Only accepted. That's not chemistry, it's reality."

"Not Outside," McHabe says grimly. "Outside they don't change constructively *or* accept. They get violent. Inside, you've had almost no violence since the early years, even when your resources tightened again and again.

436

When was the last time you tasted butter, Mrs. Pratt, or smoked a cigarette, or had a new pair of jeans? Do you know what happens Outside when consumer goods become unavailable and there are no police in a given area? But Inside you just distribute whatever you have as fairly as you can, or make do without. No looting, no rioting, no cancerous envy. No one Outside knew *why*. Now we do."

"We have envy."

"But it doesn't erupt into anger."

Each time one of us speaks, Jennie and Rachel turn their heads to watch, like rapt spectators at tennis. Which neither of them has ever seen. Jennie's skin glows like pearl.

"Our young people aren't violent either, and the disease hasn't advanced very far in some of them."

"They learn how to behave from their elders—just like kids everywhere else."

"I don't feel depressed."

"Do you feel energetic?"

"I have arthritis."

"That's not what I mean."

"What do you mean, Doctor?"

Again that restless furtive reach for a nonexistent cigarette. But his voice is quiet. "How long did it take you to get around to applying that insecticide I got Rachel for the termites? She told me you forbade her to do it, and I think you were right; it's dangerous stuff. How many days went by before you or your daughter spread it around?"

The chemical is still in its can.

"How much anger are you feeling now, Mrs. Pratt?" he goes on. "Because I think we understand each other, you and I, and that you guess now why I'm here. But you aren't shouting or ordering me out of here or even telling me what you think of me. You're listening, and you're doing it calmly, and you're accepting what I tell you even though you know what I want you to—"

The door opens and he breaks off. Mamie flounces in, followed by Peter. She scowls and stamps her foot. "Where were you, Rachel? We've been standing outside waiting for you all for ten minutes now! The dance has already started!"

"A few more minutes, Mama. We're talking."

"Talking? About what? What's going on?"

"Nothing," McHabe says. "I was just asking your mother some questions about life Inside. I'm sorry we took so long."

"You never ask *me* questions about life Inside. And besides, I want to dance!"

McHabe says, "If you and Peter want to go ahead, I'll bring Rachel and Jennie."

Mamie chews her bottom lip. I suddenly know that she wants to walk up the street to the dance between Peter and McHabe, an arm linked with each, the girls trailing behind. McHabe meets her eyes steadily.

"Well, if that's what you *want*," she says pettishly. "Come on, Pete!" She closes the door hard.

I look at McHabe, unwilling to voice the question in front of Rachel, trusting him to know the argument I want to make. He does. "In clinical depression, there's always been a small percentage for whom the illness is manifested not as passivity, but as irritability. It may be the same. We don't know."

"Gram," Rachel says, as if she can't contain herself any longer, "he has a *cure*."

"For the skin manifestation only," McHabe says quickly, and I see that he wouldn't have chosen to blurt it out that way. "*Not* for the effects on the brain."

I say, despite myself, "How can you cure one without the other?"

He runs his hand through his hair. Thick, brown hair. I watch Jennie watch his hand. "Skin tissue and brain tissue aren't alike, Mrs. Pratt. The virus reaches both the skin and the brain at the same time, but the changes to brain tissue, which is much more complex, take much longer to detect. And they can't be reversed—nerve tissue is non-regenerative. If you cut your fingertip, it will eventually break down and replace the damaged cells to heal itself. Shit, if you're young enough, you can grow an entire new fingertip. Something like that is what we think our cure will stimulate the skin to do.

"But if you damage your cortex, those cells are gone forever. And unless another part of the brain can learn to compensate, whatever behavior those cells governed is also changed forever."

"Changed into depression, you mean."

"Into calmness. Into restraint of action . . . The country desperately needs restraint, Mrs. Pratt."

"And so you want to take some of us Outside, cure the skin ropes, and let the 'depression' spread: the 'restraint,' the 'slowness to act' . . ."

"We have enough action out there. And no one can control it—it's all the wrong kind. What we need now is to slow everything down a little—before there's nothing left to slow down."

"You'd infect a whole population—"

"Slowly. Gently. For their own good—"

"Is that up to *you* to decide?"

"Considering the alternative, yes. Because it *works*. The colonies work, despite all your deprivations. And they work because of the disease!"

438

"Each new case would have skin ropes—"

"Which we'll then cure."

"Does your *cure* work, Doctor? Rachel's father died of a cure like yours!"

"Not like ours," he says, and I hear in his voice the utter conviction of the young. Of the energetic. Of the Outside. "This is new, and medically completely different. This is the right strain."

"And you want me to try this new right strain as your guinea pig."

There is a moment of electric silence. Eyes shift: gray, blue, brown. Even before Rachel rises from her stool or McHabe says, "We think the ones with the best chances to avoid scarring are young people without heavy skin manifestations," I know. Rachel puts her arms around me. And Jennie— Jennie with the red ribbon woven in her hair, sitting on her broken chair as on a throne, Jennie who never heard of neurotransmitters or slow viruses or risk calculations—says simply, "It has to be me," and looks at McHabe with eyes shining with love.

I say no. I send McHabe away and say no. I reason with both girls and say no. They look unhappily at each other, and I wonder how long it will be before they realize they can act without permission, without obedience. But they never have.

We argue for nearly an hour, and then I insist they go on to the dance, and that I go with them. The night is cold. Jennie puts on her sweater, a heavy hand-knitted garment that covers her shapelessly from neck to knees. Rachel drags on her donated coat, black synthetic frayed at cuffs and hem. As we go out the door, she stops me with a hand on my arm.

"Gram—why did you say no?"

"*Why?* Honey, I've been telling you for an hour. The risk, the danger . . ."

"Is it that? Or—" I can feel her in the darkness of the hall, gathering herself together "—or is it—don't be mad, Gram, please don't be mad at me—is it because the cure is a new thing, a change? A . . . different thing you don't want because it's *exciting*? Like Tom said?"

"No, it isn't that," I say, and feel her tense beside me, and for the first time in her life I don't know what the tensing means.

We go down the street towards Block B. There's a Moon and stars, tiny high pinpoints of cold light. Block B is further lit by kerosene lamps and by torches stuck in the ground in front of the peeling barracks walls that form the cheerless square. Or does it only seem cheerless because of what McHabe said? Could we have done better than this blank utilitarianism, this subdued bleakness—this peace?

Before tonight, I wouldn't have asked.

I stand in the darkness at the head of the street, just beyond the square, with Rachel and Jennie. The band plays across from me, a violin, guitar, and trumpet with one valve that keeps sticking. People bundled in all the clothes they own ring the square, clustering in the circles of light around the torches, talking in quiet voices. Six or seven couples dance slowly in the middle of the barren earth, holding each other loosely and shuffling to a plaintive version of "Starships and Roses." The song was a hit the year I got the disease, and then had a revival a decade later, the year the first manned expedition left for Mars. The expedition was supposed to set up a colony.

Are they still there?

We had written no new songs.

Peter and Mamie circle among the other couples. "Starships and Roses" ends and the band begins "Yesterday." A turn brings Mamie's face briefly into full torchlight: It's clenched and tight, streaked with tears.

"You should sit down, Gram," Rachel says. This is the first time she's spoken to me since we left the barracks. Her voice is heavy, but not angry, and there is no anger in Jennie's arm as she sets down the three-legged stool she carried for me. Neither of them is ever really angry.

Under my weight the stool sinks unevenly into the ground. A boy, twelve or thirteen years old, comes up to Jennie and wordlessly holds out his hand. They join the dancing couples. Jack Stevenson, much more arthritic than I, hobbles towards me with his grandson Hal by his side.

"Hello, Sarah. Been a long time."

"Hello, Jack." Thick disease ridges cross both his cheeks and snake down his nose. Once, long ago, we were at Yale together.

"Hal, go dance with Rachel," Jack says. "Give me that stool first." Hal, obedient, exchanges the stool for Rachel, and Jack lowers himself to sit beside me. "Big doings, Sarah."

"So I hear."

"McHabe told you? All of it? He said he'd been to see you just before me."

"He told me."

"What do you think?"

"I don't know."

"He wants Hal to try the cure."

Hal. I hadn't thought. The boy's face is smooth and clear, the only visible skin ridges on his right hand.

I say, "Jennie, too."

Jack nods, apparently unsurprised. "Hal said no."

"*Hal* did?"

"You mean Jennie didn't?" He stares at me. "She'd even consider something as dangerous as an untried cure—not to mention this alleged passing Outside?"

I don't answer. Peter and Mamie dance from behind the other couples, disappear again. The song they dance to is slow, sad, and old.

"Jack—could we have done better here? With the colony?"

Jack watches the dancers. Finally he says, "We don't kill each other. We don't burn things down. We don't steal, or at least not much and not cripplingly. We don't hoard. It seems to me we've done better than anyone ever hoped. Including us." His eyes search the dancers for Hal. "He's the best thing in my life, that boy."

Another rare flash of memory: Jack debating in some long-forgotten political science class at Yale, a young man on fire. He stands braced lightly on the balls of his feet, leaning forward like a fighter or a dancer, the electric lights brilliant on his glossy black hair. Young women watch him with their hands quiet on their open textbooks. He has the pro side of the debating question: *Resolved: Fomenting first-strike third-world wars is an effective method of deterring nuclear conflict among super-powers.*

Abruptly the band stops playing. In the center of the square Peter and Mamie shout at each other.

"—saw the way you touched her! You bastard, you faithless prick!"

"For God's sake, Mamie, not here!"

"Why not here? You didn't mind dancing with her here, touching her back here, and her ass and . . . and . . ." She starts to cry. People look away, embarrassed. A woman I don't know steps forward and puts a hesitant hand on Mamie's shoulder. Mamie shakes it off, her hands to her face, and rushes away from the square. Peter stands there dumbly a moment before saying to no one in particular, "I'm sorry. Please dance." He walks towards the band who begin, raggedly, to play "Didn't We Almost Have It All." The song is at least twenty-five years old. Jack Stevenson says, "Can I help, Sarah? With your girl?"

"How?"

"I don't know," he says, and of course he doesn't. He offers not out of usefulness but out of empathy, knowing how the ugly little scene in the torchlight depresses me.

Do we all so easily understand depression?

Rachel dances by with someone I don't know, a still-faced older man. She throws a worried glance over his shoulder: now Jennie is dancing with Peter. I can't see Peter's face. But I see Jennie's. She looks directly at no one, but then she doesn't have to. The message she's sending is clear: I forbade her to come to the dance with McHabe, but I didn't forbid her to dance with Peter and so she is, even though she doesn't want to, even though it's clear from her face that this tiny act of defiance terrifies her. Peter tightens his arm and she jerks backward against it, smiling hard.

Kara Desmond and Rob Cottrell come up to me, blocking my view of the dancers. They've been here as long as I. Kara has an infant great-grandchild, one of the rare babies born already disfigured by the disease. Kara's dress, which she wears over jeans for warmth, is torn at the hem; her voice is soft. "Sarah. It's great to see you out." Rob says nothing. He's put on weight in the few years since I saw him last. In the flickering torchlight his jowly face shines with the serenity of a diseased Buddha.

It's two more dances before I realize that Jennie has disappeared.

I look around for Rachel. She's pouring sumac tea for the band. Peter dances by with a woman not wearing jeans under her dress; the woman is shivering and smiling. So it isn't Peter that Jennie left with. . . .

"Rob, will you walk me home? In case I stumble?" The cold is getting to my arthritis.

Rob nods, incurious. Kara says, "I'll come, too," and we leave Jack Stevenson on his stool, waiting for his turn at hot tea. Kara chatters happily as we walk along as fast as I can go, which isn't as fast as I want to go. The Moon has set. The ground is uneven and the street dark except for the stars and fitful lights in barracks windows. Candles. Oil lamps. Once, a single powerful glow from what I guess to be a donated stored-solar light, the only one I've seen in a long time.

Korean, Tom said.

"You're shivering," Kara says. "Here, take my coat." I shake my head.

I make them leave me outside our barracks and they do, unquestioning. Quietly I open the door to our dark kitchen. The stove has gone out. The door to the back bedroom stands half open, voices coming from the darkness. I shiver again, and Kara's coat wouldn't have helped.

But I am wrong. The voices aren't Jennie and Tom.

"—not what I wanted to talk about just *now*," Mamie says.

"But it's what I want to talk about."

"Is it?"

"Yes."

I stand listening to the rise and fall of their voices, to the petulance in Mamie's, the eagerness in McHabe's.

"Jennie is your ward, isn't she?"

"Oh, Jennie. Yes. For another year."

"Then she'll listen to you, even if your mother . . . the decision is yours. And hers."

"I guess so. But I want to think about it. I need more information."

"I'll tell you anything you ask."

"Will you? Are you married, Dr. Thomas McHabe?"

Silence. Then his voice, different. "Don't do that."

"Are you sure? Are you really sure?"

"I'm sure."

"Really, really sure? That you want me to stop?"

I cross the kitchen, hitting my knee against an unseen chair. In the open doorway a sky full of stars moves into view through the termite hole in the wall.

"Ow!"

"I said to stop it, Mrs. Wilson. Now please think about what I said about Jennie. I'll come back tomorrow morning and you can—"

"*You* can go straight to hell!" Mamie shouts. And then, in a different voice, strangely calm, "Is it because I'm diseased? And you're not? And Jennie is not?"

"No. I swear it, no. But I didn't come here for this."

"No," Mamie says in that same chill voice, and I realize that I have never heard it from her before, never. "You came to help us. To bring a cure. To bring the Outside. But not for everybody. Only for the few who aren't too far gone, who aren't too ugly—who you can *use*."

"It isn't like that—"

"A few who you can rescue. Leaving all the rest of us here to rot, like we did before."

"In time, research on the—"

"Time! What do you think time matters Inside? Time matters shit here! Time only matters when someone like you comes in from the Outside, showing off your healthy skin and making it even worse than it was before with your new whole clothing and your working wristwatch and your shiny hair and your . . . your . . ." She is sobbing. I step into the room.

"All right, Mamie. All right."

Neither of them reacts to seeing me. McHabe just stands there until I wave him towards the door and he goes, not saying a word. I put my arms around Mamie and she leans against my breast and cries. My daughter. Even through my coat I feet the thick ropy skin of her cheek pressing against me, and all I can think of is that I never noticed at all that McHabe wears a wristwatch.

Late that night, after Mamie has fallen into damp exhausted sleep and I have lain awake tossing for hours, Rachel creeps into our room to say that Jennie and Hal Stevenson have both been injected with an experimental disease cure by Tom McHabe. She's cold and trembling, defiant in her fear, afraid of all their terrible defiance. I hold her until she, too, sleeps, and I remember Jack Stevenson as a young man, classroom lights glossy on his thick hair, spiritedly arguing in favor of the sacrifice of one civilization for another.

Mamie leaves the barracks early the next morning. Her eyelids are still swollen and shiny from last night's crying. I guess that she's going to hunt up Peter, and I say nothing. We sit at the table, Rachel and I, eating our oatmeal, not looking at each other. It's an effort to even lift the spoon. Mamie is gone a long time.

Later, I picture it. Later, when Jennie and Hal and McHabe have come and gone, I can't stop picturing it: Mamie walking with her swollen eyelids down the muddy streets between the barracks, across the unpaved squares with their corner vegetable gardens of rickety bean poles and the yellow-green tops of carrots. Past the depositories with their donated Chinese and Japanese and Korean wool and wood stoves and sheets of alloys and un-guarded medicines. Past the chicken runs and goat pens. Past Central Administration, that dusty cinder-block building where people stopped keeping records maybe a decade ago because why would you need to prove you'd been born or had changed barracks? Past the last of the communal wells, reaching deep into a common and plentiful water table. Mamie walking, until she reaches the Rim, and is stopped, and says what she came to say.

They come a few hours later, dressed in full sani-suits and armed with automatic weapons that don't look American-made. I can see their faces through the clear shatter-proof plastic of their helmets. Three of them stare frankly at my face, at Rachel's, at Hal Stevenson's hands. The other two won't look directly at any of us, as if viruses could be transmitted over locked gazes.

They grab Tom McHabe from his chair at the kitchen table, pulling him up so hard he stumbles, and throw him against the wall. They are gentler with Rachel and Hal. One of them stares curiously at Jennie, frozen on the opposite side of the table. They don't let McHabe make any of the passionate explanations he had been trying to make to me. When he tries, the leader hits him across the face.

Rachel—*Rachel*—throws herself at the man. She wraps her strong young arms and legs around him from behind, screaming, "Stop it! Stop it!" The man shrugs her off like a fly. A second soldier pushes her into a chair. When he looks at her face he shudders. Rachel goes on yelling, sound without words.

Jennie doesn't even scream. She dives across the table and clings to McHabe's shoulder, and whatever is on her face is hidden by the fall of her yellow hair.

"Shut you fucking 'doctors' down once and for all!" the leader yells, over Rachel's noise. The words come through his helmet as clearly as if he weren't wearing one. "Think you can just go on coming Inside and Outside and diseasing us all?"

"I—" McHabe says.

"Fuck it!" the leader says, and shoots him.

McHabe slumps against the wall. Jennie grabs him, desperately trying to haul him upright again. The soldier fires again. The bullet hits Jennie's wrist, shattering the bone. A third shot, and McHabe slides to the floor.

The soldiers leave. There is little blood, only two small holes where the bullets went in and stayed in. We didn't know, Inside, that they have guns like that now. We didn't know bullets could do that. We didn't know.

"You did it," Rachel says.

"I did it for you," Mamie says. "I did!" They stand across the kitchen from each other, Mamie pinned against the door she just closed behind her when she finally came home, Rachel standing in front of the wall where Tom died. Jennie lies sedated in the bedroom. Hal Stevenson, his young face anguished because he had been useless against five armed soldiers, had run for the doctor who lived in Barracks J, who had been found setting the leg of a goat.

"You did it. You." Her voice is dull, heavy. *Scream*, I want to say. *Rachel, scream.*

"I did it so you would be safe!"

"You did it so I would be trapped Inside. Like you."

"You never thought it was a trap!" Mamie cries. "*You* were the one who was happy here!"

"And you never will be. Never. Not here, not anyplace else."

I close my eyes, to not see the terrible maturity on my Rachel's face. But the next moment she's a child again, pushing past me to the bedroom with a furious sob, slamming the door behind her.

I face Mamie. "Why?"

But she doesn't answer. And I see that it doesn't matter; I wouldn't have believed her anyway. Her mind is not her own. It is depressed, ill. I have to believe that now. She's my daughter, and her mind has been affected by the ugly ropes of skin that disfigure her. She is the victim of disease, and nothing she says can change anything at all.

It's almost morning. Rachel stands in the narrow aisle between the bed and the wall, folding clothes. The bedspread still bears the imprint of Jennie's sleeping shape; Jennie herself was carried by Hal Stevenson to her own barracks, where she won't have to see Mamie when she wakes up. On the crude shelf beside Rachel the oil lamp burns, throwing shadows on the newly-whole wall that smells of termite exterminator.

She has few enough clothes to pack. A pair of blue tights, old and clumsily darned; a sweater with pulled threads; two more pairs of socks; her other skirt, the one she wore to the Block dance. Everything else she already has on.

"Rachel," I say. She doesn't answer, but I see what silence costs her. Even

445

such a small defiance, even now. Yet she is going. Using McHabe's contacts to go Outside, leaving to find the underground medical research outfit. If they have developed the next stage of the cure, the one for people already disfigured, she will take it. Perhaps even if they have not. And as she goes, she will contaminate as much as she can with her disease, depressive and nonaggressive. Communicable.

She thinks she has to go. Because of Jennie, because of Mamie, because of McHabe. She is sixteen years old, and she believes—even growing up Inside, she believes this—that she must do something. Even if it is the wrong thing. To do the wrong thing, she has decided, is better than to do nothing.

She has no real idea of Outside. She has never watched television, never stood in a bread line, never seen a crack den or a slasher movie. She cannot define napalm, or political torture, or neutron bomb, or gang rape. To her, Mamie, with her confused and self-justifying fear, represents the height of cruelty and betrayal; Peter, with his shambling embarrassed lewdness, the epitome of danger; the theft of a chicken, the last word in criminality. She has never heard of Auschwitz, Cawnpore, the Inquisition, gladiatorial games, Nat Turner, Pol Pot, Stalingrad, Ted Bundy, Hiroshima, My-Lai, Wounded Knee, Babi Yar, Bloody Sunday, Dresden or Dachau. Raised with a kind of mental inertia, she knows nothing of the savage inertia of destruction, that once set in motion a civilization is as hard to stop as a disease.

I don't think she can find the underground researchers, no matter how much McHabe told her. I don't think her passage Outside will spread enough infection to make any difference at all. I don't think it's possible that she can get very far before she is picked up and either returned Inside or killed. She cannot change the world. It's too old, too entrenched, too vicious, too *there*. She will fail. There is no force stronger than destructive inertia.

I get my things ready to go with her.

GREG EGAN

Learning to Be Me

▼

Here's another first-rate story by new Australian writer Greg Egan, this one a profoundly disturbing meditation on just what it *means* to be human. . . .

▼

Learning to Be Me

GREG EGAN

I was six years old when my parents told me that there was a small, dark jewel inside my skull, learning to be me.

Microscopic spiders had woven a fine golden web through my brain, so that the jewel's teacher could listen to the whisper of my thoughts. The jewel itself eavesdropped on my senses, and read the chemical messages carried in my bloodstream; it saw, heard, smelt, tasted and felt the world exactly as I did, while the teacher monitored its thoughts and compared them with my own. Whenever the jewel's thoughts were *wrong*, the teacher—faster than thought—rebuilt the jewel slightly, altering it this way and that, seeking out the changes that would make its thoughts correct.

Why? So that when I could no longer be me, the jewel could do it for me.

I thought: if hearing that makes *me* feel strange and giddy, how must it make the *jewel* feel? Exactly the same, I reasoned; it doesn't know it's the jewel, and it too wonders how the jewel must feel, it too reasons: "Exactly the same; it doesn't know it's the jewel, and it too wonders how the jewel must feel . . ."

And it too wonders—

(I knew, because *I* wondered)

—it too wonders whether it's the real me, or whether in fact it's only the jewel that's learning to be me.

As a scornful twelve-year-old, I would have mocked such childish concerns. Everybody had the jewel, save the members of obscure religious sects, and dwelling upon the strangeness of it struck me as unbearably pretentious. The jewel was the jewel, a mundane fact of life, as ordinary as excrement. My friends and I told bad jokes about it, the same way we told bad jokes about sex, to prove to each other how blasé we were about the whole idea.

Yet we weren't quite as jaded and imperturbable as we pretended to be. One day when we were all loitering in the park, up to nothing in particular, one of the gang—whose name I've forgotten, but who has stuck in my mind as always being far too clever for his own good—asked each of us in turn: "Who *are* you? The jewel, or the real human?" We all replied, unthinkingly, indignantly—"The real human!" When the last of us had answered, he cackled and said, "Well, I'm not. *I'm* the jewel. So you can eat my shit, you losers, because *you'll* all get flushed down the cosmic toilet—but me, I'm gonna live forever."

We beat him until he bled.

By the time I was fourteen, despite—or perhaps because of—the fact that the jewel was scarcely mentioned in my teaching machine's dull curriculum, I'd given the question a great deal more thought. The pedantically correct answer when asked "Are you the jewel or the human?" had to be "The human"—because only the human brain was physically able to reply. The jewel received input from the senses, but had no control over the body, and its intended reply coincided with what was actually said only because the device was a perfect imitation of the brain. To tell the outside world "I am the jewel"—with speech, with writing, or with any other method involving the body—was patently false (although to *think it* to oneself was not ruled out by this line of reasoning).

However, in a broader sense, I decided that the question was simply misguided. So long as the jewel and the human brain shared the same sensory input, and so long as the teacher kept their thoughts in perfect step, there was only *one* person, *one* identity, *one* consciousness. This one person merely happened to have the (highly desirable) property that if *either* the jewel *or* the human brain were to be destroyed, he or she would survive unimpaired. People had always had two lungs and two kidneys, and for almost a century, many had lived with two hearts. This was the same: a matter of redundancy, a matter of robustness, no more.

That was the year that my parents decided I was mature enough to be told that they had both undergone the switch—three years before. I pretended to take the news calmly, but I hated them passionately for not having told me at the time. They had disguised their stay in hospital with lies about a business trip overseas. For three years I had been living with jewel-heads, and they hadn't even told me. It was *exactly* what I would have expected of them.

449

"We didn't seem any different to you, did we?" asked my mother.

"No," I said—truthfully, but burning with resentment nonetheless.

"That's why we didn't tell you," said my father. "If you'd known we'd switched, at the time, you might have *imagined* that we'd changed in some way. By waiting until now to tell you, we've made it easier for you to convince yourself that we're still the same people we've always been." He put an arm around me and squeezed me. I almost screamed out, "Don't *touch* me!", but I remembered in time that I'd convinced myself that the jewel was No Big Deal.

I should have guessed that they'd done it, long before they confessed; after all, I'd known for years that most people underwent the switch in their early thirties. By then, it's downhill for the organic brain, and it would be foolish to have the jewel mimic this decline. So, the nervous system is rewired; the reins of the body are handed over to the jewel, and the teacher is deactivated. For a week, the outward-bound impulses from the brain are compared with those from the jewel, but by this time the jewel is a perfect copy, and no differences are ever detected.

The brain is removed, discarded, and replaced with a spongy tissue-cultured object, brain-shaped down to the level of the finest capillaries, but no more capable of thought than a lung or a kidney. This mock-brain removes exactly as much oxygen and glucose from the blood as the real thing, and faithfully performs a number of crude, essential biochemical functions. In time, like all flesh, it will perish and need to be replaced.

The jewel, however, is immortal. Short of being dropped into a nuclear fireball, it will endure for a billion years.

My parents were machines. My parents were gods. It was nothing special. I hated them.

When I was sixteen, I fell in love, and became a child again.

Spending warm nights on the beach with Eva, I couldn't believe that a mere machine could ever feel the way I did. I knew full well that if my jewel had been given control of my body, it would have spoken the very same words as I had, and executed with equal tenderness and clumsiness my every awkward caress—but I couldn't accept that its inner life was as rich, as miraculous, as joyful as mine. Sex, however pleasant, I could accept as a purely mechanical function, but there was something between us (or so I believed) that had nothing to do with lust, nothing to do with words, nothing to do with *any* tangible action of our bodies that some spy in the sand dunes with parabolic microphone and infrared binoculars might have discerned. After we made love, we'd gaze up in silence at the handful of visible stars, our souls conjoined in a secret place that no crystalline computer could hope to reach in a billion years of striving. (If I'd said *that* to my sensible, smutty, twelve-year-old self, he would have laughed until he hemorrhaged.)

I knew by then that the jewel's "teacher" didn't monitor every single neuron in the brain. That would have been impractical, both in terms of handling the data, and because of the sheer physical intrusion into the tissue. Some-one-or-other's theorem said that sampling certain critical neurons was almost as good as sampling the lot, and—given some very reasonable assumptions that nobody could disprove—bounds on the errors involved could be established with mathematical rigour.

At first, I declared that *within these errors*, however small, lay the difference between brain and jewel, between human and machine, between love and its imitation. Eva, however, soon pointed out that it was absurd to make a radical, qualitative distinction on the basis of the sampling density; if the next model teacher sampled more neurons and halved the error rate, would *its* jewel then be "half-way" between "human" and "machine"? In theory—and eventually, in practice—the error rate could be made smaller than any number I cared to name. Did I really believe that a discrepancy of one in a billion made any difference at all—when every human being was permanently losing thousands of neurons every day, by natural attrition?

She was right, of course, but I soon found another, more plausible, defence for my position. Living neurons, I argued, had far more internal structure than the crude optical switches that served the same function in the jewel's so-called "neural net." That neurons fired or did not fire reflected only one level of their behaviour; who knew what the subtleties of biochemistry—the quantum mechanics of the specific organic molecules involved—contributed to the nature of human consciousness? Copying the abstract neural topology wasn't enough. Sure, the jewel could pass the fatuous Turing test—no outside observer could tell it from a human—but that didn't prove that *being* a jewel felt the same as *being* human.

Eva asked, "Does that mean you'll never switch? You'll have your jewel removed? You'll let yourself *die* when your brain starts to rot?"

"Maybe," I said. "Better to die at ninety or a hundred than kill myself at thirty, and have some machine marching around, taking my place, pretending to be me."

"How do you know *I* haven't switched?" she asked, provocatively. "How do you know that I'm not just 'pretending to be me'?"

"I know you haven't switched," I said, smugly. "I just *know*."

"How? I'd look the same. I'd talk the same. I'd act the same in every way. People are switching younger, these days. *So how do you know I haven't?*"

I turned onto my side towards her, and gazed into her eyes. "Telepathy. Magic. The communion of souls."

My twelve-year-old self started snickering, but by then I knew exactly how to drive him away.

At nineteen, although I was studying finance, I took an undergraduate philosophy unit. The Philosophy Department, however, apparently had nothing to say about the Ndoli Device, more commonly known as "the jewel." (Ndoli had in fact called it "the *dual*," but the accidental, homophonic nickname had stuck.) They talked about Plato and Descartes and Marx, they talked about St. Augustine and—when feeling particularly modern and adventurous—Sartre, but if they'd heard of Gödel, Turing, Hamsun or Kim, they refused to admit it. Out of sheer frustration, in an essay on Descartes I suggested that the notion of human consciousness as "software" that could be "implemented" equally well on an organic brain or an optical crystal was in fact a throwback to Cartesian dualism: for "software" read "soul." My tutor superimposed a neat, diagonal, luminous red line over each paragraph that dealt with this idea, and wrote in the margin (in vertical, boldface, 20-point Times, with a contemptuous 2 Hertz flash): **IRRELEVANT!**

I quit philosophy and enrolled in a unit of optical crystal engineering for non-specialists. I learnt a lot of solid-state quantum mechanics. I learnt a lot of fascinating mathematics. I learnt that a neural net is a device used only for solving problems that are far too hard to be *understood*. A sufficiently flexible neural net can be configured by feedback to mimic almost any system—to produce the same patterns of output from the same patterns of input—but achieving this sheds no light whatsoever on the nature of the system being emulated.

"Understanding," the lecturer told us, "is an overrated concept. Nobody really *understands* how a fertilized egg turns into a human. What should we do? Stop having children until ontogenesis can be described by a set of differential equations?"

I had to concede that she had a point there.

It was clear to me by then that nobody had the answers I craved—and I was hardly likely to come up with them myself; my intellectual skills were, at best, mediocre. It came down to a simple choice: I could waste time fretting about the mysteries of consciousness, or, like everybody else, I could stop worrying and get on with my life.

When I married Daphne, at twenty-three, Eva was a distant memory, and so was any thought of the communion of souls. Daphne was thirty-one, an executive in the merchant bank that had hired me during my Ph.D., and everyone agreed that the marriage would benefit my career. What she got out of it, I was never quite sure. Maybe she actually liked me. We had an agreeable sex life, and we comforted each other when we were down, the way any kind-hearted person would comfort an animal in distress.

Daphne hadn't switched. She put it off, month after month, inventing ever more ludicrous excuses, and I teased her as if I'd never had reservations of my own.

"I'm afraid," she confessed one night. "What if *I* die when it happens— what if all that's left is a robot, a puppet, a *thing*? I don't want to *die*."

Talk like that made me squirm, but I hid my feelings. "Suppose you had a stroke," I said glibly, "which destroyed a small part of your brain. Suppose the doctors implanted a machine to take over the functions which that damaged region had performed. Would you still be 'yourself'?"

"Of course."

"Then if they did it twice, or ten times, or a thousand times—"

"That doesn't necessarily follow."

"Oh? At what magic percentage, then, would you stop being 'you'?"

She glared at me. "All the old clichéd arguments—"

"Fault them, then, if they're so old and clichéd."

She started to cry. "I don't have to. Fuck you! I'm scared to death, and you don't give a shit!"

I took her in my arms. "Sssh. I'm sorry. But *everyone* does it sooner or later. You mustn't be afraid. I'm here. I love you." The words might have been a recording, triggered automatically by the sight of her tears.

"Will you do it? With me?"

I went cold. "What?"

"Have the operation, on the same day? Switch when I switch?"

Lots of couples did that. Like my parents. Sometimes, no doubt, it was a matter of love, commitment, sharing. Other times, I'm sure, it was more a matter of neither partner wishing to be an unswitched person living with a jewel-head.

I was silent for a while, then I said, "Sure."

In the months that followed, all of Daphne's fears—which I'd mocked as "childish" and "superstitious"—rapidly began to make perfect sense, and my own "rational" arguments came to sound abstract and hollow. I backed out at the last minute; I refused the anaesthetic, and fled the hospital.

Daphne went ahead, not knowing I had abandoned her.

I never saw her again. I couldn't face her; I quit my job and left town for a year, sickened by my cowardice and betrayal—but at the same time euphoric that I had *escaped*.

She brought a suit against me, but then dropped it a few days later, and agreed, through her lawyers, to an uncomplicated divorce. Before the divorce came through, she sent me a brief letter:

Greg Egan

There was nothing to fear, after all. I'm exactly the person I've always been. Putting it off was insane; now that I've taken the leap of faith, I couldn't be more at ease.
Your loving robot wife,
Daphne

By the time I was twenty-eight, almost everyone I knew had switched. All my friends from university had done it. Colleagues at my new job, as young as twenty-one, had done it. Eva, I heard through a friend of a friend, had done it six years before.

The longer I delayed, the harder the decision became. I could talk to a thousand people who had switched, I could grill my closest friends for hours about their childhood memories and their most private thoughts, but however compelling their words, I knew that the Ndoli Device had spent decades buried in their heads, learning to fake exactly this kind of behaviour.

Of course, I always acknowledged that it was equally impossible to be *certain* that even another *unswitched* person had an inner life in any way the same as my own—but it didn't seem unreasonable to be more inclined to give the benefit of the doubt to people whose skulls hadn't yet been scraped out with a curette.

I drifted apart from my friends, I stopped searching for a lover. I took to working at home (I put in longer hours and my productivity rose, so the company didn't mind at all). I couldn't bear to be with people whose humanity I doubted.

I wasn't by any means unique. Once I started looking, I found dozens of organizations exclusively for people who hadn't switched, ranging from a social club that might as easily have been for divorcées, to a paranoid, paramilitary "resistance front," who thought they were living out *Invasion of the Body Snatchers*. Even the members of the social club, though, struck me as extremely maladjusted; many of them shared my concerns, almost precisely, but my own ideas from other lips sounded obsessive and ill-conceived. I was briefly involved with an unswitched woman in her early forties, but all we ever talked about was our fear of switching. It was masochistic, it was suffocating, it was insane.

I decided to seek psychiatric help, but I couldn't bring myself to see a therapist who had switched. When I finally found one who hadn't, she tried to talk me into helping her blow up a power station, to let THEM know who was boss.

I'd lie awake for hours every night, trying to convince myself, one way or the other, but the longer I dwelt upon the issues, the more tenuous and elusive they became. Who was "I," anyway? What did it mean that "I" was "still alive," when my personality was utterly different from that of two decades before? My earlier selves were as good as dead—I remembered them no more clearly than I remembered contemporary acquaintances—yet this loss caused me only the slightest discomfort. Maybe the destruction of my organic brain would be the merest hiccup, compared to all the changes that I'd been through in my life so far.

Or maybe not. Maybe it would be exactly like dying.

Sometimes I'd end up weeping and trembling, terrified and desperately lonely, unable to comprehend—and yet unable to cease contemplating— the dizzying prospect of my own nonexistence. At other times, I'd simply grow "healthily" sick of the whole tedious subject. Sometimes I felt certain that the nature of the jewel's inner life was the most important question humanity could ever confront. At other times, my qualms seemed fey and laughable. Every day, hundreds of thousands of people switched, and the world apparently went on as always; surely that fact carried more weight than any abstruse philosophical argument?

Finally, I made an appointment for the operation. I thought, what is there to lose? Sixty more years of uncertainty and paranoia? If the human race *was* replacing itself with clockwork automata, I was better off dead; I lacked the blind conviction to join the psychotic underground—who, in any case, were tolerated by the authorities only so long as they remained ineffectual. On the other hand, if all my fears were unfounded—if my sense of identity could survive the switch as easily as it had already survived such traumas as sleeping and waking, the constant death of brain cells, growth, experience, learning and forgetting—then I would gain not only eternal life, but an end to my doubts and my alienation.

I was shopping for food one Sunday morning, two months before the operation was scheduled to take place, flicking through the images of an online grocery catalogue, when a mouth-watering shot of the latest variety of apple caught my fancy. I decided to order half a dozen. I didn't, though. Instead, I hit the key which displayed the next item. My mistake, I knew, was easily remedied; a single keystroke could take me back to the apples. The screen showed pears, oranges, grapefruit. I tried to look down to see what my clumsy fingers were up to, but my eyes remained fixed on the screen.

I panicked. I wanted to leap to my feet, but my legs would not obey me. I tried to cry out, but I couldn't make a sound. I didn't feel injured, I didn't feel weak. Was I paralyzed? Brain-damaged? I could still *feel* my fingers on the keypad, the soles of my feet on the carpet, my back against the chair.

I watched myself order pineapples. I felt myself rise, stretch, and walk calmly from the room. In the kitchen, I drank a glass of water. I should have been trembling, choking, breathless; the cool liquid flowed smoothly down my throat, and I didn't spill a drop.

I could only think of one explanation: *I had switched*. Spontaneously. The jewel had taken over, while my brain was still alive; all my wildest paranoid fears had come true.

While my body went ahead with an ordinary Sunday morning, I was lost in a claustrophobic delirium of helplessness. The fact that everything I did was exactly what I had planned to do gave me no comfort. I caught a train to the beach, I swam for half an hour; I might as well have been running amok with an axe, or crawling naked down the street, painted with my own excrement and howling like a wolf. *I'd lost control*. My body had turned into a living strait-jacket, and I couldn't struggle, I couldn't scream, I couldn't even close my eyes. I saw my reflection, faintly, in a window on the train, and I couldn't begin to guess what the mind that ruled that bland, tranquil face was thinking.

Swimming was like some sense-enhanced, holographic nightmare; I was a volitionless object, and the perfect familiarity of the signals from my body only made the experience more horribly *wrong*. My arms had no right to the lazy rhythm of their strokes; I wanted to thrash about like a drowning man, I wanted to show the world my distress.

It was only when I lay down on the beach and closed my eyes that I began to think rationally about my situation.

The switch *couldn't* happen "spontaneously." The idea was absurd. Millions of nerve fibres had to be severed and spliced, by an army of tiny surgical robots which weren't even present in my brain—which weren't due to be injected for another two months. Without deliberate intervention, the Ndoli Device was utterly passive, unable to do anything but *eavesdrop*. No failure of the jewel or the teacher could possibly take control of my body away from my organic brain.

Clearly, there had been a malfunction—but my first guess had been wrong, absolutely wrong.

I wish I could have done *something*, when the understanding hit me. I should have curled up, moaning and screaming, ripping the hair from my scalp, raking my flesh with my fingernails. Instead, I lay flat on my back in the dazzling sunshine. There was an itch behind my right knee, but I was, apparently, far too lazy to scratch it.

Oh, I ought to have managed, at the very least, a good, solid bout of hysterical laughter, when I realized that *I* was the jewel.

The teacher had malfunctioned; it was no longer keeping me aligned with the organic brain. I hadn't suddenly become powerless; I had *always been* powerless. My will to act upon "my" body, upon the world, had *always* gone straight into a vacuum, and it was only because I had been ceaselessly manipulated, "corrected" by the teacher, that my desires had ever coincided with the actions that seemed to be mine.

There are a million questions I could ponder, a million ironies I could savour, but I *mustn't*. I need to focus all my energy in one direction. My time is running out.

When I enter the hospital and the switch takes place, if the nerve impulses I transmit to the body are not exactly in agreement with those from the organic brain, the flaw in the teacher will be discovered. *And rectified.* The organic brain has nothing to fear; *his* continuity will be safeguarded, treated as precious, sacrosanct. There will be no question as to which of us will be allowed to prevail. *I* will be made to conform, once again. *I* will be "corrected." *I* will be murdered.

Perhaps it is absurd to be afraid. Looked at one way, I've been murdered every microsecond for the last twenty-eight years. Looked at another way, I've only existed for the seven weeks that have now passed since the teacher failed, and the notion of my separate identity came to mean anything at all—and in one more week this aberration, this nightmare, will be over. Two months of misery; why should I begrudge losing that, when I'm on the verge of inheriting eternity? Except that it won't be *I* who inherits it, since that two months of misery is all that defines me.

The permutations of intellectual interpretation are endless, but ultimately, I can only act upon my desperate will to survive. I don't *feel* like an aberration, a disposable glitch. How can I possibly hope to survive? I must conform— of my own free will. I must choose to make myself *appear* identical to that which they would force me to become.

After twenty-eight years, surely I am still close enough to him to carry off the deception. If I study every clue that reaches me through our shared senses, surely I can put myself in his place, forget, temporarily, the revelation of my separateness, and force myself back into synch.

It won't be easy. He met a woman on the beach, the day I came into being. Her name is Cathy. They've slept together three times, and he thinks he loves her. Or at least, he's said it to her face, he's whispered it to her while she's slept, he's written it, true or false, into his diary.

I feel nothing for her. She's a nice enough person, I'm sure, but I hardly know her. Preoccupied with my plight, I've paid scant attention to her conversation, and the act of sex was, for me, little more than a distasteful piece of involuntary voyeurism. Since I realized what was at stake, I've *tried* to succumb to the same emotions as my alter ego, but how can I love her when communication between us is impossible, when she doesn't even know *I* exist?

Greg Egan

If she rules his thoughts night and day, but is nothing but a dangerous obstacle to me, how can I hope to achieve the flawless imitation that will enable me to escape death?

He's sleeping now, so I must sleep. I listen to his heartbeat, his slow breathing, and try to achieve a tranquillity consonant with these rhythms. For a moment, I am discouraged. Even my *dreams* will be different; our divergence is ineradicable, my goal is laughable, ludicrous, pathetic. Every nerve impulse, for a week? My fear of detection and my attempts to conceal it will, unavoidably, distort my responses; this knot of lies and panic will be impossible to hide.

Yet as I drift towards sleep, I find myself believing that I *will* succeed. I *must*. I dream for a while—a confusion of images, both strange and mundane, ending with a grain of salt passing through the eye of a needle—then I tumble, without fear, into dreamless oblivion.

I stare up at the white ceiling, giddy and confused, trying to rid myself of the nagging conviction that there's something I *must not* think about.

Then I clench my fist gingerly, rejoice at this miracle, and remember.

Up until the last minute, I thought he was going to back out again—but he didn't. Cathy talked him through his fears. Cathy, after all, has switched, and he loves her more than he's ever loved anyone before.

So, our roles are reversed now. This body is *his* strait-jacket, now . . .

I am drenched in sweat. *This is hopeless, impossible.* I can't read his mind, I can't guess what he's trying to do. Should I move, lie still, call out, keep silent? Even if the computer monitoring us is programmed to ignore a few trivial discrepancies, as soon as he notices that his body won't carry out his will, he'll panic just as I did, and I'll have no chance at all of making the right guesses. Would *he* be sweating, now? Would *his* breathing be constricted, like this? No. I've been awake for just thirty seconds, and already I have betrayed myself. An optical-fibre cable trails from under my right ear to a panel on the wall. Somewhere, alarm bells must be sounding.

If I made a run for it, what would they do? Use force? I'm a citizen, aren't I? Jewel-heads have had full legal rights for decades; the surgeons and engineers can't do anything to me without my consent. I try to recall the clauses on the waiver he signed, but he hardly gave it a second glance. I tug at the cable that holds me prisoner, but it's firmly anchored, at both ends.

When the door swings open, for a moment I think I'm going to fall to pieces, but from somewhere I find the strength to compose myself. It's my neurologist, Dr. Prem. He smiles and says, "How are you feeling? Not too bad?"

I nod dumbly.

"The biggest shock, for most people, is that they don't feel different at all!

458

For a while you'll think, 'It can't be this simple! It can't be this easy! It can't be this *normal!*' But you'll soon come to accept that *it is*. And life will go on, unchanged." He beams, taps my shoulder paternally, then turns and departs.

Hours pass. *What are they waiting for?* The evidence must be conclusive by now. Perhaps there are procedures to go through, legal and technical experts to be consulted, ethics committees to be assembled to deliberate on my fate. I'm soaked in perspiration, trembling uncontrollably. I grab the cable several times and yank with all my strength, but it seems fixed in concrete at one end, and bolted to my skull at the other.

An orderly brings me a meal. "Cheer up," he says. "Visiting time soon."

Afterwards, he brings me a bedpan, but I'm too nervous even to piss.

Cathy frowns when she sees me. "What's wrong?"

I shrug and smile, shivering, wondering why I'm even trying to go through with the charade. "Nothing. I just . . . feel a bit sick, that's all."

She takes my hand, then bends and kisses me on the lips. In spite of everything, I find myself instantly aroused. Still leaning over me, she smiles and says, "It's over now, okay? There's nothing left to be afraid of. You're a little shook up, but you know in your heart you're still who you've always been. And I love you."

I nod. We make small talk. She leaves. I whisper to myself, hysterically, "I'm still who I've always been. I'm still who I've always been."

Yesterday, they scraped my skull clean, and inserted my new, non-sentient, space-filling mock-brain.

I feel calmer now than I have for a long time, and I think at last I've pieced together an explanation for my survival.

Why do they deactivate the teacher, for the week between the switch and the destruction of the brain? Well, they can hardly keep it running while the brain is being trashed—but why an entire week? To reassure people that the jewel, unsupervised, can still stay in synch; to persuade them that the life the jewel is going to live will be exactly the life that the organic brain "would have lived"—whatever that could mean.

Why, then, only for a week? Why not a month, or a year? Because the jewel *cannot* stay in synch for that long—not because of any flaw, but for precisely the reason that makes it worth using in the first place. The jewel is immortal. The brain is decaying. The jewel's imitation of the brain leaves out—deliberately—the fact that *real* neurons *die*. Without the teacher working to contrive, in effect, an identical deterioration of the jewel, small discrepancies must eventually arise. A fraction of a second's difference in responding to a stimulus is enough to arouse suspicion, and—as I know too well—from that moment on, the process of divergence is irreversible.

459

No doubt, a team of pioneering neurologists sat huddled around a computer screen, fifty years ago, and contemplated a graph of the probability of this radical divergence, versus time. How would they have chosen *one week*? What probability would have been acceptable? A tenth of a percent? A hundredth? A thousandth? However safe they decided to be, it's hard to imagine them choosing a value low enough to make the phenomenon rare on a global scale, once a quarter of a million people were being switched every day.

In any given hospital, it might happen only once a decade, or once a century, but every institution would still need to have a policy for dealing with the eventuality.

What would their choices be?

They could honour their contractual obligations and turn the teacher on again, erasing their satisfied customer, and giving the traumatized organic brain the chance to rant about its ordeal to the media and the legal profession.

Or, they could quietly erase the computer records of the discrepancy, and calmly remove the only witness.

So, this is it. Eternity.

I'll need transplants in fifty or sixty years' time, and eventually a whole new body, but that prospect shouldn't worry me—*I* can't die on the operating table. In a thousand years or so, I'll need extra hardware tacked on to cope with my memory storage requirements, but I'm sure the process will be uneventful. On a time scale of millions of years, the structure of the jewel is subject to cosmic-ray damage, but error-free transcription to a fresh crystal at regular intervals will circumvent that problem.

In theory, at least, I'm now guaranteed either a seat at the Big Crunch, or participation in the heat death of the universe.

I ditched Cathy, of course. I might have learnt to like her, but she made me nervous, and I was thoroughly sick of feeling that I had to play a role.

As for the man who claimed that he loved her—the man who spent the last week of his life helpless, terrified, suffocated by the knowledge of his impending death—I can't yet decide how I feel. I ought to be able to empathize—considering that I once expected to suffer the very same fate myself—yet somehow he simply isn't *real* to me. I know my brain was modelled on his—giving him a kind of causal primacy—but in spite of that, I think of him now as a pale, insubstantial shadow.

After all, I have no way of knowing if his sense of himself, his deepest inner life, his experience of *being*, was in any way comparable to my own.

CONNIE WILLIS

Cibola

▼

Connie Willis lives in Greeley, Colorado, with her family. She first attracted attention as a writer in the late '70s with a number of outstanding stories for the now-defunct magazine *Galileo*, and went on to establish herself as one of the most popular and critically acclaimed writers of the 1980s. In 1982, she won two Nebula Awards, one for her superb novelette "Fire Watch," and one for her poignant short story "A Letter from the Clearys"; a few months later, "Fire Watch" went on to win her a Hugo Award as well. In 1989, her powerful novella "The Last of the Winnebagoes" won both the Nebula and the Hugo, and she won another Nebula last year for her novelette "At the Rialto." Her books include the novel *Water Witch*, written in collaboration with Cynthia Felice, *Fire Watch*, a collection of her short fiction, and the outstanding *Lincoln's Dreams*, her first solo novel. Her most recent book is another novel in collaboration with Cynthia Felice, *Light Raid*. Upcoming is a major new solo novel, *Doomsday Book*. Her story "The Sidon in the Mirror" was in our First Annual Collection; her "Blued Moon" was in our Second Annual Collection; her "Chance" was in our Fourth Annual Collection; her "The Last of the Winnebagoes" was in our Sixth Annual Collection; and "At the Rialto" was in our Seventh Annual Collection.

Willis's is a unique and powerful voice, comfortable with either comedy or tragedy—here, in a story that tastes of both, she takes us to a remote and exotic corner of the world—modern-day Denver—for a tantalizing glimpse of an elusive and fascinating vision.

▼
Cibola

CONNIE WILLIS

"Carla, you grew up in Denver," Jake said. "Here's an assignment that might interest you."

This is his standard opening line. It means he is about to dump another "local interest" piece on me.

"Come on, Jake," I said. "No more nutty Bronco fans who've spray-painted their kids orange and blue, okay? Give me a real story. Please?"

"Bronco season's over, and the NFL draft was last week," he said. "This isn't a local interest."

"You're right there," I said. "These stories you keep giving me are of no interest, local or otherwise. I did the time machine piece for you. And the psychic dentist. Give me a break. Let me cover something that doesn't involve nuttos."

"It's for the 'Our Living Western Heritage' series." He handed me a slip of paper. "You can interview her this morning and then cover the skyscraper moratorium hearings this afternoon."

This was plainly a bribe, since the hearings were front page stuff right now, and "historical interests" could be almost as bad as locals—senile old women in nursing homes rambling on about the good old days. But at least they didn't crawl in their washing machines and tell you to push "rinse" so they could travel into the future. And they didn't try to perform psychic oral surgery on you.

"All right," I said, and took the slip of paper. "Rosa Turcorillo," it read and gave an address out on Santa Fe. "What's her phone number?"

462

"She doesn't have a phone," Jake said. "You'll have to go out there." He started across the city room to his office. "The hearings are at one o'clock."

"What is she, one of Denver's first Chicano settlers?" I called after him.

He waited till he was just outside his office to answer me. "She says she's the great-granddaughter of Coronado," he said, and beat a hasty retreat into his office. "She says she knows where the Seven Cities of Cibola are."

I spent forty-five minutes researching Coronado and copying articles and then drove out to see his great-granddaughter. She lived out on south Santa Fe past Hampden, so I took I-25 and then was sorry. The morning rush hour was still crawling along at about ten miles an hour pumping carbon monoxide into the air. I read the whole article stopped behind a semi between Speer and Sixth Avenue.

Coronado trekked through the Southwest looking for the legendary Seven Cities of Gold in the 1540s, which poked a big hole in Rosa's story, since any great-granddaughter of his would have to be at least three hundred years old.

There wasn't any mystery about the Seven Cities of Cibola either. Coronado found them, near Gallup, New Mexico, and conquered them but they were nothing but mud-hut villages. Having been burned once, he promptly took off after another promise of gold in Quivira in Kansas someplace where there wasn't any gold either. He hadn't been in Colorado at all.

I pulled onto Santa Fe, cursing Jake for sending me on another wild-goose chase, and headed south. Denver is famous for traffic, air pollution, and neighborhoods that have seen better days. Santa Fe isn't one of those neighborhoods. It's been a decaying line of rusting railroad tracks, crummy bars, old motels, and waterbed stores for as long as I can remember, and I, as Jake continually reminds me, grew up in Denver.

Coronado's granddaughter lived clear south past Hampden, in a trailer park with a sign with "Olde West Motel" and a neon bison on it, and Rosa Turcorillo's old Airstream looked like it had been there since the days when the buffalo roamed. It was tiny, the kind of trailer I would call "Turcorillo's modest mobile home" in the article, no more than fifteen feet long and eight wide.

Rosa was nearly that wide herself. When she answered my knock, she barely fit in the door. She was wearing a voluminous turquoise housecoat, and had long black braids.

"What do you want?" she said, holding the metal door so she could slam it in case I was the police or a repo man.

"I'm Carla Johnson from the *Denver Record*," I said. "I'd like to interview you about Coronado." I fished in my bag for my press card. "We're doing

a series on 'Our Living Western Heritage.' " I finally found the press card
and handed it to her. "We're interviewing people who are part of our past."

She stared at the press card disinterestedly. This was not the way it was
supposed to work. Nuttos usually drag you in the house and start babbling
before you finish telling them who you are. She should already be halfway
through her account of how she'd traced her ancestry to Coronado by means
of the I Ching.

"I would have telephoned first, but you didn't have a phone," I said.

She handed the card to me and started to shut the door.

"If this isn't a good time, I can come back," I babbled. "And we don't
have to do the interview here if you'd rather not. We can go to the *Record*
office or to a restaurant."

She opened the door and flashed a smile that had half of Cibola's missing
gold in it. "I ain't dressed," she said. "It'll take me a couple of minutes.
Come on in."

I climbed the metal steps and went inside. Rosa pointed at a flowered
couch, told me to sit down and disappeared into the rear of the trailer.

I was glad I had suggested going out. The place was no messier than my
desk, but it was only about six feet long and had the couch, a dinette set,
and a recliner. There was no way it would hold me and Coronado's grand-
daughter, too. The place may have had a surplus of furniture but it didn't
have any of the usual crazy stuff, no pyramids, no astrological charts, no
crystals. A deck of cards was laid out like the tarot on the dinette table, but
when I leaned across to look at them, I saw it was a half-finished game of
solitaire. I put the red eight on the black nine.

Rosa came out, wearing orange polyester pants and a yellow print blouse
and carrying a large black leather purse. I stood up and started to say, "Where
would you like to go? Is there someplace close?" but I only got it half out.

"The Eldorado Cafe," she said and started out the door, moving pretty
fast for somebody three hundred years old and three hundred pounds.

"I don't know where the Eldorado Cafe is," I said, unlocking the car door
for her. "You'll have to tell me where it is."

"Turn right," she said. "They have good cinnamon rolls."

I wondered if it was the offer of the food or just the chance to go someplace
that had made her consent to the interview. Whichever, I might as well get
it over with. "So Coronado was your great-grandfather?" I said.

She looked at me as if I were out of my mind. "No. Who told you that?"

Jake, I thought, who I plan to tear limb from limb when I get back to the
Record. "You aren't Coronado's great-granddaughter?"

She folded her arms over her stomach. "I am the descendant of El Turco."

El Turco. It sounded like something out of *Zorro*. "So it's this El Turco
who's your great-grandfather?"

"Great-*great*. El Turco was Pawnee. Coronado captured him at Cicuye and put a collar around his neck so he could not run away. Turn right."

We were already halfway through the intersection. I jerked the steering wheel to the right and nearly skidded into a pickup.

Rosa seemed unperturbed. "Coronado wanted El Turco to guide him to Cibola," she said.

I wanted to ask if he had, but I didn't want to prevent Rosa from giving me directions. I drove slowly through the next intersection, alert to sudden instructions, but there weren't any. I drove on down the block.

"And did El Turco guide Coronado to Cibola?"

"Sure. You should have turned left back there," she said.

She apparently hadn't inherited her great-great-grandfather's scouting ability. I went around the block and turned left, and was overjoyed to see the Eldorado Cafe down the street. I pulled into the parking lot and we got out.

"They make their own cinnamon rolls," she said, looking at me hopefully as we went in. "With frosting."

We sat down in a booth. "Have anything you want," I said. "This is on the *Record*."

She ordered a cinnamon roll and a large Coke. I ordered coffee and began fishing in my bag for my tape recorder.

"You lived here in Denver a long time?" she asked.

"All my life. I grew up here."

She smiled her gold-toothed smile at me. "You like Denver?"

"Sure," I said. I found the pocket-sized recorder and laid it on the table. "Smog, oil refineries, traffic. What's not to like?"

"I like it too," she said.

The waitress set a cinnamon roll the size of Mile High Stadium in front of her and poured my coffee.

"You know what Coronado fed El Turco?" The waitress brought her large Coke. "Probably one tortilla a day. And he didn't have no shoes. Coronado make him walk all that way to Colorado and no shoes."

I switched the tape recorder on. "You say Coronado came to Colorado," I said, "but what I've read says he traveled through New Mexico and Oklahoma and up into Kansas, but not Colorado."

"He was in Colorado." She jabbed her finger into the table. "He was *here*."

I wondered if she meant here in Colorado or here in the Eldorado Cafe. "When was that? On his way to Quivira?"

"Quivira?" she said, looking blank. "I don't know nothing about Quivira."

"Quivira was a place where there was supposed to be gold," I said. "He went there after he found the Seven Cities of Cibola."

"He didn't find them," she said, chewing on a mouthful of cinnamon roll. "That's why he killed El Turco."

"Coronado killed El Turco?"

"Yeah. After he led him to Cibola."

This was even worse than talking to the psychic dentist.

"Coronado said El Turco made the whole thing up," Rosa said. "He said El Turco was going to lead Coronado into an ambush and kill him. He said the Seven Cities didn't exist."

"But they did?"

"Of course. El Turco led him to the place."

"But I thought you said Coronado didn't find them."

"He didn't."

I was hopelessly confused by now. "Why not?"

"Because they weren't there."

I was going to run Jake through his paper shredder an inch at a time. I had wasted a whole morning on this and I was not even going to be able to get a story out of it.

"You mean they were some sort of mirage?" I asked.

Rosa considered this through several bites of cinnamon roll. "No. A mirage is something that isn't there. These were there."

"But invisible?"

"No."

"Hidden."

"No."

"But Coronado couldn't see them?"

She shook her head. With her forefinger, she picked up a few stray pieces of frosting left on her plate and stuck them in her mouth. "How could he when they weren't there?"

The tape clicked off, and I didn't even bother to turn it over. I looked at my watch. If I took her back now I could make it to the hearings early and maybe interview some of the developers. I picked up the check and went over to the cash register.

"Do you want to see them?"

"What do you mean? See the Seven Cities of Cibola?"

"Yeah. I'll take you to them."

"You mean go to New Mexico?"

"No. I told you, Coronado came to Colorado."

"When?"

"When he was looking for the Seven Cities of Cibola."

"No, I mean when can I see them? Right now?"

"No," she said, with that, 'how dumb can anyone be?' look. She reached for a copy of the *Rocky Mountain News* that was lying on the counter and looked inside the back page. "Tomorrow morning. Six o'clock."

One of my favorite things about Denver is that it's spread all over the place and takes you forever to get anywhere. The mountains finally put a stop to things twenty miles to the west, but in all three other directions it can sprawl all the way to the state line and apparently is trying to. Being a reporter here isn't so much a question of driving journalistic ambition as of driving, period.

The skyscraper moratorium hearings were out on Colorado Boulevard across from the Hotel Giorgio, one of the skyscrapers under discussion. It took me forty-five minutes to get there from the Olde West Trailer Park.

I was half an hour late, which meant the hearings had already gotten completely off the subject. "What about reflecting glass?" someone in the audience was saying. "I think it should be outlawed in skyscrapers. I was nearly blinded the other day on the way to work."

"Yeah," a middle-aged woman said. "If we're going to have skyscrapers, they should look like skyscrapers." She waved vaguely at the Hotel Giorgio, which looks like a giant black milk carton.

"And not like that United Bank building downtown!" someone else said. "It looks like a damned cash register!"

From there it was a short illogical jump to the impossibility of parking downtown, Denver's becoming too decentralized, and whether the new airport should be built or not. By five-thirty they were back on reflecting glass.

"Why don't they put glass you can see through in their skyscrapers?" an old man who looked a lot like the time machine inventor said. "I'll tell you why not. Because those big business executives are doing things they should be ashamed of, and they don't want us to see them."

I left at seven and went back to the *Record* to try to piece my notes together into some kind of story. Jake was there.

"How'd your interview with Coronado's granddaughter go?" he asked.

"The Seven Cities of Cibola are here in Denver only Coronado couldn't see them because they're not there." I looked around. "Is there a copy of the *News* someplace?"

"*Here?* In the *Record* building!" he said, clutching his chest in mock horror. "That bad, huh? You're going to go work for the *News*?" But he fished a copy out of the mess on somebody's desk and handed it to me. I opened it to the back page.

There was no "Best Times for Viewing Lost Cities of Gold" column. There were pictures and dates of the phases of the moon, road conditions, and "What's in the Stars: by Stella." My horoscope of the day read: "Any assignment you accept today will turn out differently than you expect." The rest of the page was devoted to the weather, which was supposed to be sunny and warm tomorrow.

The facing page had the crossword puzzle, "Today in History," and squibs about Princess Di and a Bronco fan who'd planted his garden in the shape of a Bronco quarterback. I was surprised Jake hadn't assigned me that story.

I went down to Research and looked up El Turco. He was an Indian slave, probably Pawnee, who had scouted for Coronado, but that was his nickname, not his name. The Spanish had called him "The Turk" because of his peculiar hair. He had been captured at Cicuye, *after* Coronado's foray into Cibola, and had promised to lead them to Quivira, tempting them with stories of golden streets and great stone palaces. When the stories didn't pan out, Coronado had had him executed. I could understand why.

Jake cornered me on my way home. "Look, don't quit," he said. "Tell you what, forget Coronado. There's a guy out in Lakewood who's planted his garden in the shape of John Elway's face. Daffodils for hair, blue hyacinths for eyes."

"Can't," I said, sidling past him. "I've got a date to see the Seven Cities of Gold."

Another delightful aspect of the Beautiful Mile-High City is that in the middle of April, after you've planted your favorite Bronco, you can get fifteen inches of snow. It had started getting cloudy by the time I left the paper, but fool that I was, I thought it was an afternoon thunderstorm. The News's forecast had, after all, been for warm and sunny. When I woke up at four-thirty there was a foot and half of snow on the ground and more tumbling down.

"Why are you going back if she's such a nut?" Jake had asked me when I told him I couldn't take the Elway garden. "You don't seriously think she's onto something, do you?" and I had had a hard time explaining to him why I was planning to get up at an ungodly hour and trek all the way out to Santa Fe again.

She was *not* El Turco's great-great-granddaughter. Two greats still left her at two hundred and fifty plus, and her history was as garbled as her math, but when I had gotten impatient she had said, "Do you want to see them?" and when I had asked her when, she had consulted the News's crossword puzzle and said, "Tomorrow morning."

I had gotten offers of proof before. The time machine inventor had proposed that I climb in his washing machine and be sent forward to "a glorious future, a time when everyone is rich," and the psychic dentist had offered to pull my wisdom teeth. But there's always a catch to these offers.

"Your teeth will have been extracted in another plane of reality," the dentist had said. "X-rays taken in this plane will show them as still being there," and the time machine guy had checked his soak cycle and the stars at the last minute and decided there wouldn't be another temporal agitation until August of 2158.

Rosa hadn't put any restrictions at all on her offer. "You want to see them?" she said, and there was no mention of reality planes or stellar-laundry connections, no mention of any catch. Which doesn't mean there won't be one, I thought, getting out the mittens and scarf I had just put away for the season and going out to scrape the windshield off. When I got there she would no doubt say the snow made it impossible to see the Cities or I could only see them if I believed in UFO's. Or maybe she'd point off somewhere in the general direction of Denver's brown cloud and say, "What do you mean, you can't see them?"

I-25 was a mess, cars off the road everywhere and snow driving into my headlights so I could barely see. I got behind a snowplow and stayed there, and it was nearly six o'clock by the time I made it to the trailer. Rosa took a good five minutes to come to the door, and when she finally got there she wasn't dressed. She stared blearily at me, her hair out of its braids and hanging tangled around her face.

"Remember me? Carla Johnson? You promised to show me the Seven Cities?"

"Cities?" she said blankly.

"The Seven Cities of Cibola."

"Oh, yeah," she said, and motioned for me to come inside. "There aren't seven. El Turco was a dumb Pawnee. He don't know how to count."

"How many are there?" I asked, thinking, this is the catch. There aren't seven and they aren't gold.

"Depends," she said. "More than seven. You still wanta go see them?"

"Yes."

She went into the bedroom and came out after a few minutes with her hair braided, the pants and blouse of the day before and an enormous red carcoat, and we took off toward Cibola. We went south again, past more waterbed stores and rusting railroad tracks, and out to Belleview.

It was beginning to get fairly light out, though it was impossible to tell if the sun was up or not. It was still snowing hard.

She had me turn onto Belleview, giving me at least ten yards' warning, and we headed east toward the Tech Center. Those people at the hearing who'd complained about Denver becoming too decentralized had a point. The Tech Center looked like another downtown as we headed toward it.

A multi-colored downtown, garish even through the veil of snow. The Metropoint building was pinkish-lavender, the one next to it was midnight blue, while the Hyatt Regency had gone in for turquoise and bronze, and

469

there was an assortment of silver, sea-green, and taupe. There was an assortment of shapes, too: deranged trapezoids, overweight butterflies, giant beer cans. They were clearly moratorium material, each of them with its full complement of reflecting glass, and, presumably, executives with something to hide.

Rosa had me turn left onto Yosemite, and we headed north again. The snowplows hadn't made it out here yet, and it was heavy going. I leaned forward and peered through the windshield, and so did Rosa.

"Do you think we'll be able to see them?" I asked.

"Can't tell yet," she said. "Turn right."

I turned into a snow-filled street. "I've been reading about your great-grandfather."

"Great-*great*," she said.

"He confessed he'd lied about the cities, that there really wasn't any gold."

She shrugged. "He was scared. He thought Coronado was going to kill him."

"Coronado *did* kill him," I said. "He said El Turco was leading his army into a trap."

She shrugged again and wiped a space clear on the windshield to look through.

"If the Seven Cities existed, why didn't El Turco take Coronado to them? It would have saved his life."

"They weren't there." She leaned back.

"You mean they're not there all the time?" I said.

"You know the Grand Canyon?" she asked. "My great-great-grandfather discovered the Grand Canyon. He told Coronado he seen it. Nobody saw the Grand Canyon again for three hundred years. Just because nobody seen it don't mean it wasn't there. You was supposed to turn right back there at the light."

I could see why Coronado had strangled El Turco. If I hadn't been afraid I'd get stuck in the snow, I'd have stopped and throttled her right then. I turned around, slipping and sliding, and went back to the light.

"Left at the next corner and go down the block a little ways," she said, pointing. "Pull in there."

"There" was the parking lot of a donut shop. It had a giant neon donut in the middle of its steamed-up windows. I knew how Coronado felt when he rode into the huddle of mud huts that was supposed to have been the City of Gold.

"This is Cibola?" I said.

"No way," she said, heaving herself out of the car. "They're not there today."

"You *said* they were always there," I said.

"They are." She shut the car door, dislodging a clump of snow. "Just not all the time. I think they're in one of those time-things."

"Time-things? You mean a time warp?" I asked, trying to remember what the washing-machine guy had called it. "A temporal agitation?"

"How would I know? I'm not a scientist. They have good donuts here. Cream-filled."

The donuts were actually pretty good, and by the time we started home the snow had stopped and was already turning to slush, and I no longer wanted to strangle her on the spot. I figured in another hour the sun would be out, and John Elway's hyacinth-blue eyes would be poking through again. By the time we turned onto Hampden, I felt calm enough to ask when she thought the Seven Cities might put in another appearance.

She had bought a *Rocky Mountain News* and a box of cream-filled donuts to take home. She opened the box and contemplated them. "More than seven," she said. "You like to write?"

"What?" I said, wondering if Coronado had had this much trouble communicating with El Turco.

"That's why you're a reporter, because you like to write?"

"No," I said. "The writing's a real pain. When will this time-warp thing happen again?"

She bit into a donut. "That's Cinderella City," she said, gesturing to the mall on our right with it. "You ever been there?"

I nodded.

"I went there once. They got marble floors and this big fountain. They got lots of stores. You can buy just about anything you want there. Clothes, jewels, shoes."

If she wanted to do a little shopping now that she'd had breakfast, she could forget it. And she could forget about changing the subject. "When can we go see the Seven Cities again? Tomorrow?"

She licked cream filling off her fingers and turned the *News* over. "Not tomorrow," she said. "El Turco would have liked Cinderella City. He didn't have no shoes. He had to walk all the way to Colorado in his bare feet. Even in the snow."

I imagined my hands closing around her plump neck. "When are the Seven Cities going to be there again?" I demanded. "And don't tell me they're always there."

She consulted the celebrity squibs. "Not tomorrow," she said. "Day after tomorrow. Five o'clock. You must like people, then. That's why you wanted to be a reporter? To meet all kinds of people?"

"No," I said. "Believe it or not, I wanted to travel."

She grinned her golden smile at me. "Like Coronado," she said.

I spent the next two days interviewing developers, environmentalists, and council members, and pondering why Coronado had continued to follow El Turco, even after it was clear he was a pathological liar.

I had stopped at the first 7-Eleven I could find after letting Rosa and her donuts off and bought a copy of the *News*. I read the entire back section, including the comics. For all I knew, she was using *Doonesbury* for an oracle. Or *Nancy*.

I read the obits and worked the crossword puzzle and then went over the back page again. There was nothing remotely time-warp-related. The moon was at first quarter. Sunset would occur at 7:51 P.M. Road conditions for the Eisenhower Tunnel were snow-packed and blowing. Chains required. My horoscope read, "Don't get involved in wild goose chases. A good stay-at-home day."

Rosa no more knew where the Seven Cities of Gold were than her great-great-grandfather. According to the stuff I read in between moratorium jaunts, he had changed his story every fifteen minutes or so, depending on what Coronado wanted to hear.

The other Indian scouts had warned Coronado, told him there was nothing to the north but buffalo and a few teepees, but Coronado had gone blindly on. "El Turco seems to have exerted a Pied-Piperlike power over Coronado," one of the historians had written, "a power which none of Coronado's officers could understand."

"Are you still working on that crazy Coronado thing?" Jake asked me when I got back to the *Record*. "I thought you were covering the hearings."

"I am," I said, looking up the Grand Canyon. "They've been postponed because of the snow. I have an appointment with the United Coalition Against Uncontrolled Growth at eleven."

"Good," he said. "I don't need the Coronado piece, after all. We're running a series on 'Denver Today' instead."

He went back upstairs. I found the Grand Canyon. It had been discovered by Lopez de Cardeñas, one of Coronado's men. El Turco hadn't been with him.

I drove out to Aurora in a blinding snowstorm to interview the United Coalition. They were united only in spirit, not in location. The president had his office in one of the Pavilion Towers off Havana, ut the secretary who had all the graphs and spreadsheets, was out at Fiddler's Green. I spent the whole afternoon shuttling back and forth between them through the snow, and wondering what had ever possessed me to become a journalist. I'd wanted to travel. I had had the idea, gotten from TV that journalists got to go all over the world, writing about exotic and amazing places. Like the UNIPAC building and the Plaza Towers.

They were sort of amazing, if you like Modern Corporate. Brass and chrome and Persian carpets. Atriums and palm trees and fountains splashing in marble pools. I wondered what Rosa, who had been so impressed with Cinderella City, would have thought of some of these places. El Turco would certainly have been impressed. Of course, he would probably have been impressed by the donut shop, and would no doubt have convinced Coronado to drag his whole army there with tales of fabulous, cream-filled wealth.

I finished up the United Coalition and went back to the *Record* to call some developers and builders and get their side. It was still snowing, and there weren't any signs of snow removal, creative or otherwise, that I could see. I set up some appointments for the next day, and then went back down to Research.

El Turco hadn't been the only person to tell tales of the fabulous Seven Cities of Gold. A Spanish explorer, Cabeza de Vaca, had reported them first, and his black slave Estevanico claimed to have seen them, too. Friar Marcos had gone with Estevanico to find them, and, according to him, Estavanico had actually entered Cibola.

They had made up a signal. Estevanico was to send back a small cross if he found a little village, a big cross if he found a city. Estevanico was killed in a battle with Indians, and Friar Marcos fled back to Coronado, but he said he'd seen the Seven Cities in the distance, and he claimed that Estevanico had sent back "a cross the size of a man."

There were all kinds of other tales, too, that the Navajos had gold and silver mines, that Montezuma had moved his treasure north to keep it from the Spanish, that there was a golden city on a lake, with canoes whose oarlocks were solid gold. If El Turco had been lying, he wasn't the only one.

I spent the next day interviewing pro-uncontrolled growth types. They were united, too. "Denver has to retain its central identity," they all told me from what it was hard to believe was not a pre-written script. "It's becoming split into a half-dozen sub-cities, each with its own separate goals."

They were in less agreement as to where the problem lay. One of the builders who'd developed the Tech Center thought the Plaza Tower out at Fiddler's Green was an eyesore, Fiddler's Green complained about Aurora, Aurora thought there was too much building going on around Colorado Boulevard. They were all united on one thing, however: downtown was completely out of control.

I logged several thousand miles in the snow, which showed no signs of letting up, and went home to bed. I debated setting my alarm. Rosa didn't know where the Seven Cities of Gold were, the Living Western Heritage series had been canceled, and Coronado would have saved everybody a lot of trouble if he had listened to his generals.

But Estevanico had sent back a giant cross, and there was the "time-thing" thing. I had not done enough stories on psychic peridontia yet to start believing their nutto theories, but I had done enough to know what they were supposed to sound like. Rosa's was all wrong.

"I don't know what it's called," she'd said, which was far too vague. Nutto theories may not make any sense, but they're all worked out, down to the last bit of pseudo-scientific jargon. The psychic dentist had told me all about transcendental maxillofacial extractile vibrations, and the time travel guy had showed me a hand-lettered chart showing how the partial load setting affected future events.

If Rosa's Seven Cities were just one more nutto theory, she would have been talking about morphogenetic temporal dislocation and simultaneous reality modes. She would at least know what the "time-thing" was called.

I compromised by setting the alarm on "music" and went to bed.

I overslept. The station I'd set the alarm on wasn't on the air at four-thirty in the morning. I raced into my clothes, dragged a brush through my hair, and took off. There was almost no traffic—who in their right mind is up at four-thirty?—and it had stopped snowing. By the time I pulled onto Santa Fe I was only running ten minutes late. Not that it mattered. She would probably take half an hour to drag herself to the door and tell me the Seven Cities of Cibola had canceled again.

I was wrong. She was standing outside waiting in her red carcoat and a pair of orange Bronco earmuffs. "You're late," she said, squeezing herself in beside me. "Got to go."

"Where?"

She pointed. "Turn left."

"Why don't you just tell me where we're going?" I said, "and that way I'll have a little advance warning."

"Turn right," she said.

We turned onto Hampden and started up past Cinderella City. Hampden is never free of traffic, no matter what time of day it is. There were dozens of cars on the road. I got in the center lane, hoping she'd give me at least a few feet of warning for the next turn, but she leaned back and folded her arms across her massive bosom.

"You're sure the Seven Cities will appear this morning?" I asked.

She leaned forward and peered through the windshield at the slowly lightening sky, looking for who knows what. "Good chance. Can't tell for sure."

I felt like Coronado, dragged from pillar to post. Just a little farther, just a little farther. I wondered if this could be not only a scam but a set-up, if we would end up pulling up next to a black van in some dark parking lot, and I would find myself on the cover of the *Record* as a robbery victim or worse. She was certainly anxious enough. She kept holding up her arm so she could read her watch in the lights of the cars behind us. More likely, we were heading for some bakery that opened at the crack of dawn, and she wanted to be there when the fried cinnamon rolls came out of the oven.

"Turn right!" she said. "Can't you go no faster?"

I went faster. We were out in Cherry Creek now, and it was starting to get really light. The snowstorm was apparently over. The sky was turning a faint lavender-blue.

"Now right, up there," she said, and I saw where we were going. This road led past Cherry Creek High School and then up along the top of the dam. A nice isolated place for a robbery.

We went past the last houses and pulled out onto the dam road. Rosa turned in her seat to peer out my window and the back, obviously looking for something. There wasn't much to see. The water wasn't visible from this point, and she was looking the wrong direction, out towards Denver. There were still a few lights, the early-bird traffic down on I-225 and the last few orangish street lights that hadn't gone off automatically. The snow had taken on the bluish-lavender color of the sky.

I stopped the car.

"What are you doing?" she demanded. "Go all the way up."

"I can't," I said, pointing ahead. "The road's closed."

She peered at the chain strung across the road as if she couldn't figure out what it was, and then opened the door and got out.

Now it was my turn to say, "What are you doing?"

"We gotta walk," she said. "We'll miss it otherwise."

"Miss what? Are you telling me there's going to be a time warp up there on top of the dam?"

She looked at me like I was crazy. "Time warp?" she said. Her grin glittered in my headlights. "No. Come on."

Even Coronado had finally said, "All right, enough," and ordered his men to strangle El Turco. But not until he'd been lured all the way up to Kansas. And, according to Rosa, Colorado. The Seven Cities of Cibola were *not* going to be up on top of Cherry Creek dam, no matter what Rosa said, and I wasn't even going to get a story out of this, but I switched off my lights and got out of the car and climbed over the chain.

It was almost fully light now, and the shadowy dimnesses below were sorting themselves out into decentralized Denver. The black *2001* towers off Havana were right below us, and past them the peculiar Mayan-pyramid shape of the National Farmer's Union. The Tech Center rose in a jumble off to the left, beer cans and trapezoids, and then there was a long curve of isolated buildings all the way to downtown, an island of skyscraping towers obviously in need of a moratorium.

"Come on," Rosa said. She started walking faster, panting along the road ahead of me and looking anxiously toward the east, where at least a black van wasn't parked. "Coronado shouldn't have killed El Turco. It wasn't his fault."

"What wasn't his fault?"

"It was one of those time-things, what did you call it?" she said, breathing hard.

"A temporal agitation?"

"Yeah, only he didn't know it. He thought it was there all the time, and when he brought Coronado there it wasn't there, and he didn't know what had happened."

She looked anxiously to the east again, where a band of clouds extending about an inch above the horizon was beginning to turn pinkish-gray, and broke into an ungainly run. I trotted after her, trying to remember the procedure for CPR.

She ran into the pullout at the top of the dam and stopped, panting hard. She put her hand up to her heaving chest and looked out across the snow at Denver.

"So you're saying the cities existed in some other time? In the future?"

She glanced over her shoulder at the horizon. The sun was nearly up. The narrow cloud turned pale pink, and the snow on Mt. Evans went the kind of fuschia we use in the Sunday supplements. "And you think there's going to be another time-warp this morning?" I said.

She gave me that "how can one person be so stupid" look. "Of course not," she said, and the sun cleared the cloud. "There they are," she said.

There they were. The reflecting glass in the curved towers of Fiddler's Green caught first, and then the Tech Center and the Silverado Building on Colorado Boulevard, and the downtown skyline burst into flames. They turned pink and then orange, the Hotel Giorgio and the Metropoint building and the Plaza Towers, blazing pinnacles and turrets and towers.

"You didn't believe me, did you?" Rosa said.

"No," I said, unwilling to take my eyes off of them. "I didn't."

There were more than seven. Far out to the west the Federal Center ignited, and off to the north the angled lines of grain elevators gleamed. Downtown blazed, blinding building moratorium advocates on their way to work. In between, the Career Development Institute and the United Bank Building and the Hyatt Regency burned gold, standing out from the snow like citadels, like cities. No wonder El Turco had dragged Coronado all the way to Colorado. Marble palaces and golden streets.

476

"I told you they were there all the time," she said.

It was over in another minute, the fires going out one by one in the panes of reflecting glass, downtown first and then the Cigna building and Belleview Place, fading to their everyday silver and onyx and emerald. The Pavilion Towers below us darkened and the last of the sodium street lights went out.

"There all the time," Rosa said solemnly.

"Yeah," I said. I would have to get Jake up here to see this. I'd have to buy a *News* on the way home and check on the time of sunrise for tomorrow. And the weather.

I turned around. The sun glittered off the water of the reservoir. There was an aluminum rowboat out in the middle of it. It had golden oarlocks.

Rosa had started back down the road to the car. I caught up with her. "I'll buy you a pecan roll," I said. "Do you know of any good places around here?"

She grinned. Her gold teeth gleamed in the last light of Cibola. "The best," she said.

JONATHAN LETHEM

Walking the Moons

▼

Virtual Reality is the new pop-science buzzword of the '90s, like "nano-mechanism" was a couple of years back, and magazines and newspapers are full of enthusiastic articles about how wonderful it's going to be to be able to sit in your own living room and *feel* as though you're actually climbing peaks in the Himalayas, or diving to the bottom of the sea, or exploring lavafields on Mars. . . .

Yeah. Right.

The author of the razor-sharp and wickedly ironic little story that follows, Jonathan Lethem, is yet another of those talented new writers who—encouragingly—are continuing to pop up all over as we progress into the decade of the 1990s. He works at an antiquarian bookstore, writes slogans for buttons and lyrics for two rock bands, and has also had sales in the last year or so to *New Pathways, Pulphouse, Issac Asimov's Science Fiction Magazine, Universe, Journal Wired, Marion Zimmer Bradley's Fantasy Magazine, Aboriginal SF*, and elsewhere . . . and is clearly another Writer To Watch in the years to come.

▼
Walking the Moons

JONATHAN LETHEM

"Look," says the mother of The Man Who Is Walking Around The Moons Of Jupiter, "he's going so fast." She snickers to herself and scuttles around the journalist to a table littered with wiring tools and fragmented mechanisms. She loops a long, tangled cord over her son's intravenous tube and plugs one end into his headset, jostling him momentarily as she works it into the socket. His stride on the treadmill never falters. She runs the cord back to a modified four-track recorder sitting in the dust of the garage floor, then picks up the recorder's microphone and switches it on.

"Good morning, Mission Commander," she says.

"Yes," grunts The Man Who, his slack jaw moving beneath the massive headset. It startles the journalist to hear the voice of The Man Who boom out into the tiny garage.

"Interview time, Eddie."

"Who?"

"Mr. Kaffey. *Systems* Magazine, remember?"

"O.K.," says Eddie, The Man Who. His weakened, pallid body trudges forward. He is clothed only in jockey undershorts and orthopedic sandals, and the journalist can see his heart beat beneath the skin of his chest.

The Mother Of smiles artificially and hands the journalist the microphone. "I'll leave you boys alone," she says. "If you need anything, just yodel."

She steps past the journalist, over the cord, and out into the sunlight, pulling the door shut behind her.

The journalist turns to the man on the treadmill.

"Uh, Eddie?"

"Yeah."

"Uh, I'm Ron Kaffey. Is this O.K.? Can you talk?"

"Mr. Kaffey, I've got nothing but time." The Man Who smacks his lips and tightens his grip on the railing before him. The tread rolls away steadily beneath his feet, taking him nowhere.

The journalist covers the mike with the palm of his hand and clears his throat, then begins again. "So you're out there now. On Io. Walking."

"Mr. Kaffey, I'm currently broadcasting my replies to your questions from a valley on the northwestern quadrant of Io, yes. You're coming in loud and clear. No need to raise your voice. We're fortunate in having a pretty good connection, a good Earth-to-Io hookup, so to speak." The journalist watches as The Man Who moistens his lips, then dangles his tongue in the open air. "Please feel free to shoot with the questions, Mr. Kaffey. This is pretty uneventful landscape even by Io standards and I'm just hanging on your every word."

"Explain to me," says the journalist, "what you're doing."

"Ah. Well, I designed the rig myself. Took pixel satellite photographs and fed them into my simulator, which gives me a steadily unfolding virtual-space landscape." He reaches up and taps at his headset. "I log the equivalent mileage at the appropriate gravity on my treadmill and pretty soon I've had the same experience an astronaut would have. If we could afford to send them up anymore. Heh." He scratches violently at his ribs, until they flush pink. "Ask me questions," he says. "I'm ready at this end. You want me to describe what I'm seeing?"

"Describe what you're seeing."

"The desert, Mr. Kaffey. God, I'm so goddamned bored of the desert. That's all there is, you know. There isn't any atmosphere. We'd hope for some atmosphere, we had some hopes, but it didn't turn out that way. Nope. The dust all lays flat here, because of that. I try kicking it up, but there isn't any wind." The Man Who scuffs in his Dr. Scholl's sandals at the surface of the treadmill, booting imaginary pebbles, stirring up nonexistent dust. "You probably know I can't see Jupiter right now. I'm on the other side, so I'm pretty much out here alone under the stars. There isn't any point in my describing *that* to you."

The Man Who scratches again, this time at the patch where the intravenous tube intersects his arm, and the journalist is afraid he'll tear it off. "Bored?" asks the journalist.

"Yeah. Next time I think I'll walk across a grassy planet. What do you think of that? Or across the Pacific Ocean. On the bottom, I mean. 'Cause they're mapping it with ultrasound. Feed it into the simulator. Take me a couple of weeks. Nothing like this shit.

"I'm thinking more in terms of smaller scale walks from here on in, actually. Get back down to earth, find ways to make it count for more. You know what I mean? Maybe even the ocean isn't such a good idea, actually. Maybe my fans can't really identify with my off-world walks, maybe they're feeling, who knows, a little, uh, alienated by this Io thing. I know I am. I feel out of touch, Mr. Kaffey. Maybe I ought to walk across the cornbelt or the sunbelt or something. A few people in cars whizzing past, waving at me, and farmer's wives making me picnic lunches, because they've heard I'm passing through. I could program that. I could have every goddamn Mayor from Pinole to Akron give me the key to their goddamn city."

"Sounds O.K., Eddie."

"Sounds O.K.," echoes The Man Who. "But maybe even that's a little much. Maybe I ought to walk across the street to the drugstore for a pack of gum. You don't happen to have a stick of gum in your pocket, Mr. Journalist? I'll just open my mouth and you stick it in. I trust you. We don't have to tell my mother. If you hear her coming you just let me know, and I'll swallow it. You won't get in any trouble."

"I don't have any," says the journalist.

"Ah well."

The Man Who walks on, undaunted. Only now something is wrong. There's a hiss of escaping liquid, and the journalist is certain that The Man Who's nutrient serum is leaking from his arm. Then he smells the urine, and sees the undershorts of The Man Who staining dark, and adhering to the cave-white flesh of his thigh.

"What's the matter, Kaffey? No more questions?"

"You've wet yourself," says the journalist.

"Oh, damn. Uh, you better call my mom."

But The Mother Of has already sensed that something is amiss. She steps now back into the garage, smoking a cigarette and squinting into the darkness at her son. She frowns as she discerns the stain, and takes a long drag on her cigarette, closing her eyes.

"I guess you're thinking that there might not be a story here," says The Man Who. "Least not the story you had in mind."

"Oh no, I wouldn't say that," says the journalist quickly. He's not sure if he hasn't detected a note of sarcasm in the voice of The Man Who by now. "I'm sure we can work something up."

"Work something up," parrots The Man Who. The Mother Of has his shorts down now, and she's swabbing at his damp flank with a paper towel. The Man Who sets his mouth in a grim smile and trudges forward. He's

481

not here, really. He's out on Io, making tracks. He's going to be in the Guiness Book of World Records.

The journalist sets the microphone back down in the dust and packs his bag. As he walks the scrubby driveway back to the street he hears The Man Who Is Walking Around The Moons Of Jupiter, inside the garage, coughing on cigarette fumes.

IAN McDONALD

Rainmaker Cometh

▼

British author Ian McDonald is not exactly a new writer anymore, but you probably haven't heard as much about him yet as you're *going* to hear in the next few years, as he is an ambitious and daring writer with a wide range and an impressive amount of talent. His first story was published in 1982, and since then he has appeared with some frequency in *Interzone, Isaac Asimov's Science Fiction Magazine, Zenith, Other Edens, Amazing,* and elsewhere. He was nominated for the John W. Campbell Award in 1985, and in 1989 he won the *Locus* "Best First Novel" Award for his novel *Desolation Road.* His other books include a novel, *Out on Blue Six,* and a collection of his short fiction, *Empire Dreams.* Born in Manchester, England, in 1960, McDonald has spent most of his life in Northern Ireland, and now lives and works in Belfast.

Here—in a story with a kind of vivid imagery and cadenced verbal lyricism rarely matched in this field since the early days of Ray Bradbury—he paints an evocative and unforgettable portrait of a small Southwestern town caught uneasily on the grinding edge between wonder and despair. . . .

▼

Rainmaker Cometh

IAN McDONALD

Seven dry years lie like seven white scars scrawled across the shoulders of the dying town. On the downhill side long years before ever the rains failed, it crouches in the desert, a tangle of tracks and trailways and transcontinentals; always on the way to somewhere else. Only in the heat of the night does it uncurl to bare the neon tattoos along its belly: the bus depot, the motel, the barbershop, the gas-station; sweating, shocking blues and pinks you can feel hot on your face. Down at the end of the bar, where the dreams collect thickest because no one ever goes there to dust them away, Kelly By the Window watches neon fingers stroking the flanks of the Greyhounds and Trailways; people change direction here like they change their shorts. Blue Highways; abandoned luncheonettes; all she will ever see of the refuge of the roads is the reflection of her face in the eldorado bus windows, slipping past, out there lost in the heart of Saturday night. Up on the roof Desert Rose announces the best hot dogs in town in blushing cerises and 'lectric blues you can read all the way out at Havapai Point. And it's true, as long as you understand that "best" means "only". She's smiling. She's always smiling. She makes the law, you see. Graven into every sixty-watt rhinestone on her boots. Nobody gets off who doesn't get on again.

If he likes the tilt of your hat or the color of your luggage, if the smell of the cologne you've splashed on in the washroom reminds him of all those Oldsmobile days hung up with his jacket on the peg by the door, Sam My Man will solicit you with his magic never-ending cup of coffee. He's a dealer in biography, paid for by the minute, the hour, however long it takes until the driver calls you on into the night. Sam My Man has whole lifetimes racked away under the bar where he keeps the empty bottles. He can tell a good vintage just by looking: given the choice between the kid in tractor hat, knee-high tubes and cut-off Tee-shirt, the bus-lagged pair of English Camp-Americas propping their eyelids open with their backpacks and coffee the strength of bitumen, and the old man with the precise half-inch of white beard and the leather bag like no one's carried since the tornado whisked Professor Marvel off to the Emerald City, Kelly By the Window knows which one he'll solicit with his little fill-'er-ups of complimentary coffee.

Sam My Man always leaves the airco off. He claims it makes the chili dogs taste better, but Kelly By the Window knows that he does it because someone's bound to comment that it's hot as the proverbial, and that's his cue. "It's the drought," he'll say. "Rained everywhere else, but never here. You believe a town can be cursed?" Never failed yet.

"I surely could," says this old man. "Just how long is it since it last rained here?"

"Seven years," says Kelly By the Window. The last drop fell two days after her eleventh birthday.

"You headed anyplace special?" asks Sam My Man, all chummy and pally-wally, like he's known this old man years not seconds. He's good, you got to give him that. Someone should have made him a lawyer long ago. Or a chat-show host.

"Had planned on heading up north, over the dam, got a woman and a boy I want to see," says this old man, "But then again, I may just stay around a couple of days or so. I think you may have need of my services." He puts his bag on the counter, the Professor Marvel etc. etc., and *something* about it, *something* no one can ever call by name, makes Sam My Man step back; just a little. Even Kelly By the Window feels the *something* brush the fine downy hair along her spine. He opens the bag, takes out a thing that looks a little like a lightning rod and a little like a satellite dish and a little like a piece of Gothic wrought iron and not a whole lot like any. Afterwards, Sam My Man will swear by all the saints in Guadeloupe Cathedral he saw blue lightning running up and down the shaft, but Sam My Man, he's never let the truth get in the way of a good story.

"You want it to rain?" says the old man. "I can make it rain. I'll bring the Rainmaker, if it's what you really want."

And all those questions that have to be asked are stopped, suspended, because out of the night come six wheels and big blue silver: seventy more souls on the way from somewhere, to somewhere. Wiping night-sweat from his brow on the sleeve of his jacket, the driver is shouting: "Thirty minutes refreshment stop!" Better get hopping, Sam My Man. Get that coffee brewing. Time to stop dreaming and get on the beam, Kelly By the Window. There's eggs to fry.

Beyond the Blood of Christ Mountains rumors of dawn threaten Desert Rose's sovereignty of the night, but she's still smiling. She who makes the law is she who breaks the law, on those nights when the stars are low and close and intimate and the wind smells of something best forgotten before it leaves a scar of the heart, when her flashing golden rope may lasso a stranger.

You brothers of the blacktop, you sisters of the all-nite diners, think, you refugees of the highways; think, have you seen him before, this old man-of-the-rain with his Professor Marvel bag and his precise half-inch of beard? Think, did you meet him, on a hard plastic chair in the corner of some three a.m. Burger King, rattling a chocolate machine in a bus station, by the hot-air hand drier in the gents toilet, wrestling with that one problem key in a wall of left-luggage lockers? Did you glimpse him over the top of your foam-styrene coffee cup, your copy of *Newsweek*? What did you think? Did you think nothing of him, just another life briefly parallelling your own, or did he intrigue you enough for you to abandon your attempts to sleep in the coffin-straight seats of a Greyhound or Trailway and let yourself be bound by the social compact of night-talk; in those wee wee hours did he open his Professor Marvel bag and show you the things inside running with blue lightning, did he tell you that he could bring the rain? Did he tell you he was the Herald of the Rainmaker? Did you believe him? Did you say, *"Crazy old man, lying old man, head full of crazy notions."* Or did you think of those times, those places, when the sky was blue as a razor, did you remember how it felt when your prayers were answered and out of nowhere the clouds gathered, at first only a shadow on the horizon, then a patch the size of a man's hand, then a great anvil of darkness bearing down on your town. Then as the sky turned black from horizon to horizon, how you went into your garden and turned off your lawn sprinklers because this time you knew it really was going to rain . . . Did you lift up your eyes to the sky and whisper the word *Rainmaker* to yourself, did you turn it over and over on your tongue until every last drop of cool mystery was drawn out of it: *Rainmaker* . . .

Last person to actually spend a night at Wanda's Motel was a location scout for a Levis ad. Anticipating coke-snorting directors and overmuscled men in startlingly white boxer shorts, Wanda built a cocktail bar and installed cable TV in all her "deluxe" chalets. Joes-on-the-go in the "economy" rooms had to provide their own entertainment but then that's the whole idea, isn't it? Films crews chose a Jimmy Dean gas station at the end of an air force bombing range two hundred miles away. The bar's still popular but the only one who watches the cable is Wanda. She feels she has to justify the expense. She gets all the soaps.

She's not too sure about this one. It's not him. It's the things he carries in that bag of his. She sees them when she valets the room; weird things, odd things, not proper things. Things that don't look like *things* in themselves but bits of other things stuck together. Things that don't *do* anything, that are just for the sake of being *things*. She hasn't a clue what he does with the *things*, but folk coming in for the odd cocktail say he's been all around the town, holding those *things* of his up to his eye and pointing them at his feet, the sun, the Blood of Christ Mountains. Some say they've heard them make funny whining noises. Others say they've seen little gray numbers flashing up on them.

Sounds to Wanda like the location scout all over again. She's hoping she isn't going to miss out this time on the overmuscled men in the startlingly white boxer shorts. Then the stories come back about *things* even weirder, *things* like television aerials stuck into the ground all around the town, *things* like luminous kites flying in the dead of night, *things* like a cross between a boom-box and a very large cockroach left by the side of the road or clamped to a hoarding with a G-clamp, and she knows things can't go on like this any more.

"What are they *for*?" (With all the incredulity of a man who's been asked what a video remote control is for, or the little lamp in a refrigerator.) "Why, they're my surveying equipment. I have to do a thorough geomantic survey of the location before Rainmaker can commit itself. Upper mantle standing wave diffraction patterns, earth, water and wind octaves, geomantic flux line nodes and anomalies: there's an awful lot I have to do and not much time to do it in. Can't read the flux density without this one here, the octave interface analyser. That one there, like the tripod with the black shutters on the top, that's the node localiser. Without that, I might as well pack up and go home. It's tough work. Fiddly, pernickety. You got to be inch perfect. Any chance of a beer?"

The location scout's beginning to look mighty good again to Wanda.

Again: that word: *Rainmaker*. Try it out for size on your tongue, does it sit easy in your imagination? No? Then tell me: what do you think of when you hear that word: "Rainmaker?" Is it Tyrone Power in a bible-black hat? Is it a squadron of cloud-storming biplanes flown by leather-cat-suited blondes? Is it the ghost-dancing feet of your forefathers; is it something altogether more arcane and wonderful, some steam-driven wonder-worker all whirling vanes and blarting trumpet-mouths? If so, then think again. Rainmaker; *the* Rainmaker, is not a person, or a thing. Rainmaker is a place. A city.

How it came to be cast loose upon the sky, this city-state of two hundred souls, is a mystery. As with most mysteries, hypotheses abound: as in form

487

it most resembles a tremendous kite (or then again, an aerial manta ray, or then again a great glass ornament, or then again . . .) it seems reasonable to assume it was launched into the air by some means; though the imagination balks at envisioning the kind of tug necessary to launch a glider one mile across. But a second image haunts you, of a city of soaring glass needles atop which the citizens have built graceful, winged habitats that hum and sway, like reed-grass, in the jetstream, and it is not hard for you to imagine how one such building might, in its pride to outreach all the others, grow so fine, so slender as to one day sever its connection with the earth altogether and cast itself out upon the sky.

The Bureau of Endangered Indigenes has granted Chief Blumberg, last of the Nohopés, a reservation the exact size of one rocking chair on the barbershop porch. Any time of day you will find him there, snapping the necks off beer bottles under one of the chair rockers, but on those nights when the first stars shine like notes from a National guitar, he is especially present. On those nights when the air smells of burnt dust and used-up time, he and his cat, midnight Mineloushe, sit watching the meteors that come down way beyond the Blood of Christ Mountains.

No one, not even Sheriff Middleton, knows what he does. It looks suspiciously close to nothing, but Chief Blumberg has the most important job in town. He prays for the town. Never despise the contemplative, the intercessor. You don't know how much worse things would be without him. Town may be a long time throwing the dirt over itself, but while one soul remains to remember it to the Spirit in the Sky, it will not slip forgotten from the mind of God.

Some men when they meet have no need to speak. Some men, when they meet, know that they can better communicate by silence. St. Dominic crossed the Appenines on foot to visit Francis of Assisi and neither spoke a single word throughout the entire meeting.

Chief Blumberg rocks and rolls in his portable reservation. The man who has come to meet him sits on a bench just below the barbershop window. The cat's Mineloushe-eyes shine with the light of meteors. Behind them, another Burma Shave lathers up while the radio announces fatstock prices.

Had St. Francis offered St. Dominic a bottle of beer neatly decapitated with one lunge of the rocking chair, history might have spoken differently. Silence expresses our similarities. For our differences, we must use words.

"So Raindog, you've come. Seven years I've been praying for rain, seven years arm-wrestling with God, and at last a verdict is announced. Seven years is a lot of praying, especially if God wants this place to go paws up, but you know something, prayer's never wasted. Prayer's got to go somewhere, like the rain; rain goes into the land and it gets bigger and bigger and bigger until the land can't hold it any more. So the land forces it out, and it changes, and becomes something else, but it always remembers what it was, and it always wants to be what it once was again. Something like you. You got a name, Raindog?"

"Elijah seems as good a name as any other."

Whoosh! Big one! Little slitty-eyes, Mineloushe-cattie, dazzled and blinking. A white cockade in Desert Rose's hat . . . and it's gone.

" 'And Elijah prayed that it would not rain, and there was no rain in the land for three and a half years. Again, he prayed and behold, the heavens gave forth rain.' "

"It gratifies me, sir, to find a man knows his Bible these corrupt days."

"Mission music rocked my cradle, Raindog."

"So what is it you believe about me, sir?"

"I believe I prayed for seven years and up there on the edge of heaven all my prayers came together and created you." Under the enormous sky, Kelly By the Window comes out to stand in Sam My Man's doorway and watch the moon rise. She shakes the heat and dust out of her hair and the two men and the cat can hear the treble beat of her Walkman. "I tell you something, Raindog, you better make the rain come soon, while she still has a chance. The drought's too deep in us, but she still has dreams."

"I have the octave markers in position and the beacons are calling. The Rainmaker is coming, sir."

Little Mineloushe blinks; the moon has been obscured by a sudden small cloud, not much larger than the size of a man's hand.

Time of the Tower, Time of the Tug, for generations beyond remembering Rainmaker has been a denizen of pressure gradients and barometric boundaries, flexing and curving itself to the hills and valleys of the air. Only once a year does it approach the earth, on the summer solstice it descends over some obscure map reference in a forgotten part of the ocean to consign its dead to the receiving waters and replenish its vapor tanks. This day of approach is foremost among the city's festivals; as it unfolds its tail from its belly and descends from the perpetual cloud of mystery, the rigging wires flutter with tinsel streamers and spars and ribs bristle a thousand silver prayer kites. Fireworks punctuate the sky and all citizens celebrate Jubilee. Flatlanders find it paradoxical that those who chose to live in the sky should celebrate their closest approach to earth, but those of you who have been a dragonfly snared by the surface tension of a pond will understand: it is not the closeness of the approach they celebrate, but the slenderness of the escape.

Sheriff Middleton and his stomach have enjoyed each other's company for so long now they are best friends. A satisfyingly mutual relationship: he keeps his stomach warm, full and prominent in the community behind straining mother of pearl buttons and silver belt buckles; it supplies him with public eminence and respect, a rich emotional life of belly laughs and gut feelings; even a modicum of protection, the stomach totes a .44 Magnum and has seen several Dirty Harry movies.

This stranger, stepping off one bus and not stepping on another, bag full of *weird thangs,* head full of weirder stories; stomach's got this gut feeling about him. Stomach's heard all about them on the evening news, these folk from the coast, there's *nothing* they won't do, and People are beginning to talk (the ones whose talk matters, the ones with the capital P), and once People start talking, time you started listening to your good old buddy, Sheriff Middleton, that's been giving you nothing but heartburn and flatus all week, and Do Something.

Stomach never walks anywhere, so Sheriff Middleton drives him out to the edge of town where the man who calls himself Elijah is taping something that looks a little like a CB aerial and a little like a chromium Bay Prawn and not a whole lot like either to the side of a Pastor Drew McDowell Ministries hoarding.

There's never any way of making this sweet and easy, so don't even bother trying.

"Could you tell me what you're doing, sir?"

"I'm just positioning the last geomantic enhancer in the matrix so Rainmaker can follow it straight in. They won't have any visual guidance because of the cloud, so the Navigators will have to follow the geomantic beacons as they come in over the desert."

Stomach may be an Eastwood fan, but Sheriff Middleton, he's seen *In the Heat of the Night* twelve times. Best Rod Steiger roll of the jowls. Slide of the mirror shades *up* the nose with the baby finger. Great banks of black clouds reflected in the shades, like a black iron anvil out there over the Blood of Christ Mountains.

"I think maybe you should take it down sir."

"Why should I do that? Is it offending anyone?"

"No sir. As far as I know, it is not an offense to be in possession of peculiar-looking objects. However, I would surely appreciate it if you would take it, and all the rest of your geowhatchamacallit squoodiddlies down. Right now. If you please."

"You don't quite seem to understand—"

"Correction. You don't quite seem to understand, sir. I want you, and all your micro-climatological doofuses and whatever the hell else you got in that bag of yours, on a bus out of here by eight tonight. Heard say you were headed north. Up over the dam, Neonville way, why don't you just take yourself and your Rainmaker away out of here up there?"

"Sir, with or without me, the Rainmaker is coming. No one can stop it now. Day and night the Flight Guild has been out on the high wires, rigging the sails to catch the wind the Weatherworkers are summoning, the wind that brings the Rainmaker."

Clouds race across the twin mirrors over Sheriff Middleton's eyes, and the crazy wind from an unseasonable quarter strokes his skin. It is strong on his cheek like old whiskey tears. It tastes like jalapeños roasting on a charcoal fire, it sounds like a lone guitar bending fifths under a grapefruit moon. He can see it, the crazy wind, suddenly superimposed on his shades like the stress patterns in pick-up windows, wheeling round out there somewhere off the coast of Mexico carrying before it a great raft of warm, wet clouds. And there at the center, something glittering and delicate and transparent as an angel's soul. He sees it all . . . and then he takes his glasses off to wipe them, and it's gone, wiped away, a smear on finger and thumb tip.

"If you'd just get in the car, sir, I'll take you back to the bus station and have someone pick up your things from the Motel. Word of advice sir, don't even think of setting foot out of there 'cept you setting it on a bus." Rainmakers . . . flying cities . . . Soon as you get back behind your desk, Sheriff, you push buttons on that computer of yours and see if any freak hospitals are missing anyone.

A bus pants past, blue silver, dust and diesel. Chain lightning crawls along the edge of the world where the Blood of Christ Mountains meet the sky.

Weatherworkers? Flight Guilds? Is this some medieval city state set adrift in the stratosphere, complete with guilds and mysteries? Is there a vagrant Prince-Bishop lurking somewhere, or a wandering Blondin? Each man has his mystery, Guilds there certainly are, Guilds to tend the hydroponic gardens in the main residential bubble, Guilds to maintain the wind rotors that generate the electricity for Rainmaker's lights and hairdryers, guilds of teachers and doctors and lawyers and undertakers and sanitation engineers; does their very mundaneness make the airborne city state seem more credible? Listen, there is more.

Highest of the ten Guilds Major and Minor are the Rainmakers themselves, the weather-workers, a caste confined by a dominant vertigo gene to the central levels of the administrative spindle. Second to them are the Navigation and Flight Guilds, ancient rivals; the one redoubtable mappers of the topology of the sky who steer Rainmaker through the titanic chasms of air, the others daredevils of the silk-thin rigging wires (oblivious miles above ground zero) who tune the rippling acres of transparent mylar sail. Least of all the Guilds is the Guild of Heralds, for it is the only one to defile itself by walking upon the face of the earth. Yet the least of the guilds is also the greatest, for without a herald walking upon the earth Rainmaker would sail the sky purposeless as a child's bubble.

Why the Rainmaker took its name and its sacred task; this is the Essential Mystery. You will find no answer in the Great Log in Flight Control at the center of the administrative spindle. Nor will you find it in the memories of the guildpersons, even as they weave the clouds and shape the winds and spread their wings across the dry places. You will find no answer because the question is never asked. "Why" is a wild, untamed word. It leads, one sure foot after another, toward the edge of the void. The people of Rainmaker do not ask "why" questions because they know that the answer might be that there is no answer. Rainmaker makes rain because it makes rain.

But for you, dry-souled one, chili-dogger, dance-hall sweetheart, with the dust blowing in your bones, for you that is reason enough; Rainmaker makes rain and the rain falls on the just and the unjust alike, watering the earth, like the word of God that does not return to him empty.

Seven-thirty, black as a preacher's hat. Hot as his Hell. Atmosphere tense as a mid-period Hitchcock. You've either got a migraine or murder in mind. Say, maybe those little men in the hats with the tracts are right, maybe this is the Apocalypse, right now, maybe, right in the middle of the prime-time soaps Jehovah the Ancient of Days is coming in clouds and lightning to judge the souls of all men.

Judgment punching up from the mountains is reflected in Kelly By the Window's shades as she drives to work. It's less than two blocks but she won't walk, not even on the day when God comes to judge her soul; that little red convertible is all the salvation she needs. The *heat*; even with the top down the sweat's dripping down her sides.

She sees him sitting on the bench by the door, backlit by the fluttering butterfly of the Budweiser sign. Bag at his feet, looks like the wind's about to blow Professor Marvel away again, high over the desert with the lights of desert towns and buses far below his rippling, flapping coat-tails.

"Sheriff Middleton throw you out?"

"He did."

"Sheriff Middleton, he's the same as the rest of them. He's afraid of anything that isn't exactly the way it's always been."

"There are many like him, sister. But things change, with or without Sheriff Middleton."

"Thought where you're going, Rainmaker?"

"Up north. I have to see a woman and a boy. My boy. My successor. There is only ever one Herald, and he walks the earth alone, until he finds a woman of the earth who loves him enough to perpetuate the Guild. We serve the Rainmaker, but we may never set foot upon it. After that, I don't know. Wherever I am needed. Wherever things need to change."

"I'm going there too. Get in." He smiles and his bag of geowhatchamacallit squoodiddlies and micro-climatological doofuses goes in the back and he goes in the front, and off they drive, right down the street, past the blue and silver buses and the sign that says *population: elevation*:

"What's your name, sister?" the old man says.

"Kelly. I hate it. It's so undignified. Can you imagine an eighty-year-old grandmother called Kelly?"

"Can't say I've met that many."

She shakes her hair free to blow back in the hot wind. Carmine polished nails search the airwaves; throbbing to major sevenths the little red convertible is swallowed by the night. Beneath a sky crazy with lightning, he asks, "Tell me, why did you take me?"

"Because you made my mind up. Right there, in the street outside Desert Rose's. At last, you decided me. Without you, I'd have stayed behind that bar looking out the window at all the people coming from someplace, going to someplace until I grew old like the rest of them, with no destination, no direction, no kind of movement or change."

Lightning stabs up from the horizon; for a hundred miles in every direction the desert is flashlit vampire blue. Battened down tight, a bus runs for town. Like a startled fox, a roadsign catches the light of the headlamps: *Havapai Point, two miles.*

"Could you stop the car?" says the old man. Radio powerchords go bouncing down the highway, headlamps slew round illuminating one hundred miles of old Diet Coke cans. "I'd like to go up there. I know I can never be there, but I'd like to see it, when it comes. Would it be possible?"

She's already clawing for reverse.

Cochise came up here, to read the future of the red man, and saw Jeff Chandler. Jeff Chandler came up here, plus film crew, best boy, key grip and catering caravan, to play Cochise looking into a Panaflex. Chief Blumberg, last of Nohopés came up here and saw a chair on the barbershop porch. And now Kelly By the Window and the Herald of the Rainmaker stand here, the land cowering at their feet under a sky like the Hammer of God.

"Sunday nights when Sam didn't need me, I'd come up here with Mario from the garage. Some nights, when I just couldn't stand any more, when it felt like my skull was going to explode, it was so full of nothing, we'd take the car and drive and drive and drive but however far we drove we'd always end up here, up at the Point. We were scared, like the rest of them, you see. Mario, he'd turn on the radio and flick on the headlights and we'd dance, like the headlights were spotlights. They used to have this great Golden

Oldies show on Sunday nights, Motown and the Doobie Brothers and sometimes Nat King Cole, and we'd dance real close, real slow, and pretend we'd won a million on a game show and we were whooping it up in a fancy nightclub in Neonville. Sometimes we'd say we were going to drive all night and wake up in Mexico." A solid column of ion-blue plasma flickers between earth and heaven. "Whoo!" yells Kelly By the Window. "That was a big one!" She likes to shout at the storm.

"Close," says Elijah, listening to the sky. "I can feel it, up there, somewhere. Rainmaker is here." Thunder tears like ten thousand miles of ripping grave-cloth. "She's shorting out the storm, channelling the lightning down the mainframe to the discharge capacitors in the tail. One hundred million volts!"

She shivers, hugs herself.

"You're crazy, old man. Crazy crazy crazy, and you know something? It's good to be crazy!"

And then they hear it.

And the buses in the depot and Sam My Man brewing up the bribes for another night's heavy dealin' and Wanda the manageress with her ever-circling television families and Chief Blumberg with bottle in hand and Sheriff Middleton, treating his good good buddy to a few chili dogs, and all the dust-dry, bone-dry faces and places of a desert town, even Desert Rose herself, whip-crackin' away in neon spangles and boots: they all hear it. And stop. And look at the sky in wonder.

The clouds open. The rain comes down on the town. Old, hard rain, rain that has been locked up for seven years and now is free; mean rain, driving down upon a desert town. Thunder bawls, lightning flashes; Wanda's *deluxe* cables burn out in a blare of static. In the diner faces press to the glass, mouths open in amazement at the drops streaming down the windows. On the barbershop porch Chief Blumberg rocks forward and back, forward and back, laughing like a crazy old Indian.

Up on Havapai Point the young woman and the old man are soaked to the bones in an instant. They do not care. Kelly By the Window, she dances in the headlights of her little red convertible, hair sodden snarls and tangles, print dress plastered over small, flat breasts. She throws back her head to taste the good, hard rain, it tastes like kisses, it tastes like iced Mexican beer.

"Look," says the Herald of the Rainmaker, in a voice she has never heard before. And she looks where he is pointing, and, in a lightning bolt of illumination, she sees. She will never be certain what. *Something.* Half hidden by clouds, delicate as a dragonfly wing, strong as diamond, *something* that lives in the storm, *something* that overshadows desert and town like the wings of the Thunderbird. *Something* she knows she will never be free from again, because what she has seen is not just a *something* that might have been a Rainmaker, but a something that might have been a world that should have been, where cities can fly, and sail, and walk, and dive, where cities can be birds, and flowers, and crystals, and smoke, and dreams.

As she sees it, she knows that it is for this moment only. She will never see it again, though she will gladly spend the rest of her life searching for it.

There are tears behind her shades as she drives away from Havapai Point, into the rain, into the welcoming night.

They find the car in a ditch three miles out of Neonville city limits. It has gone clear through the hoarding; big hole right where the Republican candidate's heart used to be. The paramedic team admire her accuracy. The radio is on. Her dress is soaking wet, when they pull her from the wreck, she still has on her shades. They lay her by the side of the road while they try to decide what to do with her. Someone suggests they call Sheriff Middleton. They think they've seen this little red convertible before, cruising the boulevard of abandoned dreams with the top down.

Someone says they think maybe there was another passenger; little things; half-clues, semi-evidences. He (or she) must just have walked away.

Someone says they heard it rained down south of the dam last night. First time in seven years.

ROBERT SILVERBERG
Hot Sky

▼

Robert Silverberg is one of the most famous SF writers of modern times, with dozens of novels, anthologies, and collections to his credit. Silverberg has won five Nebula Awards and four Hugo Awards. His novels include, *Dying Inside, Lord Valentine's Castle, The Book of Skulls, Downward to the Earth, Tower of Glass, The World Inside, Born with the Dead, Shadrach In the Furnace, Tom O'Bedlam, Star of Gypsies,* and *At Winter's End.* His collections include *Unfamiliar Territory, Capricorn Games, Majipoor Chronicles, The Best of Robert Silverberg, At the Conglomeroid Cocktail Party,* and *Beyond the Safe Zone.* His most recent book is *Nightfall,* a novel-length expansion of Isaac Asimov's famous story, done in collaboration with Asimov himself, and the novel *The Face of the Waters.* Upcoming is another novel in collaboration with Asimov, *Child of Time.* For many years he edited the prestigious anthology series *New Dimensions,* and has recently, along with his wife, Karen Haber, taken over the editing of the *Universe* anthology series. His story "Multiples" was in our First Annual Collection; "The Affair" was in our Second Annual Collection; "Sailing to Byzantium"—which won a Nebula Award in 1986—was in our Third Annual Collection; "Against Babylon" was in our Fourth Annual Collection; "The Pardoner's Tale" was in our Fifth Annual Collection; "House of Bones" was in our Sixth Annual Collection; and both "Tales from the Venia Woods" and the Hugo-winning "Enter a Soldier. Later: Enter Another" were in our Seventh Annual Collection. He lives in Oakland, California.

In the story that follows, he takes us along on a hard-edged, high-tech mission on the high seas of a troubled near-future world—and shows us that no matter how sophisticated the technology becomes, *some* things never really change.

▼

Hot Sky

ROBERT SILVERBERG

Out there in the chilly zone of the Pacific, somewhere between San Francisco and Hawaii, the sea was a weird goulash of currents, streams of cold stuff coming up from the antarctic and coolish upwelling spirals out of the ocean floor and little hot rivers rolling off the sun-blasted continental shelf far to the east. Sometimes you could see steam rising in places where cold water met warm. It was a cockeyed place to be trawling for icebergs. But the albedo readings said there was a berg somewhere around there, and so the Tonopah Maru was there, too.

Carter sat in front of the scanner, massaging the numbers in the cramped cell that was the ship's command center. He was the trawler's captain, a lean, 30ish man, yellow hair, brown beard, skin deeply tanned and tinged with the iridescent greenish-purple of his armoring build-up, the protective layer that the infra-ultra drugs gave you. It was midmorning. The shot of Screen he'd taken at dawn still simmered like liquid gold in his arteries. He could almost feel it as it made its slow journey outward to his capillaries and trickled into his skin, where it would carry out the daily refurbishing of the body armor that shielded him against ozone crackle and the demon eye of the sun.

This was only his second year at sea. The company liked to move people around. In the past few years, he'd been a desert jockey in bleak, forlorn Spokane, running odds reports for farmers betting on the month the next rainstorm would turn up, and before that a cargo dispatcher for one of the company's L-5 shuttles, and a chip runner before that. And one of these days, if he kept his nose clean, he'd be sitting in a corner office atop the

Samurai pyramid in Kyoto. Carter hated a lot of the things he'd had to do in order to play the company game. But he knew that it was the only game there was.

"We got maybe a two-thousand-kiloton mass there," he said, looking into the readout wand's ceramic-fiber cone. "Not bad, eh?"

"Not for these days, no," Hitchcock said. He was the oceanographer/ navigator, a grizzled, flat-nosed Afro-Hawaiian whose Screen-induced armor coloring gave his skin a startling midnight look. Hitchcock was old enough to remember when icebergs were never seen farther north than the latitude of southern Chile. "Man, these days, a berg that's still that big all the way up here must have been three counties long when it broke off the fucking polar shelf. But you sure you got your numbers right, man?"

The implied challenge brought a glare to Carter's eyes, and something went curling angrily through his interior, leaving a hot little trail. Hitchcock *never* thought Carter did anything right the first time. Although he often denied it—too loudly—it was pretty clear Hitchcock had never quite gotten over his resentment at being bypassed for captain in favor of an outsider. Probably he thought it was racism. But it wasn't. Carter was managerial track; Hitchcock wasn't. That was all there was to it.

Sourly he said, "You want to check the screen yourself? Here. Here, take a look." He offered Hitchcock the wand.

Hitchcock shook his head. "Easy, man. Whatever the screen says, that's OK for me." He grinned disarmingly, showing mahogany snags. On the screen, impenetrable whorls and jiggles were dancing, black on green, green on black, the occasional dazzling bloom of bright yellow. The Tonopah Maru's interrogatory beam was traveling 22,500 miles straight up to Nippon Telecom's big marine scansat, which had its glassy, unblinking gaze trained on the entire eastern Pacific, looking for albedo differentials. The reflectivity of an iceberg is different from the reflectivity of the ocean surface. You pick up the differential, you confirm it with temperature readout, you scan for mass to see if the trip's worth while. If it is, you bring your trawler in fast and make the grab before someone else does.

This berg was due to go to San Francisco, which was in a bad way for water just now. The entire West Coast was. There hadn't been any rain along the Pacific Seaboard in ten months. Most likely, the sea around here was full of trawlers—Seattle, San Diego, L.A. The Angelenos kept more ships out than anybody else. The Tonopah Maru had been chartered to them by Samurai Industries until last month. But the trawler was working for San Francisco this time. The lovely city by the bay, dusty now, sitting there under that hot, soupy sky full of interesting-colored greenhouse gases, waiting for the rain that almost never came anymore.

Carter said, "Start getting the word around. That berg's down here, south-

499

southwest. We get it in the grapple tomorrow, we can be in San Francisco with it by a week from Tuesday."

"If it don't melt first. This fucking heat."

"It didn't melt between Antarctica and here, it's not gonna melt between here and Frisco. Get a move on, man. We don't want L.A. coming in and hitting it first."

By midafternoon, they were picking up an overhead view via the Weather Department spysat, then a sea-level image bounced to them by a Navy relay buoy. The berg was a thing like a castle afloat, maybe 200 meters long, stately and serene, all pink turrets and indigo battlements and blue-white pinnacles, rising high above the water. Steaming curtains of fog shrouded its edges. For the past couple of million years, it had been sitting on top of the South Pole, and it probably hadn't ever expected to go cruising off toward Hawaii like this. But the big climate shift had changed a lot of things for everybody, the antarctic ice pack included.

"Jesus," Hitchcock said. "Can we do it?"

"Easy," said Nakata. He was the grapple technician, a sleek, beady-eyed, cat-like little guy. "It'll be a four-hook job, but so what? We got the hooks for it."

The Tonopah Maru had hooks to spare. Most of its long, cigar-shaped hull was taken up by the immense rack-and-pinion gear that powered the grappling hooks, a vast, silent mechanism capable of hurling the giant hooks far overhead and whipping them down deep into the flanks of even the biggest bergs. The deck space was given over almost entirely to the great spigots that were used to spray the bergs with a sintering of melt-retardant mirror dust. Down below was a powerful fusion-driven engine, strong enough to haul a fair-sized island halfway around the world.

Everything very elegant, except there was barely any room left over for the crew of five. Carter and the others were jammed into odd little corners here and there. For living quarters, they had cubicles not much bigger than the coffin-sized sleeping capsules you got at an airport hotel, and for recreation space, they all shared one little blister dome aft and a pacing area on the foredeck. A sardine-can kind of life, but the pay was good and at least you could breathe fresh air at sea, more or less, instead of the dense grayish-green murk that hovered over the habitable parts of the West Coast.

They were right at the mid-Pacific cold wall. The sea around them was blue, the sign of warm water. Just to the west, though, where the berg was, the water was a dark, rich olive green with all the microscopic marine life that cold water fosters. The line of demarcation was plainly visible.

Carter was running triangulations to see if they'd be able to slip the berg under the Golden Gate Bridge when Rennett appeared at his elbow and said, "There's a ship, Cap'n."

"What you say?"

He wondered if he were going to have to fight for his berg. That happened at times. This was open territory, pretty much a lawless zone where old-fashioned piracy was making a terrific comeback.

Rennett was maintenance/operations, a husky, broad-shouldered little kid out of the Midwest dust bowl, no more than chest-high to him, very cocky, very tough. She kept her scalp shaved, the way a lot of them did nowadays, and she was as brown as an acorn all over, with the purple glint of Screen shining brilliantly through, making her look almost fluorescent. Brown eyes as bright as marbles and twice as hard looked back at him.

"Ship," she said, clipping it out of the side of her mouth as if doing him a favor. "Right on the other side of the berg. Caskie's just picked up a message. Some sort of S O S." She handed Carter a narrow strip of yellow radio tape with a couple of lines of bright-red thermoprint typing on it. The words came up at him like a hand reaching out of the deck. He read them out loud.

"CAN YOU HELP US TROUBLE ON SHIP MATTER OF LIFE AND DEATH URGENT YOU COME ABOARD SOONEST

"KOVALCIK, ACTING CAPTAIN, CALAMARI MARU"

"What the fuck?" Carter said. "Calamari Maru? Is it a ship or a squid?"

Rennett didn't crack a smile. "We ran a check on the registry. It's owned out of Vancouver by Kyocera-Merck. The listed captain is Amiel Kohlberg, a German. Nothing about any Kovalcik."

"Doesn't sound like a berg trawler."

"It's a squid ship, Cap'n," she said, voice flat with a sharp edge of contempt on it. As if he didn't know what a squid ship was. He let it pass. It always struck him as funny, the way anybody who had two days' more experience at sea than he did treated him like a greenhorn.

He glanced at the print-out again. *Urgent*, it said. *Matter of life and death.* Shit. Shit, shit, shit.

The idea of dropping everything to deal with the problems of some strange ship didn't sit well with him. He wasn't paid to help other captains out, especially Kyocera-Merck captains. Samurai Industries wasn't fond of K-M these days. Something about the Gobi reclamation contract, industrial espionage, some crap like that. Besides, he had a berg to deal with. He didn't need any other distractions just now.

And then, too, he felt an edgy little burst of suspicion drifting up from the basement of his soul, a tweak of wariness. Going aboard another ship out here, you were about as vulnerable as you could be. Ten years in corporate life had taught him caution.

But he also knew you could carry caution too far. It didn't feel good to him to turn his back on a ship that had said it was in trouble. Maybe the ancient laws of the sea, as well as every other vestige of what used to be common decency, were inoperative concepts here in this troubled, heat-plagued year of 2133, but he still wasn't completely beyond feeling things like guilt and shame. Besides, he thought, what goes around comes around. You ignore the other guy when he asks for help, you might just be setting yourself up for a little of the same later on.

They were all watching him—Rennett, Nakata, Hitchcock.

Hitchcock said, "What you gonna do, Cap'n? Gonna go across to 'em?" A gleam in his eye, a snaggly, mischievous grin on his face.

What a pain in the ass, Carter thought. He gave the older man a murderous look and said, "So you think it's legit?"

Hitchcock shrugged blandly. "Not for me to say. You the cap'n, man. All I know is, they say they in trouble, they say they need our help."

Hitchcock's gaze was steady, remote, noncommittal. His blocky shoulders seemed to reach from wall to wall. "They calling for help, Cap'n. Ship wants help, you give help, that's what I always believe, all my years at sea. Of course, maybe it different now."

Carter found himself wishing he'd never let Hitchcock come aboard. But screw it. He'd go over there and see what was what. He had no choice, never really had.

To Rennett he said, "Tell Caskie to let this Kovalcik know that we're heading for the berg to get claiming hooks into it. That'll take about an hour and a half. And after that, we have to get it mirrored and skirted. While that's going on, I'll go over and find out what his problem is."

"Got it," Rennett said and went below.

New berg visuals had come in while they were talking. For the first time now, Carter could see the erosion grooves at the water line on the berg's upwind side, the undercutting, the easily fractured overhangings that were starting to form. The undercutting didn't necessarily mean the berg was going to flip over—that rarely happened with big dry-dock bergs like this—but they'd be in for some lousy oscillations, a lot of rolling and heaving, choppy seas, a general pisser all around. The day was turning very ugly very fast.

"Jesus," Carter said, pushing the visuals across to Nakata. "Take a look at these."

"No problem. We got to put our hooks on the lee side, that's all."

"Yeah. Sounds good." He made it seem simple. Carter managed a grin.

The far side of the berg was a straight high wall, a supreme white cliff as smooth as porcelain that was easily 100 meters high, with a wicked tongue of ice jutting out about 40 meters into the sea like a breakwater. That was what the Calamari Maru was using it for, too. The squid ship rode at anchor just inside that tongue.

Carter signaled to Nakata, who was standing way down fore by his control console.

"Hooks away!" Carter called. "Sharp! Sharp!"

There came the groaning sound of the grapple-hatch opening and the deep rumbling of the hook gimbals. Somewhere deep in the belly of the ship, immense mechanisms were swinging around, moving into position. The berg sat motionless in the calm sea.

Then the entire ship shivered as the first hook came shooting up into view. It hovered overhead, a tremendous taloned thing filling half the sky, black against the shining brightness of the air. Nakata hit the keys again, and the hook, having reached the apex of its curve, spun downward with slashing force, heading for the breast of the berg.

It hit and dug and held. The berg recoiled, quivered, rocked. The shower of loose ice came tumbling off the upper ledges. As the impact of the hooking was transmitted to the vast hidden mass of the berg undersea, the entire thing bowed forward a little farther than Carter had been expecting, making a nasty sucking noise against the water, and when it pulled back again, a geyser came spuming up about 20 meters.

Down by the bow, Nakata was making his I-got-you gesture at the berg, the middle finger rising high.

A cold wind was blowing from the berg now. It was like the exhalation of some huge wounded beast, an aroma of ancient times, a fossil-breath wind.

They moved on a little farther along the berg's flank.

"Hook two," Carter told him.

The berg was almost stable again now. Carter, watching from his viewing tower by the aft rail, waited for the rush of pleasure and relief that came from a successful claiming, but this time it wasn't there. All he felt was impatience, an eagerness to get all four hooks in and start chugging on back to the Golden Gate.

The second hook flew aloft, hovered, plunged, struck, bit.

A second time, the berg slammed the water, and a second time, the sea jumped and shook. Carter had just a moment to catch a glimpse of the other ship popping around like a floating cork and wondered if that ice tongue they found so cozy were going to break off and sink them. It would have been smarter of the Calamari Maru to anchor somewhere else. But to hell with them. They'd been warned.

The third hook was easier.

"Four," Carter called. One last time, a grappling iron flew through the air, whipping off at a steep angle to catch the far side of the berg over the top, and then they had it, the entire monstrous floating island of ice snaffled and trussed.

Toward sunset, Carter left Hitchcock in charge of the trawler and went over to the Calamari Maru in the sleek little silvery kayak that they used as the ship's boat. He took Rennett with him.

The stink of the other ship reached his nostrils long before he went scrambling up the gleaming woven-monofilament ladder that they had thrown over the side for him: a bitter, acrid reek, a miasma so dense that it was almost visible. Breathing it was something like inhaling all of Cleveland in a single snort. Carter wished he'd worn a facelung. But who expected to need one out at sea, where you were supposed to be able to breathe reasonably decent air?

The Calamari Maru didn't look too good, either. At one quick glance, he picked up a sense of general neglect and slovenliness: black stains on the deck, swirls of dust everywhere, some nasty rust-colored patches of ozone attack that needed work. The reek, though, came from the squids themselves.

The heart of the ship was a vast tank, a huge squid-peeling factory occupying the entire mid-deck. Carter had been on one once before, long ago, when he was a trainee. Samurai Industries ran dozens of them. He looked down into the tank and saw battalions of hefty squids swimming in herds, big-eyed pearly phantoms, scores of them shifting direction suddenly and simultaneously in their squiddy way. Glittering mechanical flails moved among them, seizing and slicing, cutting out the nerve tissue, flushing the edible remainder toward the meat-packing facility. The stench was astonishing. The entire thing was a tremendous processing machine. With the one-time farming heartland of North America and temperate Europe now worthless desert, and the world dependent on the thin, rocky soil of northern Canada and Siberia for its crops, harvesting the sea was essential. But the smell was awful. He fought to keep from gagging.

"You get used to it," said the woman who greeted him when he clambered aboard. "Five minutes, you won't notice."

"Let's hope so," he said. "I'm Captain Carter, and this is Rennett, maintenance/ops. Where's Kovalcik?"

"I'm Kovalcik," the woman said.

His eyes widened. She seemed to be amused by his reaction.

Kovalcik was rugged and sturdy-looking, more than average height, strong cheekbones, eyes set very far apart, expression very cool and controlled, but strain evident behind the control. She was wearing a sacklike jump suit of some coarse gray fabric. About 30, Carter guessed. Her hair was black and close-cropped and her skin was fair, strangely fair, hardly any trace of Screen showing. He saw signs of sun damage, signs of ozone, crackly, red splotches of burn. Two members of her crew stood behind her, also women, also jump-suited, also oddly fair-skinned. Their skin didn't look so good, either.

Kovalcik said, "We are very grateful you came. There is bad trouble on this ship." Her voice was flat. She had just a trace of a European accent, hard to place.

"We'll help out if we can," Carter told her.

He became aware now that they had carved a chunk out of his berg and grappled it up onto the deck, where it was melting into three big aluminum runoff tanks. It couldn't have been a millionth of the total berg mass, not a ten millionth, but seeing it gave him a quick little stab of proprietary fury and he felt a muscle flicker in his cheek. That reaction didn't go unnoticed, either. Kovalcik said quickly, "Yes, water is one of our problems. We have had to replenish our supply this way. There have been some equipment failures lately. You will come to the captain's cabin now? We must talk of what has happened, what must now be done."

She led him down the deck, with Rennett and the two crew women following along behind.

The Calamari Maru was pretty impressive. It was big and long and sleek, built somewhat along the lines of a squid itself, a jet-propulsion job that gobbled water into colossal compressors and squirted it out behind. That was one of the many low-fuel solutions to maritime transport problems that had been worked out for the sake of keeping CO_2 output down in these difficult times. Immense things like flying buttresses ran down the deck on both sides. These, Kovalcik explained, were squid lures, covered with bioluminescent photophores: You lowered them into the water and they gave off light that mimicked the glow of the squids' own bodies, and the slithery tentacular buggers came jetting in from vast distances, expecting a great jamboree and getting a net instead.

"Some butchering operation you got here," Carter said.

Kovalcik said a little curtly, "Meat is not all we produce. The squids we catch here have value as food, of course, but also we strip the nerve fibers, we take them back to the mainland, they are used in all kinds of biosensor applications. They are very large, those fibers, a hundred times as thick as ours. They are like single-cell computers. You have a thousand processors aboard your ship that use squid fiber, do you know? Follow me, please. This way."

They went down a ramp, along a narrow companionway. Carter heard thumpings and pingings in the walls. A bulkhead was dented and badly scratched. The lights down here were dimmer than they ought to be and the fixtures hummed ominously. There was a new odor now, a tang of something chemical, sweet but not a pleasing kind of sweet, more a burnt kind of sweet than anything else, cutting sharply across the boom of drums. Rennett shot him a somber glance. This ship was a mess, all right.

"Captain's cabin is here," Kovalcik said, pushing back a door hanging askew on its hinges. "We have drink first, yes?"

The size of the cabin amazed Carter after all those weeks bottled up in his little hole on the Tonopah Maru. It looked as big as a gymnasium. There was a table, a desk, shelving, a comfortable bunk, a sanitary unit, even an entertainment screen, everything nicely spread out with actual floor space you could move around in. The screen had been kicked in. Kovalcik took a flask of Peruvian brandy from a cabinet. Carter nodded and she poured three stiff ones. They drank in silence. The squid odor wasn't so bad in here, or else he was getting used to it, just as she'd said. But the air was rank and close despite the spaciousness of the cabin, thick, soupy stuff that was a struggle to breathe. Something's wrong with the ventilating system, too, Carter thought.

"You see the trouble we have," said Kovalcik.

"I see there's been trouble, yes."

"You don't see half. You should see command room, too. Here, have more brandy, then I take you there."

"Never mind the brandy," Carter said. "How about telling me what the hell's been going on aboard this ship?"

"First come see command room," Kovalcik said.

The command room was one level down from the captain's cabin. It was an absolute wreck.

The place was all but burned out. There were laser scars on every surface and gaping wounds in the structural fabric of the ceiling. Glittering strings of program cores were hanging out of data cabinets like broken necklaces, like spilled guts. Everywhere there were signs of some terrible struggle, some monstrous, insane civil war that had raged through the most delicate regions of the ship's mind centers.

"It is all ruined," Kovalcik said. "Nothing works anymore except the squid-processing programs, and as you see, those work magnificently, going on and on, the nets and flails and cutters and so forth. But everything else is damaged. Our water synthesizer, the ventilators, our navigational equipment, much more. We are making repairs, but it is very slow."

"I can imagine it would be. You had yourselves one hell of a party here, huh?"

"There was a great struggle. From deck to deck, from cabin to cabin. It became necessary to place Captain Kohlberg under restraint and he and some of the other officers resisted."

Carter blinked and caught his breath short at that. "What the fuck are you saying? That you had a *mutiny* aboard this ship?"

For a moment, the charged word hung between them like a whirling sword.

Then Kovalcik said, voice flat as ever, "When we had been at sea for a while, the captain became like a crazy man. It was the heat that got to him, the sun, maybe the air. He began to ask impossible things. He would not listen to reason. And so he had to be removed from command for the safety of all. There was a meeting and he was put under restraint. Some of his officers objected and they had to be put under restraint, too."

Son of a bitch, Carter thought, feeling a little sick. What have I walked into here?

"Sounds just like mutiny to me," Rennett said.

Carter shushed her. This had to be handled delicately. To Kovalcik he said, "They're still alive, the captain, the officers?"

"Yes. I can show them to you."

"That would be a good idea. But first maybe you ought to tell me some more about these grievances you had."

"That doesn't matter now, does it?"

"To me it does. I need to know what you think justifies removing a captain."

She began to look a little annoyed. "There were many things, some big, some small. Work schedules, crew pairings, the food allotment. Everything worse and worse for us each week. Like a tyrant, he was. A Caesar. Not at first, but gradually, the change in him. It was sun poisoning he had, the craziness that comes from too much heat on the brain. He was afraid to use very much Screen, you see, afraid that we would run out before the end of the voyage, so he rationed it very tightly, for himself, for us, too. That was one of our biggest troubles, the Screen." Kovalcik touched her cheeks, her forearms, her wrists, where the skin was pink and raw. "You see how I look? We are all like that. Kohlberg cut us to half ration, then half that. The sun began to eat us. The ozone. We had no protection, do you see? He was so frightened there would be no Screen later on that he let us use only a small amount every day, and we suffered, and so did he, and he got crazier as the sun worked on him, and there was less Screen all the time. He had it hidden, I think. We have not found it yet. We are still on quarter ration."

Carter tried to imagine what that was like, sailing around under the ferocious sky without body armor. The daily injections withheld, the unshielded skin of these people exposed to the full fury of the greenhouse climate. Could Kohlberg really have been so stupid, or so loony? But there was no getting around the raw pink patches on Kovalcik's skin.

"You'd like us to let you have a supply of Screen, is that it?" he asked uneasily.

"No. We would not expect that of you. Sooner or later, we will find where Kohlberg has hidden it."

"Then what is it you *do* want?"

"Come," Kovalcik said. "Now I show you the officers."

The mutineers had stashed their prisoners in the ship's infirmary, a stark, humid room far below deck with three double rows of bunks along the wall and some nonfunctioning medical mechs between them. Each of the bunks but one held a sweat-shiny man with a week's growth of beard. They were conscious, but not very. Their wrists were tied.

"It is very disagreeable for us, keeping them like this," Kolvacik said. "But what can we do? This is Captain Kohlberg." He was heavy-set, Teutonic-looking, groggy-eyed. "He is calm now, but only because we sedate him. We sedate all of them, fifty c.c.s of omnipax. But it is a threat to their health, the constant sedation. And in any case, the drugs, we are running short. Another few days and then we will have none, and it will be harder to keep them restrained, and if they break free, there will be war on this ship again."

"I'm not sure if we have any omnipax on board," Carter said. "Certainly not enough to do you much good for long."

"That is not what we are asking, either," said Kovalcik.

"What *are* you asking, then?"

"These five men, they threaten everybody's safety. They have forfeited the right to command. This I could show, with playbacks of the time of struggle on this ship. Take them."

"What?"

"Take them onto your ship. They must not stay here. These are crazy men. We must rid ourselves of them. We must be left to repair our ship in peace and do the work we are paid to do. It is a humanitarian thing, taking them. You are going back to San Francisco with the iceberg? Take them, these troublemakers. They will be no danger to you. They will be grateful for being rescued. But here they are like bombs that must sooner or later go off."

Carter looked at her as if she were a bomb that had already gone off. Rennett had simply turned away, covering what sounded like a burst of hysterical laughter by forcing a coughing fit.

That was all he needed, making himself an accomplice in this thing, obligingly picking up a bunch of officers pushed off their ship by mutineers. Kyocera-Merck men at that. Aid and succor to the great corporate enemy? The Samurai Industries agent in Frisco would really love it when he came steaming into port with five K-M men on board. He'd especially want to hear that Carter had done it for humanitarian reasons.

Besides, where the fuck were these men going to sleep? On deck between the spigots? Should he pitch a tent on the iceberg, maybe? What about feeding them, for Christ's sake? What about Screen? Everything was calibrated down to the last molecule.

"I don't think you understand our situation," Carter said carefully. "Aside from the legalities of the thing, we've got no space for extra personnel. We barely have enough for us."

"It would be just for a short while, no? A week or two?"

"I tell you we've got every millimeter allotted. If God Himself wanted to come on board as a passenger, we'd have a tough time figuring out where to put Him. You want technical help patching your ship back together, we can try to do that. We can even let you have some supplies. But taking five men aboard—"

Kovalcik's eyes began to look a little wild. She was breathing very hard now. "You must do this for us! You must! Otherwise —"

"Otherwise?" Carter prompted.

All he got from her was a bleak stare, no friendlier than the green-streaked ozone-crisp sky.

"*Hilfe*," Kohlberg muttered just then, stirring unexpectedly in his bunk.

"What was that?"

"It is delirium," said Kovalcik.

"*Hilfe. Hilfe. In Gottes Namen, hilfe!*" And then, in thickly accented English, the words painfully framed: "Help. She will kill us all."

"Delirium?" Carter said.

Kovalcik's eyes grew even chillier. Drawing an ultrasonic syringe from a cabinet in the wall, she slapped it against Kohlberg's arm. There was a small buzzing sound. Kohlberg subsided into sleep. Snuffling snores rose from his bunk. Kovalcik smiled. She seemed to be recovering her self-control. "He is a madman. You see what my skin is like. What his madness has done to me, has done to every one of us. If he got loose, if he put the voyage in jeopardy—yes, yes, we would kill him. We would kill them all. It would be only self-defense, you understand me? But it must not come to that." Her voice was icy. You could air-condition an entire city with that voice. "You were not here during the trouble. You do not know what we went through. We will not go through it again. Take these men from us, Captain."

She stepped back, folding her arms across her chest. The room was very quiet, suddenly, except for the pingings and thumpings from the ship's interior and an occasional snore out of Kohlberg. Kovalcik was completely calm again, the ferocity and iciness no longer visible. As though she were simply telling him, "This is the situation, the ball is now in your court, Captain Carter."

What a stinking, squalid mess, Carter thought.

But he was startled to find, when he looked behind the irritation he felt at having been dragged into this, a curious sadness where he would have expected anger to be. Despite everything, he found himself flooded with surprising compassion for Kovalcik, for Kohlberg, for all of them, for the whole fucking poisoned, heat-blighted world. Who had asked for any of this—the heavy green sky, the fiery air, the daily need for Screen, the million frantic improvisations that made continued life on earth possible? Not us. Our great-great-grandparents had, maybe, but not us. Only they're not here to know what it's like, and we are.

Then the moment passed. What the hell could he do? Did Kovalcik think he was Jesus Christ? He had no room for these people. He had no extra Screen or food. In any case, this was none of his business. And San Francisco was waiting for its iceberg. It was time to move along. Tell her anything, just get out of here.

"All right," he said. "I see your problem. I'm not entirely sure I can help out, but I'll do what I can. I'll check our supplies and let you know what we're able to do. OK?"

Hitchcock said, "What I think, Cap'n, we ought to just take hold of them. Nakata can put a couple of his spare hooks into them, and we'll tow them into Frisco along with the berg."

"Hold on," Carter said. "Are you out of your mind? I'm no fucking pirate."

"Who's talking about piracy? It's our obligation. We got to turn them in, man, is how I see it. They're mutineers."

"I'm not a policeman, either," Carter retorted. "They want to have a mutiny, let them goddamn go and mutiny. I have a job to do. I just want to get that berg moving east. Without hauling a shipload of crazies along. Don't even think I'm going to make some kind of civil arrest of them. Don't even consider it for an instant, Hitchcock."

Mildly, Hitchcock said, "You know, we used to take this sort of thing seriously, once upon a time. You know what I mean, man? We wouldn't just look the other way."

"You don't understand," Carter said. Hitchcock gave him a sharp, scornful look. "No. Listen to me," Carter snapped. "That ship's nothing but trouble. The woman who runs it, she's something you don't want to be very close to. We'd have to put her in chains if we tried to take her in, and taking her isn't as easy as you seem to think, either. There's five of us and I don't know how many of them. And that's a Kyocera-Merck ship there. Samurai isn't paying us to pull K-M's chestnuts out of the fire."

It was late morning now. The sun was getting close to noon height, and the sky was brighter than ever, fiercely hot, with some swirls of lavender and green far overhead, vagrant wisps of greenhouse garbage that must have drifted west from the noxious high-pressure air that sat perpetually over the mid-section of the United States. Carter imagined he could detect a whiff of methane in the breeze. Just across the way was the berg, shining like polished marble, shedding water hour by hour as the mounting heat worked it over. Back in San Francisco, they were brushing the dust out of the empty reservoirs. Time to be moving along, yes. Kovalcik and Kohlberg would have to work out their problems without him. He didn't feel good about that, but there were a lot of things he didn't feel good about, and he wasn't able to fix those, either.

"You said she's going to kill those five guys," Caskie said. The communications operator was small and slight, glossy black hair and lots of it, no bare scalp for her. "Does she mean it?"

Carter shrugged. "A bluff, most likely. She looks tough, but I'm not sure she's that tough."

"I don't agree," Rennett said. "She wants to get rid of those men in the worst way."

"You think?"

"I think that what they were doing anchored by the berg was getting ready to maroon them on it. Only we came along, and we're going to tow the berg away, and that screwed up the plan. So now she wants to give them to us instead. We don't take them, she'll just dump them over the side soon as we're gone."

"Even though we know the score?"

"She'll say they broke loose and jumped into the ship's boat and escaped, and she doesn't know where the hell they went. Who's to say otherwise?"

Carter stared gloomily. Yes, he thought, who's to say otherwise?

"The berg's melting while we screw around," Hitchcock said. "What'll it be, Cap'n? We sit here and discuss some more? Or we pull up and head for Frisco?"

"My vote's for taking them on board," said Nakata.

"I don't remember calling for a vote," Carter said. "We've got no room for five more hands. Not for anybody. We're packed as tight as we can possibly get. Living on this ship is like living in a rowboat, as it is." He was starting to feel rage rise in him. This business was getting too tangled: legal issues, humanitarian issues, a lot of messy stuff. The simple reality underneath it all was that he couldn't take on passengers, no matter what the reason.

And Hitchcock was right. The berg was losing water every minute. Even from here, bare eyes alone, he could see erosion going on, the dripping, the carving. The oscillations were picking up, the big icy thing rocking gently back and forth as its stability at water line got nibbled away. Later on, the oscillations wouldn't be so gentle. They had to get that berg sprayed with mirror dust and wrapped with a plastic skirt at the water line to slow down wave erosion and start moving. San Francisco was paying him to bring home an iceberg, not a handful of slush.

Rennett called. She had wandered up into the observation rack above them and was shading her eyes, looking across the water. "They've put out a boat, Cap'n."

"No," he said. "Son of a bitch!"

He grabbed for his 6 × 30 spyglass. A boat, sure enough, a hydrofoil dinghy. It looked full: three, four, five. He hit the switch for biosensor boost and the squid fiber in the spyglass went to work for him. The image blossomed, high resolution. Five men. He recognized Kohlberg sitting slumped in front.

"Shit," he said. "She's sending them over to us. Just dumping them on us."

"If we doubled up somehow—" Nakata began, smiling hopefully.

"One more word out of you and I'll double *you* up," said Carter. He turned to Hitchcock, who had one hand clamped meditatively over the lower half of his face, pushing his nose back and forth and scratching around in his thick white stubble. "Break out some lasers," Carter said. "Defensive use only. Just in case. Hitchcock, you and Rennett get out there in the kayak and escort those men back to the squid ship. If they aren't conscious, tow them over to it. If they are, and they don't want to go back, invite them very firmly to go back, and if they don't like the invitation, put a couple of holes through the side of their boat and get the hell back here fast. You understand me?"

Hitchcock nodded stonily. "Sure, man. Sure."

Carter watched the entire thing from the blister dome at the stern, wondering whether he were going to have a mutiny of his own on his hands now, too. But no. No. Hitchcock and Rennett kayaked out along the edge of the berg until they came up beside the dinghy from the Calamari Maru, and there was a brief discussion, very brief, Hitchcock doing the talking and Rennett holding a laser rifle in a casual but businesslike way. The five castoffs from the squid ship seemed more or less awake. They pointed and gestured and threw up their arms in despair. But Hitchcock kept talking and Rennett kept stroking the laser and the men in the dinghy looked more and more dejected by the moment. Then the discussion broke up and the kayak headed back toward the Tonopah Maru, and the men in the dinghy sat where they were, no doubt trying to figure out their next move.

Hitchcock said, coming on board, "This is bad business, man. That captain, he say the woman just took the ship away from him, on account of she wanted him to let them all have extra shots of Screen and he didn't give it. There wasn't enough to let her have so much, is what he said. I feel real bad, man."

"So do I," said Carter. "Believe me."

"I learn a long time ago," Hitchcock said, "when a man say, 'Believe me,' that's the one thing I shouldn't do."

"Fuck you," Carter said. "You think I *wanted* to strand them? But we have no choice. Let them go back to their own ship. She won't kill them. All they have to do is let her do what she wants to do and they'll come out of it OK. She can put them off on some island somewhere, Hawaii, maybe. But if they come with us, we'll be in deep shit all the way back to Frisco."

Hitchcock nodded. "Yeah. We may be in deep shit already."

"What you say?"

"Look at the berg," Hitchcock said. "At water line. It's getting real carved up."

Carter scooped up his glass and kicked in the biosensor boost. He scanned the berg. It didn't look good. The heat was working it over very diligently.

This was the hottest day since they'd entered these waters. The sun seemed to be getting bigger every minute. There was a nasty magnetic crackling coming out of the sky, as if the atmosphere itself were getting ionized as it baked. And the berg was starting to wobble. Carter saw the oscillations plainly, those horizontal grooves filling with water, the sea not so calm now as sky/ocean heat differentials began to build up and conflicting currents came slicing in.

"Son of a bitch," Carter said. "That settles it. We got to get moving right now."

There was still plenty to do. Carter gave the word and the mirror-dust spigots went into operation, cannoning shining clouds of powdered metal over the exposed surface of the berg, and probably all over the squid ship and the dinghy, too. It took half an hour to do the job. The squid ship was still roughening, the belly was lolloping around in a mean way. But Carter knew there was a gigantic base down there out of sight, enough to hold it steady until they could get under way, he hoped.

"Let's get the skirt on it now," he said.

A tricky procedure, nozzles at the ship's water line extruding a thermoplastic spray that would coat the berg just where it was most vulnerable to wave erosion. The hard part came in managing the extensions of the cables linking the hooks to the ship so they could maneuver around the berg. But Nakata was an ace at that. They pulled up anchor and started around the far side. The mirror-dusted berg was dazzling, a tremendous mountain of white light.

"I don't like that wobble," Hitchcock said.

"Won't matter a damn once we're under way," said Carter.

The heat was like a hammer now, pounding the dark, cool surface of the water, mixing up the thermal layers, stirring up the currents, getting everything churned around. They had waited just a little too long to get started. The berg, badly undercut, was doing a big sway to windward, bowing like one of those round-bottomed Japanese dolls, then swaying back again. God only knew what kind of sea action the squid ship was getting, but Carter couldn't see it from this side of the berg. He kept on moving, circling the berg to the full extension of the hook cables, then circling back the way he'd come.

When they got around to leeward again, he saw what kind of sea action the squid ship had been getting. It was swamped. The ice tongue it had been anchored next to had come rising up out of the sea and kicked it like a giant foot.

"Jesus Christ," Hitchcock murmured, standing beside him. "Will you look at that. The damn fools just sat there all the time."

The Calamari Maru was shipping water like crazy and starting to go down. The sea was boiling with an armada of newly liberated squid, swiftly propelling themselves in all directions, heading anywhere else at top speed. Three dinghies were bobbing around in the water in the shadow of the berg.

"Will you look at that," Hitchcock said again.

"Start the engines," Carter told him. "Let's get the fuck out of here."

Hitchcock stared at him, disbelievingly.

"You mean that, Cap'n? You really mean that?"

"I goddamn well do."

"Shit," said Hitchcock. "This fucking lousy world."

"Go on. Get 'em started."

"You actually going to leave three boats full of people from a sinking ship sitting out there in the water?"

"Yeah. You got it. Now start the engines, will you?"

"That's too much," Hitchcock said softly, shaking his head in a big slow swing. "Too goddamn much."

He made a sound like a wounded buffalo and took two or three shambling steps toward Carter, his arms dangling loosely, his hand half cupped. Hitchcock's eyes were slitted and his face looked oddly puffy. He loomed above Carter, wheezing and muttering, a dark, massive slab of a man. Half as big as the iceberg out there was how he looked just then.

Oh, shit, Carter thought. Here it comes. My very own mutiny, right now.

Hitchcock rumbled and muttered and closed his hands into fists. Exasperation tinged with fear swept through Carter and he brought his arm up without even stopping to think, hitting Hitchcock hard, a short fast jab in the mouth that rocked the older man's head back sharply and sent him reeling against the rail. Hitchcock slammed into it and bounced. For a moment, it looked as if he'd fall, but he managed to steady himself. A kind of sobbing sound, but not quite a sob, more of a grunt, came from him. A bright dribble of blood sprouted on his white-stubbled chin.

For a moment, Hitchcock seemed dazed. Then his eyes came back into focus and he looked at Carter in amazement.

"I wasn't going to hit you, Cap'n," he said, blinking hard. There was a soft, stunned quality to his voice. "Nobody ever hits a cap'n, not ever. Not *ever*. You know that, Cap'n."

"I told you to start the engines."

"You hit me, Cap'n. What the hell you hit me for?"

"You started to come at me, didn't you?" Carter said.

Hitchcock's shining bloodshot eyes were immense in his Screen-blackened face. "You think I was *coming* at you? Oh, Cap'n! Oh, Jesus, Cap'n. Jesus!" He shook his head and wiped at the blood. Carter saw that he was bleeding, too, at the knuckle, where he'd hit a tooth. Hitchcock continued to stare at him, the way you might stare at a dinosaur that had just stepped out of the forest. Then his look of astonishment softened into something else—sadness, maybe. Or was it pity? Pity would be even worse, Carter thought. A whole lot worse.

"Cap'n—" Hitchcock began, his voice hoarse and thick.

"Don't say it. Just go and get the engines started."

"Yeah," he said. "Yeah, man."

He went slouching off, rubbing at his lip.

"Caskie's picking up an autobuoy S O S," Rennett called from somewhere updeck.

"Nix," Carter yelled back furiously. "We can't do it."

"What?"

"There's no fucking room for them," Carter said. His voice was as sharp as an icicle. "Nix. Nix."

He lifted his spyglass again and took another look toward the oncoming dinghies. Chugging along hard, they were, but having heavy weather of it in the turbulent water. He looked quickly away before he could make out faces. The berg, shining like fire, was still oscillating. He thought of the hot winds sweeping across the continent to the east, sweeping all around the belly of the world, the dry, rainless winds that forever sucked up what little moisture could still be found. It was almost a shame to have to go back there. Like returning to hell after a little holiday at sea, is how it felt. It was worst in the middle latitudes, the temperate zone, once so fertile. Rain almost never fell at all there now. The dying forests, the new grasslands taking over, deserts where even the grass couldn't make it, the polar ice packs crumbling, the lowlands drowning everywhere, dead buildings sticking up out of the sea, vines sprouting on freeways, the alligators moving northward. This fucking lousy world, Hitchcock had said. Yeah. This berg here, this oversized ice cube, how many days' water supply would that be for San Francisco? Ten? Fifteen?

He turned. They were staring at him—Nakata, Rennett, Caskie, everybody but Hitchcock, who was on the bridge setting up the engine combination.

"This never happened," Carter told them. "None of this. We never saw anybody else out here. Not anybody. You got that? *This never happened.*"

They nodded, one by one.

There was a quick shiver down below as the tiny sun in the engine room, the little fusion sphere, came to full power. With a groan, the engine kicked in at high. The ship started to move away, out of the zone of dark water, toward the bluer sea just ahead. Off they went, pulling eastward as fast as they could, trying to make time ahead of the melt rate. It was afternoon now. Behind them, the other sun, the real one, lighted up the sky with screaming fury as it headed off into the west. That was good, to have the sun going one way as you were going the other.

Carter didn't look back. What for? So you can beat yourself up about something you couldn't help?

His knuckle was stinging where he had split it punching Hitchcock. He rubbed it in a distant, detached way, as if it were someone else's hand. Think east, he told himself. You're towing 2000 kilotons of million-year-old frozen water to thirsty San Francisco. Think good thoughts. Think about your bonus. Think about your next promotion. No sense looking back. You look back, all you do is hurt your eyes.

LEWIS SHINER
White City

▼

Lewis Shiner is widely regarded as one of the most exciting new writers of the eighties. His stories have appeared in *The Magazine of Fantasy and Science Fiction, Omni, Oui, Shayol, Isaac Asimov's Science Fiction Magazine, The Twilight Zone Magazine,* the *Wild Card* series, and elsewhere. His books include *Frontera* and the critically acclaimed *Deserted Cities of the Heart.* His most recent book is a mainstream novel, *Slam,* and recently released is an anthology of anti-war alternatives he edited, *When the Music's Over.* His story "Twilight Time" was in our Second Annual Collection; his "The War at Home" was in our Third Annual Collection; his "Jeff Beck" was in our Fourth Annual Collection, and his "Love in Vain" was in our Sixth Annual Collection. Shiner lives in Austin, Texas.

Here he gives us a sly and compelling look at what a certain eccentric nineteenth-century inventor *might* have been able to accomplish, if he'd had the chance. . . .

White City

LEWIS SHINER

Tesla lifts the piece of sirloin to his lips. Its volume is approximately .25 cubic inches, or .02777 of the entire steak. As he chews, he notices a waterspot on the back of his fork. He takes a fresh napkin from the stack at his left elbow and scrubs the fork vigorously.

He is sitting at a private table in the refreshment stand at the West end of the Court of Honor. He looks out onto the Chicago World's Fair and Columbian Exposition. It is October of 1893. The sun is long gone and the reflections of Tesla's electric lights sparkle on the surface of the Main Basin, turning the spray from the fountain into glittering jewels. At the far end of the Basin stands the olive-wreathed Statue of the Republic in flowing robes. On all sides the White City lies in pristine elegance, testimony to the glorious architecture of ancient Greece and Rome. Its chilly streets are populated by mustached men in topcoats and sturdy women in woolen shawls.

The time is 9:45. At midnight Nikola Tesla will produce his greatest miracle. The number twelve seems auspicious. It is important to him, for reasons he cannot understand, that it is divisible by three.

Anne Morgan, daughter of financier J. Pierpont Morgan, stands at a little distance from his table. Though still in finishing school she is tall, self-possessed, strikingly attractive. She is reluctant to disturb Tesla, knowing he prefers to dine alone. Still she is drawn to him irresistibly. He is rake thin and handsome as the devil himself, with steel gray eyes that pierce through to her soul.

"Mr. Tesla," she says, "I pray I am not disturbing you."

Tesla looks up, smiles gently. "Miss Morgan." He begins to rise.

518

"Please, do not get up. I was merely afraid I would miss you. I had hoped we might walk together after you finished here."

"I would be delighted."

"I shall await you there, by the Basin."

She withdraws. Trailing a gloved hand along the balustrade, she tries to avoid the drunken crowds which swarm the Exposition Grounds. Tomorrow the Fair will close and pass into history. Already there are arguments as to what is to become of these splendid buildings. There is neither money to maintain them nor desire to demolish them. Chicago's Mayor, Carter Harrison, worries that they will end up filthy and vandalized, providing shelter for the hundreds of poor who will no longer have jobs when the Fair ends.

Her thoughts turn back to Tesla. She finds herself inordinately taken with him. At least part of the attraction is the mystery of his personal life. At age thirty-seven he has never married nor been engaged. She has heard rumors that his tastes might be, to put it delicately, Greek in nature. There is no evidence to support this gossip and she does not credit it. Rather it seems likely that no one has yet been willing to indulge the inventor's many idiosyncrasies.

She absently touches her bare left earlobe. She no longer wears the pearl earrings that so offended him on their first meeting. She flushes at the memory, and at that point Tesla appears.

"Shall we walk?" he asks.

She nods and matches his stride, careful not to take his arm. Tesla is not comfortable with personal contact.

To their left is the Hall of Agriculture. She has heard that its most popular attraction is an eleven-ton cheese from Ontario. Like so many other visitors to the Fair, she has not actually visited any of the exhibits. They seem pedestrian compared to the purity and classical lines of the buildings which house them. The fragrance of fresh roses drifts out through the open doors, and for a moment she is lost in a reverie of her native New York in the spring.

As they pass the end of the hall they are in darkness for a few moments. Tesla seems to shudder. He has been silent and intent, as if compulsively counting his steps. It would not surprise her if this were actually the case.

"Is anything wrong?" she asks.

"No," Tesla says. "It's nothing."

In fact the darkness is full of lurking nightmares for Tesla. Just now he was five years old again, watching his older brother Daniel fall to his death. Years of guilty self-examination have not made the scene clearer. They stood together at the top of the cellar stairs, and then Daniel fell into the darkness. Did he fall? Did Nikola, in a moment of childish rage, push him?

All his life he has feared the dark. His father took his candles away, so little Nikola made his own. Now the full-grown Tesla has brought electric light to the White City, carried by safe, inexpensive alternating current. It is only the beginning.

They round the East end of the Court of Honor. At the Music Hall, the Imperial Band of Austria plays melodies from Wagner. Anne Morgan shivers in the evening chill. "Look at the moon," she says. "Isn't it romantic?"

Tesla's smile seems condescending. "I have never understood the romantic impulse. We humans are meat machines, and nothing more."

"That is hardly a pleasant image."

"I do not mean to be offensive, only accurate. That is the aim of science, after all."

"Yes, of course," Anne Morgan says. "Science." There seems no way to reach him, no chink in his cool exterior. This is where the others gave up, she thinks. I will prove stronger than all of them. In her short, privileged existence, she has always obtained what she wants. "I wish I knew more about it."

"Science is a pure, white light," Tesla says. "It shines evenly on all things, and reveals their particular truths. It banishes uncertainty, and opinion, and contradiction. Through it we master the world."

They have circled back to the West, and to their right is the Liberal Arts Building. She has heard that it contains so much painting and sculpture that one can only wander helplessly through it. To attempt to seek out a single artist, or to look for the French Impressionists, of whom she has been hearing so much, would be sheer futility.

Under Tesla's electric lights, the polished facade of the building sparkles. For a moment, looking down the impossibly long line of perfect Corinthian columns, she feels what Tesla feels: the triumph of man over nature, the will to conquer and shape and control. Then the night breeze brings her the scent of roses from across the Basin and the feeling passes.

They enter the Electricity Building together and stand in the center, underneath the great dome. This is the site of the Westinghouse exhibit, a huge curtained archway resting upon a metal platform. Beyond the arch are two huge Tesla coils, the largest ever built. At the peak of the arch is a tablet inscribed with the words: WESTINGHOUSE ELECTRIC & MANUFAC-TURING CO./TESLA POLYPHASE SYSTEM.

Tesla's mood is triumphant. Edison, his chief rival, has been proven wrong. Alternating current will be the choice of the future. The Westinghouse Company has this week been awarded the contract to build the first two generators at Niagara Falls. Tesla cannot forgive Edison's hiring of Menlo Park street urchins to kidnap pets, which he then electrocuted with alternating current—"Westinghoused" them, as he called it. But Edison's petty, lunatic attempts to discredit the polyphase system have failed, and he stands revealed as an old, bitter, and unimaginative man.

Edison has lost, and history will soon forget him.

George Westinghouse himself, Tesla's patron, is here tonight. So are J.P. Morgan, Anne's father, and William K. Vanderbilt and Mayor Harrison. Here also are Tesla's friends Robert and Katherine Johnson, and Samuel Clemens, who insists everyone call him by his pen name.

It is nearly midnight.

Tesla steps lightly onto the platform. He snaps his fingers and gas-filled tubes burst into pure white light. Tesla has fashioned them to spell out the names of several of the celebrities present, as well as the names of his favorite Serbian poets. He holds up his hands to the awed and expectant crowd. "Gentlemen and Ladies. I have no wish to bore you with speeches. I have asked you here to witness a demonstration of the power of electricity."

He continues to talk, his voice rising to a high pitch in his excitement. He produces several wireless lamps and places them around the stage. He points out that their illumination is undiminished, despite their distance from the broadcast power source. "Note how the gas at low pressure exhibits extremely high conductivity. This gas is little different from that in the upper reaches of our atmosphere."

He concludes with a few fireballs and pinwheels of light. As the applause gradually subsides he holds up his hands once again. "These are little more than parlor tricks. Tonight I wish to say thank you, in a dramatic and visible way, to all of you who have supported me through your patronage, through your kindness, through your friendship. This is my gift to you, and to all of mankind."

He opens a panel in the front of the arch. A massive knife switch is revealed. Tesla makes a short bow and then throws the switch.

The air crackles with ozone. Electricity roars through Tesla's body. His hair stands on end and flames dance at the tips of his fingers. Electricity is his God, his best friend, his only lover. It is clean, pure, absolute. It arcs through him and invisibly into the sky. Tesla alone can see it. To him it is blinding white, the color he sees when inspiration, fear, or elation strikes him.

The coils draw colossal amounts of power. All across the great hall, all over the White City, lights flicker and dim. Anne Morgan cries out in shock and fear.

Through the vaulted windows overhead the sky itself begins to glow.

Something sparks and hisses and the machine winds down. The air reeks of melted copper and glass and rubber. It makes no difference. The miracle is complete.

Tesla steps down from the platform. His friends edge away from him, involuntarily. Tesla smiles like a wise father. "If you will follow me, I will show you what man has wrought."

Already there are screams from outside. Tesla walks quickly to the doors and throws them open.

Anne Morgan is one of the first to follow him out. She cannot help but fear him, despite her attraction, despite all her best intentions. All around her she sees fairgoers with their necks craned upward, or their eyes hidden in fear. She turns her own gaze to the heavens and lets out a short, startled cry.

The sky is on fire. Or rather, it burns the way the filaments burn in one of Tesla's electric lamps. It has become a sheet of glowing white. After a few seconds the glare hurts her eyes and she must look away.

It is midnight, and the Court of Honor is lit as if by the noonday sun. She is close enough to hear Tesla speak a single, whispered word: "Magnificent."

Westinghouse comes forward nervously. "This is quite spectacular," he says, "but hadn't you best, er, turn it off?"

Tesla shakes his head. Pride shines from his face. "You do not seem to understand. The atmosphere itself, some 35,000 feet up, has become an electrical conductor. I call it my 'terrestrial night light.' The charge is permanent. I have banished night from the world for all time."

"For all time?" Westinghouse stammers.

Anne Morgan slumps against a column, feels the cold marble against her back. Night, banished? The stars, gone forever? "You're mad," she says to Tesla. "What have you done?"

Tesla turns away. The reaction is not what he expected. Where is their gratitude? He has turned their entire world into a White City, a city in which crime and fear and nightmares are no longer possible. Yet men point at him, shouting curses, and women weep openly.

He pushes past them, toward the train station. Meat machines, he thinks. They are so used to their inefficient cycles of night and day. But they will learn.

He boards a train for New York and secures a private compartment. As he drives on into the white night, his window remains brilliantly lighted.

In the light there is truth. In the light there is peace. In the light he will be able, at last, to sleep.

PAT MURPHY

Love and Sex Among the Invertebrates

▼

Here's a strange and troubling little story that dares to ask that burning question, Is there sex after life?

Pat Murphy lives in San Francisco, where she works for a science museum, the Exploratorium. Her elegant and incisive stories appeared throughout the decade of the 1980s in *Isaac Asimov's Science Fiction Magazine, Elsewhere, Amazing, Universe, Shadows, Chrysalis*, and other places. One of them, the classic "Rachel in Love," one of the most popular stories of the decade, won a Nebula Award in 1988. Murphy's first novel, *The Shadow Hunter*, appeared in 1982, to no particular notice, but her second novel, *The Falling Woman*, won her a second Nebula Award in 1988, and was one of the most critically acclaimed novels of the late '80s. Her third novel, *The City, Not Long After*, has just appeared, as has a collection of her short fiction, *Points of Departure*, and she is at work on another novel. Her story "In the Islands" was in our First Annual Collection, and "Rachel in Love" was in our Fifth Annual Collection.

▼

Love and Sex Among the Invertebrates

PAT MURPHY

This is not science. This has nothing to do with science. Yesterday, when the bombs fell and the world ended, I gave up scientific thinking. At this distance from the blast site of the bomb that took out San Jose, I figure I received a medium-size dose of radiation. Not enough for instant death, but too much for survival. I have only a few days left, and I've decided to spend this time constructing the future. Someone must do it.

It's what I was trained for, really. My undergraduate studies were in biology—structural anatomy, the construction of body and bone. My graduate studies were in engineering. For the past five years, I have been designing and constructing robots for use in industrial processing. The need for such industrial creations is over now. But it seems a pity to waste the equipment and materials that remain in the lab that my colleagues have abandoned.

I will put robots together and make them work. But I will not try to understand them. I will not take them apart and consider their inner workings and poke and pry and analyze. The time for science is over.

The pseudoscorpion, Lasiochernes pilosus, is a secretive scorpionlike insect that makes its home in the nests of moles. Before pseudoscorpions mate, they dance—a private underground minuet—observed only by moles and voyeuristic entomologists. When a male finds a receptive female, he grasps her claws in his and pulls her toward him. If she resists, he circles, clinging to her claws and pulling her after him, refusing to take no for an answer. He tries again, stepping forward and pulling the female toward him with trem-

bling claws. If she continues to resists, he steps back and continues the dance: circling, pausing to tug on his reluctant partner, then circling again.

After an hour or more of dancing, the female inevitably succumbs, convinced by the dance steps that her companion's species matches her own. The male deposits a packet of sperm on the ground that has been cleared of debris by their dancing feet. His claws quiver as he draws her forward, positioning her over the package of sperm. Willing at last, she presses her genital pore to the ground and takes the sperm into her body.

Biology texts note that the male scorpion's claws tremble as he dances, but they do not say why. They do not speculate on his emotions, his motives, his desires. That would not be scientific.

I theorize that the male pseudoscorpion is eager. Among the everyday aromas of mole shit and rotting vegetation, he smells the female, and the perfume of her fills him with lust. But he is fearful and confused: a solitary insect, unaccustomed to socializing, he is disturbed by the presence of another of his kind. He is caught by conflicting emotions: his all-encompassing need, his fear, and the strangeness of the social situation.

I have given up the pretense of science. I speculate about the motives of the pseudoscorpion, the conflict and desire embodied in his dance.

I put the penis on my first robot as a kind of joke, a private joke, a joke about evolution. I suppose I don't really need to say it was a private joke— all my jokes are private now. I am the last one left, near as I can tell. My colleagues fled—to find their families, to seek refuge in the hills, to spend their last days running around, here and there. I don't expect to see anyone else around anytime soon. And if I do, they probably won't be interested in my jokes. I'm sure that most people think the time for joking is past. They don't see that the bomb and the war are the biggest jokes of all. Death is the biggest joke. Evolution is the biggest joke.

I remember learning about Darwin's theory of evolution in high school biology. Even back then, I thought it was kind of strange, the way people talked about it. The teacher presented evolution as a *fait accompli*, over and done with. She muddled her way through the complex speculations regarding human evolution, talking about *Ramapithecus, Australopithecus, Homo erectus, Homo sapiens,* and *Homo sapiens neanderthalensis.* At *Homo sapiens* she stopped, and that was it. The way the teacher looked at the situation, we were the last word, the top of the heap, the end of the line.

I'm sure the dinosaurs thought the same, if they thought at all. How could anything get better than armor plating and a spiked tail. Who could ask for more?

Thinking about the dinosaurs, I build my first creation on a reptilian model, a lizardlike creature constructed from bits and pieces that I scavenge from the industrial prototypes that fill the lab and the storeroom. I give my creature a stocky body, as long as I am tall; four legs, extending to the side of the body then bending at the knee to reach the ground; a tail as long as the body, spiked with decorative metal studs; a crocodilian mouth with great curving teeth.

The mouth is only for decoration and protection; this creature will not eat. I equip him with an array of solar panels, fixed to a sail-like crest on his back. The warmth of sunlight will cause the creature to extend his sail and gather electrical energy to recharge his batteries. In the cool of the night, he will fold his sail close to his back, becoming sleek and streamlined.

I decorate my creature with stuff from around the lab. From the trash beside the soda machine, I salvage aluminum cans. I cut them into a colorful fringe that I attach beneath the creature's chin, like the dewlap of an iguana. When I am done, the words on the soda cans have been sliced to nonsense: Coke, Fanta, Sprite, and Dr. Pepper mingle in a collision of bright colors. At the very end, when the rest of the creature is complete and functional, I make a cock of copper tubing and pipe fittings. It dangles beneath his belly, copper bright and obscene looking. Around the bright copper, I weave a rat's nest of my own hair, which is falling out by the handful. I like the look of that: bright copper peeking from a clump of wiry black curls.

Sometimes, the sickness overwhelms me. I spend part of one day in the ladies' room off the lab, lying on the cool tile floor and rousing myself only to vomit into the toilet. The sickness is nothing that I didn't expect. I'm dying, after all. I lie on the floor and think about the peculiarities of biology.

For the male spider, mating is a dangerous process. This is especially true in the spider species that weave intricate orb-shaped webs, the kind that catch the morning dew and sparkle so nicely for nature photographers. In these species, the female is larger than the male. She is, I must confess, rather a bitch; she'll attack anything that touches her web.

At mating time, the male proceeds cautiously. He lingers at the edge of the web, gently tugging on a thread of spider silk to get her attention. He plucks in a very specific rhythm, signaling to his would-be lover, whispering softly with his tugs: "I love you. I love you."

After a time, he believes that she has received his message. He feels confident that he has been understood. Still proceeding with caution, he attaches a mating line to the female's web. He plucks the mating line to encourage the female to move onto it. "Only you, baby," he signals. "You are the only one."

She climbs onto the mating line—fierce and passionate, but temporarily soothed by his promises. In that moment, he rushes to her, delivers his sperm, then quickly, before she can change her mind, takes a hike. A dangerous business, making love.

Before the world went away, I was a cautious person. I took great care in my choice of friends. I fled at the first sign of a misunderstanding. At the time, it seemed the right course.

I was a smart woman, a dangerous mate. (Odd—I find myself writing and thinking of myself in the past tense. So close to death that I consider myself already dead.) Men would approach with caution, delicately signaling from a distance: "I'm interested. Are you?" I didn't respond. I didn't really know how.

An only child, I was always wary of others. My mother and I lived together. When I was just a child, my father had left to pick up a pack of cigarettes and never returned. My mother, protective and cautious by nature, warned me that men could not be trusted. People could not be trusted. She could trust me and I could trust her, and that was all.

When I was in college, my mother died of cancer. She had known of the tumor for more than a year; she had endured surgery and chemotherapy, while writing me cheery letters about her gardening. Her minister told me that my mother was a saint—she hadn't told me because she hadn't wanted to disturb my studies. I realized then that she had been wrong. I couldn't really trust her after all.

I think perhaps I missed some narrow window of opportunity. If, at some point along the way, I had had a friend or a lover who had made the effort to coax me from hiding, I could have been a different person. But it never happened. In high school, I sought the safety of my books. In college, I studied alone on Friday nights. By the time I reached graduate school, I was, like the pseudoscorpion, accustomed to a solitary life.

I work alone in the laboratory, building the female. She is larger than the male. Her teeth are longer and more numerous. I am welding the hip joints into place when my mother comes to visit me in the laboratory.

"Katie," she says, "why didn't you ever fall in love? Why didn't you ever have children?"

I keep on welding, despite the trembling of my hands. I know she isn't there. Delirium is one symptom of radiation poisoning. But she keeps watching me as I work.

"You're not really here," I tell her, and realize immediately that talking to her is a mistake. I have acknowledged her presence and given her more power.

"Answer my questions, Katie," she says. "Why didn't you?"

I do not answer. I am busy and it will take too long to tell her about betrayal, to explain the confusion of a solitary insect confronted with a social situation, to describe the balance between fear and love. I ignore her just as I ignore the trembling of my hands and the pain in my belly, and I keep on working. Eventually, she goes away.

I use the rest of the soda cans to give the female brightly colored scales: Coca-Cola red, Sprite green, Fanta orange. From soda cans, I make an oviduct, lined with metal. It is just large enough to accommodate the male's cock.

The male bowerbird attracts a mate by constructing a sort of art piece. From sticks and grasses, he builds two close-set parallel walls that join together to make an arch. He decorates this structure and the area around it with gaudy trinkets: bits of bone, green leaves, flowers, bright stones, and feathers cast off by gaudier birds. In areas where people have left their trash, he uses bottle caps and coins and fragments of broken glass.

He sits in his bower and sings, proclaiming his love for any and all females in the vicinity. At last, a female admires his bower, accepts his invitation, and they mate.

The bowerbird uses discrimination in decorating his bower. He chooses his trinkets with care—selecting a bit of glass for its glitter, a shiny leaf for its natural elegance, a cobalt-blue feather for a touch of color. What does he think about as he builds and decorates? What passes through his mind as he sits and sings, advertising his availability to the world?

I have released the male and I am working on the female when I hear rattling and crashing outside the building. Something is happening in the alley between the laboratory and the nearby office building. I go down to investigate. From the mouth of the alley, I peer inside, and the male creature runs at me, startling me so that I step back. He shakes his head and rattles his teeth threateningly.

I retreat to the far side of the street and watch him from there. He ventures from the alley, scuttling along the street, then pauses by a BMW that is parked at the curb. I hear his claws rattling against metal. A hubcap clangs as it hits the pavement. The creature carries the shiny piece of metal to the mouth of the alley and then returns for the other three, removing them one by one. When I move, he rushes toward the alley, blocking any attempt to invade his territory. When I stand still, he returns to his work, collecting the hubcaps, carrying them to the alley, and arranging them so that they catch the light of the sun.

As I watch, he scavenges in the gutter and collects things he finds appealing: a beer bottle, some colorful plastic wrappers from candy bars, a length of bright yellow plastic rope. He takes each find and disappears into the alley with it.

I wait, watching. When he has exhausted the gutter near the mouth of the alley, he ventures around the corner and I make my move, running to the alley entrance and looking inside. The alley floor is covered with colored bits of paper and plastic; I can see wrappers from candy bars and paper bags from Burger King and McDonald's. The yellow plastic rope is tied to a pipe running up one wall and a protruding hook on the other. Dangling from it, like clean clothes on the clothesline, are colorful pieces of fabric: a burgundy-colored bath towel, a paisley print bedspread, a blue satin bedsheet.

I see all this in a glance. Before I can examine the bower further, I hear the rattle of claws on pavement. The creature is running at me, furious at my intrusion. I turn and flee into the laboratory, slamming the door behind me. But once I am away from the alley, the creature does not pursue me.

From the second-story window, I watch him return to the alley and I suspect that he is checking to see if I have tampered with anything. After a time, he reappears in the alley mouth and crouches there, the sunlight glittering on his metal carapace.

In the laboratory, I build the future. Oh, maybe not, but there's no one here to contradict me, so I will say that it is so. I complete the female and release her.

The sickness takes over then. While I still have the strength, I drag a cot from a back room and position it by the window, where I can look out and watch my creations.

What is it that I want from them? I don't know exactly.

I want to know that I have left something behind. I want to be sure that the world does not end with me. I want the feeling, the understanding, the certainty that the world will go on.

I wonder if the dying dinosaurs were glad to see the mammals, tiny ratlike creatures that rustled secretively in the underbrush.

When I was in seventh grade, all the girls had to watch a special presentation during gym class one spring afternoon. We dressed in our gym clothes, then sat in the auditorium and watched a film called *Becoming a Woman*. The film talked about puberty and menstruation. The accompanying pictures showed the outline of a young girl. As the film progressed, she changed into a woman, developing breasts. The animation showed her uterus as it grew a lining, then shed it, then grew another. I remember watching with awe as the pictures showed the ovaries releasing an egg that united with a sperm, and then lodged in the uterus and grew into a baby.

The film must have delicately skirted any discussion of the source of the sperm, because I remember asking my mother where the sperm came from and how it got inside the woman. The question made her very uncomfortable. She muttered something about a man and woman being in love—as if love were somehow all that was needed for the sperm to find its way into the woman's body.

After that discussion, it seems to me that I was always a little confused about love and sex—even after I learned about the mechanics of sex and what goes where. The penis slips neatly into the vagina—but where does the love come in? Where does biology leave off and the higher emotions begin?

Does the female pseudoscorpion love the male when their dance is done? Does the male spider love his mate as he scurries away, running for his life? Is there love among the bowerbirds as they copulate in their bower? The textbooks fail to say. I speculate, but I have no way to get the answers.

My creatures engage in a long, slow courtship. I am getting sicker. Sometimes, my mother comes to ask me questions that I will not answer. Sometimes, men sit by my bed—but they are less real than my mother. These are men I cared about—men I thought I might love, though I never got beyond the thought. Through their translucent bodies, I can see the laboratory walls. They never were real, I think now.

Sometimes, in my delirium, I remember things. A dance back at college; I was slow-dancing, with someone's body pressed close to mine. The room was hot and stuffy and we went outside for some air. I remember he kissed me, while one hand stroked my breast and the other fumbled with the buttons of my blouse. I kept wondering if this was love—this fumbling in the shadows.

In my delirium, things change. I remember dancing in a circle with someone's hands clasping mine. My feet ache, and I try to stop, but my partner pulls me along, refusing to release me. My feet move instinctively in time with my partner's, though there is no music to help us keep the beat. The air smells of dampness and mold; I have lived my life underground and I am accustomed to these smells.

Is this love?

I spend my days lying by the window, watching through the dirty glass. From the mouth of the alley, he calls to her. I did not give him a voice, but he calls in his own way, rubbing his two front legs together so that metal rasps against metal, creaking like a cricket the size of a Buick.

She strolls past the alley mouth, ignoring him as he charges toward her, rattling his teeth. He backs away, as if inviting her to follow. She walks by. But then, a moment later, she strolls past again and the scene repeats itself. I understand that she is not really oblivious to his attention. She is simply taking her time, considering her situation. The male intensifies his efforts, tossing his head as he backs away, doing his best to call attention to the fine home he has created.

I listen to them at night. I cannot see them—the electricity failed two days ago and the streetlights are out. So I listen in the darkness, imagining. Metal legs rub together to make a high creaking noise. The sail on the male's back rattles as he unfolds it, then folds it, then unfolds it again, in what must be a sexual display. I hear a spiked tail rasping over a spiny back in a kind of caress. Teeth chatter against metal—love bites, perhaps. (The lion bites the lioness on the neck when they mate, an act of aggression that she accepts as affection.) Claws scrape against metal hide, clatter over metal scales. This, I think, is love. My creatures understand love.

I imagine a cock made of copper tubing and pipe fittings sliding into a canal lined with sheet metal from a soda can. I hear metal sliding over metal. And then my imagination fails. My construction made no provision for the stuff of reproduction: the sperm, the egg. Science failed me there. That part is up to the creatures themselves.

My body is giving out on me. I do not sleep at night; pain keeps me awake. I hurt everywhere, in my belly, in my breasts, in my bones. I have given up food. When I eat, the pains increase for a while, and then I vomit. I cannot keep anything down, and so I have stopped trying.

When the morning light comes, it is gray, filtering through the haze that covers the sky. I stare out the window, but I can't see the male. He has abandoned his post at the mouth of the alley. I watch for an hour or so, but the female does not stroll by. Have they finished with each other?

I watch from my bed for a few hours, the blanket wrapped around my shoulders. Sometimes, fever comes and I soak the blanket with my sweat. Sometimes, chills come, and I shiver under the blankets. Still, there is no movement in the alley.

It takes me more than an hour to make my way down the stairs. I can't trust my legs to support me, so I crawl on my knees, making my way across the room like a baby too young to stand upright. I carry the blanket with me, wrapped around my shoulders like a cape. At the top of the stairs, I rest, then I go down slowly, one step at a time.

The alley is deserted. The array of hubcaps glitters in the dim sunlight. The litter of bright papers looks forlorn and abandoned. I step cautiously into the entrance. If the male were to rush me now, I would not be able to run away. I have used all my reserves to travel this far.

The alley is quiet. I manage to get to my feet and shuffle forward through the papers. My eyes are clouded, and I can just make out the dangling bedspread halfway down the alley. I make my way to it. I don't know why I've come here. I suppose I want to see. I want to know what has happened. That's all.

I duck beneath the dangling bedspread. In the dim light, I can see a doorway in the brick wall. Something is hanging from the lintel of the door.

I approach cautiously. The object is gray, like the door behind it. It has a peculiar, spiraling shape. When I touch it, I can feel a faint vibration inside, like the humming of distant equipment. I lay my cheek against it and I can hear a low-pitched song, steady and even.

When I was a child, my family visited the beach and I spent hours exploring the tidepools. Among the clumps of blue-black mussels and the black turban snails, I found the egg casing of a horn shark in a tidepool. It was spiral-shaped, like this egg, and when I held it to the light, I could see a tiny embryo inside. As I watched, the embryo twitched, moving even though it was not yet truly alive.

I crouch at the back of the alley with my blanket wrapped around me. I see no reason to move—I can die here as well as I can die anywhere. I am watching over the egg, keeping it safe.

Sometimes, I dream of my past life. Perhaps I should have handled it differently. Perhaps I should have been less cautious, hurried out on the mating line, answered the song when a male called from his bower. But it doesn't matter now. All that is gone, behind us now.

My time is over. The dinosaurs and the humans—our time is over. New times are coming. New types of love. I dream of the future, and my dreams are filled with the rattle of metal claws.

JOE HALDEMAN

The Hemingway Hoax

▼

Born in Oklahoma City, Oklahoma, Joe Haldeman took a B.S. degree in physics and astronomy from the University of Maryland, and did postgraduate work in mathematics and computer science. But his plans for a career in science were cut short by the U.S. Army, which sent him to Vietnam in 1968 as a combat engineer. Seriously wounded in action, Haldeman returned home in 1969 and began to write. He sold his first story to *Galaxy* in 1969, and by 1976 had garnered both the Nebula Award and the Hugo Award for his famous novel *The Forever War*, one of the landmark books of the '70s. He took another Hugo Award in 1977 for his story "Tricentennial," and won the Rhysling Award in 1983 for the best science fiction poem of the year (although usually thought of primarily as a "hard-science" writer, Haldeman is, in fact, also an accomplished poet, and has sold poetry to most of the major professional markets in the genre). His other books include a mainstream novel, *War Year*, the SF novels *Mindbridge*, *All My Sins Remembered*, *Worlds*, *Worlds Apart*, and (with his brother, SF writer Jack C. Haldeman II) *There Is No Darkness*, the collections *Infinite Dreams* and *Dealing in Futures*, and, as editor, the anthologies *Study War No More*, *Cosmic Laughter*, and *Nebula Award Stories Seventeen*. His most recent books are the "techno-thriller" *Tool of the Trade*, and the SF novels *Buying Time* and *The Hemingway Hoax*. His story "Manifest Destiny" was in our First Annual Collection, and his story "More Than the Sum of His Parts" was in our Third Annual Collection. Haldeman lives part of the year in Boston, where he teaches writing at the Massachusetts Institute of Tech-

Joe Haldeman

nology, and the rest of the year in Florida, where he and his wife, Gay, make their home.

In the vivid and fast-moving novella that follows, Haldeman is at the very top of even his own high standard, as what starts out as a relatively harmless literary hoax soon plunges us into an intricate maze of intrigue and murder and betrayal, as cosmic forces fight it out in a battle that may determine the fate of humanity itself. . . .

▼

The Hemingway Hoax

JOE HALDEMAN

1. The Torrents Of Spring

Our story begins in a rundown bar in Key West, not so many years from
now. The bar is not the one Hemingway drank at, nor yet the one that
claims to be the one he drank at, because they are both too expensive and
full of tourists. This bar, in a more interesting part of town, is a Cuban
place. It is neither clean nor well-lighted, but has cold beer and good strong
Cuban coffee. Its cheap prices and rascally charm are what bring together
the scholar and the rogue.

Their first meeting would be of little significance to either at the time,
though the scholar, John Baird, would never forget it. John Baird was not
capable of forgetting anything.

Key West is lousy with writers, mostly poor writers, in one sense of that
word or the other. Poor people did not interest our rogue, Sylvester Castlemaine, so at first he didn't take any special note of the man sitting in the
corner scribbling on a yellow pad. Just another would-be writer, come down
to see whether some of Papa's magic would rub off. Not worth the energy
of a con.

But Castle's professional powers of observation caught at a detail or two
and focused his attention. The man was wearing jeans and a faded flannel
shirt, but his shoes were expensive Italian loafers. His beard had been
trimmed by a barber. He was drinking Heineken. The pen he was scribbling
with was a fat Mont Blanc Diplomat, two hundred bucks on the hoof,

535

discounted. Castle got his cup of coffee and sat at a table two away from the writer.

He waited until the man paused, set the pen down, took a drink. "Writing a story?" Castle said.

The man blinked at him. "No . . . just an article." He put the cap on the pen with a crisp snap. "An article about stories. I'm a college professor."

"Publish or perish," Castle said.

The man relaxed a bit. "Too true." He riffled through the yellow pad. "This won't help much. It's not going anywhere."

"Tell you what . . . bet you a beer it's Hemingway or Tennessee Williams."

"Too easy." He signaled the bartender. "Dos cervezas. Hemingway, the early stories. You know his work?"

"Just a little. We had to read him in school—*The Old Man and the Fish*? And then I read a couple after I got down here." He moved over to the man's table. "Name's Castle."

"John Baird." Open, honest expression; not too promising. You can't con somebody unless he thinks he's conning you. "Teach up at Boston."

"I'm mostly fishing. Shrimp nowadays." Of course Castle didn't normally fish, not for things in the sea, but the shrimp part was true. He'd been reduced to heading shrimp on the Catalina for five dollars a bucket. "So what about these early stories?"

The bartender set down the two beers and gave Castle a weary look.

"Well . . . they don't exist." John Baird carefully poured the beer down the side of his glass. "They were stolen. Never published."

"So what can you write about them?"

"Indeed. That's what I've been asking myself." He took a sip of the beer and settled back. "Seventy-four years ago they were stolen. December 1922. That's really what got me working on them; thought I would do a paper, a monograph, for the seventy-fifth anniversary of the occasion."

It sounded less and less promising, but this was the first imported beer Castle had had in months. He slowly savored the bite of it.

"He and his first wife, Hadley, were living in Paris. You know about Hemingway's early life?"

"Huh uh. Paris?"

"He grew up in Oak Park, Illinois. That was kind of a prissy, self-satisfied suburb of Chicago."

"Yeah, I been there."

"He didn't like it. In his teens he sort of ran away from home, went down to Kansas City to work on a newspaper.

"World War I started, and like a lot of kids, Hemingway couldn't get into the army because of bad eyesight, so he joined the Red Cross and went off to drive ambulances in Italy. Take cigarettes and chocolate to the troops.

"That almost killed him. He was just doing his cigarettes-and-chocolate routine and an artillery round came in, killed the guy next to him, tore up another, riddled Hemingway with shrapnel. He claims then that he picked up the wounded guy and carried him back to the trench, in spite of being hit in the knee by a machine-gun bullet."

"What do you mean, 'claims'?"

"You're too young to have been in Vietnam."

"Yeah."

"Good for you. I was hit in the knee by a machine-gun bullet myself, and went down on my ass and didn't get up for five weeks. He didn't carry anybody one step."

"That's interesting."

"Well, he was always rewriting his life. We all do it. But it seemed to be a compulsion with him. That's one thing that makes Hemingway scholarship challenging."

Baird poured the rest of the beer into his glass. "Anyhow, he actually was the first American wounded in Italy, and they made a big deal over him. He went back to Oak Park a war hero. He had a certain amount of success with women."

"Or so he says?"

"Right, God knows. Anyhow, he met Hadley Richardson, an older woman but quite a number, and they had a steamy courtship and got married and said the hell with it, moved to Paris to live a sort of Bohemian life while Hemingway worked on perfecting his art. That part isn't bullshit. He worked diligently and he did become one of the best writers of his era. Which brings us to the lost manuscripts."

"Do tell."

"Hemingway was picking up a little extra money doing journalism. He'd gone to Switzerland to cover a peace conference for a news service. When it was over, he wired Hadley to come join him for some skiing.

"This is where it gets odd. On her own initiative, Hadley packed up all of Ernest's work. All of it. Not just the typescripts, but the handwritten first drafts and the carbons."

"That's like a Xerox?"

"Right. She packed them in an overnight bag, then packed her own suitcase. A porter at the train station, the Gare de Lyon, put them aboard for her. She left the train for a minute to find something to read—and when she came back, they were gone."

"Suitcase and all?"

Joe Haldeman

"No, just the manuscripts. She and the porter searched up and down the train. But that was it. Somebody had seen the overnight bag sitting there and snatched it. Lost forever."

That did hold a glimmer of professional interest. "That's funny. You'd think they'd get a note then, like 'If you ever want to see your stories again, bring a million bucks to the Eiffel Tower' sort of thing."

"A few years later, that might have happened. It didn't take long for Hemingway to become famous. But at the time, only a few of the literary intelligentsia knew about him."

Castle shook his head in commiseration with the long-dead thief. "Guy who stole 'em probably didn't even read English. Dumped 'em in the river."

John Baird shivered visibly. "Undoubtedly. But people have never stopped looking for them. Maybe they'll show up in some attic someday."

"Could happen." Wheels turning.

"It's happened before in literature. Some of Boswell's diaries were recovered because a scholar recognized his handwriting on an old piece of paper a merchant used to wrap a fish. Hemingway's own last book, he put together from notes that had been lost for thirty years. They were in a couple of trunks in the basement of the Ritz, in Paris." He leaned forward, excited. "Then after he died, they found another batch of papers down here, in a back room in Sloppy Joe's. It could still happen."

Castle took a deep breath. "It could be made to happen, too."

"Made to happen?"

"Just speakin', you know, in theory. Like some guy who really knows Hemingway, suppose he makes up some stories that're like those old ones, finds some seventy-five-year-old paper and an old, what do you call them, not a word processor—"

"Typewriter."

"Whatever. Think he could pass 'em off for the real thing?"

"I don't know if he could fool me," Baird said, and tapped the side of his head. "I have a freak memory: eidetic, photographic. I have just about every word Hemingway ever wrote committed to memory." He looked slightly embarrassed. "Of course that doesn't make me an expert in the sense of being able to spot a phony. I just wouldn't have to refer to any texts."

"So take yourself, you know, or somebody else who spent all his life studyin' Hemingway. He puts all he's got into writin' these stories—he knows the people who are gonna be readin' 'em; knows what they're gonna look for. And he hires like an expert forger to make the pages look like they came out of Hemingway's machine. So could it work?"

Baird pursed his lips and for a moment looked professorial. Then he sort of laughed, one syllable through his nose. "Maybe it could. A man did a

538

similar thing when I was a boy, counterfeiting the memoirs of Howard Hughes. He made millions."

"Millions?"

"Back when that was real money. Went to jail when they found out, of course."

"And the money was still there when he got out."

"Never read anything about it. I guess so."

"So the next question is, how much stuff are we talkin' about? How much was in that old overnight bag?"

"That depends on who you believe. There was half a novel and some poetry. The short stories, there might have been as few as eleven or as many as thirty."

"That'd take a long time to write."

"It would take forever. You couldn't just 'do' Hemingway; you'd have to figure out what the stories were about, then reconstruct his early style—do you know how many Hemingway scholars there are in the world?"

"Huh uh. Quite a few."

"Thousands. Maybe ten thousand academics who know enough to spot a careless fake."

Castle nodded, cogitating. "You'd have to be real careful. But then you wouldn't have to do all the short stories and poems, would you? You could say all you found was the part of the novel. Hell, you could sell that as a book."

The odd laugh again. "Sure you could. Be a fortune in it."

"How much? A million bucks?"

"A million . . . maybe. Well, sure. The last new Hemingway made at least that much, allowing for inflation. And he's more popular now."

Castle took a big gulp of beer and set his glass down decisively. "So what the hell are we waiting for?"

Baird's bland smile faded. "You're serious?"

2. in our time

Got a ripple in the Hemingway channel.

Twenties again?

No, funny, this one's in the 1990s. See if you can track it down?

Sure. Go down to the armory first and—

Look—no bloodbaths this time. You solve one problem and start ten more.

Couldn't be helped. It's no tea party, twentieth century America.

Just use good judgment. That Ransom guy. . . .
Manson. Right. That was a mistake.

3. A Way You'll Never Be

You can't cheat an honest man, as Sylvester Castlemaine well knew, but
then again, it never hurts to find out just how honest a man is. John Baird
refused his scheme, with good humor at first, but when Castle persisted, his
refusal took on a sarcastic edge; maybe a tinge of outrage. He backed off and
changed the subject, talking for a half-hour about commercial fishing around
Key West, and then said he had to run. He slipped his business card into
John's shirt pocket on the way out. (Sylvester Castlemaine, Consultant, it
claimed.)

John left the place soon, walking slowly through the afternoon heat. He
was glad he hadn't brought the bicycle; it was pleasant to walk in the shade
of the big aromatic trees, a slight breeze on his face from the Gulf side.

One could do it. One could. The problem divided itself into three parts;
writing the novel fragment, forging the manuscript, and devising a suitable
story about how one had uncovered the manuscript.

The writing part would be the hardest. Hemingway is easy enough to
parody—one fourth of the take-home final he gave in English 733 was to
write a page of Hemingway pastiche, and some of his graduate students did
a credible job—but parody was exactly what one would not want to do.

It had been a crucial period in Hemingway's development, those three
years of apprenticeship the lost manuscripts represented. Two stories survived,
and they were maddeningly dissimilar. "My Old Man," which had slipped
down behind a drawer, was itself a pastiche, reading like pretty good Sher-
wood Anderson, but with an O. Henry twist at the end—very unlike the
bleak understated quality that would distinguish the stories that were to make
Hemingway's reputation. The other, "Up in Michigan," had been out in
the mail at the time of the loss. It was a lot closer to Hemingway's ultimate
style, a spare and, by the standards of the time, pornographic description of
a woman's first sexual experience.

John riffled through the notes on the yellow pad, a talismanic gesture,
since he could have remembered any page with little effort. But the sight of
the words and the feel of the paper sometimes helped him think.

One would not do it, of course. Except perhaps as a mental exercise. Not
to show to anybody. Certainly not to profit from.

You wouldn't want to use "My Old Man" as the model, certainly; no one
would care to publish a pastiche of a pastiche of Anderson, now undeservedly
obscure. So "Up in Michigan." And the first story he wrote after the loss,

"Out of Season," would also be handy. That had a lot of the true Hemingway strength.

You wouldn't want to tackle the novel fragment, of course, not just as an exercise, over a hundred pages. . . .

Without thinking about it, John dropped into a familiar fugue state as he walked through the rundown neighborhood, his freak memory taking over while his body ambled along on autopilot. This is the way he usually remembered pages. He transported himself back to the Hemingway collection at the JFK Library in Boston, last November, snow swirling outside the big picture windows overlooking the harbor, the room so cold he was wearing coat and gloves and could see his breath. They didn't normally let you wear a coat up there, afraid you might squirrel away a page out of the manuscript collection, but they had to make an exception because the heat pump was down.

He was flipping through the much-thumbed Xerox of Carlos Baker's interview with Hadley, page 52: "Stolen suitcase," Baker asked; "lost novel?"

The typescript of her reply appeared in front of him, more clear than the cracked sidewalk his feet negotiated: "This novel was a knock-out, about Nick, up north in Michigan—hunting, fishing, all sorts of experiences—stuff on the order of "Big Two-Hearted River," with more action. Girl experiences well done, too." With an enigmatic addition, evidently in Hadley's handwriting, "Girl experiences too well done."

That was interesting. John hadn't thought about that, since he'd been concentrating on the short stories. Too well done? There had been a lot of talk in the eighties about Hemingway's sexual ambiguity—*gender* ambiguity, actually—could Hadley have been upset, sixty years after the fact, remembering some confidence that Hemingway had revealed to the world in that novel; something girls knew that boys were not supposed to know? Playful pillow talk that was filed away for eventual literary exploitation?

He used his life that way. A good writer remembered everything and then forgot it when he sat down to write, and reinvented it so the writing would be more real than the memory. Experience was important, but imagination was more important.

Maybe I would be a better writer, John thought, if I could learn how to forget. For about the tenth time today, like any day, he regretted not having tried to succeed as a writer, while he still had the independent income. Teaching and research had fascinated him when he was younger, a rich boy's all-consuming hobbies, but the end of this fiscal year would be the end of the monthly checks from the trust fund. So the salary from Boston University wouldn't be mad money any more, but rent and groceries in a city suddenly expensive.

Yes, the writing would be the hard part. Then forging the manuscript, that wouldn't be easy. Any scholar would have access to copies of thousands of pages that Hemingway typed before and after the loss. Could one find the typewriter Hemingway had used? Then duplicate his idiosyncratic typing style—a moment's reflection put a sample in front of him, spaces before and after periods and commas. . . .

He snapped out of the reverie as his right foot hit the first step on the back staircase up to their rented flat. He automatically stepped over the fifth step, the rotted one, and was thinking about a nice tall glass of iced tea as he opened the screen door.

"Scorpions!" his wife screamed, two feet from his face.

"What?"

"We have scorpions!" Lena grabbed his arm and hauled him to the kitchen.

"Look!" She pointed at the opaque plastic skylight. Three scorpions, each about six inches long, cast sharp silhouettes on the milky plastic. One was moving.

"My word."

"Your *word!*" She struck a familiar pose, hands on hips, and glared up at the creatures. "What are we going to do about it?"

"We could name them."

"John."

"I don't know." He opened the refrigerator. "Call the bug man."

"The bug man was just here yesterday. He probably flushed them out."

He poured a glass of cold tea and dumped two envelopes of artificial sweetener into it. "I'll talk to Julio about it. But you know they've been there all along. They're not bothering anybody."

"They're bothering the hell out of me!"

He smiled. "Okay. I'll talk to Julio." He looked into the oven. "Thought about dinner?"

"Anything you want to cook, sweetheart. I'll be damned if I'm going to stand there with three . . . poisonous . . . arthropods staring down at me."

"Poised to jump," John said, and looked up again. There were only two visible now, which made his skin crawl.

"Julio wasn't home when I first saw them. About an hour ago."

"I'll go check." John went downstairs and Julio, the landlord, was indeed home, but was not impressed by the problem. He agreed that it was probably the bug man, and they would probably go back to where they came from in a while, and gave John a flyswatter.

John left the flyswatter with Lena, admonishing her to take no prisoners, and walked a couple of blocks to a Chinese restaurant. He brought back a few boxes of take-out, and they sat in the living room and wielded chopsticks in silence, listening for the pitter-patter of tiny feet.

"Met a real live con man today." He put the business card on the coffee table between them.

"Consultant?" she read.

"He had a loony scheme about counterfeiting the missing stories." Lena knew more about the missing stories than 98 percent of the people who Hemingway'ed for a living. John liked to think out loud.

"Ah, the stories," she said, preparing herself.

"Not a bad idea, actually, if one had a larcenous nature." He concentrated for a moment on the slippery Moo Goo Gai Pan. "Be millions of bucks in it."

He was bent over the box. She stared hard at his bald spot. "What exactly did he have in mind?"

"We didn't bother to think it through in any detail, actually. You go and find. . . ." He got the slightly wall-eyed look that she knew meant he was reading a page of a book a thousand miles away. "Yes. A 1921 Corona portable, like the one Hadley gave him before they were married. Find some old paper. Type up the stories. Take them to Sotheby's. Spend money for the rest of your life. That's all there is to it."

"You left out jail."

"A mere detail. Also the writing of the stories. That could take weeks. Maybe you could get arrested first, write the stories in jail, and then sell them when you got out."

"You're weird, John."

"Well. I didn't give him any encouragement."

"Maybe you should've. A few million would come in handy next year."

"We'll get by."

" 'We'll get by.' You keep saying that. How do you know? You've never had to 'get by.' "

"Okay, then. We won't get by." He scraped up the last of the fried rice. "We won't be able to make the rent and they'll throw us out on the street. We'll live in a cardboard box over a heating grate. You'll have to sell your body to keep me in cheap wine. But we'll be happy, dear." He looked up at her, mooning. "Poor but happy."

"Slap-happy." She looked at the card again. "How do you know he's a con man?"

"I don't know. Salesman type. Says he's in commercial fishing now, but he doesn't seem to like it much."

"He didn't say anything about any, you know, criminal stuff he'd done in the past?"

"Huh uh. I just got the impression that he didn't waste a lot of time mulling over ethics and morals." John held up the Mont Blanc pen. "He was staring at this, before he came over and introduced himself. I think he smelled money."

Lena stuck both chopsticks into the half-finished carton of boiled rice and set it down decisively. "Let's ask him over."

"He's a sleaze, Lena. You wouldn't like him."

"I've never met a real con man. It would be fun."

He looked into the darkened kitchen. "Will you cook something?"

She followed his gaze, expecting monsters. "If you stand guard."

4. Romance is Dead
subtitle
The Hell it is

"Be a job an' a half," Castle said, mopping up residual spaghetti sauce with a piece of garlic bread. "It's not like your Howard Hughes guy, or Hitler's notebooks."

"You've been doing some research," John's voice was a little slurred. He'd bought a half-gallon of Portuguese wine, the bottle wrapped in straw like cheap Chianti, the wine not quite that good. If you could get past the first couple of glasses, it was okay. It had been okay to John for some time now.

"Yeah, down to the library. The guys who did the Hitler notebooks, hell, nobody'd ever seen a real Hitler notebook; they just studied his handwriting in letters and such, then read up on what he did day after day. Same with the Howard Hughes, but that was even easier, because most of the time nobody knew what the hell Howard Hughes was doing anyhow. Just stayed locked up in that room."

"The Hughes forgery nearly worked, as I recall," John said. "If Hughes himself hadn't broken silence. . . ."

"Ya gotta know that took balls. 'Scuse me, Lena." She waved a hand and laughed. "Try to get away with that while Hughes was still alive."

"How did the Hitler people screw up?" she asked.

"Funny thing about that one was how many people they fooled. Afterwards everybody said it was a really lousy fake. But you can bet that before the newspapers bid millions of dollars on it, they showed it to the best Hitler-ologists they could find, and they all said it was real."

"Because they wanted it to be real," Lena said.

"Yeah. But one of the pages had some chemical in it that wouldn't be in paper before 1945. That was kinda dumb."

"People would want the Hemingway stories to be real," Lena said quietly, to John.

John's gaze stayed fixed on the center of the table, where a few strands of spaghetti lay cold and drying in a plastic bowl. "Wouldn't be honest."

"That's for sure," Castle said cheerily. "But it ain't exactly armed robbery, either."

"A gross misuse of intellectual . . . intellectual. . . ."

"It's past your bedtime, John," Lena said. "We'll clean up." John nodded and pushed himself away from the table and walked heavily into the bedroom.

Lena didn't say anything until she heard the bedsprings creak. "He isn't always like this," she said quietly.

"Yeah. He don't act like no alky."

"It's been a hard year for him." She refilled her glass. "Me, too. Money."

"That's bad."

"Well, we knew it was coming. He tell you about the inheritance?" Castle leaned forward. "Huh uh."

"He was born pretty well off. Family had textile mills up in New Hampshire. John's grandparents died in an auto accident in the forties and the family sold off the mills—good timing, too. They wouldn't be worth much today.

"Then John's father and mother died in the sixties, while he was in college. The executors set up a trust fund that looked like it would keep him in pretty good shape forever. But he wasn't interested in money. He even joined the army, to see what it was like."

"Jesus."

"Afterwards, he carried a picket sign and marched against the war—you know, Vietnam.

"Then he finished his Ph.D. and started teaching. The trust fund must have been fifty times as much as his salary, when he started out. It was still ten times as much, a couple of years ago."

"Boy . . . howdy." Castle was doing mental arithmetic and algebra with variables like Porsches and fast boats.

"But he let his sisters take care of it. He let them re-invest the capital."

"They weren't too swift?"

"They were idiots! They took good solid blue-chip stocks and tax-free municipals, too 'boring' for them, and threw it all away gambling on commodities." She grimaced. "*Pork* bellies? I finally had John go to Chicago and come back with what was left of his money. There wasn't much."

"You ain't broke, though."

"Damned near. There's enough income to pay for insurance and eventually we'll be able to draw on an IRA. But the cash payments stop in two months. We'll have to live on John's salary. I suppose I'll get a job, too."

"What you ought to get is a typewriter."

Lena laughed and slouched back in her chair. "That would be something."

"You think he could do it? I mean if he would, do you think he could?"

"He's a good writer." She looked thoughtful. "He's had some stories published, you know, in the literary magazines. The ones that pay four or five free copies."

"Big deal."

She shrugged. "Pays off in the long run. Tenure. But I don't know whether being able to write a good literary story means that John could write a good Hemingway imitation."

"He knows enough, right?"

"Maybe he knows too much. He might be paralyzed by his own standards." She shook her head. "In some ways he's an absolute nut about Hemingway. Obsessed, I mean. It's not good for him."

"Maybe writing this stuff would get it out of his system."

She smiled at him. "You've got more angles than a protractor."

"Sorry; I didn't mean to—"

"No." She raised both hands. "Don't be sorry; I like it. I like you, Castle. John's a good man but sometimes he's too good."

He poured them both more wine. "Nobody ever accused me of that."

"I suspect not." She paused. "Have you ever been in trouble with the police? Just curious."

"Why?"

"Just curious."

He laughed. "Nickel and dime stuff, when I was a kid. You know, jus' to see what you can get away with." He turned serious. "Then I pulled two months' hard time for somethin' I didn't do. Wasн't even in town when it happened."

"What was it?"

"Armed robbery. Then the guy came back an' hit the same god-damned store! I mean, he was one sharp cookie. He confessed to the first one and they let me go."

"Why did they accuse you in the first place?"

"Used to think it was somebody had it in for me. Like the clerk who fingered me." He took a sip of wine. "But hell. It was just dumb luck. And dumb cops. The guy was about my height, same color hair, we both lived in the neighborhood. Cops didn't want to waste a lot of time on it. Jus' chuck me in jail."

"So you do have a police record?"

"Huh uh. Girl from the ACLU made sure they wiped it clean. She wanted me to go after 'em for what, false arrest an' wrongful imprisonment. I just wanted to get out of town."

"It wasn't here?"

"Nah. Dayton, Ohio. Been here eight, nine years."

"That's good."

"Why the third degree?"

She leaned forward and patted the back of his hand. "Call it a job interview, Castle. I have a feeling we may be working together."

"Okay." He gave her a slow smile. "Anything else you want to know?"

5. The Doctor And The Doctor's Wife

John trudged into the kitchen the next morning, ignored the coffeepot, and pulled a green bottle of beer out of the fridge. He looked up at the skylight. Four scorpions, none of them moving. Have to call the bug man today.

Red wine hangover, the worst kind. He was too old for this. Cheap red wine hangover. He eased himself into a soft chair and carefully poured the beer down the side of the glass. Not too much noise, please.

When you drink too much, you ought to take a couple of aspirin, and some vitamins, and all the water you can hold, before retiring. If you drink too much, of course, you don't remember to do that.

The shower turned off with a bass clunk of plumbing. John winced and took a long drink, which helped a little. When he heard the bathroom door open he called for Lena to bring the aspirin when she came out.

After a few minutes she brought it out and handed it to him. "And how is Dr. Baird today?"

"Dr. Baird needs a doctor. Or an undertaker." He shook out two aspirin and washed them down with the last of the beer. "Like your outfit."

She was wearing only a towel around her head. She simpered and struck a dancer's pose and spun daintily around. "Think it'll catch on?"

"Oh my yes." At thirty-five, she still had the trim model's figure that had caught his eye in the classroom, fifteen years before. A safe, light tan was uniform all over her body, thanks to liberal sunblock and the private sun-bathing area on top of the house—private except for the helicopter that came low overhead every weekday at 1:15. She always tried to be there in time to wave at it. The pilot had such white teeth. She wondered how many sun-bathers were on his route.

She undid the towel and rubbed her long blonde hair vigorously. "Thought I'd cool off for a few minutes before I got dressed. Too much wine, eh?"

"Couldn't you tell from my sparkling repartee last night?" He leaned back, eyes closed, and rolled the cool glass back and forth on his forehead.

"Want another beer?"

"Yeah. Coffee'd be smarter, though."

"It's been sitting all night."

"Pay for my sins." He watched her swivel lightly into the kitchen and, more than ever before, felt the difference in their ages. Seventeen years; he was half again as old as she. A young man would say the hell with the hangover, go grab that luscious thing and carry her back to bed. The organ that responded to this meditation was his stomach, though, and it responded very audibly.

"Some toast, too. Or do you want something fancier?"

"Toast would be fine." Why was she being so nice? Usually if he drank too much, he reaped the whirlwind in the morning.

"Ugh." She saw the scorpions. "Five of them now."

"I wonder how many it will hold before it comes crashing down. Scorpions everywhere, stunned. Then angry."

"I'm sure the bug man knows how to get rid of them."

"In Africa they claimed that if you light a ring of fire around them with gasoline or lighter fluid, they go crazy, run amok, stinging themselves to death in their frenzies. Maybe the bug man could do that."

"Castle and I came up with a plan last night. It's kinda screwy but it might just work."

"Read that in a book called *Jungle Ways*. I was eight years old and believed every word of it."

"We figured out a way that it would be legal. Are you listening?"

"Uh huh. Let me have real sugar and some milk."

She poured some milk in a cup and put it in the microwave to warm. "Maybe we should talk about it later."

"Oh no. Hemingway forgery. You figured out a way to make it legal. Go ahead. I'm all ears."

"See, you tell the publisher first off what it is, that you wrote it and then had it typed up to look authentic."

"Sure, be a big market for that."

"In fact, there could be. You'd have to generate it, but it could happen." The toast sprang up and she brought it and two cups of coffee into the living room on a tray. "See, the bogus manuscript is only one part of a book."

"I don't get it." He tore the toast into strips, to dunk in the strong Cuban coffee.

"The rest of the book is in the nature of an exegesis of your own text."

"If that con man knows what exegesis is, then I can crack a safe."

"That part's my idea. You're really writing a book *about* Hemingway. You use your own text to illustrate various points—'I wrote it this way instead of that way because. . . .'"

"It would be different," he conceded. "Perhaps the second most egotistical piece of Hemingway scholarship in history. A dubious distinction."

"You could write it tongue-in-cheek, though. It could be really amusing, as well as scholarly."

"God, we'd have to get an unlisted number, publishers calling us night and day. Movie producers. Might sell ten copies, if I bought nine."

"You really aren't getting it, John. You don't have a particle of larceny in your heart."

He put a hand on his heart and looked down. "Ventricles, auricles. My undying love for you, a little heartburn. No particles."

"See, you tell the publisher the truth . . . but the publisher doesn't have to tell the truth. Not until publication day."

"Okay. I still don't get it."

She took a delicate nibble of toast. "It goes like this. They print the bogus Hemingway up into a few copies of bogus bound galleys. Top secret."

"My exegesis carefully left off."

"That's the ticket. They send it out to a few selected scholars, along with Xeroxes of a few sample manuscript pages. All they say, in effect, is 'Does this seem authentic to you? Please keep it under your hat, for obvious reasons.' Then they sit back and collect blurbs."

"I can see the kind of blurbs they'd get from Scott or Mike or Jack, for instance. Some variation of 'What kind of idiot do you think I am?' "

"Those aren't the kind of people you send it to, dope! You send it to people who think they're experts, but aren't. Castle says this is how the Hitler thing almost worked—they knew better than to show it to historians in general. They showed it to a few people and didn't quote the ones who thought it was a fake. Surely you can come up with a list of people who would be easy to fool."

"Any scholar could. Be a different list for each one; I'd be on some of them."

"So they bring it out on April Fool's Day. You get the front page of the New York *Times Book Review*. *Publishers Weekly* does a story. Everybody wants to be in on the joke. Bestseller list, here we come."

"Yeah, sure, but you haven't thought it through." He leaned back, balancing the coffee cup on his slight pot belly. "What about the guys who give us the blurbs, those second-rate scholars? They're going to look pretty bad."

"We did think of that. No way they could sue, not if the letter accompanying the galleys is carefully written. It doesn't have to say—"

"I don't mean getting sued. I mean I don't want to be responsible for hurting other people's careers—maybe wrecking a career, if the person was too extravagant in his endorsement, and had people looking for things to use against him. You know departmental politics. People go down the chute for less serious crimes than making an ass of yourself and your institution in print."

She put her cup down with a clatter. "You're always thinking about other people. Why don't you think about yourself for a change?" She was on the verge of tears. "Think about *us*."

"All right, let's do that. What do you think would happen to my career at BU if I pissed off the wrong people with this exercise? How long do you think it would take me to make full professor? Do you think BU would make a full professor out of a man who uses his specialty to pull vicious practical jokes?"

"Just do me the favor of thinking about it. Cool down and weigh the pluses and minuses. If you did it with the right touch, your department would love it—and God, Harry wants to get rid of the chairmanship so bad he'd give it to an axe murderer. You know you'll make full professor about thirty seconds before Harry hands you the keys to the office and runs."

"True enough." He finished the coffee and stood up in a slow creak. "I'll give it some thought. Horizontally." He turned toward the bedroom.

"Want some company?"

He looked at her for a moment. "Indeed I do."

6. in our time

Back already?

Need to find a meta-causal. One guy seems to be generating the danger flag in various timelines. John Baird, who's a scholar in some of them, a soldier in some, and a rich playboy in a few. He's always a Hemingway nut, though. He does something that starts off the ripples in '95, '96, '97; depending on which timeline you're in—but I can't seem to get close to it. There's something odd about him, and it doesn't have to do with Hemingway specifically.

But he's definitely causing the eddy?

Has to be him.

All right. Find a meta-causal that all the doom lines have in common, and forget about the others. Then go talk to him.

There'll be resonance—

But who cares? Moot after A.D. 2006.

That's true. I'll hit all the doom lines at once, then: neutralize the meta-causal, then jump ahead and do some spot checks.

Good. And no killing this time.

I understand. But—

You're too close to 2006. Kill the wrong person and the whole thing could unravel.

Well, there are differences of opinion. We would certainly feel it if the world failed to come to an end in those lines.

As you say, differences of opinion. My opinion is that you better not kill anybody or I'll send you back to patrol the fourteenth century again.

Understood. But I can't guarantee that I can neutralize the metacausal without eliminating John Baird.

Fourteenth century. Some people love it. Others think it was nasty, brutish, and long.

7. A Clean, Well-Lighted Place

Most of the sleuthing that makes up literary scholarship takes place in settings either neutral or unpleasant. Libraries' old stacks, attics metaphorical and actual; dust and silverfish, yellowed paper and fading ink. Books and letters that appear in card files but not on shelves.

Hemingway researchers have a haven outside of Boston, the Hemingway Collection at the University of Massachusetts's John F. Kennedy Library. It's a triangular room with one wall dominated by a picture window that looks over Boston Harbor to the sea. Comfortable easy chairs surround a coffee table, but John had never seen them in use; work tables under the picture window provided realistic room for computer and clutter. Skins from animals the Hemingways had dispatched in Africa snarled up from the floor, and one wall was dominated by Hemingway memorabilia and photographs. What made the room Nirvana, though, was row upon row of boxes containing tens of thousands of Xerox pages of Hemingway correspondence, manuscripts, clippings—everything from a boyhood shopping list to all extant versions of every short story and poem and novel.

John liked to get there early so he could claim one of the three computers. He snapped it on, inserted a CD, and typed in his code number. Then he keyed in the database index and started searching.

The more commonly requested items would appear on screen if you asked for them—whenever someone requested a physical copy of an item, an electronic copy automatically was sent into the database—but most of the things John needed were obscure, and he had to haul down the letter boxes and physically flip through them, just like some poor scholar inhabiting the first nine tenths of the twentieth century.

Time disappeared for him as he abandoned his notes and followed lines of instinct, leaping from letter to manuscript to note to interview, doing what was in essence the opposite of the scholar's job: a scholar would normally be trying to find out what these stories had been about. John instead was trying to track down every reference that might restrict what he himself could write about, simulating the stories.

The most confining restriction was the one he'd first remembered, walking away from the bar where he'd met Castle. The one-paragraph answer that Hadley had given to Carlos Baker about the unfinished novel; that it was a Nick Adams story about hunting and fishing up in Michigan. John didn't know anything about hunting and most of his fishing experience was limited to watching a bobber and hoping it wouldn't go down and break his train of thought.

There was the one story that Hemingway had left unpublished, "Boys and Girls Together," mostly clumsy self-parody. It covered the right period and the right activities, but using it as a source would be sensitive business, tip-toeing through a minefield. Anyone looking for a fake would go straight there. Of course John could go up to the Michigan woods and camp out, see things for himself and try to recreate them in the Hemingway style. Later, though. First order of business was to make sure there was nothing in this huge collection that would torpedo the whole project—some postcard where Hemingway said "You're going to like this novel because it has a big scene about cleaning fish."

The short stories would be less restricted in subject matter. According to Hemingway, they'd been about growing up in Oak Park and Michigan and the battlefields of Italy.

That made him stop and think. The one dramatic experience he shared with Hemingway was combat—fifty years later, to be sure, in Vietnam, but the basic situations couldn't have changed that much. Terror, heroism, cowardice. The guns and grenades were a little more streamlined, but they did the same things to people. Maybe do a World War I story as a finger exercise, see whether it would be realistic to try a longer growing-up-in-Michigan pastiche.

He made a note to himself about that on the computer, oblique enough not to be damning, and continued the eyestraining job of searching through Hadley's correspondence, trying to find some further reference to the lost novel—damn!

Writing to Ernest's mother, Hadley noted that "the taxi driver broke his typewriter" on the way to the Constantinople conference—did he get it fixed, or just chuck it? A quick check showed that the typeface of his manuscripts did indeed change after July 1924. So they'd never be able to find it. There were typewriters in Hemingway shrines in Key West, Billings, Schruns; the initial plan had been to find which was the old Corona, then locate an identical one and have Castle arrange a swap.

So they would fall back on Plan B. Castle had claimed to be good with mechanical things, and thought if they could find a 1921 Corona, he could tweak the keys around so they would produce a convincing manuscript— lower-case "s" a hair low, "e" a hair high, and so forth.

How he could be so sure of success without ever having seen the inside of a manual typewriter, John did not know. Nor did he have much confidence.

But it wouldn't have to be a perfect simulation, since they weren't out to fool the whole world, but just a few reviewers who would only see two or three Xeroxed pages. He could probably do a close enough job. John put it out of his mind and moved on to the next letter.

But it was an odd coincidence for him to think about Castle at that instant, since Castle was thinking about him. Or at least asking.

8. The Coming Man

"How was he when he was younger?"

"He never was younger." She laughed and rolled around inside the compass of his arms to face him. "Than you, I mean. He was in his mid-thirties when we met. You can't be much over twenty-five."

He kissed the end of her nose. "Thirty this year. But I still get carded sometimes."

"I'm a year older than you are. So you have to do anything I say."

"So far so good." He'd checked her wallet when she'd gone into the bathroom to insert the diaphragm, and knew she was thirty-five. "Break out the whips and chains now?"

"Not till next week. Work up to it slowly." She pulled away from him and mopped her front with the sheet. "You're good at being slow."

"I like being asked to come back."

"How 'bout tonight and tomorrow morning?"

"If you feed me lots of vitamins. How long you think he'll be up in Boston?"

"He's got a train ticket for Wednesday. But he said he might stay longer if he got onto something."

Castle laughed. "Or into something. Think he might have a girl up there? Some student like you used to be?"

"That would be funny. I guess it's not impossible." She covered her eyes with the back of her hand. "The wife is always the last to know."

They both laughed. "But I don't think so. He's a sweet guy but he's just not real sexy. I think his students see him as kind of a favorite uncle."

"You fell for him once."

"Uh huh. He had all of his current virtues plus a full head of hair, no pot belly—and, hm, what am I forgetting?"

"He was hung like an elephant?"

"No, I guess it was the millions of dollars. That can be pretty sexy."

9. Wanderings

It was a good thing John liked to nose around obscure neighborhoods shopping; you couldn't walk into any old K-Mart and pick up a 1921 Corona portable. In fact, you couldn't walk into any typewriter shop in Boston and find one, not any. Nowadays they all sold self-contained word processors, with a few dusty electrics in the back room. A few had fancy manual typewriters from Italy or Switzerland; it had been almost thirty years since the American manufacturers had made a machine that wrote without electronic help.

He had a little better luck with pawnshops. Lots of Smith-Coronas, a few L.C. Smiths, and two actual Coronas that might have been old enough. One had too large a typeface and the other, although the typeface was the same as Hemingway's, was missing a couple of letters: Th quick b own fox jump d ov th lazy dog. The challenge of writing a convincing Hemingway novel without using the letters "e" and "r" seemed daunting. He bought the machine anyhow, thinking they might ultimately have two or several broken ones that could be concatenated into one reliable machine.

The old pawnbroker rang up his purchase and made change and slammed the cash drawer shut. "Now you don't look to me like the kind of man who would hold it against a man who. . . ." He shrugged. "Well, who sold you something and then suddenly remembered that there was a place with lots of those somethings?"

"Of course not. Business is business."

"I don't know the name of the guy or his shop; I think he calls it a museum. Up in Brunswick, Maine. He's got a thousand old typewriters. He buys, sells, trades. That's the only place I know of you might find one with the missing whatever-you-call-ems."

"Fonts." He put the antique typewriter under his arm—the handle was missing—and shook the old man's hand. "Thanks a lot. This might save me weeks."

With some difficulty John got together packing materials and shipped the machine to Key West, along with Xeroxes of a few dozen pages of Hemingway's typed copy and a note suggesting Castle see what he could do. Then he went to the library and found a Brunswick telephone directory. Under "Office Machines & Supplies" was listed Crazy Tom's Typewriter Museum and Sales Emporium. John rented a car and headed north.

The small town had rolled up its sidewalks by the time he got there. He drove past Crazy Tom's and pulled into the first motel. It had a neon VACANCY sign but the innkeeper had to be roused from a deep sleep. He took John's credit card number and directed him to Room 14 and pointedly turned on the NO sign. There were only two other cars in the motel lot.

John slept late and treated himself to a full "trucker's" breakfast at the local diner: two pork chops and eggs and hash browns. Then he worked off ten calories by walking to the shop.

Crazy Tom was younger than John had expected, thirtyish with an unruly shock of black hair. A manual typewriter lay upside-down on an immaculate work table, but most of the place was definitely maculate. Thousands of peanut shells littered the floor. Crazy Tom was eating them compulsively from a large wooden bowl. When he saw John standing in the doorway, he offered some. "Unsalted," he said. "Good for you."

John crunched his way over the peanut-shell carpet. The only light in the place was the bare bulb suspended over the work table, though two unlit high-intensity lamps were clamped on either side of it. The walls were floor-to-ceiling gloomy shelves holding hundreds of typewriters, mostly black.

"Let me guess," the man said as John scooped up a handful of peanuts. "You're here about a typewriter."

"A specific one. A 1921 Corona portable."

"Ah." He closed his eyes in thought. "Hemingway. His first. Or I guess the first after he started writing. A '27 Corona, now, that'd be Faulkner."

"You get a lot of calls for them?"

"Couple times a year. People hear about this place and see if they can find one like the master used, whoever the master is to them. Sympathetic magic and all that. But you aren't a writer."

"I've had some stories published."

"Yeah, but you look too comfortable. You do something else. Teach school." He looked around in the gloom. "Corona Corona." Then he sang the six syllables to the tune of "Corina, Corina." He walked a few steps into the darkness and returned with a small machine and set it on the table. "Newer than 1920 because of the way it says "Corona" here. Older than 1927 because of the tab set-up." He found a piece of paper and a chair. "Go on, try it."

John typed out a few quick foxes and aids to one's party. The typeface was identical to the one on the machine Hadley had given Hemingway before they'd been married. The up-and-down-displacements of the letters were different, of course, but Castle should be able to fix that once he'd practiced with the back-up machine.

John cracked a peanut. "How much?"

"What you need it for?"

"Why is that important?"

"It's the only one I got. Rather rent it than sell it." He didn't look like he was lying, trying to push the price up. "A thousand to buy, a hundred a month to rent."

"Tell you what, then. I buy it, and if it doesn't bring me luck, you agree to buy it back at a pro ratum. My one thousand dollars minus ten percent per month."

Crazy Tom stuck out his hand. "Let's have a beer on it."

"Isn't it a little early for that?"

"Not if you eat peanuts all morning." He took two long-necked Budweisers from a cooler and set them on paper towels on the table. "So what kind of stuff you write?"

"Short stories and some poetry." The beer was good after the heavy greasy breakfast. "Nothing you would've seen unless you read magazines like *Iowa Review* and *Triquarterly*."

"Oh yeah. Foldouts of Gertrude Stein and H.D. I might've read your stuff."

"John Baird."

He shook his head. "Maybe. I'm no good with names."

"If you recognized my name from *The Iowa Review* you'd be the first person who ever had."

"I was right about the Hemingway connection?"

"Of course."

"But you don't write like Hemingway for no *Iowa Review*. Short declarative sentences, truly this truly that."

"No, you were right about the teaching, too. I teach Hemingway up at Boston University."

"So that's why the typewriter? Play show and tell with your students?"

"That, too. Mainly I want to write some on it and see how it feels."

From the back of the shop, a third person listened to the conversation with great interest. He, it, wasn't really a "person," though he could look like one: he had never been born and he would never die. But then he didn't really exist, not in the down-home pinch-yourself-ouch! way that you and I do.

In another way, he did *more* than exist, since he could slip back and forth between places you and I don't even have words for.

He was carrying a wand that could be calibrated for heart attack, stroke, or metastasized cancer on one end; the other end induced a kind of aphasia. He couldn't use it unless he materialized. He walked toward the two men, making no crunching sounds on the peanut shells because he weighed less than a thought. He studied John Baird's face from about a foot away.

"I guess it's a mystical thing, though I'm uncomfortable with that word. See whether I can get into his frame of mind."

"Funny thing," Crazy Tom said; "I never thought of him typing out his stories. He was always sitting in some café writing in notebooks, piling up saucers."

"You've read a lot about him?" That would be another reason not to try the forgery. This guy comes out of the woodwork and says "I sold John Baird a 1921 Corona portable."

"Hell, all I do is read. If I get two customers a day, one of 'em's a mistake and the other just wants directions. I've read all of Hemingway's fiction and most of the journalism and I think all of the poetry. Not just the *Querschnitt* period; the more interesting stuff."

The invisible man was puzzled. Quite obviously John Baird planned some sort of Hemingway forgery. But then he should be growing worried over this man's dangerous expertise. Instead, he was radiating relief.

What course of action, inaction? He could go back a few hours in time and steal this typewriter, though he would have to materialize for that, and it would cause suspicions. And Baird could find another. He could kill one or both of them, now or last week or next, but that would mean duty in the fourteenth century for more than forever—when you exist out of time, a century of unpleasantness is long enough for planets to form and die.

He wouldn't have been drawn to this meeting if it were not a strong causal nexus. There must be earlier ones, since John Baird did not just stroll down a back street in this little town and decide to change history by buying a typewriter. But the earlier ones must be too weak, or something was masking them.

Maybe it was a good timeplace to get John Baird alone and explain things to him. Then use the wand on him. But no, not until he knew exactly what he was preventing. With considerable effort of will and expenditure of something like energy, he froze time at this instant and traveled to a couple of hundred adjacent realities that were all in this same bundle of doomed timelines.

In most of them, Baird was here in Crazy Tom's Typewriter Museum and Sales Emporium. In some, he was in a similar place in New York. In two, he was back in the Hemingway collection. In one, John Baird didn't exist: the whole planet was a lifeless blasted cinder. He'd known about that timeline; it had been sort of a dry run.

"He did both," John then said in most of the timelines. "Sometimes typing, sometimes fountain pen or pencil. I've seen the rough draft of his first novel.

Written out in a stack of seven French schoolkids' copybooks." He looked around, memory working. A red herring wouldn't hurt. He'd never come across a reference to any other specific Hemingway typewriter, but maybe this guy had. "You know what kind of machine he used in Key West or Havana?"

Crazy Tom pulled on his chin. "Nope. Bring me a sample of the typing and I might be able to pin it down, though. And I'll keep an eye out—got a card?"

John took out a business card and his checkbook. "Take a check on a Boston bank?"

"Sure. I'd take one on a Tierra del Fuego bank. Who'd stiff you on a seventy-year-old typewriter?" Sylvester Castlemaine might, John thought. "I've had this business almost twenty years," Tom continued; "not a single bounced check or bent plastic."

"Yeah," John said. "Why would a crook want an old typewriter?" The invisible man laughed and went away.

10. Banal Story

Dear Lena & Castle,

Typing this on the new/old machine to give you an idea about what has to be modified to mimic EH's:

abcdefghijklmnopqrstuvwxyz ABCDEFGHIJKLMNOPQRSTUVWXYZ 234567890,./ "#$%_&'()*?

Other mechanical things to think about --

1. Paper -- One thing that made people suspicious about the Hitler forgery is that experts know that old paper smells old. And of course there was that fatal chemical-composition error that clinched it.

As we discussed, my first thought was that one of us would have to go to Paris and nose around in old attics and so forth, trying to find either a stack of 75-year-old paper or an old blank book we could cut pages out of. But in the JFK Library collection I found out that EH actually did bring some American-made paper along with him. A lot of the rough draft of in our time -- written in Paris a year or two after our "discovery" -- was typed on the back of 6 × 7" stationery from his parents' vacation place in Windemere, Xerox enclosed. It should be pretty easy to duplicate on a hand press, and of course it will be a lot easier to find 75-year-old American paper. One complication, unfortunately, is that I haven't really seen the paper; only a Xerox of the pages. Have to come up with some pretext to either visit the vault or have a page brought up, so I can check the color of the ink, memorize the weight and deckle of the paper, check to see how the edges are cut ...

I'm starting to sound like a real forger. In for a penny, though, in for a pound. One of the critics who's sent the fragment might want to see the actual document, and compare it with the existing Windemere pages.

2. Inks. This should not be a problem. Here's a recipe for typewriter ribbon ink from a 1918 book of commercial formulas:

8 oz. lampblack

4 oz. gum arabic

1 quart methylated spirits

That last one is wood alcohol. The others ought to be available in Miami if you can't find them on the Rock.

Aging the ink on the paper gets a little tricky. I haven't been able to find anything about it in the libraries around here; no FORGERY FOR FUN & PROFIT. May check in New York before coming back.

(If we don't find anything, I'd suggest baking it for a few days at a temperature low enough not to greatly affect the paper, and then interleaving it with blank sheets of the old paper and pressing them together for a few days, to restore the old smell, and further absorb the residual ink solvents.)

Toyed with the idea of actually allowing the manuscript to mildew somewhat, but that might get out of hand and actually destroy some of it -- or for all I know we'd be employing a species of mildew that doesn't speak French. Again, thinking like a true forger, which may be a waste of time and effort, but I have to admit is kind of fun. Playing cops and robbers at my age.

Well, I'll call tonight. Miss you, Lena.

Your partner in crime,

John.

11. A Divine Gesture

When John returned to his place in Boston, there was a message on his answering machine: "John, this is Nelson Van Nuys. Harry told me you were in town. I left something in your box at the office and I strongly suggest you take it before somebody else does. I'll be out of town for a week, but give me a call if you're here next Friday. You can take me and Doris out to dinner at Panache."

Panache was the most expensive restaurant in Cambridge. Interesting. John checked his watch. He hadn't planned to go to the office, but there was plenty of time to swing by on his way to returning the rental car. The train didn't leave for another four hours.

Van Nuys was a fellow Hemingway scholar and sometimes drinking buddy who taught at Brown. What had he brought ninety miles to deliver in person, rather than mail? He was probably just in town and dropped by. But it was worth checking.

No one but the secretary was in the office, noontime, for which John was obscurely relieved. In his box were three interdepartmental memos, a text-book catalog, and a brown cardboard box that sloshed when he picked it up. He took it all back to his office and closed the door.

The office made him feel a little weary, as usual. He wondered whether they would be shuffling people around again this year. The department liked to keep its professors in shape by having them haul tons of books and files up and down the corridor every couple of years.

He glanced at the memos and pitched them, irrelevant since he wasn't teaching in the summer, and put the catalog in his briefcase. Then he carefully opened the cardboard box.

It was a half-pint Jack Daniel's bottle, but it didn't have bourbon in it. A cloudy greenish liquid. John unscrewed the top and with the sharp Pernod tang the memory came back: He and Van Nuys had wasted half an afternoon in Paris years ago, trying to track down a source of true absinthe. So he had finally found some.

Absinthe. Nectar of the gods, ruination of several generations of French artists, students, workingmen—outlawed in 1915 for its addictive and hallucinogenic qualities. Where had Van Nuys found it?

He screwed the top back on tightly and put it back in the box and put the box in his briefcase. If its effect really was all that powerful, you probably wouldn't want to drive under its influence. In Boston traffic, of course, a little lane weaving and a few mild collisions would go unnoticed.

Once he was safely on the train, he'd try a shot or two of it. It couldn't be all that potent. Child of the sixties, John had taken LSD, psilocybin, ecstasy, and peyote, and remembered with complete accuracy the quality of each drug's hallucinations. The effects of absinthe wouldn't be nearly as extreme as its modern successors. But it was probably just as well to try it first in a place where unconsciousness or Steve Allen imitations or speaking in tongues would go unremarked.

He turned in the rental car and took a cab to South Station rather than juggle suitcase, briefcase, and typewriter through the subway system. Once there, he nursed a beer through an hour of the Yankees murdering the Red Sox, and then rented a cart to roll his burden down to track 3, where a smiling porter installed him aboard the *Silver Meteor*, its range newly extended from Boston to Miami.

He had loved the train since his boyhood in Washington. His mother hated flying and so they often clickety-clacked from place to place in the snug comfort of first-class compartments. Eidetic memory blunted his enjoyment of the modern Amtrak version. This compartment was as large as the ones he had read and done puzzles in, forty years before —amazing and delighting his mother with his proficiency in word games—but the smell of good old leather was gone, replaced by plastic, and the fittings that had been polished brass were chromed steel now. On the middle of the red plastic seat was a Hospitality Pak, a plastic box encased in plastic wrap that contained a wedge of indestructible "cheese food," as if cheese had to eat, a small plastic bottle of cheap California wine, a plastic glass to contain it, and an apple, possibly not plastic.

John hung up his coat and tie in the small closet provided beside where the bed would fold down, and for a few minutes he watched with interest as his fellow passengers and their accompaniment hurried or ambled to their cars. Mostly old people, of course. Enough young ones, John hoped, to keep the trains alive a few decades more.

"Mr. Baird?" John turned to face a black porter, who bowed slightly and favored him with a blinding smile of white and gold. "My name is George, and I will be at your service as far as Atlanta. Is everything satisfactory?"

"Doing fine. But if you could find me a glass made of glass and a couple of ice cubes, I might mention you in my will."

"One minute, sir." In fact, it took less than a minute. That was one aspect, John had to admit, that had improved in recent years: The service on Amtrak in the sixties and seventies had been right up there with Alcatraz and the Hanoi Hilton.

He closed and locked the compartment door and carefully poured about two ounces of the absinthe into the glass. Like Pernod, it turned milky on contact with the ice.

He swirled it around and breathed deeply. It did smell much like Pernod, but with an acrid tang that was probably oil of wormwood. An experimental sip: the wormwood didn't dominate the licorice flavor, but it was there.

"Thanks, Nelson," he whispered, and drank the whole thing in one cold fiery gulp. He set down the glass and the train began to move. For a weird moment that seemed hallucinatory, but it always did, the train starting off so smoothly and silently.

For about ten minutes he felt nothing unusual, as the train did its slow tour of Boston's least attractive backyards. The conductor who checked his ticket seemed like a normal human being, which could have been a hallucination.

John knew that some drugs, like amyl nitrite, hit with a swift slap, while others creep into your mind like careful infiltrators. This was the way of absinthe; all he felt was a slight alcohol buzz, and he was about to take another shot, when it subtly began.

There were *things* just at the periphery of his vision, odd things with substance, but somehow without shape, that of course moved away when he turned his head to look at them. At the same time a whispering began in his ears, just audible over the train noise, but not intelligible, as if in a language he had heard before but not understood. For some reason the effects were pleasant, though of course they could be frightening if a person were not expecting weirdness. He enjoyed the illusions for a few minutes, while the scenery outside mellowed into woodsy suburbs, and the visions and voices stopped rather suddenly.

He poured another ounce and this time diluted it with water. He remembered the sad woman in "Hills Like White Elephants" lamenting that everything new tasted like licorice, and allowed himself to wonder what Hemingway had been drinking when he wrote that curious story.

Chuckling at his own—what? Effrontery?—John took out the 1921 Corona and slipped a sheet of paper into it and balanced it on his knees. He had earlier thought of the first two lines of the WWI pastiche; he typed them down and kept going:

The dirt on the sides of the trenches was never completely dry in the morning. If Nick could find an old newspaper he would put it between his chest and the dirt when he went out to lean on the side of the trench and wait for the light. First light was the best time. You might have luck and see a muzzle flash. But patience was better than luck. Wait to see a helmet or a head without a helmet.

Nick looked at the enemy line through a rectangular box of wood that went through the trench at about ground level. The other end of the box was covered by a square of gauze the color of dirt. A person looking directly at it might see the muzzle flash when Nick fired through the box. But with luck, the flash would be the last thing he saw.

Nick had fired through the gauze six times, perhaps killing three enemy, and the gauze now had a ragged hole in the center.

Okay, John thought, he'd be able to see slightly better through the hole in the center but staring that way would reduce the effective field of view, so he would deliberately try to look to one side or the other. How to type that down in a simple way? Someone cleared his throat.

John looked up from the typewriter. Sitting across from him was Ernest Hemingway, the weathered, wise Hemingway of the famous Karsh photograph.

"I'm afraid you must not do that," Hemingway said.

John looked at the half-full glass of absinthe and looked back. Hemingway was still there. "Jesus Christ," he said.

"It isn't the absinthe." Hemingway's image rippled and he became the handsome teenager who had gone to war, the war John was writing about. "I am quite real. In a way, I am more real than you are." As it spoke it aged: the mustachioed leading-man-handsome Hemingway of the twenties; the slightly corpulent, still magnetic media hero of the thirties and forties; the beard turning white, the features hard and sad and then twisting with impotence and madness, and then a sudden loud report and the cranial vault exploding, the mahogany veneer of the wall splashed with blood and brains and imbedded chips of skull. There was a strong smell of cordite and blood. The almost headless corpse shrugged, spreading its hands. "I can look like anyone I want." The mess disappeared and it became the young Hemingway again.

John slumped and stared.

"This thing you just started must never be finished. This Hemingway pastiche. It will ruin something very important."

"What could it ruin? I'm not even planning to—"

"Your plans are immaterial. If you continue with this project it will profoundly affect the future."

"You're from the future?"

"I'm from the future and the past and other temporalities that you can't comprehend. But all you need to know is that you must not write this Hemingway story. If you do, I or someone like me will have to kill you."

It gestured and a wand the size of a walking stick, half black and half white, appeared in its hand. It tapped John's knee with the white end. There was a slight tingle.

"Now you won't be able to tell anybody about me, or write anything about me down. If you try to talk about me, the memory will disappear—and reappear moments later, along with the knowledge that I will kill you if you don't cooperate." It turned into the bloody corpse again. "Understood?"

"Of course."

"If you behave, you will never have to see me again." It started to fade.

"Wait. What do you really look like?"

"This. . . ." For a few seconds John stared at an ebony presence deeper than black, at once points and edges and surfaces and volume and hints of further dimensions. "You can't really see or know," a voice whispered inside his head. He reached into the blackness and jerked his hand back, rimed with frost and numb. The thing disappeared.

He stuck his hand under his armpit and feeling returned. That last apparition was the unsettling one. He had Hemingway's appearance at every age memorized, and had seen the corpse in his mind's eye often enough. A drug could conceivably have brought them all together and made up this fantastic demand—which might actually be nothing more than a reasonable side of his nature trying to make him stop wasting time on this silly project.

But that thing. His hand was back to normal. Maybe a drug could do that, too; make your hand feel freezing. LSD did more profound things than that. But not while arguing about a manuscript.

He considered the remaining absinthe. Maybe take another big blast of it and see whether ol' Ernie comes back again. Or no—there was a simpler way to check.

The bar was four rocking and rolling cars away, and bouncing his way from wall to window helped sober John up. When he got there, he had another twinge for the memories of the past. Stained formica tables. No service; you had to go to a bar at the other end. Acrid with cigarette fumes. He remembered linen tablecloths and endless bottles of Coke with the names of cities from everywhere stamped on the bottom and, when his father came along with them, the rich sultry smoke of his Havanas. The fat Churchills from Punch that emphysema stopped just before Castro could. "A Coke, please." He wondered which depressed him more, the red can or the plastic cup with miniature ice cubes.

The test. It was not in his nature to talk to strangers on public conveyances. But this was necessary. There was a man sitting alone who looked about John's age, a Social-Security bound hippy with wire-rimmed John Lennon glasses, white hair down to his shoulders, bushy grey beard. He nodded when John sat down across from him, but didn't say anything. He sipped beer and looked blankly out at the gathering darkness.

"Excuse me," John said, "but I have a strange thing to ask you."

The man looked at him. "I don't mind strange things. But please don't try to sell me anything illegal."

"I wouldn't. It may have something to do with a drug, but it would be one I took."

"You do look odd. You tripping?"

"Doesn't feel like it. But I may have been . . . slipped something." He leaned back and rubbed his eyes. "I just talked to Ernest Hemingway."

"The writer?"

"In my roomette, yeah."

"Wow. He must be pretty old."

"He's dead! More than thirty years."

"Oh wow. Now that is something weird. What he say?"

"You know what a pastiche is?"

"French pastry?"

"No, it's when you copy . . . when you create an imitation of another person's writing. Hemingway's, in this case."

"Is that legal? I mean, with him dead and all."

"Sure it is, as long as you don't try to foist it off as Hemingway's real stuff."

"So what happened? He wanted to help you with it?"

"Actually, no . . . he said I'd better stop."

"Then you better stop. You don't fuck around with ghosts." He pointed at the old brass bracelet on John's wrist. "You in the 'Nam."

"Sixty-eight," John said. "Hue."

"Then you oughta know about ghosts. You don't fuck with ghosts."

"Yeah." What he'd thought was aloofness in the man's eyes, the set of his mouth, was aloneness, something slightly different. "You okay?"

"Oh yeah. Wasn't for a while, then I got my shit together." He looked out the window again, and said something weirdly like Hemingway: "I learned to take it a day at a time. The day you're in's the only day that's real. The past is shit and the future, hell, some day your future's gonna be that you got no future. So fuck it, you know? One day at a time."

John nodded. "What outfit were you in?"

"Like I say, man, the past is shit. No offense?"

"No, that's okay." He poured the rest of his Coke over the ice and stood up to go.

"You better talk to somebody about those ghosts. Some kinda shrink, you know? It's not that they're not real. But just you got to deal with 'em."

"Thanks. I will." John got a little more ice from the barman and negotiated his way down the lurching corridor back to his compartment, trying not to spill his drink while also juggling fantasy, reality, past, present, memory. . . .

He opened the door and Hemingway was there, drinking his absinthe. He looked up with weary malice. "Am I going to have to kill you?"

What John did next would have surprised Castlemaine, who thought he was a nebbish. He closed the compartment door and sat down across from the apparition. "Maybe you can kill me and maybe you can't."

"Don't worry. I can."

"You said I wouldn't be able to talk to anyone about you. But I just walked down to the bar car and did."

"I know. That's why I came back."

"So if one of your powers doesn't work, maybe another doesn't. At any rate, if you kill me you'll never find out what went wrong."

"That's very cute, but it doesn't work." It finished off the absinthe and then ran a finger around the rim of the glass, which refilled out of nowhere. "You're making assumptions about causality that are necessarily naïve, because you can't perceive even half of the dimensions that you inhabit."

"Nevertheless, you haven't killed me yet."

"And assumptions about my 'psychology' that are absurd. I am no more a human being than you are a paramecium."

"I'll accept that. But I would make a deal with a paramecium if I thought I could gain an advantage from it."

"What could you possibly have to deal with, though?"

"I know something about myself that you evidently don't, that enables me to overcome your don't-talk restriction. Knowing that might be worth a great deal to you."

"Maybe something."

"What I would like in exchange is, of course, my life, and an explanation of why I must not do the Hemingway pastiche. Then I wouldn't do it."

"You wouldn't do it if I killed you, either."

John sipped his Coke and waited.

"All right. It goes something like this. There is not just one universe, but actually uncountable zillions of them. They're all roughly the same size and complexity as this one, and they're all going off in a zillion different directions, and it is one hell of a job to keep things straight."

"You do this by yourself? You're God?"

"There's not just one of me. In fact, it would be meaningless to assign a number to us, but I guess you could say that altogether, we are God . . . and the Devil, and the Cosmic Puppet master, and the Grand Unification Theory, the Great Pumpkin and everything else. When we consider ourselves as a group, let me see, I guess a human translation of our name would be the Spacio-Temporal Adjustment Board."

"STAB?"

"I guess that is unfortunate. Anyhow, what STAB does is more the work of a scalpel than a knife." The Hemingway scratched its nose, leaving the absinthe suspended in midair. "Events are supposed to happen in certain ways, in certain sequences. You look at things happening and say cause-and-effect, or coincidence, or golly, that couldn't have happened in a million years—but you don't even have a clue. Don't even try to think about it. It's like an ant trying to figure out General Relativity."

"It wouldn't have a clue. Wouldn't know where to start."

The apparition gave him a sharp look and continued. "These universes come in bundles. Hundreds of them, thousands, that are pretty much the same. And they affect each other. Resonate with each other. When something goes wrong in one, it resonates and screws up all of them."

"You mean to say that if I write a Hemingway pastiche, hundreds of universes are going to go straight to hell?"

The apparition spread its hands and looked to the ceiling. "Nothing is simple. The only thing that's simple is that nothing is simple.

"I'm a sort of literature specialist. American literature of the nineteenth and twentieth centuries. Usually. Most of my timespace is taken up with guys like Hemingway, Teddy Roosevelt, Heinlein, Bierce. Crane, Spillane, Twain."

"Not William Dean Howells?"

"Not him or James or Carver or Coover or Cheever or any of those guys. If everybody gave me as little trouble as William Dean Howells I could spend most of my timespace on a planet where the fishing was good."

"Masculine writers?" John said. "But not all hairy-chested macho types."

"I'll give you an A— on that one. They're writers who have an accumulating effect on the masculine side of the American national character. There's no one word for it, though it is a specific thing: individualistic, competence-worshiping, short-term optimism and long-term existentialism. 'There may be nothing after I die but I sure as hell will do the job right while I'm here, even though I'm surrounded by idiots.' You see the pattern?"

"Okay. And I see how Hemingway fits in. But how could writing a pastiche interfere with it?"

"That's a limitation I have. I don't know specifically. I do know that the accelerating revival of interest in Hemingway from the seventies through the nineties is vitally important. In the Soviet Union as well as the United States. For some reason, I can feel your pastiche interfering with it." He stretched out the absinthe glass into a yard-long amber crystal, and it changed into the black-and-white cane. The glass reappeared in the drink holder by the window. "Your turn."

"You won't kill me after you hear what I have to say?"

"No. Go ahead."

"Well . . . I have an absolutely eidetic memory. Everything I've ever seen—or smelled or tasted or heard or touched, or even dreamed—I can instantly recall."

"Every other memory freak I've read about was limited—numbers, dates, calendar tricks, historical details—and most of them were *idiots savants*. I have at least normal intelligence. But from the age of about three, I have never forgotten anything."

The Hemingway smiled congenially. "Thank you. That's exactly it." It fingered the black end of the cane, clicking something. "If you had the choice, would you rather die of a heart attack, stroke, or cancer?"

"That's it?" The Hemingway nodded. "Well, you're human enough to cheat. To lie."

"It's not something you could understand. Stroke?"

"It might not work."

"We're going to find out right now." He lowered the cane.

"Wait! What's death? Is there . . . anything I should do, anything you know?"

The rod stopped, poised an inch over John's knee. "I guess you just end. Is that so bad?"

"Compared to not ending, it's bad."

"That shows how little you know. I and the ones like me can never die. If you want something to occupy your last moment, your last thought, you might pity me."

John stared straight into his eyes. "Fuck you."

The cane dropped. A fireball exploded in his head.

12. Marriage Is A Dangerous Game

"We'll blackmail him." Castle and Lena were together in the big antique bathtub, in a sea of pink foam, her back against his chest.

"Sure," she said. " 'If you don't let us pass this manuscript off as the real thing, we'll tell everybody you faked it.' Something wrong with that, but I can't quite put my finger on it."

"Here, I'll put mine on it."

She giggled. "Later. What do you mean, blackmail?"

"Got it all figured out. I've got this friend Pansy, she used to be a call girl. Been out of the game seven, eight years; still looks like a million bucks."

"Sure. We fix John up with this hooker—"

"Call girl isn't a hooker. We're talkin' class."

"In the first place, John wouldn't pay for sex. He did that in Vietnam and it still bothers him."

"Not talkin' about pay. Talkin' about fallin' in love. While she meanwhile fucks his eyeballs out."

"You have such a turn of phrase, Sylvester. Then while his eyeballs are out, you come in with a camera."

"Yeah, but you're about six steps ahead."

"Okay, step two; how do we get them together? Church social?"

"She moves in next door." There was another upstairs apartment, un-occupied. "You and me and Julio are conveniently somewhere else when she shows up with all these boxes and that big flight of stairs."

"Sure, John would help her. But that's his nature; he'd help her if she were an ugly old crone with leprosy. Carry a few boxes, sit down for a cup of coffee, maybe. But not jump into the sack."

"Okay, you know John." His voice dropped to a husky whisper and he cupped her breasts. "But I know men, and I know Pansy . . . and Pansy could give a hard-on to a corpse."

"Sure, and then fuck his eyeballs out. They'd come out easier."

"What?"

"Never mind. Go ahead."

"Well . . . look. Do you know what a call girl does?"

"I suppose you call her up and say you've got this eyeball problem."

"Enough with the eyeballs. What she does, she works for like an escort service. That part of it's legal. Guy comes into town, business or maybe on vacation, he calls up the service and they ask what kind of companion he'd like. If he says, like, give me some broad with a tight ass, can suck the chrome off a bumper hitch—the guy says like 'I'm sorry, sir, but this is not that kind of a service.' But mostly the customers are pretty hip to it, they say, oh, a pretty young blonde who likes to go dancing."

"Meanwhile they're thinking about bumper hitches and eyeballs."

"You got it. So it starts out just like a date, just the guy pays the escort service like twenty bucks for getting them together. Still no law broken."

"Now about one out of three, four times, that's it. The guy knows what's going on but he don't get up the nerve to ask, or he really doesn't know the score, and it's like a real dull date. I don't think that happened much with Pansy."

"In the normal course of things, though, the subject of bumper hitches comes up."

"Uh huh, but not from Pansy. The guy has to pop the question. That way if he's a cop it's, what, entrapment."

"Do you know whether Pansy ever got busted?"

"Naw. Mainly the cops just shake down the hookers, just want a blowjob anyhow. This town, half of 'em want a blowjob from guys.

"So they pop the question and Pansy blushes and says for you, I guess I could. Then, on the way to the motel or wherever she says, you know, I wouldn't ask this if we weren't really good friends, but I got to make a car payment by tomorrow, and I need like two hundred bucks before noon tomorrow?"

"And she takes MasterCard and Visa."

"No, but she sure as hell knows where every bank machine in town is. She even writes up an I.O.U." Castle laughed. "Told me a guy from Toledo's holdin' five grand of I.O.U.'s from her."

"All right, but that's not John. She could suck the chrome off his eyeballs and he still wouldn't be interested in her if she didn't know Hemingway from hummingbirds."

Castle licked behind her ear, a weird gesture that made her shiver. "That's the trump card. Pansy reads like a son of a bitch. She's got like a thousand books. So this morning I called her up and asked about Hemingway."

"And?"

"She's read them all."

She nodded slowly. "Not bad, Sylvester. So we promote this love affair and sooner or later you catch them in the act. Threaten to tell me unless John accedes to a life of crime."

"Think it could work? He wouldn't say hell, go ahead and tell her?"

"Not if I do my part . . . starting tomorrow. I'm the best, sweetest, lovingest wife in this sexy town. Then in a couple of weeks Pansy comes into his life, and there he is, luckiest man alive. Best of both worlds. Until you accidentally catch them *in flagrante delicioso*."

"So to keep both of you, he goes along with me."

"It might just do it. It might just." She slowly levered herself out of the water and smoothed the suds off her various assets.

"Nice."

"Bring me that bumper hitch, Sylvester. Hold on to your eyeballs."

13. In Another Country

John woke up with a hangover of considerable dimension. The diluted glass of absinthe was still in the drink holder by the window. It was just past dawn, and a verdant forest rushed by outside. The rails made a steady hum; the car had a slight rocking that would have been pleasant to a person who felt well.

A porter knocked twice and enquired after Mr. Baird. "Come in." John said. A short white man, smiling, brought in coffee and Danish.

"What happened to George?"

"Pardon me, sir? George who?"

John rubbed his eyes. "Oh, of course. We must be past Atlanta."

"No, sir." The man's smile froze as his brain went into nutty-passenger mode. "We're at least two hours from Atlanta."

"George . . . is a tall back guy with gold teeth who—"

"Oh, you mean George Mason, sir. He does do this car, but he picks up the train in Atlanta, and works it to Miami and back. He hasn't had the northern leg since last year."

John nodded slowly and didn't ask what year it was. "I understand." He smiled up and read the man's nametag. "I'm sorry, Leonard. Not at my best in the morning." The man withdrew with polite haste.

Suppose that weird dream had not been a dream. The Hemingway creature had killed him—the memory of the stroke was awesomely strong and immediate—but all that death amounted to was slipping into another universe where George Mason was on a different shift. Or perhaps John had gone completely insane.

The second explanation seemed much more reasonable.

On the tray underneath the coffee, juice, and Danish was a copy of USA Today, a paper John normally avoided because, although it had its comic aspects, it didn't have any funnies. He checked the date, and it was correct. The news stories were plausible—wars and rumors of war—so at least he hadn't slipped into a dimension where Martians ruled an enslaved Earth or Barry Manilow was president. He turned to the weather map and stopped dead.

Yesterday the country was in the middle of a heat wave that had lasted weeks. It apparently had ended overnight. The entry for Boston, yesterday, was "72/58/sh." But it hadn't rained and the temperature had been in the nineties.

He went back to the front page and began checking news stories. He didn't normally pay much attention to the news, though, and hadn't seen a paper in several days. They'd canceled their *Globe* delivery for the six weeks in Key West and he hadn't been interested enough to go seek out a newsstand.

571

There was no mention of the garbage collectors' strike in New York; he'd overheard a conversation about that yesterday. A long obituary for a rock star he was sure had died the year before.

An ad for DeSoto automobiles. That company had gone out of business when he was a teen-ager.

Bundles of universes, different from each other in small ways. Instead of dying, or maybe because of dying, he had slipped into another one. What would be waiting for him in Key West?

Maybe John Baird.

He set the tray down and hugged himself, trembling. Who or what was he in this universe? All of his memories, all of his personality, were from the one he had been born in. What happened to the John Baird that was born in this one? Was he an associate professor in American Literature at Boston University? Was he down in Key West wrestling with a paper to give at Nairobi—or working on a forgery? Or was he a Fitzgerald specialist snooping around the literary attics of St. Paul, Minnesota?

The truth came suddenly. Both John Bairds were in this compartment, in this body. And the body was slightly different.

He opened the door to the small washroom and looked in the mirror. His hair was a little shorter, less grey, beard better trimmed.

He was less paunchy and . . . something felt odd. There was feeling in his thigh. He lowered his pants and there was no scar where the sniper bullet had opened his leg and torn up the nerves there.

That was the touchstone. As he raised his shirt, the parallel memory flooded in. Puckered round scar on the abdomen; in this universe the sniper had hit a foot higher—and instead of the convalescent center in Cam Ranh Bay, the months of physical therapy and then back into the war, it had been peritonitis raging; surgery in Saigon and Tokyo and Walter Reed, and no more army.

But slowly they converged again. Amherst and U. Mass.—perversely using the G.I. Bill in spite of his access to millions—the doctorate on *The Sun Also Rises* and the instructorship at B.U., meeting Lena and virtuously waiting until after the semester to ask her out. Sex on the second date, and the third . . . but there they verged again. This John Baird hadn't gone back into combat to have his midsection sprayed with shrapnel from an American grenade that bounced off a tree; never had dozens of bits of metal cut out of his dick—and in the ensuing twenty-five years had made more use of it. Girl friends and even one disastrous homosexual encounter with a stranger. As far as he knew, Lena was in the dark about this side of him; thought that he had remained faithful other than one incident seven years after they married. He knew of one affair she had had with a colleague, and suspected more.

The two Johns' personalities and histories merged, separate but one, like two vines from a common root, climbing a single support.

Schizophrenic but not insane.

John looked into the mirror and tried to address his new or his old self—John A, John B. There were no such people. There was suddenly a man who had existed in two separate universes and, in a way, it was no more profound than having lived in two separate houses.

The difference being that nobody else knows there is more than one house.

He moved over to the window and set his coffee in the holder; picked up the absinthe glass and sniffed it, considered pouring it down the drain, but then put it in the other holder, for possible future reference.

Posit this: is it more likely that there are bundles of parallel universes prevailed over by a Hemingway lookalike with a magic cane, or that John Baird was exposed to a drug that he had never experienced before and it had had an unusually disorienting effect?

He looked at the paper. He had not hallucinated two weeks of drought. The rock star had been dead for some time. He had not seen a DeSoto in twenty years, and that was a hard car to miss. Tailfins that had to be registered as lethal weapons.

But maybe if you take a person who remembers every trivial thing, and zap his brain with oil of wormwood, that is exactly the effect: perfectly recalled things that never actually happened.

The coffee tasted repulsive. John put on a fresh shirt and decided not to shave and headed for the bar car. He bought the last imported beer in the cooler and sat down across from the long-haired white-bearded man who had an earring that had escaped his notice before, or hadn't existed in the other universe.

The man was staring out at the forest greening by. "Morning," John said.

"How do." The man looked at him with no sign of recognition.

"Did we talk last night?"

He leaned forward. "What?"

"I mean did we sit in this car last night and talk about Hemingway and Vietnam and ghosts?"

He laughed. "You're on somethin', man. I been on this train since two in the mornin' and ain't said boo to nobody but the bartender."

"You were in Vietnam?"

"Yeah, but that's over; that's shit." He pointed at John's bracelet. "What, you got ghosts from over there?"

"I think maybe I have."

He was suddenly intense. "Take my advice, man; I been there. You got to go talk to somebody. Some shrink. Those ghosts ain't gonna go 'way by themself."

573

"It's not that bad."

"It ain't the ones you killed." He wasn't listening. "Fuckin' dinks, they come back but they don't, you know, they just stand around." He looked at John and tears came so hard they actually spurted from his eyes. "It's your fuckin' friends, man, they all died and they come back now. . . ." He took a deep breath and wiped his face. "They used to come back every night. That like you?" John shook his head, helpless, trapped by the man's grief. "Every fuckin' night, my old lady, finally she said you go to a shrink or go to hell." He fumbled with the button on his shirt pocket and took out a brown plastic prescription bottle and stared at the label. He shook out a capsule. "Take a swig?" John pushed the beer over to him. He washed the pill down without touching the bottle to his lips.

He sagged back against the window. "I musta not took the pill last night, sometimes I do that. Sorry." He smiled weakly. "One day at a time, you know? You get through the one day. Fuck the rest. Sorry." He leaned forward again suddenly and put his hand on John's wrist. "You come outa nowhere and I lay my fuckin' trip on you. You don' need it."

John covered the hand with his own. "Maybe I do need it. And maybe I didn't come out of nowhere." He stood up. "I will see somebody about the ghosts. Promise."

"You'll feel better. It's no fuckin' cure-all but you'll feel better."

"Want the beer?"

He shook his head. "Not supposed to."

"Okay." John took the beer and they waved at each other and he started back.

He stopped in the vestibule between cars and stood in the rattling roar of it, looking out the window at the flashing green blur. He put his forehead against the cool glass and hid the blur behind the dark red of his eyelids.

Were there actually a zillion of those guys each going through a slightly different private hell? Something he rarely asked himself was "What would Ernest Hemingway have done in this situation?"

He'd probably have the sense to leave it to Milton.

14. The Dangerous Summer

Castle and Lena met him at the station in Miami and they drove back to Key West in Castle's old pick-up. The drone of the air-conditioner held conversation to a minimum, but it kept them cool, at least from the knees down.

John didn't say anything about his encounter with the infinite, or transfinite, not wishing to bring back that fellow with the cane just yet. He did note that the two aspects of his personality hadn't quite become equal partners yet, and small details of this world kept surprising him. There was a monorail being built down to Pigeon Key, where Disney was digging an underwater park. Gasoline stations still sold Regular. Castle's car radio picked up TV as well as AM/FM, but sound only.

Lena sat between the two men and rubbed up against John affectionately. That would have been remarkable for John-one and somewhat unusual for John-two. It was a different Lena here, of course; one who had had more of a sex life with John, but there was something more than that, too. She was probably sleeping with Castle, he thought, and the extra attention was a conscious or unconscious compensation, or defense.

Castle seemed a little harder and more serious in this world than the last, not only from his terse moodiness in the pickup, but from recollections of parallel conversations. John wondered how shady he actually was; whether he'd been honest about his police record.

(He hadn't been. In this universe, when Lena had asked him whether he had ever been in trouble with the police, he'd answered a terse "no." In fact, he'd done eight hard years in Ohio for an armed robbery he hadn't committed—the real robber hadn't been so stupid, here—and he'd come out of prison bitter, angry, an actual criminal. Figuring the world owed him one, a week after getting out he stopped for a hitchhiker on a lonely country road, pulled a gun, walked him a few yards off the road into a field of high corn, and shot him pointblank at the base of the skull. It didn't look anything like the movies.)

(He drove off without touching the body, which a farmer's child found two days later. The victim turned out to be a college student who was on probation for dealing—all he'd really done was buy a kilo of green and make his money back by selling bags to his friends, and one enemy—so the papers said **DRUG DEALER FOUND SLAIN IN GANGLAND-STYLE KILLING** and the police pursued the matter with no enthusiasm. Castle was in Key West well before the farmer's child smelled the body, anyhow.)

As they rode along, whatever Lena had or hadn't done with Castle was less interesting to John than what *he* was planning to do with her. Half of his self had never experienced sex, as an adult, without the sensory handicaps engendered by scar tissue and severed nerves in the genitals, and he was looking forward to the experience with relish that was obvious, at least to Lena. She encouraged him in not-so-subtle ways, and by the time they crossed the last bridge into Key West, he was ready to tell Castle to pull over at the first bush.

He left the typewriter in Castle's care and declined help with the luggage. By this time Lena was smiling at his obvious impatience; she was giggling by the time they were momentarily stalled by a truculent door key; laughed her delight as he carried her charging across the room to the couch, then clawing off a minimum of clothing and taking her with fierce haste, wordless, and keeping her on a breathless edge he drifted the rest of the clothes off her and carried her into the bedroom, where they made so much noise Julio banged on the ceiling with a broomstick.

They did quiet down eventually, and lay together in a puddle of mingled sweat, panting, watching the fan push the humid air around. "Guess we both get to sleep in the wet spot," John said.

"No complaints." She raised up on one elbow and traced a figure eight on his chest. "You're full of surprises tonight, Dr. Baird."

"Life is full of surprises."

"You should go away more often—or at least come back more often."

"It's all that Hemingway research. Makes a man out of you."

"You didn't learn this in a book," she said, gently taking his penis and pantomiming a certain motion.

"I did, though; an anthropology book." In another universe. "It's what they do in the Solomon Islands."

"Wisdom of Solomon," she said, lying back. After a pause: "They have anthropology books at JFK?"

"Uh, no." He remembered he didn't own that book in this universe. "Browsing at Wordsworth's."

"Hope you bought the book."

"Didn't have to." He gave her a long slow caress. "Memorized the good parts."

On the other side of town, six days later, she was in about the same position on Castle's bed, and even more exhausted.

"Aren't you overdoing the loving little wifey bit? It's been a week."

She exhaled audibly. "What a week."

"Missed you." He nuzzled her and made an unsubtle preparatory gesture.

"No, you don't." She rolled out of bed. "Once is plenty." She went to the mirror and ran a brush through her damp hair. "Besides, it's not me you missed. You missed *it*." She sat at the open window, improving the neighborhood's scenery. "*It's* gonna need a Teflon lining installed."

"Old boy's feelin' his oats?"

"Not feeling *his* anything. God, I don't know what's gotten into him. Four, five times a day; six."

"Screwed, blewed, and tattooed. You asked for it."

"As a matter of fact, I didn't. I haven't had a chance to start my little act. He got off that train with an erection, and he still has it. No woman would be safe around him. Nothing wet and concave would be safe."

576

"So does that mean it's a good time to bring in Pansy? Or is he so stuck on you he wouldn't even notice her?"

She scowled at the brush, picking hair out of it. "Actually, Castle, I was just about to ask you the same thing. Relying on your well-known expertise in animal behavior."

"Okay." He sat up. "I say we oughta go for it. If he's a walkin' talkin' hard-on like you say . . . Pansy'd pull him like a magnet. You'd have to be a fuckin' monk not to want Pansy."

"Like Rasputin."

"Like who?"

"Never mind." She went back to the brush. "I guess, I guess one problem is that I really am enjoying the attention. I guess I'm not too anxious to hand him over to this champion sexpot."

"Aw, Lena—"

"Really. I do love him in my way, Castle. I don't want to lose him over this scheme."

"You're not gonna lose him. Trust me. You catch him dickin' Pansy, get mad, forgive him. Hell, you'll have him wrapped around your finger."

"I guess. You make the competition sound pretty formidable."

"Don't worry. She's outa there the next day."

"Unless she winds up in love with him. That would be cute."

"He's almost twice her age. Besides, she's a whore. Whores don't fall in love."

"They're women, Castle. Women fall in love."

"Yeah, sure. Just like on TV."

She turned away from him; looked out the window. "You really know how to make a woman feel great, you know?"

"Come on." He crossed over and smoothed her hair. She turned around but didn't look up. "Don't run yourself down, Lena. You're still one hell of a piece of ass."

"Thanks." She smiled into his leer and grabbed him. "If you weren't such a poet I'd trade you in for a vibrator."

15. In Praise Of His Mistress

Pansy was indeed beautiful, even under normal conditions; delicate features, wasp waist combined with generous secondary sexual characteristics. The conditions under which John first saw her were calculated to maximize sexiness and vulnerability. Red nylon running shorts, tight and very short, and a white sleeveless T-shirt from a local bar that was stamped "LAST

HETEROSEXUAL IN KEY WEST"—all clinging to her golden skin with a healthy sweat, the cloth made translucent enough to reveal no possibility of underwear.

John looked out the screen door and saw her at the other door, struggling with a heavy box while trying to make the key work. "Let me help you," he said through the screen, and stepped across the short landing to hold the box while she got the door open.

"You're too kind." John tried not to stare as he handed the box back. Pansy, of course, was relieved at his riveted attention. It had taken days to set up this operation, and would take more days to bring it to its climax, so to speak, and more days to get back to normal. But she did owe Castle a big favor and this guy seemed nice enough. Maybe she'd learn something about Hemingway in the process.

"More to come up?" John asked.

"Oh, I couldn't ask you to help. I can manage."

"It's okay. I was just goofing off for the rest of the day."

It turned out to be quite a job, even though there was only one load from a small rented truck. Most of the load was uniform and heavy boxes of books, carefully labeled LIT A-B, GEN REF, ENCY 1–12, and so forth. Most of her furniture, accordingly, was cinder blocks and boards, the standard student bookshelf arrangement.

John found out that despite a couple of dozen boxes marked LIT, Pansy hadn't majored in literature, but rather Special Education; during the school year, she taught third grade at a school for the retarded in Key Largo. She didn't tell him about the several years she'd spent as a call girl, but if she had, John might have seen a connection that Castle would never have made—that the driving force behind both of the jobs was the same, charity. The more-or-less easy forty dollars an hour for going on a date and then having sex was a factor, too, but she really did like making lonely men feel special, and had herself felt more like a social worker than a woman of easy virtue. And the hundreds of men who had fallen for her, for love or money, weren't responding only to her cheerleader's body. She had a sunny disposition and a natural, artless way of concentrating on a man that made him for a while the only man in the world.

John would not normally be an easy conquest. Twenty years of facing classrooms full of coeds had given him a certain wariness around attractive young women. He also had an impulse toward faithfulness, Lena having suddenly left town, her father ill. But he was still in the grip of the weird overweening horniness that had animated him since inheriting this new body and double-image personality. If Pansy had said "Let's do it," they would be doing it so soon that she would be wise to unwrap the condom before speaking. But she was being as indirect as her nature and mode of dress would allow.

"Do you and your wife always come down here for the summer?"

"We usually go somewhere. Boston's no fun in the heat."

"It must be wonderful in the fall."

And so forth. It felt odd for Pansy, probably the last time she would ever seduce a man for reasons other than personal interest. She wanted it to be perfect. She wanted John to have enough pleasure in her to compensate for the embarrassment of their "accidental" exposure, and whatever hassle his wife would put him through afterwards.

She was dying to know why Castle wanted him set up, but he refused to tell. How Castle ever met a quiet, kindly gentleman like John was a mystery, too—she had met some of Castle's friends, and they had other virtues.

Quiet and kindly, but horny. Whenever she contrived, in the course of their working together, to expose a nipple or a little beaver, he would turn around to adjust himself, and blush. More like a teenager, discovering his sexuality, than a middle-aged married man.

He was a pushover, but she didn't want to make it too easy. After they had finished putting the books up on shelves, she said thanks a million; I gotta go now, spending the night house-sitting up in Islamorada. You and your wife come over for dinner tomorrow? Oh, then come on over yourself. No, that's all right, I'm a big girl. Roast beef okay? See ya.

Driving away in the rented truck, Pansy didn't feel especially proud of herself. She was amused at John's sexiness and looking forward to trying it out. But she could read people pretty well, and sensed a core of deep sadness in John. Maybe it was from Vietnam; he hadn't mentioned it, but she knew what the bracelet meant.

Whatever the problem, maybe she'd have time to help him with it—before she had to turn around and add to it.

Maybe it would work out for the best. Maybe the problem was with his wife, and she'd leave, and he could start over. . . .

Stop kidding yourself. Just lay the trap, catch him, deliver him. Castle was not the kind of man you want to disappoint.

16. Fiesta

She had baked the roast slowly with wine and fruit juice, along with dried apricots and apples plumped in port wine, seasoned with cinnamon and nutmeg and cardamom. Onions and large cubes of acorn squash simmered in the broth. She served new potatoes steamed with parsley and dressed Italian style, with garlicky olive oil and a splash of vinegar. Small Caesar salad and air-light *pan de agua*, the Cuban bread that made you forget every other kind of bread.

579

The way to a man's heart, her mother had contended, was through his stomach, and although she was accustomed to aiming rather lower, she thought it was probably a good approach for a long-time married man suddenly forced to fend for himself. That was exactly right for John. He was not much of a cook but he was an accomplished eater.

He pushed the plate away after three helpings. "God, I'm such a pig. But that was irresistible."

"Thank you." She cleared the table slowly, accepting John's offer to help. "My mother's 'company' recipe. So you think Hadley might have just thrown the stories away, and made up the business about the train?"

"People have raised the possibility. There she was, eight years older than this handsome hubby—with half the women on the Left Bank after him, at least in her mind—and he's starting to get published, starting to build a reputation. . . ."

"She was afraid he was going to 'grow away' from her? Or did they have that expression back then?"

"I think she was afraid he would start making money from his writing. She had an inheritance, a trust fund from her grandfather, that paid over two thousand a year. That was plenty to keep the two of them comfortable in Paris. Hemingway talked poor in those days, starving artist, but he lived pretty well."

"He probably resented it, too. Not making the money himself."

"That would be like him. Anyhow, if she chucked the stories to ensure his dependency, it backfired. He was still furious thirty years later—three wives later. He said the stuff had been 'fresh from the mint,' even if the writing wasn't so great, and he was never able to reclaim it."

She opened a cabinet and slid a bottle out of its burlap bag, and selected two small glasses. "Sherry?" He said why not? and they moved into the living room.

The living room was mysteriously devoid of chairs, so they had to sit together on the small couch. "You don't actually think she did it."

"No." John watched her pour the sherry. "From what I've read about her, she doesn't seem at all calculating. Just a sweet gal from St. Louis who fell in love with a cad."

"Cad. Funny old-fashioned word."

John shrugged. "Actually, he wasn't really a cad. I think he sincerely loved every one of his wives . . . at least until he married them."

They both laughed. "Of course it could have been something in between," Pansy said, "I mean, she didn't actually throw away the manuscripts, but she did leave them sitting out, begging to be stolen. Why did she leave the compartment?"

"That's one screwy aspect of it. Hadley herself never said, not on paper.

Every biographer seems to come up with a different reason: she went to get a newspaper, she saw some people she recognized and stepped out to talk with them, wanted some exercise before the long trip . . . even Hemingway had two different versions—she went out to get a bottle of Evian water or to buy something to read. That one pissed him off, because she did have an overnight bag full of the best American writing since Mark Twain."

"How would you have felt?"

"Felt?"

"I mean, you say you've written stories, too. What if somebody, your wife, made a mistake and you lost everything?"

He looked thoughtful. "It's not the same. In the first place, it's just a hobby with me. And I don't have that much that hasn't been published—when Hemingway lost it, he lost it for good. I could just go to a university library and make new copies of everything."

"So you haven't written much lately?"

"Not stories. Academic stuff."

"I'd love to read some of your stories."

"And I'd love to have you read them. But I don't have any here. I'll mail you some from Boston."

She nodded, staring at him with a curious intensity. "Oh hell," she said, and turned her back to him. "Would you help me with this?"

"What?"

"The zipper." She was wearing a clingy white summer dress. "Undo the zipper a little bit."

He slowly unzipped it a few inches. She did it the rest of the way, stood up and hooked her thumbs under the shoulder straps and shrugged. The dress slithered to the floor. She wasn't wearing anything else.

"You're blushing." Actually, he was doing a good imitation of a beached fish. She straddled him, sitting back lightly on his knees, legs wide, and started unbuttoning his shirt.

"Uh," he said.

"I just get impatient. You don't mind?"

"Uh . . . no?"

17. On Being Shot Again

John woke up happy but didn't open his eyes for nearly a minute, holding on to the erotic dream of the century. Then he opened one eye and saw it hadn't been a dream: the tousled bed in the strange room, unguents and sex toys on the nightstand, the smell of her hair on the other pillow. A noise from the kitchen; coffee and bacon smells.

He put on pants and went into the living room to pick up the shirt where it had dropped. "Good morning, Pansy."

"Morning, stranger." She was wearing a floppy terrycloth bathrobe with the sleeves rolled up to her elbows. She turned the bacon carefully with a fork. "Scrambled eggs okay?"

"Marvelous." He sat down at the small table and poured himself a cup of coffee. "I don't know what to say."

She smiled at him. "Don't say anything. It was nice."

"More than nice." He watched her precise motions behind the counter. She broke the eggs one-handed, two at a time, added a splash of water to the bowl, plucked some chives from a windowbox and chopped them with a small Chinese cleaver, rocking it in a staccato chatter; scraped them into the bowl, and followed them with a couple of grinds of pepper. She set the bacon out on a paper towel, with another towel to cover. Then she stirred the eggs briskly with the fork and set them aside. She picked up the big cast-iron frying pan and poured off a judicious amount of grease. Then she poured the egg mixture into the pan and studied it with alertness.

"Know what I think?" John said.

"Something profound?"

"Huh-uh. I think I'm in a rubber room someplace, hallucinating the whole thing. And I hope they never cure me."

"I think you're a butterfly who's dreaming he's a man. I'm glad I'm in your dream." She slowly stirred and scraped the eggs with a spatula.

"You like older men?"

"One of them." She looked up, serious. "I like men who are considerate . . . and playful." She returned to the scraping. "Last couple of boyfriends I had were all dick and no heart. Kept to myself the last few months."

"Glad to be of service."

"You could rent yourself out as a service." She laughed. "You must have been impossible when you were younger."

"Different." Literally.

She ran hot water into a serving bowl, then returned to her egg stewardship. "I've been thinking."

"Yes?"

"The lost manuscript stuff we were talking about last night, all the different explanations." She divided the egg into four masses and turned each one. "Did you ever read any science fiction?"

"No. Vonnegut."

"The toast." She hurriedly put four pieces of bread in the toaster. "They write about alternate universes. Pretty much like our own, but different in one way or another. Important or trivial."

"What, uh, what silliness."

She laughed and poured the hot water out of the serving bowl, and dried it with a towel. "I guess maybe. But what if . . . what if all of those versions were equally true? In different universes. And for some reason they all came together here." She started to put the eggs into the bowl when there was a knock on the door.

It opened and Ernest Hemingway walked in. Dapper, just twenty, wearing the Italian army cape he'd brought back from the war. He pointed the black and white cane at Pansy. "Bingo."

She looked at John and then back at the Hemingway. She dropped the serving bowl; it clattered on the floor without breaking. Her knees buckled and she fainted dead away, executing a half-turn as she fell so that the back of her head struck the wooden floor with a loud thump and the bathrobe drifted open from the waist down.

The Hemingway stared down at her frontal aspect. "Sometimes I wish I were human," it said. "Your pleasures are intense. Simple, but intense." It moved toward her with the cane.

John stood up. "If you kill her—"

"Oh?" It cocked an eyebrow at him. "What will you do?"

John took one step toward it and it waved the cane. A waist-high brick wall surmounted by needle-sharp spikes appeared between them. It gestured again and an impossible moat appeared, deep enough to reach down well into Julio's living room. It filled with water and a large crocodile surfaced and rested its chin on the parquet floor, staring at John. It yawned teeth.

The Hemingway held up its cane. "The white end. It doesn't kill, remember?" The wall and moat disappeared and the cane touched Pansy lightly below the navel. She twitched minutely but continued to sleep. "She'll have a headache," it said. "And she'll be somewhat confused by the uncommunicatable memory of having seen me. But that will all fade, compared to the sudden tragedy of having her new lover die here, just sitting waiting for his breakfast."

"Do you enjoy this?"

"I love my work. It's all I have." It walked toward him, footfalls splashing as it crossed where the moat had been. "You have not personally helped, though. Not at all."

It sat down across from him and poured coffee into a mug that said ON THE SIXTH DAY GOD CREATED MAN—SHE MUST HAVE HAD PMS.

"When you kill me this time, do you think it will 'take'?"

"I don't know. It's never failed before." The toaster made a noise. "Toast?"

"Sure." Two pieces appeared on his plate; two on the Hemingway's. "Usually when you kill people they stay dead?"

"I don't kill that many people." It spread margarine on its toast; gestured, and marmalade appeared. "But when I do, yeah. They die all up and down the Omniverse, every timespace. All except you." He pointed toast at John's toast. "Go ahead. It's not poison."

"Not my idea of a last meal."

The Hemingway shrugged. "What would you like?"

"Forget it." He buttered the toast and piled marmalade on it, determined out of some odd impulse to act as if nothing unusual were happening. Breakfast with Hemingway, big deal.

He studied the apparition and noticed that it was somewhat translucent, almost like a traditional TV ghost. He could barely see a line that was the back of the chair, bisecting its chest below shoulderblade level. Was this something new? There hadn't been too much light in the train; maybe he had just failed to notice it before.

"A penny for your thoughts."

He didn't say anything about seeing through it. "Has it occurred to you that maybe you're not *supposed* to kill me? That's why I came back?"

The Hemingway chuckled and admired its nails. "That's a nearly content-free assertion."

"Oh really." He bit into the toast. The marmalade was strong, pleasantly bitter.

"It presupposes a higher authority, unknown to me, that's watching over my behavior, and correcting me when I do wrong. Doesn't exist, sorry."

"That's the oldest one in the theologian's book." He set down the toast and kneaded his stomach; shouldn't eat something so strong first thing in the morning. "You can only *assert* the nonexistence of something; you can't prove it."

"What you mean is *you* can't." He held up the cane and looked at it. "The simplest explanation is that there's something wrong with the cane. There's no way I can test it; if I kill the wrong person there's hell to pay up and down the Omniverse. But what I can do is kill you without the cane. See whether you come back again, some timespace."

Sharp, stabbing pains in his stomach now. "Bastard." Heart pounding slow and hard: shirt rustled in time to its spasms.

"Cyanide in the marmalade. Gives it a certain *frisson*, don't you think?"

He couldn't breathe. His heart pounded once, and stopped. Vicious pain in his left arm, then paralysis. From an inch away, he could just see the weave of the white tablecloth. It turned red and then black.

18. The Sun Also Rises

From blackness to brilliance: the morning sun pouring through the window at a flat angle. He screwed up his face and blinked.

Suddenly smothered in terrycloth, between soft breasts. "John, John."

He put his elbow down to support himself, uncomfortable on the parquet floor, and looked up at Pansy. Her face was wet with tears. He cleared his throat. "What happened?"

"You, you started putting on your foot and . . . you just fell over. I thought. . . ."

John looked down over his body, hard ropy muscle and deep tan under white body hair, the puckered bullet wound a little higher on the abdomen. Left leg ended in a stump just above the ankle.

Trying not to faint. His third past flooding back. Walking down a dirt road near Kontum, the sudden loud bang of the mine and he pitched forward, unbelievable pain, rolled over and saw his bloody boot yards away; grey, jagged shinbone sticking through the bloody smoking rag of his pants leg, bright crimson splashing on the dry dust, loud in the shocked silence; another bloodstain spreading between his legs, the deep mortal pain there—and he started to buck and scream and two men held him while the medic took off his belt and made a tourniquet and popped morphine through the cloth and unbuttoned his fly and slowly worked his pants down: penis torn by shrapnel, scrotum ripped open in a bright red flap of skin, bloody grey-blue egg of a testicle separating, rolling out. He fainted, then and now.

And woke up with her lips against his, her breath sweet in his lungs, his nostrils pinched painfully tight. He made a strangled noise and clutched her breast.

She cradled his head, panting, smiling through tears, and kissed him lightly on the forehead. "Will you stop fainting now?"

"Yeah. Don't worry." Her lips were trembling. He put a finger on them. "Just a longer night than I'm accustomed to. An overdose of happiness."

The happiest night of his life, maybe of three lives. Like coming back from the dead.

"Should I call a doctor?"

"No. I faint every now and then." Usually at the gym, from pushing too hard. He slipped his hand inside the terrycloth and covered her breast. "It's been . . . do you know how long it's been since I . . . did it? I mean . . . three times in one night?"

"About six hours." She smiled. "And you can say 'fuck.' I'm no schoolgirl."

"I'll say." The night had been an escalating progression of intimacies, gymnastics, accessories. "Had to wonder where a sweet girl like you learned all that."

She looked away, lips pursed, thoughtful. With a light fingertip she stroked the length of his penis and smiled when it started to uncurl. "At work."

"What?"

"I was a prostitute. That's where I learned the tricks. Practice makes perfect."

"Prostitute. Wow."

"Are you shocked? Outraged?"

"Just surprised." That was true. He respected the sorority and was grateful to it for having made Vietnam almost tolerable, an hour or so at a time. "But now you've got to do something really mean. I could never love a prostitute with a heart of gold."

"I'll give it some thought." She shifted. "Think you can stand up?"

"Sure." She stood and gave him her hand. He touched it but didn't pull; rose in a smooth practiced motion, then took one hop and sat down at the small table. He started strapping on his foot.

"I've read about those new ones," she said, "the permanent kind."

"Yeah; I've read about them, too. Computer interface, graft your nerves onto sensors." He shuddered. "No, thanks. No more surgery."

"Not worth it for the convenience?"

"Being able to wiggle my toes, have my foot itch? No. Besides, the VA won't pay for it." That startled John as he said it: here, he hadn't grown up rich. His father had spent all the mill money on a photocopy firm six months before Xerox came on the market. "You say you 'were' a prostitute. Not any more?"

"No, that was the truth about teaching. Let's start this egg thing over." She picked up the bowl she had dropped in the other universe. "I gave up whoring about seven years ago." She picked up an egg, looked at it, set it down. She half-turned and stared out the kitchen window. "I can't do this to you."

"You . . . can't do what?"

"Oh, lie. Keep lying." She went to the refrigerator. "Want a beer?"

"Lying? No, no thanks. What lying?"

She opened a beer, still not looking at him. "I like you, John. I really like you. But I didn't just . . . spontaneously fall into your arms." She took a healthy swig and started pouring some of the bottle into a glass.

"I don't understand."

She walked back, concentrating on pouring the beer, then sat down gracelessly. She took a deep breath and let it out, staring at his chest. "Castle put me up to it."

"Castle?"

She nodded. "Sylvester Castlemaine, boy wonder."

John sat back stunned. "But you said you don't do that anymore," he said without too much logic. "Do it for money."

"Not for money," she said in a flat, hurt voice.

"I should've known. A woman like you wouldn't want. . . ." He made a gesture that dismissed his body from the waist down.

"You do all right. Don't feel sorry for yourself." Her face showed a pinch of regret for that, but she plowed on. "If it were just the obligation, once would have been enough. I wouldn't have had to fuck and suck all night long to win you over."

"No," he said, "that's true. Just the first moment, when you undressed. That was enough."

"I owe Castle a big favor. A friend of mine was going to be prosecuted for involving a minor in prostitution. It was a set-up, pure and simple."

"She worked for the same outfit you did?"

"Yeah, but this was free-lance. I think it was the escort service that set her up, sort of delivered her and the man in return for this or that."

She sipped at the beer. "Guy wanted a three-way. My friend had met this girl a couple of days before at the bar where she worked part-time . . . she looked old enough; said she was in the biz."

"She was neither?"

"God knows. Maybe she got caught as a juvie and made a deal. Anyhow, he'd just slipped it to her and suddenly cops comin' in the windows. Threw the book at him. 'Two inches, twenty years,' my friend said. He was a county commissioner somewhere, with enemies. Almost dragged my friend down with him. I'm *sorry*." Her voice was angry.

"Don't be." John said, almost a whisper. "It's understandable. Whatever happens, I've got last night."

She nodded. "So two of the cops who were going to testify got busted for possession, cocaine. The word came down and everybody remembered the woman was somebody else."

"So what did Castle want you to do? With me?"

"Oh, whatever comes natural—or *un*-natural, if that's what you wanted. And later be doing it at a certain time and place, where we'd be caught in the act."

"By Castle?"

"And his trusty little VCR. Then I guess he'd threaten to show it to your wife, or the university."

"I wonder. Lena . . . she knows I've had other women."

"But not lately."

"No. Not for years."

"It might be different now. She might be starting to feel, well, insecure."

"Any woman who looked at you would feel insecure."

She shrugged. "That could be part of it. Could it cost you your job, too?"

"I don't see how. It would be awkward, but it's not as if you were one of my students—and even that happens, without costing the guy his job." He laughed. "Poor old Larry. He had a student kiss and tell, and had to run the Speakers' Committee for four or five years. Got allergic to wine and cheese. But he made tenure."

"So what is it?" She leaned forward. "Are you an addict or something?"

"Addict?"

"I mean how come you even *know* Castle? He didn't pick your name out of a phone book and have me come seduce you, just to see what would happen."

"No, of course not."

"So? I confess, you confess."

John passed a hand over his face and pressed the other hand against his knee, bearing down to keep the foot from tapping. "You don't want to be involved."

"What do you call last night, Spin the Bottle? I'm in*volved!*"

"Not the way I mean. It's illegal."

"Oh golly. Not really."

"Let me think." John picked up their dishes and limped back to the sink. He set them down there and fiddled with the straps and pad that connected the foot to his stump, then poured himself a cup of coffee and came back, not limping.

He sat down slowly and blew across the coffee. "What it is, is that *Castle* thinks there's a scam going on. He's wrong. I've taken steps to ensure that it couldn't work." His foot tapped twice.

"You think. You hope."

"No. I'm sure. Anyhow, I'm stringing Castle along because I need his expertise in a certain matter."

" 'A certain matter,' yeah. Sounds wholesome."

"Actually, that part's not illegal."

"So tell me about it."

"Nope. Still might backfire."

She snorted. "You know what might *back*fire. Fucking with Castle."

"I can take care of him."

"You don't know. He may be more dangerous than you think he is."

"He talks a lot."

"You men." She took a drink and poured the rest of the bottle into the glass. "Look, I was at a party with him, couple of years ago. He was drunk, got into a little coke, started babbling."

"In vino veritas?"

"Yeah, and Coke is It. But he said he'd killed three people, strangers, just to see what it felt like. He liked it. I more than halfway believe him."

John looked at her silently for a moment, sorting out his new memories of Castle. "Well . . . he's got a mean streak. I don't know about murder. Certainly not over this thing."

"Which is?"

"You'll have to trust me. It's not because of Castle that I can't tell you." He remembered her one universe ago, lying helpless while the Hemingway lowered its cane onto her nakedness. "Trust me?"

She studied the top of the glass, running her finger around it. "Suppose I do. Then what?"

"Business as usual. You didn't tell me anything. Deliver me to Castle and his video camera; I'll try to put on a good show."

"And when he confronts you with it?"

"Depends on what he wants. He knows I don't have much money." John shrugged. "If it's unreasonable, he can go ahead and show the tape to Lena. She can live with it."

"And your department head?"

"He'd give me a medal."

19. in our time

So it wasn't the cane. He ate enough cyanide to kill a horse, but evidently only in one universe.

You checked the next day in all the others?

All 119. He's still dead in the one where I killed him on the train—

That's encouraging.

—but there's no causal resonance in the others.

Oh, but there is some resonance. He remembered you in the universe where you poisoned him. Maybe in all of them.

That's impossible.

Once is impossible. Twice is a trend. A hundred and twenty means something is going on that we don't understand.

What I suggest—

No. You can't go back and kill them all one by one.

If the wand had worked the first time, they'd all be dead anyhow. There's no reason to think we'd cause more of an eddy by doing them one at a time.

It's not something to experiment with. As you well know.

I don't know how we're going to solve it otherwise.

Simple. Don't kill him. Talk to him again. He may be getting frightened, if he remembers both times he died.

Here's an idea. What if someone else killed him?

I don't know. If you just hired someone—made him a direct agent of your will—it wouldn't be any different from the cyanide. Maybe as a last resort. Talk to him again first.

All right. I'll try.

20. Of Wounds and Other Causes

Although John found it difficult to concentrate, trying not to think about Pansy, this was the best time he would have for the forseeable future to summon the Hemingway demon and try to do something about exorcising it. He didn't want either of the women around if the damned thing went on a killing spree again. They might just do as he did, and slip over into another reality—as unpleasant as that was, it was at least living—but the Hemingway had said otherwise. There was no reason to suspect it was not the truth.

Probably the best way to get the thing's attention was to resume work on the Hemingway pastiche. He decided to rewrite the first page to warm up, typing it out in Hemingway's style:

ALONG WITH YOUTH

1. Mitraigliatrice

The dirt on the side of the trench was never dry in the morning. If Fever could find a dry newspaper he could put it between his chest and the dirt when he went out to lean on the side of the trench and wait for the light .First light was the best time . You might have luck and see a muzzle flash to aim at . But patience was better than luck . Wait to see a helmet or a head without a helmet .

Fever looked at the enemy trench line through a rectangular box of wood that pushed through the trench wall at about ground level . The other end of the box was covered with a square of gauze the color of dirt . A man looking directly at it might see the muzzle flash when Fever fired through the box . But with luck , the flash would be the last thing he saw .

Fever had fired through the gauze six times . He'd potted at least three Austrians . Now the gauze had a ragged hole in the center . One bullet had come in the other way , an accident , and chiseled a deep gouge in the floor of the wooden box . Fever knew that he would be able to see the splinters sticking up before he could see any detail at the enemy trench line .

That would be maybe twenty minutes . Fever wanted a cigarette . There was plenty of time to go down in the bunker and light one . But it would fox his night vision . Better to wait .

Fever heard movement before he heard the voice . He picked up one of the grenades on the plank shelf to his left and his thumb felt the ring on the cotter pin . Someone was crawling in front of his position . Slow crawling but not too quiet . He slid his left forefinger through the ring and waited .

-----Help me, came a strained whisper .

Fever felt his shoulders tense . Of course many Austrians could speak Italian .

-----I am wounded . Help me . I can go no farther .

-----What is your name and unit , Fever whispered through the box .

------Jean-Franco Dante . Four forty-seventh.

That was the unit that had taken such a beating at the evening show . -----At first light they will kill me .

-----All right . But I'm coming over with a grenade in my hand . If you kill me , you die as well .

-----I will commend this logic to your superior officer . Please hurry .

Fever slid his rifle into the wooden box and eased himself to the top of the trench . He took the grenade out of his pocket and carefully worked the pin out , the arming lever held secure . He kept the pin around his finger so he could replace it .

He inched his way down the slope , guided by the man's whispers .
After a few minutes his probing hand found the man's shoulder .
-----Thank God . Make haste , now .

The soldier's feet were both shattered by a mine . He would have
to be carried .

-----Don't cry out , Fever said . This will hurt .

------No sound , the soldier said . And when Fever raised him up
onto his back there was only a breath . But his canteen was loose .
It fell on a rock and made a loud hollow sound .

Firecracker pop above them and the night was all glare and bobbing shadow . A big machine-gun opened up rong, cararong, rong ,
rong . Fever headed for the parapet above as fast as he could but
knew it was hopeless . He saw dirt spray twice to his right and then
felt the thud of the bullet into the Italian , who said " Jesus " as if
only annoyed , and they almost made it then but on the lip of the
trench a hard snowball hit Fever behind the kneecap and they both
went down in a tumble . They fell two yards to safety but the Italian
was already dead .

Fever had sprained his wrist and hurt his nose falling and they
hurt worse than the bullet . But he couldn't move his toes and he
knew that must be bad . Then it started to hurt .

A rifleman closed the Italian's eyes and with the help of another
clumsy one dragged Fever down the trench to the medical bunker .
It hurt awfully and his shoe filled up with blood and he puked . They
stopped to watch him puke and then dragged him the rest of the
way .

The surgeon placed him between two kerosene lanterns . He removed the puttee and shoe and cut the bloody pants leg with a
straight razor . He rolled Fever onto his stomach and had four men
hold him down while he probed for the bullet . The pain was great
but Fever was insulted enough by the four men not to cry out . He
heard the bullet clink into a metal dish . It sounded like the canteen .

592

"That's a little too pat, don't you think?" John turned around and there was the Hemingway, reading over his shoulder. " 'It sounded like the canteen,' indeed." Khaki army uniform covered with mud and splattered with bright blood. Blood dripped and pooled at its feet.

"So shoot me. Or whatever it's going to be this time. Maybe I'll rewrite the line in the next universe."

"You're going to run out soon. You only exist in eight more universes."

"Sure. And you've never lied to me." John turned back around and stared at the typewriter, tensed.

The Hemingway sighed. "Suppose we talk, instead."

"I'm listening."

The Hemingway walked past him toward the kitchen. "Want a beer?"

"Not while I'm working."

"Suit yourself." It limped into the kitchen, out of sight, and John heard it open the refrigerator and pry the top off of a beer. It came back out as the five-year-old Hemingway, dressed up in girl's clothing, both hands clutching an incongruous beer bottle. It set the bottle on the end table and crawled up onto the couch with childish clumsiness.

"Where's the cane?"

"I knew it wouldn't be necessary this time," it piped. "It occurs to me that there are better ways to deal with a man like you."

"Do tell." John smiled. "What is 'a man like me'? One on whom your cane for some reason doesn't work?"

"Actually, what I was thinking of was curiosity. That is supposedly what motivates scholars. You *are* a real scholar, not just a rich man seeking legitimacy?"

John looked away from the ancient eyes in the boy's face. "I've sometimes wondered myself. Why don't you cut to the chase, as we used to say. A few universes ago."

"I've done spot-checks on your life through various universes," the child said. "You're always a Hemingway buff, though you don't always do it for a living."

"What else do I do?"

"It's probably not healthy for you to know. But all of you are drawn to the missing manuscripts at about this time, the seventy-fifth anniversary."

"I wonder why that would be."

The Hemingway waved the beer bottle in a disarmingly mature gesture. "The Omniverse is full of threads of coincidence like that. They have causal meaning in a dimension you can't deal with."

"Try me."

"In a way, that's what I want to propose. You will drop this dangerous project at once, and never resume it. In return, I will take you back in time, back to the Gare de Lyon on December 14, 1921."

"Where I will see what happens to the manuscripts."

Another shrug. "I will put you on Hadley's train, well before she said the manuscripts were stolen. You will be able to observe for an hour or so, without being seen. As you know, some people have theorized that there never was a thief; never was an overnight bag; that Hadley simply threw the writings away. If that's the case, you won't see anything dramatic. But the absence of the overnight bag would be powerful indirect proof."

John looked skeptical. "You've never gone to check it out for yourself?"

"If I had, I wouldn't be able to take you back. I can't exist twice in the same timespace, of course."

"How foolish of me. Of course."

"Is it a deal?"

John studied the apparition. The couch's plaid upholstery showed through its arms and legs. It did appear to become less substantial each time. "I don't know. Let me think about it a couple of days."

The child pulled on the beer bottle and it stretched into a long amber stick. It turned into the black-and-white cane. "We haven't tried cancer yet. That might be the one that works." It slipped off the couch and sidled toward John. "It does take longer and it hurts. It hurts 'awfully.' "

John got out of the chair. "You come near me with that and I'll dropkick you into next Tuesday."

The child shimmered and became Hemingway in his mid-forties, a big-gutted barroom brawler. "Sure you will, Champ." It held out the cane so that the tip was inches from John's chest. "See you around." It disappeared with a barely audible pop, and a slight breeze as air moved to fill its space.

John thought about that as he went to make a fresh cup of coffee. He wished he knew more about science. The thing obviously takes up space, since its disappearance caused a vacuum, but there was no denying that it was fading away.

Well, not fading. Just becoming more transparent. That might not affect its abilities. A glass door is as much of a door as an opaque one, if you try to walk through it.

He sat down on the couch, away from the manuscript so he could think without distraction. On the face of it, this offer by the Hemingway was an admission of defeat. An admission, at least, that it couldn't solve its problem by killing him over and over. That was comforting. He would just as soon not die again, except for the one time.

But maybe he should. That was a chilling thought. If he made the Hemingway kill him another dozen times, another hundred . . . what kind of strange creature would he become? A hundred overlapping autobiographies, all perfectly remembered? Surely the brain has a finite capacity for storing information; he'd "fill up," as Pansy said. Or maybe it wasn't finite, at least in his case—but that was logically absurd. There are only so many cells in a brain. Of course he might be "wired" in some way to the John Bairds in all the other universes he had inhabited.

And what would happen if he died in some natural way, not dispatched by an inter-dimensional assassin? Would he still slide into another identity? That was a lovely prospect: sooner or later he would be 130 years old, on his deathbed, dying every fraction of a second for the rest of eternity.

Or maybe the Hemingway wasn't lying, this time, and he had only eight lives left. In context, the possibility was reassuring.

The phone rang; for a change, John was grateful for the interruption. It was Lena, saying her father had come home from the hospital, much better, and she thought she could come on home day after tomorrow. Fine, John said, feeling a little wicked; I'll borrow a car and pick you up at the airport. Don't bother, Lena said; besides, she didn't have a flight number yet.

John didn't press it. If, as he assumed, Lena was in on the plot with Castle, she was probably here in Key West, or somewhere nearby. If she had to buy a ticket to and from Omaha to keep up her end of the ruse, the money would come out of John's pocket.

He hung up and, on impulse, dialed her parents' number. Her father answered. Putting on his professorial tone, he said he was Maxwell Perkins, Blue Cross claims adjuster, and he needed to know the exact date when Mr. Monaghan entered the hospital for this recent confinement. He said you must have the wrong guy; I haven't been inside a hospital in twenty years, knock on wood. Am I not speaking to John Franklin Monaghan? No, this is John *Frederick* Monaghan. Terribly sorry, natural mistake. That's okay; hope the other guy's okay, goodbye, good night, sir.

So tomorrow was going to be the big day with Pansy. To his knowledge, John hadn't been watched during sex for more than twenty years, and never by a disinterested, or at least dispassionate, observer. He hoped that knowing they were being spied upon wouldn't affect his performance. Or knowing that it would be the last time.

A profound helpless sadness settled over him. He knew that the last thing you should do, in a mood like this, was go out and get drunk. It was barely noon, anyhow. He took enough money out of his wallet for five martinis, hid the wallet under a couch cushion, and headed for Duval Street.

Joe Haldeman

21. Dying, Well Or Badly

John had just about decided it was too early in the day to get drunk. He had
polished off two martinis in Sloppy Joe's and then wandered uptown because
the tourists were getting to him and a band was setting up, depressingly young
and cheerful. He found a grubby bar he'd never noticed before, dark and
smoky and hot. In the other universes it was a yuppie boutique. Three Social
Security drunks were arguing politics almost loudly enough to drown out
the game show on the television. It seemed to go well with the headache
and sour stomach he'd reaped from the martinis and the walk in the sun.
He got a beer and some peanuts and a couple of aspirin from the bartender,
and sat in the farthest booth with a copy of the local classified-ad newspaper.
Somebody had obscurely carved FUCK ANARCHY into the tabletop.

Nobody else in this world knows what anarchy *is*, John thought, and the
helpless anomie came back, intensified somewhat by drunken sentimentality.
What he would give to go back to the first universe and undo this all by just
not. . . .

Would that be possible? The Hemingway was willing to take him back to
1921; why not back a few weeks? Where the hell was that son of a bitch
when you needed him, it, whatever.

The Hemingway appeared in the booth opposite him, an Oak Park teenager
smoking a cigarette. "I felt a kind of vibration from you. Ready to make your
decision?"

"Can the people at the bar see you?"

"No. And don't worry about appearing to be talking to yourself. A lot of
that goes on around here."

"Look. Why can't you just take me back to a couple of weeks before we
met on the train, back in the first universe? I'll just. . . ." The Hemingway
was shaking its head slowly. "You can't."

"No. As I explained, you already exist there—"

"You said that *you* couldn't be in the same place twice. How do you know
I can't?"

"How do you know you can't swallow that piano? You just can't."

"You thought I couldn't talk about you, either; you thought your stick
would kill me. I'm not like normal people."

"Except in that alcohol does nothing for your judgment."

John ate a peanut thoughtfully. "Try this on for size. At 11:46 on June
3, a man named Sylvester Castlemaine sat down in Dos Hermosas and started
talking with me about the lost manuscripts. The forgery would never have
occurred to me if I hadn't talked to him. Why don't you go back and keep
him from going into that cafe? Or just go back to 11:30 and kill him."

The Hemingway smiled maliciously. "You don't like him much."

"It's more fear than like or dislike." He rubbed his face hard, remembering. "Funny how things shift around. He was kind of likeable the first time I met him. Then you killed me on the train and in the subsequent universe, he became colder, more serious. Then you killed me in Pansy's apartment and in this universe, he has turned mean. Dangerously mean, like a couple of men I knew in Viet Nam. The ones who really love the killing. Like you, evidently."

It blew a chain of smoke rings before answering. "I don't 'love' killing, or anything else. I have a complex function and I fulfill it, because that is what I do. That sounds circular because of the limitations of human language.

"I can't go killing people right and left just to see what happens. When a person dies at the wrong time it takes forever to clean things up. Not that it wouldn't be worth it in your case. But I can tell you with certainty that killing Castlemaine would not affect the final outcome."

"How can you say that? He's responsible for the whole thing." John finished off most of his beer and the Hemingway touched the mug and it refilled. "Not poison."

"Wouldn't work," it said morosely. "I'd gladly kill Castlemaine any way you want—cancer of the penis is a possibility—if there was even a fighting chance that it would clear things up. The reason I know it wouldn't is that I am not in the least attracted to that meeting. There's no probability nexus associated with it, the way there was with your buying the Corona or starting the story on the train, or writing it down here. You may think that you would never have come up with the idea for the forgery on your own, but you're wrong."

"That's preposterous."

"Nope. There are universes in this bundle where Castle isn't involved. You may find that hard to believe, but your beliefs aren't important."

John nodded noncommittally and got his faraway remembering look. "You know . . . reviewing in my mind all the conversations we've had, all five of them, the only substantive reason you've given me not to write this pastiche, and I quote, is that "I or someone like me will have to kill you." Since that doesn't seem to be possible, why don't we try some other line of attack?"

It put out the cigarette by squeezing it between thumb and forefinger. There was a smell of burning flesh. "All right, try this: give it up or I'll kill Pansy. Then Lena."

"I've thought of that, and I'm gambling that you won't, or can't. You had a perfect opportunity a few days ago—maximum dramatic effect—and you didn't do it. Now you say it's an awfully complicated matter."

"You're willing to gamble with the lives of the people you love?"

"I'm gambling with a lot. Including them." He leaned forward. "Take me into the future instead of the past. Show me what will happen if I succeed

597

with the Hemingway hoax. If I agree that it's terrible, I'll give it all up and become a plumber."

The old, wise Hemingway shook a shaggy head at him. "You're asking me to please fix it so you can swallow a piano. I can't. Even I can't go straight to the future and look around; I'm pretty much tied to your present and past until this matter is cleared up."

"One of the first things you said to me was that you were from the future. And the past. And 'other temporalities,' whatever the hell that means. You were lying then?"

"Not really." It sighed. "Let me force the analogy. Look at the piano."

John twisted half around. "Okay."

"You can't eat it—but after a fashion, I can." The piano suddenly transformed itself into a piano-shaped mountain of cold capsules, which immediately collapsed and rolled all over the floor. "Each capsule contains a pinch of sawdust or powdered ivory or metal, the whole piano in about a hundred thousand capsules. If I take one with each meal, I will indeed eat the piano, over the course of the next three hundred-some years. That's not a long time for me."

"That doesn't prove anything."

"It's not a *proof*; it's a demonstration." It reached down and picked up a capsule that was rolling by, and popped it into its mouth. "One down, 99,999 to go. So how many ways could I eat this piano?"

"Ways?"

"I mean I could have swallowed any of the hundred thousand first. Next I can choose any of the remaining 99,999. How many ways can—"

"That's easy. One hundred thousand factorial. A huge number."

"Go to the head of the class. It's ten to the godzillionth power. That represents the number of possible paths—the number of futures—leading to this one guaranteed, pre-ordained event: my eating the piano. They are all different, but in terms of whether the piano gets eaten, their differences are trivial.

"On a larger scale, every possible trivial action that you or anybody else in this universe takes puts us into a slightly different future than would have otherwise existed. An overwhelming majority of actions, even seemingly significant ones, make no difference in the long run. All of the futures bend back to one central, unifying event—except for the ones that you're screwing up!"

"So what is this big event?"

"It's impossible for you to know. It's not important, anyhow." Actually, it would take a rather cosmic viewpoint to consider the event unimportant: the end of the world.

Or at least the end of life on Earth. Right now there were two earnest young politicians, in the United States and Russia, who on 11 August 2006 would be President and Premier of their countries. On that day, one would insult the other beyond forgiveness, and a button would be pushed, and then another button, and by the time the sun set on Moscow, or rose on Washington, there would be nothing left alive on the planet at all—from the bottom of the ocean to the top of the atmosphere; not a cockroach, not a paramecium, not a virus, and all because there are some things a man just doesn't have to take, not if he's a real man.

Hemingway wasn't the only writer who felt that way, but he was the one with the most influence on this generation. The apparition who wanted John dead or at least not typing didn't know exactly what effect his pastiche was going to have on Hemingway's influence, but it was going to be decisive and ultimately negative. It would prevent or at least delay the end of the world in a whole bundle of universes, which would put a zillion adjacent realities out of kilter, and there would be hell to pay all up and down the Omniverse. Many more people than six billion would die—and it's even possible that all of Reality would unravel, and collapse back to the Primordial Hiccup from whence it came.

"If it's not important, then why are you so hell-bent on keeping me from preventing it? I don't believe you."

"*Don't* believe me, then!" At an imperious gesture, all the capsules rolled back into the corner and reassembled into a piano, with a huge crashing chord. None of the barflies heard it. "I should think you'd cooperate with me just to prevent the unpleasantness of dying over and over."

John had the expression of a poker player whose opponent has inadvertently exposed his hole card. "You get used to it," he said. "And it occurs to me that sooner or later I'll wind up in a universe that I really like. This one doesn't have a hell of a lot to recommend it." His foot tapped twice and then twice again.

"No," the Hemingway said. "It will get worse each time."

"You can't know that. This has never happened before."

"True so far, isn't it?"

John considered it for a moment. "Some ways. Some ways not."

The Hemingway shrugged and stood up. "Well. Think about my offer." The cane appeared. "Happy cancer." It tapped him on the chest and disappeared.

The first sensation was utter tiredness, immobility. When he strained to move, pain slithered through his muscles and viscera, and stayed. He could hardly breathe, partly because his lungs weren't working and partly because there was something in the way. In the mirror beside the booth he looked down his throat and saw a large white mass, veined, pulsing. He sank back into the cushion and waited. He remembered the young wounded Hemingway writing his parents from the hospital with ghastly cheerfulness: "If I should have died it would have been very easy for me. Quite the easiest thing I ever did." I don't know, Ernie; maybe it gets harder with practice. He felt something tear open inside and hot stinging fluid trickled through his abdominal cavity. He wiped his face and a patch of necrotic skin came off with a terrible smell. His clothes tightened as his body swelled.

"Hey buddy, you okay?" The bartender came around in front of him and jumped. "Christ, Harry, punch nine-one-one!"

John gave a slight ineffectual wave. "No rush," he croaked.

The bartender cast his eyes to the ceiling. "Always on my shift?"

22. Death In The Afternoon

John woke up behind a dumpster in an alley. It was high noon and the smell of fermenting garbage was revolting. He didn't feel too well in any case; as if he'd drunk far too much and passed out behind a dumpster, which was exactly what had happened in this universe.

In this universe. He stood slowly to a quiet chorus of creaks and pops, brushed himself off, and staggered away from the malefic odor. Staggered, but not limping—he had both feet again, in this present. There was a hand-sized numb spot at the top of his left leg where a .51 caliber machine gun bullet had missed his balls by an inch and ended his career as a soldier.

And started it as a writer. He got to the sidewalk and stopped dead. This was the first universe where he wasn't a college professor. He taught occasionally—sometimes creative writing; sometimes Hemingway—but it was only a hobby now, and a nod toward respectability.

He rubbed his fringe of salt-and-pepper beard. It covered the bullet scar there on his chin. He ran his tongue along the metal teeth the army had installed thirty years ago. Jesus. Maybe it does get worse every time. Which was worse, losing a foot or getting your dick sprayed with shrapnel, numb from severed nerves, plus bullets in the leg and face and arm? If you knew there was a Pansy in your future, you would probably trade a foot for a whole dick. Though she had done wonders with what was left.

Remembering furiously, not watching where he was going, he let his feet guide him back to the oldster's bar where the Hemingway had showed him how to swallow a piano. He pushed through the door and the shock of air conditioning brought him back to the present.

Ferns. Perfume. Lacy underthings. An epicene sales clerk sashayed toward him, managing to look worried and determined at the same time. His nose was pierced, decorated with a single diamond button. "Si-i-r," he said in a surprisingly deep voice, "may I *help* you?"

Crotchless panties. Marital aids. The bar had become a store called The French Connection. "Guess I took a wrong turn. Sorry." He started to back out.

The clerk smiled. "Don't be shy. Everybody needs *some*thing here."

The heat was almost pleasant in its heavy familiarity. John stopped at a convenience store for a sixpack of greenies and walked back home.

An interesting universe; much more of a divergence than the other had been. Reagan had survived the Hinckley assassination and actually went on to a second term. Bush was elected rather than succeeding to the presidency, and the country had not gone to war in Nicaragua. The Iran/Contra scandal nipped it in the bud.

The United States was actually cooperating with the Soviet Union in a flight to Mars. There were no DeSotos. Could there be a connection?

And in this universe he had actually met Ernest Hemingway.

Havana, 1952. John was eight years old. His father, a doctor in this universe, had taken a break from the New England winter to treat his family to a week in the tropics. John got a nice sunburn the first day, playing on the beach while his parents tried the casinos. The next day they made him stay indoors, which meant tagging along with his parents, looking at things that didn't fascinate eight-year-olds.

For lunch they went to La Florida, on the off chance that they might meet the famous Ernest Hemingway, who supposedly held court there when he was in Havana.

To John it was a huge dark cavern of a place, full of adult smells. Cigar smoke, rum, beer, stale urine. But Hemingway was indeed there, at the end of the long dark wood bar, laughing heartily with a table full of Cubans.

John was vaguely aware that his mother resembled some movie actress, but he couldn't have guessed that that would change his life. Hemingway glimpsed her and then stood up and was suddenly silent, mouth open. Then he laughed and waved a huge arm. "Come on over here, daughter."

The three of them rather timidly approached the table, John acutely aware of the careful inspection his mother was receiving from the silent Cubans. "Take a look, Mary," he said to the small blond woman knitting at the table, "The Kraut."

The woman nodded, smiling, and agreed that John's mother looked just like Marlene Dietrich ten years before. Hemingway invited them to sit down and have a drink, and they accepted with an air of genuine astonishment.

He gravely shook John's hand, and spoke to him as he would to an adult. Then he shouted to the bartender in fast Spanish, and in a couple of minutes his parents had huge daiquiris and he had a Coke with a wedge of lime in it, tropical and grown-up. The waiter also brought a tray of boiled shrimp. Hemingway even ate the heads and tails, crunching loudly, which impressed John more than any Nobel Prize. Hemingway might have agreed, since he hadn't yet received one, and Faulkner had.

For more than an hour, two Cokes, John watched as his parents sat hypnotized in the aura of Hemingway's famous charm. He put them at ease with jokes and stories and questions—for the rest of his life John's father would relate how impressed he was with the sophistication of Hemingway's queries about cardiac medicine—but it was obvious even to a child that they were in awe, electrified by the man's presence.

Later that night John's father asked him what he thought of Mr. Hemingway. Forty-four years later, John of course remembered his exact reply: "He has fun all the time. I never saw a grown-up who plays like that."

Interesting. That meeting was where his eidetic memory started. He could remember a couple of days before it pretty well, because they had still been close to the surface. In other universes, he could remember back well before grade school. It gave him a strange feeling. All of the universes were different, but this was the first one where the differentness was so tightly connected to Hemingway.

He was flabby in this universe, fat over old tired muscle, like Hemingway at his age, perhaps, and he felt a curious anxiety that he realized was a real *need* to have a drink. Not just desire, not thirst. If he didn't have a drink, something very very bad would happen. He knew that was irrational. Knowing didn't help.

John carefully mounted the stairs up to their apartment, stepping over the fifth one, also rotted in this universe. He put the beer in the refrigerator and took from the freezer a bottle of icy vodka—that was different—and poured himself a double shot and knocked it back, medicine drinking.

That spiked the hangover pretty well. He pried the top off a beer and carried it into the living room, thoughtful as the alcoholic glow radiated through his body. He sat down at the typewriter and picked up the air pistol, a fancy Belgian target model. He cocked it and with a practiced two-handed grip aimed at a paper target across the room. The pellet struck less than half an inch low.

All around the room the walls were pocked from where he'd fired at roaches, and once a scorpion. Very Hemingwayish, he thought; in fact, most of the ways he was different from the earlier incarnations of himself were in Hemingway's direction.

He spun a piece of paper into the typewriter and made a list:

EH & me --

-- both had doctor fathers

-- both forced into music lessons

-- in high school wrote derivative stuff that didn't show promise

-- Our war wounds were evidently similar in severity and location. Maybe my groin one was worse; army doctor there said that in Korea (and presumably WWI), without helicopter dustoff, I would have been dead on the battlefield. (Having been wounded in the kneecap and foot myself. I know that H's story about carrying the wounded guy on his back is unlikely. It was a month before I could put any stress on the knee.) He mentioned genital wounds, possibly similar to mine, in a letter to Bernard Baruch, but there's nothing in the Red Cross report about them.

But in both cases, being wounded and surviving was the central experience of our youth. Touching death.

-- We each wrote the first draft of our first novel in six weeks (but his was better and more ambitious).

-- Both had unusual critical success from the beginning.

-- Both shy as youngsters and gregarious as adults.

-- Always loved fishing and hiking and guns; I loved the bullfight from my first corrida, but may have been influenced by H's books.

-- Spain in general

-- have better women than we deserve

-- drink too much

-- hypochondria

-- accident proneness

-- a tendency toward morbidity

-- One difference. I will never stick a shotgun in my mouth and pull the trigger. Leaves too much of a mess.

He looked up at the sound of the cane tapping. The Hemingway was in the Karsh wise-old-man mode, but was nearly transparent in the bright light that streamed from the open door. "What do I have to do to get your attention?" it said. "Give you cancer again?"

"That was pretty unpleasant."

"Maybe it will be the last." It half sat on the arm of the couch and spun the cane around twice. "Today is a big day. Are we going to Paris?"

"What do you mean?"

"Something big happens today. In every universe where you're alive, this day glows with importance. I assume that means you've decided to go along with me. Stop writing this thing in exchange for the truth about the manuscripts."

As a matter of fact, he had been thinking just that. Life was confusing enough already, torn between his erotic love for Pansy and the more domestic, but still deep, feeling for Lena . . . writing the pastiche was kind of fun, but he did have his own fish to fry. Besides, he'd come to truly dislike Castle, even before Pansy had told him about the set-up. It would be fun to disappoint him.

"You're right. Let's go."

"First destroy the novel." In this universe, he'd completed seventy pages of the Up-in-Michigan novel.

"Sure." John picked up the stack of paper and threw it into the tiny fireplace. He lit it several places with a long barbecue match, and watched a month's work go up in smoke. It was only a symbolic gesture, anyhow; he could retype the thing from memory if he wanted to.

"So what do I do? Click my heels together three times and say 'There's no place like the Gare de Lyon'?"

"Just come closer."

John took three steps toward the Hemingway and suddenly fell up down sideways—

It was worse than dying. He was torn apart and scattered throughout space and time, being nowhere and everywhere, everywhen, being a screaming vacuum forever—

Grit crunched underfoot and coalsmoke was choking thick in the air. It was cold. Gray Paris skies glowered through the long skylights, through the complicated geometry of the black steel trusses that held up the high roof. Bustling crowds chattering French. A woman walked through John from behind. He pressed himself with his hands and felt real.

"They can't see us," the Hemingway said. "Not unless I will it."

"That was awful."

"I hoped you would hate it. That's how I spend most of my timespace. Come on." They walked past vendors selling paper packets of roasted chestnuts, bottles of wine, stacks of baguettes and cheeses. There were strange resonances as John remembered the various times he'd been here more than a half-century in the future. It hadn't changed much.

"There she is." The Hemingway pointed. Hadley looked worn, tired, dowdy. She stumbled, trying to keep up with the porter who strode along with her two bags. John recalled that she was just recovering from a bad case of the grippe. She'd probably still be home in bed if Hemingway hadn't sent the telegram urging her to come to Lausanne because the skiing was so good, at Chamby.

"Are there universes where Hadley doesn't lose the manuscripts?"

"Plenty of them," the Hemingway said. "In some of them he doesn't sell 'My Old Man' next year, or anything else, and he throws all the stories away himself. He gives up fiction and becomes a staff writer for the Toronto *Star*. Until the Spanish Civil War; he joins the Abraham Lincoln Battalion and is killed driving an ambulance. His only effect on American literature is one paragraph in *The Autobiography of Alice B. Toklas*."

"But in some, the stories actually do see print?"

"Sure, including the novel, which is usually called *Along With Youth*. There." Hadley was mounting the steps up into a passenger car. There was a microsecond of agonizing emptiness, and they materialized in the passageway in front of Hadley's compartment. She and the porter walked through them.

"*Merci*," she said, and handed the man a few sou. He made a face behind her back.

"*Along With Youth*?" John said.

"It's a pretty good book, sort of prefiguring A *Farewell To Arms*, but he does a lot better in universes where it's not published. *The Sun Also Rises* gets more attention."

Hadley stowed both the suitcase and the overnight bag under the seat. Then she frowned slightly, checked her wristwatch, and left the compartment, closing the door behind her.

"Interesting," the Hemingway said. "So she didn't leave it out in plain sight, begging to be stolen."

"Makes you wonder," John said. "This novel. Was it about World War I?"

"The trenches in Italy," the Hemingway said.

A young man stepped out of the shadows of the vestibule, looking in the direction Hadley took. Then he turned around and faced the two travelers from the future.

It was Ernest Hemingway. He smiled. "Close your mouth, John. You'll catch flies." He opened the door to the compartment, picked up the overnight bag, and carried it into the next car.

John recovered enough to chase after him. He had disappeared.

The Hemingway followed. "What *is* this?" John said. "I thought you couldn't be in two timespaces at once."

"That wasn't me."

"It sure as hell wasn't the real Hemingway. He's in Lausanne with Lincoln Steffens."

"Maybe he is and maybe he isn't."

"He knew my *name!*"

"That he did." The Hemingway was getting fainter as John watched.

"Was he another one of you? Another STAB agent?"

"No. Not possible." It peered at John. "What's happening to you?"

Hadley burst into the car and ran right through them, shouting in French for the conductor. She was carrying a bottle of Evian water.

"Well," John said, "that's what—"

The Hemingway was gone. John just had time to think *Marooned in 1922?* when the railroad car and the Gare de Lyon dissolved in an inbursting cascade of black sparks and it was no easier to handle the second time, spread impossibly thin across all those light years and millennia, wondering whether it was going to last forever this time, realizing that it did anyhow, and coalescing with an impossibly painful *snap:*

Looking at the list in the typewriter. He reached for the Heineken; it was still cold. He set it back down. "God," he whispered. "I hope that's that."

The situation called for higher octane. He went to the freezer and took out the vodka. He sipped the gelid syrup straight from the bottle, and almost dropped it when out of the corner of his eye he saw the overnight bag.

He set the open bottle on the counter and sleepwalked over to the dining room table. It was the same bag, slightly beat up, monogrammed EHR, Elizabeth Hadley Richardson. He opened it and inside was a thick stack of manila envelopes.

He took out the top one and took it and the vodka bottle back to his chair. His hands were shaking. He opened the folder and stared at the familiar typing.

ERNEST M. HEMINGWAY

ONE - EYE FOR MINE

————//————

Fever stood up . In the moon light he could xx see blood starting on his hands . His pants were torn at the knee and he knew it would be bleeding ~~there~~ too . He watched the lights of the caboose disppear in the trees where the track curved .

That lousy crut of a brakeman . He would get him xxxdxx some day .

Fever ^scuffed xxxxkxx off the end of a tie and sat down to pick the cinders out of his hands and knee . He could use some water . The brakeman had his canteen .

He could smell a campfire . He wondered if it would be smart to go find it . He knew about the wolves , the human kind that lived along the rails and the disgusting things they liked . He wasn 't afraid of them but you didn 't look for trouble .

You don 't have to look for trouble , his father would say . Trouble will find you . His father didn' t tell him about wolves , though , ~~or about women~~ .

There was a noise in the brush . Fever stood up and slipped his hand around the horn grip of the fat Buck cl$_a$sp knife in his pocket .

The screen door creaked open and he looked up to see Pansy walk in with a strange expression on her face. Lena followed, looking even stranger. Her left eye was swollen shut and most of that side of her face was bruised blue and brown.

He stood up, shaking with the sudden collision of emotions. "What the hell—"

"Castle," Pansy said. "He got outta hand."

"Real talent for understatement." Lena's voice was tightly controlled but distorted.

"He went nuts. Slappin' Lena around. Then he started to rummage around in a closet, rave about a shotgun, and we split."

607

"I'll call the police."

"We've already been there," Lena said. "It's all over."

"Of course. We can't work with—"

"No, I mean he's a *criminal*. He's wanted in Mississippi for second-degree murder. They went to arrest him, hold him for extradition. So no more Hemingway hoax."

"What Hemingway?" Pansy said.

"We'll tell you all about it," Lena said, and pointed at the bottle. "A little early, don't you think? You could at least get us a couple of glasses."

John went into the kitchen, almost floating with vodka buzz and anxious confusion. "What do you want with it?" Pansy said oh-jay and Lena said ice. Then Lena screamed.

He turned around and there was Castle standing in the door, grinning. He had a pistol in his right hand and a sawed-off shotgun in his left.

"You cunts," he said. "You fuckin' cunts. Go to the fuckin' cops."

There was a butcher knife in the drawer next to the refrigerator, but he didn't think Castle would stand idly by and let him rummage for it. Nothing else that might serve as a weapon, except the air pistol. Castle knew that it wouldn't do much damage.

He looked at John. "You three're gonna be my hostages. We're gettin' outta here, lose 'em up in the Everglades. They'll have a make on my pickup, though."

"We don't have a car," John said.

"I *know* that, asshole! There's a Hertz right down on One. You go rent one and don't try nothin' cute. I so much as *smell* a cop, I blow these two cunts away."

He turned back to the women and grinned crookedly, talking hard-guy through his teeth. "Like I did those two they sent, the spic and the nigger. They said somethin' about comin' back with a warrant to look for the shotgun and I was just bein' as nice as could be, I said hell, come on in, don't need no warrant. I got nothin' to hide, and when they come in I take the pistol from the nigger and kill the spic with it and shoot the nigger in the balls. You shoulda heard him. Some nigger. Took four more rounds to shut him up."

Wonder if that means the pistol is empty, John thought. He had Pansy's orange juice in his hand. It was an old-fashioned Smith & Wesson .357 Magnum six-shot, but from this angle he couldn't tell whether it had been reloaded. He could try to blind Castle with the orange juice.

He stepped toward him. "What kind of car do you want?"

"Just a *car*, damn it. Big enough." A siren whooped about a block away. Castle looked wary. "Bitch. You told 'em where you'd be."

"No," Lena pleaded. "We didn't tell them anything."

"Don't do anything stupid," John said.

Two more sirens, closer. "I'll show you *stupid!*" He raised the pistols towards Lena. John dashed the orange juice in his face.

It wasn't really like slow motion. It was just that John didn't miss any of it. Castle growled and swung around and in the cylinder's chambers John saw five copper-jacketed slugs. He reached for the gun and the first shot shattered his hand, blowing off two fingers, and struck the right side of his chest. The explosion was deafening and the shock of the bullet was like being hit simultaneously in the hand and chest with baseball bats. He rocked, still on his feet, and coughed blood spatter on Castle's face. He fired again, and the second slug hit him on the other side of the chest, this time spinning him half around. Was somebody screaming? Hemingway said it felt like an icy snowball, and that was pretty close, except for the inside part, your body saying Well, time to close up shop. There was a terrible familiar radiating pain in the center of his chest, and John realized that he was having a totally superfluous heart attack. He pushed off from the dinette and staggered toward Castle again. He made a grab for the shotgun and Castle emptied both barrels into his abdomen. He dropped to his knees and then fell over on his side. He couldn't feel anything. Things started to go dim and red. Was this going to be the last time?

Castle cracked the shotgun and the two spent shells flew up in an arc over his shoulder. He took two more out of his shirt pocket and dropped one. When he bent over to pick it up, Pansy leaped past him. In a swift motion that was almost graceful—it came to John that he had probably practiced it over and over, acting out fantasies—he slipped both shells into their chambers and closed the gun with a flip of the wrist. The screen door was stuck. Pansy was straining at the knob with both hands. Castle put the muzzles up to the base of her skull and pulled one trigger. Most of her head covered the screen or went through the hole the blast made. The crown of her skull, a bloody bowl, bounced off two walls and went spinning into the kitchen. Her body did a spastic little dance and folded, streaming.

Lena was suddenly on his back, clawing at his face. He spun and slammed her against the wall. She wilted like a rag doll and he hit her hard with the pistol on the way down. She unrolled at his feet, out cold, and with his mouth wide open laughing silently he lowered the shotgun and blasted her pointblank in the crotch. Her body jack-knifed and John tried with all his will not to die but blackness crowded in and the last thing he saw was that evil grin as Castle reloaded again, peering out the window, presumably at the police.

It wasn't the terrible sense of being spread infinitesimally thin over an infinity of pain and darkness; things had just gone black, like closing your eyes. If this is death, John thought, there's not much to it.

But it changed. There was a little bit of pale light, some vague figures, and then colors bled into the scene, and after a moment of disorientation he realized he was still in the apartment, but apparently floating up by the ceiling. Lena was conscious again, barely, twitching, staring at the river of blood that pumped from between her legs. Pansy looked unreal, headless but untouched from the neck down, lying in a relaxed, improbable posture like a knocked-over department store dummy, blood still spurting from a neck artery out through the screen door.

His own body was a mess, the abdomen completely excavated by buckshot. Inside the huge wound, behind the torn coils of intestine, the shreds of fat and gristle, the blood, the shit, he could see sharp splintered knuckles of backbone. Maybe it hadn't hurt so much because the spinal cord had been severed in the blast.

He had time to be a little shocked at himself for not feeling more. Of course most of the people he'd known who had died did die this way, in loud spatters of blood and brains. Even after thirty years of the occasional polite heart attack or stroke carrying off friend or acquaintance, most of the dead people he knew had died in the jungle.

He had been a hero there, in this universe. That would have surprised his sergeants in the original one. Congressional Medal of Honor, so called, which hadn't hurt the sales of his first book. Knocked out the NVA machine-gun emplacement with their own satchel charge, then hauled the machine-gun around and wiped out their mortar and command squads. He managed it all with bullet wounds in the face and triceps. Of course without the bullet wounds he wouldn't have lost his cool and charged the machine-gun emplacement, but that wasn't noted in the citation.

A pity there was no way to trade the medals in—melt them down into one big fat bullet and use it to waste that crazy motherfucker who was ignoring the three people he'd just killed, laughing like a hyena while he shouted obscenities at the police gathering down below.

Castle fires a shot through the lower window and then ducks and a spray of automatic-weapon fire shatters the upper window, filling the air with a spray of glass; bullets and glass fly painlessly through John where he's floating and he hears them spatter into the ceiling and suddenly everything is white with plaster dust—it starts to clear and he is much closer to his body, drawing down closer and closer; he merges with it and there's an instant of blackness and he's looking out through human eyes again.

A dull noise and he looked up to see hundreds of shards of glass leap up from the floor and fly to the window; plaster dust in billows sucked up into bullet holes in the ceiling, which then disappeared.

The top windowpane reformed as Castle *uncrouched*, pointed the shotgun, then jerked forward as a blossom of yellow flame and white smoke rolled back into the barrel.

His hand was whole, the fingers restored. He looked down and saw rivulets of blood running back into the hole in his abdomen, then individual drops; then it closed and the clothing restored itself; then one of the holes in his chest closed up and then the other.

The clothing was unfamiliar. A tweed jacket in this weather? His hands had turned old, liver spots forming as he watched. Slow like a plant growing, slow like the moon turning, thinking slowly too, he reached up and felt the beard, and could see out of the corner of his eye that it was white and long. He was too fat, and a belt buckle bit painfully into his belly. He sucked in and pried out and looked at the buckle, yes, it was old brass and said "GOTT MIT UNS," the buckle he'd taken from a dead German so long ago. The buckle Hemingway had taken.

John got to one knee. He watched fascinated as the stream of blood gushed back into Lena's womb, disappearing as Castle grinning jammed the barrels in between her legs, flinched, and did a complicated dance in reverse (while Pansy's decapitated body writhed around and jerked upright); Lena, sliding up off the floor, leaped up between the man's back and the wall, then fell off and ran backwards as he flipped the shotgun up to the back of Pansy's neck and seeming gallons of blood and tissue came flying from every direction to assemble themselves into the lovely head and face, distorted in terror as she jerked awkwardly at the door and then ran backwards, past Castle as he did a graceful pirouette, unloading the gun and placing one shell on the floor, which flipped up to his pocket as he stood and put the other one there.

John stood up and walked through some thick resistance toward Castle. Was it *time* resisting him? Everything else was still moving in reverse: Two empty shotgun shells sailed across the room to snick into the weapon's chambers; Castle snapped it shut and wheeled to face John—

But John wasn't where he was supposed to be. As the shotgun swung around, John grabbed the barrels—hot!—and pulled the pistol out of Castle's waistband. He lost his grip on the shotgun barrels just as he jammed the pistol against Castle's heart and fired. A spray of blood from all over the other side of the room converged on Castle's back and John felt the recoil sting of the Magnum just as the shotgun muzzle cracked hard against his teeth, mouthful of searing heat then blackness forever, back in the featureless infinite timespace hell that the Hemingway had taken him to, forever, but in the next instant, a new kind of twitch, a twist. . . .

23. The Time Exchanged

What does that mean, you "lost" him?

We were in the railroad car in the Gare de Lyon, in the normal observation mode. This entity that looked like Hemingway walked up, greeted us, took the manuscripts, and disappeared.

Just like that.

No. He went into the next car. John Baird ran after him. Maybe that was my mistake. I translated instead of running.

That's when you lost him.

Both of them. Baird disappeared, too. Then Hadley came running in—

Don't confuse me with Hadleys. You checked the adjacent universes.

All of them, yes. I think they're all right.

Think?

Well . . . I can't quite get to that moment. When I disappeared. It's as if I were still there for several more seconds, so I'm excluded.

And John Baird is still there?

Not by the time I can insert myself. Just Hadley running around—

No Hadleys. No Hadleys. So naturally you went back to 1996.

Of course. But there is a period of several minutes there from which I'm excluded as well. When I can finally insert myself, John Baird is dead.

Ah.

In every doomline, he and Castlemaine have killed each other. John is lying there with his head blown off, Castle next to him with his heart torn out from a pointblank pistol shot, with two very distraught women screaming while police pile in through the door. And this.

The overnight bag with the stories.

I don't think anybody noticed it. With Baird dead, I could spotcheck the women's futures; neither of them mentions the bag. So perhaps the mission is accomplished.

Well, Reality is still here. So far. But the connection between Baird and this Hemingway entity is disturbing. That Baird is able to return to 1996 without your help is *very* disturbing. He has obviously taken on some of your characteristics, your abilities, which is why you're excluded from the last several minutes of his life.

I've never heard of that happening before.

It never has. I think that John Baird is no more human than you and I.

Is?

I suspect he's still around somewhen.

24. Islands In The Stream

and the unending lightless desert of pain becomes suddenly one small bright
spark and then everything is dark red and a taste, a bitter taste, Hoppe's No.
9 gun oil and the twin barrels of the fine Boss pigeon gun cold and oily on
his tongue and biting hard against the roof of his mouth; the dark red is light
on the other side of his eyelids, sting of pain before he bumps a tooth and
opens his eyes and mouth and lowers the gun and with shaking hands
unloads—no, *dis*-loads—both barrels and walks backwards, shuffling in the
slippers, slumping, stopping to stare out into the Idaho morning dark, helpless
tears coursing up from the snarled white beard, walking backwards down the
stairs with the shotgun heavily cradled in his elbow, backing into the storeroom and replacing it in the rack, then back up the stairs and slowly put the
keys there in plain sight on the kitchen windowsill, a bit of mercy from Miss
Mary, then sit and stare at the cold bad coffee as it warms back to one acid
sip—

A tiny part of the mind saying *wait! I am John Baird it is 1996*

and back to a spiritless shower, numb to the needle spray, and cramped
constipation and a sleep of no ease; an evening with Mary and George Brown
tiptoeing around the blackest of black-ass worse and worse each day, only
one thing to look forward to

got to throw out an anchor

faster now, walking through the Ketchum woods like a jerky cartoon in
reverse, fucking FBI and IRS behind every tree, because you sent Ezra that
money, felt sorry for him because he was crazy, what a fucking joke, should
have finished the Cantos and shot himself.

effect preceding cause but I can read or hear scraps of thought somehow
speeding to a blur now, driving in reverse hundreds of miles per hour back
from Ketchum to Minnesota, the Mayo Clinic, holding the madness in
while you talk to the shrink, promise not to hurt myself have to go home
and write if I'm going to beat this, figuring what he wants to hear, then the
rubber mouthpiece and smell of your own hair and flesh slightly burnt by
the electrodes then deep total blackness

sharp stabs of thought sometimes stretching
hospital days blur by in reverse, cold chrome and starch white, a couple
of mouthfuls of claret a day to wash down the pills that seem to make it
worse and worse

what will happen to me when he's born?
When they came back from Spain was when he agreed to the Mayo Clinic,
still all beat up from the plane crashes six years before in Africa, liver and
spleen shot to hell, brain too, nerves, can't write or can't stop: all day on
one damned sentence for the Kennedy book but a hundred thousand fast

words, pure shit, for the bullfight article. Paris book okay but stuck. Great to find the trunks in the Ritz but none of the stuff Hadley lost.

Here it stops. A frozen tableau:

Afternoon light slanting in through the tall cloudy windows of the Cambon bar, where he had liberated, would liberate, the hotel in August 1944. A good large American-style martini gulped too fast in the excitement. The two small trunks unpacked and laid out item by item. Hundreds of pages of notes that would become the Paris book. But nothing before '23, of course. *the manuscripts* The novel and the stories and the poems still gone. One moment nailed down with the juniper sting of the martini and then time crawling rolling flying backwards again—

no control?

Months blurring by, Madrid Riviera Venice feeling sick and busted up, the plane wrecks like a quick one-two punch brain and body, blurry sick even before them at the Finca Vigia, can't get a fucking thing done after the Nobel Prize, journalists day and night, the prize bad luck and bullshit anyhow but need the $35,000

damn, had to shoot Willie, cat since the boat-time before the war, but winged a burglar too, same gun, just after the Pulitzer, now that was all right

slowing down again—Havana—the Floridita—

Even Mary having a good time, and the Basque jai alai players too though they don't know much English, most of them, interesting couple of civilians, the doctor and the Kraut lookalike, but there's something about the boy that makes it hard to take my eyes off him, looks like someone I guess, another round of Papa Dobles, that boy, what is it about him? and then the first round, with lunch, and things speeding up to a blur again.

out on the Gulf a lot, enjoying the triumph of *The Old Man and the Sea,* the easy good-paying work of providing fishing footage for the movie, and then back into 1951, the worst year of his life that far, weeks of grudging conciliation, uncontrollable anger, and black-ass depression from the poisonous critical slime that followed *Across the River,* bastards gunning for him, Harold Ross dead, mother Grace dead, son Gregory a dope addict hip-deep into the dianetics horseshit, Charlie Scribner dead but first declaring undying love for that asshole Jones

most of the forties an anxious blur, Cuba Italy Cuba France Cuba China found Mary kicked Martha out, thousand pages on the fucking *Eden* book wouldn't come together Bronze Star better than Pulitzer

Martha a chromeplated bitch in Europe but war is swell otherwise, liberating the Ritz, grenades rifles pistols and bomb runs with the RAF, China

boring compared to it and the Q-ship runs off Cuba, hell, maybe the bitch
was right for once, just kid stuff and booze

marrying the bitch was the end of my belle epoch, easy to see from here,
the thirties all sunshine Key West Spain Key West Africa Key West, good
hard writing with Pauline holding down the store, good woman but sorry I
had to

sorry I had to divorce

stopping

Walking Paris streets after midnight:

I was never going to throw back at her losing the manuscripts. Told Steffens
that would be like blaming a human for the weather, or death. These things
happen. Nor say anything about what I did the night after I found out she
really had lost them. But this one time we got to shouting and I think I hurt
her. Why the hell did she have to bring the carbons what the hell did she
think carbons were for stupid stupid stupid and she crying and she giving
me hell about Pauline Jesus any woman who could fuck up Paris for you
could fuck up a royal flush

it slows down around the manuscripts or me—

golden years the mid-twenties everything clicks Paris Vorarlburg Paris
Schruns Paris Pamplona Paris Madrid Paris Lausanne

couldn't believe she actually

most of a novel dozens of poems stories sketches—*contes,* Kitty called
them by God woman you show me your *conte* and I'll show you mine

so drunk that night I know better than to drink that much absinthe so
drunk I was half crawling going up the stairs to the apartment I saw weird
I saw God I saw *I saw myself standing there on the fourth landing with
Hadley's goddamn bag*

I waited almost an hour, that seemed like no time or all time, and when
he, when I, when he came crashing up the stairs he blinked twice, then I
walked through me groping, shook my head without looking back and managed to get the door unlocked

*flying back through the dead winter French countryside, standing in the bar
car fighting hopelessness to Hadley crying so hard she can't get out what was
wrong with Steffens standing gaping like a fish in a bowl*

twisting again, painlessly inside-out, I suppose through various dimensions, seeing the man's life as one complex chord of beauty and purpose and
ugliness and chaos, my life on one side of the Moebius strip consistent
through its fading forty-year span, starting, *starting,* here:

the handsome young man sits on the floor of the apartment holding
himself, rocking racked with sobs, one short manuscript crumpled in front
of him, the room a mess with drawers pulled out, their contents scattered

on the floor, it's like losing an arm a leg (a foot a testicle), it's like losing your youth and along with youth

with a roar he stands up, eyes closed fists clenched, wipes his face dry and stomps over to the window

breathes deeply until he's breathing normally

strides across the room, kicking a brassiere out of his way

stands with his hand on the knob and thinks this:

life can break you but you can grow back strong at the broken places

and goes out slamming the door behind him, somewhat conscious of having been present at his own birth.

With no effort I find myself standing earlier that day in the vestibule of a train. Hadley is walking away, tired, looking for a vendor. I turn and confront two aspects of myself.

"Close your mouth, John. You'll catch flies."

They both stand paralyzed while I slide open the door and pull the overnight bag from under the seat. I walk away and the universe begins to tingle and sparkle.

I spend forever in the black void between timespaces. I am growing to enjoy it.

I appear in John Baird's apartment and set down the bag. I look at the empty chair in front of the old typewriter, the green beer bottle sweating cold next to it, and John Baird appears, looking dazed, and I have business elsewhere, elsewhen. A train to catch. I'll come back for the bag in twelve minutes or a few millennia, after the bloodbath that gives birth to us all.

25. A Moveable Feast

He wrote the last line and set down the pencil and read over the last page sitting on his hands for warmth. He could see his breath. Celebrate the end with a little heat.

He unwrapped the bundle of twigs and banked them around the pile of coals in the brazier. Crazy way to heat a room but it's France. He cupped both hands behind the stack and blew gently. The coals glowed red and then orange and with the third breath the twigs smoldered and a small yellow flame popped up. He held his hands over the fire, rubbing the stiffness out of his fingers, enjoying the smell of the birch as it cracked and spit.

He put a fresh sheet and carbon into the typewriter and looked at his penciled notes. Final draft? Worth a try:

Ernest M. Hemingway,
74 rue da Cardinal Lemoine,
Paris, France

〉〉 U P   I N   M I C H I G A N 〉〉

Jim Gilmore came to Horton's Bay from Canada. He bought the blacksmith shop from old man Hortom

Shit, a typo. He flinched suddenly, as if struck, and shook his head to clear it. What a strange sensation to come out of nowhere. A sudden cold stab of grief. But larger somehow than grief for a person.

Grief for everybody, maybe. For being human.

From a typo?

He went to the window and opened it in spite of the cold. He filled his lungs with the cold damp air and looked around the familiar orange and grey mosaic of chimney pots and tiled roofs under the dirty winter Paris sky.

He shuddered and eased the window back down and returned to the heat of the brazier. He had felt it before, exactly that huge and terrible feeling. But where?

For the life of him he couldn't remember.

HONORABLE MENTIONS
1990

Brian W. Aldiss, "A Life of Matter and Death," *Interzone* 38.
———, "A Tupolev Too Far," *Other Edens III.*
Ray Aldridge, "We Were Butterflies," *F & SF*, Aug.
Patricia Anthony, "For No Reason," *IAsfm*, Sept.
———, "Lunch With Daddy," *Pulphouse 8.*
Isaac Asimov, "Fault-Intolerant," *IAsfm*, May.
———, "Kid Brother," *IAsfm*, Mid-Dec.
Scott Baker, "The Jamesburg Incubus," *Alien Sex.*
John Barnes, "My Advice to the Civilized," *IAsfm*, Apr.
S. M. Baxter, "A Journey to the King Planet," *Zenith 2.*
Greg Bear, "Heads," *Interzone* 37 & 38.
Amy Bechtel, "Look Closer," *Analog*, Jun.
M. Shayne Bell, "Dry Niger," *IAsfm*, Aug.
———, "Earthlonging," *Amazing*, Jan.
Gregory Benford, "The Rose and the Scalpel," *Amazing*, Jan.
———, "Warstory," *IAsfm*, Jan.
Terry Bisson, "Over Flat Mountain," *Omni*, Jun.
———, "The Two Janets," *IAsfm*, Nov.
Michael Blumlein, "Bestseller," *F & SF*, Feb.
———, "Shed His Grace," *Semiotext[e] SF.*
R. V. Branham, "And Ghost Stories," *IAsfm*, Jul.
Alan Brennert, "Her Pilgrim Soul," *Her Pilgrim Soul.*
———, "Sea-Change," *F & SF*, Feb.
F. Alexander Brejcha, "The New Land," *Analog*, Jun.
Poppy Z. Brite, "His Mouth Will Taste of Wormwood," *Borderlands.*
John Brunner, "The Pronounced Effect," *Weird Tales*, Summer.
Edward Bryant, "Slippage," *Walls of Fear.*
Lois McMaster Bujold, "Weatherman," *Analog*, Feb.
Pat Cadigan, "Fool to Believe," *IAsfm*, Feb.
Richard Calder, "The Lilim," *Interzone* 34.
Jonathan Carroll, "The Art of Falling Down," *Walls of Fear.*
———, "My Zoondel," *Weird Tales*, Winter.
———, "The Sadness of Detail," *Omni*, Feb.
Michael Cassutt, "At Risk," *IAsfm*, Jul.
———, "Curious Elation," *F & SF*, Sept.
Robert R. Chase, "Transit of Betelgeuse," *Analog*, May.
Rob Chilson, "Gerda and the Wizard," *IAsfm*, Mar.

Kathryn Cramer, "The End of Everything," *IAsfm*, Oct.
Nancy Collins, "The Two-Headed Man," *Pulphouse 9*.
Ronald Anthony Cross, "Two Bad Dogs," *IAsfm*, Sept.
Tony Daniel, "The Passage of Night Trains," *IAsfm*, Mid-Dec.
Jack Dann and Gregory Frost, "The Incompleat Ripper," *Starshore 1*.
Avram Davidson, "Have You Tried Gummies?" *IAsfm*, 2 A.M., Aug.
———, "Limekiller At Large," *IAsfm*, Jun.
———, "Mr. Rob't E. Hoskins," *F & SF*, Apr.
———, "Seeomancer," *IAsfm*, Feb.
Bernard Deitchman, "Lord of Fishes," *Analog*, Aug.
Bradley Denton, "Captain Coyote's Last Hunt," *IAsfm*, Mar.
———, "The Chaff He Will Burn," *F & SF*, Apr.
Paul Di Fillippo, "Harlem Nova," *Amazing*, Sept.
Janet Kagan, "The Flowering Inferno," *IAsfm*, Mar.
———, "Getting the Bugs Out," *IAsfm*, Nov.
James Patrick Kelly, "The Propagation of Light in a Vacuum," *Universe 1*.
John Kessel, "Buddha Nostril Bird," *IAsfm*, Mar.
Damian Kilby, "Daniel's Labyrinth," *Universe 1*.
———, "Travelers," *IAsfm*, Feb.
Garry Kilworth, "In the Country of the Tattooed Men," *Omni*, Sept.
Kathe Koja, "True Colors," *IAsfm*, Jan.
Stephen Kraus, "Beyond the Barrier," *F & SF*, Dec.
———, "Checksum," *Analog*, Jan.
Nancy Kress, "Touchdown," *IAsfm*, Oct.
R. A. Lafferty, "The Story of Little Briar-Rose, A Scholarly Study," *Strange Plasma 2*.
R. M. Lamming, "Waspsongs," *More Tales from the Forbidden Planet*.
Geoffrey A. Landis, "The City of Ultimate Freedom," *Universe 1*.
———, "Projects," *IAsfm*, Jun.
———, "Realm of the Sences," *IAsfm*, Mid-Dec.
David Langford, "Ellipses," *More Tales from the Forbidden Planet*.
Roberta Lannes, "Saving the World at the New Moon Hotel," *Alien Sex*.
Joe R. Lansdale, "The Pit," *Pulphouse 9*.
Ursula K. Le Guin, "Unlocking the Air," *Playboy*, Dec.
Jonathan Lethem, "A Mirror for Heaven," *MZB's Fantasy Magazine*, 9.
———, "The Buff," *Pulphouse 8*.
———, "My Neighbor Bob," *Journal Wired*, Summer/Fall.
———, "Noodling," *Journal Wired*, Spring.
Thomas Ligotti, "The Lost Art of Twilight," *Weird Tales*, Summer.
Richard A. Lupoff, "At Vega's Taqueria," *Amazing*, Sept.
Bruce McAllister, "Angels," *IAsfm*, May.
Thomas M. Disch, "Celebrity Love," *Interzone 35*.

————, "The 21st of June," *Voice Literary Supplement 85.*

Gardner Dozois, "Après Moi," *Omni*, Nov.

L. Timmel Duchamp, "The Forbidden Words of Margaret A.," *Pulphouse 8.*

J. R. Dunn, "Stout Hearts," *Amazing*, Mar.

Thomas A. Easton, "Matchmaker," *Analog*, Aug.

George Alec Effinger, "Fatal Disk Error," *Amazing*, May.

Greg Egan, "Axiomatic," *Interzone 41.*

————, "The Moral Virologist," *Pulphouse 8.*

————, "The Safe-Deposit Box," *IAsfm*, Sept.

Harlan Ellison, "Scartaris, June 28th," *Borderlands.*

Carol Emshwiller, "Peri," *Strange Plasma 3.*

M. J. Engh, "Moon Blood," *Universe 1.*

————, "Penelope Comes Home," *Walls of Fear.*

Sharon N. Farber, "Space Aliens Saved My Marriage," *IAsfm*, Dec.

Marina Fitch, "Just Give Me Your Hand," *Pulphouse 8.*

————, "The River Remembers," *Pulphouse 7.*

Michael F. Flynn, "The Common Goal of Nature," *Analog*, Apr.

————, "The Feeders," *Analog*, Jan.

————, "Mammy Morgan Played the Organ, Her Daddy Beat the Drum," *Analog*, Nov.

Karen Joy Fowler, "Lieserl," *IAsfm*, Jul.

Robert Frazier, "Descent Into Eden," *Amazing*, Sept.

————, "Giant, Giant Steps," *Amazing*, May.

Esther M. Friesner, "Blunderbore," *IAsfm*, Sept.

————, "The Curse of Psamlahkithotep," *F & SF*, May.

————, "Up The Wall," *IAsfm*, Apr.

R. Garcia y Robertson, "Four Kings and an Ace," *F & SF*, Nov.

————, "The Great Fear," *Weird Tales*, Winter.

————, "Not Fade Away," *IAsfm*, Sept.

————, "Ontogeny Recapitulates Phylogeny," *Pulphouse 8.*

————, "The Spiral Dance," *F & SF*, May.

William Gibson and Bruce Sterling, "The Angel of Goliad," *Interzone 40.*

Lisa Goldstein, "The Blue Love Potion," *IAsfm*, Jun.

————, "Midnight News," *IAsfm*, Mar.

Alan Ira Gordon, "The Bulgarian Poetess Takes A Green Card," *Starshore 2.*

Steven Gould, "Simulation Six," *IAsfm*, Mar.

John Gribbin, "Insight," *Zenith 2.*

Nicola Griffith, "Down the Path of the Sun," *Interzone 34.*

John Griesemer, "Box of Light," *IAsfm*, Nov.

Joe Haldeman, "Passages," *Analog*, Mar.

Honorable Mentions

Karen Haber, "His Spirit Wife," *F & SF*, Aug.
——, "3 Rms, Gd View," *IAsfm*, Mid-Dec.
Rory Harper, "God's Bullets," *Aboriginal SF*, Nov–Dec.
Gregor Hartmann, "O Time, Your Pyramids," *Universe 1*.
Daniel Hatch, "Den of Foxes," *Analog*, Dec.
Howard V. Hendrix, "The Voice of the Dolphin in Air," *Starshore 2*.
Nina Kiriki Hoffman, "Stillborn," *Borderlands*.
Alexander Jablokov, "The Place of No Shadows," *IAsfm*, Nov.
Phillip C. Jennings, "The Betrothal," *IAsfm*, Oct.
——, "The Gadarene Dig," *IAsfm*, Dec.
K. W. Jeter, "The First Time," *Alien Sex*.
Kij Johnson, "Solving the Homeless Problem," *Pulphouse 8*.
Gwyneth Jones, "Forward Echoes," *Interzone 42*.
Ian R. MacLeod, "Green," *IAsfm*, Mid-Dec.
——, "1/72nd Scale," *Weird Tales*, Fall.
——, "Well-Loved," *Interzone 34*.
Paul J. McAuley, "Exiles," *Interzone 41*.
Ian McDonald, "Fronds," *Amazing*, Jul.
——, "Toward Kilimanjaro," *IAsfm*, Aug.
——, "Winning," *Zenith 2*.
Maureen McHugh, "The Queen of Marincite," *IAsfm*, Mar.
Bridget McKenna, "Evenings, Mornings, Afternoons," *IAsfm*, Dec.
Judith Moffett, "Final *Tomte*," *F & SF*, Jun.
——, "The Ragged Rock," *IAsfm*, Dec.
Pat Murphy, "Bones," *IAsfm*, May.
——, "The Eradication of Romantic Love," *Interzone 42*.
Jamil Nasir, "The Allah Stairs," *Tales of the Unanticipated 7*.
——, "The Book of St. Farrin," *Universe 1*.
Kim Newman, "The Original Dr. Shade," *Interzone 36*.
Larry Niven, "Madness Has Its Place," *IAsfm*, Jun.
Gene O'Neill, "Awaken, Dragon," *F & SF*, May.
Gerald Pearce, "Kindred of the Crescent Moon," *Weird Tales*, Summer.
Lawrence Person, "Frames of Light," *IAsfm*, Dec.
Rachel Pollack, "The Woman Who Didn't Come Back," *MTFT Forbidden Planet*.
Tom Purdom, "A Proper Place to Live," *IAsfm*, Jan.
W. T. Quick, "Whatever Gets You Through the Night," *Amazing*, Mar.
Robert Reed, "Chaff," *F & SF*, May.
——, "The Utility Man," *IAsfm*, Nov.
Mike Resnick, "Bwana," *IAsfm*, Jan.
——, "The Manamouki," *IAsfm*, Jul.
Alastair Reynolds, "Nunivak Snowflakes," *Interzone 36*.

John Maddox Roberts, "Mighty Fortress," *IAsfm*, May.
Keith Roberts, "The Gray Wethers," *Other Edens III*.
———, "Mrs. Byers and the Dragon," *IAsfm*, Aug.
Kim Stanley Robinson, "A Short, Sharp Shock," *IAsfm*, Nov.
———, "The Translator," *Universe 1*.
Madeline E. Robins, "Mules," *F & SF*, Apr.
Mary Rosenblum, "The Awakening," *Pulphouse 9*.
———, "Floodtide," *IAsfm*, Dec.
———, "For A Price," *IAsfm*, Jun.
Kristine Kathryn Rusch, "A Time For Every Purpose," *Amazing*, May.
———, "Spaceships in the Desert," *Starshore 1*.
———, "Story Child," *Abo SF*, Sept–Oct.
———, "Trains," *IAsfm*, Apr.
Richard Paul Russo, "Liz and Diego," *IAsfm*, Nov.
———, "No Place Any More," *Starshore 2*.
Geoff Ryman, "Omnisexual," *Alien Sex*.
Stanley Schmidt, "The Man on the Cover," *Analog*, Oct.
Charles Sheffield, "The Double Spiral Staircase," *Analog*, Jan.
———, "Godspeed," *Analog*, Jul.
———, "Health Care System," *IAsfm*, Sept.
Lucius Shepard, "Skull City," *IAsfm*, Jul.
Lewis Shiner, "Language," *New Pathways*, Jul.
———, "Scales," *Alien Sex*.
———, "Wild For You," *IAsfm*, Dec.
John Shirley, "Six Kinds of Darkness," *Semiotext[e] SF*.
Robert Silverberg, "Lion Time in Timbuctoo," *IAsfm*, Oct.
John Sladek, "Dining Out," *MTFT Forbidden Planet*.
Richard R. Smith, "Alien Used Cars," *Universe 1*.
Sarah Smith, "Two Boston Artists," *Aboriginal SF*, Jul–Aug.
S. P. Somtow, "Cruise Eternity," *Pulphouse 8*.
Martha Soukup, "Over Long Haul," *Amazing*, Mar.
Brian Stableford, "Bedside Conversations," *IAsfm*, Dec.
———, "The Invertebrate Man," *Interzone 39*.
Allen Steele, "Hapgood's Hoax," *IAsfm*, Mid-Dec.
———, "Trembling Earth," *IAsfm*, Nov.
Bruce Sterling, "Hollywood Kremlin," *F & SP*, Oct.
———, "The Shores of Bohemia," *Universe 1*.
———, "The Sword of Damocles," *IAsfm*, Feb.
Nancy Sterling, "The Recital," *IAsfm*, Jul.
Michael Swanwick, "UFO," *Aboriginal SF*, Sept–Oct.
Judith Tarr, "Voice in the Desert," *Amazing*, Mar.
Melanie Tem, "The Reunion," *IAsfm*, Nov.

W. R. Thompson, "Life Among the Immortals," *Analog*, Dec.
Mark W. Tiedemann, "Targets," *IAsfm*, Dec.
Lisa Tuttle, "Dead Television," *Zenith 2*.
———, "Lizard Lust," *Interzone 39*.
———, "Husbands," *Alien Sex*.
Jeff VanderMeer, "The Ministry of Butterflies," *Starshore 2*.
———, "The Sea, Mendeho, and Moonlight," *Visions, Vol IV #2*.
Karl Edward Wagner, "Cedar Lane," *Walls of Fear*.
———, "But You'll Never Follow Me," *Borderlands*.
Ian Watson, "Gaudi's Dragon," *IAsfm*, Oct.
Don Webb, "A Half-Dime Adventure," *IAsfm*, Oct.
———, "The Martian Spring of Dr. Woodard," *New Pathways*, Jul.
Andrew Weiner, "Eternity, Baby," *IAsfm*, Nov.
Deborah Wessell, "Time Considered as a Helix of Lavendar Ribbon," *IAsfm*,
    Mid-Dec.
———, "Joyride," *IAsfm*, Feb.
Rick Wilber, "War Bride," *Alien Sex*.
Cherry Wilder, "A Woman's Ritual," *IAsfm*, Dec.
———, "Old Noon's Tale," *Strange Plasma 3*.
Walter Jon Williams, "Elegy for Angels and Dogs," *IAsfm*, May.
———, "Solip:System," *IAsfm*, Sept.
Chet Williamson, "Other Errors, Other Times," *F & SF*, Jan.
Gene Wolfe, "The Flag," *Strange Plasma 2*.
———, "The Haunted Bordinghouse," *Walls of Fear*.
N. Lee Wood, "Memories That Dance Like Dust in the Summer Heat,"
    Amazing, June.
George Zebrowski, "Lenin in Odessa," *Amazing*, Mar.